AD NOMAD

The Case Histories
Of Dane Bacchus

A Novel

Eric Jay Sonnenschein

Hudson Heights Press
New York

Ad Nomad, the Case Histories of Dane Bacchus
© 2011 by Eric Jay Sonnenschein

ISBN: 9780983194743

For my wife, Marilyn and my daughter, Amanda

Rob:
First book
to you,
my friend,
with the,
wild ideas,

Acknowledgements

I wish to thank my wife, Marilyn Oran Sonnenschein, for her unwavering support and help, my daughter, Amanda, for designing the cover of this book, and Ralph Gabriner for the photograph.

CONTENTS

"The great decisions of human life have as a rule far more to do with the instincts and other mysterious, unconscious factors than with conscious will and well-meaning reasonableness...Each of us carries his own life-form—an indeterminable form which cannot be superseded by any other." GF Jung

This novel is a work of fiction, not a record of fact. The situations, characters, locations, and institutions depicted here are products of the author's imagination, or used fictitiously. Any resemblance to events, institutions, locations, or people, living or dead, is coincidental.

AD NOMAD 1
THE OLDEST JUNIOR COPYWRITER IN THE WORLD

Case 1-A

PRE-EXISTING CONDITION

1. THE PASSION AND THE PARACHUTE

Dane Bacchus sat at his desk and faced the harvest of a spring semester, one hundred final exams to read. He told himself it was no big deal. He would pace himself, read ten—make it five—blue books, then break. He would take many breaks, so his mind would not wander—or overheat. At this rate, he would finish by sundown.

He picked up paper #1.

Crash! Bang! Boom! That is the sound of a auto accident. No, not an ordinary auto accident, but a alcohol related auto accident...

Maybe the reader should be drunk, Dane thought. But it was 10 AM and he didn't drink.

Driving under the influence of alcohol is deafinitely a serious offense. The reason is because some body could be hurt or killed. When people are drinking they get so drunk. Everything gets blurry.

Dane graded the test and moved to the next.

Students that plagiarizes a term paper or cheats on an exam should be given a written test to determine his or her failure of the class.

Sometimes plagiarism might be best, Dane conceded. He paused to indulge a moment of mind cleansing resentment. After twelve years at the university and as a full-time instructor for six, he was still teaching remedial sections. He coped with it only because it provided time to write. But now the seventh year loomed. After seven years, university rules barred him from a full-time job. He reread the letter from the Dean: "The committee agrees that Professor Bacchus is an enthusiastic and effective teacher, but the Handbook requires that the next year be his last."

He was so close to a literary breakthrough. If only he could keep his job for the foreseeable future, he would endure reams of academic ineptitude. All he needed was income enough to support his wife and young daughter. But no, the Handbook denied him!

Dane stared at the leaning tower of blue books, which seemed no shorter, despite his efforts. At least he had a job for one more year. He eyed the test booklet at the top of the pile reluctantly and delved into it. Dane sighed with relief. The student chose to write about "Flowers for Algernon." How bad could that be?

Self respect is something everybody's got to have. But when you have a learning or mental disability of reality, good luck with that. It's like self respect sometimes gets the rong image. In our society   people dont except you for who you are but more like what you are.

Enough! Dane scooped up the tower of blue books and heaved it. Tests landed in a disheveled heap on the bedroom floor. Dane concluded that if he flung the exams a thousand times, the result would never be as disordered as their contents.

"What's going on?" Becky asked. "Why are finals on the floor?"

"I had a meltdown," Dane explained.

"Then I shouldn't show you this. The health plan won't pay for that doctor's visit."

"What?" Dane read the document. Becky's last visit to a doctor, which Dane had insisted upon when she experienced dizzy spells, was not covered because his plan stipulated one checkup per year.

Dane stared at the explanation of benefits and at the blue paper around his feet, and considered his next move—toward the telephone in the kitchen. "This can't be right," he muttered. "I'll take care of it."

He dialed the university human resources department. He would remind them that it might be his last year but it was premature to pull the plug on his benefits. His conversation with human resources followed a familiar trajectory. He bewailed the unjust charge to an administrator whose most salient qualification was patience. She pointed out that his plan allowed only one wellness visit per year, which had been his choice. When Dane accepted culpability for his putrid lack of foresight, the woman rewarded him with the good news that he could modify his plan next year in an open enrollment period.

"But there won't be a next year!" Dane blurted.

Like a geyser, his truth spouted from the bedrock of denial. He knew it was futile to grovel for nonexistent security. Dead air filled the phone line like nerve gas. The human resources officer surmised that Dane was terminally ill or planning suicide. He, meanwhile, saw himself as a human lemming approaching a malevolent future in lockstep with an irrelevant past. The stable ground of a decade split under him. From its terrifying maw issued a harrowing question: What would he do next to support his family?

If he continued to teach, he could look forward to eking out a small and unstable income from several low-paying, part-time jobs at many institutions. He needed a new career but teaching was the only work Dane had done for years. Could he do anything else? He had no choice. His daughter was four, his family needed more living space and he was their sole support.

Desperation is a gale that shakes complex questions into simple answers. As Dane recognized the vast dimensions of his uncertainty, his mind was plunged into frenzy. Out of this chaos, came a moment of coherence and purpose. To quiet his nerves, he flipped through a magazine that had arrived in the mail. Facing an article on the sewers of Paris was an ad whose headline read: *Buses tell the best stories.*

"Becky, look!"

His finger jabbed the glossy page; his jaws twitched but he could not speak.

Becky looked over his shoulder.

"*Buses tell the best stories.* It's good. But it sounds familiar!"

"Because I wrote it! It's my ad!" Dane shouted.

From the sideboard he extracted his old zip up portfolio. "There it is, see? *Buses tell the best stories.*"

Years before, Dane had tried breaking into advertising and wrote this headline for his "book." It won his teacher's praise but no job came of it. Now the concept returned to taunt—or invite—him. Dane was bitter that his idea was stolen but he viewed it as a providential sign providing direction, even salvation. It was *the burning bus* exhorting him to stop teaching others to write, and to go forth into ADVERTISING.

Reasons against attempting this exploit piled as high as the blue books, but Dane was transfixed by the ad in *Global World* Magazine. The headline, *Buses tell the best stories*, decoded, meant YOUR FUTURE IS ADVERTISING. It was a message he could not ignore.

Case 1-B
THE ADVANGELIST

2. BODY ODOR MAKES A COMEBACK

Dane's previous attempt to break into advertising, fourteen years before, had come unexpectedly in the heat of inspiration and had died predictably in cold criticism and general indifference.

He was in a clerical position at *Lumbago Associates*, a small firm that sold advertising space in non-profit science magazines. It was his first full-time, dead-end job after scraping by as a writer and journalist, and he quickly learned that if he wanted to succeed and make more money, he, too, would have to sell ad space, which he despised. The only work Dane liked at *Lumbago Associates* was the occasional copywriting assignment that came his way when the partners were too busy to write. The copy often amounted to no more than 25 words about a lab product or device, but the task was vaguely creative and engaged Dane's interest.

His creativity awakened, Dane tore out magazine ads he admired and analyzed them. He foraged for photographs, wrote copy and rubbed on headlines from sheets of *Lettraset*. When he had done

6

fifteen ads, he bought a leather portfolio and looked for a job.

Dane cold-called major agencies and asked for "the creative director," but administrative assistants brushed him off like a gnat. After being telephone fodder, Dane modified his approach. He asked for creative directors by name and sent them his résumé.

One creative director offered Dane an interview. He claimed he had hired many men with unconventional jobs, including cab drivers, garbage collectors and morgue workers. Dane was euphoric for a week, but on the morning of the interview, his train was slow and he had to run a half mile from the station to the agency. Despite his strenuous effort to be on time, Dane arrived five minutes late, soaked in perspiration, only to be told his interviewer had gone to breakfast.

The creative director returned at 9:30. He was a suave, older man with thick, well-coiffed silver hair, stylish attire and a confident aura that exuded money and power like designer cologne. He seemed to step out of an ad! He probably had a silver *Porsche* or *Jag* to match his hair and impressed young women by driving it top down.

The dashing creative director welcomed Dane with an extended hand and guided him to his office. He apparently bore no grudge against his latest "street find" for arriving five minutes late.

When Dane was seated, the creative director talked about himself.

"I'm a learner, a lover, and a liar," he said, "Not necessarily in that order."

The creative director paused, expecting a witty rejoinder or at least a raucous guffaw from his junior copywriter candidate, but Dane emitted a nervous chuckle that resembled a cough.

The creative director rifled through Dane's book. He stopped at the *Heineken* ad, with its photograph of Dane in a tee shirt swilling from a bottle.

"Nobody wants to see a slob drinking beer," the creative director remarked.

"I thought slobs were the target audience for beer, sir," Dane

7

replied.

"Yes, but they don't *know* they're slobs. They think the drinkers of *other* beers are slobs."

"Oh, I get it," Dane said as he pretended to take notes with a pen he forgot to bring on an invisible piece of paper on his lap. He was miffed that the creative director called him a slob.

The creative director flipped through Dane's soup campaign, which featured Dane's girlfriend, Becky, smiling winsomely as she sipped a wholesome spoonful.

"Your sister's cute, but she could lose a few pounds," the creative director opined.

"She's not a model. She was doing me a favor," Dane replied, his face flushed with anger. How dare this man insult Becky! Dane wanted to leap on the desk and pummel the creative director in the dying name of chivalry, but he felt fairly certain that it would not help him get the job.

The creative director now focused on a men's cologne ad showing a man and woman on a beach. "This could be it," Dane thought. He barely breathed.

"This ad could help body odor make a comeback," the creative director predicted.

"You don't like two people in love walking on a beach, sir?"

"Not really," the creative director retorted bluntly.

The creative director closed the binder. "Dan, you need to be harder on yourself. I want you to go through this book and keep only the best work. Then do more ads like it."

3. VALEDICTORY BEER

Dane was encouraged. All he needed to land an advertising job was to write more and better ads. He enrolled in a *Network for Learning* class. His teacher was a copywriter named Hal Runny, a soft-spoken ex-journalist from Oregon with horn-rimmed glasses.

Hal rode his bike to work through rush hour traffic for a daily dose of life-and-death, which he claimed "added flavor to his burger."

Hal was more than an advertising teacher; he was an *Advangelist* and his class was a revival.

The *Advangelist* imbued his four students with respect for the inner reality of package goods, the lives they touched, the problems they solved and the benefits they conferred. Speaking in proverbs that zinged like headlines, he taught that "products are more than useful items on grocery shelves, but living brands that fulfill the lives and illuminate the minds of consumers and manufacturers!" It was, he affirmed, "the copywriter's noble task to make brands manifest to the world." Hal described with homespun solemnity the comparative goodness of a *Wendy's* burger, the pathos of his wife's *dishpan hands* and his gratitude for the dishwashing liquid that protected them with healing aloe.

Hal's promotional zeal filled Dane with the spirit of advertising. He now had the conviction that brings vitality to ambition. Dane was so inspired by the *Advangelical* approach that he signed up for a second session. This was when he had a conceptual breakthrough. He created three campaigns for his book. The best was for *Happy Trails Bus Lines*. It was a series of Americana photos from the '50s: a hipster on a bus, a diner waitress and a geezer with his fiddle. The headline read: "Buses tell the best stories" and the body copy told each person's reason for being on that bus: adventure, ambition, pleasure. Hal immediately perceived Dane's quantum leap. The *Advangelist* proclaimed that the advertising gods had smiled on his apostle and called the bus campaign an act of genius. During the last class, Hal told Dane he was "ready to go out there and get a job." To celebrate, the mentor invited the protégé to a neighborhood bar for a valedictory beer.

In a dark *Blarney Stone* tavern, the veteran copywriter imparted to Dane his ultimate thoughts about advertising and media. "You know what scares me most?" Hal said. "While we sit here swilling beer, people's perceptions of reality are being warped by self-absorbed Hollywood types, who lie around swimming pools and have no sense of reality. In advertising, we use the most popular of these bogus perceptions to sell products."

A silence settled over the two men in the bar as Hal's dark wisdom fermented in Dane's mind. The mentor's deflating rumination was not the uplifting send-off Dane expected. "You really believe advertising is warmed over crap?" Dane asked. "You always sounded positive about what you're doing. How can you believe in it, if you think it's a lie?"

"How could I not?" Hal countered quietly. "There's truth in lies."

"What are you saying?" Dane asked the *Advangelist*. The protégé stared hard at his mentor. Was it possible that the worm of cynicism had subverted Hal's beautiful faith in the redemptive power of products and unique sales propositions? Dane was taking *Advangelism* too seriously. He could not straddle a contradiction and move forward; he could not admit he was in a venal pursuit, motivated by greed. He needed to believe he was embarked on a noble and worthwhile enterprise. Perhaps noting the deranged zealotry in Dane's eyes, Hal fine-tuned his message.

"Believe it or not, even minds and hearts corrupted by non-stop deception respond to a clearly-stated truth," Hal said. "That can be your mission, your niche. Dane, I've had by-lines on award winning articles, but they pale next to writing a great campaign. You're capable of great work. So go out there and do it."

Out of the bleakness of his vision of pool-side apocalypse, Hal found the perfect pitch to call Dane to action. In short, he was a professional ad man.

"I'll give it all I have," Dane promised.

Brimming with pride and conviction, Dane phoned the creative director who had seen his book to set up a second interview. Dane was teaching mornings at a business school, so the creative director agreed to meet him at 2 PM. Dane arrived twenty minutes early to show that he had learned lesson #1 about being on time. At two o'clock the receptionist dialed the creative director's extension. No answer. "He probably hasn't returned from lunch. He should be here shortly."

By 2:30 the creative director was still out.

His assistant emerged. She said she had no idea what happened to the creative director. Dane saw this as a test and chose to wait. At five o'clock, agency people rushed through the reception area. They glanced at Dane with curiosity and pity. The creative director's assistant came out in her coat.

"You're still here?" she asked.

"I was supposed to meet the creative director and no one called to cancel," Dane replied.

"He was out for the afternoon," she said. "So I guess the meeting's cancelled."

Dane left with the assistant, who seemed neither shocked nor sympathetic about his predicament. Dane, however, was confused. What message was the creative director trying to send him? Should he phone the man and ask for another meeting? As Dane grappled with these questions, he asked himself a more general one: how did he feel about the way the creative director treated him? Was this the norm in advertising?

Dane did not let the creative director's brush-off deter him. He continued to peddle his portfolio to find that elusive first job. He interviewed with a rising woman copywriter, who asked him to converse with her in baby talk for a car ad she was working on. Dane said he did not know baby talk and left her office without a job. He was actually fluent in baby talk, but for him it was the language of love and he spoke it only with Becky.

Advertising remained an impassible frontier for Dane. He found a teaching position. In three years, he and Becky married, and five years later, they had a daughter.

Case 1-C

MADISON AVENUE COCKTAIL

4. THE ORACLE

More than a decade had passed since Dane's last pass at advertising. It was always a tough field to break into and probably no easier now. Dane ransacked his memory for one advertising professional he could call to advise him how to proceed or whether to proceed at all.

One name came to mind. Thor Kevorksen was someone Dane knew marginally from college. They became better acquainted at an alumni cocktail party after they graduated. During their 40-proof conversation, Kevorksen revealed how he landing his first job—by imitating a seal at an interview. At that time Dane wanted to write books and movies. Kevorksen chortled that books and movies were more elaborate forms of advertising—money-making entertainments devised to exploit human emotions.

If Dane reached Kevorksen, he would tell him, "You were right," and Thor would surely help him because people like nothing more than to have their judgment validated. But since the debate occurred twenty years before, Kevorksen had probably retired. Even if he was still in the industry, the odds were against finding him at the same agency.

When Dane phoned Kevorksen that afternoon, he viewed the call as an instrument of fate like *I Ching* or a *Ouiji Board*. If Kevorksen was the rare person who stayed at the same agency for twenty years, Dane would read this as a sign that his cockeyed plan could succeed. If Kevorksen was unreachable, Dane would seek another career. He phoned the agency and asked for Thor. Without hesitation, the operator connected him, and half a ring later Kevorksen picked up and blurted his name, "Thorkvorksen!" so fast that he did not swallow the two names so much as rear-end one with the other.

It was a miracle that his one contact was the most stable man in advertising and Dane could not contain his euphoria. In this one sign, Dane read his destiny and his success. He identified himself with a dramatic gasp and pause, as if his name were the answer to Kevorksen's unspoken question. Kevorksen recalled Dane but before he could abort the conversation, Dane's mouth went into overdrive. He told Kevorksen the entire back-story behind this impromptu interruption of his day. Thor responded with rapid, caffeinated "Uh huhs," and "Yeah, yeahs," which anticipated a redemptive punch line to a long setup. Dane sensed that the conversation was going well but he had to deliver his message. Closing his eyes, he dropped his bomb.

"I want to get into advertising!" Pause. "But I'm probably too old to start, right?"

"You're not too old. Your timing is excellent," Kevorksen replied. "Remember, the largest audience is our generation."

Of course! Why hadn't Dane thought of it? They were *baby busters*, the baby boomers' younger siblings, who tagged along to demonstrations but were too young to be drafted, who listened to '60s music but were too young for love-ins, who inherited the counter-culture like a cool hand-me-down only to store it away in the conservative era of deflated expectations and conformity that ensued. They missed the war but suffered its aftermath—an economic slow-down fueled by higher gas prices, a larger workforce and fewer jobs. They were underachievers, regardless how hard they tried.

Now by a brilliant twist of history, the demographic that made it hard for Dane to get a job at 22 might sustain him when he was 42. Once Kevorksen confirmed that Dane's hunch about an advertising career was not delusional, he offered to review Dane's "book." Thor proposed and cancelled many meeting times but delay did not discourage Dane. It enhanced his intuition that he had made a powerful contact. A date was finally set for a month later. Dane fantasized, against years of contrary experience, that one meeting with Kevorksen would land him a job.

5. THE AGE OF TIN

Exhilarated by the possibility of a new career, Dane poured over books about advertising, including the classics—*Reality in Advertising, Confessions of an Advertising Man,* and *From those Wonderful Folks Who Brought You Pearl Harbor.* He learned that he was not falling into a volatile and tawdry business, but a venerable industry with a long tradition, aesthetic standards, and a canon of lore. With his new field came fresh purpose and a new *Valhalla* of heroes. His enthusiasm grew as he discovered that advertising was more than non-stop drinking, spouting headlines between belches, and hallucinating brand characters before passing out. It was psychology, sociology, cultural anthropology. This widely reviled field rewarded hard work, respected intelligence, and indulged the eccentricity and freedom associated with creativity.

Dane's neighbor, Doris, was an advertising copywriter. Doris looked perpetually harassed. However, given the embryonic state of his fresh ambition, Dane took care not to infer her unhappy appearance from her occupation. Doris had studied puppetry and Cro-Magnon semiotics, not writing or business. She started on Madison Avenue comparatively late in life, taking night classes at *The Institute of Design* and landing her first job in her late 30s. Yet, despite her belated start and brief career, Doris had some prestigious positions on her résumé. Since Dane was past his 30s, knowing another late-starter made his goal seem tangible. The most inspirational and irrelevant of questions doubled his resolve, "If she can do it, why can't I?"

How many ill-fated plans start with this competitive query! So many reasons may explain why another person is doing what you are not—aptitude, viewpoint, a personality trait, family background, an academic pursuit, or work experience that provides special insight about a product or marketing, in general. Or luck.

When Dane encountered Doris in the neighborhood, he

rhapsodized about his advertising aspirations, brimming over with all he was learning about the field. He shared anecdotes and theories from books he read and asked Doris to describe her experiences. She responded to his exuberance with a pitying expression that implied, "You poor fool!" She told the fable of her big break, how after four courses, she had a teacher who liked her work and recommended her for a position. Doris recounted this without affect as if ticking off events that led to a coronary bypass.

"I don't get it," Dane said. "You've got the best job in the world and you're miserable. You're paid to think and write creatively every day and always about something different. Advertising is the most creative profession. Writers use words. Artists use colors and design. Movie-makers use film. But a copywriter uses them all and writes ads, billboards, letters, brochures and commercials."

Doris stared at Dane through her large glasses with a buzz-killing gaze. "You're excited about a new career. You read about advertising in its golden age. But I'm in the trenches, doing car dealership ads. Believe me, it's no golden age. It's the age of tin. And I'm the goat."

Doris's disillusionment was no antidote to Dane's ardor. He thought she was "playing it cool" because she was in a club he wanted to crash. He envied his neighbor's nonchalance about something he craved so badly. A perquisite of getting what you wanted was that you could be cynical about it. He wondered if the day would ever come when he would be blasé about advertising. He promised himself it would never happen. If he was ever hired as a copywriter, he would never take the job for granted.

As Dane absorbed the lessons of great advertising thinkers—Rosser Reeves, David Ogilvy, George Lois, and Jerry de la Femina—he created new concepts to supplement the best ones from years before. He asked his university students to pose for him in jeans, sneakers and boots for a new apparel campaign to update his portfolio. He wanted to impress Thor Kevorksen.

6. THE EVALUATION

After several postponements, Dane went to the fabled ninth floor of one of the top ten advertising conglomerates in the world and sat on the low, black leather couches that sucked his body in like quicksand. The receptionist, a woman in her 70s, regaled him with stories of her fashion model youth back in the day. Thor Kevorksen emerged, nervous, spindly, with a pot belly and thinning blond hair. He raced toward Dane from across the lobby, his hand extended stiffly like a poker. He shook Dane's hand and led him back to his corner office.

"So it's been twenty years," Kevorksen said, "How've you been?"

"I'm alive."

"So I'm not hallucinating. *Quelle* relief! So...let's look at your book."

The warm segment of this reunion was over. Kevorksen was letting Dane know that their remote connection was good for a professional assessment of his work and some advice. Dane fumbled to open the portfolio. Kevorksen flipped the pages with nervous fingers; his eyes gave each concept intense scrutiny; they were not looking at or over, but into and behind, like x-rays. When he liked something, he asked Dane about it, or went, "Umm, nice." When he disapproved he made a terse remark. When he came to Dane's *GAS-X* ad in which Dane was photographed wearing a gas-mask, he said, "One rule in the antacid category is 'Don't make fart jokes.'" When Kevorksen came to Dane's toothpaste concept—of a great toothy dinosaur fish suspended from the ceiling of the Museum of Natural History—he declared, "Dinosaurs are death. They make products seem out of date."

Within two minutes, Thor had reviewed Dane's twenty pieces of creativity and closed the book. He looked at Dane seriously.

"So, you want to be in advertising."

"Yes," Dane replied, unbearably eager for Thor's appraisal.

"You want to sell soap and suppositories."

"More than anything."

"We go back a long way so I'll give you my short speech. When I started looking for a job, one interviewer asked what my college major was. I told him it was American Studies. 'Ah, good,' he said. 'Advertising *is* American studies.' He told me I'd learn more about America than I ever wanted to."

"What did you learn, Thor?"

"That America is a land of hemorrhoids and halitosis, of dry hair and oily skin, of bad gums and tooth decay, of high blood pressure and low energy. So why do you want to be in advertising, Dane?"

"To make money?"

Thor blinked and pondered for a moment. Dane wondered if it was the wrong answer.

"That works. So...your book...Half of this is amateurish drivel. A quarter of it is semi-decent and derivative. But a quarter of it shows promise. I like the bus ad."

"It was the first one I ever did—"

"—what you have here won't get you a job," Thor interrupted Dane to prevent him from feeling good about himself, "My advice is keep working on your book and take a course at *The Institute of Design*."

Dane was disappointed that Kevorksen would not even offer him a low-level, hands-on, junior job, but he could not argue with his one contact.

"Can I show you my new stuff when I create it?"

"Any time," Kevorksen said. "Come back in a few months."

7. SCHOOL FOR ADS

"How good do you want to be?" *The Institute of Design* challenged Dane on the subway train every day in January. Another ad with a sad harlequin consoled him, "Are you lost? We'll help you find yourself!" while another series of ads featured everyday artists—a man covered in tattoos, a graffiti artist with a spray can and a public wall, and a woman in a cluttered, wildly decorated apartment—urging him to "turn (his) genius into a job." Registration for the city's colleges and universities was in full swing, and *The Institute of Design*, widely known as *ID*, always produced the most compelling ads with messages that penetrated the static in the brain and stirred it with desire.

ID was an unavoidable proving ground for a job in advertising. Various people in the business had advised Dane that he must go there to learn the craft and make indispensable connections. Dane balked each time. *ID* classes were taught by Madison Avenue professionals, a notoriously cynical and vituperative cadre. They had seen it all and would have the power to anoint or destroy people for sport. Dane was never willing to put his ego in this all-or-nothing situation, but now that he faced unemployment, his ego would have to fend for itself.

Dane attended an open house for the advertising program at *ID* on a cold January night. The auditorium was SRO. Most of the crowd was in business attire, heading home from work. The mood in the room was fraught with anticipation, exhaustion and discontent.

The program was supposed to open with a short video describing the vaunted advertising program. Lights, titles, music—*darkness*. After a few failed attempts to resuscitate the obligatory, ice breaking, crowd-inspiring video overture, the lights came on and two speakers were introduced. The first to speak was a creative director of art: a bald, intense man, modestly dressed and soft-spoken. The expression in his eyes suggested that he spoke to his audience from a great distance—the far end of a long career. He delivered a succinct account of his long, circuitous path to his current position and admitted that on most days he performed tedious, uncreative tasks. But after a day of "killing work" he sometimes had time to immerse himself in a creative project that redeemed the tedium.

The art director concluded his talk with a short discourse on the use of pattern and discontinuity in art direction to make ads "pop." It was an unassuming and persuasive performance.

The second speaker, a copywriter in his late 20s, slouched in his seat and never left it. His shaved head hung from his neck and he shielded his eyes from the lights to protect a hangover. His cheeks were mottled by razor burns and stubble and a wrinkled shirt billowed over his torso and the wide, tomato-stained thighs of his jeans. His appearance, so far exceeding studied neglect, suggested that rules of business appearance no longer applied to him since he belonged to an elite caste, obeyed a higher authority, and possessed a freedom that exempted him from cleanliness and sobriety.

The copywriter stumbled and mumbled through his introductory remarks as if talking gibberish to himself, and punctuated each inarticulate passage by scratching his crotch. On first impression, this lack of preparation was calculated to offend his listeners with how little they would learn from him. The ultimate effect, however, was to reach deep into the longings of his audience, trapped in their service-economy conformity and restraint. He held out an elusive promise—that if his listeners were good enough they could also be slobs with impunity. In advertising, how you looked meant nothing and what was in your head and in your heart, everything. Through studied sloth, the copywriter conveyed another less appealing truth: a creative had no time for personal grooming. One must turn over one's soul day and night to market-driven demons. This was performance advertising and he was an animated billboard for the life and lifestyle of an advertising creative—The Rock Star Copywriter.

Suddenly, like thunder rumbling in a fog, the Rock Star Copywriter raised a strong voice steeped in righteous belligerence. "I, too, was once, confused about my career path!" he cried, startling the dormant crowd. "I was bitter and angry. I drank too much. I was desperate for a job that didn't make me want to kill people, including myself. Was it possible to pay bills and express my inner being? I had no idea but I was willing to die finding out. I was like you!"

He squinted and pointed out into the semi-dark auditorium in an accusatory manner that made Dane respond, "I hope not."

"My father was a fireman," The Rock Star Copywriter continued. "Maybe that's why I had a burning need to create. I lived at home, worked as a traffic guy in an agency, and schlepped all day, pushing jobs around from office to office. Man, was I pissed! I wasted a lot of time and money in bars, drinking and carelessly throwing darts. Some actually hit people and I had to do community service."

The Rock Star Copywriter paused for the light, nervous laughter that rose from the audience like the last carbonated bubbles from a flat soda. "But then one day my life changed. I was reborn. My mom started it. She said, 'Sonny, you always had a way with words...why don't you write for a living?' So I bought a book called *So You Want to Be a Creative,* by Margaret Dumont, the Hall of Fame creative recruiter. I read it cover to cover and then backwards. Yeah, that's right! And if you're not totally brain-dead *when I'm finished talking* you'll get your butts over to the nearest Barnes and Noble and buy it, too.

"I did what the book told me to do.

"I enrolled in *The Institute of Design* and that's what you'll do if you're smart. I'll never forget it. My first teacher was this little bald Greek guy. Our first assignment was to go home and write a campaign. I stayed up nights, beating my brains out for concepts and headlines. When I showed up for the next class, I was damn proud of what I'd done. So the little Greek guy points at the wall. 'Who did this ad?' he asks. He was pointing at my concept. I was so excited, I nearly pissed myself. 'I did it,' I croaked. 'This is the worst piece of shit on this wall,' he said. 'No, it's the worst piece of shit I have ever seen!' He tore my ads from the wall and ripped them up so slowly I could hear each paper fiber split. Then he tossed the bits of paper in the air so my work showered on me like confetti.

"I was depressed and humiliated. I didn't want to go back. I thought I was a deluded piece of crap, but my mom warned me I'd better not quit—I had talent and *more importantly* she paid for the class. So I did the next assignment and put my concepts on the wall. The little Greek guy looked over all the work and he pointed to one concept. 'Who did this?' he demanded. It was mine. 'This is the best work on the wall. No, it's the best I have ever seen from a student!'"

"And it was the same concept from the previous week," The art director onstage interjected.

The audience laughed. Was this rehearsed? The Rock Star Copywriter scowled.

"I took four classes here, got my book together and had four offers before I was finished. This business has lifted me higher than I've ever been and it's dropped me lower than I ever thought I could sink. One week I'm shooting a commercial in Malibu, staying in the bungalow where four major celebrities OD'ed; the next, I'm fired and on my ass in the street. Through it all, I never stopped believing in myself or forgot I was a creative. It may mean nothing in this world but in this business, it's everything. Once you're a creative you're a creative all the way.

"I was interviewing at *Applebaum and Flinder* with the top guy— ya know, Flinder. I'd already had a few interviews, so I'm in his office, thinking Famous Flinder's gonna make an offer. He looks at one ad, shuts my book and says, 'I hate your work. It's not very good.' He expected me to leave with my legs between my tail. Well, I got up and shouted in his face, 'You think you're God and everybody's an ant you can step on. Well, I'm no ant and you can't step on me!' So he said, 'You're hired.'"

"And he put you on the Raid account," the art director quipped.

The silence in the auditorium shattered into hundreds of pieces of laughter while the Rock Star Copywriter glowered.

"I love my life. You know how I spend my day? Ten o'clock I get to the office. I eat a Danish, have my coffee, and look over the paper. At eleven, I play Frisbee in front of the office building. Afternoons I go to meetings and take in a movie. At six, I eat lunch. In the evening, I start writing. And I go until dawn. Creativity is my life. I feel like the luckiest guy in the world that I get paid to create something that has never been before. That's what it means to be a creative and that's why I love it. I guarantee that if you take my class you can call me at three in the morning to tell me your great idea. And just one more thing—when people tell me, 'Advertising isn't brain surgery' I totally disagree. You see, what I do is like brain surgery. If you're going to be successful in this business you'd better know your way around the human brain."

"Everybody wears scrubs where he works," the art director quipped. The audience laughed. The show was over.

The Rock Star Copywriter fielded questions. Dane asked if he thought it could take ten classes at *ID* "to finally get it" and write concepts that would get him hired. The Rock Star Copywriter replied that if it took ten classes Dane should think about another line of work. Then he added that an intelligent guy like Dane should be able to do it in three classes, or even two. "If you can do it in one, you must be a genius."

"Then I'll just have to be a genius," Dane thought. He would soon be out of a teaching job and one class at *ID* was all he could afford.

8. CLASS ACTS

The open house did not encourage Dane, but an advertising class was unavoidable, so he perused the catalogue for a course that seemed right for him. It was imperative to choose well since he had little time to work with and less money to invest.

The course titles were bizarre. *Create Naked* declared that "fresher than fresh breath won't help. You need a book that will win respect..." Another course, *The One*, assured transcendence over hard reality, "Fifteen books an hour come across the creative director's desk each day. So you want to be *The One*?" Still another, titled

Maximum Exposure, promised that guest creative directors would review student work. "We can't guarantee a job but you never know. After all, why have a killer book if you can't get the right people to see it? A warning followed: "No head cases or slackers." This course cost the most—and it was closed.

Create Naked intrigued Dane. It was taught by Perry Winkel, a creative supervisor at *Gadwyn, Dinkinger and Mirmalino,* an award-winning boutique agency Dane never heard of. In his blurb, Winkel admonished his readers that "when you go into the big interview you are always naked, whether you wear *Armani* or *Levis.* A firm handshake, super-white teeth, and a shoe shine will not land your dream job. This course will teach you how to create smart, job-winning ads every time."

As a college professor, Dane had written course descriptions. He recognized in Winkel's paragraph a balance of Madison Avenue flash and academic thoughtfulness. It exploited a common fear: who never had the humiliating dream of being naked in a public place? Yet under the hucksterism was a commitment to teach advertising like serious writing.

Dane dialed Winkel. A meek, nervous voice answered. Its tone was not tough and provocative like the course description but quavering and fragile. Perry assured Dane that his class would include exercises to overcome writer's block. He cupped the receiver to tell a colleague, *'I'll be there in a minute. I'm on the phone!'* Winkel resumed his discussion with Dane in a taut whisper. "Massive layoffs...can't talk. But really, take this course. It'll be fun. I can help...give you job hunting tips." Dane said *Create Naked* was at the top of his list. "Okeedokee," Perry Winkel replied and hung up. It was the deal-breaker. Dane could not take a class with anyone who said, "Ookeedokee."

For two weeks, Dane searched for a class. After several calls and unanswered voice mails, Dane finally made a solid contact. Brandon Houlihan, who taught a class titled *Creative Clinic,* worked on major accounts at *BYOB*, a hallowed agency. Houlihan sounded like a warm and congenial human being, not an irascible psycho poseur. "This is the guy you would want to work with," Dane thought. He reviewed the course description. Three creatives would teach the class—a creative director, a senior art director and a copywriter. Having three teachers appealed to Dane. Three opinions of his work gave him better odds against ego demolition.

Dane tried to register but the class was full. The *ID* administrator said he would need the instructors' permission to enroll. Dane saw this obstacle as a sign that he had found a popular course with the right teachers.

It was a bitterly cold winter. The class convened east of Second Avenue—three trains and a long walk—at 6 PM. In shoe-boots with long toes and raised heels, Dane pounded the sidewalk like he was trying to leave his footprints in the concrete. Advertising was his only career option and he faced extinction. Middle-aged and starting over, he would submit his talent to notoriously arrogant people with tyrannical views and vague aesthetics. Desperate to succeed, Dane resolved to ace this class and impress the teachers. But he would need toughness and resilience to learn from the class without being damaged by it if it went badly.

9. THE THREE STOOGES

Dane entered a large, bleak room that must have once been an art studio. It was full of people in business attire, waiting for the teachers to show. After fifteen minutes, three husky men traipsed into the room in single file—short, medium and tall. The oldest, shortest and roundest of the three was Dick Billings, the creative director. His face was red, not from windburn or exercise, but agitation. Dick wore a perpetual grimace, as if imminent disaster were his constant companion. The tallest of the crew was Buzz Dingblatz, a burly, curly-haired man with a pasty face and thick glasses, who looked like an extra in a disaster movie. The man in the middle was Brandon Houlihan, with whom Dane had spoken. He was dark-haired and robust, with the self-assurance of a prosperous bartender.

The three teachers bobbed and weaved before their eager multitude of students, avoiding one another like intelligent billiard balls. Dane saw that they were unprepared to teach the first class and were committing *timeocide*—mowing down the minutes with depraved indifference. They believed the first class was a waste since there was no student work to evaluate, but without planned remarks, exercises or handouts to fill the gap, they faced the perdition of teaching without a plan—they had to improvise.

The troika delivered their autobiographies and recounted anecdotes about the quirks of the business. Buzz Dingblatz, the art director, worked his way into the major agency from a design studio. His partner, Brandon Houlihan, was a traffic coordinator when Dingblatz lost his partner. Houlihan's boss asked Buzz, "Why don't you give this guy a shot?" Buzz and Houlihan were so compatible that clients asked if they were married.

The creative director, red-faced Dick, talked quietly out of the side of his mouth, like one half of him had something to say the other half did not want to hear. The highlight of the first class was Dick's story about a commercial he wrote featuring a smart dog and a TV star. The commercial was smart and funny and had *Clio* written all over it. The product manager loved the spot and they found a brilliant canine to star in it. Then, just before the shoot, the client insisted on hiring his favorite TV star, an action-oriented actor, famous for car chases and stunts, to play opposite the smart dog.

"It ruined the commercial," Dick moaned, "The actor was unprofessional—and bad—while the dog was spot on. He was a consummate professional and would get this resigned look, as if to say, 'Why me?'

"Hard as we tried, we couldn't salvage it. Afterwards, friends in the business would say, 'Great spot! But what's the actor doing there?' Every time I think of it, it gets me right here." Dick tapped his chest and winced. "But that's our business. Heartbreak and acid indigestion are occupational hazards. It's tough getting great work done—or even good work. When it happens it's a miracle. But we keep fighting. I tell my guys all the time to keep their heads up, no matter how many times they get shot down."

The first assignment was to promote a music and video superstore on Times Square. The three teachers dismissed the class with the exhortation, "Go out there and write good ads!"

After the first session, the teachers signed Dane into the class, and he wasted no time optimizing his opportunity. The ensuing afternoon, he reconnoitered the superstore, took photographs, and carefully observed its dimensions and offerings, then devised not one but three campaigns, each with a different tone and mood.

The second class had the voltage of an opening night. Every student hoped to be the one who "had it," for the teachers from BYOB to be "blown away" by their work. Concepts were taped to the walls. One by one, Dane's classmates were disabused of their dream of "making it," slammed by criticism and ridicule. When the teachers came to Dane's nine ads on the wall, they asked who had done them all. Dane proudly raised his hand, believing his industry would be commended.

"Don't ever do three campaigns again!" Dick, the red-faced creative director, rebuked him.

"I'm sorry," Dane replied. "I didn't know which direction was best. I hoped you'd guide me. In Confessions of an Advertising Man, David Ogilvy advised going into a presentation with more than one campaign."

"David Ogilvy?" Dick grimaced as if Dane had activated his heartburn. "You're comparing yourself to David Ogilvy?"

"I was just taking a page from his book," Dane said.

"Is David Ogilvy teaching the class?" Buzz Dingblatz, the burly art director, asked.

"I don't see him here," Houlihan, the dart-playing copywriter, added.

The three teachers "critiqued" Dane's work on the wall. They were energetic and organized in their assaults. They focused on Dane's "redeeming social value concept," in which a suicide hotline operator, a cop and a psychiatrist each claimed in a rhyming headline how the superstore reduced suicide, crime and depression in New York.

"Is the rhyming headline your attempt at rap?" Dingblatz, the art director, jeered.

"It's a mnemonic device," Dane said.

"A moronic device?" Dingblatz chortled.

"Mnemonic. It helps people remember."

"Rhyme is never used in ads," Houlihan, the beer-bellied copywriter, added.

"Isn't that a good reason to use it?" Dane asked.

"Not if it's bad rhyme," red-faced Dick, the creative director, joined in. "Anyway, suicide, crime and mental illness should never appear in ads. It's in bad taste."

"When did taste become a benchmark for advertising?" Dane asked. That stopped the argument.

"Just don't do three campaigns again," Dick Billings said.

Dane felt dejected and confused. After trying so hard to choose the right class, he found himself in a bloated cohort of 45 students with three instructors who thought little of his ability and hated him. But it was too late to change. Even if he did, what guarantee did he have that another teacher would be more receptive? Since calculation and chance brought him here, he would stay. He did not speculate that this experience foreshadowed worse to come.

For several weeks Dane dragged himself to class with ads he liked, which the teachers reviled. His one consolation was that they were tough on other students, too. Maybe they were captious in order to weed out thin-skinned dilettantes. The next week confirmed his hypothesis. Fifteen students had dropped out.

Creative reviews were a clumsy ballet. The three teachers paced and ambled with enough lumbering agility not to crash into each other while dissecting the creative offerings on the wall. Each critique was a springboard for personal tangents about people, incidents and favorite ads. The teachers' free associations were so *free* that after 10 minutes, they paused, blinked and asked which ad they were assessing.

This was slapstick education so Dane dubbed them "The Three Stooges."

Yet while Dane belittled the three instructors, he wanted nothing more than to be anointed "The Fourth Stooge." He tried to make himself more likeable by asking questions after class. His stratagem seemed to pay off. Red-faced Dick, the creative director, praised one of his ads as smart and funny. "If you can do 11 more ads like this I can find you a job at any agency," he told Dane.

Dane would have been ecstatic about Dick's good review if he understood why the captious creative director liked this particular ad, which he considered quiet and dry. At any rate, even if he could replicate one ad 11 times without being called a self-cloning *El Redundo*, didn't repetition kill creativity?

Despite his reservations, Dane viewed Dick Billings' approval as a propitious sign that he was "getting it," which prompted him to send a query letter to creative directors in 50 agencies, including Billings, soliciting an entry-level job. After one class, red-faced Dick told Dane that he had received the letter and pointed out to him that he misspelled David Ogilvy's name. This seemed more significant to him than the content of the letter, which he characterized as "cheeky." Dick told Dane that he should find the right way to sell himself.

"How do I do that?" Dane asked eagerly, sensing that at last he would learn something of value.

"Sell yourself. Not your shirt," red-faced Dick replied, flicking

Dane's baggy chemise with disdain.

10. THE ALIENATOR

For several weeks, the class lurched toward its conclusion without incident. Dane's concepts received favorable but tepid notice that made him feel less than optimistic about his prospects. He tried to get on the teachers' good sides, but their bad sides were turned to him at all times. Worry and frustration overwhelmed his internal filtration system and reached toxic levels.

Dane became needlessly contentious. During one session the class discussed an assignment for a GPS tracking system. One student wrote the headline, "Map-makers hate our guts." "The Three Stooges" thought this idea was brilliant since they claimed that most people hated reading maps. That did not sound right to Dane.

"What about the nine million members of the *National Geographic Society* who love maps?" he asked. "The NGS even offers one as a premium."

Houlihan, the copywriter, was furious. "That's what's wrong with this class. There are too many lawyers. Who cares about *National Geographic* readers? What the fuck does that have to do with a GPS?"

"Plenty," Dane replied, "*National Geographic* readers are affluent and likely to travel. Market research would probably target them as your audience. And don't forget the millions of AAA members. They're also avid map-readers."

"*That's it, I've had it. We're the teachers and if you don't like it here, then leave!*" red-faced Dick cried, his flush deepening to crimson, his neck pulsing like an infection.

"I paid for the class," Dane objected. "You're teachers. Do you expect us to passively agree with everything you say and never ask a question or make a relevant point? What kind of education is that? I'm raising a legitimate advertising issue and you're going ballistic. You have to know your audience, right?"

They rolled their eyes and told him he was "full of shit." They would not physically eject Dane and he would not be intimidated.

Meanwhile, the other students did not understand Dane's attitude. They did not demand give-and-take in a creative class. They had a mature view of advertising. They saw it as a business. Bosses gave orders and underlings carried them out—without discussion—or were fired.

Dane viewed this protocol as anti-creative. He saw "The Three Stooges" as corporate tyrants and his cynical peers as poseurs, who craved creative jobs but lacked *creative* spirit. They in turn saw Dane as a self-defeating trouble-maker.

This peer animosity finally surfaced in class. Buzz Dingblatz , the burly art director, perused one of Dane's dog food concepts and said, "I know you guys don't want to hear this, but I like this ad."

Now it was as big as a billboard: The advertising class hates Dane. It was not surprising. Many of his classmates worked long hours in low-level agency jobs and did not always do the assignments. They thought Dane did extra to show them up or to psyche them out, and took revenge by complaining about him. They asked the teachers if "something could be done" about Dane. "The Three Stooges" did all they could to accommodate these concerned students by discouraging him consistently and by vigilantly denigrating his work.

Eventually, Dane could bear it no more. Hostilities erupted with the tourism ads.

Dane believed he would ace the tourism assignment. He selected a country where he had served in the Peace Corps, so he knew the subject well—a prerequisite to great advertising. He tried various approaches, focusing on adventure, food and interactions with people—all reasons tourists pay thousands of dollars on their vacations.

"The Three Stooges" loved an ad promoting Turkey. A student had sketched a tourist bending over as a Turkish soldier inserted an automatic weapon up his butt. "The Three Stooges" laughed hilariously at this. Dane saw the lewd appeal of the cartoon, but did not understand why seeing someone sodomized by a gun would persuade anyone to visit Turkey. Later, red-faced Dick reviewed Dane's ads, which showed tourists interacting with native people and indigenous animals, and blurted, "I can't figure these out."

"Imagine a gun up someone's ass and you'll get it," Dane gibed.

"These ads suck!" Dick shouted, "If Val Sambucca taught this class he'd light a match to them and hurl them out the window."

"Yeah, a *Madison Avenue Cocktail!*" Buzz Dingblatz intoned, giving Dick a high-5.

"I'd like to see you try," Dane muttered.

11. MADISON AVENUE COCKTAIL

The next week "The Three Stooges" brought in a fourth man.

"We've invited a special guest," Dick announced. "You've heard of him. Who hasn't? Give it up for Val Sambucca."

Val Sambucca, a.k.a. *The Flamethrower*, was the celebrated creative director from *Sambucca and Slivovitz*, the last independent high-concept boutique shop on the planet. He was famous for a car dealership commercial that showed a young couple driving down the highway in their vehicle with a male voice-over saying, "You are witnessing highway robbery. These people paid sticker price for their minivan..." Sambucca was notorious for abusing students at *ID* and creatives at his agency.

The class, reduced to a third of its original number, applauded loudly for *The Flamethrower*, a short, paunchy man with furtive eyes and a twisted proboscis that had encountered many fists. Sambucca flexed and pointed nervously on the balls of his feet and rubbed his nose vigorously. He looked voracious, yet food was not the object of his appetite. He was after *fresh ego*. Everyone in the room knew why he came. He was the hit man brought in to take Dane, his attitude, and his concepts down.

"Val's been on a teaching sabbatical and he told us at the *One Club* how much he misses classroom interaction. So we told him to come in and have fun," Buzz Dingblatz said.

Sambucca stammered a few perfunctory remarks. He was uncomfortable ad-libbing without a straight-man—the students' creative efforts. The legend abruptly turned to the concepts on the wall and started to critique. Before commenting on a campaign he asked who wrote it. After marinating a few ads in tepid bile, Sambucca glanced at the teachers for a signal. He came to Dane's work and the teachers nodded.

"Who did this ad?"

"I did," Dane said.

He stared at Dane. "What were you thinking?"

Dane started to explain his thought process when Sambucca interrupted. "I didn't ask you what you were thinking because I wanted to know what you were thinking. I asked what you were thinking, as in *'What the fuck were you thinking?'* To which the best response would have been, *'Not too fucking much!'* What is this? You call this a headline? This ad should not be on the wall. This ad should never have been conceived. This copy wastes the paper it's written on. It insults the tree that gave its life for the paper. This concept abuses the eyes that read it. Let's put this ad to good use."

Sambucca ripped Dane's ad from the wall, crumbled the paper, extracted his gold *Dunhill* lighter and struck the flint, emitting sparks and a reek of lighter fluid. As if protected by divine toner, Dane's crumpled ad failed to light. Sambucca flicked his lighter repeatedly until he burned the hairs on his forefinger and scorched a corner of the sheet. Before his concept was cremated, Dane leaped from his seat and lunged at Sambucca.

"Barbecue the ad and you eat it!" Dane yelled.

The Flamethrower had a reputation to protect and was impervious to threats. He took his pyrotechnics as seriously as Macy's on the 4th of July and did not relent. He applied his lighter flame again to the conceptual wad as Dane grabbed his arm. They struggled. Dane pinned Sambucca's wrist and the lighter fell from his hand. The five-time *Clio* winner smashed the charred, crumpled concept in Dane's face as if to make him eat his words. Infuriated by this upgrade in degradation, Dane wrestled his adversary to the floor, pinned his arms and stuffed the charred ad in the mad guru's mouth.

"Your work is not only bad, it tastes bad!" Sambucca shouted.

"In your garbage mouth everything tastes bad!" Dane retorted.

When the squirming and fisticuffs on the floor had abated, "The Three Stooges" pried Dane off of Sambucca.

"This man is in the Advertising Hall of Fame! You can be expelled from *ID* for this!" red-faced Dick ranted. "You'll never work in this town!"

"You and he can go to prison for what he did!" Dane replied. "Setting fires in a building with no working fireplace is arson! And everyone here is a witness!"

Neither Sambucca nor "The Three Stooges" ever considered the legal ramifications of their mischief. They now regarded one another with teeth-gnashing panic. Yet even when faced with possible felony charges, they invoked the First Amendment. They claimed that lighting student work and tossing it from windows was protected speech; furthermore, it was Sambucca's trademarked teaching style. "If the First Amendment doesn't protect you from shouting, 'Fire!' in a crowded room, it won't protect you from setting the fire," Dane pointed out. They grew quiet after that and red-faced Dick Billings reclaimed his sheepish, worried look.

They told Dane they would forget about the fracas if he would.

The fireball incident altered the mood of the class. By the last session in late April, only five students remained of the original 45. The room, once packed like a rush hour train, had become drafty. Just one student found the teachers' favor, a self-described hack, who drew concepts deftly with magic markers. Though Dane attended every session and completed every assignment, he had little sense of accomplishment, only pride in his diligence and stamina. He gave himself credit for not giving up like 40 others in the class, but thought that maybe he should have, since the consensus was that he would not succeed at this difficult, new career.

Dane left the last class by himself and headed west on 23rd Street, his gait less emphatic than ten weeks before. He had lost his swagger and looked beaten up, if not beaten down. He had fought *The Institute of Design* to a stand-off, but holding his own offered dubious consolation since the ordeal did not result in a job.

At one of the many corners Dane crossed that evening, another of the five class finishers stood next to him while they waited for the light to change. In ten weeks, Dane and this classmate never spoke but now they walked together and discussed their plans. Dane's fellow "alumnus" was a filmmaker who needed a real job. He had many friends in advertising and was more conservative in every way than Dane ever was. Before their paths diverged, the ex-classmate had a few parting words for Dane.

"One thing I'll say about you, man, is you're coming from a different place. That's a real advantage in this business. I didn't always like where you were coming from, but it was always original."

Dane received this comment as his final grade. It was a mixed review that promised conflict, difficulty and a happy ending. "The Three Stooges" gave Dane a B-.

Case 1-D
HAVE BOOK, WILL HIRE

12. SIX MONTH CHECKUP/2nd OPINION

After *The Institute of Design*, Dane felt prepared to revisit Thor Kevorksen and show him what he had done in six months. He was confident that Thor would be impressed by his commitment and offer him a job, or recommend him for one at his own agency. After a month of postponements, Thor finally sat with Dane in his office and flipped through his book. The old protégé watched his reluctant mentor blink, wince and furrow his brow. He measured each sporadic guffaw and cringed when Kevorksen shook his head sternly.

Moments later, Kevorksen closed the book with ritual precision and looked Dane in the eye.

"You've made significant progress," Thor said. "The book is getting there."

"Getting there?" Dane repeated like a sad parrot. "It's not there yet?"

"No. But you're close," Kevorksen nodded effusively.

Kevorksen maintained that Dane had three good campaigns, as opposed to the one he started with, but it was still not enough. Dane needed one more campaign and a few "one-offs" or single ads. In his financial uncertainty, Dane perceived "close" as a light year away. He controlled his dejection by exhaling in short puffs through his nose. Kevorksen noticed this and frowned with concern.

"Are you okay?" he asked his old protégé.

"Oh, yeah," Dane reassured him. "This is how I process bitter disappointment."

"Oh, that's neat," Kevorksen said. "But like I said, you're really close. There's a lot of good stuff. It just needs...a little more."

"Thor, that's great, but I mean, I wondered if I couldn't get an entry level job with my good stuff and then get better on the job...You know, I have a family and my teaching job is almost over."

Kevorksen smiled at Dane with wistful eyes and pursed lips, like he was about to tell a seven-year old he could not give him a cookie.

"No, that's not how it works, Dane. I wish it were. But *believe* me, when *it's there*, you'll get the job. All you need is tweaking and a more professional feel. You know, better art direction."

"That's all? How can I get better art direction?" Dane asked.

"You'll have to find an art director who'll work with you."

"Can you recommend anyone?"

"No. Sorry. All the art directors I know are so busy."

Dane thanked Kevorksen for his help but cursed him under his breath. It was his luck to have a mentor who saved the worst news till last and finished with one final daunting task. How would Dane find an art director if he did not work at an agency?

Doris, his depressed neighbor, had an agency job, so Dane asked her to recommend an art director. She said art directors she knew were too busy, but one studio artist might be available. He was always in trouble for changing art directors' layouts and making unsolicited design suggestions. Since he was angling to become an art director, he might be willing to work with Dane.

"That's terrific!" Dane replied. Doris looked at him quizzically, unsure why he was enthusiastic.

"He changes headlines and body copy, too," she reminded Dane, as if he had not understood the first time.

"That's okay. He's an ambitious underdog. He has passion, like me!"

Doris sighed.

"He's terrible but he's all I can come up with. Here is his contact information. Make sure he doesn't change your concepts or your words. If he does, call him on it."

13. THE SEAGULL & THE GARLIC KNOT

Lance Brubaker worked in the studio of Wyatt-Knight, a hip mainstream agency. The décor at Wyatt-Knight was someone's idea of the creative process, an adult's kindergarten nostalgia. Splotches of primary color covered the rubberized linoleum walls and floors as if buckets of poster paint had been heaved at them. The walls were festooned with crayon doodles and scarred by rubber bumps, craters, and fuzzy coral-like protuberances, making it resemble a synthetic vertical reef.

Contrary to most agencies, the Wyatt-Knight production studio was the neatest space in the complex. Lance Brubaker sat in the middle of it, a large, affable man insulated by earphones and sunglasses and hovering over his computer like a caveman over fire.

Lance and Dane strolled to the South Street wharf, occupied benches facing the harbor, chewed garlic knots, and mused on life. Lance said he hailed from a small Pennsylvania town, where he starred as a high school swimmer and soccer player.

"Swimming tore up my shoulder and soccer blew out my knee," Lance reflected. "But what hurt most was winter swim practice at 5 AM. That first dive in the freezing pool was like smashing into a pane of glass naked."

Lance's dad worked long hours at his butcher shop on Main Street. He loathed young Lance's addiction to TV and video games. "Ha! I learned everything I know today from TV and video games and I make more money than my old man ever did," Lance cracked ironically, heaving half a garlic knot on the river. "I still play video games, only now it's with *InDesign*, *Illustrator* and *Photoshop*. And TV is where I get my ideas."

A seagull swooped down and retrieved the garlic knot Lance had tossed on the water. The enterprising bird perched on a railing and pecked at the morsel as Dane and Lance reviewed each other's work. Lance liked Dane's concepts and agreed to help him bring the portfolio to a more professional level—with layouts and logos.

After their collaboration pact, the two men shared quiet time staring at the East River, which eddied and churned before them.

"I can't wait to be a full-fledged creative," Lance said. "Then I can act like my shit doesn't stink."

"Yeah," Dane agreed, as if this were a universal aspiration.

The seagull that nibbled Lance's garlic knot took wing and suddenly plunged into the churning river.

Dane and Lance rarely met after that first meeting. When Lance needed images for layouts Dane researched them at the Public Library. Dane enjoyed rummaging for photographs and was pleased when Lance approved the ones he found. Lance did not change Dane's concepts as much as Doris had predicted, except for the dog food campaign which "The Three Stooges" loved. Lance put the race dog pictures under filters so they were in lurid red, sickly black and white, and X-ray. He drained the color from the dogs' fur so they looked like ghoulish monsters.

Dane asked Lance to restore the colors but the designer resisted.

"You don't want race dogs in your book," Lance insisted. "You'd have the ASPCA and PETA all over your ass. Those dogs are gruesomely mistreated."

Dane met Lance in June and expected a professional-looking book and a job by fall. But the project, so close to completion in summer, dragged on for months. Lance was as hard to pin down as Kevorksen. Dane phoned his collaborator once a week but his calls were never returned. He wondered if Lance was angry, or wanted compensation. When he caught him on the phone after weeks of trying, he was so relieved that he forgot his anger. Dane brooked Lance's exotic excuses for not delivering the ads—strained thumb ligaments from a foosball tournament, a rare fungus contracted from his wife, a rash from agency toilet paper—since he could ill afford to antagonize him.

In mid-winter, nine months after the seagull died from the garlic knot, Lance said the portfolio was nearly done. Only one ad needed a final detail—*Buses tell the best stories*—which Dane had done in *The Advangelist's* class. Kevorksen claimed it was Dane's best. Now it needed a logo to make it look like a real ad and Dane had no idea where to find one. Then he recalled he had taken a long bus trip years before. Fortunately, Dane traveled so seldom that the bus tag with the logo was still looped around the valise handle. Even luckier, the *Happy Trails Bus Line* had not changed its logo. Dane clipped the tag and phoned Lance.

"So put them in the mail and I'll get them next week," Lance said.

"I need to get this done. I'll come up to your house," Dane

replied.

"You care so much that you'll come all the way up here? OK. I'll drop the logo into the layout while you wait."

Dane and Becky drove to Lance's house in Tarrytown. It was a cottage halfway up a steep hill. Its nicest feature was a skylight that made Lance's attic office bright and warm. Lance inserted the last detail on the first and best ad campaign Dane had ever done. Now the concepts looked like ads and Dane could shop the portfolio like he was serious about a job.

Lance had one more gift for Dane. It was the name of a creative recruiter, who had helped him in the past. Lance told Dane to use his name when he called her.

14. A SLAP IN THE FACE

Connie Melman's slogan was "I don't find jobs. I make careers." She worked for a recruiting firm in the Flatiron district where many agencies had migrated for cheaper space. Dane tried to relax in the waiting room. This would be the first time he showed off his new improved portfolio. He scavenged the coffee table by the couch for reading matter and found a new issue of *Ad Age*. A large post-it was affixed to it with a bold-faced message: "If you steal this magazine, you will never work again." Dane turned the pages of the magazine nervously. He was afraid that he would accidentally defile it and disqualify himself from future employment. He put down the magazine and kept himself loose by rubbing his jaws and slapping his face.

"When you get tired of doing that, may I have a whack?" Connie Melman asked.

Dane petted his face quickly and less sharply to make it seem that he was subjecting himself to a self-induced skin enhancement therapy.

"I saw it in *Maxim*," he said, so she would think he learned the behavior from a cool magazine, rather than making it up, himself.

Dane had no need to worry about authenticating his story because Connie was not listening. The petite, high-powered woman had no time to learn about his peccadilloes. She brought Dane to a small meeting room and trumpeted her life story while Dane waited for her to review his portfolio.

"So, first let me tell you about Connie. I've been in this business for twenty years. My husband's Mel Melman, the chief creative officer of GLOBOS, one of the biggest agencies on the planet. See the sign on the wall? Go on, read it! 'Beware of Connie!' Commit that to memory and live by it. I know everybody, so if you ever think of crossing me, stop thinking—or you will never, *ever* work anywhere. But Connie comes with benefits. I am extremely good to people I represent. I get them the best jobs and the most money," Connie paused. "So now you know about Connie. It's your turn. Where's your résumé?"

"I didn't bring one," Dane said.

"No résumé?" Connie asked with astonishment.

"I have no previous advertising experience so the résumé seemed irrelevant," Dane said.

"Irrelevant? *It's your friggin' résumé.* When is a résumé irrelevant at an interview?" Connie demanded irascibly. "Answer: *Never!* How can I talk to you if I don't know anything about you?"

"You could ask me questions?" Dane asked contritely.

"What were you thinking? I cannot believe a man of your age and experience would come to a meeting without a résumé."

Dane plunged from confidence to imbecility in seconds. He started to justify his thought process to show Connie how smart he really was, but this only confirmed his impaired judgment. She glared at him like he was a panhandler with bad breath and body odor. Dane stopped talking. It was unbearable for him to think he had blown this interview. How could he forget a simple thing like a résumé? He seemed wired differently from the people he dealt with. His only salvation was to be contrite and appeal to her humanity.

"I'm sorry. I thought it would be a presumptuous waste of your time to show you a résumé full of teaching jobs. Clearly, I was wrong to try to read your mind. But I brought my book, which I worked on with Lance. Can I show it to you?"

"What good is it with no résumé?" creative recruiter snapped.

Connie darted from the room to take a call and left Dane to wallow in remorse. Later she flipped through his portfolio like it was an old *Cosmo* in a hair salon and acknowledged that it was good. "Still, with no résumé there is no way I can present you to my clients," she said. "The market's tight. You're a beginner trying to break in. That's a tough sell. I have openings for elite, drop drawer, crème de la crème creatives—senior writers, creative directors. Juniors come in rarely."

"What would you advise me to do?"

"*Sell yourself,*" she said. "You have a good *gut.*"

"I do? How can you tell?"

"I feel it in my gut that you have a good *gut.* Use it."

As Dane left Connie's office he chided himself for squandering another chance. He had made a poor impression on an important recruiter and she would never help him. Connie *had* unexpectedly complimented his instincts, though such praise belied his failure to bring a résumé to their meeting. However, when Dane replayed the interview from the distance of a few city blocks, he agreed with Connie about his gut. The proof was ironically his missing résumé. Despite Connie's angry diatribe, she conceded that she could not help him since he lacked experience, which his work history confirmed.

The headhunter's rejection did not shake Dane's commitment to advertising. His toughness and self-belief would have made legendary football coaches and American self-help gurus proud. Despite a B- in his only class at *ID*, a mentor unwilling to hire or recommend him, and no recruiter to help find him work, Dane had no doubt he would succeed. Self-belief does not always feed on facts, but where does self-belief wander into self-delusion?

Had Dane crossed the line?

Case 1-E

INTERVIEWS, MENUS & A TAKE-HOME EXAM

15. FIRST INTERVIEWS

For their daughter's sixth birthday party, Dane and Becky could only afford to invite half of her kindergarten classmates. This led to civil war in the class, made mortal enemies of some parents, and complicated Iris's school days. Dane and Becky shielded her from this fall out, but Dane felt guilty for it. His work choices had harmed his daughter and his unemployment benefits were running out.

As Iris posed happily in her new velvet dress, euphoric about her party and oblivious to her family's money problems, Dane smiled through his guilt and assessed his options. He would market his two books—a novel and an ad portfolio—and grab the first opportunity he received. Dane took a sacred vow. If he found an advertising job first he would work at this career diligently for 20 years to support Iris until she was grown—and forget about his creative writing.

To fulfill this promise, Dane went on a job-blitz for two months. Dane put his "gut" into action. He had no leads so he cold-called several agencies. He often connected with an automated voice telling him that if he knew his party's extension, which he never did, he could dial it at any time, or hold the line and wait for the operator. When he managed to get through to live receptionists, he pumped them for names of creative directors, supplicated their assistants and delivered copies of his book—a small, vinyl binder with plastic sleeves. In reception areas where he left his book, he noted his competitors' slick, leather-bound, zippered binders and hard cases—and wondered if his modest offering could compete.

After weeks of cold response to his feverish effort, Dane felt like he was staring up the side of a skyscraper that must be scaled. At last, a human resources director phoned to arrange an interview. Dane was nervous and excited. He wore his one suit that was too tight and arrived at the agency a half hour early. The receptionist gave him an application form to occupy his time and a recruiter finally greeted him.

Dane wrestled with his facial muscles to hide his disappointment. His interviewer was a newly hired junior recruiter, nervous and unsure. She ushered him to an airless room, nodded vapidly at his book, posed probing questions like, "What was your favorite job and why?" and scribbled in the margins of his résumé. Dane wore a starched shirt. During the tedious interview, his back started to itch. At first, Dane rubbed his back against the chair like he had seen Baloo, the bear in Disney's *The Jungle Book* do. He thought he was being subtle but the junior recruiter's eyes widened as she watched him move up and down in the chair. Dane felt he needed to explain. "My shirt, it's got too much starch..."

She smiled tautly and said it was okay. But Dane knew it wasn't. His junior interviewer continued to ask him highly conceptual questions she must have learned in human resources camp, like what experience in his life fulfilled him the most.

"Besides scratching my back?" Dane joked. The junior recruiter did not laugh. Meanwhile his back itch persisted, so Dane reached around to scratch it. However, his sleeves were so tight that when he bent his arm, the underarm seam ripped loudly. He did not know how much he had damaged the jacket but the interviewer's stunned expression made him blush. Again, he felt compelled to explain. "I didn't do what you think I did. That was my sleeve ripping."

"No worries. We're almost done here," the junior recruiter said.

After a half hour, she drew a deep breath, told Dane this was a pre-screening interview, promised he would hear of any openings, and pressed the "down" elevator button for him. Dane tried to derive something positive from the fiasco. "Now you know what it's like to be a practice dummy," he told himself as he walked against the cold wind.

Each day Dane followed up with places he had left his portfolio. "Has my book been seen?" he inquired of creative managers, who replied that they heard nothing; the creative department was out; there were no openings; a hiring freeze was in effect. In his youth, this magnitude of indifference would have made Dane quit, but now he could not concede defeat. And despite the apparent futility of his quest, Dane was exhilarated, intoxicated by his despair.

16. CHINESE MENU

Doris, the depressed copywriter, once again provided a lift. She gave Dane the phone number of her favorite recruiter, Albert Griffin, a voluble New York native who took Dane's call and immediately complained about his heartburn. When Griffin interviewed Dane, he liked his book. He praised his ads for their humanity and maintained that one—a *Gas-X* concept in which Dane wore a gas mask—cut to the heart of heartburn.

"Really, is that you in the mask? It is! I see the resemblance. That ad is so good, so honest, *and so real.* I have to laugh. But it also gets me right here," Griffin said as he pressed his chest with his splayed palm and belched. "Ah. That's it. Excuse me. My bicarbonate just kicked in."

It was fitting that this *Gas-X* ad now gave Dane job-seeking relief. Griffin loved the same concept which Kevorksen, Dane's mentor, derisively dismissed as a lowly "fart joke." Dane felt vindicated; he had been right all along and everything he experienced up to this point seemed like gratuitous grief. This was what "clicking" with someone could do.

Griffin promised to help Dane. At the end of the interview the talent recruiter asked him if he was serious about advertising. One of Griffin's cousins had married a famous author, who wrote copy before publishing several bestsellers. Dane nodded wistfully at the anecdote and secretly hoped Griffin was foretelling his fate.

In a week, Griffin sent Dane on his first real job interview, at *Peebles and Rigoletto*—a reputable shop with award-winning creative. Dane interviewed with a veteran whose eyes were subdued by disappointment.

"Are you sure you want to be in advertising?" the weary veteran asked, "It's like wallowing in a pile of crap with worms in your gut. Is that what you want?"

"Yes," Dane replied enthusiastically, thinking it was a trick question. "That's exactly what I want. I'm not afraid of dirt, nematodes or a good challenge."

Dane was sure he aced that interview.

Griffin was blasé when he told Dane that the interviewers at *Peebles and Rigoletto* liked Dane but hired someone else—another of Griffin's copywriters! The headhunter spared him the details but warned Dane that rejection was part of the business. In Griffin's casual tone, Dane heard a callous subtext, "You had your chance and didn't score. You let me down."

Dane needed a second interview but Griffin was not forthcoming. Dane tried contacting the headhunter. He needed Griffin to tell him, "I believe in you." When Griffin took his call after several days, Dane detected that the recruiter's attitude toward him had changed. Griffin told Dane he needed experience.

"It's like school," Griffin observed. "You need kindergarten to get into first grade. Write an ad for a Chinese take-out—a flier or menu. Then you can put it in your book and people will think you're professional."

Chinese menu? Was Griffin joking? It sounded like a step backward into the primeval peat bog of advertising, an evolutional phase before handbills for psychics. Dane felt demeaned but he could not argue with his only advocate in the industry, so he collected take-out menus for study. When a take-out manager noticed Dane's interest in his menu, he handed him a stack of them and encouraged

45

him to give them to friends and neighbors. He even offered Dane free fried rice for his effort.

17. THE DREAM

Just when Dane seemed to have lost Griffin as his only advocate, Ella Bolden, a glamorous young recruiter, reviewed his portfolio, page by page, smiled from time to time, and closed it.

"Your book is highly conceptual," she said, "You're a real writer, it's in your blood."

"You liked the book?" he asked incredulously.

Ella smiled for the first time.

"I like most of the campaigns in it and there wasn't anything I hated. You did something really interesting with *Blimpie*. You actually made it seem like a cool place to eat at two in the morning."

"Yeah, well that's my niche—giving mystique to goods and services poor people can afford."

Ella sighed. "Not every agency is right for every person. Frankly, I don't have any clients who are right for you."

"No?" Dane asked. He experienced a familiar sensation of much internal weeping.

"Actually, no headhunter can help you now. Most agencies hire juniors from within to save money. But I have no doubt you can get hired on your own."

"You don't think I'm delusional for believing I can get a job?"

"You're not delusional at all. This is your dream," she defended him from his doubts. "People will pay attention. Show them your book and don't sell yourself short by calling yourself a beginner. There's nothing junior about you."

"I'm old, right?"

"That's not what I meant. You're a real writer. Let people know advertising is your dream."

His dream. These words from a woman who barely knew him

sounded oracular to Dane. He considered her proposition uneasily. He had always wanted material well-being, to spend without worry. In advertising he could make real money. Did this make advertising his dream? It was creative but anonymous. It was a job. He could be like other people taking trains and living in offices. Maybe this *was* what he wanted—to fit in. Like an enzyme, Ella the Headhunter's suggestion worked inside him. Out of it, Dane created the ad campaign that mattered most—*to sell advertising to himself*. If he convinced himself he was serious, maybe others would believe him. Dane perceived copywriting as creativity without glory. But what if he conceived a great campaign that revolutionized advertising? He would be famous. He could even change how people think. If this were possible, then advertising might become his dream.

18. THE TEST

With renewed ardor, Dane called unfamiliar agencies, became fluent in voice mail, forced conversation on secretaries and assistants and the few creative directors he caught on the fly. One of these rare individuals took precious moments from his busy schedule to relate to Dane how much he hated his book. Dane was like an inebriated boxer swinging haymakers at imaginary foes.

Advertising required contacts. Since Dane had none he needed to believe his constant activity would be rewarded. However, his submissions were random and he could not keep the agencies straight in his head. They were names and lobbies. As his job hunt lost traction, he lost patience. He craved a clear assessment of where he stood. Even "No" was better than an ongoing "to be determined." He was exposing a character flaw for corporate life: a low tolerance for uncertainty.

One agency, WIF Advertising, on 42nd Street, near the UN, had his portfolio for a few weeks. One morning, in a spate of frustration, Dane phoned WIF and asked for the creative director. A woman answered. He rambled that his book had been at WIF for a month and he had heard nothing. He wanted the book returned to him because he could not afford to leave it where there was no interest.

"The president of the agency just gave your portfolio to the creative director. He wants to meet you. Are you sure you want it back?"

Dane felt foolish. He had become so programmed for failure that he was deaf to success. Although he was unsure to whom he was speaking, or who the creative director was, he remembered what to say.

"No, of course not."

"So you're available to meet the creative director?"

"Yes."

"Then I'll have to get back to you with the details."

Dane was too stunned to be excited. He had been in such a funk that he did not allow himself to hope.

The next Tuesday Dane appeared in the dark lobby of WIF Advertising, where an angry receptionist reported his arrival. A tall blond woman came out to meet Dane and escorted him to his appointment. This was Deirdre Ryan, the office manager, who had spoken to Dane on the phone. "So here you are," she said, smiling at Dane like she knew him.

"You're meeting Paul Wittman. He is a partner, executive vice president and chief creative officer of the agency. His brother, Maury, is the chief executive officer. Good luck." Deirdre brought him to Paul Wittman's office, waited until the agency co-owner got off the phone, and announced, "Paul, this is your eleven o'clock appointment."

Paul Wittman was ten years younger than Dane, impeccably groomed and attired. He was imperious and friendly by turns like a feudal lord used to having absolute authority. His father had owned the agency and Paul and his brother, Maury, worked there every summer of their youth. Wittman appreciated his status, but behind his Teddy Roosevelt spectacles, his blue eyes betrayed resentment. He scowled like a man who had been deprived of a sense of his merit because he never submitted to the tests by which ordinary people earn it. He observed Dane wearily, as if the forty-something bedraggled man was one more burden to deal with. Then he lifted Dane's portfolio from his desk and dropped it.

"We do real estate advertising here. My client owns a residential property downtown. It's the next up and coming neighborhood for young singles...the Wall Street district. Here's what I need: a brochure by tomorrow morning. Can you do it?"

Dane promised to deliver. Wittman's eyes responded without belief, anticipation, or enthusiasm, yet his need for a brochure was sufficiently great to suspend disbelief and give this human question mark a chance. He briefed Dane on the building, the audience and the tone he wished to convey.

"Can you have this done by 11 A.M, tomorrow morning?

"Yes," Dane said without hesitation.

"I'll expect you then."

For Dane, the assignment was more than an opportunity to succeed; it was a feast of creative possibilities and he could not get home fast enough to gorge himself. He was invited not simply to write headlines and body copy but to create a world. He imagined the young financial analyst he was writing for, a presumptuous man, sure of his talents but insecure in his status. His reader was new in the city and had an enormous appetite for life coupled with a soft spot for comfort and convenience. This young professional wanted a place close to work, with quiet nights and abundant amenities—a large space, a new kitchen, an exhilarating harbor view, state-of-the-art electric wiring for his computer and appliances, and a health club for fitness and women. This was the young man Dane might have been had he come to the city with a job, marketable skills or money. As Dane wrote late into the night, he assumed the character of the suave building and of the savvy realtor who revealed its secrets to the

49

apartment hunter like a worldly Virgil guiding Dante through hell. Oh, the client would love this!

Stoked by high levels of inspired desperation, Dane needed all night and most of the morning to complete his task. He took three trains and dashed three long blocks from Grand Central to make his 11 o'clock deadline. When he arrived two minutes early with perspiration streaming down his face, Paul Wittman was waiting in the lobby with his hand out. Even so, the agency co-owner looked shocked to see Dane. His expectations were so low that Dane exceeded them by showing up. Dane gained confidence from this small victory.

"So you have my brochure?" Wittman demanded with the imperious tone of an employer.

Dane reached into his briefcase and extracted the manuscript. The grimacing agency partner accepted the stapled sheets and led Dane back to his office. While Dane watched, Wittman read the brochure. Within a few paragraphs Wittman laughed. Then he smiled and laughed again. When he finished the manuscript, he looked up and smiled at Dane.

"This is great. I love this. It's fresh; it has a point of view. It has the *right* point of view," he said. "I'll show it to the client. So, now, I told you I'd give you what you want if you wrote the brochure. What do you want?"

"A job," Dane said.

"What kind of job?"

Dane knew he had to ask for something so modest that Wittman would not refuse.

"Junior copywriter. That's all I want."

Wittman nodded as if weighing the proposal on scales in his brain.

"That sounds feasible. What kind of salary are you looking for?"

"How much will you pay?"

"No, no. Tell me what you want."

Again Dane felt the need to be circumspect. Wittman was prosperous but he ran a small agency and had to control payroll.

"How about thirty thousand?"

Wittman stroked his chin and squinted. "Let me think about that. Heck. It sounds reasonable. Okay, it's a deal. You earned it."

It was momentous for Dane, but he did not want to simply enjoy it; he needed to build on it. Wittman had mentioned that the same client had two buildings and needed two brochures. To secure his place and show off his talents, Dane asked Wittman if he could write the second brochure. The agency partner told Dane it was unnecessary—he already had the job. But Dane insisted that he wanted to do it, so Wittman briefed him on the second project. Dane completed it overnight and returned the following morning. By that time Wittman had client feedback on the first brochure.

"The client loved your copy! They want us to put the manuscript into layout as is."

Wittman read Dane's second manuscript and he liked it more than the first. He brought Dane together with a diminutive, young art director named Saroja, who drew a flower on her forehead with a makeup pencil. Together they brainstormed the covers for two brochures. Paul approved them and sent them to the client.

The next week, Dane started his first job in advertising.

Case 1-F
ADTHROPOLOGY

19. THE NEW WORLD

"This is your new home," Deirdre Ryan said as she showed him into a conference room next door to Paul Wittman's office. At the end of a long table cluttered with newspapers and old equipment a desktop computer and printer awaited him. The room was a dark storage dump, cluttered by boxes and computer parts. Dane gazed out the window at a skyscraper with art deco brick patterns across Second Avenue and at the slender trees abutting the curb. He listened to the sluice of traffic and repeated, "I'm an advertising creative. I'm a copywriter."

For the first hours of his first day nothing happened. Dane wondered if he really had a job. The world he conquered was a dusty, cluttered room. His audition and success were not a week old, yet after a few hours Dane felt anxious and vulnerable, alone on an island perilously close to an alien mainland.

New colleagues walked by his makeshift office sporadically. They peered in, grinned and pointed at Dane as if he were a new zoo animal. This was because Wittman circulated a memo announcing Dane's hire, in which he exhorted employees to introduce themselves and use his services. They went halfway, stopping by Dane's dark cave without saying hello.

Dane's insecurity was acute. The ebb and flow of advertising and office life were unfamiliar. He never factored idleness into a job. He was the first full-time copywriter at WIF. He had earned his position in the classic manner—by selling his work to a client. He deserved to be where he was: *so where was he?*

Maury Wittman, the agency president and Paul's brother, handed Dane an assignment: to write a headline for a photograph of a seductive woman in a short skirt, leaning against a brick wall. The ad was for an apartment complex but Dane was unclear about the message. Hookers live here? Dane wrote a page of headlines and heard no more about it.

Later in the week Mildred Walters, an executive with the look and manner of a wealthy society woman, handed Dane a small assignment. Mildred had an affluent East Side clientele, which included elite real estate brokers and developers. She asked Dane for taglines. Dane wrote two pages of slogans and put them on her desk. The next day, Mildred recorded a message on Dane's voice mail, "Dane, I've reviewed your taglines. Unfortunately, none are adequate." She sighed. "What a shame that you could not do this one thing for me." Within 30 seconds, the triumphs that brought Dane to WIF were rubble.

Dane retreated to his dark office and observed the life of the agency through passing figures and cacophonous bursts of language, like a shopkeeper watching street traffic with craving eyes. Was he wise to leave teaching for this misadventure in which you could be smart enough to get a job and too stupid to keep it? Under this fear lay a deeper one. He had no teaching career to go back to. He must succeed at advertising.

As he wallowed in despair, Paul Wittman appeared in the doorway. "Congratulations!" he proclaimed. "The client loved everything, especially your copy."

Later Wittman summoned Dane to his office. He was on the phone with the real estate mogul, who wanted Dane to write a mission statement for his company and a speech for his son's *Bar Mitzvah*. Dane hurried from the office to write the first draft of the mission statement. Then he turned to the *Bar Mitzvah* speech. He made it so poignant that his eyes misted near the end. It was his best work but he felt cheated because he could not put it in his portfolio. When he returned to Paul's office to read both pieces to his boss, Wittman threw up his hands and laughed, "Relax, Dane! You have the job."

On the train platform that Friday evening, Dane ended his first week in an aura of security and bliss. His commercial triumph after years of literary failure redeemed his long struggle and confirmed his faith. Finally someone appreciated his writing. Yet fresh success opened a festering wound. Why had editors and agents spurned his work to which he devoted so much time, love and effort for many years while Wittman and a real estate mogul loved two brochures dashed off in two evenings? Were his new patrons unsophisticated boobs or were publishing professionals stultifying dolts?

Or was advertising his true medium? Dane sensed that he had finally made the crucial transition from teaching and underemployment to a full-time job. He could support his family. For a moment he felt truly free.

20. DIM SUM AND DIMMER

In his dark, makeshift office cluttered with cast-off computer parts, Dane agonized over his tenuous position but resolved to make the most of it. He internalized the mantra-like lexicon of real estate advertising and learned to use buzzwords and catchphrases like "breath-taking views" and "granite countertops" so fluently that he transformed clichés to figures of poetry.

It was not a dream job at a top shop but he could do great work and replace the homemade concepts in his portfolio with produced pieces. Griffin's derisive advice echoed in his head—he must have printed materials to show he was professional. First Dane edited the brochures in layout, poring over every word, map and caption to eliminate mistakes. Finally he and the art director, Saroja, reviewed the matchprint, the last version before the brochure went to press. Dane was signing off on it when a studio artist asked about the spelling of *dim sum*. In a sentence about Chinatown it was spelled *dim sun*. Dane thought it was correct but *Webster's International* disagreed.

"Dim sun, din sum! How could I be so ignorant!" Dane berated himself. Why didn't he write *Peking duck*? At least he could spell it! Dane measured his dilemma: if he called out the mistake, they would need a new matchprint for $400 and he would be fired. If he let it slide, a captious reader might catch *dim sun* and complain. The brochures would be recalled. The agency would eat the cost of another printing, and Dane would lose his job and reputation. This was when Dane's judgment saved him. He calculated the odds that a Moroccan realtor would know how to spell a Chinese dumpling. They were small. Anyway, Dane could argue that *"Dim sun"* was technically not incorrect because American spelling only approximated Chinese

phonetics. He signed off on the matchprint and held his breath...for weeks.

The dreaded complaint about the misspelled culinary delight, a brochure recall, and his subsequent firing never took place. The gaffe went unnoticed. Dane saw this as a propitious sign that he was on his way up, invulnerable and unstoppable.

21. FIRST EXPLORATION

At WIF, Dane's work and its value were determined by Paul Wittman, a moody and mercurial autocrat. Wittman never defined Dane's role because a staff copywriter was unprecedented at WIF. Dane came along when Wittman was most vulnerable. A real estate speculator had promised lucrative, new business, but Wittman was tired and made only a cursory effort to service the mogul's account, when Dane trudged in with incongruous enthusiasm. Handing a major project to a middle-aged rookie was Wittman's impulsive way of tossing the business to fate.

The cost of Dane's good fortune was that he depended completely on Wittman, who had considered firing Dane from the moment he hired him. All that saved the oldest junior copywriter from dismissal was the agency partner's superstition. He viewed Dane like a winning lottery ticket; his copy made him money once, so it could happen again.

Dane sensed his boss's ambivalence and worried about being fired, but remained grateful for the job. The dark room he occupied abutted Wittman's office. Dane frequently walked in to share with the Executive Vice President a headline or concept. He wished to demonstrate his productivity and to justify his hire. Dane also thought it was a good idea to *hang* with his benefactor to show his loyalty. However, Wittman felt uncomfortable with Dane's intrusions. One morning when Dane entered Wittman's office, the agency owner glanced up from his reading and brayed, "Would you please not barge into my office?"

Dane apologized but was humiliated to be upbraided for bad manners. He had made a mistake. Reporting to his boss was no sign of respect but a rude imposition. In his isolation he relied on Paul for work and conversation more than he should. He was only *the junior copywriter* and the Co-principal/Chief Creative Officer did not wish to hang with him. His benefactor was not his pal.

In the tough environment of WIF, Dane needed more allies. Paul and his brother owned the agency but Dane sensed that much of the agency's revenue was generated by the account executives. During a lull, he walked from office to office, like a peddler, soliciting assignments from other account people. Si Grossberg, a short, stout executive with a long pony-tail and a Hawaiian shirt, peered at Dane over his glasses.

"You want to help?" Si asked. "Find me a hot, young babe for tonight!"

His assistant, an austere woman, who looked like she stepped out of Greek tragedy, added with rolling eyes, "But don't tell his wife."

Next Dane approached Christine, an attractive woman with a growing clientele. "No. We're good, thanks," she said briskly, her arms crossed like a "Do not..." sign.

Finally, Dane walked up to Al Vortman, the most successful recruitment ad executive. Vortman stood over the desk of his assistant with a pile of invoices in one hand and the stem of his eyeglasses between his teeth. Dane asked Vortman if he needed copy support.

"Support!" Vortman repeated as if hearing the word for the first time. "You want to give me support?"

The tall, pear-shaped man, whose small, bald head, curly fringe hair and proboscis made him look like Big Bird's brother, stared at Dane as if to pity his ignorance. He turned to his assistant.

"He wants to know if I need support. *Support!* You came to the right guy," Vortman said. "I got a hernia the size of a baseball!"

Dane grinned uneasily at Vortman's medical disclosure. He was unsure whether to laugh or commiserate with the bird-man's ailment. Vortman's small dark eyes taunted Dane's social confusion.

"You think my hernia's funny?" Vortman grimaced.

"No, not at all. I didn't think you were serious," Dane replied.

"I'm not," Vortman replied with the same baleful countenance.

"Then congratulations, I guess," Dane said. "Do you need a copywriter?"

"Sorry, Mack. My stuff writes itself."

Ten minutes later Dane was back in his makeshift office, feeling superfluous again.

22. A CLANDESTINE BRIEFING

Dane liked to think of the small conference room as his office but people were always barging in to use the laminator, to forage in boxes or to jerk around computer monitors. One afternoon, Dane returned from lunch and walked in on the Wittman brothers eating sushi. While the smell of raw fish and mustard afflicted his nostrils, Deirdre Ryan stepped inside. "Do you mind if I do some filing?" she asked breathlessly.

Before Dane could respond, the statuesque woman with the low-cut dress dropped a stack of folders on the table.

"So, how are you getting along?" Deirdre asked.

"I'm still learning," Dane said.

"If you have questions, just ask," she replied as she picked up the files she came with and left.

One afternoon Deirdre entered the conference room and closed the door. She asked Dane if he could keep a secret. "You're a writer— tell me what you think."

She opened a *Network for Learning* booklet, like the one where he had found his first advertising class years before. One page was bookmarked. The header read: "Travel writing."

"I've always dreamed of being a travel writer, of going around the world and writing about it all—the sites I saw and the food I ate. What do you think?" Deirdre asked.

"It's an interesting goal. Have you done any writing?"

"Only the schlock they ask me to do here. I was thinking of taking this course. What do you think?"

"It looks good. If you ever need anyone to look at your writing, I'd be glad to," Dane said.

"Aren't you nice? I might take you up on that."

Deirdre strutted to the door and turned to him.

"I have an idea. I want to write a travel book about bed and breakfasts across the United States. It would be like *Blue Highways* but I'd call it *Blue Sheets*."

"Great title!" Dane said.

Her eyes glowed from his praise. "Aren't you nice?"

After that initial encounter, Deirdre found other occasions to visit Dane's provisional office. She did not need to devise creative pretexts. It was the storage bin for the entire agency.

"So, how are you getting along?" she asked.

"Not as busy as I'd like to be," he said.

"I can explain that to you...but not here. One day, I'll tell you the story."

Becky warned Dane against big lunches, so he bought a yogurt at a supermarket down the street and ate it in the Tudor City courtyard.

One afternoon, while he sat on a bench with his yogurt, a woman in a raincoat and sunglasses walked by suspiciously unaccompanied by a dog, and sat next to him.

"It's good to see you're getting your calcium," the woman said to him.

He turned aghast and saw that it was Deirdre Ryan.

"Don't acknowledge me," she said. "We're two random strangers on a bench. What I'm about to tell you must remain confidential. You may have wondered why the account executives are not giving you work. It's simple. The account people hate the Wittmans and Paul Wittman hired you. Ergo, they hate you. It's simple math."

"Thanks for the heads up," Dane said gloomily.

"My pleasure," she said. "You have a right to know why you are experiencing difficulties. Now do you want to know why they hate the Wittmans?"

Before Dane could decline, Deirdre explained that the account people at WIF had worked for themselves until Maury and Paul went on a shopping spree and bought them out. Now they worked for the Wittmans. The account people brought in their own business and managed their accounts while the Wittmans provided services—an office, telephones, computers, a studio and a billing department. The account people in turn paid the Wittmans a cut of their profits. The executives saw Dane's copywriting as another "service" for which the Wittmans wanted them to pay a steep fee.

"So now you understand why the account people hate the Wittmans and view themselves as peons paying blood money to *the man*," Deirdre said. "And why they see you as *the man's* monkey."

"Yes, this is all clear now, thank you."

"I know I can trust your discretion because I am the only friend you've got," Deirdre said. "And just so you know, I take no sides, I don't judge. I like the Wittmans even if they have not given me a raise in three years." Deirdre stood up and straightened her raincoat. "This conversation never happened." She wiped a smudge from her raincoat with annoyance.

"You're paying for my dry cleaning."

23. DEFENDING TURF

One morning only weeks after he was hired, Dane found a young man in the lobby with a portfolio hanging from his arm. He was tall, thin and well-dressed. Dane identified the visitor as a younger version of himself, although Dane was neither well-mannered nor well-dressed as a young man. The portfolio in the young man's hand meanwhile tagged him as a copywriter. Dane's projection switched to resentment and concern. Betty the receptionist had not arrived so the visitor turned to Dane.

"Do you know Mildred Walters?"

"Yes."

"Can I leave this here?"

Dane now saw the young man as his competitor. This was the problem of reinventing himself a generation late. Dane was pitted against men or women who could have been his children—or nephews and nieces.

"I'll take care of it," Dane said.

When the young man left, Dane put the portfolio on Betty's counter with a note: "For Mildred."

Dane felt threatened and violated. He was starving for work and clinging to his job, but Mildred didn't care. She was trying to hire a young man with less experience than he had! His first impulse was to heave the portfolio in the *Papaya Boy* dumpster but he did not want to hurt the writer, who was like him—only twenty-two years younger. Dane needed a more effective and mature way to protect his domain or he would be like a medieval king of France—all title and no turf. He aimed to write for the entire agency, to be the go-to scribe they asked for to give eloquence to their incoherence. Now he was only known as Paul's private copywriter, or, as Evan, an obnoxious junior account executive, had the gall to call him, "the unemployed staff copywriter."

"I have to stop being the office joke," Dane muttered. He sauntered into Paul's office, oblivious to the fact that he was barging in.

Paul looked up, sensed that Dane was "off" like a rabid animal, so he deployed his trusted defense—feigned friendliness.

"So, Dane, there you are! How are you?" Wittman asked.

"Fine," Dane replied. "Can we talk for a second?"

"Sure thing. Are you keeping busy?"

This question, which often unnerved Dane, now rankled him.

"No, I'm not busy. You want to know why? Because your esteemed colleague, Mildred Walters, assigns copywriting assignments to an outside freelancer."

Paul Wittman had trained as an actor and did not miss his chance to improvise a riff that ran from eye-popping, jaw-dropping shock to pucker-lipped, brow-creasing outrage.

"This will not stand," he snarled. "You are the copywriter. I'll take care of this."

Now Dane could *see* Paul do what he *heard* Paul do all day. The agency owner pressed two numbers, held the receiver away from his face—turning the phone from an instrument of communication to a weapon of intimidation—and *paged.*

"Mildred Walters. Call Paul."

When she did not respond, Paul left a stern message on her voice mail and gave Dane a peace sign.

Later that day, Dane saw Mildred leave Paul's office, visibly distraught. By the end of the week, she had recuperated enough to stop Dane in the hall.

"I know what you did. It was reprehensible."

"You threaten my job and my family by hiring freelancers and you call me reprehensible!" Dane replied.

"That is my business."

"You work for WIF—and I'm the copywriter—so it's my business, too."

"Nice," Mildred said, "It won't help you. But you already know this."

She walked off smartly. Dane had prevented Mildred from hiring a freelancer but it was a pyrrhic victory since she would never give him work and would always be his enemy.

24. SMALL VICTORIES

Failure is a singular catastrophe but success accumulates in a myriad of small efforts and events. For two months Paul gave Dane a series of projects and Dane responded splendidly, indulging his imagination, usually going overboard and landing on his feet.

A new client who converted small manufacturing buildings into luxury lofts in Gramercy, Chelsea and the Village needed to intrigue a select clientele with million dollar lofts of a thousand square feet. Paul assigned Dane to write three brochures. Dane approached each slender volume like a collection of poetic sketches in which every facet and nuance of the building and its locality was revealed in a photograph, a word, a passage. He wandered neighborhoods, absorbed the mood and life of the streets, and took detailed notes about all that he perceived.

He noted trees blossom in pocket parks, studied rows of Greek revival houses with stone and brick facades, shoulder to shoulder like subway passengers; strolled down quiet side streets lined by storefronts with faded awnings and odd signs, and sampled pizza from shops redolent of basil, tomatoes and garlic. He admired the façades of magnificent churches built from the funds of faithful immigrants on the model of old world basilicas; they now served new communities with soup kitchens, thrift shops and off-off Broadway theaters. Though Dane wrote of million dollar lofts, he did not confine his prose to cathedral ceilings, oak floors, granite counters, copper splash-backs, Viking stoves and Sub-Zero refrigerators. He opened the French windows in these brochures to the sensations, spirit, and humanity of the cobblestone streets and let the city pour in.

When the brochures were done, Dane was summoned to jury duty. He could not build on his momentum. Rather than be idle at WIF, he twiddled his thumbs in the glutted jury room and worried for three days that he would be usurped and forgotten.

He had good news when he returned to work. Deirdre Ryan told him that Wittman was behaving strangely, laughing and clapping his hands in his office. When she burst in to see what was wrong, Paul was kicking back and smiling with a manuscript in hand. "Are you okay?" she asked her boss. I'm reading Dane's copy," Wittman replied. Later, Paul told Dane that his brochures were exciting.

There were other highlights. Dane received a last minute assignment to write a magazine ad for a hospital. The excitement and anxiety of doing a major full-page ad under such a tight deadline gave Dane palpitations. His teeth hurt and he felt a tingling in his arm. He thought he was having a heart attack. His first impulse was to pace the office, as if he could fend off death by out-walking it. "I can't drop dead now. I'm getting paid next Friday. And this is too big an opportunity. I have to write this ad."

After pacing the conference room and drinking the water cooler dry, he felt better and a headline came to him: "You don't have to open a heart to heal it." The client loved the ad and it ran in *Time Magazine* the next month.

Those were the bright moments between the dark matter of days and weeks when Dane waited for work in the cluttered conference room. Despite occasional good reviews, Dane steeled himself for termination before each payday on alternate Fridays. His idleness preyed on his sanity and self-esteem but was a humorous sideshow for the agency.

Dane's fear of firing was more than paranoid. He viewed his niche at WIF scientifically: He was a transplanted organ; while he had not been rejected by WIF, he was not accepted. Common sense suggested that his underemployment, Paul's moods, and the hostility of his colleagues would inexorably result in his termination.

25. A TASK NOT IN THE JOB DESCRIPTION

Although Dane was next door to Paul's office, the owner insisted on paging him.

63

"Dane, call Paul!"

He stared at the phone like it was a pistol, closed his eyes and lifted the receiver to his head.

"Dane," Paul said. "Can you swing by?"

Dane stood up and walked eight paces until he stood at the agency co-owner's door.

"So there you are,'" Wittman said cheerfully.

"I've been here all day," Dane said defensively.

"I paged earlier but you were out."

"I must have been in the men's room."

Dane was so rigidly intent on maintaining his frozen composure that Paul's voice hummed in his consciousness. He waited for verbal cues like "it isn't working..." When he did not hear them, he listened for a clue to this meeting's agenda. There was none. Paul simply wanted to talk.

"Are you keeping busy?'

Once again, the question impaled Dane. He did not know how to answer it with indemnity. If he was truthful, he would be fired. If he lied, he would be found out and fired.

"I could do more," Dane replied.

"Have you spoken with the account people?" Paul asked.

"Yes, with limited success," Dane admitted.

"Hmmm," the chief creative officer nodded to simulate concern and raised one eyebrow behind his Teddy Roosevelt glasses to simulate thought, then glanced at his *Rolex*.

"I have to rush," Wittman said. "We'll talk. But I'd like you to do something for me."

Dane swallowed hard. "What is it?"

It was a summer Friday. The sky darkened with an impending thunderstorm.

"I'm vacationing in Spain for a few weeks. Before I take off I need you to witness me sign my will," Paul said.

"Sure, no problem!" Dane agreed cheerfully. It was a morbid

request but to Dane it sounded like a reprieve.

26. ADTHROPOLOGY

Now that Paul was out of the office, Dane knew he could not be fired.

Dane had only one assignment. He wrote headline after headline for SPACEFINDERS, an agency that guaranteed an apartment for anyone who qualified. Around him WIF business proceeded per usual, in curses, shouts, taunts, laughs and frantic questions.

Paul's vacation left Dane alone and unsupervised, which permitted him to become acquainted with the agency environment. He ambled about and unobtrusively observed office life at various times of the day so as not to modify behavior while gawking at it. He inventoried the sights, smells, sounds and dimensions of the place with the method of an earnest social observer.

WIF occupied three sides of a rectangle on the second floor of a modest, glass and steel office building, one flight up from a hotdog stand called *Papaya Boy*, whose confused effluvium of spiced beef filler and fruit drinks permeated the agency's air supply. Dane was ambivalent about the proximity of this fast food favorite. Nostalgia was irresistible. When he was a young ad salesman trying to get his bearings in New York, *Papaya Boy* was an oasis—one of the few places where he could afford to eat. Those were not happy times but they were full of dreams. Now when Dane bit into a crisp casing and savory juices squirted over his tongue, he tasted the 22-year-old's hope and longing. But nostalgia had a downside. As delicious as *Papaya Dog's* products were, their pungent odors were down-scale, making it hard for WIF employees to view themselves as upwardly mobile professionals. Dane noticed that he felt lethargic and reeked of garlic after *Papaya Boy*. He also gained weight and Becky warned him of the danger of self-indulgence. He switched back to yogurts from a nearby grocery.

WIF's employees were slow to reveal themselves to Dane. They showed occasional flamboyance—shouts, crass jokes, obscene gestures—but for the most part they had the reticence of oppressed people who believed that self-expression and collegiality could only lead to firing. Work week fatigue compelled them to save energy and limit their gestures. Even so, some people made strong impressions. Betty, the receptionist and an aspiring veterinarian, had a perpetual scowl, suggesting that her passion for animals stemmed in part from her hatred of humans. Julius, the studio manager, a divorced 50-year-old grandfather, ate voraciously because he aspired to weigh 200 lbs—although he stood 5'6"—in the belief that it would make him more substantial. And Al Vortman, the largest grossing account executive, proclaimed, while relieving himself at the men's room urinal, "This is the highlight of my day."

Each afternoon between 12:30 and 1 PM the account executives congregated around reception and traded crude insults with Betty. She impugned their virility while they vilified her chastity. Whenever Dane observed this social ritual en route to the men's room, he marveled at the consistency of mutual abuse—apparently political correctness had not come to WIF—and he wondered what motivated it. Did lunchtime hunger trigger hostility or did personal attacks stimulate appetite?

The invective, it turned out, was incidental. Dane passed reception once as the mailman arrived and witnessed an extraordinary event—a postal feeding frenzy. Like a ravenous pack, several account executives tugged at the stack of mail, passed it, and rifled through envelopes, looking for checks that clients promised were "in the mail." This was the ignominious back end of the agency life cycle—bringing in clients was hard; getting paid was harder.

To collect from deadbeat clients, WIF had Nuno, the collections specialist, an accomplished weekend painter, whose portrait of Maury Wittman, hanging in the conference room, assured his ongoing employment. Nuno was one of the few who talked to Dane, perhaps because he sensed in him a kindred outsider. He confided to Dane that up to 20% of WIF accounts went into collections and he was doing a good job if he collected on half of those. Nuno never worried about keeping busy. The Wittmans and the account people constantly complained to him as if he, not the clients, failed to pay.

At times Dane needed to escape to the only place out of range of the crackling intercom, but even the men's room was no save haven. It was a sad, narrow enclosure with three little cubicles and two urinals. As he stood at one urinal, Al Vortman was spending the best part of his day at the next one.

"So, giving it a cool drink?" Vortman asked. Dane had no answer for that. "Nice facilities, right?" Vortman continued. "I hope you realize you're pissing into a priceless antique. These urinals go back to the introduction of indoor plumbing."

Dane laughed. Vortman was harping on his usual theme—the shabbiness and discomfort of the WIF offices and the Witmans' indifference to improving them. The toilet stalls were worse than the urinals—dilapidated, cramped and affording little privacy. The door of one cubicle had no latch. To keep it closed you had to press your foot against it.

One day, Dane sat behind the defective door and Donny, a bilious Brooklynite, who worked in the publications room, burst in, crying out for emergency relief.

"Bad fried rice," he gasped and jiggled Dane's latch, then pushed against the door. "I'm dying! Please! *Help me!*"

Dane's foot met Danny's door pressure from inside with equal force, barring the desperate man. If Dane had spoken up, Danny would have respected his right to finish. However, Dane observed a rule of silence while sitting on the can. He believed that speaking at the moment of relief polluted "the sanctity of the act"—a quasi-religious concept rooted in the humiliation of his past. During his stint at *Lumbago Associates*, the science magazine advertising firm, a garrulous salesman named Jim Mackey noted Dane's sneakers under the partition and joked at a staff meeting that Dane must have been the guy in the next stall. Dane denied it with a red face but the damage was done—people knew he crapped!

Now Donny called out to another colleague. "The door is friggin' jammed! Will you help me?"

"Sure."

The two men heaved their collective bulk at Dane's stall door, ripping it from its hinges, and landing on Dane. The potty-crashers sprawled, thrashed and scrambled to their feet, trampling and elbowing Dane as his body curled against the pipes and water tank. Only being painfully smacked in the mouth and suffocating under the man crush distracted the junior copywriter from his shame.

"Couldn't you see I'm in here?" Dane cried out.

"My bad, Dude," Donny said. "But why didn't you say something?"

Dane could not admit that he kept a silent vigil in the john to prevent his bowel movements from becoming a hot topic around the water cooler. Instead, he gave what he considered a more measured response. "I was meditating."

"Meditating?" Donny yelled. "Did you hear that? He was meditating!" That was it. For two weeks, Dane, "The Flushing Maharishi," was the #1 topic in office toilet humor.

27. THE COPYWRITER'S NEW CLOTHES

During the hiatus, Dane also tried to improve his appearance. For years as a college instructor, he dressed like a beggar because teachers and students shared a culture of poverty and studied neglect. In advertising, nobody studied so it was just neglect. "Shabby isn't cool or respected here, son. Trendy rules," Evan, the obnoxious junior account executive, said. "Keep looking like crap and people will think you're a weird guy doing research, not a serious creative. I know it hurts, but hey, I'm trying to help."

Dane found himself at the crossroads between stale perpetuation and reinvention. With a few months of steady income to draw from, Dane shopped for new clothes.

It was an upgrade he was going for, not an overhaul. He did not aspire to Paul Wittman's high-end designer look, yellow ties with little pig motifs, but he hoped to look at least contemporary within a modest budget. Becky was a master shopper. While the summer clearance sales were in swing, she escorted Dane to the outlet centers in New Jersey and helped him find attractive casual summer wear. He bought two shades of khaki pants and several polo shirts in teal, eggplant purple, coral, sage and bottle green, and a light cotton plaid shirt for times he felt like buttons.

Dane finally thought he looked the part of an up-and-coming junior copywriter of a certain age. However, like most innovations, his new look solved one problem and spawned another. Dane wanted his wonderful shirts to look perpetually new, for their rich dyes to endure. Yet he knew with great foreboding that he would perspire in the infernal summer heat and that the shirts would smell. They would need to be washed and would lose their vibrant colors and soft textures.

To prevent this natural disaster, Dane might have followed the example of Evan, the obnoxious junior account executive, who wore a T-shirt under his polo shirt to absorb perspiration. But Dane thought it looked "stupid" to wear one casual shirt under another. It was tantamount in his mind to wearing a sweater under a sweater or a coat under a coat. He dealt with the problem in his own way, by lumbering slowly through hot subway tunnels and down city streets. He pulled his shirt away from his torso, tucked napkins behind his neck to absorb hot-under-the-collar dampness, and ducked into bank lobbies for air conditioning. However, the last tactic prompted aggressive customer service representatives to scare him off with offers of 10-year certificates of deposit at 1% interest rate.

Despite Dane's clever tactics, torrid subways and concrete streets made him sweat. When he arrived at his office, he sensed the new shirt with its rich dye hovering close to his wet torso. If he continued to wear the shirt normally, it would absorb his sweat like a sponge, stink and discolor. He must act decisively and fast. He closed his office door, pulled the shirt carefully over his head to minimize body contact and laid it on the chair. While he wrote headlines he glanced at the shirt like it was a sick patient. He wondered if he had rescued it in time to preserve its cleanliness and hue. "Damn it, why did I have to wear a nice shirt on such a hot day? I can't wear anything nice. My life doesn't allow for it," Dane lamented bitterly.

As he stroked the shirt to gauge its dryness, his door opened and Deirdre Ryan was staring at him. She had dropped many hints to Dane that he should invite her to lunch but now her eyes bulged at his half nudity. "This is not what it looks like," Dane said. "This is bare-chested bonding. I learned it when my daughter was born. By baring my chest at the office I feel more committed to the work."

"*Committed.* Yes. That thought crossed my mind," Deirdre said.

Before this incident Dane was considered weird at WIF. Now he was believed to be a semi-nudist. Yet even this did not mitigate his isolation.

Later Dane devised a "more acceptable" way to preserve the freshness of his polo shirts. As soon as he arrived at WIF he dampened several paper towels in the men's room and planted them in various strategic locations on his body—between his neck and his collar, on his back and under his armpits. Often he forgot to remove the towels. When he came to a meeting, one colleague said, "Dane, your wet towels are showing."

28. WORKING CLASS HERO

One afternoon at lunchtime Maury Wittman threw a party for Gary, the chief of operations. A burly man with a shaggy moustache and a ponytail, Gary had been with the agency for thirty years, and worked his way up from messenger to glorified maintenance man. The festivities were in the lobby and centered on a 6-foot-long hero on a table. Maury Wittman gave a speech about how long Gary had served at WIF. He declared that his father had the utmost respect for Gary.

Maury brandished an envelope.

"It isn't a watch," he said, eliciting a laugh. "It's an all expenses-paid seven-day tour of Italy. That's right, so Gary and Lucille can visit the land of their ancestors...But Gary, don't get any ideas about staying there. We need you here to install the new windows."

During the laughter, Maury handed Gary the envelope. Gary grinned and looked askance in embarrassment. His wife had sneaked into the city to surprise him.

"Crossing the ocean will be a piece of cake," Mrs. Gary said. "It took me two hours to get into the city!"

"Now you know what I go through every friggin' day," Gary chided her.

Jake Ribosky stepped forward. A portly salesman from the Bronx who wore ties nearly as wide as he was, Ribotsky had worked at WIF almost as long as the guest of honor.

"Congratulations, Gary," Ribotsky said. "The AC sucks. When will you fix it?"

The employees laughed. Gary promised to talk to the building superintendent.

"It's just like Gary to solve problems at his own party," Maury Wittman quipped.

Then most of the employees rushed to the long table to honor Gary by eating his sandwich. The mega-baguette was thick, crusty and coated with sesame seeds. It was filled with deli meats and cheeses so the Hindus, Moslems, vegetarians and Kosher-keeping Jews at WIF, half of the staff, settled for sodas.

After the party dwindled, some revelers stood by the reception counter.

"How long till you get your sandwich?" Jake Ribotsky asked Al Vortman, the big-earning, Big Bird look-alike.

"I decided to roll over my sandwich into several post-retirement hamburgers," Vortman replied. "That way I don't have to pay taxes on the condiments."

"Thanks for telling me," Ribotsky replied. "I'll mention it to my estate planner."

"You're better off telling your mortician!" Vortman said.

Everyone laughed.

'It's great that Gary got...errr...recognized," Jake Ribotsky said, "But one thing I don't get...Why all the deli meat? It gives me gas."

"Yeah, why they order that?" Saroja, the Hindu art director, demanded. "They could order something for different people."

"I'll tell you why," said Al Vortman, chewing on his eyeglass stem. "It's brilliant corporate finance. If up to 40% of the sandwich is uneaten, the Wittmans can claim the uneaten sandwich as a business expense. Then they donate the leftovers to a homeless shelter and reap a charitable deduction. And after three or four half-eaten sandwiches, they get a significant tax write-off. The Wittmans are always thinking."

"In other words, they're cheap!" Ribotsky said.

Everyone laughed for ten seconds, then realizing the seditious nature of their mirth, stopped abruptly and scattered to their respective jobs.

29. AN ABSOLUT BRAINSTORM

When Paul returned from his vacation, he asked Dane what he'd done for three weeks.

"I wrote headlines and tags for two projects," Dane said.

"By yourself?"

"Yes."

"That's grim."

Paul had an uncanny way of stating the truth and doing nothing about it. He collected the twenty pages Dane wrote and never mentioned them again.

Paul put Dane and the other creatives to work on a major business pitch. A national rental company specializing in furnished apartments for relocating executives was about to open communities in the New York area. These communities were designed for people with no time to find a house or apartment; they had electrical installations and amenities, such as spas and swimming pools. Convenience was their core benefit.

Dane worked with Saroja, his first art director. They were stuck on a headline. Dane hunted for verbs with the prefix "re." *Recharge, resuscitate, revitalize.* Saroja, who spoke English with an unintelligible accent, was a tough critic. When Dane called out a verb, Saroja shook her head and leafed through a thesaurus.

"Should I use your Pantone book to come up with colors?" Dane asked resentfully.

"*Hey man,* I seen plenty of writers use a thesaurus," Saroja said.

The art director's taunt motivated Dane. The right words soon came to him: "*Why resort to a rental? Rent a resort.*"

Paul stared at the words without speaking. He repeated them under his breath and screwed up his face, like he was squeezing the line until it yielded the same message new and improved. Then he thanked Dane for his work and went to the pitch. Several months later the real estate company hired WIF and used Dane's headline for the first ad, which appeared in every local paper's real estate section.

Gradually, Paul called Dane in on major projects. He asked him to brainstorm a concept for a landmark building. The new owners were seeking an agency and WIF was a finalist. All creatives mustered in Maury Wittman's office. Arlen Lesser, the freelance creative director, was there, along with Paul and Saroja, the art director.

"I want everybody to think," Maury, the president, said, "Close your eyes and your mouths and just *think.*"

Dane was wary of closing his eyes in a crowded room. The last time he did so, he was standing at a bus station urinal with a picked pocket and wet shoes. It occurred to him that this "quiet time" could be a practical joke to see who was stupid enough to close his eyes. He squinted and found that everyone else's eyes were shut.

Someone opened his mouth to yawn but Maury preemptively pressed his finger to his lips and said, "Shhhh."

After five minutes the agency president opened his eyes, blinked miserably and admitted that his brain was fried.

"I got it! I got it!" Arlen shouted like an overeager outfielder on a softball team.

"The Grand Canyon!!!" Arlen announced as if he had invented it.

"The Grand Canyon?" Paul asked skeptically.

Arlen waved his hand to indicate that Paul didn't understand. Arlen gazed upward at a forty-degree angle, the head-tilt reserved for visionaries and ecstatic saints.

"We superimpose the building over a shot of the Grand Canyon. The headline reads: *Experience the Wonder of New York.*"

Maury rubbed his temples as if grinding the idea in his head. Paul squinted skeptically.

"You're comparing the Helmsley building to the Grand Canyon? It's no wonder of the world," Paul remarked.

The brainstorming session adjourned when Maury complained that his head hurt and he was seeing polka dots, two warning signs of stroke. Paul, Saroja and Dane formed a team and had an idea. Why not turn the skyscraper into a branding icon like the *Absolut* bottle? Dane had seen the building lit in the shape of a cross during the Christmas holidays. They could *Photoshop* lit windows in the building in the form of various symbols: A question mark, an exclamation point, and a *V* for victory sign.

Paul presented the concept at the business pitch. He reported afterward that the client liked their idea but said it didn't give him a "stiffy." Although the client forgave WIF for his lack of sexual arousal and invited the Wittmans to present again, Maury and Paul could not get over the client's snub. *"Didn't give him a stiffy*...Maybe Viagra is the concept he needs!"* Paul grumbled.

Dane was unsure if WIF won this account. Many pitches had a similar outcome. People hyperventilated over new business. Yet, when it disappeared, nobody said where it went, until suddenly months later the business was back and work conceived months before was produced. Dane wondered how he could build a reputation with such dubious opportunities.

Case 1-G
DUMBO MON AMOUR

30. DUMB AND DUMBO

The Wittman brothers rarely missed a corporate leadership trend. They read that Fortune 500 company high echelon managers went on retreats for team-building and strategy-making, so as the high echelon of WIF, they went whitewater rafting. Before their trip, Paul paged Dane. "Dane, see Paul."

As usual, Dane expected to be fired. But after their usual conversation about how busy Dane was not, Paul had exciting news.

"I'm running late but something big is about to happen and I want you to work on it."

"Big? You do? Great!" Dane spoke in short words to cut down on his loquacity because Wittman had criticized him for rambling. But Paul was now in a mood for effusive grandiloquence to match the grandeur of the project. He winced at Dane's monosyllabic drivel. How had he hired such a feckless individual?

"It's a huge opportunity," Wittman continued. "Instead of branding a building, we're branding a neighborhood. Have you heard of DUMBO?"

"The elephant?"

"No. It's the hottest new neighborhood in New York, the next SOHO. It stands for 'down under the Manhattan Bridge overpass.' Ram Vaklemptis, the guy who invented SOHO, owns buildings in DUMBO and wants to give it the same hype. Your work has been great and I thought you should be in on this."

"You did? That's great. I mean thanks," Dane stammered.

Paul shook his head at Dane's inarticulate babbling.

"Don't thank me. You earned it. I want you to work with Arlen."

"Arlen Lesser? Why do I have to work under him?" Dane protested. "My work's the selling point with clients."

"Don't be arrogant," Paul said. "Arlen's a genius. He coined the term 'gold coast' in Florida. Then he coined 'gold coast' for Connecticut."

"Genius," Dane muttered.

"Arlen knows a lot. You can learn from him."

"I have an infallible gut," Dane said.

"That's why you're here. But Arlen has 25 years of experience."

Paul slipped on his designer backpack and patted Dane on the arm on his way out.

"You'll get there."

Dane needed to create a campaign that would bring him success and immortality. Every copywriter was stalking the concept, headline, tagline, icon that would make him famous—"Just do it," *The Jolly Green Giant*, *Speedy Alka Seltzer*, a Cockney gecko, or a middle-aged man squeezing toilet paper. The DUMBO pitch was his ticket to transcendence but Arlen, the senior consultant, stood in his path. Dane needed to move Arlen aside...but how? The Wittman brothers believed in Arlen. He was the big idea man who branded empires by hyperventilating pithy phrases. Arlen's *Methodist Hospitals* campaign slapped headlines on city buses that read: "Wheezing in Woodside," "Flu in Flushing," "Gastritis in Greenpoint" and "Acid reflux in Astoria."

DUMBO lurked in the corner of Dane's mind where imagination

and ambition coiled like passionate lovers. The DUMBO visit would take place on Friday. All week Dane created concepts and headlines on his own since art directors' time was considered too precious to waste on him. He dismissed the slight. When he conceived the winning idea, he would enter the Advertising Hall of Fame. It was no Nobel Prize but he would take it. Dane heard nothing from Arlen until Friday, when the short, great man showed up in a silk jacket that flowed down to his knee caps. He introduced himself to Dane, though they had recently worked together. Arlen's red face reeked of his after-shave, *Water Polo*. He hunched like he was ducking a missile.

The main topic of conversation on the way to DUMBO was its name. DUMBO evoked flying elephants and a white elephant was slang for a fiasco. Would it be possible to come up with another name? No, Vaklemptis, the developer, was attached to it.

Arlen revealed his idea. Since DUMBO was on the waterfront how cool would it be to do an "On the Waterfront" campaign with stills from the movie classic?

"Will longshoremen live in DUMBO?" Dane asked, "These lofts go for a million bucks."

"People know the movie," Arlen said, "It could give the area immediate recognition. Plus I can get my friend Bud Shulberg to write the DUMBO ads."

"Is Bud Shulberg alive?" Dane asked.

"It makes no difference," Arlen said.

Arlen's plan left everyone speechless. He filled this void with another story from the annals of his life.

"So I wrote this campaign for an apartment complex in Washington. This garden community was on an island in the Potomac near the Memorial Bridge. You been to D.C.? It's the nation's capital. *Beautiful*. The developers could not give these units away—and real estate was hot! So I saw an article in the *Post* claiming women in D.C. outnumbered men by 3-1. *Bingo!* I did an ad showing young men pushing shopping carts over the Memorial Bridge to this new island community. The headline read: *Most Single Men Per Capita in Washington*. The place filled up in weeks."

"Were there really so many single men?"

"Who knew? Who cared?" Arlen jeered.

"If it wasn't true the women would move out."

"But I moved on. I'm the copywriter, not the landlord."

The drive was fast. One claim the DUMBO realtors made was true—the neighborhood was close to Manhattan. DUMBO looked deserted except for a long line of addicts waiting for methadone at a drug center.

The WIF cohort's destination was "The Bell Tower," the first of several factory buildings Vaklemptis would convert into luxury dwellings. "The Bell Tower" was a rugged, ten story bastion of white concrete which was once a toilet paper factory. The builder was an English immigrant with a fondness for "Big Ben," so he had a bell tower designed for the roof. The bells originally sounded to announce the time of day, to make the company and its product seem important, and to remind workers of "the mother country." When the factory went out of business, the bells were dismantled. They were now simulated by a computer synthesizer connected to the elevator's electric system, and were played on special occasions.

The developer, Ram Vaklemptis, arrived at "The Bell Tower" with casual grandeur. He was a sixty-something urban pioneer with the remote cool of a shaman. The self-anointed "Father of SOHO" had transformed an industrial ghetto into the most chic neighborhood on earth and would need all his magic to turn the same trick with DUMBO. If he succeeded, his genius would be chiseled in stone. If he failed, history would dub him the *Doofus of DUMBO* and his SOHO success would go down as a lucky footnote. Vaklemptis had a dusty appearance and a fresh smell, which Dane identified as baby powder. The crusty developer had sprinkled talc on his construction togs to appear dirty while smelling clean.

Vaklemptis shook everyone's hands but lost interest when he

came around to Dane, who wondered why he was snubbed. Was he wearing respect repellent? True, the junior copywriter exuded low status. No question, he was a middle-aged guy in jeans and long hair with a camera around his neck, who conjured up a bad actor playing an oafish tourist. Vaklemptis had sound reasons for slighting him but Dane shoved his insignificance in the mogul's face. He snapped pictures, asked questions, cheerfully told Vaklemptis, "I'm the junior copywriter!" and offered his hand to the client, who shook it because he did not know what else to do.

Arlen engaged Vaklemptis in a lively dialogue. Dane observed that the two men closely resembled one another, from the curly, gray hair to the narrow, guarded eyes to the hunched shoulders and bow-legged gaits. Even more remarkable than their physical likeness were their rapid jaw movements as they jabbered incessantly. They could have been brothers or tribesmen. But what tribe would that be?

The WIF troupe rode a construction elevator up to the bell tower loft on the 11th floor where Dane took photographs.

The views of the harbor and downtown Manhattan inspired Dane. Downtown skyscrapers thrust skyward in a parabola of steel and concrete like a gleaming inversion of Niagara Falls. The power of construction made rock flow out of rock. Dane shot a roll of film and outlined ideas for a concept whose headlines flashed across his mind like captions for the skyline that filled his eyes.

If real estate was the treasure of New York, the harbor was its source. The city was a world but the rivers, harbor and the ocean beyond were the world from which it emerged. DUMBO was a sleepy Brooklyn waterfront but first it was the nexus of sky and water. Dane's campaign would show how a DUMBO resident experienced and transcended New York through the bell tower's spectacular views. He spoke the headline that translated the rapture of the senses into the first commandment of real estate: *Location, location, sensation! New York Living and Beyond.*

After Dane clicked his pictures on the terrace he ambled through the interior space. "The lofts are huge," he thought. "But with no people, there is no world." In New York, space sold better than sex, but what if he blended space and sex? Dane imagined a world for DUMBO: a furnished loft, its owners wearing robes on the balcony on a Sunday morning after a night of passionate love-making, surveying all that their eyes possessed—the splendor of Manhattan, river, harbor. They would remove their bathrobes in the heat and stretch their arms skyward so that the sunlight and salt air embraced their suntanned bodies. He listened to the man's thoughts, "A jug of wine, a crusty baguette—and *Dumbo*." Yes, there was a headline. And the woman: she spoke her piece in French, "*Mon Cheri, la vie est belle à DUMBO.*" Then she switched to Italian, "*La vita! L'amore! La DUMBO!*" Dane was overwhelmed by the rapture of his fantasy. The subject of his second campaign would be the sexy denizens of DUMBO. He would call it "La Dolce DUMBO!"

31. THE HUNCHBACK OF NOTRE DUMBO

On Monday Dane wanted Saroja, the art director, to do layouts for his concept but she had injured her hand opening a can of dog food and was out of action. Dane cut out pictures and glued them to paper under his headlines like he had done as a student. He was so confident of his concept that he did not care about his crude techniques.

In the Wittmans' absence, Arlen called the creative review that afternoon and ran the meeting. His work was professionally art-directed and mounted on foam board, with the best color output. He had done three approaches: "A Loftier Way to Live," "DUMBO: the Next Right Move" and finished with his tour de force, "When the Bell Tower Chimes, It's Time for Dumbo." Arlen was ebullient about the last concept because it incorporated all of the property's features: the building, the neighborhood and the bell tower. It included a photograph of a group of hip people staring at the reflection of the bell tower in the East River.

After Dane presented his concept, "Location, location, sensation!" and explained the thinking behind it, he paused before the main event—"La Dolce DUMBO!"

He set the scene, describing in detail the naked people on their bell-tower condo balconies as they toasted the harbor with glasses of *Dom Perignon*, fed one another chocolate dipped strawberries, and lifted their glasses to the rising sun.

When he finished, the room was silent; his colleagues' mouths were agape.

"Very interesting," Arlen said, "Okay, so let's get rolling on my ads."

"Wait!" Dane countered as he came out of his self-induced erotic trance. "You said we needed different viewpoints. Now that you have them, you're going with your point of view three times over?"

"It's not a democracy," Arlen replied. "And it has nothing to do with who did the ads. If you came up with something outstanding I'd say so. It's the work that counts..."

"The work *should* count but you have the delusion that your work is genius," Dane cried. "This campaign needs real ideas, not warmed over clichés. Let Paul decide."

"Paul isn't here. I'm the boss," Arlen said.

"You can't do this!" Dane exclaimed. "We need an idea equal to the majestic views. Your ego is getting in the way."

"Your attitude is in the way!" Arlen said.

"Don't you see? We need *La Dolce Dumbo!* Dane cried "What are you offering the people? *When the bell tower chimes it's time for DUMBO!* What does that mean?"

Dane performed his interpretation of Arlen's favorite line by lumbering around the room stooped like a hunchback, swinging his arms, crying, "*Ding-dong-ding-dong!*" until he noticed in his peripheral view that his colleagues were staring at him aghast.

No one in that room had ever seen this before at WIF—or

anywhere else. What would Dane do next? In the apprehensive silence, Dane intuited that he had gone too far.

"Are you finished?" Arlen asked.

"Yes," Dane said gratefully since it allowed him to minimize the damage.

"We need to talk," Arlen said and stomped off. Dane followed him out but Arlen did not talk to Dane. He wanted him to think about what he had done.

Dane was in a panic. He believed Arlen was phoning Paul to have him fired. This was the only pretext Paul needed. "How could I be so stupid?" Dane asked himself rhetorically. "It's a job!" Later Arlen appeared at Dane's squalid office. Dane was relieved to see him and greeted him with a friendly, "Hello!"

"I wanted to be fair," Arlen said. "I described your work over the phone to Maury. He also hated it."

Under the guise of sportsmanship, Arlen slashed Dane's ego again, triggering another outpouring of Dane's anger.

"Described my work? That's ridiculous!"

Arlen shook his fist at Dane before storming off. "You'll never work in this town when I'm finished with you!"

32. BUS POP

Dane was sick with rage and frustration—at Arlen, at himself, at everything. He had lost his chance to ascend to advertising greatness and he might have lost his job.

He was meeting Becky and Iris after Iris's ballet class. How could he face them after putting their financial security at risk? He took a bus up to Lincoln Center. At a stop near Columbus Circle, a stocky biker type with tattoos pushed Dane aside as he moved to the bus exit. Infuriated by the man's rudeness, Dane shoved him in the back. The strong man turned and landed a hard blow to Dane's arm and ribs as he stepped down. Then he challenged Dane to fight in the street.

Dane knew there was no reason to brawl with this man but after being pushed around at work, he couldn't tolerate being bullied on a bus. Besides, his arm and ribs were throbbing and he needed to retaliate. Dane stepped off the bus and the two men circled one another. Dane assumed a boxing stance, his body angled to his opponent. He bobbed, he weaved—and he kept his distance.

Dane's aggressive adversary soon dispensed with the sweet science and went into street fight mode. He lunged like a wrestler, swung at Dane's head with an open hand like a mauling bear, and dealt a glancing, scraping blow at Dane's head with his fingernails. Dane sidestepped, backed away and threw a wild kick he learned years before in a complementary kung fu class. Although the kick lacked sufficient force and aim to inflict anything but laughter, and never approached its target—his opponent's groin—it made contact just below the man's knee, causing him to lose his balance. The burly bruiser stumbled and fell hard on the pavement, landing on his arms and wrists. He screamed in pain and writhed on the ground, swearing he'd kill the "skinny bastard that did this" to him.

Dane gasped and clutched his ribs. He was sure the man had cracked them with his first punch. He staggered uptown to meet Becky and Iris at Lincoln Center. The pain dealt by the ruffian's blows screamed its reproach at Dane's reckless anger.

All the pain and swelling directed Dane's thoughts to the real source of his anger. For the past month his career at WIF had gained momentum. It seemed possible that he would do big things; his reinvention would be complete. Now he was trapped as a second-stringer, reporting to Arlen, getting squashed by Arlen. The resident genius had to justify the money he was paid and so did the Wittmans who paid him. Dane was the reliable economy copywriter. Regardless what he did, he would be viewed at WIF as the world's oldest junior copywriter.

Becky immediately noticed the scratch on Dane's forehead and his strained breathing. He said he fell on the sidewalk so she would

83

not worry. That night Dane could not sleep. His body ached but it was nothing compared with his anguish over risking his job and career for a DUMBO building. "You idiot," he thought, "You have a family. Remember why you're in advertising in the first place." Dane swore he would be cooler in the future, if there was a future, and would never again risk his job for ideas.

The next day no one was around to fire Dane or note his contrition. The Wittman brothers and Arlen went to the pitch without him. For the first time, other people in the agency looked Dane in the eye with friendliness. Was this how they showed sympathy for his exclusion from the pitch after he worked so hard on it? Maybe they respected him for standing up for himself. Or they recognized him as one of them...the low-paid, voiceless help.

When the pitch team returned—the Wittmans, Arlen and Saroja—they quickly dispersed—grim and tight-lipped—and closed their office doors. Dane's behavior was never mentioned. Apparently, he was an afterthought, a status for which he was grateful. Dane was smart enough to say nothing but was glad the pitch had gone badly since a poor outcome validated his excluded work and eclipsed his extreme behavior. He was not proud of his selfish attitude but he could not repress it. He was 44 years old and viewed Arlen's failure as his only chance for success.

33. AFTERMATH

"Dane. See Paul."

It was the phone page that always made Dane sick. It did not sound like the Paul who laughed at his copy, but the tyrant Paul who answered to no one and made up rules as he went along.

Dane straightened his shoulders. He expected to be axed and wanted to make a dignified appearance like the soldiers marching to their executions in *Paths of Glory*. For two months, when each payday passed without a call to Wittman's office, Dane thought he actually had a chance of lasting twenty weeks—the threshold for unemployment benefits.

But this was no payday. It was Wednesday. The DUMBO pitch had gone badly on Tuesday and Dane had acted out on Monday. It was a perfect day for payback. In the fallout of failure, Paul could blame Dane for everything. Paul was on the phone when he noticed Dane standing in the doorway. He waved his hand and pointed to the chair on the other side of the desk. A voice in Dane cried, "Don't sit. Run. Save yourself."

When the call was over, Paul observed Dane analytically as if attempting to understand a newly discovered hominid.

"So, Dane."

"Yes?"

"*Oy*, what am I going to do with you?"

"Give me a big assignment so I can be on the cover of *Ad Age*?"

Paul sighed. A smirk curled his lips just as his lunch arrived at the end of Deirdre's manicured fingertips. She dropped it on Paul's desk, gave Dane an impatient glance and walked out. Paul extracted an aromatic chicken *parm* sandwich from the bag and took a voracious bite.

"Dane, what happened with you and Arlen...it wasn't good."

"It wasn't?"

"No."

"I was only defending my ideas. I wanted you to get that business."

"I appreciate that you care. But insubordination? Arguing? This is not good."

"I didn't realize I was insubordinate since Arlen was not technically my boss."

Paul ruminated the sandwich and the thought. Yes, Dane had scored points. Wittman studied the world's oldest junior copywriter. Dane winced with every labored breath from the ribs he bruised in his bus stop beat-down. He seemed less pushy and more sympathetic.

"Okay. This is what we're going to do. We'll move you to another office. You'll be working with Roger. We'll see how that goes, okay?"

"Sure."

"And don't make enemies."

"I won't," Dane promised. For that moment Dane meant it. His hands were shaking in his pockets. When he closed the door of the conference room, he laughed. He had escaped termination again. Making enemies seemed to be the price of making his way but he was given the second chance for which he prayed. Now he must honor his pledge never to risk his job for his ego. He would take opportunities when given, cooperate and do what was asked of him.

Although he was banished to the nether end of the office, far from his benefactor and from the source of his creative tasks, Dane was in a state of grace.

"*Yes!*" he exulted. "*I am a survivor!*"

Case 1-H
SMOKE GETS IN YOUR EYES

34. IN THE CLOSET

Dane was evicted from the dusty conference room he shared with discarded computer parts, as Paul decreed, but his exile was only part of an agency-wide expansion. The Wittmans sent out a special bulletin that WIF would take over a vacant office suite and occupy the entire second floor. This prompted a wave of optimism. It meant growth, prosperity and more room for everyone.

His new workspace was a former supply closet abutting the creative director's corner office, on the opposite end of the floor from Paul. It did not denote promotion so much as detention. Sufficient space was provided for Dane, a desk and a book-case. When he tipped his chair it leaned against the wall behind him.

Despite its punitive dimensions, the office cell provided

unforeseen benefits. It was near the studio so Dane was among creative people and beyond Paul's supervision. Perhaps now he could separate himself from the Wittmans and craft his own image with the account people. His nook was secluded, too. If he got drowsy at four, he shut his door and took short naps. But when he opened his door, a plume of smoke drifted out of the creative director's office next door and filled the hallway.

People seemed to forget about Dane in his new locale but when he thought he was safe from the others, they flushed him out. Once while his head was bowing and his chin tipping over his chest, the door opened and banged against the corner of his desk. Dane started, his chair tilted back, his knees smacked his desk and he fell out of his chair in agony. It was Deirdre Ryan wanting to know if everything was all right.

35. ADVERTISEMENTS FOR HIMSELF

Dane accepted his closet office and demotion with quiet patience and good will. He had learned his lesson after the DUMBO debacle. He was intent on keeping his job and being a good employee.

Even so, in the tiny room, he could not prevent a colony of thoughts from festering in the anaerobic recesses of his subversive brain. He had been dumped in an obscure corner, he remained Wittman's personal copywriter, and he barely made a living. Creative assignments trickled in—name a new building here and do some signage there—but these tasks were neither here nor there. They would not make advertising pay off. He still earned less than his teaching salary.

Idleness was Dane's persistent problem in large part because he was a diligent worker. A messy desk made him nervous, so when he received an assignment he worked overtime to complete it.

To keep his mind and self-esteem alive and advertise his skills, Dane wrote proverbs and taped them to his door. One morning he arrived at his closet office and his proverbs were gone. Dane asked if anyone had seen his proverbs. He was told to see Gary.

"Talk to Paul," Gary said.

"I personally had your proverbs removed," Paul said.

"But why? Dane said. "They're creative and wise."

"They did not reflect the agency's work. We post only our creative."

"You've violated my First Amendment rights," Dane pointed out.

"You can write what you want," Paul replied. "But it's my right not to have it posted. I don't want them representing the agency to clients."

As if clients were strolling by Dane's closet!

Was it possible that Dane had been in his first advertising job for only six months and it felt like he had been there for years?

36. GREEN ACRES

Over time Dane's exile to the other end of the WIF offices went from liberating to tedious. He was on Paul's version of probation.

It was 4 PM. Dane tilted back against the office wall a foot behind him. He inhaled cigarette smoke from the creative director's office when Alfonse, the psychopathic designer, opened the adjacent door to return to the studio. Julius, the studio manager, reprimanded Alfonse and Alfonse shouted back. Dane was idle, tired and uninspired. The job that had meant so much to him felt like a dead end. Why did his dreams end this way? WIF was shaping up as a garbage heap to him, and advertising as a fiasco, when Paul Wittman's voice came over the intercom. "Dane, see Paul."

Now Dane was immune to this summons. He no longer expected to be fired. Or he was so dispirited that he wished to be put out of his misery.

When he entered Wittman's office, the benevolent despot was using chopsticks to slurp up *Udon* noodles from a Styrofoam container.

"So, Dane, are you busy?"

Dane no longer felt chest pains when asked this question. He concluded that Wittman already knew the answer and was toying with him.

"I have something for you. It's *Green Acres*. They've been my client for years and I don't have time anymore. I'm bequeathing it to you."

It was an odd gift, Dane's first account. *Green Acres* was a 55 and older community with houses, pools, tennis courts, a golf course, a community center, and a hyperactive activities office that was always planning "exciting" events and parties for its residents, which it promoted via newspaper ads to prospective home-buyers.

Dane wrote advertorials about these events once a month—in October, it was Oktoberfest, in November, the annual Thanksgiving Plymouth re-enactment and visit to a turkey farm. In December *Green Acres* held a ballroom dance competition and *Scandinavian Night* featuring meatballs and *gravlax*, and in February, it was a Valentine's Day romantic lunch at a New York bistro.

In December, Dane wrote:

> December is winter's gate, poised before the cold and the holidays, when people's thoughts turn to warmth and indoor entertainment...
>
> December's main event, Scandinavian Night, will offer a festive blend of food, music and dance—a typical recipe for Green Acres parties. After a savory full course meal of frikedeller (fried meat dumplings), raggmunk (potato pancakes), kottbullar (meatballs), red cabbage, and ris almande, there will be another Norse ritual—the "Swedish Lucia" in which a woman carries a cake with candles into a dark room singing 'Santa Lucia'...Most ideas for Green Acres come from residents, says Margaret Atwater, the recreation director, and Scandinavian night is no

exception...

Dane relished his detailed descriptions of *Green Acres* events. He peopled the galas with lewd geezers and women with hair and nails done every week, all working hard to enjoy their golden years. He staged an imaginary choir of Swedish virgins in white robes singing *Santa Lucia* while lusty men with potbellies and ponytails ogled them and popped meatballs in the mouths of sexy grandmothers in skimpy dance costumes. Dane all but tasted the *gravlax* and the gherkins. The burn of *aquavit* coursing down his throat was so real to him that he coughed.

When Dane snapped out of his creative reverie, he realized he was only 11 years younger than the *Green Acres* minimum age. Paul Wittman had given him this account because he believed Dane would fit right in with *Green Acres*. It was his "retirement" settlement from the agency—and he seemed to need one, with his short afternoon naps.

The *Green Acres* account was a call to action. If he was eleven years away from a retirement community he had better do something with his life—*and fast*.

When Dane's pieces were approved, he placed them in every New Jersey newspaper where the *Green Acres* developers advertised. Simultaneously, he sent poems he had written recently to a literary magazine.

A few weeks later, he received a letter from the magazine: two of his poems had been accepted for publication.

37. PERFORMANCE ART

Dane's success with his poems revived his spirit but in a few days he was unsatisfied and agitated again. It was like stepping out into daylight after a good movie in a dark theater. Dane roused himself from his torpor. He could no longer submit quietly to solitary confinement in his closet office. He had an inexorable urge to connect with the world around him.

Now free of Wittman's influence, he let his WIF colleagues know who he really was—not the world's oldest junior copywriter, but the world's youngest immortal poet. He spent more time in the studio and became friendly with Julius, the studio manager.

By appealing to Julius's better nature, Dane was free to hang out in the studio, a vast improvement over sitting alone in his closet. There, Dane bantered with designers and mechanical artists who produced the ads that made WIF profitable. The artists were always busy with nerve-wracking drudgery and enjoyed Dane's patter. Account executives, bounding in and out, badgered Julius and squawked at the artists to produce their jobs on deadline. "Oh, Julius is eating his lunch. That's a higher priority than getting my friggin' work done," Al Vortman jeered. "Here, Julius, can I hold your sandwich for you while you stuff your face? I'll do anything to make your life easier!"

"Here's something else you can hold for me," Julius retorted, cupping his crotch. "And you can eat it, too!"

Amid the banter and pressure, Dane made friends with the studio people. Cal was 6'8" and a former folk singer. Diane was the attractive girlfriend of a star deejay on a major FM station. The only artist who objected to Dane's presence was Alfonse, a squat, chain-smoking curmudgeon who loved golf so much that he played in the snow. He once rode the bus with Dane to the Port Authority and confided that in his two years at WIF the Wittmans never learned his name or once said hello. "That's okay," he growled, "I got no respect for those clowns anyway."

The publication of Dane's poems revived his hope for creative success. Each day he extracted the magazine from his briefcase and read his poems, but soon Dane wanted more. Walt Whitman had declared that great poets need great audiences. Dane would settle for *any* audience. He had performed his work at bookstore *open mic* events when he was a professor with free time. Was the recent publication of his work a portent that he should read publicly again? Maybe the overheated art studio was his venue and reading for its culture-starved artists was his lucky break.

Dane devised a short act. He would enter the studio, recite his shorter poems and withdraw suddenly, like he was doing a *guerilla* poetry reading. He performed the act a few times and Cal and Diane found it entertaining. They laughed hard and applauded before Dane made a fast exit. He knew he could not linger or Julius would intervene because he had to keep the studio profitable and poetry readings might interfere with this objective.

Dane soon added a costume to the performance. He slicked down his middle-parted hair and wore punched out plastic glass frames and a baggy, tweed jacket. He recited his verse in a nasal voice, with pompous pauses, and lifted a finger with pseudo-solemnity. Alfonse, who sat in the rear of the studio with his back to the door and a mirror propped nearby so he could anticipate an attack, shouted, "Shut up!"

"Hey," Cal said, "We're listening."

Dane continued with the next verse.

"Get a job!" Alfonse shouted.

Julius entered when he heard Alfonse barking and told Dane he should probably save his poems for open *mics* in the East Village. Dane was shut down in another extraneous attempt to be creative at WIF.

38. BREAKTHROUGH, BREAKDOWN

Dane's cancelled poetry event created a buzz. People heard of his antics. The WIF staff sensed that here was a subversive talent and a downtrodden, oppressed peon like themselves, who had to sacrifice his creativity, just like they sacrificed their hard-earned commissions to the Wittmans.

Finally there was a breakthrough. Christine, the young and successful recruitment executive, gave Dane an assignment. This alone was no triumph; on the contrary, it was an unmitigated failure. Nothing Dane wrote pleased Christine. She dismissed him briskly. "Do you consider yourself a professional?" she asked. Being vilified publicly this way could have fatally damaged anyone's career, and Dane's was already on life-support. Yet, negative publicity from the right person can often be more effective than the best publicity from the wrong one. WIF was far more negative than most corporate cultures; it was ruled by feuds, not alliances. Here, you were judged on the basis of your enemies, not your friends. Christine had many enemies, and when other recruitment executives heard her eviscerate Dane's reputation, they suddenly liked and respected him.

Every month the WIF staff convened in the main conference room to celebrate employee birthdays. The birthday song was sung, two cakes were cut and everyone received a piece. There was always a portion left over from each cake. "This is a demonstration of shrewd management," Al Vortman said. "See those two leftover pieces of cake? Management has a plan to save them in a freezer. They'll carry them over until next month and reduce cake expenditures by 15%. You don't believe me? Bill Gates invited the Wittmans to speak at his business summit in Switzerland. They'll lead seminars and share this remarkable practice with world leaders."

"They'll call it *Let them eat cake...but no seconds,*" Dane replied.

Dane had appreciated Vortman's sarcastic business analysis for some time and now Vortman reciprocated by smiling wryly at Dane's retort. He even chuckled a little and scratched the fringe of hair around his bald pate. It signified a victory for the world's oldest junior copywriter since Vortman rarely responded to anyone's humor but his own.

WIF's top earner was so impressed with Dane that he asked him if he was available to write ads for a major new client. *"Absolutely!"* Dane replied. Vortman asked Dane if he had experience with recruitment ads. Dane had no experience with classifieds beyond reading them, but was so eager for work that if he had been offered an assignment handing out toilet paper in the men's room, he would have asked when he could start. He assured Vortman that recruitment ads were his specialty. Vortman did not believe him but agreed to show him the basics.

Dane's first assignment was an innocuous Systems Analyst ad, which the client inexplicably loved. This led to a Field Specialist ad and an Operations Chief ad. In a month Dane wrote ads to recruit for every position in the company, including Chief Financial Officer and Chief Executive. Dane's 20 classified ads were inserted in publications in all major markets.

Vortman and his partner were getting rich with this client and Dane contributed to the success in mysterious ways. Not that he wasn't working hard. Vortman would spend an hour struggling to articulate what he wanted in a headline, which always came down to "Be a part of our system." Or "Work with our system." After chewing his glass frame stems to *Twizzlers*, Vortman threw up his arms and shouted at Dane that he should know what to write—*he was the writer!* When Dane produced several alternatives, Vortman pondered these short, apparently perfunctory ads like abstruse physics equations, before issuing his edict. "No, it's not right...it should be loftier. But not so far out there that nobody believes it."

This assignment did not fool Dane into believing he was doing anything creative but it reassured him that he could keep his job for another month. Writing recruitment copy also won him the respect of other account executives. He felt he finally fit in at WIF. He was no longer *the* freak, just another freak.

For reasons unknown, Dane's want ads were highly successful. He had a baffling knack for writing *Great opportunity for the right person*. Business was so good that Vortman induced the Wittmans to buy Dane a fax machine for his apartment in case a recruitment ad emergency required that he write from home.

The Wittmans might have used Dane's breakthrough as a bridge to their disgruntled vassals, but Paul Wittman had other ideas.

Paul paged Dane in a stern voice, *"Call Paul."*

"So I hear you've been writing copy for Vortman."

"Yes."

"How's that been going?"

"Very well. They like my work," Dane boasted.

"I'm glad to hear it. You've been busy. So how many hours have you worked?"

"I don't know exactly. A lot."

"You mean, you haven't been filling out timesheets?" Paul asked.

"Was I supposed to?"

"Of course!" Paul said. "How do you think we get paid around here?

Dane should have known success would lead to disaster. Now that Dane wrote for someone other than Paul, he was supposed to bill his time like a studio artist. Paul ordered Dane to account for every hour he worked on Vortman's business and to submit the timesheet, which Wittman would tender to Vortman as an invoice. Finally, Paul's original plan to turn Dane's copywriting into a profit center might succeed.

Did Vortman understand this arrangement? He may have assumed he was doing Dane and the Wittmans a favor by giving the junior copywriter something to do. Meanwhile, Dane felt like a traitor and a spy. He was friendly with Vortman and his partner, Josh. They treated him like a human being and appreciated his work. Now he would make them wish they hadn't.

It was Dane's first encounter with timesheets but not Vortman's. When WIF's biggest earner saw the timesheet and Wittman's bill for Dane's copy, he stormed around the office spasmodically, bumping into furniture, waving the crumpled invoice like it was a severed limb. He thrust the printouts under Dane's face and jabbed at the numbers.

"Did you know about this?" he cried.

"Paul told me to report my time."

"You spent this many hours on those ads?"

"Probably more," Dane said. "That goes back six weeks."

"You blood-sucking parasite!" Vortman shouted. "I wrote those ads. You don't know the first thing about recruitment ads."

"That's a lie," Dane said. "I've answered thousands of them."

Vortman stared at Dane with venomous intensity before he waddled off, waving a letter opener and vituperating in the hallway. "They charge us for these humping desks and these stinking phones and this crap studio!" Vortman shouted, "Now they're bleeding us dry with an incompetent copywriter! Here, just get it over with!" He stuck out his arm and drew the letter opener across his veins. Nothing happened. "Even the letter opener is a cheap, substandard rip off!" he concluded.

Dane was humiliated by Vortman's tirade and disappointed to lose a potential friend and colleague. However, he felt worse for what he did to Vortman's personality. For months after the billing event, Vortman was always red-faced and ranting; yet he lost the sparks of humor that lit his darkness. He no longer took joy in his urination or bantered with Betty, the receptionist, about his lost virility and her lost virtue. Paying for Dane's copywriting, which he claimed he never needed, was the provocation that set loose every one of his resentments and wreaked carnage on his soul.

This event affected Dane in other ways. He experienced first-hand a side of business which he had previously only glimpsed at and overheard; it was combat and people often got hurt. For one, his growing credibility with the recruitment executives was destroyed and their area was off-limits. He was forced to reroute his office traffic pattern to avoid Vortman. He could no longer enter the studio for more than a moment or walk the long corridor without looking askance. WIF had become his private Yugoslavia—a once unified domain carved into hostile zones.

One afternoon, Dane walked into the men's room. Vortman was standing at the urinal. As soon as he saw Dane, his face reddened and he muttered curses under his breath.

Vortman grew more agitated and he could not relieve himself. He discharged his anger at Dane. "See what you did? You've ruined the best part of my day!" Vortman gulped. His body trembled and jerked. He turned spasmodically and discharged at Dane, before collapsing on the floor of the tiny men's room. Betty called 911. Dane had to wash the last of his new polo shirts which he had saved from the previous summer.

39. ROGER OVER AND OUT

Hate forms a bond as strong as love. Since nearly 90% of WIF was enemy territory to Dane, he retreated to his closet office. And since he was a hated person at the agency, he formed an alliance with its resident misanthrope, Roger Garber, the creative director of art, whose office was conveniently next door.

Garber was a brilliant, disillusioned man who smoked all day and let account people's demands carom off his hard façade while he stared at a monitor, tweaking layouts with fleet-fingered ease. Garber was a Pratt alumnus and a veteran of prestigious agencies, but his eyesight was weak, his lenses dense, and his eye sockets limned by crow's feet, leathery as scars. Divorced, a chain smoker and a Ponzi scheme investor, Roger was an apotheosis of self-loathing.

Yet, despite his faults, Garber was WIF's creative guru. He never concealed his scorn for the Wittmans, whom he considered bean counters and poseurs, nor viewed his job as anything but the last chapter in his book of bad luck, a life sentence for the crime of being alive.

Garber liked Dane because he perceived him to be a luckless misfit on a lower rung of life. As a neighborly gesture, Garber asked Dane to write headlines for an ad campaign he was doing for an obscure restaurant near JFK airport, where a four-star New York chef had fled to escape the pressure. Still guilt-ridden for making Vortman sick with timesheets, Dane asked Roger if he would need to bill his time.

"Bill as much as you want. It's for the Wittmans," Roger replied.

Dane believed he had found a creative ally in Roger but aside from their discontent, they were not kindred spirits. Elements in Roger's personality made Dane uneasy. While they brainstormed, Roger bragged to Dane that he was a high-class hack. "I have a repertoire of twenty layouts," he said. "When I get an assignment, I analyze which approach works best. It's that easy. These people don't know the difference. They like it better if they've seen it a thousand times."

"Don't you want to try something new—just to prove you can do it?"

"No," Roger said.

To be an unabashed hack, Roger needed an off-setting virtue— like making a lot of money. In his mind, this sanitized his corruption. By contrast, Dane was too indigent to take pride in being an uninspired sellout. Out of psychological necessity, he aspired to be great. When he showed discomfort at Roger's admission, Roger put a mentoring spin on his cynicism.

"It sounds canned and formulaic but you can't be any other way or the work kills you," Roger said. He leaned forward until his thick glasses blurred his eyes into gray puddles. "Don't let it kill you, Dane."

One bond Roger and Dane shared was their mutual hatred of Arlen Lesser. Arlen was always barging into Roger's office, making imperious demands. One afternoon, Lesser stormed in, stuttered inarticulate orders for last-minute layouts, smacked his hands, snapped his fingers, shouted, "Chop, chop!" and stormed off in confusion.

Roger knew Dane loathed the itinerant creative director of copy even more than he did and enjoyed teasing him.

"I just saw your friend, Arlen. He sends his regards," Garber asked.

"Arlen should have his own action movies," Dane remarked. "*Blow hard.* The sequel would be *Blow harder.*"

Roger laughed.

"They pay him $90,000 to blow hard," Roger remarked. "Think about it when you get your paycheck."

Dane needed Garber's alliance. He had alienated everyone else. Yet he knew Roger reported on Arlen's lucrative compensation, not to sympathize with him, but to trigger his emotional meltdown. Dane shrugged coolly and deprived Roger of his entertainment, but the disclosure of Arlen's $90,000 retainer secretly did Roger's work, killing Dane's gratitude for his inadequate paycheck. Yet how could he demand a raise when he was not busy enough to justify more money—or even his current salary? As long as Paul underemployed him and used Arlen as a creative director, Dane was stuck where he was.

After the restaurant ad, Dane and Roger received a new assignment, a full-page spread for *Green Acres*. They had teamed successfully before but the *Green Acres* ad was different. *Green Acres* was a brand Dane knew well. He had authored several *Green Acres* advertorials and believed himself an expert on the 55+-year-old mind. At any rate, he thought he knew the topic better than Roger did and expected a more equal partnership than before. However, for Roger the power structure was unchanged. He expected *his* junior copywriter to defer to him.

After nearly losing his job in the DUMBO showdown, Dane vowed to accept his abject position and never risk his livelihood for an idea. In this spirit of resignation, Dane would have accepted subservience to Roger with due humility. However, remorse has an expiration date and Dane's had passed. He was angry and impatient with his mediocre situation. Dane's abused ego was highly volatile. A deficit of money and respect inflamed it and a thwarted creative opportunity made it explode.

When Dane spilled his ideas to Roger, with marketing rationales for each of them, the creative director exhaled smoke from his nostrils. When Dane coughed, Roger said, "This is what I think." And that was that.

Dane had considered Roger a fellow traveler who respected his intellect and talent. Now Roger showed he was a dictator like Arlen Lesser. Dane felt doubly betrayed.

He hoped that Paul would reverse Roger and endorse his concepts but Paul believed the *Green Acres Estates* client had no taste anyway, so why should he further alienate his disgruntled creative director by overriding him? He supported Roger's ideas and Dane saw one more creative opportunity squandered.

Dane reached a personal milestone. He was more frustrated than ever. "You were not meant to create!" the world screamed at him. If only he accepted this mantra in his heart he might be happy. He could give rave reviews to derivative movies, lavish praise on tuneless tunes, and tell Arlen and Roger how brilliant they were. Life would be easy.

40. CLEARING THE AIR

However, ego-suppressive therapy came with significant risks— total personality destruction. Dane could not suppress his ego or deny his creative drive. As a result, he despised Roger, his former friend and newest oppressor, as much as Arlen. Yet this hatred burned hotter since it was exacerbated by daily contact. Arlen did his damage and disappeared for months, whereas Roger was next door and ineluctable. Each time Roger's door opened, smoke billowed into the hall to trigger Dane's rancor.

Roger suffocated Dane's lungs and his creativity. He and Alfonse, the poetry-hating snow-golfer, huddled silently over Roger's desk, sucking and belching smoke fifteen times a day like peasants supping in a hut. When Roger's door opened, smoke rolled out like a fog. Dane coughed and was reminded of the botched ad and his banned poetry readings. Roger and Alfonse would not stop at spoiling his creative opportunities; they must also ruin his health.

In his closet office, Dane wheezed and seethed with feeble wrath. How could he change the situation? The WIF rule about smoking was: "Do it behind closed doors."

Of course, this rule had as much effect as a cigarette filter. Smoke was airborne, it defied enclosures. Dane coughed constantly. His clothes and skin reeked of Roger's fumes. He overcame his fresh loathing of Roger and asked the creative director if he could smoke less indoors or keep his door closed more often. Roger curtly recited his mantra, "I close my door when I smoke, which I have a right to do. Now get out."

Dane called the city government and learned about the laws governing cigarettes in the workplace. Technically Roger was in the right. He could smoke in his office behind closed doors if such was the company rule, since each firm determined its own smoking policy. Dane's only option to improve his air quality was to persuade the Wittmans to make WIF a smoke-free workplace. Dane circulated a petition. He canvassed the office like he had done when begging for work, explained the situation and cadged signatures. Even Mildred Walters, who denied him crumbs of creative assignments, signed his petition. After an hour Dane had obtained forty signatures among fifty employees. He submitted the petition to Paul Wittman, who was impressed by Dane's initiative but warned him *again* not to make enemies—advice which in Dane's case always came too late.

Two days later Dane found a memo on his desk that had been distributed to every employee. Effective the following Monday, there would be no smoking at WIF. Anyone who wished to smoke would need to do so outside the building.

It was a stunning coup for Dane. He was in advertising strictly for the money but had inadvertently become a political activist and public health advocate. People who never spoke to him now thanked him for his efforts. Once reviled and ridiculed, he was now a respected member of the WIF community. Despite his status as a low-wage flunkey, Dane demonstrated the long-lost innate leadership his fifth grade teacher claimed he had. Maybe not keeping a good man down and cream rising to the top were not mere clichés.

For one Thursday afternoon—the day of the edict—Dane felt good about himself. He knew without being told (but was told anyway by several colleagues) that Roger and Alfonse, the two smoking malcontents, were furious with him. Roger was conveniently absent for a few days. However, when he returned, he glared balefully at Dane and spewed expletives at him, loudly declaring him a backstabbing bastard-asshole.

People wondered if Roger would finally quit in protest of this final affront to his indispensability. They could not foresee the fallout of going smoke-free.

41. BAD DÉCOR

When Dane arrived on Monday, Gary, the office manager, told him he had moved his personal effects to another office at the far end of the floor. It was the first reprisal for Dane's anti-smoking activism. The Wittmans were appeasing Roger, who had threatened to quit if he had to be next door to "that backstabbing prick."

Dane was warned about the new office. It had problems, including excessive summer heat, a glass wall along the hallway and a tendency to flood from a faulty AC unit. But Dane was determined to see his new office as a victory. It was thrice the size of his closet office and he immediately saw a creative opportunity to transform the glass wall along the hallway into the world's largest construction paper mosaic. He foraged sheets of colored Xerox paper—green, yellow, pink, and blue—and taped them like tiles to the glass expanse. Within hours, Dane had turned the transparent surface into an opaque wall that resembled a childish Mondrian and afforded optimal privacy.

Deirdre Ryan, the office administrator, had written Dane out of her personal romance novel and was seen making out at office functions with an account executive. However, she now recognized that fate placed Dane near her office for another amorous assault. Perhaps this was an augury that he would leave his family and accompany her on a long-overdue vacation tour of lovely New England bed and breakfasts, the promotional brochure for which she now held in her hand.

Deirdre found a way to be close to Dane and to lord it over him, as well. As soon as he had mounted his construction paper mural, Deirdre came by to complain.

"The construction paper must come down," she said.

"Why? I just put it up. It looks great," Dane said.

"It looks tacky and it violates the WIF rule on office décor," she said.

"What rule? I can't work with people walking by and looking in," Dane said. "I need privacy in which to create."

"Create?" Deirdre laughed. "Is that you've been doing?"

Dane blushed at his admittedly grandiose job description.

They struck a compromise. Deirdre provided thicker, better quality paper squares in tasteful shades of brown and beige.

42. SCRAPS

Paul Wittman called Dane into his office. Almost a year had passed since Dane walked in with his landmark real estate brochures. He had been with the mercurial Wittman long enough to be unfazed by his paradoxical management style. Wittman could be counted on to hire a man only to let him languish, to promote his creativity only to suppress it, and to ban smoking only to punish the man who instigated the ban. Being summoned to Paul's office no longer produced dread but curiosity.

"I've called you in, Dane, because we have more work from *National Luxury Rentals*. They want a tagline to brand all of their promotional pieces as well as a new ad. I want you to work closely with Arlen."

"That's an oxymoron," Dane pointed out, "Arlen doesn't work closely with anyone. At best he just steals ideas."

"Yeah, yeah, yeah. Dane, you've been in advertising for over nine months but you're still not reborn as an advertising man. This business is all about collaboration."

Deirdre Ryan appeared at the door with a large paper bag between her manicured fingers. She held it far from her body as if it contained a feral animal, but it was only Paul's take-out breakfast. Along with running the office, pacifying clients, supervising production, and planning her boss's travel, Deirdre ordered and brought him his meals. The aroma of fried egg quickly suffused the office. Deirdre dropped the bag on Paul's desk and rushed out to remove her dignity from the compromising act.

Paul tucked into his breakfast—an egg white omelet with Monterey jack cheese, cherry tomatoes and *fines herbes,* pan-fried red potatoes and a container of Tropicana orange juice. As Paul shared his advertising wisdom and a creative brief with Dane between plastic forkfuls of fried egg white, Steve Pomodoro, director of creative services, walked in.

"Saroja is a difficult woman," Steve announced, as if imparting strange news.

"She's worth it," Paul said flatly.

Pomodoro received this message.

"I am 100% committed to working with her!" Pomodoro said.

"Steve, sit," said Paul, who preferred eating in company, especially when his company was not joining him. "Steve-o, how would you like to work with Dane on a new project?"

"Cool," Pomodoro said with his well-known positive energy. Pomodoro had arrived on the WIF scene as an emergent star. In strictly personal terms, the director of creative services was impressive. Tall, athletic, a devoted son, who played golf with his dad,

Pomodoro strode the halls with the vitality and purpose of a linebacker, performing even mundane movements such as standing and sitting like an action hero. Pomodoro was also a *can-do* executive with innovative ideas, such as introducing plastic job folders—a huge hit. In addition to his many gifts, Steve had the most important trait of a true leader. He was unabashed about sharing his personal life with his colleagues. When he arrived at WIF, he courageously "put it out there" that he was undergoing a revolutionary hair growth procedure using computer-guided nano-needles to transplant hair from his buttocks to his scalp. For months the staff marked the passage of their lives by the growth of Pomodoro's coiffure, only to note wistfully that both progressed too slowly. Mabel, a pretty woman in accounts payable, lamented, "*Isss* such a shame...Steve *iss* such a handsome man."

Dane liked Pomodoro but when he looked at his head, he could not avoid the thought that it was a piece of his ass.

After his propitious start, Pomodoro was a casualty of the Wittmans' penchant for blaming employees for their mistakes. He was cruising with a perfect record until the SPACEFINDERS brochures were produced. Paul Wittman and his art directors thought white cardboard was *too yesterday* for their trendy SPACEFINDERS client so they chose pale green stock. When photographs were printed on green cardboard, the models' skin tones had a morbid verdure. Paul Wittman was irate. "You've made a luxury building look like a morgue!" he lambasted Pomodoro.

As director of creative services, it was not Pomodoro's job to make impractical decisions—only to make them work. He was blamed for the fiasco and because he accepted blame, he became a trusted employee.

Now Paul Wittman briefed Dane and Pomodoro about the *National Luxury Rentals* campaign. However, Pomodoro was distracted. He could not take his eyes off of his boss's breakfast.

When Wittman made a business point and asked for Pomodoro's

opinion, he had to shout, "Steve!" to startle him from a trance.

"I'm sorry, Paul. Your breakfast looks so delicious," Pomodoro said with watery eyes and a slack jaw.

"It is. You want some? Here, I'm finished with it," Paul said.

Wittman passed the aluminum container with its scraps of egg white omelet and untouched home fries to Pomodoro and looked on with amusement as the director of creative services wolfed down his breakfast remains. When he was done, they discussed the next assignment.

43. A CREATIVE FANTASY

The new project was unprecedented for WIF. It was bigger than a building or even a residential complex. This was a condo resort and spa with a dozen golf courses in the mountains of New Jersey.

Pomodoro, Saroja, and Dane brainstormed pitch concepts together. The unique selling point of these condos was that they were all situated on a golf course, so that a resident could roll out of bed to play nine holes. Pomodoro in particular appreciated this amenity since he often drove long distances to play golf on weekends.

Rather than have people close their eyes and scribble down ideas according to WIF tradition, Dane suggested that the team truly collaborate. He took the lead by asking questions, eliciting ideas. Saroja offered some. So did Pomodoro. Dane transcribed their thoughts on a flip-chart and by posing more questions, he induced Saroja and Steve to see how their ideas connected and formed larger themes. Dane also offered his own thinking and asked for feedback. While the session was in full-pitch, Pomodoro exclaimed, "This is fun!"

Spontaneously, Dane applied teaching methods to brainstorming. He realized that this had been missing from his advertising experience thus far because supervisors showed little interest in involving everyone in the creative process—or because no process was in place.

44. ANNIVERSARY

It was the one year anniversary of Dane's first day on the job. He could track his progress by the distance of twenty feet between the dusty conference room where he started and his musty new digs.

Much had happened at WIF in a year. Betty, the angry receptionist, got pregnant and married, and several recruitment executives claimed to be the father of her child, prompting ribald arguments. Perhaps in response to the slander, Betty filed a worker's compensation grievance against WIF, alleging that the toxic environment made her too sick to work. Deirdre Ryan was furious. "That whore," she muttered. "This place makes me sick but you don't see me staying home to collect!"

That afternoon, Deirdre Ryan opened Dane's door and peeked in.

"Do you have a moment, Dane?"

"Sure," he said. "What's on your mind?"

"You are," Deirdre replied as she sashayed to Dane's desk and leaned over to whisper. The office administrator made sure that her designer scent "Lust" filled the junior copywriter's congested nostrils and that her full breasts filled his eyes like two plump pastries on a tray. "You've been here a year but instead of being promoted you're regressing."

"Please don't remind me," Dane ruefully replied.

Dane was staring at the same ad with a seductive woman Maury Wittman gave him to work on when he arrived at WIF the year before. Now under its headline, "Do you love where you live?" Dane was rewriting Wittman's twenty words of body copy for the tenth time.

Deirdre sighed heavily with the hint of a purr to suggest impatient desire.

"Do you want to go on like this?" she asked. "Don't you want to advance in your career?"

"You mean, get another job?"

"No, keep this one," Deirdre insisted with droll annoyance. She smiled indulgently at Dane like he was a difficult child. "I just talked to Paul."

"You did? What about?" Dane asked.

She chuckled as if Dane were playing dumb to be cute, rather than just being dumb.

"About you, silly. I convinced him to give you a better position with more responsibility and a real future."

"What could that be?" Dane asked with foreboding.

"Starting next week, you're the new copy chief!" Deirdre replied with a throaty hush of excitement.

"Copy chief? What is that?"

Deirdre inhaled deeply to show intense bosom heaving and replied, "You'll find out."

For Deirdre, "copy chief" was code for inserting herself in Dane's life by currying his gratitude and affection. For Dane, being the copy chief meant he would no longer be involved solely with his own piddling copy, but with the entire agency's verbiage. He would be responsible for every word written at WIF to ensure that it reflected client changes and was accurate in every way. The more this sank into Dane's porous brain matter, the heavier it became. "Copy chief" sounded less like a promotion than a cruel punishment. Deirdre had cleverly foisted one of her burdens on Dane. And with good intentions or sweet revenge, she gave the job a title that conferred no honor, prestige or pride.

If anyone asked what he did, Dane would answer, "I'm a copy chief!" It sounded like a fatuous job featured on *Mr. Rogers Neighborhood.*

"Who is that at our door? Oh, it's the Copy Chief. Hello, Mr. Copy Chief. Did you bring us some copy today?"

"Yes, I did, Mr. Rogers..."

Copy chief required a spiffy hat...Dane could design it: An eyeshade with rolls of paper sprouting from the band.

"Gee, that's great, Deirdre, thanks for thinking of me," Dane said.

"Anything for my favorite junior copywriter. Oh, excuse me, my favorite *copy chief.*" Deirdre shimmied her shoulders as if shivering with excitement at the mention of Dane's elevated status.

"By the way, Dane, what did you think of that bed and breakfast brochure?" she asked. "You've traveled, haven't you?"

"I was in the Peace Corps twenty years ago, if that's what you mean."

Just then, Maury Wittman opened the door. "Deirdre, can I see you about those reports?" He turned to Dane. "How's the body copy coming?"

"Great!" Dane said. "I'm down to 18 words."

"Super, drop it off on my desk when you're down to 15."

45. WELCOME TO MY RICE PADDY

The first response to Dane's first act as copy chief came one day after the memo announcing his promotion.

It was an unqualified disaster.

Dane had no idea what he was supposed to do.

SPACEFINDERS complained about the brochure he had reviewed. A paragraph from page 10 had not been moved to page 15, per agreement. A "the" on page 12 had not been moved to page 10 and changed to "an." Meanwhile page 13 had not been switched with page 9, thus impeding the flow of ideas. *It was a communications mess!*

Now Dane had no choice but to be initiated in the tribe of WIF—he too must take his turn as scapegoat and become a trusted, if not respected, employee. He must undergo Paul Wittman's eye-rolling interrogations and have his intelligence belittled on a daily basis—in open meetings, behind closed doors and behind his back. Yet, Dane viewed his fate with perspective. If young boys of an Amazon tribe were willing to insert their hands in gloves infested with biting ants as a rite of manhood, he reasoned that he could endure the WIF rite of passage to feed his family.

A year had passed since Dane became a professional copywriter, yet he felt less substantial now, not more so. Each day he seemed lighter as if there were less of him. Was his spirit leaving his body? No doubt.

One Monday morning, Dane found his office flooded with black water. Kenny, a collections specialist from Trinidad, who once assured Dane that no one ever got fired at WIF and then was let go a few months later, had occupied this space. Dane recalled Kenny's complaint that the room flooded when the air conditioner was shut off on weekends. Dane removed his shoes and socks and waded in. He could not use the computer while standing in the swamp, so he squatted on his chair. Deirdre Ryan admonished him. "Dane Bacchus, get down! You can't work that way. It's unprofessional."

"And this office is professional? What else can I do?"

Dane made a spectacle of himself, hoping his intolerable work conditions would shame the Wittmans into improving them, although there was no precedent for this.

"Get out of there. It's against WIF rules. Have you read the manual?" Deirdre reproached him.

Dane vacated his office until the building's maintenance man sucked up the water with an industrial vacuum cleaner.

When the mephitic liquid was drained, the office reeked of moldy synthetic carpet. Dane inhaled the noxious air as Maury Wittman changed the copy on the seductive woman ad *again*. The indecipherable black scribbles on the paper looked like disgusting nematodes. One year after starting this career, Dane reflected that he had regressed financially, his creative writing had atrophied, and he was now transcribing the doodles of an egomaniac in a mildewed, glass-walled office. It was time for lunch.

He went out for yogurt and returned to find an unexpected

message on his voice mail. It was from Ella Bolden, the beautiful recruiter who had encouraged Dane more than a year ago but had not returned his calls since. Her message was garbled but Dane understood this much: Ella had something interesting to discuss with him so he should call her back immediately. Dane was more perplexed than excited. Excitement requires background and anticipation, and this message was without precedent.

"Hello!" Ella greeted him warmly, effusively like she always knew they would be having this conversation. "Do you know anyone at Green Advertising? No? It's a pharmaceutical agency. They're interested in seeing your book. Are you interested?"

Interest did not come close to describing Dane's emotion. Later that afternoon Ella phoned him again. She had searched all over for Dane's book when someone from Green Advertising informed her that it had already been delivered to them and they wished to interview Dane immediately.

Dane wore the only sport jacket he had—a corduroy blazer—to his interview at the pharmaceutical agency. It was the hottest day so far that year and he perspired heavily. Afterwards, his interviewer said he would get back to him.

The next Tuesday, Ella phoned Dane with a torrent of good news. Another creative director from Green Advertising had seen and liked his book and wanted to meet him. By freakish luck, Dane and this creative director had the same alma mater and both worked as teachers overseas after college. He interviewed Dane and promptly offered him a job.

46. RESIGNATION

Two weeks after his first interview for the new position, Dane appeared in Paul Wittman's office doorway, careful not to enter.

"Do you have a moment?" he asked Paul with exaggerated respect.

"Yeah, sure," Paul said, tilting his head. Dane seemed different. He wondered what had gotten into the junior copywriter.

Dane handed Paul an envelope. Paul examined the envelope quizzically and smiled at Dane.

"What is this?" Wittman asked, believing it was a practical joke.

"Read it," Dane urged him.

After Paul read the letter, he studied Dane's eyes like a detective.

"How long has this been going on?"

"How long has what been going on?" Dane asked.

"Your discontent. Have you thought out the consequences? You have a family, right? How will you support them if you quit?"

Dane laughed.

"I was offered another job."

"What?" The stupefaction on Paul's face almost made Dane's thirteen months at WIF worthwhile. The reward for being underestimated is the chance to prove one's value. A smirk twisted Paul's lips. Of course, this was a practical joke. Or the world's oldest junior copywriter was delusional.

"So how much are they paying you to leave?"

No stain is as hard to remove as a preconceived notion. Paul believed Dane was staging this resignation to grab more money. He would quote a figure only a few thousand more than his current salary, Paul would top it, and Dane would be back where Wittman wanted him—only at a higher price. No problem: he could fire him later.

"Sixty thousand," Dane replied.

Paul's reaction to the 100% salary increase gave Dane almost as much joy as his hire. Wittman was stunned and embarrassed since he would not and could not pay that much to keep Dane.

During the awkward pause, Dane lost his desire to flaunt his higher market value in Wittman's face. He had been tortured for the better part of the year by his boss's haughty indifference but before all of that, Wittman had given him his first "break."

"I want to thank you for making this opportunity possible," Dane told Paul. "You were the only person in advertising who gave me a chance. This new job, this bigger salary, is not against you—it's because of you. And I'll always be grateful."

In Dane's last two weeks, Maury made sure to change the copy of his seductive woman ad several more times to remind Dane of what he would be missing. Mildred Walters, who never gave Dane even a headline to write, stopped him in the hall, "So you're leaving. How is Paul taking it?"

"Like he takes everything else. It's business." Dane said. "And by the way, why do you care? You haven't given me any reason to stay."

In fact, Dane never considered Wittman's feelings. He viewed the past year as an apprenticeship—a long ordeal to which he was deliberately subjected. Dane never thought his agony was only partly induced by WIF and Wittman. In the heady time of two weeks notice, the job world's version of an international terminal between departure and destination, Dane sensed freedom, escape and progress. He enjoyed WIF when he knew it was not his destiny.

The next year, while driving in the city, Dane noticed his headlines stenciled on the shade of a SPACEFINDERS window and experienced an exhilarating split-second of immortality.

AD NOMAD 2
WRITER OF RECORD

Case 2-A
NO KENNEL FOR OLD DOGS

1. MIXED RECEPTION

Dane sat in the lobby of Green Healthcare Advertising as the receptionist paged his new supervisor several times without success. If Dane had not held the offer letter in his hand, he might have wondered if the new job was a fantasy in his head.

The office manager noticed Dane becoming a couch fixture and concluded that he was an office equipment salesman. She asked Dane his business with dry formality in order to dismiss him. She grimaced when he said he was the new copywriter waiting to start his new job. Something was terribly wrong, she said, as she disappeared behind a door.

"By terribly wrong, did she mean me?" he thought. It was plausible, but Dane was too excited to be disheartened. After 15 months in the agency above *Papaya Dog*, Green Healthcare was advertising as he pictured it. Even the lobby exuded intensity.

When Dane had waited long enough to hear the young receptionist's prolific domestic troubles, the woman who mistook Dane for a salesman led him to his new cubicle, apologizing profusely for the inhospitality he encountered.

"This is not how things are done at GHA!" she exclaimed as if there had been better days before. "This won't happen again!"

It was a safe promise, Dane thought. How many first days could he have at Green Advertising? Dane did not take his indifferent welcome personally. After thirteen months at WIF Advertising, he was inured to being treated as insignificant. He viewed it as a first impression he had to overcome.

Dane sat in his cubicle along a row of cubicles in a vast fluorescent-lit room. He was impervious to the lack of space and privacy. His cubicle was no smaller in his mind than a launching pad.

Around him sat attractive, youthful people, including a petite woman with a gold post in her nose. They all sipped coffee and stared at computer screens. Everyone looked relaxed and no one seemed to work.

This was how Dane had visualized office life years ago when he was scuffling on the street as an aspiring writer: a clean, carpeted paradise where attractive, well-educated people enjoyed AC. Only now he could not fully savor the moment because he experienced it a generation late.

2. MEET YOUR MENTOR

Landon LeSeuer, a.k.a. *The Savior*, the suave man who hired Dane, suddenly appeared by his cubicle and gave him a warm hello. "So, there you are! Sorry I wasn't here to meet you. Everyone knows I don't show up before ten."

Landon was handsome and neat; he wore faded jeans and a polo shirt that fit perfectly. Landon "fit" in every way. He had a corporate face. Each feature was naturally selected not to stand out as an individual but to work well in a team. As a teacher and world-traveler for years, Landon had a ready-to-wear diplomacy that smoothed away every hard edge of human interaction. Within seconds, Dane forgot that Landon had made him wait an hour, and anticipated becoming his friend.

"There are two kinds of writers in this business," Landon told Dane in his office. "Consumer writers like us and science writers, who bond with molecules. Yes, they are mutants who love data, footnotes, annotations, *p* values. *Now, now!* Don't look so worried. It isn't rocket science. You'll be fine. What you'll be working on isn't high science. We're putting you on medicated diapers and a heartworm medication for starters. Don't worry, I'll protect you."

"Why do I need protection?" Dane wondered. *"Does he think I have diaper rash or heartworm?"* As strange as these suggestions

were, he could not imagine any other reason for needing protection in this convivial environment with carpeting, cubicles and a cappuccino machine.

A young man in a cubicle outside Landon's office fretted over a clinical article. Austin Weebler was a junior copywriter and Landon's protégé, a recent college grad with a BS in chemistry. Youth and academic degree partly explained why Weebler was a junior copywriter—*pedigree* did the rest. Austin's mother was a legendary copywriter, whose thirty second commercials convinced Americans that soda was a wholesome beverage and that dogs preferred gourmet kibble. Landon was grooming Austin to be a science writer while he tutored him in advertising.

Dane received his first assignment: to rewrite a brochure about a heartworm medication. It was a simple task and Dane attacked it with disproportionate vigor to impress his supervisor. Landon reviewed Dane's work that afternoon and told Dane he had done well. He asked Dane to write several headlines and taglines for the same product. Dane complied and Landon praised him again. Yet Dane did not feel he had broken a creative sweat. Were these small assignments Landon's way of gently breaking in his new copywriter and imbuing him with confidence before a major trial?

At day's end, Landon told Dane he would be out of the office on business for a few days and for two weeks on vacation. While he was out, Dane could introduce himself to other groups and help out if necessary.

The next day Dane's heartworm medication copy came back to him in a layout scrawled with red circles and unintelligible words. The editor had proposed alternative phrasings and inserted punctuation changes. Emboldened by Landon's praise, Dane stormed to the editor to protest. She was bent over her desk and stared up at him as if to say, "Who are you and why are you disturbing me?"

She was not Dane's preconceived idea of an editor. She wore a turban, a polka dot dress, a circle of scarlet lipstick, and had a boa draped over her cubicle partition. He asked the flamboyant editor to explain her changes, which she was in no mood to defend. "If you don't agree with the changes "stet" them," she said.

Dane had won his first skirmish, defending his stylistic integrity in a paragraph about heartworm.

3. FOSTER PROTÉGÉ

Dane did not lose an opportunity to bond with his benefactor because he had none. Landon LeSeuer promised to take Dane to lunch, introduce him to colleagues, and show him the neighborhood, but always exempted himself at the last moment due to a meeting or prior engagement. Landon had worked at Green Healthcare Advertising through several corporate incarnations and name changes. He was popular, knew everyone, and booked himself for lunch weeks in advance.

At twice his former income, Dane was a foster protégé again— hired by someone he rarely saw and plunked down among strangers with whom he had little in common.

Landon wished to reward and develop Dane's talent, not befriend him. He delegated the big brother role to Austin Weebler, a man half Dane's age. The junior copywriter took Dane on a grand tour, pointing out departments and places of interest, in particular the men's rooms, where Dane heard the unmistakable sounds of retching, gagging and moaning.

"What is that?" Dane asked young Weebler.

"Oh, that? Men puking their guts out," his guide replied casually.

"Is there a bug going around?" Dane inquired.

"Nah," Weebler answered. "It's just a business pitch and a few product launches. Barfing is fairly normal around here. Everybody does it. It's like part of the culture. They say you've only truly worked at Green when you've thrown up at least once."

"Interesting," Dane said queasily.

He had misgivings about Weebler's reliability as a guide. Young Austin was bright and affable but he sniffled like a cocaine addict. He was pale, blinked frequently, grinned for no apparent reason and guffawed in response to serious statements. Austin had other quirks. He preferred to stand even while reading, due to Gluteal Deficit Disorder, a condition that caused painful sitting. Weebler explained that it was a rare side effect of his anti-depression medication.

Austin guided Dane through the Flatiron district. It was one of the perks of working at Green. This job meant more than money or a title; it also provided a vibrant street life and great lunches. WIF had *Papaya Dog*, *miso* at a Korean deli, and supermarket yogurt, but Flatiron offered Dane a world of lunch choices—market buffets, brick-oven pizza stands, *artesenal* sushi, organic Chinese, Syrian falafel, and Thai "to die for." During the walking tour, young Weebler invited Dane to break California rolls with him at an expensive sushi place. Dane declined with the excuse that raw fish was suspect during summer months. The real reason was that Dane's low-income apprenticeship at WIF left him with a permanent spending disability, Hand-Wallet Disease, a post-traumatic stress syndrome related to poverty. Despite doubling his salary, Dane retained the mind-set of the oldest living junior copywriter who could not afford more than a cup of a soup and a slice of bread.

Dane asked Austin to break *falafel* with him but the junior copywriter said Middle Eastern food was contraindicated with his medication. Austin ordered sushi to go while Dane salivated on line for a $3 falafel sandwich from *Sunshine Falafel*. With his fat sandwich tightly inserted in a bag, Dane found a bench in Union Square and ate a herniated pita full of deep fried garbanzo balls. Rivulets of tahina poured between his fingers and tomato bits tumbled on his pants as dogs frolicked nearby.

Weebler confided to Dane that he was clueless about advertising and was "standing on feet of jello." Despite his illustrious advertising mother, he reached out for guidance. Dane admitted that he, too, was trying to figure it all out. He was reluctant to play Austin's advisor since Landon probably reserved the role for himself. It was a scruple Dane would pay for later.

4. THE BOYS AND THE PRICE OF NUDITY

This teeming new world was irresistible to Dane. He explored the entire floor like a tourist in an exotic capital. Weebler, a veteran of six months at Green Healthcare Advertising, teased Dane that he behaved like a puppy. Dane was mortified. He was too old to be frisky and wide-eyed, but this at last was big-time advertising with a wide array of humanity and he could not temper his enthusiasm.

Dane's new neighbors were all juniors in the agency like Dane but they were juniors in *all* respects—in their 20s and 30s. Dane's cubicle-neighbor, Carl, an art director with black-rimmed glasses, resembled a befuddled father in a 1950s Disney movie. He drank himself into a stupor every night in a Williamsburg bar. One morning Carl stumbled into the office with white tape on his glasses. He had sat on them before passing out on his bed at 4 AM. Across the way, a loud, young art director, Danielle, was always shouting on the phone, "That's the bottom line!" and "You're the best!" Across from Dane sat Bettina Rios, a petite, long-haired Peruvian beauty, who teased Dane about how much a man should pay to see her nude: a topic on her favorite reality show. "A million dollars?" she asked. "I would do it for a million dollars!"

Dane soon had significant down time, but his experience at WIF taught him how to respond. He circulated from office to office, meeting people and foraging for work. In one office, several strapping, young men yelled obscenities at each other. One had another in a headlock and delivered a "nuggy," rubbing the man's scalp with his knuckles. The *nuggy*-giver was Eton Krassweiler, who, at 29, was the youngest creative director in medical advertising history. He looked up from his roughhousing and glared balefully at

Dane.

"What do you want?"

"You need help? I'm up," Dane said softly.

"No, I've got this under control," Krassweiler snarled, rolling his eyes as he struggled with his squirming victim, a senior writer.

"I meant work. Do you need writing help?"

"He's looking for work," Krassweiler jeered in a high nasal voice. "No work, old man."

Austin whispered to Dane that this group was known as *The Boys*. They were the hot creative guns of the agency who had won six pitches in a row. Nobody got in their way or questioned them about anything.

Dane believed Green Healthcare Advertising was a significant step in his rise to advertising supremacy. Great things could happen to him here if Eton Krassweiler and *The Boys* did not stunt his growth. They were a gang like those he scrapped with in elementary school and high school. As with any potential enemy, Dane gathered information about *The Boys* and soon had a profile.

The Boys came to Green as protégés of a charismatic creative director who abruptly quit and left them to advance his teachings. They evolved into a priestly creative cult, a corporate neoplasm segregated from other staffers by a membrane of disdain. Green management, believing *the Boys* to be gifted, supported this separation to nurture their creative purity.

Eton Krassweiler, *The Boys'* leader, was an *enfant terrible* with a voracious appetite for food, success and adolescent mayhem. He and his posse of rowdy men moved *en masse* through Green Advertising and bivouacked in his office, where they did most of their creative work. Behind a slammed door, Krassweiler conducted brainstorming sessions. When he was bored, he tossed people and things, bolted from the office, and shouted, "I got to take a dump!"

With their boorish elitism, *The Boys* reminded Dane of the Rock Star Copywriter at *The Institute of Design* orientation, who scratched his gonads like a non-conformist genius with scabies. Their reputation for brilliance gave them license to abuse others and a monopoly on new business pitches.

Dane realized he was in a caste system similar to pick-up basketball. The best players could dribble and shoot while everyone else on the court rebounded, passed and watched. Dane despised these advertising wunderkinds for their surly insolence, but envied their gilded reputations and aura of success. It must be great, he thought, to be able to say and do anything with impunity and to be truly valued.

5. THE PROCESS

Other than the size and energy of Green Healthcare Advertising, the most important major difference to which Dane needed to adapt was the work flow. As the only copywriter at WIF Dane *was* the process. His creative output went from his computer to his printer to Paul and to the art director.

At Green, projects crossed many desks and departments in sequence. All work had to be documented. It was tedious but everyone admitted that it was an improvement over the botched jobs, litigation, chaos and money routinely lost prior to the current system.

Dane had to learn and follow process—fast. It went like this.

The writer's copy went to a supervisor, an account person and a client. When a client approved the copy, it was "dropped" into a folder for word processing. From there, the manuscript went into layout and all changes were scrawled on the most recent layout, called "The Bible."

Process was simple but Dane was often slow when it came to simple. It was a new concept for him and he needed to develop a new skill set.

Sylvia Bittman, the traffic manager, made sure he did. Sylvia was a swaggering woman with matted hair and black eyes—a born overseer. Sylvia told Dane he needed to drop his latest copy.

"Drop the copy?" Dane said. "What do you mean?"

"You're joking! Drop the friggin' copy. It's easy."

Dane had no idea what to do. He could ask Sylvia for an explanation and receive another demeaning diatribe or respond in a joking way by resorting to *Occam's razor:* the simplest explanation must be right.

He dropped the heavy folder Sylvia had given him on the floor. Papers scattered everywhere. Dane's joke fell flat.

"You idiot!" Sylvia screamed. "What do you think you're doing? Are you stupid? Where did Landon find you? At a soup kitchen? Are you making more work for me? You think this is funny? You'd better pick it up!"

Sylvia stormed off and Dane tagged along. He suspected that wherever she went he would need to defend himself.

They found the threshold of Landon's office. Dane had not seen him in weeks and did not know he was around.

"Landon, do you know what your new writer just did? He dumped a job jacket on the floor."

"No!" Landon replied with ironic gravity. "That is an unusual approach."

"Landon, would you please explain our process to your writer? I don't have the time!" Sylvia replied irascibly.

"Yes, yes, of course," Landon agreed. Sylvia was already gone.

"High strung, isn't she?" *The Savior* said before returning to his e-mail. "Oh, and by the way, Dane, you'll be in your new office next Monday."

"Really? That's great!" Dane said.

"You deserve it," Landon replied. "Your work has been very good."

"Thanks...So how do I drop the manuscript in the folder?" Dane asked.

"Call IT. They'll help you."

And that was the process.

6. OLD DOGS, NEW TRICKS

Process notwithstanding, Dane achieved the corporate symbol of success—his own office—in impressive time and this personal milestone inspired him to learn the creative idiom of this new advertising genre with comparable speed. One assignment won him special notice. It involved branding, the core of pharmaceutical advertising.

Since pharmaceutical products were regulated by company medical and legal committees and the FDA, word play and double entendres were off limits to the copywriter because they could mislead, confuse or seduce the patient. Humorous headlines were likewise taboo, deemed inappropriate for products to treat sick and dying.

To overcome these impediments, pharmaceutical advertising exploited visual branding elements like icons, images and logos. An image implied what a headline could never say. Dane was assigned to create a new character for a popular antibiotic. For a year, the brand's creative team had laid waste to every bug-killing concept, dependability symbol and power icon. Flyswatters, frogs with obscenely long flypaper tongues, vintage cars, lighthouses, jets, and super-heroes that pummeled villains with names like *Strep-monster* and *Flagellin,* had all lived and died.

With his fertile imagination, Dane invented a Saluki dog catching a rabbit in the desert, a rattlesnake assaulting a prairie dog and a lifeguard rescuing a child from a sea teeming with aquatic bacteria.

The lifeguard was the winner.

Dane was thrilled but the reason for his triumph was no food for pride.

The antibiotic treated children's respiratory infections, so the client liked having a lifeguard who saved children. The lifeguard also presented various tactical opportunities, including coloring books, boy and girl lifeguard dolls, comic books—for distribution to sick children at pediatricians' offices—and cartoon commercials.

Adults could also love the lifeguard. Men might appreciate a female lifeguard in a one-piece and women would go for a buff male lifeguard.

"It's got legs," Landon LeSeuer complimented Dane. One of the young female junior executives handed Dane an unforeseen compliment.

"I guess you *can* teach old dogs new tricks!"

7. NO KENNEL FOR OLD DOGS

If Dane was an old dog at Green Healthcare, he was not the only one in the kennel. His partner, Stan Bushkin, was more qualified for this distinction. Bushkin was a decade older than Dane.

When Landon was out—which was often—Bushkin was Dane's creative supervisor. His office was next door to *the Boys*, but he occupied the opposite end of the creative spectrum.

Bushkin was rotund and slovenly with coarse hair and a jowly face that conveyed boyish mischief. He was from the golden age of advertising and its creative, carefree ethos endured in him as a pulse. In Bushkin's pre-digital prime, concepts were drawn with markers and type was set by hand. He won awards as an art director but had to relearn everything when computers, scanners and software rendered mechanical processes obsolete.

In the yin and yang of creators and refiners, Bushkin was a creator. Witty and versatile, he drew vivid comps and crafted headlines that read like punch lines, and would have been productive if asked to conceive new ads. However, his talents were useless in medical advertising, where original work was rarely done. Bushkin was lost when told to redo old ads. His hands and jowls trembled when he showed his layouts to Gaines Burger, the captious creative director who appeared in the office as seldom as possible and reinforced his status by criticizing everything that was done in his absence.

Other than such awkward moments, Bushkin acted like a mascot in semi-retirement. He exuded delight to have a full-time job and spent much of his time playing hide and seek and perusing *eBay*.

When Bushkin did not rhapsodize about shopping at wholesale clubs or buying his cousin's apartment for cheap, he entertained Dane with horror stories about his freelance debacles. One time Bushkin was called in to save a huge account. He worked for 48 straight hours churning out concepts. The agency lost the business anyway and the bitter creative director berated Bushkin and refused to pay him.

On Monday mornings Bushkin told Dane in a dreamlike tone how he and his wife spent their weekend.

"We went to *Costco* on Saturday. You ever go to *Costco*? No? What's wrong with you? We bought a 32 oz slab of lox."

"Did you have people over for brunch?" Dane asked.

"Why would we do that?"

"Because you bought so much lox. Who ate it all?"

Bushkin stared at Dane incredulously like he was hopelessly slow.

"We did. We ate it while we watched cable."

As partners, Dane and Bushkin tried to develop rapport. They often went out for lunch and sauntered around the farmer's market at Union Square.

Because Dane had a penchant for falafel sandwiches, Bushkin called him "Baba Ghanoush." Before they returned to the office one afternoon, Bushkin let Dane tag along when he purchased shoe laces at the store where his orthotics were made. Dane knew this moment was significant since Bushkin wouldn't share his bad feet with just anyone.

Yet Bushkin was more complex than a regressive old man with flat feet. He believed he was hired for his funny, award-winning consumer campaigns, so he wracked his brain to produce uproarious drug ideas—for incontinent men without prostates and women with cancer. He trawled for goofy pictures and devised droll headlines to make sick patients and distraught caregivers laugh.

Dane admired Bushkin's boisterous wit but he already sensed after only a month at Green that *funny* and *edgy* were not the right tone for selling healthcare products. This audience did not consist of truck-driving, beer-guzzling sports lovers looking for a cheap laugh but patients and physicians seeking information and a reason to believe. Creativity needed to be confined to dryly clever concepts and headlines—and then only for drugs treating non-life-threatening diseases.

Understanding the patient's emotional state was Dane's strength. He sympathized with the pain, the shame and the earnest desire for relief— and aimed for the trenchant phrase to sum up the audience's response to a disease. Bushkin thought Dane's dry, laconic statements were not advertising.

Dane and Bushkin were able to coexist with their differences until they collaborated on an ad for adult diapers which targeted urologists and family doctors with incontinent patients. During one brainstorming session for medicated diapers, Bushkin let his imagination go.

"*Baba Ghanoush*, how about we have two women talking? One says, 'Where did you buy those diapers? They're so chic!'" Bushkin said in a falsetto voice.

"Diapers are not chic," Dane replied. "They keep incontinent people from peeing on the floor so they avoid humiliation."

"Sick people are people, too," Bushkin protested. "They like to laugh."

"Not at themselves," Dane pointed out.

"What about this?" Dane asked. "It's vanilla but it may work. You have a woman in a white dress and summer bonnet. The headline reads: "Now you can wear your summer whites.""

"What's that?" Bushkin yelled.

"Women want to be stylish but they can't if they're worried about leakage. With our product, they don't have to worry," Dane explained. "We can also put her in a tennis outfit and a white pant suit."

"No!" Bushkin shouted. He stood up and shook his fist at Dane, then reached for the nearest projectile, a half-empty coffee cup, and hurled it at the wall. "What are you doing here?" Bushkin blurted furiously. "You don't know how to write. Your ads aren't funny! They're not even clever!"

This was a milestone in Dane's career. He had been disrespected and ignored many times but never told to his face that he lacked talent. Though he was stunned by Bushkin's insult, his fights at WIF taught him to renounce anger. He explained himself calmly to his partner, who implacably shook his fist at Dane and shouted, "Get out!"

Dane retreated to his office to process what had just transpired. *Was he in trouble?* He knew cheap jokes were irrelevant to selling drugs but Bushkin was from the *Golden Age*. He was out of touch, yet possessed a nobler aesthetic! He once sold *Miller Light*!

In Bushkin's diatribes, Dane heard echoes of *The Institute of Design*, of "The Three Stooges" and Sal Sambucca with his *Madison Avenue Cocktail*, and even of Arlen Lesser at WIF—all traditional ad men. Dane conceded that he might not have been hired in the Golden Age; no doubt, he fit in better with aluminum or tin. Yet, he also knew he would surpass Bushkin in medical advertising *if Bushkin did not have him fired first!*

What if Bushkin reported to Landon that Dane was strictly aluminum or tin and Bushkin refused to work with him? It might raise questions about the quality and authenticity of Dane's portfolio.

At WIF, Dane was banished to a closet after three months and to an office rice paddy after ten. Was the pattern repeating itself after only two months at Green?

Such speculations spun in his head until they gave him vertigo. He did not know what to do so he went to lunch.

8. PUNGENT LUNCH

While one famous character had breakfast at *Tiffany's* to feel better, Dane improved his outlook with lunch at the farmer's market in Union Square. There he tried to lose himself in the vitality of the people and the variety of foods.

On Mondays, Wednesdays and Fridays, upstate farmers, coastal fishmongers, and local tradesmen plied their wares and Dane purchased tart organic apples and molar-cracking pretzels.

After his fight with Bushkin, Dane stopped at the concession of a Korean *kimchee* vendor—a market newcomer. Dane tasted the *kimchee*. It was the best he ever had. It reminded him of a simpler time when he was a graduate student tutoring Korean children at their Flushing apartment and inhaled pungent cabbage fermenting in a flower box on their terrace. Nostalgic for when he was poor but appreciated, Dane bought a container of *kimchee* and returned to the office.

He closed his door and pried open the plastic top, eager to taste the funky delicacy. It was like opening *Pandora's Box* of shit. Out of doors, the *kimchee* aroma mingled with other smells and dissipated rapidly in the chill air; in a restaurant it was a pungent fanfare to Korean feasting. But Dane's *kimchee* offended the impersonal business setting, permeating the stale air of the sealed office with a fleet and feculent stench.

Dane closed the container and waved his arms to sweep away the spreading effluvium but was helpless against it. Unable to expel the smell, he fled to locate an antidote. After hiding the *kimchee* in a paper bag in the fridge, he foraged for air spray. From halfway across the office floor, he heard Danielle, the loud art director, shout, "Ass odor!" It was a safe bet she wasn't thinking, "Prized Korean condiment."

However, the loud woman's accusatory cries gave Dane an idea. If he joined the loud protest against the *kimchee* smell, people might look elsewhere for the culprit; the ploy often worked for flatulent subway riders.

Dane raced to the chief administrator's office and found a can of *Lysol*, then returned to his office, hoping to eliminate the *kimchee* odor before most of his office neighbors returned from lunch. Too late. A crowd had gathered outside his door. They were sniffing through clogged sinuses as if morbidly attracted to the stench or curiously seeking the carcass from which it came.

"Excuse me. I have a *kimchee* situation here," Dane said as he sprayed relentlessly, insouciant of the public health risk of discharging so many disinfectant droplets into the air supply.

He feared that the word would circulate that he had an episode of fecal incontinence, which was doubtless the worst impression one could make in a corporate milieu.

Later he discovered a printed sign on his closed door:

Men's Room Out of Order.

As befitting an ad agency, the message was professionally typed in Helvetica. Graffiti was scrawled on the margins: *The copy stinks. So does the writer.*

Dane shut his office door and held his head in his hands. What possessed him to eat fermented cabbage for lunch? Couldn't he have a normal food with a familiar smell like everyone else? That night, Dane brought home his container of *kimchee*. When he peeled off the lid in the kitchen, Becky made him close the container and eat its fetid contents in the hallway by an open window.

9. PITCH OUT

After Dane's *kimchee* experience, he received a new assignment— a drug indicated for fecal incontinence. The irony was not lost on Dane.

Was it mere coincidence that his first assignments were for heartworm, adult diapers and fecal incontinence? Dane worried that he was being type-cast as the senior writer with senior problems. Did the *kimchee* incident fuel this impression?

Landon never told Dane he was being tested. This was the Green Way. All writers underwent a rigorous probation, in which they were expected to work themselves up from the humblest body part to the loftiest. Only after a writer proved himself in the bowels was he allowed to write about the heart, lungs and brain.

Dane had no idea of this. All he knew was that his career was progressing slowly. After two months, he had an office at Green Healthcare but no reputation. Even so, he made the most of his fecal incontinence assignment for a drug called *Conteyne*. Dane's gut told him that nobody, including a patient with fecal incontinence, wanted to see or think of feces. Thus, he transposed the problem—untimely delivery—to a different context—cargo transport. He conceived an ad in which a truck, seen from behind, loses its load of boxes, which obstruct the road. The boxes are gift-wrapped, which further idealizes the problem. The headline read: Avoid untimely deliveries. *Conteyne*.

Landon gave the ad several deep head nods, signifying that he liked the *Conteyne* concept. "Yes," he said. "This is very good, Dane. The gift boxes are a nice touch. They almost bring a tear to the eye."

Dane was growing in confidence but along his sense of creative prowess was stalked by restlessness. He craved a more significant assignment to show off his talent.

Finally, an important pitch came to Green for a landmark cancer drug. Only some people were asked to contribute and Dane was not one of them. It was unclear who picked the team and why but Dane was in agony. Meanwhile, *The Savior* was out of town and could not help him. Now Dane was certain he was stereotyped as old and stale. In addition, his exclusion triggered painful childhood flashbacks. When he was ten, he often went to a field where neighborhood boys played football. While the games were in progress, Dane watched patiently and hoped a player would drop out or drop dead, so the teams would be uneven and he could play. One player finally left but as Dane ran onto the field, other boys walked off. The game was over.

Dane was in a funk. Unexpectedly, Bushkin came to his office to cheer him up.

"Don't worry about those guys," he said. "You've got what it takes."

Bushkin's gesture seemed sincere; yet, it reminded Dane of his diatribe weeks before. Dane wondered if Bushkin's caustic assessment of his talent had been candid and correct. Maybe he should not be a copywriter.

Austin Weebler, Landon's protégé, also noted that Dane was excluded from the action.

"So are you working on the pitch?" Austin Weebler asked.

"No," Dane told the quirky junior copywriter.

"That's dumb. You come here from a mainstream agency and everybody knows you have an amazing book. Why did they put me on this and not you?" Weebler asked.

Dane shrugged.

"Hey, that doesn't mean you can't play a part. We can still brainstorm, you and me. You'd be helping me out and they'll see what you can do."

At first, Dane balked. Instinct told him exclusion from a project was like a strikeout in baseball—irrevocable. And Weebler was probably using him so he would have more to show at creative reviews.

Or maybe Weebler was trying to be friends. Dane knew it was better to have an ally than an enemy, and even an unofficial creative opportunity was better than none at all. He agreed to help Weebler.

Austin explained the drug: it destroyed head and neck tumors. Unlike lymphomas, leukemia, or ovarian cancer, head and neck tumors were often outcomes of unhealthy behavior. Head and neck cancer patients were typically heavy smokers and drinkers. "Irresponsible slobs" was how Austin described them. They were thought to bring cancer on themselves. Many had neoplasms the size of oranges.

This physical detail gave Dane an idea: a photograph of an old hand holding a grapefruit with a simple headline reading "This was the size of the tumor in my neck. Now I live without it."

Weebler wrote the headline excitedly and hurried to the creative review. Dane expected to hear nothing more about the pitch.

Later Austin appeared in his office. "At the creative review, they really liked your idea of the hand holding the orange. They're going to test it. So I told them, 'Dane Bacchus came up with that idea.'"

Dane had hoped for this outcome but was now dissatisfied with it. Despite his being left off the pitch, his idea forced its way in. His talent was vindicated, yet the victory was empty. He was not invited to join the pitch team. While agency excitement surged at the prospect of new business, he felt more dejected. Had he come this far to be left out of the game—again, just like when he was ten?

10. PROBATION

While others did vital creative tasks, Dane was saddled with daily maintenance work usually delegated to juniors and beginners. He copied by hand changes from client faxes onto the most recent layout. Dane reviewed each new round against the previous one to ensure all changes were made. Dane hated the tedium. He chose advertising because it promised creative work. Could he pretend he was more than a glorified clerk?

One afternoon, while the excitement of the pitch percolated around Dane, the junior account person on the adult diapers account, Maureen Fitzrooney, delivered a heavy folder full of corrections for his review. Dane's face contorted in an involuntary scowl as if Maureen had delivered a bag of soiled diapers.

"What is it now?" he asked the young woman.

"It's the changes," Maureen said as she dropped the heavy folder on his desk.

"It's time to change the diapers," Dane cracked, oblivious to Maureen's grimace and what it portended.

At around that time, Dane's probationary period was over. At last, he would qualify for health insurance.

Late one afternoon, Landon phoned him to come to his office. Dane had no cause for concern, but *The Savior's* voice was tight and unusually serious, and, unlike Paul Wittman, Landon had never summoned him by phone to his office before.

The door was closed. Dane knocked and was asked to enter the dimly lit room. Landon sat on his couch and the director of human resources, Sue Larimore, was next to him. Sue was a lounge singer by night but now she glowered like a bouncer.

"We've heard disturbing things about how you relate to members of your team," she said. "We can't tell you who complained but you've been described as uncooperative and unpleasant."

Dane was stunned. Just moments before, he had been sitting back and taking stock of his success. He planned to celebrate his anniversary that evening with Becky. Now he appeared to be losing his job.

"You're not losing your job," Landon said as if reading Dane's mind. Dane was not reassured. The mention of a firing suggested its possibility.

The human resources officer asked Dane if he recalled doing or saying anything inappropriate. Dane struggled for composure.

"I can't believe this," Dane said haltingly. "I thought I was doing well. I get along with everyone."

He noted that his interrogators were sympathetic.

"Dane, sometimes we men seem aggressive without meaning to," Landon said. "Women can read even a tone of voice or a passing facial expression as macho, chauvinistic, misogynistic abuse. In a team environment where we often work closely and under pressure, we need to take extreme care with the signals we send."

If Dane could have seen his facial expression at that moment, he might have wished to send more intelligent signals. His mouth was open. He looked dumbfounded or just dumb as he learned how he was betrayed by his behavior. "I try to be pleasant at all times," he pleaded, "But my face has a mind of its own."

Landon nodded sympathetically. He never had this problem and felt twice as much compassion for the poor wretch who did. Meanwhile, the human resources director, who, as a lounge singer, knew people best in dark rooms, studied Dane in the fading autumn light.

"Dane, before advertising you were a writer and teacher. You were autonomous. It must be hard to adapt to advertising, which is collaborative," she remarked.

The human resources executive's casual observation triggered immense pain, like a cold instrument pressing a chronic wound. Dane had tried to forget his prior life as a writer and teacher. He needed to prove he could be as creative in advertising, where money was to be made, as he had been in literature, where only poverty thrived. He argued with himself that art and survival were not enemies. A good salary, a respectable title and a vibrant ambience anesthetized the pain of subordination. Now the human resources director probed his hiding place where subversive longings and old demons awaited release. He felt like a fraud.

"No, no," Dane protested, "I love working with other people. That's part of the fun."

He hoped they believed him after the human resources director's direct hit exposed his guilt. He had probably lashed out at someone recently because he wanted to be a creative hero instead of a team-player doing the grunt work.

When the meeting was over, Landon asked Dane if he was okay. Dane was relieved to still be employed but was close to tears. Despite being forgotten for the first hour of his first day and excluded from the pitch, Dane was comfortable at Green. He never cringed before each payday, believing it would be his last—until now. He realized that regardless how genteel the workplace seemed, he was always one complaint away from termination.

Case 2-B
BRANDING INCONTINENCE

11. THE WORKSHOP

Green Healthcare Advertising strived to be more than a workplace. Top management was committed to the vision of a holistic job experience. "Hard work" was banished from the agency vocabulary and replaced by the slogan, "Heart work," with the variation, "Work is where the heart is." Both iterations appeared prolifically on posters in lobbies, corridors, and on old-fashioned campaign buttons, distributed to employees under every plausible pretext. The aim was to instill in staff-members a sense of family and fun.

Parties were weekly happenings at Green. Other agencies needed reasons to celebrate, but at Green, the prevailing concept was, "Celebrate and reasons will follow."

In this festive culture, popular holidays presented ideal opportunities to foster lasting collegial bonds while stressing the creative verve that distinguished advertising from other industries. During "Green Halloween," for instance, the featured event was the annual creative pumpkin contest, in which every employee was invited to carve and design his own, unique pumpkin. All finished jack-o'-lanterns were later displayed on a large conference table near the glass doors in a festive profusion of three-dimensional design.

During Dane's first "Green Halloween," Landon was represented not by a pumpkin caricature, like other Green notables, but by an empty space and a card reading "OOTO" (Out of the office). This gag derided *The Savior* for his many business trips. Although Dane suffered from his mentor's frequent absences, he felt considerable loyalty for him and was incensed by this public ridicule.

Dane removed the card from the display and showed it to Landon.

"Ah," *The Savior* said with wry amusement. "Someone is impugning my good name. Thank you, Dane!"

"It was the probably *The Boys*," Dane said. "They act like they own the place."

Landon nodded and gave Dane an appraising and sympathetic look.

"This has been a difficult time of adjustment for you, hasn't it? I'll be out of town for a week. I need you to attend a branding workshop in my place. What do you know about urinary incontinence?"

It was one of those trick questions to which there was no comfortable answer in medical advertising.

Nevertheless, a week after Dane's near-firing (he believed only his tears saved him), Dane was rewarded for defending his mentor's reputation. He received a creative assignment—direct mail letters to women suffering from urinary incontinence—and earned a spot in a brand-identity workshop for an injectable product used to treat the embarrassing condition. This workshop would bring together the client and the finest minds in urinary incontinence marketing. When it was over, a device comprised of collagen, a needle, and a syringe would possess a brand identity, a positioning statement, and the basis for an ad campaign.

Green's urology client had never advertised its products because urologists understood and trusted them without promotion. However, the manufacturer now faced competition from major pharmaceutical firms that outspent it in sales forces, marketing materials, and physician-oriented events. Since Green's client had only developed technical literature to support its products, it needed the full advertising treatment Green Advertising provided—branding workshops, positioning laboratories, and brand character constructions.

A branding workshop was a combination of college literary seminar, religious séance and nursery school. Account managers did PowerPoint presentations, led the group in analytical discussions, and facilitated creative collages with magazine pictures, glue, sparkles, feathers and other arts supplies. There were short writing exercises with sentences that began: "Dr. Urologist says, "When I relieve a patient's incontinence, I feel like...." Answers included Louis Pasteur, Albert Schweitzer, Mother Theresa, and House.

From these creative exercises, insights and perceptions emerged. Participants formed more than an image for their product; they imbued it with a soul, an identity, a personality and a spiritual life. A brand character was born; an advertising strategy was charted.

It was nothing less than miraculous for a needle, a syringe and collagen.

Dane was no neophyte in this prestigious specialty. He had done brand research for his adult diaper product. In one session, he took notes behind a two-way mirror while venal pediatricians on their lunch hour were asked, "If Disposable Diaper X drove into this room what make of car would Disposable Diaper X be driving?" Dane could barely refrain from laughing.

However, this urology brand character workshop was high profile compared to disposable diaper research. Dane found himself in a brightly lit corporate boardroom with clients, the highest agency officials and catered lunch. He would need to participate, create concepts, propose ideas, and eat neatly.

In order to give the product a brand character, everyone needed to be clear about the audience—in this case, urologists. Who were these specialists? How did they view themselves? What make of car did they drive?

"They have inferiority complexes," claimed a consulting psychotherapist, who had many urologists as patients. A nurse, who had worked with urologists for 25 years, corroborated this profile. She said her employers often labeled themselves, "plumbers in white coats." However, a guest urologist countered that he and his peers enjoyed "stellar" self-esteem and considered themselves "masters of the urinary tract." Later, the clients described urologists by the vehicles they drove, the beverages they drank and their favorite foods, TV programs, musical selections, hair colors, and vacation destinations, as documented in secret videos taken by sales reps during complimentary dinners and events.

Based on this input, agency people and their clients wrote statements depicting urologists' psyches and perspectives. Clients and ad people enjoyed workshops because everyone involved believed that they were doing something more interesting, more stimulating and more important than devising a cartoon character or a generic sounding logo. That would come later.

At the end of three days, the client and agency understood who urologists really were. Most were self-described plumbers of the medical trade—self-deprecating and unpretentious. Yet, within their generic low self-esteem lurked the individual need for affirmation, validation and respect. They yearned to be thought masters of their specialty.

The brand workshop reminded Dane of his teaching days and he thrived in its seminar structure. In the long and painful gestation of the brand character, he played the role of male midwife, helping others to articulate their ideas, then rephrasing them, providing insights, and building consensus. Dane had a strong voice in crafting the brand character statement, positioning statement and brand aspiration statement. But he did not stop there. He gave the brand character its first words, suggested which schools the brand character would attend and what it would look like and do in twenty years. Account people and clients nodded appreciatively when Dane spoke and he made a substantial impression.

12. A BREAKTHROUGH IN INCONTINENCE

The news of Dane's contribution to the incontinence workshop reached Landon when he returned from his travels.

The creative director called Dane into his office. Dane was once again on his guard. He had no idea why Landon summoned him, which increased his nervousness. Had a client or an agency satrap complained that Dane talked too much at the workshop, or that he slobbered over his salad?

Landon hunched over his computer in the dark room. A classic reading lamp on the corner of his desk cast a disk of light over his handsome profile.

"Take a seat, Dane."

The situation seemed dire. Dane withdrew within himself, deep beneath his tingling exterior. On the surface, he felt a feverish chill on his skin, and experienced the scene as if from afar. Peristalsis rumbled through his intestinal tract. All of his reading about fecal incontinence appeared like a teletype across his consciousness. He tightened his sphincter for control.

"Dane, I want to apologize. When I called you in here last month, it was because Maureen Fitzrooney filed a serious complaint against you. From what I had come to know about you, it was hard to believe her allegations. However, as a matter of HR policy, we needed to take her complaint seriously, especially since you were in the probationary period. As it turns out, you were right to protest your innocence. Maureen is no longer with the agency. She had a plethora of her own issues and a penchant for complaining about others. So please, accept my apology and let's put that behind us."

"I will, Landon. I just want to be worthy of your confidence."

"You are, Dane. That's why I've called you in. I had to be sure about you, that you could handle pressure. You have been tested as thoroughly as a condom. You have held up splendidly."

"Tested? I mean, thank you, Landon."

The Savior regarded Dane with pride and trust. His manner was at once paternal and fraternal, with a soupçon of grandeur and gravitas befitting a feudal lord confiding in his vassal.

"Dane, you've passed five of the six trials of pharma. First, you showed the inflated ego of a true writer by defending trivial heartworm copy from an editor while having the good manners not to insult her tawdry attire. Second, you passed the bad partner test. When Bushkin, an advertising dinosaur, denigrated your talents, you did not retaliate with profanity or violence. In your third trial, you kept your cool when you were passed over for a pitch and never protested when your concept won the business without your receiving credit for it. For your fourth trial, you handled the human resources accusation of inappropriate conduct toward a female colleague without calling the accuser a bitch. And most recently, you sat for three days in a urinary incontinence workshop without wetting yourself."

Landon paused, perhaps expecting Dane to laugh at his uncharacteristic attempt at crude humor. But Dane could not believe Landon was capable of crassness and thought he was hearing things. "Of course, *je plaisante!*" Landon continued. "In fact, you contributed with your typical brilliance. You've worked your way up the anatomical ladder—from pet parasites to human intestines and now to the urinary tract. You've written movingly on fecal incontinence. Your concept with the truck losing its load of Christmas gifts on the road still makes me nod with wry approval. For this you merit extra credit. I have only one more task for you to carry out. If it goes as well as I expect it will, you'll receive the assignment you were born to have."

"Yes, thank you," was all Dane could say. Had he really done all of that in four months? He was awestruck by his own industry.

"Now you know more than you ever wanted to about urologists and stress incontinence. So I need you to create a powerful message and campaign for the product, a collagen injectable that prevents involuntary leakage."

"That's...wonderful, Landon. Thank you. I won't disappoint you."

"*De rien!* I know you won't," Landon replied cheerfully.

Landon's use of French idioms always reassured Dane and buoyed his spirits. No doubt it recalled his undergraduate days, when he studied French philosophy and was the Big Existentialist on Campus. *Sacré bleu!* Those were the good times, when nothingness was a cool idea and not the story of his life.

For a week, Dane pondered the assignment, struggling for the words, images—and voice—of stress incontinence—an embarrassing problem afflicting millions of women, as well as men after prostate surgery. It might not lend itself to humor but it was not life-threatening, so he could be creative with it.

On the evening of the *Silver Pill* Awards annual wine, cheese and crudités party, Dane was more anxious than usual. It was a sign of inspiration inflating in his brain. Of course, when he experienced this torment it seemed that nothing good could come of it. He felt heavy, uneasy and dull, like a frustrated failure. His colleagues were heading out to *the Silver Pills* party. They cajoled Dane to stop working so they could hit the shindig in a "creative show of force." Despite their pressure, Dane could not stop writing headlines and doodling on his pad. The more his workmates coaxed him, the more rooted he was to his chair. He was so agitated that he perspired from the conflicting pressure to stay and to leave.

When his colleagues finally gave up on him and left, Dane experienced great calm and relief, such as he had rarely felt. Out of the relaxed sphincter of his imagination, headlines emerged, then visuals. He had that rare creative event—a total eclipse of the mind. Words and images came together in a complete concept and this one concept then suggested two more for a perfect campaign.

Dane wrote the visual ideas and headlines in large, crude letters— a child's emphatic penmanship—before bolting for the *Silver Pills* party. Spent and serene, he had a dull headache—a creative concussion—but enjoyed the industry schmooze because he had cause to celebrate, although he kept it to himself. He knew his incontinence work was good; no, better than good. Incontinence would never be seen quite the same way again.

When he presented these concepts to the client later that week, in Green's main conference room, everyone was pleased. Afterwards, Landon left the room with Dane and whispered, "That's *your* work. You should be proud. Great job! Come to my office. I need to speak with you."

13. DANE RECEIVES HIS REWARD

Even in the ecstasy of triumph, Dane was grim and businesslike as he walked into his mentor's office. A tower of folders stood on the corner of *The Savior's* desk.

"You've done everything I've asked of you," LeSeuer said. "I couldn't be prouder. You have proven yourself worthy of the assignment I had in mind when I hired you."

Landon prepared to lift the stack of folders from his desk but flinched.

"I've been having trouble with my back," he admitted. "Please take the folders."

Dane lifted the tower of folders and held it before him. Landon placed his hands under the stack so that the two men simultaneously bore the folders for ten seconds. Then LeSeuer released his grip, leaving Dane to carry the stack of bulging folders alone.

"This is the most significant business pitch I ever won, Dane, and I've won more than my share. This drug is expected to gross $8 billion per year. I'm handing it over to you."

The stack Dane held rigidly before him measured forty inches high and weighed sixty lbs. It contained every study, government submission of data, internal document, FDA letter, and clinical trial protocol related to *Refluxydyl,* the next blockbuster GERD

(Gastroesophogeal reflux disease) medication to be launched. Dane's arms trembled under the unstable weight. Yet he summoned all his strength to remain strong and still. He understood the importance of this moment. It was tantamount to the dubbing of a knight or the changing of a guard. He even imagined it was like Jacob receiving Isaac's birthright. Dane felt he must be worthy of this investiture and the solemn trust it signified. He held the tower of documents steady to demonstrate to Landon his strength and purpose. If he laid it on the desk or let his arms so much as flinch he would show his mentor that he lacked the will and toughness for this job.

"Dane, you are now the writer of record," Landon said. "You will be an expert on everything pertaining to this product and this account. I know you are ready."

Dane's arms were twitching now and the stack hung low in his weary arms. When *The Savior* concluded his remarks, he nodded, smiled warmly and said, "Go forth and read every word in that stack...Just kidding."

When the brief ceremony was over, Dane carried off the voluminous stack of documents, which swung low before him like an elephant trunk. He walked as fast as he could to his office, believing that if he took his time he would have a hernia and drop it all in front of everyone, resulting in a moment to rival the office *kimchee* fiasco, now recorded in agency annals.

Case 2-C
GERDMASTER

14. THE LORD OF REFLUXYDYL

As Dane subdivided the document tower into several low-rise units and scattered them on diverse office surfaces, Dane assumed writing responsibility for the multimillion dollar launch of *Refluxydyl*, the sexy next generation proton pump inhibitor (PPI) and a presumptive multi-billion dollar blockbuster drug.

It was the most important new launch at Green and arguably in the entire pharmaceutical industry. Dane had triumphed over heartworm, and fecal and urinary incontinence, but now he had to battle GERD, a.k.a. acid reflux disease, a much larger and more lucrative therapeutic area, populated by many drugs of divergent strengths and modes of action.

This was the marketing story.

Esophogard, a hugely popular and profitable drug, would soon go off-patent and its manufacturer faced the loss of $8 billion in revenue. The drug company hoped to replace its juggernaut with a new drug, which was the same molecule trimmed in half—an *enantiomer*.

The unproven theory behind the *enantiomer* was that it worked better than the original molecule and had fewer side effects. It was steak without gristle. But was a leaner molecule a meaner one?

Refluxydyl presented two significant marketing problems. First, it was no more effective than the soon-to-be-generic product it would replace. Secondly, it would cost three times more than the generic. Equal strength at three times the cost was a hard sell.

However, Dane saw *Refluxydyl* only as an enormous opportunity. The launch of *Refluxydyl* was his chance to create something important. Though he had achieved some success by becoming the writer of record on a blockbuster account, Dane aspired to advertising greatness. He posed himself the challenge of creating the winning concept, something uniquely his. To accomplish this, he must only write a powerful, enduring headline and a compelling visual based on a real product benefit.

In advertising terms, it was a daunting challenge. Since *Refluxydyl* worked no better than the drug it would replace, Dane needed to provide another compelling reason for doctors and patients to switch. People often believed that new was better than old, and that evolution produced improvement. However, the new drug was no breakthrough, only the next phase in a progression. Meanwhile, the client wished to avoid depicting *Esophogard*, the older drug, as passé since it remained the most popular drug in its class, and would gross billions before going off-patent. The new drug must not cannibalize the old one, but be identified with it. To this end, *Refluxydyl* had the same branding colors as *Esophagard* and the pills and packages were to bear an unmistakeable family resemblance.

In Dane's view, this was no revolution but an orderly succession. People felt comfortable with gradual change; now how could it be expressed?

One evening in the subway, Dane stood by a pole when a sentence occurred to him that was so simple and pure, it was appalling it had not come sooner. Dane fumbled in his pocket for a pen, only to realize he had no paper handy. This was no time to scrounge for a scrap in his briefcase; any distraction would break the delicate strand of words. He let go of the pole and started writing on his hand but the pen was dry. He put the pen tip in his mouth to moisten it, moved it violently across his palm until the ink flowed, and staggered around the subway car, scrawling precious words on the parchment of his skin. When the train lurched to a stop, Dane stumbled on a seated passenger's foot and fell, driving the ballpoint deep into his hand. Dane shouted out in pain, removed the pen and resumed writing.

"Are you okay?" one kindly passenger inquired.

"Fine," Dane said automatically, unwilling to impede the flow of the line with an extraneous word. As blood seeped from his self-inflicted stigmata, Dane crouched on the subway floor and scribbled the last three words of his verbal formula. He completed the breakthrough line and licked away the blood to protect it.

"Where *Esophaguard* left off, *Refluxidyl* takes off."

Dane visualized a sprinter handing off a purple baton with the *Refluxidyl* logo on it to a stronger, sleeker runner.

The time, effort and internal turmoil he needed to arrive at this simple solution astonished him. It was more like excavation than creation. Tons of debris had to be hauled from his mind to find this concept. But now that he had it, it seemed to have always been there.

In this sense, advertising was an art. Before a work came into being it was impossible to imagine it; yet once it existed, one could not imagine the world without it. Now Dane was free to enjoy his weekend. He and Becky took Iris to a classmate's birthday party at a skating rink. When the birthday girl threw up, Dane saw this as a sign that he must pay for his divine insight with an act of kindness. He helped the astonished parents clean the mess.

At the next creative review the walls of a conference room were festooned with pictures and headlines on paper scraps. Within the agency, Dane's concept was identified as a winner. Landon predicted that they would see *Where Esophagard left off, Refluxydyl takes off* for years to come.

No sooner had the buzz from Dane's concept subsided than three members of the client's product team broke protocol and barged into the creative review, two weeks ahead of the agency presentation. They liked Dane's concept and headline but the client's branding director focused on a picture Bushkin had discovered. It was a flame cupped between two hands. It had no headline because Bushkin no longer had a writing partner. The clients needed none. They fixated on this stock image as if it were a sacred icon and identified in its luminous mystery the brand essence of *Refluxydyl*.

The Green creative team scrambled to perfect this image even while developing other concepts. Bushkin emerged from creative irrelevance to assert his Golden Age genius, while Dane saw his major opportunity to make a name for himself aborted.

15. THE LADY OF REFLUXYDYL

Green Healthcare Advertising was the fifth largest pharmaceutical advertising agency in the world, but the acid reflux launch forced it to grow. The studio and creatives needed to work 24/7 to satisfy the client's indefatigable quest for the concept that would make *Refluxydyl* a blockbuster.

Stan Bushkin, the art supervisor, was so happy to have a job that he took orders from his boss, Gaines Burger, and did not dare to be proactive. However, launching an $8 billion brand demanded leadership, initiative and organizational prowess.

A new art supervisor was brought on to "help" Bushkin.

Gwen Maxon was a tall, large-boned woman with a musical voice, a sharp eye, deep reservoirs of energy and will and a vast network of designers, retouchers, production people, and art directors whose talents she could tap at a moment's notice. When Gwen introduced herself to Dane on her first day, she seemed tentative and quiet. She spent the greater part of her first day in the lady's room throwing up. Everybody saw this as a propitious sign; Gwen was clearly off to a good start. When her stomach settled, Gwen lived up to her overture and became the powerhouse of the *Refluxidyl* launch.

A fifteen-year veteran, Gwen knew all phases of advertising and worked with ferocious purpose. She could often be found stooped over her computer, working out the details of a layout so intently that if spoken to, she answered in the monotone of an oracle. Work, however, was merely one outlet for Gwen's persona. She had childlike powers of observation and loved to laugh and carry on. Her light spirit was unstable, though. When crossed or harassed, Gwen's large brown eyes widened and rolled and her voice contracted into a tremulous whisper more intimidating than a shout.

One morning, the acid reflux team sat in their team conference room waiting for a status meeting to begin and for Stan Bushkin to show up. After fifteen minutes the goateed and rotund Gaines Burger arrived.

The creative director of art informed the team solemnly that he had news to tell them before they heard it elsewhere. Bushkin had been fired.

Burger filled the stunned silence that ensued by eulogizing Bushkin as a great guy and a talented man, who simply did not have the right personality or skill set for the hands-on, day-to-day leadership needed at that moment on this team.

At Green, employees were terminated humanely. They were not barred from their offices, ushered out by security guards and told their possessions would be shipped to them later. Bushkin lumbered around the offices until noon like a man experienced in all things, including job loss. He shook hands and said his good-byes. He told Dane he had a bright future. Dane found it ironic that Bushkin was fired soon after discovering the client's favorite concept.

16. MAIDEN PRESENTATION

The first major presentation for the client took place a week before Christmas at the company headquarters west of Philadelphia. Dane and Gwen had arranged 19 concepts on 16 x 24 corkboard panels in order of presentation and fine-tuned their remarks. People patted his shoulder and told him not to be nervous. There was no need; Dane was confident. He knew he could fall back on his dormant teaching skills.

Dane and Gwen took a train to Philadelphia with Landon LeSeuer and his partner, Gaines Burger, for the three o'clock meeting. They were supposed to leave at 11 AM but Gaines insisted that noon was early enough. When they arrived in Philadelphia at 2 PM, Landon insisted on using the men's room. "I learned long ago not to make myself uncomfortable for clients," he remarked with casual sagacity.

By 2:10 PM their limo was en route to the company headquarters twenty miles west. The highways were choked with holiday shoppers so they took back roads that meandered at 30 mph. When Dane watched the car clock approach 3 o'clock, his mood plunged from nervous to despondent. By making the client wait, his supervisors were dooming his chance to shine. Dane recalled the interview when he blew his chances by arriving at 9:05. Was he cursed?

Forty-five minutes late, Dane and Gwen rushed into the dark conference room with two huge canvas cases on their shoulders. Eighteen hostile drug company employees awaited them. It was the last Friday before Christmas and they wanted their weekends to begin. With their heads down, Dane and Gwen set up the concept boards along the walls, avoiding eye contact with their hosts and ignoring their barbed remarks. Dane and Gwen presented the work and smoothly exchanged parts like TV anchor-people. When they were done, the clients applauded vigorously. The amount and quality of the creative work impressed them. In praising the creative team's diligence, however, they admonished Landon and Gaines never to be late again.

On the way home, the mood was jubilant. The creative directors congratulated Dane and Gwen for their presentation. They made jokes about being late.

News of the *Refluxidyl* success traveled. Dane tasted agency celebrity. The account management team use his "runners" concept as a textbook example of the "generational theme"—a template for the new age of Me-2 drugs, in which new compounds were the virtually same as old ones.

17. DANE AND GWEN: A SUCCESSUAL RELATIONSHIP

The brilliant success of the presentation exhilarated Dane. He and Gwen had rescued the account from a debacle and transformed it. Dane shared the triumph with Gwen—and felt differently about her. He respected her talent, her warm voice with its bright notes, and her confidence. She had poise under pressure and was a natural improviser—always in the moment. Most of all, Gwen was strong and competent, someone on whom he could rely.

Dane and Gwen made several business trips to the clients'

headquarters in Philadelphia. They would rendezvous at Penn Station when the concessions were opening and take an early morning train. Dane always carried a large canvas case with foam board concepts on his shoulder. The new partners drank coffee and ate Danishes on the train and rehearsed their presentations, which were often well-received. The marketing of *Refluxidyl* moved swiftly to the first round of testing.

This partnership was special to Dane. He knew it because he usually hated early mornings, yet looked forward to rising two hours early to make the train with Gwen. He was attracted to Gwen in a new way. It was a *successual* attraction.

Years before Dane had dated a woman copywriter, who claimed that successful advertising people cared more about business than about sex. Success was not just an aphrodisiac for them; it *was* sex. At the time, Dane thought it was twisted but now he felt the same way. He was smitten with Gwen because he had success with her and wanted more. He was attentive to her and as proprietary as a husband.

In advertising, this was a normal and healthy phenomenon. Buzz Dingblatz, who taught Dane's class at *The Institute of Design,* joked that a client often asked him where his girlfriend, Houlihan, was. Partnership was an arranged relationship, at once random and passionate.

Dane and Gwen's *successual* relationship deepened in the fertility of time. They were together in trains, stations, cars, arriving, departing, and waiting. In Philadelphia, Gwen introduced Dane to *Anne's* pretzels. "After every client meeting I treated myself to one of these. The proof is here!" she said, patting one ample buttock. She laughed. "I didn't care. They're so good!" Dane laughed along. He enjoyed Gwen's spontaneity and her ingenuous self-mockery. She had the confidence to laugh at herself—and mean it.

As they rolled through New Jersey, Gwen reminisced that she often took that train years before with a partner "she loved" at another agency. Their client had been unusually sadistic, which was saying a lot in a business marked by cruelty and abuse. She would storm in late to presentations, call Gwen's work crap and stomp out.

Going on business trips with his partner was Dane's idea of how advertising should be. Even Gwen's adoring accounts of a beloved former partner did not diminish his contentment. Dane was not jealous of Gwen's work memories. He knew her affection for an ex-partner was an accretion of joys, torments, adrenaline and exhaustion, over moments and years. She might eventually feel the same way about Dane. But in his view, what they had now was perfect. Gwen knew failure with her previous partners; with Dane, she had only success. And more would come.

This was the beauty of a *successual* relationship, which distinguished it from a sexual bond. With sex, the past compromised the present, but with success, the past was irrelevant; only now and later mattered. And while sex rarely improved in time, success compounded.

However, a *successual* relationship was no safer than any other in certain respects. On one morning train to Philly, Gwen whispered excitedly, "Look, there's L—!" She pointed at a former rock star nearby, whose shaggy, magenta hair and multiple piercings identified her as having gone over-the-hill to below sea level. Dane was acutely jealous. He wanted Gwen to be more energized about their work, their partnership and their success than about a played-out performer—*but she wasn't*. The success Gwen laid at his feet she turned into a doormat.

Gwen thrust the past in Dane's face and made him look at it. She exposed their winning streak in the mirror of his deep seated ambitions. He once aimed for an artist's fame and respect but settled for a paycheck and an adman's low status and transient achievements. Now he had to live with the compromise.

After round one of testing, two campaign concepts were front-runners—Dane's "Runners" and the departed Bushkin's "Glowing hand." Dane believed he would have a transcendent success to transport him from late-blooming journeyman to industry superstar, agency owner and hall-of-famer. He had a perfect advertising trifecta: great partner, blockbuster account, winning campaign. His career could not get better.

And it didn't, not for now. Success was a large planet with immense gravitational force. As Dane's desires approached their object, they disintegrated in the intense gravity of the heavenly body.

18. THE WORM IN THE DREAM

At a client meeting before the second round of testing, the product manager remarked that *Left off...takes off*, Dane's headline, might imply that *Refluxidyl* was third line therapy—to be prescribed only when other drugs in its class failed to work. Since PPI's were remarkably effective as second-line therapy, *Refluxydyl* as a third-line drug would be rarely prescribed. Rather than a multi-billion dollar blockbuster, *Refluxydyl* would be fortunate to make $100 million.

All twenty people on the client side worried in unison. They had not considered this interpretation; nor had doctors in research. But if one person could imagine it, others might. *Left off...takes off* meant "passing the baton" to most people, but if it meant "last resort" to anyone, *Refluxidyl* sales would decline.

"*Left off...takes off* can mean 'hand-off,'" the product manager remarked. "But it can also mean 'hold off.'"

Foreheads around the conference table creased as one, eyebrows arched, and eyes welled with calculation and concern. Like a worm, the product manager's suggestion gnawed at the *Refluxydyl* team's confidence in Dane's concept.

"Nobody's even implied *hold off!*" Dane pleaded—nicely. "The doctors love these words, this idea!"

"Yes, but we can't risk *Refluxydyl* being mistaken for a third line therapy. We need to convert six million *Esophogard* users!" the product manager replied patiently as Landon put his hand on Dane's shoulder to defuse a meltdown.

Dane was in shock. Language, his most trusted and beloved faculty, betrayed him as his fine headline was twisted and inverted by medical marketing. It was a common fate. In pharmaceutical advertising, each slogan was a chemical compound, every phrase a molecule, analyzed and evaluated in denotations and connotations.

The product manager had seen a small crack in his headline. It related to how drugs are prescribed, the process of step therapy, or *fail first* in managed care. To treat a condition like acid reflux, doctors were expected to start a patient on first line therapy—a medicine that was effective, safe, accessible and cheap. To treat heartburn, a doctor might have a patient try an antacid like TUMS or an H2 blocker like *Zantec*. If first line therapy failed, the doctor could prescribe a second-line therapy, like *Esophagard*—more powerful and more expensive. If a second-line therapy failed, doctors could prescribe a third-line therapy. The product team worried that "Where Esophagard left off, Refluxydyl takes off" could be taken to mean that Refluxydyl should be prescribed only if *Esophagard* did not work. This would result in a marketing disaster.

It was too late to kill Dane's concept so it was presented for the first round of research. In the morning session, doctors overwhelmingly ranked "Left off... takes off" first. This worried the product manager. She told the moderator to ask doctors if *Left off...takes off* suggested third line therapy.

Once the question was raised, doctors conceded that the phrase could mean "third line therapy." This was how research went all day. Of the ten doctors who ranked *Left off...takes off* first, six said the headline could mean "third-line therapy." Dane's breakthrough was broken by the power of suggestion.

"It's ridiculous," he lamented later to Gwen. "They put the idea in the doctors' heads and acted like it was there all the time."

Gwen stared at her screen as she worked assiduously on a layout that had to go out.

"I understand how you feel," Gwen said. "You want to be the hero. I once had a concept that looked like a sure winner. Finally, after years of dressing up other people's stuff, I'd have my own idea out there. So a creative director was envious. She put it in the client's head that the concept could be seen another way. Poof! It was gone. Honey, that's the way it goes. Oh, well, try again..."

19. BITTER PILL

Advertising does not bury its dead concepts. It does not mourn its heroes. It has no heroes. Advertising moves on—and on—without loyalty, gratitude, memory, or remorse. Advertising stares ahead and worships the next chance—and the next—to plant short phrases in public places.

When a concept goes down, no moment of silence marks its passing. People hear of it like the tolling of bells or the rumor of free food in the kitchenette. Pavlov's creative minds salivate with the opportunity to spawn new ideas.

Although "Where *Esophogard* left off, *Refluxydyl* takes off" lingered on the morphine-drip of research, the client's lingering doubt about Dane's exquisite headline triggered new rounds of brainstorming. A client's over-thinking made Dane look incompetent. The creative assignment was no longer his. It had become too big and important for his imagination.

The client ordered Landon to deploy every available resource on *Refluxydyl*. Copywriters and art directors from across Green's many divisions were pressed into service. Freelancers were mustered like mercenaries, briefed for ten minutes on *Refluxydyl*, and set loose on Dane's domain.

Nobody told Dane that when his concept went down, he went down with it, falling from Brahmin to pariah, from sanctity to filth. He was unready to be cold leftovers for fridge removal on the last

Friday of the month. He was the writer of record and would take on all comers.

20. THE LONELINESS OF THE WRITER OF RECORD

The first forfeit Dane paid for having his concept aborted was that he had no creative partner. During this moment of upheaval, he was like a jockey without a horse.

He wrote pages of ideas, headlines and visuals and went to Gwen's office to discuss them, but she was too busy managing art and production to brainstorm with Dane. Gwen accepted the sheets of paper and promised to look at them. When he heard nothing, Dane stopped by her office, but Gwen was either on the phone or at meetings.

"Have you looked at the concepts?" He asked when he found her.

"No, I'm sorry. I'm up to my eyeballs with studio issues," Gwen replied.

The *Refluxydyl* client had an obsessive need to suck the universe dry of ideas and litter the world with them; Green's creatives were up to the challenge, producing concepts non-stop for *Refluxidyl*. Many of these contributors were newly promoted junior creatives who had started only months before as office assistants.

Dane was trampled by the creative rush. He looked on bitterly as writers and art directors were matched en masse, like a cult wedding, while he toiled alone. Dane was not "in a good place." He had been there before—key stroking ideas on 8x11 paper while rivals produced glossy print outs with rich images and bold type. Dane faced the prospect that another person's concept would represent *Refluxydyl*. As the writer of record, he would be condemned to pen body copy under an alien headline.

Desperate to prevent this outcome, Dane tortured his mind to devise another brilliant concept and courted Gwen to design it. He often stopped by her office with a concept in hand.

"You want to hear my idea?"

"I'd love to," Gwen replied graciously. "But I'm late for a meeting."

Noting his dejection, she added brightly, "You're so prolific. I'll put it with your other ideas."

She opened the top drawer of her desk and inserted Dane's latest idea on top of the stack of ideas he had been giving her for weeks.

In that gesture Dane recognized his updated status on the *Refluxydyl* team. His concepts were dead and Gwen's desk drawer was the coffin in which they were buried. Was Gwen the undertaker? Was she too busy or did she starve his spirit and kill his career slowly with smiles and evasions?

No. Dane knew Gwen was not to blame. She was always more than his partner. She had a bigger title, more responsibility and far more experience. As group art supervisor, Gwen headed the account. She organized her studio contacts brilliantly to accommodate a client who would pay any amount for creative output. Gwen transformed the *Refluxidyl* team into an agency within the agency. She was the queen of the Green ants, and Dane was a drone.

"We're partners," Dane pleaded. "Everybody else has a partner and they're all on this account. Except for me—the writer of record!"

"It *is* ironic. I'm sorry," Gwen replied sympathetically.

"When will we concept again?" he asked.

"I wish I knew," she said.

"At creative reviews I tape my headlines and stick figures to the wall and they're ignored. Words need art. You've got to help me."

She laughed. "Don't you think I want to? It's more fun than this. Look, I'll hire a freelance art director to work with you, so you'll have someone to play with!"

It was a kinky professional gesture. Dane's partner not only permitted him to work with another art director but signed off on it. It was as if his wife, unavailable for sex, paid for prostitutes.

One art director Gwen recruited for Dane had won awards for

Volvo, IBM, and *NFL* commercials. He must have felt over-qualified for *Refluxydyl* because he sat in Dane's office and never lifted his pen even to doodle while Dane plied him with ideas.

Finally, the art star seemed to emerge from a long trance. "I got it!" he said. He drew a football and insisted it was the perfect symbol for *Refluxidyl.*

"A football?" Dane asked with perplexity and nodded so he would not seem stupid.

"What do people do when they watch football? Eat food that gives them heartburn. It's a no-brainer. You can't lose," the rent-a-genius explained.

Dane suggested that they keep working, that a better idea might lie in wait in the abscesses of their minds. But the art director superstar insisted that no more thinking was necessary—and it might be harmful. They had their "big idea." The advertising gods had been kind to them. It would tempt misfortune to be greedy.

"Chill brother!" the rent-a-genius said. He spent the remainder of the afternoon on his cell, planning his birthday party. "Keep it real!" he told Dane. "What does that mean?" Dane asked. "I dunno. But I live by it," the rent-a-genius said.

Later, the account vice president reviewed the football ad on the wall and reproached Dane, "A football? Really, Dane?"

21. IN FLAGRANTE DESCRIPTO

One afternoon Dane stopped by Gwen's office to beg her to collaborate. Her door was closed so he knocked. "Come in," the art group supervisor called out in her warm, musical voice that never failed to lift his spirits just a little.

When Dane opened the door, he found his partner at her desk chatting with two junior creatives. The young writer had been recently promoted from office assistant and the art director was Carl, the degenerate who constantly sat on his hipster glass frames during drunken stupors.

"Come in, Dane. We were looking at concepts," Gwen said.

"Perfidious woman," Dane thought.

Spread out on his partner's floor were reams of concepts in 11x17 color printouts.

Dane saw clouds in the Pantone shade of *Refluxydyl* purple, a purple giant and a man with purple lips playing a purple harmonica. Two midgets mugged in purple wrestling outfits, one on the other's impish shoulders.

"Hey, I used that man with the purple banjo!" Dane cried, affronted by their plagiarism of his plagiarism.

Dane seethed. Why did his partner humor the young copywriter and art director? Did such mediocrity deserve encouragement? Of course, she was flirting, having her fun while he, the writer of record, played the creative cuckold, typing worthy concepts by the ton to be buried in the coffin of her drawer. The writer of record had no art director, yet this untried junior with no book, no experience, and no *Institute of Design* class—who never saved his work from being torched and tossed from a window—was prancing around on his own creative team.

"What do you think of this work, Dane?" Gwen asked.

"Frankly, it's ludicrous and derivative. You can take two of anything and color them purple...and what does it mean?"

The junior creatives took their cue to leave.

"What's wrong, Dane?" Gwen asked in her soothing voice that spoke to the four-year-old in him. "You sound upset. Is anything wrong?"

"You claim you have no time to work with me. Then I find you schmoozing with junior creatives. They have partners. I don't!"

"Excuse me!" Gwen replied. Her eyes widened and rolled in their sockets as her temper flared. Dane knew he was in trouble. "I have a demanding husband at home and now one at work?"

"I'm not your husband!"

"Precisely! Dane, what do you want from me?"

"I want you to be my partner. I'm the writer of record and I want an art partner!"

"Fine!" Gwen turned to the screen and slammed the keys with her fingers, then swept the papers from the desk with a backstroke of her arm.

"Dane, I thought you had aspirations to be a supervisor. Shouldn't you look at what others are doing? Shouldn't you mentor the less experienced?"

"I *am* one of the less experienced!" he reminded her.

Gwen glanced at her watch.

"We'll have this discussion some other time."

"Some other time!—that should be my tagline!" Dane blurted and stormed out.

In his office, Dane laid his head on his stack of *Refluxydyl* "New drug application" documents like a primary school child giving himself a time out. He was as forlorn as he had ever been. Gwen was right. He knew he should apologize. But what good would it do? He had given her every reason not to work with him.

Gwen had him pegged. He behaved like a needy house-husband. Now she would file for professional divorce because Dane was a 'head case" with an "attitude problem." Then Dane realized that his *successual relationship* with Gwen had been over for awhile. When the success was gone, she moved on. The writer of record on a blockbuster drug launch was left with a blockbuster heartache.

22. PROVED, IMPROVED

Dane's agony was not about to go away. It was chronic, degenerative, and systemic, migrating from one disaster to another. Everything up until now was an appetizer for the putrid entrée that awaited him.

A new cohort of freelancers was hired. One freelancer was a

40ish woman from Westchester named Jenna. She was known as "Queen Cobra" back when she ran the Bangkok office of *Boshko & Benershke*, once the most creative shop in Southeast Asia. Jenna had been around the world, writing award-winning copy for major global brands like *XOXO* shower products, *Zeus* lambskin sheaths, *Yugo* and *Dr. Shill's* anti-itch powder. She wore oversized tinted glasses and had long, dark hair with a white stripe down the middle. When Jenna huddled over her copy, a skunk seemed to be sleeping on her head.

On her first day, Jenna studied the creative output on the wall. She immediately focused on Dane's *Left off...takes off* concept.

"Intriguing," she said. "This is the way to go but it's not there yet." She set out to perfect his concept.

It was a new experience for Dane—and a new threat. People typically liked or hated his ideas. Jenna was the only person who ever set out to out-Dane him.

"Nobody can do me better," he told himself with more pride than confidence. "I've drilled the well dry."

For a week, Jenna sat lotus-style on the floor of the free-lancers' room, scribbling and scratching out headlines. Finally, "Queen Cobra" and her art director showed a simple ad with two pills on it. The capsule on the left was *Esophogard*, going off patent. Underneath it was the word "Proved" in Times-Roman, 72 pt. Next to it was a longer *Refluxydyl* capsule. Below it was the word, "Improved."

Proved. Improved.—a simplification of *Left off...takes off*— quickly morphed from sensation to contagion and rocketed to #1 launch headline.

Account people adored it. Doctors muttered it under their breath. The chief executive at *Refluxydyl's* drug company, who had craved a "Think Small"-style ad since he was an ad-struck child, was ecstatic.

Dane's morale plunged to bathyscaphic depths. Jenna pumped up his idea and rode it like an elephant. Damn it all! Dane could have been riding high. He, too, had a "pill concept" but Gwen swore she would never do a drug ad with pills in it.

"And by the way," Dane pointed out to anyone with ears, "*Proved. Improved.* makes a false claim." Data showed that *Refluxidyl* had better results than its predecessor—but only at twice the dosage! The FDA would never let this stand.

The writer of record was an angry prophet, unheeded amid the widespread rejoicing over the glorious mantra, *Proved. Improved.* Only one person hearkened to Dane and believed his prophecy: Gwen.

She was in more pain than he was. As the art supervisor, Gwen would be making those pills look good for a very long time.

Here was the basis for a *successual* reconciliation. Dane and Gwen would never have what they had before but they were old allies who needed each other now. Together in Gwen's office with the door closed, they commiserated.

"I begged you to do the pill concept, but, no, that would have been too easy!" Dane fulminated.

"Pill ads are cheesy," Gwen replied.

"People love cheese!" Dane snapped back. "Especially when it's proved and improved cheese."

"So do rats and mice," Gwen rejoined.

"Get used to hating pills in ads. You'll be seeing them for years!"

Gwen stared at Dane abstractedly like he was a pill on a billboard. Suddenly, her eyes widened and rolled in their sockets. Dane feared he had set her off—*again!*

"There won't be pills in my ads," Gwen growled. "Let's think."

Together, Dane and Gwen mobilized their brains and struggled to top *Proved, Improved.* They came up with "GERD be gone: The Next Generation."

People smiled and nodded but it wasn't nearly as cute as *Proved. Improved.* Once you had $E=MC^2$ could you ever be happy with $a^2+b^2=c^2$?

For hours Dane and Gwen muttered and shouted word couplings that might be as darling, simple and direct as *Proved. Improved.* This was no longer creativity but concept radiation.

"A tank and a Pope-mobile! Dane shouted.

"An ostrich and an emu!" Gwen snapped back.

"A purple dromedary and a purple camel. The extra hump!

"Genius. Ingenious."

"Hey, that's good! What about star, super-star?"

"Oh, yes!" he yelled. "Mortal. Immortal. That's it!"

"It provides heartburn relief, not everlasting life!" Gwen pointed out.

While they performed this mutual concept extraction, shouts and laughter burst from the adjacent office. *The Boys* were at work and play. The thud of a body slam echoed from the wall.

"What *are* they doing?" Dane asked.

"It's a perpetual office party," Gwen replied.

"Have you said anything to them?" Dane asked.

"In passing. Nicely. They got louder."

On cue, the dry wall thundered from another body thump. Gwen's "Golden Pencil" award wobbled on her side of the sheetrock and fell. A radiator pipe hissed, punctuated by a groan and giggles.

"Fine, refine!" Dane shouted to drown out the ruckus next door.

Someone crowed next door. A chair collided with a file cabinet. A groan was trailed by a torrent of curses.

"Shut up!" Dane shouted, pounding the wall with his fist.

"Fuck you!" was the response, punctuated by a fist clouting the wall.

"Don't start a war," Gwen warned.

"You don't think we can take them on?" Dane retorted, smiling. Gwen was a big woman with a fiery temper. He liked their chances against anyone.

Gwen grimaced. "I have too much to do."

"You suck!" a male voice bellowed next door.

"No, you suck!" a voice responded.

Pause.

"You suck!" a chorus of men shouted. It sounded like an angry reunion of *The Village People*.

Dane could no longer tolerate the relentless ruckus, nor pretend it did not disrupt his thoughts.

He burst from Gwen's office and knocked on Krassweiler's door. No answer. A yowl of pain issued from inside, followed by giggles.

Dane opened the door. Krassweiler had Austin Weebler, Landon's junior copywriter, in a headlock. Austin laughed, vermillion-faced, while he struggled to break the hold.

"You're having way too much fun!" Krassweiler shouted, heaving young Weebler at the wall.

"Hey, watch out!" a writer shouted when Austin's body crashed next to him.

"Could you guys keep it down?" Dane requested.

"Sorry we woke you from your nap!" Krassweiler jeered.

"We're working," Dane said.

"*Oh, they're working*," Krassweiler repeated ironically. "I didn't know you guys had work." The leader of *The Boys* glowered. "Why don't you run along to your office and relieve yourself?"

Abashed by this reference to his *kimchee* disaster, Dane withdrew to Gwen's office and resumed.

"*Credible. Incredible.*"

23. GRAMMATICAL CASTRATION & OTHER THINGS THAT STINK

The next morning, Dane smelled a fetid odor in his office, emanating from a desk drawer. He found a plastic baggy of melted feces with a specimen tag reading, "Winning concept."

That was not the only embellishment. On Dane's bookshelf, amid plants and nick-knacks, sat a novelty plastic troll, its hands grasping a soft-eraser erection. A tag tied to its leg read, "What I do best."

It was definitely an inside job, Dane thought. He had not watched *The Maltese Falcon* twenty times for nothing. Someone was sending him a message.

At the *Refluxydyl* team status meeting, Dane made an announcement.

"Someone left a bag of crap in my desk."

"The cleaning service is not doing their job," Gaines Burger replied crisply.

"It's not a custodial matter," Dane said. "A bag of crap should not be in my desk."

"As much as I want to talk about your crap, Dane, we have other crap to discuss," Gaines said. "Something important has come up."

"We all know '*Proved. Improved.*' tested extraordinarily well," Landon said. "The client loves it. It looked like our launch-headline-apparent.

"Now there's a glitch. An editor on the client side vetoed '*Proved. Improved.*' Apparently 'Proved' is grammatically incorrect as a past participle. It must be replaced by 'Proven.'"

"Did you ever hear of anything so insane?" Gaines Burger, the creative director of art, asked with rhetorical outrage as he emerged from silent shock. "Like grammar matters. When was advertising ever grammatical?"

"Like *never!*" the team agreed.

"The meaning of the ad remains intact," Landon continued as Gaines Burger covered his head with his hands.

"*Proven. Improved.* has no balls!" Gaines Burger cried.

"True, the grammatically correct version lacks laser phrasing," Landon said.

"*Proved. Improved.* was hyper-connective communication. It by-passed the brain and went right to the heart," Gaines Burger expatiated.

"We're all sorry for the loss, Gaines, but we must go on," Landon said.

"Wait. Did Cybil call their top guy? He had a hard on for *Proved. Improved*," Gaines suggested.

"He's traveling in seclusion," Landon reported.

"I think I have his in-flight cell number! I'll get it," Gaines Burger bellowed, slapped his hands and lunged for the door.

"Sit down, Gaines. We've tried every channel, every frequency, and every device. *Refluxydyl*'s top management will not override an editorial decision. *Proven. Improved.* must be replaced."

"Why was I ever born!" Gaines asked. This question prompted a wave of speculation in the room.

When the meeting was adjourned, Dane knew he had to suppress all smiles and flatten the spring in his step. Green's creative directors and account people were in despair. A second status meeting was scheduled as a *Proved. Improved.* support group. A therapist from Green's sibling medical education agency provided grief counseling.

Typical questions were posed at an open coping session. "How could a client tamper so irresponsibly with the creative? How could grammar get in the way of a great ad? But they all distilled to this: Why did bad things happen to good advertising?

Dane was more than relieved; he was elated. It was the best he felt since he conceived, *"Left off. Takes off."* For the first time since his concept was killed, he no longer took its death personally, since it was clearly a common outcome. The failure of "Queen Cobra's" concept felt almost as good as success. He knew his reaction was petty and he was ashamed of it. Had advertising corrupted him or revealed the corruption already there?

Either way, he could not let it fester. Dane pined for change. He knew he must escape this toxic environment and seek a healthier one. The belief that such an atmosphere existed in advertising sustained him.

Case 2-D
OFFICE VIGILANTE

24. LOCKED OUT, ACT OUT

Now that the enemy concept was routed by editorial intervention, Dane's status as the writer of record was reinforced, his judgment vindicated. He and Gwen reconciled, their mutual strife creating a more durable bond. In a corporate setting, Dane showed something more important than talent—toughness—and did something more impressive than produce a headline of genius—he survived one.

With time running out on selecting a launch concept, Green and the *Refluxydyl* manufacturer reverted to Bushkin's *Glowing Hands*, the image of hands cupping a mysterious light—the client's original favorite. Dane wrote a headline that grew more vapid and meaningless with every regulatory review. No one was happy with the campaign, but all creatives were satisfied that it was the client's fault.

Dane felt more secure now than he had for months. He exuded confidence and calm. He expected the work to go more smoothly.

Unfortunately, when he banged on Gwen's wall and interrupted *The Boys'* violent revelry, he antagonized them. The melting turd in his desk was no isolated prank, signifying the end of hostilities. It was a calling card. The *pitch-meisters'* perfect record had been marred by recent losses and there were fewer pitches. Eton Krassweiler, the alpha boy, was restless. The great predator fed on vast quantities of raw opportunity. When he was underfed, he prowled for mischief. He had become so bored of late that door-slamming no longer satisfied him. He now flew into violent fits, body-slamming his crew-members at all times. In their disgruntled down time, *The Boys* perceived Dane's aura of success and took offense.

One evening when Dane was working late, he returned from the men's room to find his office door locked. The maintenance men had left for the weekend and were not at their favorite Friday after-work watering hole. An experienced lock-picker, working in the studio, helped Dane gain entry. The incident was blamed on an overzealous cleaning woman.

The following week Dane was locked out of his office when he arrived at work and a third time while he chatted with a colleague down the hall.

Dane was sure he was in a sequel to *Melted Feces and Priapic Troll*, titled *Locked Door*, starring *The Boys*. Still, he brushed it off. Then, one afternoon, he stopped by his office after lunch to retrieve a file he needed for a meeting, and found his door locked. Now the prank sabotaged his work and he could no longer maturely ignore it. He needed to be bold.

He stormed into Krassweiler's office. It was full of younger creatives—men *and* women. Before Dane opened his mouth to speak, his intrusive presence made the co-ed gang go silent. They regarded him with fear. If *the Boys* had an aptitude for closing doors Dane knew how to open them.

"Somebody in this room is locking my office door!" he announced sharply. "This bullshit behavior is not funny and it's got to stop *now*."

The ten people crowded in the office were stunned by his raid. The slack jaws, wide eyes and gaping mouths of the ordinarily swaggering, young creatives testified to Dane's powers of intimidation.

Dane withdrew to his office, pleased to have stood up for himself and confident that his office door would never be locked again. As he applied himself to more headlines and slogans, Krassweiler bounded into his office, leaned over his desk and stuck his large face in front of Dane, tempting him to punch it. Dane forswore the bait.

"Who the hell are you coming to my office and threatening my group members?" Krassweiler demanded with theatrical vehemence.

"Who the hell are you to barge into my office and shout in my face?" Dane countered calmly, yet with enough resonance that anyone could hear he was not backing down.

"I am a respected employee at this agency—that's who!" Krassweiler shouted.

"Then act like one," Dane replied.

"Who are you to tell me how to act? I bring money into this agency, money that pays your pathetic salary."

"I was going to ask for a raise," Dane pointed out.

Krassweiler was trying to regain the face he lost when Dane violated his sovereign domain and scared his "tough" team members speechless.

"What are you trying to prove, old man? You're a laughingstock. How does it feel to know you'll always be second-string, lower than a man a generation younger?"

"It could feel better," Dane admitted candidly, determined not to let Krassweiler anger him.

"Yeah. Well, it's not going to. Get this. You will never work on a pitch while I'm here. You'll be a copy janitor and pretend you're a writer."

Trash-talk works like many drugs. It is more effective as it accumulates. The power of an insult, meanwhile, is proportionate to how accurately it describes the recipient's situation. A good insult erodes self-esteem, whereas a great insult taps self-perception.

Krassweiler was a master of insults. He laid them on with speed, volume and precision. By calling Dane a janitor, he reinforced Dane's perception of his inferior status and of Krassweiler's success as a permanent obstacle to his progress.

Dane was clinging to self-control; Krassweiler tried to make him lose it. The young creative director was face to face with Dane, breathing garlic-rich lunch in his face, reinforcing his disdain and Dane's subservience. Then Krassweiler belched. It was the office version of a "face wash" in ice hockey—when one player stuffs his smelly glove in an adversary's face—the ultimate provocation.

Dane understood that if he backed down he would be humiliated but if he became violent Krassweiler would have him fired.

"If I'm a janitor I should remove the trash," Dane said. He pulled Krassweiler by the collar, threw him over the desk and landed an uppercut squarely on the creative director's nose. Krassweiler tumbled and crashed head first against the bookcase, bringing plant pots, books and papers down on him. From the broken bric-a-brac the truculent creative *wunderkind* snagged Dane's arm with one hand and flailed at him with the other, smacking his eye.

"I'm talking to your supervisor!" Krassweiler shouted. "What do you think will happen when he learns what you've done?"

Dane returned to his rational corporate senses and recognized the trouble he was in. His only hope of keeping his job was to frame Krassweiler as the aggressor. Eton smacked him in the groin from his cramped sprawl but Dane pulled away and bolted from his office, shouting, "Krassweiler's had an accident!"

Cubicle dwellers nearby did their utmost to ignore Dane's outcry. Krassweiler, who had scrambled to his feet, pounced on Dane from behind and put him in a head lock to choke him into submission. Dane thrust his elbow into Krassweiler's solar plexus, stamped on his foot and drove him backward against the plasterboard wall, where he had him pinned. At that point, other colleagues interceded to stop the fight. Krassweiler's crew members peeled Dane off of their leader, who touched his nose, saw blood on his finger and wagged it at Dane.

"You're finished! I am a respected employee of this agency. You can't make me bleed!" Krassweiler threatened.

"You assaulted me in my office!" Dane countered.

"I'm talking to your supervisor. What will Landon say? He'll fire your sorry ass!"

"Let's *both* talk to him," Dane agreed. He walked away from Krassweiler and headed to Landon's office. Krassweiler did not know what else to do so he followed.

"You can't lead me around like an animal! I'm a respected employee of this agency!" Krassweiler objected.

"Then behave like one!" Dane replied.

When they entered Landon's office, Dane stated his grievance.

"Landon, with all the pranks, cliques and bullies around here, it's like high school revisited!" Dane declaimed.

Landon raised his eyes from his monitor and regarded Dane with measured consternation. "Really! I had no idea."

Dane summarized the situation, hitting all the low points—the locked door, his exasperated response and Krassweiler's office invasion—before the young creative director gave his side.

"Your employee has behaved outrageously, Landon!" Krassweiler cried. "He has falsely accused every member of my group and created ill will. Then he assaulted me in his office."

"*His* office?" Landon asked suspiciously.

Krassweiler was on the verge of vehement protest when he paused as if he had forgotten something. He took stock of his appearance. His shirt was ripped and his face was streaked with dirt from Dane's fallen plants. He lost his swagger and looked beaten, which was bad enough. But he absolutely could not have his crew perceive him as a victim or hear him whine for justice from a colleague he ridiculed.

"Like I said, Landon, Dane is out of control because he doesn't make enough money to pay his bills," Krassweiler said.

Dane and Landon exchanged a baffled look at this *non sequitur*. Krassweiler had abandoned his argument and was now demeaning Dane's income, the corporate version of his manhood. He was also implying that Landon was too cheap to give Dane a raise. The moment passed. Landon promised Krassweiler he would investigate, which was his code for "nothing will get done and all will be forgiven and forgotten." The young creative director sneered and walked off, dissatisfied.

Krassweiler was an inveterate juvenile delinquent but he was also, as he claimed, "a highly respected employee of Green Healthcare Advertising." He demanded retribution. Dane was summoned to human resources, where the new vice president of HR, Fiona

Dumbarton, a plump, English woman with wet-looking hair that gave her a coming-out-of-the-shower freshness, inquired what had occurred in his office. Dane presented himself as the victim of relentless abuse. Fiona listened attentively and prescribed a remedy. "Dane, I want you to tell Eton how terribly sorry you are for the misunderstanding. Assure him that you only want to do a good job, and then express the hope that you can put all this nonsense behind you and get along like the teammates you are."

Since Dane was the party whose door was repeatedly locked, who found melted feces in his desk and a lewd troll in his bookcase, and whose office was trashed, he refused to "make nice" with Krassweiler. Fiona did not press him to do so. The HR director viewed Dane and Krassweiler as two members of the same childish tribe and hoped they would both find employment elsewhere. However, to resolve the matter, she determined that Krassweiler was the more important miscreant and placed Dane on probation.

25. DANE'S SECRET TORMENTOR REVEALED

After his raid on Krassweiler's office, Dane's door was treated with respect. It was left open while he was out.

Then the door was locked again.

Dane's anger was tapped. Now he was merely curious. Who would repeatedly do such an asinine thing after the ugliness that transpired? Dane asked the three people in cubicles closest to his office if they had seen anyone behaving suspiciously around his door.

Bettina, the art buyer from Uruguay, a petite, young woman with a gold stud in her nose, came to Dane's office when security had opened his door and told him she would give a special discount to see her topless—only $50.

"Bettina, I can't. It's wrong and it violates the employee manual."

"But I need money. Anyway, I'm more than worth it."

"You're much more than worth it," Dane replied with due

chivalry. "Look, I'll give you twenty if you tell me who's been locking my door."

Okay, she agreed, before whispering the name. "It's Austin."

Good natured, pasty-faced, depression-medication-taking Weebler? Since Landon was out of the office too often to mentor him and Dane never lunched with him on high-priced sushi, Weebler fell into the wrong crowd. He was seduced by the violence and immaturity of *The Boys*. Now he was "pledging" with them to join their pack. But since he had no creative flair to offer the gang, he performed pranks to obtain their respect.

When Dane suggested to Landon that Austin Weebler was involved in his door lockings, *The Savior* called in his protégé who swore his innocence. Like a doting absentee father, Landon thought his son's word was sufficient.

Dane finally confronted Weebler.

"Why did you lock me out of my office?"

"I didn't do it," the young copywriting star replied.

"You were seen doing it."

"It wasn't me. Maybe it was somebody who looks like me."

"Nobody looks like you."

"Thanks, Dane. You think I'm unique?" Weebler asked.

"Uniquely disturbed. You once welcomed me. Now you lock me out of my office. Why?"

"Because...because...you wouldn't eat sushi with me."

"Do you think this is funny?"

"It *is* kind of hilarious," Weebler admitted.

"You mean, humiliating. When I leave my office, I wonder when I'll get back in. I felt at home at Green but you killed it."

"Sorry," Austin said. "I should have been more sensitive...but it was just so funny—your face when you realized you were locked out!"

"Tragic if it happens to you, but hilarious when it happens to me," Dane retorted. He was about to punish Weebler with a stern explanation of the Mel Brooks adage about comedy, when young

Austin winced and gripped his chest. "I really need water. I have bad heartburn."

Dane suspected the mischievous junior copywriter of squirming out of the confrontation but he looked truly ill, so he let him go.

26. INAPPROPRIATE CONTACT & A GRISLY DISCOVERY

Now that the launch concept was in place, it needed to be applied to a plethora of marketing items, including promotional premiums like pens, prescription pads, calendars, and paper-weights; informational pieces, such as sales aids, brochures, and direct mail letters; and packaging, including bottle labels and boxes. As the writer of record, Dane wrote copy for every item and needed to sign off on each project before it left the agency.

Although his creative satisfaction index had hit a 52 week low, Dane was spending on average 12 hours a day at the office. After editors reviewed a piece, Dane evaluated their remarks and answered their queries, then handed off the layout to the art director, account person and studio, where changes were flowed into new layouts. Even an inconspicuous error triggered a new round of changes. And if anyone procrastinated, a piece scheduled to go out by end of day might sit on a desk until 5 or 6 PM, resulting in a very long night.

As the process hijacked his life, Dane habitually stayed at the office until anywhere from 9 PM to midnight. He was like an organ of the agency body. Jobs circulated through him. He imparted his enzyme here or stripped away a molecule there.

However, Dane adapted to the grind of medical writing, its succession of late nights and artistic dead ends. Though greatness was unlikely to be achieved here, Dane found other compensations. He came to appreciate the grim camaraderie of colleagues who habitually worked late, each with a different motive. Some were workaholics; others feared their empty apartments. There were perk-people who dawdled late enough to qualify for free dinners and later still for free cab rides home. What the night shift shared were fluorescent light overlapping shadow, the reek of hot feet, a plaintive quiet and the patient fight against fatigue.

What Dane experienced in the bleary-eyed, head-aching, feet-sniffing late nights at Green was a sense of one-ness with the heartbeat of humanity, of having reached the molten core of existence. It was a comfort to live, work and suffer like most people in the world. Dane would have considered this a spiritual compensation and been satisfied with it.

One evening, a piece requiring paltry changes disappeared between 7 PM and 10 PM. When an hour passed and the traffic person did not stop by his office, Dane searched for her. She had gone to dinner. When she returned, she belched and reproved Dane for his aggressiveness, as Sarah Bittman instructed her to do. She told him the layout he was "hot for" was with an editor.

"You'll have to wait patiently," she admonished Dane as if he were a five-year-old. "That's why they pay you the big bucks."

"But there were only a few tiny corrections—a comma here, a colon there!" Dane said. "How can that take three hours?"

"People all work differently," the traffic girl replied. "You want it to be perfect, don't you?"

At approximately 10 PM Dane thought the process was stuck, something had gone awry. The job was just an envelope with a logo and the words, "Learn about GERD" on the flap. How much could be wrong with it? He left his office to investigate, starting with the account executive, who was out of her office. Dane noticed a paperback on the floor with an intriguing title, *The Account Manager's Guide*. The subtitle read: "How to Get Anybody to Do Anything Anytime!"

A spoiler on the cover promised success to anyone who followed the precepts set forth in the slender tome. Dane was curious to illuminate his long hours of drudgery. He opened to the middle of the book and read a random passage:

Take the pressure off yourself by putting it on everyone else...Stay on balance by knocking everyone else off theirs. Give others less time to think so you have more time to act. Keep people guessing to keep them alert. Talent and intelligence produce good work; adrenaline produces great work. Tell your creatives to get it done yesterday, so you can look at it next week and the client can see it a month later. Employees work best under tight deadlines and intense stress, and ask fewer questions. Never accept one or two drafts when you can ask for ten. The more you ask for, the better you get. Make people work late as often as you can. It will make the work seem more important.

Dane was stunned and angry. He felt like a tool. He had accepted late nights because he believed they were necessary. But working late and endless revisions had nothing to do with process or a job well done. It was about control; the agency intended the job to consume his life until the job was everything and he would do anything to keep it. Writing about drugs was like being on one.

Now Dane would get answers about the lost envelope, sign off and head home. It was 11 o'clock. He had renounced the hope of dinner and a quiet evening with his family but he might salvage a few hours of sleep. He went to the editor's office. The door was closed. He knocked. There was no answer. He opened the door and found the editor, an older man and a freelancer, slumped over his desk. A dark stream of blood crossed from his ear across his cheek and down into a dark pool on the envelope layout.

The paramedics said he had suffered a massive hemorrhage at around 8:30 PM. Death followed shortly thereafter.

Dane barely knew the dead editor. Still, he was shaken by his demise. The man was a jazz saxophonist just scraping by. Sympathy aside, Dane could not help thinking, "I could have been out of here, if only he were scheduled for nine!"

However, death, like agency work, was rarely convenient. Sarah

Bittman insisted that the piece go out that night. Another editor would need to review it. That morning, Dane came home at 4 AM and returned to work at 10.

27. RETURN OF THE HEADHUNTER

Later that day, Dane's phone rang.

"Dane, Albert Griffin. Do you have a few moments to talk?"

"Do I ever! How did you find me?"

"I find everyone. I'm a vulture. That makes you or your job dead meat."

Dane was never happier to hear from a scavenger. Like all headhunters, Griffin had a telepathic instinct for his clients' employment troubles. Yet, his appearance was a sign of hope. It meant the end of one opportunity and the start of another. Dane had not heard from Griffin since his third month at WIF, when the recruiter proposed a "once-in-a-lifetime-you'll-never-stop-thanking-me" opportunity to take a junior copywriter position in Shanghai, China, which included a generous relocation package. When Dane was offered the job and turned it down, Griffin excommunicated him. Now, nearly two years later, all was apparently forgiven.

"So I hear you're doing big things—on heartburn, of all things. Ha-ha! You and I and heartburn go back awhile, right, Dane? I always knew you'd be a success. So, is your agency taking good care of their star copywriter? Are you happy?"

Dane was slow to respond due to exhaustion.

"I see," Griffin continued. "So you're open to change, a better salary, a bigger title. Do I hear you right?"

Dane remained speechless. Since the death of *Left off...takes off* and his *Refluxydyl* reversals, he had been discontented and restless but hearing the headhunter describe his emotions in such detail made him feel vulnerable.

"I hear you," Griffin said. "Well, let me tell you something. I've

179

got a few openings for someone with your experience and skills. Would you be interested?"

Dane cleared his throat. Did he dare to divulge his subversive yearnings when his phone could be tapped, his conversations taped?

"That's what I thought," Griffin concluded. "I'll tell you more later and set up the interviews."

"Thanks for thinking of me, Albert," Dane stammered.

"How could I forget the man in the gasmask? Talk to you later, kiddo."

Dane took Griffin's fortuitous call as more than a sign of deliverance. He saw it as a confirmation that he had not prostituted his talents after all, but found his true calling. Writing had brought him hardship until now, but after a year at Green Advertising his creative reputation was so widely known that various agencies were willing to throw more money at his gifts. When Griffin phoned him the next day, Dane agreed to an interview.

28. INTERVIEW WITH A MAN WHO LOOKS LIKE A VAMPIRE

Griffin sent Dane on an interview. Dane scheduled it around lunch. Regardless how close the other agency was, he knew he would be out longer than an hour, but no one at Green noted his absence. He had doubled his income but his perceived value was what it had been at WIF.

The job search was conspiratorial and exhilarating—and it depressurized his relationships with colleagues. Dane no longer craved their affirmation or hated them for withholding it. He did not care if they nodded vacuously at his opinions and declined to collaborate with him. If they ignored his value, the joke was on them. He was hot.

Well, closer to room temperature. Dane intrigued other agencies because he was the perfect human resource—a copywriter with one year of experience. At that point in his career, he did not need to be taught or paid too much. Creative managers also liked conducting job interviews because it filled the down time between meetings. And best of all, discontented job seekers provided spicy insights about competing agencies.

Dane's first interview was with Giles Bubis, who owned a small agency. Bubis had switched from copywriting to client services because it seemed more creative. Everything about Bubis was stiff, from his dark suit to his ravaged face, which was as cold and grim as the wet clay of a fresh grave.

Bubis asked Dane why he wanted to leave Green. Dane blathered about needing more challenge and creative freedom. Bubis stared at Dane with bemusement and slid an article across his desk. The piece described a clinical study for a hypertension drug.

"I want a writer who can read an article like this, pick out the main points and turn it into a selling message...in ten minutes," Giles said, "Can you do that?"

"I can learn fast enough," Dane said brashly.

"You can learn it fast enough but can you do it long enough? Over and over for years? That's what I need." Bubis emphasized each "over" until the word turned like a greasy chicken on a rotisserie. The grim man's monotone matched his stiffness and made Dane shudder. Bubis was telling Dane the story of his life and foretelling Dane's future.

To cut the morbid tension, Dane glanced around the office. His eyes stopped on a pair of brown shoes perched between statuettes and folders on a shelf. Dane asked Bubis about the shoes.

The stiff muscles of Bubis's face trembled for a second.

"Those are the bowling shoes of my client's late father. When his father died, he said, 'I want you to have them.'"

"Do you bowl?" Dane asked.

"No," Bubis snapped. "That's not the point. My client and I are so close that he would give me his only father's bowling shoes. I treasure them more than all of my awards...You're new in this business. How can you understand?"

In the post-interview debrief, Griffin told Dane that he and Bubis were not a good fit, but he phoned with a new opportunity—writing about asthma. Dane gasped with excitement. He would finally graduate from the gastrointestinal and urinary tracts to the loftier lungs. The interview was scheduled for late morning. To clear this time with his colleagues at Green, Dane called in sick and promised to come in late. The moment he arrived at Green, he skulked to the men's room and repeatedly rammed his forefinger down his throat so he would be heard gagging and retching to pay off his "sick story." Another employee was puking in the next stall, so Dane's self-induced gagging harmonized nicely. No one suspected his exit strategy; on the contrary, his colleagues believed that by vomiting in the men's room, Dane had finally become one of them.

Case 2-E
THE GUINEA PIG & THE WHISTLE BLOWER

29. PLEASE DON'T EAT THE DRUG SAMPLES!

One afternoon Dane returned from a particularly tasty falafel lunch to find an email, subject-line: URGENT, on top of his inbox. He had just returned from an interview and thought the email was for him alone—his job search had been found out and he would be fired.

He finally had the courage to open it.

It has come to our attention that drug samples are missing. Clients provide these to assist in package design and copy. These drugs are not recreational and have no pleasurable side effects. They can, however, be harmful...If you have taken these drugs for your own use or resale, please realize that you are violating Green Advertising rules and state and federal law. If you know anything about these thefts please respond to this email.

The lack of pleasurable side-effects made the theft of these drugs peculiar. Even if an employee pilfered them for treatment, was it possible that one person had osteoporosis, diabetes type 2, arthritis, *and* heart-worm—or knew individuals and dogs with all of these diseases? And if such an employee existed, he surely knew no sample dose could effectively treat these illnesses.

To diffuse an embarrassing matter, management investigated under cover, but their efforts were unavailing.

Dane was at the office late one evening when he found Austin Weebler in the men's room, gripping the sides of a sink. He was shaking badly. Dane asked him if he was all right. "Yeah, I'm okay," Austin replied. "It's just a bug."

Later that week Austin had an incident with a client. He was presenting a clinical piece when the client challenged his use of data. Weebler tried to explain but the client taunted, "Do the math!" Austin bowed his head and chuckled. "I know the math. And here's something else I know...*biofeedback!* My fist hits your mouth and there's an improvement." He lunged at the client and swung his fist many times in the area of his head, shouting, "Let's see if your drug can manage this!"

At that point, Weebler collapsed into a twitching, unconscious heap.

Such behavior called for summary termination but Weebler's unconscious twitching saved his job. Witnesses ascribed his violent act to a neurological event. It was believed that he had discontinued his anti-depressant, resulting in panic and rage. Colleagues forgave Austin in a company-signed get-well card. They believed he was a fine, young writer whose mind could not be wasted. Even the pummeled client welcomed Austin back on the account when his condition improved.

Weebler confirmed the agency's story. He claimed that his anti-depressant had interacted with his athlete's foot powder.

Hospital toxology tests, however, contradicted Weebler's account.

Significant traces of drugs Austin wrote about were in his tissue: osteoporosis, diabetes type 2, arthritis and heartworm medications mingled in his cells. It was clear that Weebler had been on the sample-stealing crime spree.

Management's fervent support for Weebler initially puzzled Dane but their clemency toward young Austin soon made strategic sense. He was a walking side effect of drugs in which he had expertise. Agency and clients defended him to protect their interests.

Unclear was the star junior copywriter's motive for taking the toxic cocktail. Why did a young man with a promising career abuse drugs for overeating couch potatoes, people with brittle bones or aching joints, and parasite-infested dogs?

Some speculated that Weebler's depression turned suicidal when his new friends, *The Boys,* derided him for never crafting a clever headline or concept. They had also made insensitive remarks about Austin's mother, how she caused Austin's depression by feeding him gourmet kibble, and obtained his job for him by performing unmentionable acts with Landon.

Dane was out of the gossip stream that circulated at Green as reliably as recycled air. These popular rumors never reached his ears. He believed he triggered Weebler's drug binge by confronting him for his door locking prank.

"This is what happens when you make a big deal about things!" Dane berated himself.

30. GUILT COUNSELING

Dane was in a funk about Weebler's condition. He initiated lively discussions about the drug-binger's motives in the kitchenette, elevator bank, lavatories, status meetings and any other common space where Green people congregated. Such public expressions of conscience disturbed his colleagues and disrupted the office.

Landon called Dane in for a chat on one of the rare days he was in.

"You've been here a year, haven't you?" *The Savior* asked.

"Yes." Dane froze inside. "Is he going to fire me—*now*?"

"You know what I like most about this job besides the money, travel, profit sharing and extensive vacation time?" Landon asked Dane. "Learning about my people. You've surprised me, Dane. I never imagined how much you care about others. You've grown as a writer and as a human being."

"That's weird because I feel like a slime ball," Dane replied.

"It could be a chemical imbalance. There must be something to take for that!"

"I'm not ill, Landon. I feel guilty," Dane said. "I worked with Austin Weebler. I accused him of locking me out of my office. We had words. I think I may have contributed to his collapse."

"That's nonsense! No one is at fault for Austin," Landon said. "Least of all Austin. Hypochondria is an occupational hazard for medical writers. Every employee contract should come with a warning: 'This job may be psychosomatic.' When you write about diseases, it's natural to think you have one."

"So you're saying Austin overdosed on the meds he wrote about because he believed he had osteoporosis, diabetes, and heartworm?" Dane asked in disbelief.

"Yes. Along with yeast infections and endometriosis. But mostly, Austin was guilt-ridden for writing about other peoples' misery and death."

"Then why don't all copywriters take drugs they write about?"

"Lack of access, courage, or interest, I suppose," Landon explained. "Austin is unusual. He's a hypochondriac who loves chemistry. Most writers imagine symptoms but they're afraid to take drugs they write about. Austin sees drugs as molecules and he is unafraid."

Dane nodded as if head shaking would distribute Landon's story throughout his brain.

"I've been reading about people who self-treat for imaginary diseases," Dane said. "Munchausen's by Proxy Syndrome seems to fit."

Landon nodded energetically. "It works for me."

31. A LAB RAT'S TWISTED MOTIVES

Advertising must give its audience a reason to believe and Dane had one or two. Austin Weebler suffered from imaginary illness and delusional self-treatment.

Though Dane sought lasting relief from guilt, Landon's interpretation did not persuade him. One Friday after work, Dane visited Weebler at the hospital.

When Dane walked into his room, Austin's eyes widened and a smile crossed his pasty face.

"Hey, puppy man! Getting into your office okay?"

"Of course, you're not around!" Dane cracked. "Why did you do this?"

Weebler looked away. "You wouldn't believe me."

"Was it because of me?" Dane blurted.

Weebler grinned at Dane. "You don't have kyphosis."

"I know I don't have dowager's hump. That's not the point," Dane replied impatiently.

"But it is the point! I did it for women who do! And for people who wheeze. And for dogs with heartworm."

"How could poisoning yourself help these diverse populations?"

"See, it's like this, *Puppy Man*. Some people don't respect you, but I do. You know why? Because you come to work each day to write the best ad campaign ever written. That's integrity. For me, integrity means knowing what I write is true. Drugs aren't always effective, but they should be safe. If I write that it's safe, I have to know it's safe."

"So you used yourself as a guinea pig."

"I'm a walking, talking side-effect," Weebler croaked. He could barely speak. The osteoporosis medication had affected his vocal cords.

"But why would you use yourself to prove this?"

"My mom could get osteoporosis. Can I tell my mom that a drug will help her when it's going to make her sick and die?"

He wagged his finger to entreat Dane to come closer.

"That drug you work on sells itself," Weebler whispered.

"What do you mean?"

"Look who's buying it. And why."

Weebler drew Dane closer so he could whisper in his ear.

"The purple folder. It's in Landon's office."

Dane nodded vaguely. As he turned to leave he detected a weak tugging on his shirt cuff.

"Don't turn your back—," Weebler whispered hoarsely, and took a long time trying to swallow, "—on the truth." Then Weebler's eyes closed.

32. THE PURPLE FOLDER

Although Austin Weebler was apparently raving, Dane believed him. He left the hospital committed to finding the purple folder.

He sneaked into Landon's office, closed the door and turned on the lamp over Landon's desk. *The Savior* had been gone for weeks. He was in the East Asian office, teaching Indonesian copywriters how to write about medicated diapers for pediatricians.

Among coded folders on the hard drive, Dane found one titled "purple." Landon's aversion to computers, passwords, and user names made the "purple folder" easy to access. Dane glossed over a list of emails and documents. Finally he came to one titled "Pentimento" and opened it.

"K-rations: source of protein and GERD. $2 billion k-ration initiative."

Dane stared at the screen, stunned by the magnitude of a

conspiracy. The holding company that launched *Refluxidyl* also marketed pork and beans, canned sausages, microwaveable scrambled eggs and sausage containers, as well as breath mints, all of which were, Dane knew, risk factors for immediate and prolonged acid reflux. For this reason, one government document urged the prompt launch of *Refluxydyl* as "crucial to national security."

The implications were appalling. Brave soldiers, lured to military service by patriotism, glory or a college education they could not otherwise afford, faced hostile fire from the enemy and esophagus-scorching friendly fire from their grateful nation. Depraved criminals received a nutritious last meal before execution, yet our fighting forces ate fast food that triggered acid reflux, bloating, constipation and headaches.

Dane looked up. The traffic manager, Sylvia Bittman, observed his transgression with rapacious curiosity.

"Hi," Dane said with a meek grin on his flushed face.

"Did Landon ask you to use his computer?" Sylvia inquired.

"Yes, in fact. He needed information which I'm finding for him."

"When did Landon contact you?" Sylvia asked.

"This afternoon," Dane said.

"He must have been up in the middle of the night because he's eighteen hours away," Sylvia countered suspiciously.

"Yes, in fact, he complained he was tired after being out with clients. You know how Asian businessmen like to party," Dane replied.

"I have no experience with Asian party animals," Sylvia Bittman said curtly as if this were one more deprivation in her long list. "Be sure to shut it down before you leave."

Sylvia despised Dane, yet now he that he gave her all she needed to have him terminated, she lost interest in prosecuting his lying, trespassing self. Did she actually believe him or was she letting him believe she did before she returned to her office to report him? Either way, Dane had already been caught in the act, so he completed his treachery in progress and downloaded the purple folder onto his flash drive as leverage if Green Advertising acted against him.

33. TO BLOW THE WHISTLE OR TO SWALLOW IT

As Dane rode the subway home, he felt the memory stick dangling at the end of a string against his bare chest, like a protective amulet. It contained the power of information.

He pondered his next move. What he could he do with this information to inflame public opinion, make public officials blush, stammer and resign, and bring a duplicitous government into crisis?

He had signed a confidentiality agreement pledging never to share business information with anyone. Given the sensitive legal and political nature of this disclosure, the contents of the purple folder could only be dispatched to an entity sufficiently powerful to ensure his and his family's safety. The Justice Department was his first resort, but could the government be trusted to investigate a conspiracy at its highest level?

As the crushing complexity and danger of his situation became clear, so did the futility of whistle-blowing. Dane's whistle was like a toy in a child's party favors. It would issue a shrill little sound. His fear started to talk. It asked Dane if loose cannon disclosures were the right response to a matter of national security. He considered the problem from another angle. While facing dismemberment, death and government rations, soldiers might need strong acid reflux relief. Was it ethical to put Americans in the field with acid reflux only to deny the most effective relief and damn the cost?

Dane phoned a major newspaper. He believed he had a front page story but he was put through to the health section. The reporter who interviewed him was more interested in writing an article on whether proton pump inhibitors really worked. She and her husband both suffered from acid reflux, resulting from a career's worth of vending machines. She told Dane she would talk to her editor and get back to him.

Dane was dissatisfied with the response of the serious journalist at a reputable paper, so he phoned a tabloid. There, he spoke with a reporter working on a feature about barbecues, with a sidebar on associated health risks.

"So, would you say *acid reflex* is a major risk for people?" the reporter asked. "Yes? On a scale of one to ten, how much risk is there of dying from acid *reflex* if you eat barbecue every night?"

"I'm not talking about barbecue!" Dane pleaded. "I'm telling you about a government conspiracy in which our fighting men and women are being given acid reflux deliberately to enrich the makers of GERD medications! Doesn't corruption of that magnitude mean a thing to you?"

Dane's query prompted a long silence. Dane hoped he had finally gotten through to this reporter.

"Would you say taking a *Refluxydyl* pill before the barbecue would provide protection from *acid reflex*...you know, like the pill?" the reporter asked.

Dane slammed the phone. He was putting his career and his life at risk to expose acid reflux and its treatment as part of a government conspiracy to enrich a drug company, but for the fourth estate, severe heart burn was no more than a lifestyle story.

He finally resorted to contacting a national tabloid magazine. Surely, these masters of sensationalism and scandal would feast on the sordid implications of the purple folder.

It was a bull's eye. While Dane was on hold with an editor, enthusiastically considering a feature with the headline, 'Government belly bomb plot exposed!" Landon appeared in the doorway.

"Dane," Landon said. "*Mon ami*, we have to talk."

"But I thought you were in Guam," Dane stammered, shocked and guilty to see his boss standing there.

"No, no," Landon said. "I'm here. So, I know what you know."

"But I don't..."

Landon cut him off with a "Tut, Tut" and flashed his puckish smile. *"Ce n'est pas grave.* Everybody knows it. Relax. Nothing will happen. All is forgiven. I told you, I'll protect you."

"But it *is* serious," Dane said. He was impervious to Landon's French expressions and promises of security now.

"Death is serious. Heartburn is not serious," *The Savior* replied in his wise and mellow tone.

"It's all a big lie!" Dane shouted to penetrate his mentor's laissez-faire attitude.

"Are you fighting for truth and justice in the pharmaceutical industry? How can you fight for something that never was?" *The Savior* asked with his worldly smile.

"Men are...are getting acid reflux needlessly—"

"—And cured. We sell the drugs. Don't be shocked, *mon vieux.* If we have a plan that makes some people ill to make them better, it's only smart marketing. Where's the harm?"

LeSeuer's eyes expressed a far-off laughter. He was an old soul whose sole conviction was that the *Refluxidyl* affair was nothing more than a burp in cosmic indigestion.

"So, *ça va? Tout va bien?* We're cool?" Landon asked, "Because we have to be cool."

"Sure, we're cool," Dane conceded. Since whistle-blowing had not worked out for him, he was relieved to resume as a medical copywriter.

34. CHOPPED LIVER

Nevertheless, Dane felt that he had failed to redeem Weebler's brave sacrifice. Dane experienced guilt and disorientation for hours.

"You weak and venal dog!" he taunted himself in the men's room mirror as Carl, the bibulous art director, walked in. "You won't get any argument from me," Carl said as he planted himself at a urinal and discharged his three lunch hour beers.

Soon Dane's self-accusations ceded to doubts. Was the purple folder real? Weebler was rumored to be comatose, even brain dead. Some claimed he was in line for an experimental esophageal transplant—if the procedure even existed—while others claimed his esophagus was irreparably damaged by the osteoporosis medications he ingested. Dane wondered if anyone so sick and delusional, so physically scarred and professionally compromised, was coherent. He convinced himself that he hallucinated Austin's testimony. It must have been another distorted daydream—his frustrated creativity pushing to the surface.

However, Dane's orgy of guilt, rationalization and moral ambivalence came to a full stop later that day, when an email slapped him out of his self-flagellation. It announced that two junior copywriters who were office assistants when Dane arrived at Green were promoted to copywriters. They had reached the same level in three months that he occupied after a year.

Exclusion and degradation were staples of Dane's day. Yet, he felt lucky to be at Green Healthcare Advertising. He enjoyed yoga classes, pulse and blood pressure readings, as well as other wellness initiatives, which management instituted to make employees feel at home so they would work longer. He was proud of his position, but now he viewed his title as trash and himself as a sap. How did this happen and what could he do?

He remained obtuse in office politics, yet he knew instinctively that storming into Landon's office to demand a promotion hours after being exonerated for flagrantly violating agency policies would be poorly timed. He was a trespasser, a classified documents thief, a would-be whistle-blower and an insubordinate liar, so he was not a prime candidate for promotion and a raise.

This moment was especially bitter for Dane since he had no one to share it with. If Bushkin had not been terminated they might have sauntered to the park, slobbered over falafels and commiserated with one another over their mistreatment. Fortunately, other colleagues at

Green Advertising, who occupied lowly positions, noted Dane's open moping and reached out to him in his moment of bad attitude. They related painful stories of working hard and well for the privilege of continuing to work hard and well. Dane found solace with one such colleague, Beatrice Merriweather, a designer and a Buddhist, who was on such a high spiritual plane that she never wore deodorant, making her an iconoclast among professional women.

Beatrice revealed to Dane the situational truth, "Those junior copywriters must have received other offers, so Green promoted them to keep them here."

"Loyalty, hard work and performance don't count? Do I have to threaten to leave before I can get what I deserve?"

"See Seymour Payne," Beatrice said.

35. THE WORLD'S GREATEST LIVING JUNIOR ART DIRECTOR

Seymour Payne was a legend at Green Advertising many spoke of but few had seen. Dane met him a few times in the kitchenette but never knew who he was. Seymour would fill the coffee filter with two packages of coffee and brew it all into one cup. He said it was all that kept him awake.

Payne had been at Green Advertising for fifteen years after a career at the best agencies on Madison Avenue. As these shops disappeared or were folded into conglomerates, he extended his career at Green as a junior art director, a rank he had held twenty years before. Green Advertising was thrilled to have the great Seymour Payne with his incomparable eye and innovative design at a bargain price.

Fifteen years later Payne remained a junior art director. No one considered promoting him, although he worked on the most important business with younger, less experienced art directors, who were his supervisors. When Seymour demanded a raise, his bosses smiled at his tirades. He had no leverage. Who else would hire him?

One time Payne was assigned an office with two junior art directors. Management thought he would be a wonderful mentor. Seymour made noises all day. He grunted, groaned, hummed and burst into sound bytes of Winston Churchill while he worked. His protégés could not be in a room with him, so Seymour was left alone after that. He clung to his job and amused himself. If you worked late, you might see Seymour in his office doorway with a mango in each hand and a "strange look" on his face.

Dane found Seymour in his office hunched over his putter, about to tap a ball into a paper cup four feet away. The ball rolled into the cup. The craggy legend glanced at Dane without a trace of surprise like he had drained that putt a thousand times.

"Years of practice, I'm ashamed to say," the advertising legend said. "What can I do for you?

Dane introduced himself and summarized his situation.

"You seem hurt and surprised," Seymour said, "Don't waste your emotion on this cesspool. If you want respect in this business, do yourself a favor and forget about it. You're a commodity so auction your ass."

Seymour opened a file cabinet to extract a bottle of *Drambuie*. He poured two cups of the Scotch liqueur, which he and Dane drained, and two refills. After the libation, Seymour emitted a deep cough that seemed to expel the dust and demons of a long career spent in polluted office air.

"They call this creative," he said. "Accountants are the real creatives at this agency. Have you figured it out yet? You can lie, cheat, steal and falsify your timesheets all you want and keep your job. You can be incompetent, lose business and keep your job. You can squeeze mangoes while female colleagues walk to the lady's room; they'll make you take sensitivity training—but you'll keep your job. The only way you lose your job is to have a creative thought—and the audacity to fight for it. Leave this place. Leave them all. Don't for a second be fool enough to believe loyalty, individuality and creativity exist in these places. You'll do fine."

36. END GAME

Being promoted at a pharmaceutical agency paralleled how drug dealers increased their drug earnings. By threatening to withdraw the product, you increased its value.

Griffin called with more opportunities. A number of agencies were interested in Dane and wished to lure him away from Green. He enjoyed his popularity and believed he might deserve it, but he also suspected that he was the beneficiary of an error in the labor market, which conferred inordinate value on mid-level copywriters.

Dane entertained offers from two agencies and turned down a third. It was an exciting time. He seemed to have a dimension nobody at Green could see. He wondered if Landon and his colleagues knew his secret and wanted him to leave.

Yet as he composed his letter of resignation, Dane remained unsure that he would leave Green. Despite his problems and resentments, Dane had many friends at the agency. He had learned much, succeeded often, and made many mistakes. He had transgressed and been forgiven. It was a strange but nurturing environment.

Finally Dane received an irresistible opportunity. A freelancer he had worked with was now a creative director at another agency. He offered Dane a promotion to senior copywriter, a 33% salary increase, and an assortment of interesting clients and projects.

Dane entered Landon's office.

"*Salut,* Dane! Écoute! I have to run to a meeting. Is this an emergency? Can it wait until next week? *The Savior* expostulated.

"No," Dane said. "It will only take a second."

He whipped out the envelope and handed it to Landon with crisp formality. It amused Dane how swiftly LeSeuer paused, how suddenly he made the time to deal with him. When Landon opened the letter, there was no wisdom in his eyes and no smirk in his youthful visage.

"Is it because of the locked door?"

"No."

"Is it because of the purple folder?

"No."

"Then what is it?"

"They're giving me more money and a better position."

"Oh. That. Don't sign anything. I'll talk to Rupert."

Rupert Mainwaring, the new creative director, was an Australian who had sold his small agency to Green and joined the multinational agency as a creative director. He was promoted to the flagship office to squash cliquishness and shenanigans, and unite everyone. Mainwaring devised an organizational concept—interlocking circles like the Olympics logo. Each circle symbolized a group and all groups linked in "unchained synergy." Rupert spent tens of thousands to animate his concept because research showed that cartoon characters were more trusted than humans.

After Dane resigned in the morning, he waited all day for Mainwaring to make a counter-offer. Finally the creative director called him in. When Dane entered his office, the Australian chief creative officer stood in the corner, wearing a green flannel body suit, a purple cape and a yellow coxcomb with bells on his head—the costume of *The Green Dreamer*—the animated character he created to symbolize unity. Mainwaring believed that when he wore these superhuman, yet likeable togs, his powers of persuasion were irresistible.

"Close the door, would you, mate?"

"OK," Dane said, ducking out of the office and shutting the door behind him. He thought he had caught the creative director in a private moment.

"No, come back and sit down!" Mainwaring called after him.

Dane took a chair and rationalized the creative director's appearance. Of course, Mainwaring had just returned from a video shoot to promote Green as "Agency of the Year." It was better than an alternative explanation: that Dane was having a hypoglycemic hallucination from starving all day.

At first, Mainwaring stared out the window at Fifth Avenue, looking depressed and disoriented. In this attitude, he seemed fairly normal to Dane despite the get up. Suddenly, the chief creative officer turned, leaped on his chair and onto his desk, did a jig and wagged his finger at Dane, who leaned back in his chair until it tipped. The resigning copywriter sprawled on the floor, scrambled to his feet, and crouched defensively.

"What's wrong, Dane. Are you feeling odd—insecure, perhaps?"

"Uh, no, not really!" Dane said.

"Ummm, but you're leaving us. You don't want to do that, do you? You like it here. We like having you here. So why are you leaving?"

"I have a family. I need to make more money. Surely you understand that."

"I do?" Mainwaring asked as he continued to stare out the window. "Yes, ummm, I do, yes. More money."

"Isn't that why you came here and left your family on the other side of the planet?" Dane asked.

Mainwaring was affronted to be discussed. He narrowed his eyes and took his measure of Dane. "Yes, money is always in the equation. But it was more than that for me. I wanted the challenge, the chance to make things happen, to shape events, to have an impact...Don't you want that?"

"Yes, I do. But that's not happening for me here."

Mainwaring laughed dryly. "You have to earn it."

"If I haven't earned a promotion I don't know who has," Dane replied angrily. "Some guys in this department with three months experience have my title and salary!"

"All right. I'm offering you senior writer and a raise of ten thousand dollars. How's that sound?"

Dane had been offered $25, 000 to leave Green Advertising and now $10,000 to stay—the difference was less than Mainwaring spent on his cartoon. Dane knew what he had to do.

"Thank you for your offer, but I can't accept it," Dane said.

"Well, good meeting you. Good luck," the chief creative officer said.

What a gift this Mainwaring had, Dane thought, to make a man wait all day, insult him, and wish him well. That was advertising!

The next morning, Landon asked Dane if Rupert made a counter-offer. Dane said he had.

"Did you take it?"

"I couldn't. It was $15,000 less," Dane said.

Landon furrowed his eyebrows. For once, *The Savior* appeared perplexed by human behavior. "Why did they make a counter-offer if they weren't going to match the offer you had?

"I don't know. You're in management. You tell me."

Treachery, insubordination, procedure violations and fighting did not end Dane's employment at Green Advertising. It ended for a few thousand dollars.

AD NOMAD 3
GRANDMAS GONE WILD
& OTHER ACTS OF GENIUS

Case 3-A

AESTHETIC VS. ASSTHETIC

1. CREATIVE COMMUNE

When Dane was hired at Integrimedicom, it seemed like a brilliant career move. Integrimedicom was consumer-oriented. He could write commercials and expand his repertoire.

Integrimedicom presented a wholesome work environment, mellow with minimal politics. No one had their own account. Clients, products and projects were shared by the entire department.

"We're small," Sheldon, the executive creative director, explained when Dane started. "We all have to be ready to jump in at any time."

Communal creativity with no ownership or egos at first appealed to Dane. This could be heaven on Madison Avenue—civilized colleagues, no lock outs, fistfights, or backbiting strife. The department even took him out to lunch with the man he would replace, who resigned "to get serious about his career."

Integrimedicom occupied the seventh floor of an old office building at the crossroads of Lower Manhattan, in proximity to the Holland Tunnel, where Soho, Little Italy and Tribeca converged or divided, depending on your point of view. Across Avenue of the Americas to the west, New York reached for the rest of America in a ganglion of ramps, Canal Street and Grand—a narrow passage dilating to a hectic estuary of traffic. The offices of this new, yet classic small agency were level with the roof line of Soho—black tar beaches from which water-towers jutted like industrial pagodas.

In his capacious office along a broad corridor, Dane sat with his back to the window. Messy leftover manuscripts covered his desk like the droppings of a corporate bird. Changes had been made to an obsolete version. Editors with hatchet haircuts caviled at him to test his mettle and dedication. Would he stick long enough to rectify the mess and earn his pay? When he had time, Dane went down into the streets to the north and east—for pizza rustica slices topped by rosemary, onions and coins of fried potato or quarts of Chinese noodle soup with hot red oil floating on the surface.

Integrimedicom was an agency that apparently observed a different set of rules from the rest of the advertising world. Its proximity to Chinatown was palpable in its creative philosophy. It was like a cloister facing east, its staff a sect with paychecks, and the communal creativity they practiced was a rigorous discipline demanding self-control and self-denial.

Yet in many respects, this cloister was like a plantation, where Sheldon and Nadine, the creative directors, were lord and lady and all others, serfs.

Sheldon was an amazing octogenarian and a fifty-year advertising veteran. He was a worrier, not a warrior. Before each morning's status meeting, he popped the lid off an aspirin bottle and said, "Never too early for *Excedrin.*"

Unlike Green, where creative assignments were initiated with pompous briefings and consummated with festive reviews, Sheldon and Nadine managed their business with serenity and simplicity, quietly circulating projects, shuffling partners and evaluating work behind closed doors.

What you started creatively at Integrimedicom, you rarely finished and what you finished passed through so many hands that you were a caretaker, never a creator.

"It's all about process here," Sheldon advised Dane on the day he started. "The result takes care of itself."

With a family to support, survival was Dane's primary objective. He repeated a mantra, "This is a good place. These are nice people. You're paid a lot." When he was not saying this, he tried to keep his mouth shut.

Dane's paycheck more than compensated for a coolie's lack of fulfillment. Two years before, he earned $20,000 as a senior lecturer—and the university would not rehire him at that pittance!

Now his income was five times what he made as a teacher. He had reached the salary a butcher at Victor's Meat Market once foretold for him while he quartered his chicken. Dane personified the advertising dream luring many to the industry, and achieved it in classic advertising style—with talent, luck and shrewd job moves.

Money transformed Dane's life in small, yet significant ways. He once dreaded bills but now enjoyed paying them! He signed checks with bravado, as if to taunt, "You want a piece of me, utility? Take that, credit card company! I can handle every bill, fee, and charge you send."

Stability was Integrimedicom's most alluring seduction. Dane's colleagues had been there for years. Their contentment as creative cogs suggested that individual achievement was an illusory striving ending in futility and pain. Integrimedicom had become for them a spiritual citadel where creatives attained agency Nirvana—freedom from a tortured craving for personal recognition and from the clash of egos which inevitably resulted in painful loss of income. Sheldon was a visionary dispensing enlightenment to those who poured their souls into boxes, slogans and shelf talkers. If truth in advertising was dead, perhaps Dane had found at Integrimedicom a shining paradox— security in advertising.

2. A COPYWRITER FOR CHRISTMAS

In Dane's second week, Roscoe, an art director, stopped by his office before their presentation. Roscoe carried several concepts they had worked on for a commercial—Dane's first television assignment.

The commercial was for *Donaral,* the most trusted medication for menopausal symptoms and the largest selling product for *American Pharmacon.* Roscoe rhapsodized about a television shoot and outlined the review process. Each team presented script concepts to Sheldon and Nadine, who selected their favorite concept for development.

"You'll see how it works," Roscoe said confidently like he already knew he and Dane were a cinch to shoot the commercial.

Dane viewed this early partnership with Roscoe as a sign of Sheldon's and Nadine's confidence in him. Roscoe was a top-flight designer and the godfather of Nadine's children. If Dane impressed Roscoe, Nadine and Sheldon would favor him. Yet, collaborating with Roscoe held significant risk.

The bald curmudgeon should have had "Dangerous Explosives" stamped on his skull. Maybe he hid it under the stocking cap which he pulled over his eyelids like a wooly condom. When he worked, Roscoe glared at his monitor like a crazed derelict, his blotched face knotted like a fist. Festivities also set Roscoe on edge. When the department took Dane to lunch on his first day, Roscoe threw a breadstick into his minestrone bowl and bolted without explanation.

At their first brainstorming session, Roscoe stared at Dane and dared him to have an idea. Dane knew he had better show his creativity and strategic insight, so he blurted a concept: policewomen in uniform, judges in robes and construction workers in orange bibs all conveying one message: Women with tough jobs have tough menopausal symptoms. This appealed to the working woman's feminine side. One headline read, "You earn like a man and you burn like a woman."

Roscoe nodded. "That covers hot flashes," he said. Dane sensed he had Roscoe's approval, if not his respect. After this salvo, Dane deferred to Roscoe, with his years of experience in television and print. When Dane expressed self-doubt, Roscoe responded kindly, "No worries. You're doing fine."

Then they hit an impasse.

Roscoe hated Dane's favorite headline and refused to show it. Dane implored him to compromise.

"Let it go!" Roscoe rebuked him. "Be professional. When I say, 'No,' it's no."

Dane chafed at this interpretation of "professional" but

swallowed his indignation. Commercials were new to him. Maybe Roscoe knew better.

When Dane and Roscoe presented their work, Sheldon perused one concept. "This could be *the one* but it needs a better headline." He closed his eyes and recited one. *It was Dane's headline—the one Roscoe rejected.*

Dane had repressed his ego all week to accommodate Roscoe. Now it detonated.

"That's my headline!" Dane cried.

"What?" Sheldon asked. "I just said it."

"I wrote it but *he* vetoed it!"

"You unprofessional scumbag!" Roscoe excoriated Dane. "I won't work with him again!"

The volatile art director stormed out of Sheldon's office.

Jousting with Roscoe was unexceptional. Even equable Sheldon, whom Roscoe once called a chipmunk and a *putz*, argued with him. However, Dane's fight with Roscoe was remarkable for its speed and rancor.

Nadine, who had viewed the new copywriter as her Christmas gift to *Uncle* Roscoe, now regarded Dane like she had to return him for store credit.

"You have to trust your partner," she rebuked him.

"Yes," Sheldon added, "Trust, err...the essence of partnership."

"He said my headline sucked. He has no taste!" Dane replied.

"Trust trumps taste," Sheldon corrected Dane, quoting from his own unwritten text, *The Book of Sheldon*. "Taste is a sensation; trust is an unchanging truth. I have written many headlines Nadine vetoed and I have killed many of her layouts."

"My layouts never die!" Nadine interjected. "But if one did, I would handle it."

Dane still had no inkling that his pairing with Roscoe was no vote of confidence but a live sacrifice to Roscoe, who, like an Aztec priest, routinely tore promising headlines from the heads of new copywriters and served them, pulsating with articulate energy, to Sheldon. Now, because the sacrificial copywriter spoke out of turn, the rite was disrupted. Sheldon asked Dane to stay behind. They needed to talk.

3. THE BEE AND THE FLOWER

"We have an efficient creative eco-system here," the genial creative director explained. "Everyone works together. We can't have people hating each other."

"But it was a great headline," Dane said, "—which you confirmed by coming up with the same one."

"Dane, this is irrelevant. We do things differently here," Sheldon said, bracing his left wrist with his right hand. At first, Dane thought Sheldon clutched his wrist as a sign of strength or osteoarthritis. But his wrist was tired due to the heavy Swiss watch which encircled it. "I know my earring and good hair make me look young but I've been in this business for fifty years. Nadine and I have 85 years of combined experience. We know our clients. At Integrimedicom we share ideas and bring them together. Like bees, we collect pollen from flowers. You may not be the flower type."

Sheldon stated his observation with profundity, as if the bee and flower were *yin and yang* and knowing which one you were was the litmus of creative identity. Dane despised passivity but loved his income. He confronted his first moment of truth. After implying his boss was a plagiarist, he knew contrition was a must.

"I want to be a flower, Sheldon," Dane pleaded. "But I also want to do great work."

"You do, Dane. But creativity is not holding on, it's letting go," Sheldon said, quoting himself from *The Book of Sheldon*, his unofficial oral tradition of Integrimedicom wisdom. "We don't force ideas or cling to them. We let them come to us."

Sheldon was adept at having ideas come to him, Dane thought. That was the problem.

Nadine poked her head in the doorway. "Shel, we're late for the overactive bladder patients and menopausal women focus group interface."

"Yes, excuse me, Dane" Sheldon replied. "There is learning when those groups collide."

Nadine agreed. "Cross-pollinating brands may provide multiple orgasms...I meant promotional opportunities."

"We know what you meant. Will they let us order from that four-star restaurant?" Sheldon asked. Before Sheldon and Nadine left for research, Sheldon called in Leslie Goldfarb, the most senior and lowest ranking art director.

"Goldfarb, would you team with Dane? Roscoe is working on another project."

Goldfarb escorted Dane to his office. The wiry, white-haired art director was an advertising veteran of 25 years. For six of those years he had been hanging on at Integrimedicom. This was Dane's best job to date but for Goldfarb it was a parking lot.

Although Goldfarb evinced the self-effacing wisdom of one who accepted a stalemate with life, the former photographer and top-flight art director might have qualified in some minds as a defeated has-been. Within the hierarchy of Integrimedicom, teaming with Goldfarb was a demotion, but Dane liked the wiry art director with the weary eyes. Goldfarb moved loosely, languidly like water, and despite a self-confessed lack of taste—the man loved cheap thrillers, smoothies and chick flicks, and conceded that he wasn't deep—he had dignity and a subtle energy. As with scribes of old, Goldfarb's knowledge of his craft, of life's rhythms and the sun's warmth, were written in the composure of his face and his forbearing eyes. Most agency people hoarded experience like a personal deodorant while sharing cynicism freely. Not Goldfarb. Battered, not bitter, he was candid and inspired trust.

"Do you think Sheldon came up with your headline because he's a mind-reader?" Goldfarb asked. *"It was a set up! A mini-conspiracy!*

Roscoe thought your headline was too *good* for you, so he gave it to Sheldon, who pretended it was his."

"A conspiracy to steal my concept? I didn't know a conspiracy could be so small."

"Where have you been? Do you read the papers? The internet?" Goldfarb inquired, his eyes peering at Dane as if he were searching for intelligent life in him. "There is no democracy anymore. It's one big conspiracy. There are conspiracies at the highest level and they trickle down to your concept. It's trickle-down conspiracy!"

"Okay. So they conspired to steal my work. Did they expect me not to react? How can I make a name for myself if people steal my ideas?"

Goldfarb probed his molars with his finger to remove sticky candy.

"They don't care about your career. They're paying you."

"What kind of place is this?" Dane asked.

"You're finding out."

4. HOW COPYWRITING GOT ITS NAME

For two weeks after his run-in with Roscoe, Dane disciplined his ego with drudgery. Each day he practiced the rigor of executing projects others started. He embraced the process by moving kits, stickers, pens, and other innocuous items to production. When copy was to be written, Dane transcribed pre-approved language from earlier versions and took pleasure and pride in how well he could do this elementary school task.

He believed his diligence and self-mastery were noted and rewarded when a creative assignment finally came his way. It was like a feast day erupting from the flatline of routine. The department convened and Sheldon and Nadine took turns reading the ten page creative brief.

Dane now teamed with Goldfarb, the old master of self-abasement. Goldfarb was a mental yogi. He could make his ego very small so it seemed not to exist. He also put it through contortions. When Goldfarb's talents were impugned, his layouts defamed and his designs vilified, he showed no emotion. With these qualities in mind, Sheldon assigned Goldfarb to be Dane's partner. "Les, I want you to mentor Dane in the ways of Integrimedicom. Teach him to let go, rather than to hold on."

Goldfarb smiled. "I don't know if it can be taught. It's a special gift to have your ego squashed like a bug—and not care."

The humble art director and the arrogant copywriter collaborated well. When Dane struggled for the right words, he stared out the mullioned windows at Soho's rooftop water towers while Goldfarb, the ego-control yogi, sat on the sill, soaking up winter sun and conserving energy for his long trek back to Connecticut. When Dane blurted a headline Goldfarb liked, the yogi smiled and said, "Nice. I like it!" When Dane proposed a concept Goldfarb hated, the wily art director said, "Eh!" and they explored further. It was a partnership.

On the eve of the creative review, Dane and Goldfarb had seven concepts with headlines and tags. Goldfarb taped them to his wall. The partners sat back and savored their work.

"I feel good about this, Dane," Goldfarb said. "We have some winners."

"The world encompassed in a toilet bowl is pure genius," Dane admitted. "It says it all about overactive bladder."

Suddenly Ronny, the copywriter, walked into the office. He wore black framed glasses and a plaid shirt buttoned to the collar. Ronny was from overseas and had extensive pharmaceutical experience. He had survived one year at the fabled I.M. Pecker, a venerable agency where the legendary Seymour Glom and his lieutenant, Dex Pez, stood at reception at 9 AM, checking who came in a minute late so they could fire them.

"Sup?" Ronny asked, scoping the office. "Got your shit on the wall to see if it stinks? I mean *sticks*."

"We're in good shape," Goldfarb said. "How about you?"

"Been working on the motherfuggin' recall letter for defective *Vulcan Shield* IUDs. No chance to brainstorm, man."

"How's your ass?" Goldfarb asked.

Ronny was unusually broad around the pelvis. Painful growths had been surgically removed from his anus, which now required 24/7 protection. The brilliant immigrant smacked his rump, causing a plastic wad around his hips to gasp pneumatically.

"Still got stitches. Can't enjoy my dump," Ronny said.

"Ass injuries are the worst," Goldfarb said sympathetically.

"A good crap was once my shining bliss but toilet seats are no longer thrones. They are rings of fire," said the non-native master of metaphor. "I need a powdered donut: baby powder, not *Krispy Kreme.*"

"*Krispy Kreme* should pay you NOT to say that," Goldfarb retorted, grimacing.

"I should sue these *muvvahs,*" Ronny replied, by which he meant Integrimedicom, Inc., "The chairs kill my ass, man."

As the agency gossip, Ronny was always pumping for information. When he had it, he spread it like manure. He had a passion for scams, posing as a student for a phony discount subscription to the *Wall Street Journal* and announcing his birthday several times a year, so his memory-challenged colleagues would buy him lunch on a quarterly basis. With the amount he saved on food and news, Ronny claimed he was able to buy a *Rolex*, which he wore on special occasions like payday. Calling his Swiss watch "an investment," he held his arm against his chest to protect his investment from smacking walls.

Ronny viewed copywriting in terms of caste. He deduced that only Sheldon and Nadine, the creative directors, had creative license, although they compelled all staffers to devise concepts, headlines and tags. This confusing dilemma for most creatives was for Ronny a technicality. He knew his duty was to fall short creatively, so Sheldon and Nadine would laugh, believe themselves to be geniuses and value Ronny as a creatively deficient employee.

For this reason, Ronny never agonized over blank paper or wracked his brain for ideas. When a creative review loomed, he circulated like cholesterol in colleagues' offices, took mental notes of their work and copied the headlines and concepts he liked.

As Ronny scanned the layouts on the wall, Dane recognized him as a threat. He told Goldfarb to remove their concepts—but too late. Sensing his cue to exit, Ronny rubbed his nose, waved and ambled away.

The next day Ronny and his teammate presented their work first. When Dane and Goldfarb followed, Sheldon and Nadine laughed.

"Another toilet bowl world!" Nadine chided. "You couldn't have an original idea?"

"The toilet bowl world is ours!" Dane shouted.

"We just saw it," Sheldon remarked.

"And plagiarizing Ronny of all people! He doesn't have a creative bone," Nadine jeered.

Dane looked at Ronny's concept, then at Goldfarb.

"He stopped by our office yesterday and stole it from *us*. We should have removed everything from the wall!" Dane replied hotly.

"Calm down," Goldfarb whispered.

"It could be a coincidence," Sheldon conciliated. "Simultaneous brainstorms are common as with most weather systems."

"Some ideas are so obvious, everybody has them," Nadine added.

"A toilet bowl world is fresh and not obvious. I didn't plagiarize it!" Dane shouted.

Sheldon was shocked by Dane's vehemence. Even Nadine was taken aback.

"Call in Ronny," Nadine said. She pretended to mediate while goading Dane. Everyone knew Ronny stole ideas. It was deemed an honor since he was a discriminating thief. But Nadine had something special planned. She wanted Dane to confront Ronny and go berserk.

After a quiet week, she deserved to be entertained! She had decided Dane was a bad fit and wanted him gone. If Dane lost control, Sheldon would have to fire him to ensure office harmony and security.

Ronny appeared. He wore his *Rolex*, as he always did for a creative presentation, and held his left wrist in front of him. Sheldon happened to be wearing his *Rolex* as well.

"Nice watch," Sheldon told Ronny, flattered by his subordinate's mimicry.

"Thank you, sir," Ronny replied. "It is only stainless steel, not plated gold like yours."

"You'll get there," Sheldon reassured him.

"Have you seen this before?" Nadine asked, indicating the disputed concept.

The resourceful permanent resident stared at the printout without expression or recognition.

"No way. These eyes never made visual contact with that object. Absolutely not!" Ronny insisted.

"He's covering his ass!" Dane cried.

Sheldon and Nadine looked at one another.

"You showed us this concept ten minutes ago," Nadine said, rolling her eyes.

"I did? Oh, yeah," he said. "You make an excellent point. If I wrote it, I must have seen it."

"You saw it, all right," Dane cried. "In Goldfarb's office."

"It's hard not to see things and be influenced," Ronny conceded calmly. "I might have dreamed it, too. My dreams are full of crap."

"If it's crap, why did you take credit for it?" Dane blurted. Goldfarb restrained him.

"I was only doing my job. I am a copywriter. It is my job to copy and to write," Ronny said unequivocally, as if quoting an eternal truth from a holy text of plagiarism.

Sheldon dismissed Ronny.

Goldfarb negotiated the awkward aftermath. He explained that he and Dane created the concepts and Ronny saw them on the wall. Sheldon and Nadine accepted the story but rather than apologize to Dane for accusing him of plagiarism, they admonished him for making a scene.

"You'll give yourself a stroke if you get worked up over such a trifle," Nadine said, as if concerned for the mental health she did her utmost to undermine.

"It's my integrity," Dane explained, his hands and voice shaking. "When I present work, it's mine. That's my guarantee, my bond."

"Integrity is to believe in but professional courtesy is to bond with," Sheldon sanctimoniously quoted himself. He asked Dane to stay behind—*again*. A nervous grin gripped Dane's facial muscles, as he poised for castigation or termination.

"Dane, your work is outstanding but your interaction is unacceptable."

"I'm sorry, Sheldon. I have to defend my reputation; it's all I have."

"Without colleagues who will work with you, you have even less!" Sheldon replied. The creative director averted his eyes from Dane to multi-task on his computer monitor. He studied *LL Bean* online while meting out discipline.

"How well do you know Ronny?" Sheldon asked. "My guess is not at all. Ronny appears to be a thief. In fact, he is a cultural victim. Ronny knows he has a problem. He borrows other people's ideas without permission. We're aware of it. He's getting help. But why does he have this problem? Ronny is sublimating his people's long history of subjugation and accommodation. His ethnic group is very old and it only survived by 'copying' a succession of dominant cultures. First it was the Babylonians, then the Assyrians, then the Medes, followed by Persians, Arabs, Kazakhs, Mongols, Turks, the French, the British and now the Americans. His people have copied so many cultures that now nobody knows much about them. It's in Ronny's cultural DNA to copy."

"I had no idea, really!" Dane replied, playing along with Sheldon's exotic strain of racial guilt. He wondered if "Ronny and the culture of plagiarism" was one more parable from the *Book of Sheldon*.

"Things are not always as they appear," Sheldon said sententiously.

"No," Dane agreed. He strongly suspected that Sheldon was talking crap, but it was the sweetest crap he ever heard because it did not include the words, "You're fired."

5. FOUR RULES OF NOBLE CONDUCT

Dane's anger over Ronny's plagiarism passed swiftly but deposited a residue of fear. Having his work stolen diminished his career but protecting it seemed far worse. When he denounced Ronny, he defended a concept which could die in days, whereas his job might not last as long. Ronny had seniority, minority status and was a victim of history—a human resources triple-threat. By accusing Ronny, Dane incriminated himself.

Worst of all, Dane had violated the Integrimedicom code—*again*.

Pride in his work was a self-destructive attitude which put his career at risk, but expunging it could do irreversible harm. If Dane renounced intellectual property, he might kill his creative spirit, which he would need for the afterlife, life after advertising. Dane believed advertising was his Babylon, a transient affliction, and that he was a "bird of passage" who would return to writing, his impecunious passion.

The senior copywriter wished to renounce ambition for security and a paycheck but craved recognition. Discontent surged in him like peptic acid after his twice-weekly falafels until he asked himself the Integrimedicom question that dispelled all anguish for a time. "Why am I complaining? I have a window office with plants on the sill and a view of Soho."

Dane was embroiled in a career-threatening conflict between

transcendence and the job. Creative fulfillment, which he craved, came in moments—at conception, peer acceptance, and wider approval—but a job spread over time like eternal butter on infinite bread. Transcendence meant nothing in a job. By forgetting this, Dane put himself in continual dread of losing it. Could he find transcendence in his work? To find out, Dane needed to go within.

He rectified his previous errors by practicing Integrimedicom's *Four Rules of Noble Conduct*—work on everything, collaborate with anyone, own nothing, offend no one—as specified in a human resources memorandum titled "Professionalism" and transcribed by the Committee for Professional Standards from the *Book of Sheldon*. Dane accepted hack work with enthusiasm, undertook menial projects with servile humility, and kept his head down and his mind occupied.

When changes came from clients, Dane copied them on the most recent lay-out, titled *The Bible*, with the painstaking pride of a Sumerian scribe. If he altered even a word to feel like a real writer, the account executive badgered him to transcribe the changes verbatim. Plagiarism was preferred to paraphrase since clients put their trust in pre-approved verbiage. Ronny was probably right. Copywriters were hired to copy.

Dane put in long hours to prove his diligence so Sheldon and Nadine would consider him worthy of his hire. He was going in the right direction—but only crawling there. These measures were too subtle to repair the image he had created as an ambitious loner. He needed a bolder gesture of subservience and ego-denial. Since he had made a poor impression by defending his work from theft, he needed to show he had gone beyond petty possessiveness.

During the next creative free-for-all, Dane wrote headlines and taped them to the walls of his office, then left the door open so Ronny and others could come in and steal freely. Dane waited but no one came. "I probably scared them off with all of my ownership issues," he muttered. If his thieving colleagues would not walk in and help themselves to his ideas under his willing nose, he would deliver the stolen goods. Dane stopped by Ronny's office with pages of headlines and asked him about his recuperating anus. Ronny shrugged. "At least I can fart pain-free," the suffering plagiarist conceded. Dane nodded sympathetically and "misplaced" the stack of headlines on Ronny's desk.

Then Dane barged into Sheldon's office to ask which expensive watch he should buy on installment from a pawnbroker. "I can't help you with pawnbrokers," Sheldon replied. Dane thanked him profusely for his expertise and left a stack of headlines on a chair before he left.

Dane dropped pages on the desks and chairs in every colleague's office and waited for harvest. So they would know the work was his, he key stroked every word in his signature *Tahoma* font. After leaving his donations, he toiled on his own headlines, tags and body copy.

At the next creative review, Dane looked for his headlines and concepts among those presented by his colleagues, but no one had stolen so much as one headline, tag—or word. Dane was stunned and offended. What a perverse lot his Integrimedicom colleagues were— they would steal but would not accept a gift.

Perhaps he had made it too easy for them. Maybe they mistrusted the handout headline that appeared mysteriously on their desks, as if it were a Halloween apple with an embedded razor blade or a suspicious suitcase in a public place. After 9/11, everyone was on alert. Soon signs might be posted around the office: "If you find suspicious copy, call security."

Dane was frustrated by the difficulty of giving away his creative bounty but he did not relent. Perhaps his colleagues needed a greater challenge. Maybe they preferred to find great headlines willy-nilly as in a scavenger hunt. For the next assignment, Dane littered his clever pages in public places—on the floors of toilet stalls, kitchenette counters and conference tables. He printed copies and left them on the printers. He waited to be plundered. However, at the next creative review, Dane was the only one to present Dane's work.

He was more despondent and frustrated than usual as the

Integrimedicom way remained an elusive concept.

"I can't give it away!" He lamented. "Maybe I'm not meant for selfless creativity."

6. THREE LITTLE WORDS

By testifying to Ronny's transgression, Goldfarb saved Dane's job. In recognition of this, Sheldon and Nadine dissolved their partnership.

Dane was now paired with Gordon Palmisano, the associate creative director of art. Palmisano had a dour countenance and an austere manner. Goldfarb speculated that it was because Palmisano was disappointed on his wedding night—and never recovered. Around this soft, morbid core formed a gnarly crust. Palmisano held strong views on many things for a very long time and was averse to compromise. The bulbous roots of a rubber plant, which he had purchased when he arrived at Integrimedicom fifteen years before, now traversed his office floor like boa constrictors. Palmisano drew inspiration from them as he squeezed the life out of his writing partner's copy.

"Sheldon and Nadine want to see us," he told Dane. It related to a project they had done weeks before.

Sheldon and Nadine sat in his corner office, gossiping about Beulah Muschamp, a spokeswoman for *Donaral*. The aging pop diva had a commercial where she said she shrank two inches and lost two of her five octaves before taking *Donaral*. Singing at a recent corporate function, *Beulah* hit a high C and shattered the *Donaral* marketing director's champagne glass in mid-sip, cutting his tongue and lips. A diabetic who used an insulin pump while binging on donuts, the marketing director bled profusely because he was on an anti-platelet therapy for atherosclerosis.

Nadine was listing the sexual favors the marketing director could no longer render his wife when Sheldon noticed Palmisano and Dane loitering in the doorway. With a mortified nod, he invited them in. Nadine's loquacity having run its course, Sheldon told the creative team why they were summoned.

Several 11x17 color concepts from weeks before lay across Sheldon's desk. They were for the makers of *Uribilox*, a 24-hour slow-release pill to stop overactive bladder, a disease Sheldon proudly claimed to have invented. Before overactive bladder entered medical books, a persistent urge to urinate was not considered an illness, but part of aging, like senility. People without bladder control stayed close to toilets and tried to hide their problem out of shame.

Then Sheldon and the makers of *Urbilox* transformed a humiliating problem into a dignified disease, which was sympathetic and treatable. Brochures, hotlines and questions to ask your doctor supplanted shame and ridicule.

"The client chose your concept for their annual meeting," Sheldon explained.

"All right!" Dane bellowed and pumped his fist. In that impulsive gesture, Dane undid weeks of progress he had made to become a selfless high-paid peon. It was hard to undo a lifetime of uncorroborated self-love.

"Can we improve it?" Sheldon asked.

"Come up with better words," Nadine said.

"The client didn't like the words?" Dane asked.

"What the client *likes* doesn't count here," Nadine declared. "Only what we think matters. The client pays us because we're experts."

Dane knew he was in trouble when Sheldon and Nadine acted like aesthetic gurus rather than client-pleasing prostitutes.

"*Imagine, Innovate. Inspire* are three little words," Dane pleaded.

"They're big words but the *ideas* are small," Nadine replied, her eyes fixed on Dane's crotch. "Maybe we need smaller words but bigger ideas. Like *Think, wish, dream.*"

"Imagine, Innovate. Inspire are fine words," Dane replied indignantly.

"They're egotistical words.   They all start with *I,*" Nadine snapped.

Everything can be improved," Palmisano added.

"We'll help you," Sheldon said with paternal alacrity.

We'll help you were the three and a half little words Dane dreaded most. They meant his words would die, but only after he was tortured in the vain attempt to save them. The creative directors wanted to own every creative act. A cold light flared in Palmisano's dark eyes, like a nova in a distant galaxy, as he anticipated the fun. Dane had battled him for these words. Now Palmisano would get his thesaurus-thumping revenge.

"It's your copy, Dane. Sheldon said. You have the last word."

In what sounded like a burping match, Sheldon, Nadine, and Palmisano blurted alternatives for the three word sequence.

"Investigate. Integrate. Invigorate," Nadine said.

"Nice," Sheldon replied.

"Initiate. Eliminate. Illuminate," Palmisano said.

"Too dark," Nadine said.

"Direct. Connect. Protect," Sheldon said.

"That says it all," Nadine said.

When every effort to change his words was exhausted, Dane said, "I like my copy."

"Are you sure?" Sheldon asked with furrowed brow.

"Yes."

Dane left Sheldon's office with his three words intact. He won the skirmish. Yet in the solitude of his office, he did not feel victorious, only insecure. Integrimedicom offered no place or support for personal satisfaction. The very air rejected it.

"What did you do this time?" Dane berated himself. All ad agencies shared one immutable truth. The creative director had more clout than a copywriter. Dane realized that he might have put his job and family's welfare in peril—*again.*

7. AESTHETIC VS ASSTHETIC

Goldfarb, Dane's guide in the ways of Integrimedicom, appeared in the doorway. His eyes were closed. He had been up since 5 AM. He had biked to his town's YMCA, swum a quarter mile, biked to his town's train station, then hiked two miles from Grand Central to Integrimedicom—and it was now late afternoon.

When Dane saw his mentor and said, "Hey!" Goldfarb's eyelids snapped open and his eyes were bright with mirth. Dane was startled.

"*Three words!* Not even a sentence," Goldfarb said. "Would it have killed you to let Sheldon have a word?"

"So you heard! No! *Yes!*" Dane slumped over his desk and pulled on his thinning hair. He was divided against himself. "It wouldn't have killed me but it would have killed the headline."

Goldfarb smiled at the torment of the younger man.

"You're weak," Goldfarb chided. "What is a headline? Words on paper! You are a master of words but you let words master you."

"I do, don't I?" Dane admitted. "I'm so stupid!" He smacked his forehead.

"Not stupid. Just handicapped by a hypertrophic ego. Hey, how do you like *hypertrophic* coming from me?"

"It's beautiful...But it wasn't my big ego this time, Goldfarb. I was compelled by an aesthetic law," Dane replied.

"You mean *assthetic.*"

"If I changed one word, I had to change them all, and the line would die," Dane argued.

"Words don't die, oh *Wordy One,*" Goldfarb said as he pulled a yogurt and a plastic spoon from the deep pocket of his cargo pants. "They are reborn a billion times in a billion mouths from a billion minds, most of which are empty."

"Spoken like an art director who failed English composition,"

Dane countered. "Words produce combinations, like stones that lean on each other in precarious balance. A headline rejects a new word like a body rejects a transplant."

"And an agency passes a new copywriter like a stone."

"You're right," Dane conceded. "So what can I do?"

"I've taught you what I know," Goldfarb said. "But I'm an art director, a click-meister, playing with type, images and layout. You need to learn from another copywriter. What about your neighbor, McAdam? He'll teach you all you need to know about being a writer at Integrimedicom."

By fighting for himself, Dane had not gained confidence but lost his nerve. Were words worth such agony? Dane vowed never to fight for language again. Only the job mattered—the license to write for money. He would learn from McAdam.

8. THE ROLE MODEL

Goldfarb was right. No one exemplified the creative philosophy of Integrimedicom more completely than James McAdam. In the next office, McAdam hacked away at brochures about menopause based on internet articles he copied, pasted, discarded and forgot—a method which led to last-minute havoc when facts needed to be checked and sources found.

McAdam embodied Integrimedicom's ideals. He grinned fatuously, spoke softly, drank heavily and worked long into the night.

His father was the legendary founder of an award-winning agency, but James rebelled against all that McAdam Sr. stood for—originality, excellence and success—only to create a new standard. James disappeared every afternoon for beer and volleyball with friends, then returned to his office and toiled into the night. This regimen permitted him to bill a ridiculous number of hours to capricious clients.

McAdam's unique schedule also made him an elusive colleague.

Dane, for one, rarely saw him. At meetings McAdam seldom spoke. When Dane worked late he passed McAdam's office to see Integrimedicom's paragon at work—and to learn in candid glimpses how success could be achieved.

But McAdam's process repelled a simple read. Each night he pecked on a keyboard on his lap, as if guarding the mystery of the wordsmith's creative act. With white socks crossed on his desk and his red face glowing in a yellow pool of lamp light, McAdam was a luminous icon in the dark. He smiled at the keys and evinced no sign of effort. His brow never furrowed from strain; he did not frown, pause, or check his monitor. He knew his words so well that he did not need to confirm them with his eyes.

Dane stood in the doorway and studied McAdam, immersed in his task. "If only my work were this easy," he thought.

McAdam suddenly glanced up. He nodded casually at Dane as if a colleague staring at him from the hallway were normal behavior.

"Hey! Working late?" McAdam asked.

"Of course," Dane said. "Sorry for bothering you. I couldn't help but notice how you go about your business. It seems effortless."

"I can do this in my sleep. In fact, I *am* sleeping," McAdam said.

"You must have good dreams because you're smiling."

"It's the booze. I'm a happy hack," McAdam admitted.

Dane laughed. He identified McAdam him as that rare individual Maslow described: a self-actualized human, perfectly suited to his environment and work.

One morning, the creative wing of Integrimedicom was in a panic. Babette, the vice president of client services, was screaming. Nadine paced and looked overwrought. Sheldon gulped down aspirins and gripped his Swiss watch like a squeeze toy. Sid Gorfine, the agency president, was on the creative floor, smacking his leather pants with hyperactive wrath.

"McAdam's in trouble," Goldfarb said.

James McAdam's career had advanced because he amiably did

what he was told. Recently, Babette and her client pressured him to insert a map he found on the internet into a brochure. When the agency's unauthorized use was detected by the atlas publisher, James was cited for copyright infringement.

Dane was disoriented. Only weeks after he submitted to the values of Integrimedicom, its business was under siege and his role model was in disgrace. Dane had to deprogram himself to his default setting of integrity. He hoped McAdam's plagiarism would shock Integrimedicom out of its stealing ways so Dane could be openly original again.

However, by week's end, Integrimedicom had paid the atlas publisher a licensing fee and a five-figure settlement and order was restored. McAdam accepted full responsibility but rather than lose his job, he was promoted to vice president! In an email announcing the promotion, Sheldon described McAdam as the consummate team player and praised him for his initiative and accountability.

The culture of larceny returned and Dane resumed trying to emulate McAdam—a serial beer drinker who sacrificed evenings, talent and reputation for the team—in order to fit in. McAdam was Sheldon's favorite and Nadine teased him about his alcohol abuse. If only Dane could be like McAdam!

Dane had to think like McAdam and put McAdam*ism* into practice. To achieve this, he needed to devise a project or test. One finally came to him. He would turn the stress incontinence brochure he had written at Green into an overactive bladder brochure he was working on at Integrimedicom. It was a brilliant way to save time. Stress incontinence and overactive bladder differed but had a similar result—involuntary urination, diapers and embarrassment. Who would notice or care that the copy was borrowed from another source? After regulatory committees filtered the language, all brochures sounded alike, anyway.

By cutting and pasting copy from the previous document into a new template, and altering a few details and phrasings, Dane composed a new brochure in an hour. The crime was so easy and perfect—Dane had plagiarized himself. While musing on his felonious innovation, he had a transformative idea. If he applied his experiment to all products and conditions, he would write the universal patient brochure template. It would describe every disease in vague language, offer a page or two of treatment options and conclude with the same mealy-mouthed advice "to see your doctor." Only the diseases, product descriptions and charts would be left blank.

The thrill of scamming himself and the pharmaceutical world lasted ten minutes, after which Dane experienced a let down. He sensed that one-copy-fits-all might be what the world wanted but it cheated him of what he loved most—the thrill of writing something new each time, even if the originality was sucked out of it by account services, clients and regulatory panels. All diseases were not alike, even if they were talked about in similar ways and had similar outcomes.

As Dane debated whether to carry out his mass-deception, just to see if it worked, the traffic manager dumped a folder bulging with copy on his desk for his review and signature.

At that moment, Dane knew he could not be like McAdam, even if it meant making his life easier. He pushed through the slow, tedious changes by thinking about the new overactive brochure he was writing.

Case 3-B
AN OLD LADY AND A DOG

9. EASY & SLEAZY

Dane's employment followed the pathology of a chronic disease—inflammations and remissions. After the *Battle for Three Words* he recoiled, but when he was not terminated, he relaxed.

Weeks passed. Dane made significant progress in learning the

Integrimedicom culture. He did not protest or flinch when his ideas were stolen. He took it as a compliment when his headlines showed up in colleagues' work. He perceived it as a power that yielded a benefit; his colleagues took credit for his concepts but they needed him to produce them. His influence invisibly grew.

Since Palmisano had failed to change even one of Dane's three words, Dane was reassigned to Goldfarb in the free-for-all to create a new campaign for *Hyalny*, an injectable synovial fluid for osteoarthritic knees. Dane and Goldfarb focused on the simplicity and ease of therapy. As opposed to pill-popping everyday for temporary pain relief, HYALNY required only three shots, spaced days apart, and provided months of knee pain relief. "The *easy* way to OA pain relief. *Hyalny*" was the headline Dane wrote to convey this message.

"Injections aren't easy," Nadine remarked, dismissing the idea. The following morning Nadine and Sheldon showed the work they would present to the client. One of their concepts had a group of old surfers. The headline read, "It's *easily* the most amazing thing in knee pain relief... *Hyalny*."

After the meeting, Goldfarb seethed with indignation as he and Dane walked to Chinatown for lunch.

"*Easy* was your idea and they stole it," Goldfarb remarked sharply. "Sheldon lacks integrity. That would never happen at DOA. If *easy* was your word, nobody else could use it.

"Words can't be owned," Dane pointed out.

"*Easy* was your idea!" Goldfarb insisted. "Nadine said it sucked. Then Sheldon used it like it was his all along."

'That's what they do," Dane said. "You said it, yourself."

"It's wrong!" Goldfarb retorted as a pedicab from a stand on Grand nearly ran into him.

"I can use *easy* in the tag as in *Easy does it with Hyalny*," Dane reassured Goldfarb.

"No, Sheldon owns *easy* now," Goldfarb concluded as if the rights to the word were irrevocably lost.

Dane found it strange that Goldfarb, who usually did as he was told and was candid about lacking conviction in such matters, inveighed against Sheldon's word theft. Dane had better headlines, concepts and storyboards stolen and was blasé over losing *easy.* He attributed his indifference to a hard-won maturity but his nonchalance disturbed Goldfarb most.

They lunched on chicken and broccoli at *Uncle Tung's,* a Chinese restaurant on Lafayette Street that looked like an old banquet hall. The misdeeds of Sheldon and Nadine made Goldfarb nostalgic for his better days.

"At DOA, people didn't steal ideas," Goldfarb said. "Creativity was sacred. Nobody changed anything. I'm sorry you never experienced that."

Dane listened without envy as if Goldfarb were telling a historical anecdote from "before his time." He wondered why Goldfarb made him dwell on the mediocrity of his experience.

"Maybe I'm better off not knowing what I've missed," Dane said. "I have to appreciate what I have."

"It hurts to see hear you say that. You used to get mad when you were ripped off," Goldfarb replied.

"I need the job."

"It's a trap," the sagacious art director warned. "If you give away your ideas you'll have nothing left. You'll keep your job but never get another one. That's how they get you."

The old seed of restlessness, sown by an unlikely source, quickened in Dane's mind.

10. CONSPIRACY THEORY

In the next round to produce a new campaign for *Hyalny,* Dane and Goldfarb devised a concept in which an older couple carried shopping bags with unusual enthusiasm—by jumping in the air. It was the last thing a person with osteoarthritis of the knee was likely to do. The headline read, "I get around!" This was the applied art of advertising—a popular phrase repurposed for the consumer world.

Nadine and Sheldon meanwhile proudly unveiled their new concept: "an old lady and a dog."

"An old lady and a dog can't lose," Sheldon said.

"When did an old lady and a dog become a concept?" Becky asked Dane that night when he recounted this episode. "They can't be serious."

Sheldon and Nadine presented the new *Hyalny* work to the client at the drug company's corporate headquarters. When they returned, they convened everyone in the conference room.

"Dave Bruburger, the orthopedic division director, liked your concepts," Nadine told Dane and Goldfarb.

"Yes!" Dane blurted involuntarily, pumping his fist. He could never purge himself of the habit of celebrating minor accomplishments in the manner of a game show contestant.

Nadine and Sheldon regarded one another with disgust.

"What was Bruberger smoking?" Nadine asked Sheldon.

"Crack. I heard he's been reassigned," Sheldon replied, as if the executive had been demoted for liking Dane's and Goldfarb's ad.

"But 'an old lady and a dog' will also be tested," Nadine announced.

The showdown between "I get around!" and "an old lady and a dog" took place in a research facility in Philadelphia. Many interviewees, all with osteoarthritis of the knee, responded warmly to "an old lady and a dog" but a majority identified with jubilant grocery shoppers jumping and singing a Beach Boys lyric.

The second round of research took place in Chicago and there was no budget for Dane and Goldfarb to attend. They had to watch it on a webcast from the corporate boardroom. Goldfarb was glum.

"What's wrong?" Dane asked. "This is great. We get to watch people respond to our work on TV. It's like a reality show."

"You think so, huh? That's our work. We should be there. I

don't like it," Goldfarb said.

Nevertheless, Dane and Goldfarb pulled their plush, upholstered chairs close to the monitor and waited for the screen to stop being blue. Goldfarb had recently had a few thousand dollars of overdue dental work so he did not bring popcorn. Instead, he brought soy chips from the *Gourmet Garage*. Dane popped *Gummy Bears*.

The first interview was set for 1 PM but the screen stayed blue. Suddenly an image popped on the monitor. "Here we go!" Dane said.

They saw a still shot of an empty room devoid of furniture, windows and voices. It looked like a restroom or stairwell. Dane's anticipation grew. Five minutes passed. Nothing changed. Dane's excitement fermented into apprehension.

"It's like a Warhol movie I once saw," Goldfarb said. "I didn't like it. It was too deep."

"Maybe the first interviewee is late or didn't show," Dane speculated hopefully.

"We're the ones who didn't show!" Goldfarb blurted, irritated by Dane's naiveté. "Can't you see? It's a conspiracy!"

"Conspiracy? For what? Against whom?" Everyday, Goldfarb told Dane about an article or book he read about some arcane group responsible for every depredation and disaster, including JFK, El Niño, 9/11, global warming and mad cow disease.

Goldfarb gave Dane an incredulous look. "*For* 'an old lady and a dog' and *against* us!"

A half hour passed. Still the creative team held their position before the flat screen. The less they saw the more attention they paid, in case they were missing something or hallucinating the emptiness.

"Maybe it's on a premium channel. Or pay-per-view!" Dane suggested.

"We shouldn't have to pay. It's our work!" Goldfarb cried. "No, like I said, it's a conspiracy. I've studied these things. This has all the markings of a covert op funded by a right wing think tank and sanctioned by the Trilateral Commission."

"All for a synovial fluid injectable ad? How are national interests served by that?"

Goldfarb looked at Dane sadly.

"They'll stop at nothing for 'an old lady and a dog.'"

After an hour, by tacit agreement that the show was not improving, Dane and Goldfarb stood up to leave.

"I don't drink but I should reconsider," Goldfarb said.

Later Sheldon and Nadine emailed the creative team: "Ooops! They put the camera in the wrong spot. But great work, guys. They loved everything."

"Wrong room—*right!*" Goldfarb said. "Sounds like the Warren Commission all over again! *Wrong* room, *one* bullet!"

The testing firm released its top-line research report. "An old lady and a dog" had tested better with women over seventy, the target audience, and would be the campaign concept. Goldfarb's and Dane's improbable winning streak ended in predictable defeat. They left the meeting in silence.

"You knew that was going to happen," Goldfarb said later. "They always get their way. I was afraid you would lose your cool. But you were strong."

"Stunned is more like it."

"The writer you replaced was fragile. He shouted and threw things."

"Sounds healthy," Dane replied, who envied his predecessor and hated his own passivity.

"Losing your temper is weak," Goldfarb replied. "You have to stay strong."

Self-control did not make Dane feel strong. When his concepts were defeated by chicanery, he lost faith in competition. Worse, he no longer believed creative content mattered. If "an old lady and a dog" was going to win every time, how could he continue?

Case 3-C
YOUR BEST MOVE: ADMIT YOU'RE A HERMAPHRODITE

11. QUEEN NADINE'S *HE*-REM

Dane was in crisis and his struggle was apparent to everyone. He thought he could keep his professional grief a private matter, but colleagues could be vultures, circling over floundering conviction and dying fire. His sadness was palpable in elevators, corridors, lobbies and conference rooms. Nadine sensed Dane wavering and stepped up her effort to flush him from Integrimedicom.

Nadine was expert in the arts of alienation. She gave Dane more tedious assignments, changed headlines on ads under the mere suspicion that he wrote them, and made him stay late to shepherd projects he had never seen.

Unlike some people Dane knew, whose hatred masked love or fear, Nadine's loathing of Dane was pure and deep. During his first interview, Nadine pointed out to Sheldon that none of the concepts in Dane's portfolio had been produced. When Nadine dismissed Dane to go home for Thanksgiving, she told him to enjoy his turkey since he would be keeping his job—it was the first time he thought he could lose it.

Goldfarb was familiar with Nadine's bad side. He had done hard time in the harsh tundra of her wrath when she first appeared at Integrimedicom, before he groveled out of her scorn into her benign indifference. He told Dane to get her to like him by laughing at her jokes.

It was easy for Goldfarb to say but impossible for Dane to do. He did not know how to curry favor with someone who despised him and his banter was bad. Poor social skills aside, Dane feared Nadine. He had seen her before—in mythology books. She was a contemporary Cybele, the fertility goddess, whose male priests gelded themselves in a religious frenzy to roast their nuts on her fiery altar.

Nadine had not always been an implacable earth goddess; she evolved into the role. She began as an ambitious and industrious art director who aimed to succeed with talent alone. Then she worked for a demanding and attractive woman whom everyone hated but feared. She was everything Nadine thought she did not want to be until she overheard a male colleague say, "She's a bitch but you *know* she's wearing sexy underwear."

That crude remark revealed to Nadine what she wanted most: to be worshipped so she could be four times as effective with half the effort. But since she could not command with attraction, she hurled herself on her male subordinates with high decibel aggression.

Each man on staff played a role in Nadine's *he*ram of male misfits. Sheldon was the beloved, senile father; Goldfarb, the impotent uncle; Ronny, the masturbating cousin; Roscoe, the sadistic, gay brother; Palmisano, the incestuous half-brother, who might kill himself from self-loathing. Rex, the traffic manager, was the servant sex toy. Dane did not know his role yet.

He would find out—at the Christmas luncheon.

Under the guise of family feeling, Nadine exploited the staff's weakness for free food by organizing departmental lunches. These rites had a liturgy—the cover of *People* magazine or a bizarre internet story. Nadine was the lady at court and these were her courtiers. She raised an issue and they humored her by discussing it.

Nadine arranged the annual Christmas luncheon at *Big Dong*, Soho's own cafeteria style Chinese restaurant. As the creative team ate meat over rice, Nadine introduced the weird story *du jour*: hermaphrodites had fallen in love and had a wedding at *Taco Bell*.

"So Dane, what do you think?" she asked.

"I still like *Taco Bell*."

"You have to respect a man who's true to his fast food," Sheldon opined.

"No, I don't," Nadine retorted, tossing a Dane a disgusted glance. "I meant isn't it amazing how much sex hermaphrodites can have?

But if you have two genitals, does it mean you have to have sex twice to be satisfied? That's not fair. I can't have it once with regularity."

"Regularity is a problem," Sheldon quipped.

"*Toilet humor* from you, Shel, I never..."

"You're a bad influence," the executive vice president admitted.

"What fascinates me about hermaphrodites is that when they're horny they can do themselves—with no hands, right, Ronny?" Nadine persisted.

"A firm handshake is a sure sign of too much jerking-off," Ronny replied, with his head down as he shoveled food in his mouth with a plastic spoon.

"Of course, even a hermaphrodite has to get it hard to get it in. And that isn't easy, is it Goldfarb?"

"No, not easy, Nadine!" Goldfarb answered with loud, empty cheer.

"I think it would be great for a hermaphrodite to work for me," Nadine said. "You know why, Dane?"

"No," Dane replied as he braced himself for the innuendo that he was a hermaphrodite.

"Because if I told him to fuck himself, he could do it!"

The first laughter came like a tide of sewage after a long rainfall but crested short of inundation.

"It would make your job more fulfilling, right Nadine?" Dane shot back.

Sheldon guffawed. *"Touché."*

As Dane absorbed Nadine's hostile glare, he wondered if they would ever get along or even coexist.

12. DOWN BY NADINE

After *Big Dong*, Nadine was more determined to oust Dane. She seemed to taunt him, "You wish I weren't here but HERE I AM." And now that Goldfarb was Dane's partner again, he was also in her cross-hairs.

Nadine routinely reviled their work in imperious monologues that precluded rebuttal and discussion. Nadine knew everything about advertising so she was a lethal critic. She reviled type-face, pictures, layout and copy, and saved her diatribes for day's end so Goldfarb and Dane would have a long night.

"But, Nadine, I followed your design template and direction!" Goldfarb pleaded.

"Are you saying this pile of shit is my fault?" Nadine lashed out.

Her eyes were so wide in their shallow sockets that only a miraculous counterforce kept them from rolling down her cheeks. "The layout sucks and it's not even *yours!* Is that what we pay you for? *Stale mediocrity?* If you're bad, at least have the balls to be original, okay?"

"Yes, Nadine, I'll redo the ad," Goldfarb acquiesced.

Nadine tapped on her *Blackberry* without acknowledging his capitulation.

Dane knew Nadine persecuted Goldfarb on his account but Goldfarb would not let him take the blame.

"That's Nadine," Goldfarb sighed. "When she started here, she hated everything I did. I told Sheldon I thought Nadine wanted me fired. Sheldon said it couldn't be true...that Nadine was a good person. Later Nadine called me in and said, 'I know what you did. Sheldon is too busy. Nobody cares...' She backed off but I have to keep her happy."

Goldfarb lifted four boxes of candies out of his backpack. "Every year Nadine sells sweets for her kids' school and I buy them. With my bad teeth! When she calls for a birthday lunch, I go, even if I pay twice as much as I should to subsidize her drinks."

For most office workers 5 PM was the hour of salvation but Dane dreaded it, because Nadine always waited until that moment when he was wrapping up his day to tell him he had to stay late on a client call or to sign off on a piece still in editorial.

Nadine never checked up on Dane after business hours. She had Rex, the traffic coordinator, do enforce her orders. Nadine was Sheldon's muscle and Rex was hers. Rex had studied military coming-of-age movies and did a brilliant impersonation of a dapper Hollywood drill sergeant in European suits, wide ties and tasseled *Bally* loafers. He claimed he made the traffic department shine so Integrimedicom would be proud. Nobody knew what he was talking about.

Rex also extemporized about giving back to the community but what was he giving back—bloated job folders? He made Sheldon and Nadine laugh when he claimed his dad threatened to divorce his mom if she did not take DONARAL because menopause made her nasty. Rex spoke in the deep voice and long cadences of a lay-minister, but had the flirtatious manner and macho swagger of an expert in getting laid.

He patrolled Dane's office every night to ensure that Dane did his job.

"When can I go home?" Dane would ask.

"When the job is done!" Rex replied imperiously.

"Is the last round coming anytime soon?"

"I'll let you know," Rex replied.

"Do I have to stay?"

"Are you are a professional?"

Dane nodded.

"Then you know the answer."

"But is this piece really going out tonight?"

"*O-o-o-h, yeah.* Count on it!"

With a raised eyebrow and a crisp turn, Rex swaggered out.

More than once, Dane stayed at the office until midnight waiting for an omitted comma on a piece that never went out. He thought of complaining to Sheldon but Goldfarb warned him off. "This is what they pay us for. Complaining is the one thing that will get you fired."

Rex was a lady's man who wanted to command the respect of

men. When Dane walked past Rex in the hall, he looked the traffic manager in the eye and nodded. Rex responded by grabbing his crotch.

"What does crotch-grabbing mean?" Dane asked Goldfarb, who lived in Winton, Ct. but grew up in the Bronx and thus had street credentials, in Dane's mind.

"Can't help you," Goldfarb admitted. "Maybe he likes you?"

"Couldn't he just say, 'Yo'?"

"Maybe he likes you more than 'Yo'."

One afternoon Dane entered Nadine's office to inquire about a correction she made, which he could not decipher. Rex was draped across her couch, with his legs crossed at the knee. He stroked his bald head abstractedly as if pleasuring his head. The mood was so intimate that Dane apologized for interrupting it.

That evening Dane worked late. The piece had to go out and major issues needed resolution—logos, typefaces and layout—Nadine's domain.

When Rex had delivered the latest round to Dane, he warned that it was "hot" and required prompt attention. Dane had questions and waited for Rex to return. When Rex did not make his rounds, Dane phoned the traffic manager and reached his voice mail, then hunted for him in the halls without success.

Babette Mamenger, the account supervisor, appeared in Dane's office, holding her jumbo tumbler full of diet *Sprite* in her gloved hands. Babette's black gloves were no ostentation or fashion statement. They concealed bleeding cuticles, a side effect of a seizure medication she was taking.

"So you've got the hot job! Why is it on your desk?" Babette demanded, pointing at the ten pounds of paper in a five pound bag.

"Rex never came back for it," Dane replied dolefully.

"I want to sign off already," Babette snapped. "I need to blow this pop stand at ten. It's my tenth wedding anniversary. We're dancing at *The Rainbow Room*."

"I want to leave, too," Dane replied. "But only Nadine can answer these queries."

Babette grabbed the folder and led Dane to Nadine's office, where a sliver of light shone under the door.

"Knock," Babette said.

Dane tapped on the door.

No answer.

"Knock hard," Babette said.

Dane rapped a little harder. He thought he heard Nadine saying, "Right there. That's it."

"She must be working on a layout," Dane whispered. "Maybe we should come back."

"I'm not missing midnight supper in the stars for this!"

Babette opened the door wide, prompting a scream, a thump and a deep, involuntary curse from under the desk.

Nadine lay back in her ergonomic chair, face flushed, eyes glassy and disoriented. Her blouse was unbuttoned, exposing pale breasts and hard nipples. Her skirt was bunched up around her hips.

"Damn! My head!" Rex's manly baritone bellowed from under the desk.

"We need you to sign off," Babette said as nicely as she could.

"I will! Just get out."

"I have to be out of here at ten."

"Get the fuck out!"

"Should I close the door?" Dane asked.

"Get out!"

"I guess that's a yes," Dane whispered.

He closed the door.

As they walked away, Babette smirked.

"Every woman has her own way of treating vaginal dryness."

Case 3-D
RESEARCH: THE MOST CREATIVE ADVERTISING

13. JOB RELATED ILLNESS

Like many diseases Dane wrote about, his situation at Integrimedicom steadily deteriorated. With nothing of interest to do, and a lot of it, he experienced a common affliction—he hated his job. Before entering the building each morning, he stared at five *bas reliefs* on the façade above the doors. They were WPA-style representations of impassive workers fixated on their work, sculpted with Paleolithic roundness and a smooth absence of detail. Dane imagined stories for these figures and the truth they imbued, their devotion to labor. It was his only creative exercise of the day.

Dane's morning ritual was well-known among his colleagues. Nadine mocked him and gossiped about his quirk. Babette, the account director, also noted Dane's absorption in the sculptural reliefs as he paced before the building. One morning she stopped to ask him, "Have you lost your way?"

Throughout the day, Dane waxed nostalgic about old jobs and scouted for a new one. One afternoon he saw Landon LeSeuer in the street and asked how things were going. Dane had left Green a year before but his stint there was already cast in the amber afterglow of false positive memories. Trying to escape his present in a delusional past, Dane nearly asked Landon for a job but his former boss reassured him that he had done well to leave: there were major layoffs at Green and no new business.

Dane walked back to Integrimedicom feeling more trapped and desperate.

Desperation is the beginning of the end for most people but for Dane it was only a beginning. Others in his abject position might have been crushed and fled to a new field but Dane's creative will was like a mutant bacterium overcoming lethal toxins—adapting and evolving into a stronger life form.

It was Dane's good luck that Integrimedicom was worse off than he was. Clients were leaving, accounts were scaling back and the agency had nothing in its pipeline to replenish them. Leads were few and invitations to pitch were so rare that they were joyous occasions during which people dashed about excitedly as if the business were already won.

It was a time for fear—and flux. Old processes were ineffectual and old dogmas in doubt. The old order needed new ideas—*anyone's* ideas. This was good news for bottom-feeders like Dane. He was summoned from his dungeon of drudgery, where he had been forgotten, and re-introduced to the quorum of his colleagues.

"Meeting in the conference room!" Babette Mamenger, the account services director, called from the hallway as she clapped her gloved hands.

Dane saved the case study he was writing about a woman with overactive bladder, who urinated on her wedding gown and refused to go anywhere until her doctor prescribed *Uribilox*.

He rose stiffly from his chair and hobbled into the hallway. Just as Landon LeSeuer had observed, medical writers tended to internalize diseases they described and to imagine symptoms—Dane was highly susceptible to this occupational hazard. His job problems aggravated his medical empathy, transforming him into a psychosomatic mess. He limped on pseudo-arthritic knees, sat after a few steps due to illusory leg cramps and experienced extraneous urges to urinate. He expressed his frustrated creativity in imaginary diseases, which became his principal mode of expression.

"Oh, my aching legs!" Dane moaned, echoing his letter to patients with intermittent claudication.

"Come on, we're late," Goldfarb exhorted him.

"I'll be there in a minute. Nature calls!" Dane replied, afflicted by a sudden twinge of overactive bladder like the December bride in his patient brochure.

After standing at a urinal for no real reason, Dane's delusional aching knees intervened and persuaded him to sit in the conference room.

14. THE MOTHER AND THE MEGALOMANIAC

Sid Gorfine, the self-proclaimed father of direct-to-consumer advertising and CEO of Integrimedicom, now a subsidiary of a global network to which had he sold his agency years before, built his reputation on one insight: gullible consumers, with a little information, could obtain any drug they wanted if an advertiser made them want it.

In recognition of this landmark discovery, the advertising establishment paid Gorfine its highest honor. It heralded his success, studied and adapted his methods—and left him fighting for his job. When his improbable theory became standard practice, Sid learned that imitation is not only advertising's sincerest flattery, but its most lethal weapon. Advanced biologic drugs for cancer and arthritis were now sold on the 6 o'clock news and during sports programs. Gorfine was a shoo-in for the Pharma Advertising Hall of Fame in Parsippany, New Jersey, but the success of his ideas had unintended side effects that were destroying his agency.

Portly and disheveled, Sid stood before the packed conference room, conducting research for a business pitch to a baby needs company. His silk shirt was missing buttons, his leather pants were unzipped and mustard dappled his tie. Angelina, an office assistant, newly returned from maternity leave, sat beside Sid, as the in-house expert on a new mother's attitudes.

"What are your needs?" Sid asked Angelina. Her eyes were closed and she did not respond.

"What are your needs?" Sid repeated testily. His expert seemed to be a somnambulist.

The father of consumer drug advertising clapped his hands close to Angelina's ears and her eyes shot open with fright.

"I could use sleep," she replied candidly.

"What are your needs for the baby?" Gorfine badgered her.

"What do you mean?" She asked.

"When you buy a baby bottle, a formula, baby food, or diapers, what goes through your mind?"

"I look for price. 'Cause baby things are so expensive."

"That is not your first concern, is it?" Sid demanded.

"I want my baby to be healthy and safe. I want to keep things simple."

"Yes!" Sid raised his arms to signal a conceptual touchdown. "Simple as a mother's trust. Simple and strong as a mother's love! But sweet as a mother's milk..."

Sid's eyes shut tight. Perspiration beaded above his upper lip and streamed down from his bald pate over his face. His lips quivered.

"I love it when Sid brainstorms," Goldfarb whispered. "Nobody gets wet but Sid."

Suddenly Sid's eyelids snapped open like haunted window shades and he gazed at an audience only he could see.

'That's it!" Sid proclaimed. "Simple, soft and strong as a mother's loving and lovable love!"

"It's a bit long," Sheldon, the executive creative director, remarked as he fingered the diamond dangling from his ear.

"You creatives can wordsmith it!" Sid retorted with a peremptory wave of his hand.

Anyone who believed an interruption would brake Sid's train of thought hadn't been riding it long.

"So we're inside Mommy's head," Sid's finger eddied in the air, "But we haven't completed the branding circle."

He aimed his key chain laser pointer at a wall projection of the four-gated branding wheel, whose gates were guarded by three-headed dogs. Each dog icon had a word caption. The four words were "Envision," "Empower," "Endow" and "Embody."

240

Sid pointed to "Embody."

"We can't put baby to bed," he chuckled, "until we're in baby's head...So, what is baby thinking?" Sid asked Angelina.

Her eyes pleaded for direction.

"Feed me. Change me... Mommy?" she guessed.

Sid shook his head violently. "You call yourself a mother! What is baby thinking?"

Chastened yet convinced that her 4% raise depended on a correct response, Angelina tried again.

"*Ehhhh! Grrr. Ehhh.* That's what my baby says."

Everyone laughed. Sid dropped a pile of books on the table to restore order.

"That's what you hear but what is baby saying?"

Encouraged by the audience response, Angelina took a risk.

"He's thinking, *Mommy feed me. Waaaah! Mommy, clean me. I'm cold and wet. I have stinky poopie!*" Angelina improvised in a tiny, high-pitched voice.

Angelina's performance was no fluke. After playing the Mother Superior in her high school's production of "The Sound of Music," Angelina attended night acting classes at the Herbert Rogoloff studio—as part of Integrimedicom's tuition reimbursement program—where she specialized in *sensitivity to stimuli* and *belief in imaginary circumstances.*

"You're not a real mother!" Gorfine scoffed.

Angelina's mouth quivered. "It's not true. I am a real mother..." Suddenly, her eyes teared. "*Yes*, it's true. I am a bad mother. But what can I do? I have to work!"

She bawled and covered her face.

"Can you believe Sid?" Goldfarb whispered. "He convinced a mother he knows more about her baby than she does."

The room was silent as if the air itself were holding Sid's ire like a mist. Then, out of the pall, one small voice could be heard.

"*Love me forever, Mommy! Love me soft like a blankee. Rub*

my nose with a hankie, Mommy. Pat my soft little baby tooshie."

It was the high-pitched, lisping voice of "Little Sid," Gorfine's inner child. Sid held his fists small and tight by his face and shook them like an infant. Coughs cluttered the silence to disguise the irrepressible laughter humming in the closed air.

"Soft as my mommy! Sweet like Mommy's milk! Mommy, love me always purely! Smile at me pretty Mommy, I love you, Mommy, love me, love me love me!" Sid cried. His fists were clenched, his cheeks quivered, his rigid body hopped. Sweat beads flew from Sid's creased forehead. Then his shaking stopped. Sid opened his eyes and glowered at his staff. "See where we're going with this? This client has a line of baby products and we can brand every last sucker..."

Angelina sat at the front table, spent and wet-faced like a used towel. Dane could not bear the sight of a new mother, and a working one at that, looking lost and distraught. With indignation inflaming every nerve fiber, Dane shot to his feet before he could reason with himself.

"Excuse me, but what you're doing isn't research," Dane declaimed. "It's performance art."

Sid blinked at Dane. His mouth opened and closed but no words emerged. Not one of his research meetings had been disrupted in twenty years. He was stunned and so depleted by his performance that he had no response.

"What right do you have to make a mother cry?" Dane demanded. "Isn't giving birth hard enough? Have you ever done it? I was with my wife when she gave birth and I'll tell you something, Sid: unlike the stunt you just pulled, there was nothing fake about it. Giving birth is a brave act...And I can't sit by and let you trash someone who's done it..."

Dane heard the echo of his voice trail off and realized that it was the only sound in the room. He was also the only one standing, now that Sid collapsed in his chair. Dane feared the silence; it made him consider what he was doing, so he stammered on.

"I saw my daughter being born. My wife screamed for hours. I saw the pulsing vagina and throbbing hemorrhoids till I thought they would burst. Any man who says he knows motherhood more than a mother is lying."

Dane paused. He had no idea what he would say next but his hands and knees were shaking and his mouth was too dry to produce more language, so he sat down. His colleagues were dumbstruck at witnessing a career suicide.

"I think we can all go now," Babette said. "Thank you for coming."

15. UNEXPECTED FALLOUT

The stampede from the room was thunderous.

After his puzzling outburst, Dane sat deflated in his chair and skulked back to his office to absorb what he had just done. His knack for making enemies had metastasized beyond the creative department. Dane-hatred would creep into every corner of the agency like mold or fungus, become ubiquitous and unanimous, and Nadine would have him fired by consensus.

"Why did I do that?" he asked himself repeatedly.

Before his protest of one, Dane hoped research would provide egress from his creative doldrums—the challenge and advancement lacking in his writing job. He recognized that headlines and concepts were no longer transcendent vehicles. To become an advertising giant he might need other tools. Research generated messages from consumers' insights and helped consumers make wise choices. Good research would justify his paycheck and give his career new "legs."

Sid Gorfine's presentation detonated in the middle of Dane's new career path. Dane observed with horror how research could be abused. Worse, his new success route was road-blocked by another buffoon.

Babette Mamenger came to Dane's office that evening just as he prepared to leave. He had two thoughts when he saw her: that he had stayed too long and would surely be fired.

"I liked the way you stood up to Sid and defended Angelina," Babette said. "It took guts and compassion."

"Thanks," Dane replied blandly as he waited for the bad news.

Babette was the executive vice president and account services director of Integrimedicom. Because of her special relationship with the DONARAL franchise manager, Babette controlled the account that provided 80% of agency revenues and brought in new projects on a regular basis.

"I like what you've been doing for the mail campaign and brochure," Babette told Dane in her cigarette-leathered voice. "I saw your "HRT, WHY ME?" brochure and swore a woman wrote it. How do you write a woman's point of view with such sensitivity? Are you gay?"

"No."

"Cross-dresser?"

"No."

"Live with your mom?"

"No."

"Oh," she replied skeptically. Some people liked to solve crosswords each day; Babette enjoyed solving people in the same way, but Dane stumped her. "Well, you're talented, regardless."

Babette asked Dane to come to her office. She fired up a clove cigarette, which she considered healthier than tobacco, and tossed some papers across the desk.

"The letters you wrote. I had some ideas. Can we discuss them?"

"Sure," Dane sighed. Babette had a reputation for working until all hours.

"This letter needs something. How does this sound? You're an active woman so stay that way."

"That works," Dane said.

"It's crap," Babette replied, relishing the harsh critique even at her own expense. "I'm no writer. How would you improve it?"

Dane felt himself sinking in the quicksand of another late night creative argument. If Dane defended his words, Babette would retaliate with endless alternatives. If he agreed to her changes, she would revert to an earlier version. It was mutual verbal masturbation. They put the three words "vital, active and strong" in divers combinations until they couldn't pronounce the words.

"How about, 'You're v-v-v-vital. You're a-a-a-ctive. You're s-s-s-strong. And you have the best hours—*years*—ahead," Dane said. His lips trembled as he fought to squelch a yawn.

"They're not superwomen," Babette whined before taking a long pull from her diet *Pepsi*. "What about: *'You're an active woman and now you can stay that way'*."

"Great!" he said. "I love it!"

She peeled off her gloves to expose her hands. Blood seeped from her cuticles like red oil, a side effect of her seizure medication.

"You're just yessing me! I'm trying to help you. Do you have any passion left...any *balls*?"

"It's 11 PM. I've been here since nine this morning!" Dane replied. "You have every right to taunt my manhood. I'll even join in!"

"I'm asking for your creativity. Which is more than anyone in your department is doing. You're at a dead end!"

"I am?" Dane asked with surprise. He thought he was the only one who knew.

"You're a phony," Babette said, scratching flakes of dried blood from her cuticles like old nail polish.

"Why? Because I'll never go through menopause?"

"No. Because you pretend a paycheck is all you want. You've been writing this stuff for months but do you have the slightest idea what menopause is like? I want you at research. See how this beautiful writing of yours plays with real women."

Dane felt a jolt. He wanted ardently to go home but Babette was offering the salvation of his advertising dream. He braced himself for another grueling ride through the eye of a brainstorm.

"Go home!" Babette said.

16. RESEARCH & BARBEQUE

Dane was relieved to be let off so easily. He did not realize that this evening marked his turning point at Integrimedicom. He had won Babette's sympathy and respect—a major coup. As the highest ranking woman at Integrimedicom and Nadine's worst enemy, Babette was Dane's ideal ally.

Nadine despised Babette with her bleeding fingers, nasal voice, clunky jewelry, tumblers of diet soda, and deep-seated insecurity. She viewed Babette as an inferior being who worked hard because she had no children and no life. Yet, regardless how often Nadine insulted her, Babette never acknowledged the blows or lashed out at Nadine.

When Babette saw Dane staring at the *bas reliefs* on the façade that morning, she recognized that he was depressed and understood why; Nadine's talent for making people miserable was no secret to her. Babette also believed Dane was "old school"—he craved initiative and competition and thirsted for recognition. Dane was ideal for her purposes. She decided to recruit him as an undercover creative operative to take down Nadine.

The research facility was near the Charlotte, North Carolina airport. Dane hated flying so Babette sat next to him to calm his nerves. She told him about her ailments and how she wanted a child but thought she could never have one. Her two-hour monologue made Dane forget his fear of flight and consider skydiving.

The client, a hyperactive woman who typically conducted business with Babette on her cell during rush hour, paced the observation room, playing with post-its. "Look," she announced, showing a post-it on a letter. "No more same old boring direct mail. We'll slap colorful post-its on it with messages like: *Hot flashes be gone!* Women will love them!"

Babette's job was to tell the client how brilliant that was and she did it brilliantly.

Two of the first three interviewees never showed. The third, a dignified, middle-aged woman, said she had a hysterectomy when she was 35.

"Damn," Babette muttered. "They're not supposed to have hysterectomies. This is for women going through natural menopause."

"Pooh! Use it anyway," the client said.

The next woman was in her 40s and experiencing perimenopause. She was soft-spoken and sedate with a refined accent. The interviewer asked about her health and attitude toward menopause. "You know, my mama went through change of life and she never took pills," the woman said, "Not a one. It's natural, it's part of life," she said. "I'm not afraid of aging and I'm not about to put anything in my body to make me feel something that isn't real."

"Oh, shut up!" the client yelled at the two-way mirror. "She's poison! Get her out of here!"

Only two of first nine women who reviewed Dane's menopause materials were in the right category and both were hostile to hormone replacement therapy. The others had hysterectomies or were too old. The tenth and last interviewee was tall and elegant, had broad shoulders, a jutting jaw—and a lump in her neck.

"She's a man!" Dane whispered to Babette.

"Really?" Babette squinted through the glass. "No one will notice. I love her hair."

The transvestite answered questions about hot flashes and vaginal dryness with expertise and gave insightful responses to the promotional materials. He was their best subject.

The psychologist/moderator was unconcerned about the authenticity of his subjects. He would write a report and bind it in leatherette; his clients would call it research and base marketing decisions on it. Meanwhile, the psychologist knew what was important. He insisted that the team have North Carolina barbecue for lunch. Platters were rolled in and two days of tedious research were forgiven in a binge of chicken and ribs.

During the flight home, Babette slipped into the seat next to Dane.

"So, how do you like research?

"It's creative," Dane replied.

"We got paid, right? Listen, you were helpful and I appreciated it. The client liked you. So your time has come. Creative, research...they're sideshows. Now you can do something really big. Advertising, PR...I can't tell you more, but just be ready."

Case 3-E
GRANDMAS GONE WILD

17. OUR EXPERT ON VAGINAL DRYNESS

A few months later, Babette escorted a new client through the offices of Integrimedicom, introducing creatives at their desks like animals in their habitat. She stopped in Dane's doorway and pointed at his wide stare and hunched shoulders.

"Dane Bacchus is our expert on vaginal dryness," Babette announced with a stage whisper and a flourish of her gloved hand as if protecting his sacred concentration from her tawdry showmanship.

Raising his eyes from the monitor, Dane grimaced to improvise the character of *Expert in Vaginal Dryness*—a crabby man for whom a woman's biological clock was no abstraction, but a cluster of disagreeable symptoms to which he was often exposed. He capped off his performance by smiling and waving at Babette and her guest, suggesting the hope of imminent relief.

Babette was too seasoned at handling clients to let such nuances be perceived. Dane's hand flourish swept the empty space vacated by two grinning women.

Expert on Vaginal Dryness.

Dane muttered the epithet like it was a plaid sports jacket he was trying on from the clearance rack of an off-price department store. *Expert on Vaginal Dryness* had a ring to it if you forgot the meaning of the words. "Is this how you want your obit to read?" He asked himself. It struck him how often his obituary had become his point of reference.

Yet these were the best of times for Dane at Integrimedicom. After the trip to North Carolina, he was promoted to chief writer of DONARAL and Babette singled him out for creative projects. He had input in every initiative. But once the exhilaration of good treatment wore off, Dane was restless and uneasy again. He had been through the worst of Integrimedicom and now the best—and did not feel much different.

Expert on Vaginal Dryness.

Dane always wanted to be an expert—but not on menopause. He was squeamish about the condition, though exempt from it. In truth, Babette overrated him. He was no more an expert on atrophic vaginitis, mood swings, or hot flashes than a butcher was a biologist. His only skill was to arrange the words in novel combinations.

Besides, there was so much more to Dane than menopause. He could not be tethered to one ailment when a universe of sickness was his to explore. He had produced a staggering amount of original copy in recent weeks, on products treating an array of debilitating conditions.

The letter on his monitor, for instance, was about painful leg cramps due to intermittent claudication—poor circulation in the legs—mainly affecting aged people:

"Are you able to walk only a short distance before you feel painful cramping in your legs? Does this discomfort interfere with your active lifestyle? Now there is something you can do. Talk to your doctor about STRIDALL. To help you get started on STRIDALL we have attached a $10 coupon to help pay for your first prescription. And to thank you for taking this important first step, we have enclosed a pedometer and a walking diary so you can tell your doctor how far you walk each day. We congratulate you for taking this first BIG step toward getting back your active life."

Dane's bleary eyes dilated with demented pride. This letter to octogenarians about a drug that reduced leg cramps incorporated every direct-to-consumer element: insincere enthusiasm to contrast with the decrepitude of his audience; a reference to active life—ancient history for many of these patients; an exhortation to talk to their doctors; and a vapid expression of vacuous hope that they would walk again pain-free. To top it off, the walking diary and pedometer were tokens of appreciation his readers would never appreciate. *Perfect.* When he was done, Dane wondered if the piece would be opened and read or jettisoned. Would his readers use the pedometer and write their walking distances in their diaries? After all the art and irony, this was the most impact he could hope to make. Dane emailed the leg pain letter and dropped his head in his hands, to collect what thoughts were left inside.

Yes, this was success, yet fulfillment still eluded him. Under Nadine's censure, the challenge had been to keep and endure his job. Now that the job was easy and pleasant, Dane wanted more.

The inarticulate public address interrupted his respite, announcing a meeting that would be equally inarticulate. Dane wondered why agencies had so many meetings since they rarely conveyed information effectively and distracted people from their work. Perhaps the key purpose of meetings was to keep individuals from being alone with their despair.

18. RAY BOB LIVE!

Babette Mamenger rang a cowbell and stood in the hallway shrieking, "Brain donors in the main conference room! Pizza!"

That morning Dane had discovered a gray blob on his desk with a cardboard certificate requesting a donation. The gray blob was a plastic brain. The certificate was an organ donor card asking Dane and all employees to donate their brains to Integrimedicom.

It was the agency's introduction to Integrimedicom's new president, Ray Bob Blassingame. Sid Gorfine had abruptly retired after his baby needs presentation caused permanent regression. There was another plausible reason for Sid's departure. Integrimedicom recently lost 15% of its income when SPECTREX, an ADHD drug, fired the agency for unfocused advertising. Ray Bob Blassingame was installed in Sid's place. Ray Bob had worked on the agency side, the client side and the regulatory side. He had all sides covered. At noon he had something special planned.

The new president of Integrimedicom stood at the head of the conference table. Ray Bob was a short, wiry man with a red nose and several strands of red hair in an extreme pull over. Steaming boxes were stacked in front of him like a leaning lectern of Pizza.

"Look you guys. I swear on this stack of pizzas that this agency will make our numbers. Our guys in London saw our numbers last year and frankly they got ill all over them. Not only were we off our growth projection of 15%; hell, we were down 15% from last year. In their view, that wasn't tea and crumpets, dudes, it was more like reeking old stout. I said they weren't seeing the big picture, how the industry was down 16% so we were ahead of the pack. That dog didn't hunt; it didn't even go bow-wow. *"So you're alpha dog in a pack of losers!"* the London guys said. They made it clear the same lame excuse would never fly again.

"This year, top management expects 23% growth. That's pie in the sky or pie in the face, depending on your perspective. But the bottom line reads as follows: I stuck my scrawny neck out there for you guys because in my gut, I know you can deliver the pizza. There, I said it. It's out there. Pressure builds. You're wondering, *'How do we do this?'* First, I want you to look at the face in the mirror and instead of getting violently ill, ask yourself, 'Am I doing what it takes to meet my commitments?' Because at the end of the day, that's all she wrote. Amateur hour is over. It's prime time to be a professional or don't let the door hit you on the way out. It's time to take off the gloves and the training wheels and step up to the plate. Accountability is the new deal. Innovation and initiative are the coin of the realm. It's time to put *fun* back into functional. Not a day goes by that I don't ask the Lord why he didn't make me a foot taller, so I'd be the biggest damn point guard in the NBA. And the best looking. Ha-Ha! It's a tough world out there. I drove my *Beamer* in today and a dignified woman in a Mercedes gave me the finger!"

"That was me, Ray," Nadine quipped. Everybody laughed.

"Oh, yeah? You're fired...Nah, I love ya, Dina, just kidding. So this woman in a Mercedes gives me the finger and I roll down my window and say, 'Honey, you shoulda bought a Beamer!'"

More laughter. The pizza was losing its heat; its sweet, greasy aroma was a faint memory. The creative department would join the ranks of blue collar, bust-ass wage slaves, eating cold pizza while they worked.

"You professionals don't need to hear me blow smoke out of my—mouth. So listen up. Our client, *American Pharmacon*, has a product that keeps this good ship lollypop rolling down the river...you know it well, DONARAL. Pure grade female donkey piss...but it works and it's been working for fifty years...which is longer than I've been on God's green earth. So they want something special from us. An anniversary. A birthday party. A 50th birthday for the best little menopause symptom relief medication that ever was. We're part of history. Is that great or what? A fifty-year-old drug for fifty year old women...But I'm not writing copy. That's your job. So my last words to you guys are," Ray Bob paused, his chin upturned, his mouth half open, his fingers extended like two knives, "What the hell were those last words? Oh yeah! Wake up and smell the pizza!"

19. A CAMPAIGN OF HIS OWN

Ray Bob took two slices from the top box, slapped them on a paper plate and retreated through the closest door, leaving the agency "lunch and think" session to Babette.

This was a milieu in which Dane excelled. When it was an official brainstorm with an easel, a pad and a magic marker he was transformed into the eager fifth grader who raised his hand for every question.

More was needed here than a clever headline or tactic. The DONARAL client was seeking a massive promotional campaign which would incorporate public relations, medical and consumer advertising, targeting doctors and patients.

"What about a huge writing contest?" Dane asked rhetorically. "Women love to write. Language and visual processing happens throughout the female brain. Words and images work together in perfect metaphors."

Dane paused to catch his breath. He noted that his female colleagues were intrigued by this characterization of their mental faculties.

"Women love expressing emotion," he continued, "—and we know this product has made a strong emotional connection with women. So we promote a national essay contest. We ask women to describe how DONARAL has improved their lives and offer a luxurious grand prize. A week in Hawaii. A photo shoot with celebrities."

"And a coffee table book," Babette said, "With all the menopausal super stars!"

"Yeah, and Annie Leibovitz can shoot it," Nadine said.

"I like it," Babette said. "Women write copy for a woman's product. What could be more authentic and persuasive than that?"

Within ten minutes, Dane brought English composition to advertising, enrolled millions of women in a copywriting sweepstakes, and became the lead writer of a national campaign.

This project was different from anything he had undertaken. It could not be wrested from him like a line of copy. It was on a par with the *Jolly Green Giant, Chiquita Banana,* and the *GEICO gecko.* Dane finally had the big idea to lift him from a journeyman to an advertising legend.

Once the client and PR firm agreed on the DONARAL 50th birthday campaign idea, Dane devised several concepts to advertise the event. No other teams were involved. He collaborated on ads, billboards and direct mail with an art director handpicked by Nadine to provide a woman's viewpoint.

They attended focus groups where women evaluated ad concepts and openly discussed hot flashes in business meetings, mood swings that wrecked marriages and other menopausal nightmares DONARAL was indicated to prevent. Most of the women in these groups warned against making the DONARAL birthday campaign a self-aggrandizing corporate affair; at the same time, they promised to support a meaningful event that helped women better understand and cope with menopause.

These women's attitudes about DONARAL and menopause inspired Dane and increased his enthusiasm about the project. Once again, he felt he was doing more than earning a living. He witnessed firsthand that advertising could do more than promote a product; it could address health issues and change social attitudes. He was helping to send a message to women at home and in the workforce, women who were harassed and even ashamed of the natural changes their bodies were undergoing, that their lives not only extended, but had value, beyond reproduction.

20. RENTING SUCCESS

By summer's end, Dane was writing for successful osteoarthritis and menopause campaigns, and was the go-to guy in leg cramps and overactive bladder. Within ten months of his hire, Dane was the most important copywriter at Integrimedicom.

It seemed the right moment to take a short vacation with his family. Since his summer plans had waited until the last moment, they had to book five days at a musty motel in eastern Long Island, where they occupied a tiny room and splashed around in a shallow pool shaped like a dolphin. In the evenings they ate shell-fish and contracted gastroenteritis.

When Dane returned to Integrimedicom, he learned that Sheldon and Nadine had tested another concept while he was gone. It was a picture of a leather photo album with DONARAL 50th Anniversary embossed on its cover.

"How could you let them do this?" he asked Goldfarb.

"*Let them?*" Goldfarb protested. "I didn't have to let them! They've been dying to get their hands on this project but you controlled it—until you took a break."

"So I can never take a vacation without being stabbed in the back?"

"That's it! Or be like me. Accept how things are and don't care!"

Regardless how much he accomplished at Integrimedicom, Dane realized he only rented success. Nadine and Sheldon were ruthless competitors who drew on the talent of the entire department. They could even induce Goldfarb to work against him.

Fortunately, the leather book concept did not perform as well as the four aging sorority sisters holding hands and skipping, so Dane's ownership of the DONARAL gala stayed intact.

21. A NIGHT FOR THE AGED

The DONARAL 50th birthday campaign made history. Ads ran in publications soliciting women's essays. Hundreds of thousands of women responded. Dane, Nadine, and Sheldon were able to bill hundreds of hours by reading essays. The client selected the grand winners based on age, race, region, and novelty of story. One DONARAL testimonial came from a 70-year old show-girl. The most exotic DONARAL user was a nurse.

Six months after Dane first proposed the contest, the 50th birthday celebration took place and the 12 contest winners arrived in New York. They went on a whirlwind tour of receptions, a photo shoot, a day of beauty and an awards dancer and dinner event.

Dane was invited to the gala dinner. He could say with some justification that this was his party.

Yet, as soon as he walked into the banquet room, Dane finally understood what Randy Newman meant in "Mama Told Me Not to Come."

This gala was the end result of his imagination. When he read the essays and met their authors, he believed his creativity had a purpose—to empower women to live and achieve beyond their reproductive years. So why did melancholy fill the room like air freshener?

He looked around. Where are the men? Honorees were invited to bring along "significant others," yet few husbands, sons or brothers were in attendance. There was no sense that men were despised, unwanted or excluded—they were just absent. Was there no place for men in the lives of these fulfilled women? Dane would soon find out.

His first task was to greet the contest winners—the twelve inspiring women who believed age was just a number and attributed their youthfulness and success to DONARAL. He shook hands with a nurse from Alaska, who blended modern medicine with shamanism, and then fulfilled her life-long dream of racing in the Iditarod; a Native American mother of ten; a world-renown surgeon; a federal judge; an operator of gourmet soup kitchens; a 66-year-old who earned a Ph.D. and gave all the credit to DONARAL for raising her I.Q.; and a hospice worker who used the gift of extended youth to give comfort to the dying.

At the end of the reception line stood Elaine, the 70-year-old star

of her community theater's production of *Follies* and the founder of
the Rockerettes, a silver-haired chorus line of long-legged, high-
kicking senior women, who toured retirement communities across the
U.S. and even performed in the Grand Canyon.

"I remember you!" Dane said as he shook Elaine's hand. "I loved
your story. And here you are."

"And here you are!" she said, touched by his enthusiasm. "Aren't
you sweet?"

"You were an inspiration," Dane said. "You helped me believe in
the product—not that I would ever take hormone replacement
therapy."

"I'm glad I inspired you," she replied as she stared into his eyes.

"I hope I have the vitality to achieve something when I'm your
age."

"Oh, I have vitality," she said. "Age is just a number."

"He has your number," said Joyce, the Alaskan tundra nurse and
Iditarod racer, who was on Dane's other side.

The two women clashed with dueling sneers. Seeing how this
might go, Dane excused himself from their company and drifted to
the far end of the ballroom, where he waited for people to settle before
sitting at an empty table.

As he waited for soup to be served, Babette approached with a
posse of awards winners in tow.

"There you are! Why are you sitting alone? You didn't already
offend someone and embarrass yourself, the agency and our client,
did you?"

"No, no," one woman said. "He was charming."

"That's what I like to hear. I brought you company."

The women surrounded Dane, poised to occupy his table.

"Were you trying to shake us? You should know better," Elaine,
the senior showgirl, said. She posed before him in her spangled gown
with the slit up to her hip and the décolletage down to her solar
plexus.

Dane helped each woman into her chair.

"What a gentleman!" Elaine remarked. "I love that."

"You love anything that moves," said Joyce, the Alaskan nurse.

"These gestures just put people in a festive mood," Dane said.

"They put me in the mood," Elaine said.

"You're always in the mood," the Alaskan nurse quipped.

The high-kicking Rockerette smiled at the Alaskan nurse and turned to Dane.

"Manners are a lost art. I love them because I'm just an old-fashioned girl," she said.

"That means she doesn't put out on the first date unless she's horny," quipped the Alaskan nurse, "—which is always."

The Alaskan nurse and Iditarod racer may have come off as peculiarly acerbic and rude for a guest of honor at a glittering affair. As she would later explain in her journal, she had swallowed too much seal blubber while caring for sick Inuits to sit back and watch her glamorous co-winner waylay the one unescorted man at the gala.

The show-girl scowled at her heckler, "We're having a conversation."

"Is that what you call it?"

Elaine smiled at Dane. She chuckled when he smiled back.

"Will you dance with me?" Elaine asked.

Dane pressed his back against the chair and tried to ignore the question.

"Let's dance. Don't be shy. Other people are dancing, we'll blend in."

"I shouldn't. I'm working."

"Tonight it's your job to have fun!"

The *Rockerette* leaned forward and jiggled her breasts to demonstrate that, real or otherwise, they were there.

"You're afraid your colleagues will tease you for dancing with an old broad?"

Dane was ashamed at how right she was so he escorted *the*

Rockerette to the dance floor.

The orchestra struck up a medley of Lawrence Welk classics. The floor was crowded with women in formal wear dancing with each other. Dane guided Elaine to the middle so they would go unnoticed. He coaxed his feet to do the box step he had once learned at a middle school cotillion. Elaine was an expert ballroom dancer. She told him to relax and she would talk him through the steps. By the third song, Dane forgot his manifold embarrassments.

"So, what are *your* fantasies?" Elaine asked Dane as she pressed against him during the fox trot.

"I'm living my fantasy," Dane replied.

"Aren't you sweet?" she cooed and touched his hand.

"I mean being here, conceiving a national campaign—and with such a positive message. This was my fantasy."

"You're lucky," Elaine said.

Elaine draped her arms around Dane and pressed tightly against him.

"I know what men want," she whispered.

"*You do?*" he gasped, creating separation between them.

Dane was saved from Elaine's response by microphone feedback, which introduced the awards ceremony. Ordinarily Dane despised such proceedings but now he clung to every grandiloquent tribute and found refuge from Elaine's flirtation in frequent rounds of lusty applause until his palms were as raw as they were in adolescence.

He surveyed the banquet hall. At the next table, Babette and the DONARAL franchise manager were matching stunts. She removed her gloves to show off her bleeding cuticles while he pressed his insulin pump, gorged himself on pastries and sweated profusely.

After the meal was over, Dane left his table, said good-bye to Babette and Nadine and headed toward the opulent lobby.

"Hello! Elaine called after him. "You forgot something."

Dane patted his jacket and pants to ensure that his wallet and phone were in his pockets.

"This is what you forgot."

It was a card with her phone number.

"Call me if you're ever in Arizona—or if you're scheduling an event."

"Thank you."

She accompanied Dane into the lobby. Near the elevators, she asked if he would escort her up to her floor. There had been incidents in the hotel, women accosted in the corridors and ice rooms. She told Dane she shared a room with another essay winner, a woman minister who distributed condoms in Zambia.

"Take me, take me," she whispered. "I know what men want."

"It's flattering but I can't," Dane said.

"When you're an old man and your pants are up to your nipples, you'll regret it."

"If I live that long," Dane conceded modestly.

Joyce, the Iditarod racer, came up behind them.

"When you left your sorbet uneaten, the spirits told me what you were up to," the Alaskan nurse said shamanistically.

'He asked me for my card," the Rockerette replied.

"And I ate your sorbet! I see through your sequins, lady. You've been all over him like peanut butter on Ritz crackers, you old vamp!"

"Age is just a number, you old seal!" Elaine answered.

"That hair isn't even real!" Joyce taunted.

To prevent the Alaskan nurse from proving her point, Elaine pounced on her and the two strong women tumbled to the marble floor of the four-star hotel, where they improvised the inaugural DONARAL gladiatorial—rolling, kicking, flailing, punching and clawing.

Bystanders in the lobby aimed their cell phones at the fight like spontaneous paparazzi, tussling with each other for position as they feasted on the moment with photos and videos.

"Mush! Mush, alpha bitch!" the Alaskan nurse cried out, reverting to her Iditerarod, dog-handling experience as she gained an advantage over the *Rockerette.*

Dane thought he should try to stop the fight to prevent injury, impropriety and negative publicity. However, if he became entangled with their bodies, he might look like a sexual pervert trying to make a public threesome. Dane was saved from taking action by one more human eruption in the lobby. With the orchestra playing the final strains of champagne music and the clients safely away in their corporate limousine, Babette staggered back into the hotel lobby, where she found Nadine talking to a handsome bellhop. Babette had skipped her epilepsy meds for this evening so she could imbibe and was sufficiently pixilated to shout at Nadine, "I can't have children because I'm sick. Having kids is just a number. I'm more woman than you are."

"You're a pathetic incompetent!" Nadine sneered.

"You're a phony. You don't even use DONARAL. I do! You two-faced bitch!" Babette cried.

At Integrimedicom, Nadine would have ignored the insult but in a four-star hotel she was acutely aware of her reputation. Nadine slapped Babette, who retaliated by swatting Nadine's face with her black gloves. The two women grabbed hold of one another's coats and lost their balance. When they fell to the carpet, Babette's body started to thrash.

"Put your fingers in her mouth!"

The Alaskan nurse's health care instincts superseded her competitive pride. She pried herself free of the *Rockerette* and assisted Babette. The mood after the gala quickly degenerated from slapstick to somber as the hotel staff surrounded the fallen vice-president of account services in order to shield guests from the terror of epilepsy, prevent more lurid footage and avert a lawsuit.

22. GRANDMAS GONE WILD

After a quiet night for mayhem in the City, the front pages of the next morning's tabloids splashed cell-phone photographs of the *Rockerette* and the Alaskan nurse wrestling on the floor of the 4-Star Hotel under the headline," GRANDMAS GONE WILD!"

The story mentioned that the female gladiators were in town for the DONARAL 50th anniversary celebration as winners of the "Age is just a number" essay contest entered by *millions* of women worldwide.   On the inside pages, a smaller photograph showed the undercard—Babette grappling with Nadine. Dane imagined how the DONARAL product team felt about having their dignified event depicted as a woman's wrestling match. He left the office and took a long walk to Chinatown for noodle soup, unable to sit still for the repercussions. After all he had done and been through at Integrimedicom, he would finally be fired over this embarrassing fracas.

But nothing happened when he returned and he was at a loss. After three years in advertising, Dane had not fully grasped its mercurial ways. DONARAL's public relations and advertising budgets were in the millions but could never buy a fraction of the media coverage the old drug now received. News shows worldwide picked up the DONARAL story because of the raw footage of the Rockerette grappling with the Alaskan nurse. In 24 hours, millions of people knew about DONARAL and witnessed its putative effects. For every viewer who laughed, three others believed that DONARAL must be a wonder drug to make these older women fight so hard. Thousands of women in their age bracket wished to try DONARAL, to feel physical passion again or simply to thrash an aggravating neighbor. DONARAL's 1-800 number was inundated by calls; the website crashed from the number of visitors seeking the free trial offer.

The DONARAL account was flying that week as prescriptions soared by 2000%. The product team was in a superb mood. After one day off, Babette returned to the office, bruised but undeterred, with several pieces of new business. *American Pharmacon* loved the gala, loved the publicity, and was even moved by Babette's fit. They wanted to extend and expand the campaign, to the point of sponsoring a martial arts event for older women.

Case 3-F
PROMISCUOUS GOLDFISH

23. DISPOSSESSED

With such a spectacular outcome to his campaign, Dane had every reason to believe he could ride his triumph right onto the cover of *Pharm Annals,* the bible of medical advertising, as "The Genius behind GRANDMAS GONE WILD!"

When he strolled into the DONARAL status meeting after the gala, he braced himself for a standing ovation. Instead, there was nowhere for him to sit. The conference room was a bloated infection of displaced advertising folk. Dane had made DONARAL relevant again but was now reduced to competing for business scraps with every other copywriter.

It was no reflection on Dane. Despite the DONARAL triumph, Integrimedicom was in crisis.

Another client was lost. *Prunastadil* took its flat sales and disgusting side effects elsewhere. The *Prunastadil* commercials were legendary. An austere doctor in a white lab coat recited the product's effectiveness at producing weight loss and explained how it removed fat from the blood stream, only to conclude that *Prunastadil* was associated with side effects like greasy stools and fecal incontinence.

Was it shocking that *Prunastadil* fell short of sales targets?

The client blamed Integrimedicom for the debacle. They claimed their agency of record had given poor direction, although it was documented that Babette, Sheldon and Nadine first advised against a doctor commercial, and secondly, against having a doctor read the gruesome fair balance. Due to the mention of greasy stools, the media group could not buy air time during the all-important evening news hour when people were eating dinner.

"We begged them to use a woman and a dog!" Nadine lamented.

"We were firm on that point!" Sheldon added, jabbing the conference table nonviolently with his forefinger.

"They said a woman and a dog had no relevance!" Nadine cried between swigs of microbrewery diet non-alcoholic ale.

"Irrelevance is irrelevant!" Ray Bob replied. "When your news is greasy stools, relevance is the enemy, Jack!"

"Greasy stools! I hate my life!" Nadine bewailed.

The fate of *Prunastadil* was another indictment against Sheldon and Nadine, and one more indication that Integrimedicom must change, with Dane in the vanguard. Who would fail to note that he succeeded while they failed?

However, Dane's success did not bring him reward but more suffering. When a large account like *Prunastadil* died, its team migrated to a living one to survive. Since the DONARAL business was booming, everyone in the creative department flocked to it to feed on its billable hours. In accordance with Integrimedicom principles, Sheldon and Nadine allocated the DONARAL hours among all staffers, capping them for each person. Since Dane had already exceeded the cap, he had to find his hours elsewhere.

24. A TIME FOR HEROES

On the verge of becoming an industry icon, Dane was an agency afterthought. A wave of insecurity, dejection and defeat rolled over him as he foraged for work. Every compromise and accomplishment of the past eighteen months was expunged.

Ronny meanwhile handled scarcity with finesse. In dry spells, he walked the hallways of Integrimedicom, begging for open job numbers from his colleagues so he could bill time. He never even learned the names of these accounts.

Dane could have copied Ronny, who was not proprietary about

his groveling. He could have hustled for job numbers but it bothered him to take credit for work he did not do. He waited for a legitimate assignment and endured the slow, gnawing pangs of idleness, while playing *Javanoid*, a game his nine-year daughter, Iris, taught him.

One afternoon, two men with crew cuts and square jaws came to Integrimedicom. Ronny walked out between them with his arms pinioned to his sides. He was under investigation for improperly receiving a student prescription to the *Wall Street Journal,* in a federal sting to purge white collar corruption.

After Ronny's arrest, Dane no longer considered billing time to jobs he was not working on. Just when Dane was sure he could no longer delay submitting his empty timesheets, he was given a chance to be a hero. Integrimedicom's holding company threw the agency a life-line and its most critical opportunity to date—the SLOJAC account.

The creative department was mustered. Ray Bob stood at the head of the table. There was no stack of hot pizza boxes, only a few greasy bags of garlic knots. Dane remembered his lunch with Lance Brubaker at the South Street Seaport, in particular, the dead seagull. Was this a sign, four years later, that Dane had come full circle to his dismal origin?

"Guys, the bad news is we're not making our numbers. The good news is we still have two weeks. It's truth or dare time. The *truth* is we need more business and I *dare* you to do the best work of your lives—to reach higher and work smarter. The alternative is—damn!— *there is no alternative!*

"Life is an ultimatum," Ray Bob continued after a long pause in which his eyes closed and he appeared to sleep. "If we don't live we die. Winning is an ultimatum, too; losing is not an option. Everybody in this room is a winner. Now we get to prove it! We've been given an opportunity to pick up some new business. Our sister agency, BLT, just blew it with SLOJAC, the premature ejaculation drug. They're consumer guys. Sure, they know a ton about shooting their loads *but what do they know about drugs?* They tried edgy: *Some guys don't know when to get off!* and *Making love or making a mess?* Then they tried—what was it? Oh yeah: *Is sex something you want to remember or wish you could forget?"* Ray Bob chuckled, coughed in his fist, and regained his sober mien.

"Personally, I like that one but the client hated it and fired the agency. So now it's up to us to save the business for our parent company. Who says advertising is no place for heroes? I drag my butt here every morning from Hershey, PA. Now I want each of you to click on your inner heroes. Dudes, I'm not asking for everything you've got because we all know that won't cut it. We need *more* than you've got. Save your agency. Save your holding company. Save our jobs!"

Ray Bob's Adam's apple bounced as hard as the basketball he once dribbled off his foot in the state Class DD high school consolation game. The CEO of Integrimedicom tugged on his collar, causing his clip-on tie to fall to the floor. He stared at the entertainment console at the far end of the room with visionary conviction—blue eyes wide, blood-shot, dilated by panic—then glanced at his watch, jammed his clip-on tie into his collar, muttered he was late and bolted.

The CEO's premature exit before discussing the background slides for SLOJAC was an apt introduction to the new drug Integrimedicom would launch.

Babette delivered the details of the brief.

"This is a very exciting opportunity and an exciting drug. Anything that prolongs sexual intercourse has to be exciting, right?" There was a deep groan from the back of the room, resonating more pain than pleasure. "I guess someone's already excited," Babette resumed. "Can you please hold your questions—and comments—until the end? This is a launch of firsts and mosts. SLOJAC is the world's first drug indicated for premature ejaculation. And PE is the most common sexual problem to affect men. Did you know PE affects one out of every three men? You guys know who you are," she said, winking.

The men looked around. Their eyes communicated either, "Who, me?" or "Not me!" depending on their degree of confidence. It was like Dane's health class in middle school when the teacher asked all the boys who masturbated to raise their hands.

"But here's the problem," Babette continued. "Premature ejaculation has no global definition. Is it less than five minutes? Is it less than two minutes? Or is it just bad sex nobody's happy with? The drug is terrific. It's a super-refined, ninth-generation SSRI that goes to work in an hour, gets in and out of the body fast and has few side effects. But selling SLOJAC alone won't make it. We have to advocate for the disease...to make it a health concern of epidemic proportions, not just one more drug company conspiracy to sell drugs nobody needs.

"It's important for us to show sensitivity. PE is not life-threatening but it hurts—*a lot*. It ruins lives, destroys relationships, makes grown men cry and makes women bite their lips *till they bleed*," Babette's fist pressed her gut as if she were having a cramp and she emitted an involuntary, muffled cry before re-boarding her train of thought. "People have been laughing about premature ejaculation for years. We need to make them *stop*."

"I know the perfect writer for this job," Nadine declared. "Dane Bacchus!"

A nervous titter filled the room; people did not know whether to be envious or contemptuous, whether to jeer or cheer.

Dane also teetered on the high wire of ambivalence. Should he blush or beam? Within seconds, he stood up to set his personal record straight.

"I just want to say that my ejaculations are always timely," he said.

This self-defense released the raucous laughter in everyone's hearts and filled the room like helium in a birthday balloon. But Dane could not appreciate his moment of comic triumph. It occurred to him that he might have been pegged all along as a premature ejaculator, which explained his lack of status and respect, and that no one would believe anything to the contrary.

"Everything about this drug is fast. It's fast-acting, fast-clearing and the launch is happening fast," Babette warned. "We usually test messages, do mood boards, focus groups and rounds of creative, but we'll have to deliver creative to the client in two weeks. Here is a DVD of the research. Watch it over the weekend and have something by Monday."

25. ALL IN THE TIMING

SLOJAC was Dane's most dangerous assignment to date although he did not know it. On the surface, this project started like the rest.

With slide decks and DVDs under one arm, Dane left the meeting burdened by the symptoms of a new creative challenge— disorientation and a headache. His brain swirled with ideas hacked into sentence fragments. He had to invent a fresh and intelligent concept but would have settled for something merely intelligible at that moment. His pencil wandered over the paper. "Ejaculation. Premature. Shame. Worry."

"You know this stuff!" Dane pleaded with himself. "This is your domain."

As words formed in Dane's mind, fate smacked him in the brain. How uncanny that of all diseases, he should create for this one! SLOJAC could be life-changing and career-defining. Dane was excited—*not over-excited*—but premature ejaculation was an area of expertise, like vaginal dryness, which he never asked for.

"Forget what you know!" he berated himself. "It's just another condition."

Dane gripped his head and pulled his hair. This was an imprudent emotional act. He had just started using *Rogaine* and was uprooting new growth.

He knew that every subject should be viewed with dispassion—like a rare cancer of which he had no experience. Was this possible now? Premature ejaculation was not intermittent claudication, overactive bladder, hot flashes or other conditions Dane wrote about—miseries particular to women and the aged. As Babette said, nearly all men had experienced premature ejaculation. PE had touched Dane, as well. Was detachment plausible with such memories? He could neither forget, nor renounce his bond with PE sufferers. His empathy was a danger to him.

Every conqueror in history had a special weapon. The Greeks had the Trojan horse, the Romans, the blunt sword and the English, the long bow. Nadine had SLOJAC and she wielded it on Dane. Rather, she let Dane wield SLOJAC on himself; using his strength against him. He was born to lead the SLOJAC account. It promised challenge and greatness. It was his destiny and doom.

Goldfarb recognized Dane's peril. He had seen this story play out before. It was the oldest Integrimedicom tactic in the *Book of Sheldon*: the heroic delusion, the *Save Integrimedicom* bit. Every veteran knew there was no saving Integrimedicom; the agency was going nowhere but it was never lost. It was a circle always spinning on its axis of problems and solutions, fabrications and truths.

Dane was in torment. At first, Goldfarb supposed it was the writing process—the universal agony of starting to think. But it grew worse. Wracked by the internal forces of intuition, knowledge and creativity applied to a painful and too-familiar subject, Dane was ripping at his innards, cursing himself as elements in his mind pushed to the articulate surface.

"Hey, take it easy. It's just another pitch," Goldfarb warned Dane.

"No, this could be the one."

"You say that about everything. You beat your brains in and Sheldon and Nadine will end up with a woman and a dog."

"Not this time. A woman and a dog can't ejaculate prematurely."

"That's true," Goldfarb conceded. "But if they could it would be a great act."

Dane was oblivious to Goldfarb. He was in a cage in his head where problem was bloodied by solution and insight was tortured until it talked.

"I got it," Dane cried out. "Business and sex are about timing. In business, it's better to be early. In sex, early is a disaster. The early worm doesn't get the bird!"

"Not bad!" Goldfarb said. "But no man sees his penis as a worm."

"Red-butt bonobos, you're right! I need something more."

Dane read out loud from *The Premature Ejaculation Handbook* by Jack Comerford, PhD.

"Premature ejaculation (*Ejaculo Praecox* for the smart set) is a paradox, a common problem but an unsolved mystery."

"So is that our headline? The paradox of premature ejaculation?" Goldfarb asked. "It's a little deep, don't you think? What do I know? I'm not deep."

"But a paradox is an enigma," Dane mused.

"So we show a guy jerking off at the foot of the Sphinx?"

"Listen!" Dane said. "Where is it? Hmmm. *Dum da da da dum da da*...Here it is...'There are many misconceptions about premature ejaculation. The following are NOT typically causes: overexcitement; a history of fast, public or dangerous sex, as in cars, elevators or on roller-coasters; performance anxiety; guilt about sex or pleasure; worry about holding an erection; unresolved relationship issues; life stress...'

"*Yes!* I knew it was more complicated than doing multiplication in my head!" Dane shouted, pumping his fist. He once despaired when he made it only to 3x3.

"Look, Dane. You sure you want to do this? You're too close to it. You know too much."

"That's my power! In advertising, it's all about knowing the product and the consumer."

"*Yeah, yeah!* That's a myth. It's better to know nothing."

"Oh, man, this is great stuff," Dane ejaculated. "Listen: 'Research indicates that pelvic muscles are in a hyperactive state in men with premature ejaculation.' Does that sound familiar?"

"I got to take a leak," Goldfarb said.

"Exactly! It's overactive bladder all over again!" Dane yelled. "Spastic muscles twitch out of control. The premature ejaculator isn't excited. He's a tire pump gone wild!!!"

Goldfarb squirmed in the doorway and bolted for the men's room. When he returned, Dane had the premature ejaculation DVD on pause.

For fifteen minutes they watched ordinary men and women reveal how premature ejaculation wrecked their lives. One scholar-athlete made out with his girlfriend after practice. He ejaculated during foreplay and ran up a dry cleaning bill, which he paid for by fixing games with local gamblers. When his teammates found out about his PE they humiliated him by squirting *Elmer's Glue* all over his locker. He quit the team, lost his chance for a scholarship and became an alcoholic and woman abuser out of shame and frustration. Another man, who participated in a clinical trial, related how he timed himself with a stop-watch for a month and had a breakdown when he could never break the 30-second mark. Meanwhile, the wife of a premature ejaculator spoke through tears about how her husband's sexual obsession migrated from the size of his penis to the length of his intercourse. Rather than whisper sweet nothings in her ear, he ticked off the seconds of his love-making. "I was like a launching pad!" she cried.

When the video was done, Goldfarb stretched. "That movie could have used popcorn," he said.

Dane was impervious to Goldfarb's extraneous remarks. He was stunned and stirred by the testimonial DVD. He had read about and experienced the red face of premature ejaculation but hearing its many voices transported it from the realm of embarrassment to an ego-smashing, relationship-crushing hell. This was when Dane had a penetrating insight.

"None of those people had faces!" he said.

"It's a legal thing," Goldfarb said.

"The subjects' faces are pixilated to protect their identities," Dane muttered. "Out of shame. But what if we could end that? How great would that be?"

"You mean, a world with no hunger or premature ejaculation?"

"Yes."

"Where all sex is perfection?" Goldfarb asked.

"Yes!"

Goldfarb whistled and burst into song, *"Imagine there's no premature ejaculation, no coitus interruptus, too!"*

"That could be our commercial!" Dane said. "That's SLOJAC!"

It was Dane's first creative breakthrough.

The campaign was titled "Faces of Premature Ejaculation." Goldfarb sketched a layout for a three page concept—a teaser cover and a two-page spread. On the cover the faces were blurred to show that PE was a serious and humiliating condition. Turn the page and the faces were in focus, happy and relaxed. In this problem/solution story, premature ejaculation was the villain and SLOJAC, the hero.

When they were done, Goldfarb shook his head and smiled at Dane. "Kiddo, I really thought you were lost. But this is your best work yet."

Dane smiled sheepishly. He felt drained and empty. However, this time the creative solution did not bring him its usual peace and satisfaction. After his creative release, old demons returned.

26. A LOAD ON HIS MIND

That night Dane slept fitfully, plagued by dreams of overexcitement. He woke up crying out.

"Are you okay?" Becky asked.

"Can we make love?" Dane asked.

"But I'm sleeping," Becky replied groggily.

"Please, it's important."

Becky rolled over and Dane proceeded to time himself. He made it to just over a minute before he lost count falling asleep. Timing intercourse worked like counting sheep for him. Instead of feeling reassured about premature ejaculation, he added narcolepsy to his list of problems.

When Dane and Goldfarb showed their concepts, Sheldon and Babette were impressed by *The Faces of Premature Ejaculation*. Nadine chortled that she knew Dane was the right man for the job.

The clients disagreed. They said *The Faces of PE* was depressing. The drug company wanted to promote SLOJAC as a relationship drug to help couples more fully enjoy themselves.

Dane and Goldfarb had prepared for this setback with an alternative campaign that featured men on stilts, pogo sticks, a bronco, a mechanical bull, and hanging from rings—activities where longevity mattered. The tagline, "Keep on Keeping On," conveyed hope and persistence.

When "Keep on Keeping On" was presented, Sheldon, Babette and the entire launch team stood and applauded.

The SLOJAC product team also enjoyed the concept. They had a good laugh but when their hilarity subsided to coughs, they said the tone was too playful and that the concept implied an over-promise. They did not want people to think SLOJAC would help them ride bulls or walk on stilts. They were also concerned that people sought medical help only for a "serious disease" and would take a drug to enhance sex only if it improved relationships, not merely performance.

This increased the pressure on Dane. One week remained to deliver a new campaign. Prowling the streets for inspiration, he noticed men and women jogging and shooting hoops. On a handball

court, a man and woman smacked a ball at each other. Dane
envisioned a new campaign focused on men and women playing
together. "Make it last!" put sex in the context of shared activities,
wholesome fun and healthy relationships. PE would be broadened
from a male problem to a couples' issue.

Dane and Goldfarb sent several executions to the client, who
liked this approach but wanted something else.

Another idea came to Dane, object-oriented and funky:
photographs of large men releasing heavy objects—medicine balls, a
shot put, or a huge stone. The headline, "Release the load," would tell
men to stop worrying about PE and do something about it.

The SLOJAC marketing team loved "Release the load."

Then, out of nowhere the director of urology marketing overruled
them. He had a vision in the shower: a man on a bicycle holding a
bowl with a goldfish. The agency people were perplexed. How did
goldfish pertain to premature ejaculation? The director of marketing
explained that "a man, a bike and a goldfish" had tested extremely
well for an HIV medication the previous year, so it would not need to
be re-tested, which would save time and money. Anyway, why
shouldn't "a man, a bike and a goldfish" work as well for premature
ejaculation as it had for HIV?

When he was told to write body copy for 'a man, a bike and a
goldfish,' Dane said, "You're kidding. We have to push back."

"The client loves it. We should embrace it," Sheldon said.

"This happens all the time," Nadine added.

"What is the connection between 'a man, a bike and a goldfish'
and premature ejaculation?" Dane asked.

"Don't be so literal," Ray Bob interjected. "It oozes healthy
lifestyle."

"You're too close to it," Sheldon said. "Lighten up."

"How can I? Premature ejaculation destroys lives!" Dane cried.
"'A man, a bike and a goldfish' says nothing about the problem or the
product."

"You're over-excited," Ray Bob said. "I know premature ejaculation can be a bitch, man. We've all been there with a leaky water gun. But we've got to get beyond the personal now."

"This is not about my water-gun!" Dane argued. "SLOJAC can be the biggest drug since Viagra. *Bigger*. Viagra was for old guys. SLOJAC is for *all* guys. We need something more than a man on a bike with a goldfish."

"There is no time!" Ray Bob pleaded. "Look, you've done great work but now it's time to do what the client says. We need you to write the most kick-ass premature ejaculation copy ever written for 'a man, a bike and a goldfish.' Take off the training wheels and step up to the plate!"

"It makes no sense!" Dane pleaded.

Ray Bob read the *can't-do* spirit in Dane's eyes. He exhaled hotdog breath in his favorite copywriter's face and spoke urgently, "Listen, big guy! When I was third string guard on the worst high school team in Pennsylvania history I learned one priceless lesson. Sometimes you shoot. Other times you pass. And sometimes you take a charge. The game is on the line. You take the charge, we get the ball. We're counting on you. Remember: shooting your load too soon in the sack is embarrassing. Shooting it too soon in business is expensive."

It was a speech more appropriate to *Hooters* than *Hoosiers* but it worked. Dane went from petulant to professional and pledged to write the best damned copy ever written for "a man, a bike and a goldfish."

27. PROMISCUOUS FISH

A week later, "a man, the bike, and a goldfish" were ready for regulators. The agency brass sat back smugly, poised for a big win. How could they lose? They were giving the client what they wanted.

Early on, one regulator, a Russian scientist, chastised the agency.

"I cannot believe you guys. You are unbelievable. You use goldfish for an HIV medication and I tell you many times not to go there, that goldfish are filthy beasts and bowl is metaphor for unprotected sex. So now again you serve up disgusting fish! But this time you exploit tiny carps to sell drug for premature ejaculation for more sex. Do you not understand English?"

"With all due respect, we meant 'a man, a bike and a goldfish' to be life-affirming. We portrayed them with taste and dignity," Sheldon replied respectfully.

"These goldfish are naked! They cavort in a bowl, engage in orgies. Clearly this ad promotes unsafe sex and raunchy life-style," the scientist regulator pushed back.

Dane never liked "a man, a bike and a goldfish," as a concept but he considered them chaste. It seemed absurd that such insipid icons were lewd to anyone. Yet, he never intended to defend the morality of goldfish until Sheldon implored him with a fervent nod to be a character reference.

"These fish are not naked," Dane interjected. "They wear scales. And while goldfish are prolific defecators, they are no more licentious than other beasts."

"How can you make this claim? Goldfish live in water, which is associated with bathhouses, co-ed showers, hot-tubs and nudist beaches!" the Russian scientist insisted.

"Goldfish were never role models." Dane argued. "They are popular pets."

The regulators were outraged by Dane's impudence and went offline to deliberate.

In a week they delivered their verdict in a terse email: no man, bike and goldfish need apply. Integrimedicom returned to concept development. While no one explicitly blamed Dane for the fiasco, Sheldon and Nadine appropriated the project. They gave the concept their classic touch, replacing the man with an elderly woman, the bike with a basket, and the goldfish with a dog. The client approved and submitted it to regulatory.

"This I like!" proclaimed the Russian scientist. "'Old lady and dog' are perfectly anti-promiscuous!" The regulators swiftly approved the revamped concept. 'An old woman and a dog' saved another Integrimedicom launch.

However, they could not save SLOJAC. The FDA rejected its new drug application. In the government's view, premature ejaculation was not a legitimate medical problem and making men have longer intercourse offered no health benefit. In the wake of this devastating ruling, men on bikes with goldfish, heaving men, sports couples, and men on stilts were buried in a mass grave and forgotten.

Dane was too dejected to react.

28. GOING FACIAL

Soon after the SLOJAC debacle, two clinical studies showed that *Donoral* had no effect on brain function or on heart health. If women felt smarter or more vital it was all in their heads. While the studies ripped the premise of the recent 50th birthday gala, they were limited in scope and merely nipped at the myth of DONARAL, leaving its main therapeutic and safety claims intact.

The following week, a major government trial studying the health benefits of DONARAL was shut down two years prior to its scheduled end-date when an unacceptably high number of women taking it were diagnosed with tumors, heart disease and blood clots. Only a month after its birthday gala, DONARAL plunged from miracle drug to a black box warning, indicating deadly risk. News spread from the medical community to the mainstream media. A national magazine cover story about DONARAL sent the drug company's stock into a single-digit abyss. Within days, prescriptions trickled to nothing.

No meetings were called at Integrimedicom. The client did not ask the agency for promotional tactics to deny these reports or to spin them in a positive way.

A pall gathered over the agency. The one healthy account to which everyone had gravitated was dry. Integrimedicom was on life-support.

One afternoon, Dane returned to his office with a container of Chinese noodle soup when he noted Sheldon's corner office door was shut. While Dane poured hot pepper oil into the steaming soup, his phone rang.

"Dane, can you come to my office?" Sheldon asked in a subdued voice.

"May I finish my soup?" Dane asked as his brain linked the solemn tone, the vague invitation and the closed door. He guessed that if he did not eat before the meeting, he would not want to eat afterward.

"Yes, but come in right afterward," Sheldon replied.

When Dane entered the corner office, three corporate vice presidents awaited him. Sheldon stared at papers on his desk like a TV anchorman before a commercial break. He glanced at Dane, then lowered his eyes. Nadine sat on a couch against one wall. The director of human resources, a hunched woman dressed in black, leaned on the edge of Sheldon's desk. The three executive vice presidents stared at Dane like he'd been disfigured in an accident.

"Dane, we have traveled the same path and our journey has been full of discovery and event. But now our paths diverge," Sheldon said.

Since Dane did not respond, Sheldon felt the need to translate.

"We have to let you go," the creative director continued. "You've been a fine colleague. You've done a great job but we've lost business and we've been ordered to make cuts."

Silence.

"It's the rule at Integrimedicom. The last to come must be the first to go," Sheldon explained.

They studied his face for signs of acknowledgement.

"Oh," Dane said.

Dane was acutely aware of his hot cheeks, the tautness of his jaws. Job-related dystonia, a general rigidity, gripped his limbs. His entire being contracted into one question, "Why are you doing this to me?" Was it because of *Prunastadil*'s "greasy stools" and the discredit of DONARAL? Or was it because he failed to purchase even one box of candies to support Nadine's children's daycare center?

"We've all gone through this," Sheldon said.

"We've all been there," Nadine added.

"You'll receive a severance package," the human resources director assured him flatly.

Dane's mind was like a ransacked room, with thoughts and sentences scattered, broken and disordered. Out of the shambles, he uttered the one thought left intact. "It's not my fault the agency is losing business. My work has been successful."

"Yes. We're glad we hired you and we're sorry you have to go," Sheldon said.

"So why am I being laid off?"

"It's not you," Nadine added. "It's the business."

Nadine told a fable. It was Christmas and Nadine expected a bonus but received a pink slip instead. "Quite a bonus!" she laughed and slapped her hands. "Good times!"

"If we can do anything, just call," Sheldon said. "Even when you're not with us, we're always with you."

"We're family," Nadine affirmed.

The human resources director, with her black eyes and fine, long beak, leaned against Sheldon's desk, poised like a raptor to bear off the carcass of Dane's employment to her administrative nest of separation papers, benefits explanations, rights, privileges, a booklet on how to handle a "reduction in force" and best wishes for a great future.

The humiliation of facing colleagues who considered him expendable and the strain of guarding his emotions proved so heavy that Dane sank into the couch, wishing to flee but unable to do more than blink.

Put your stuff in a trash bag, he thought. *A good thing you didn't keep your plants. Everything for a reason. What will they think when they see the trash bag in the subway and when I'm walking home?*

He reflected bitterly that everyone else had worked here forever whereas he lasted less than two years. What was his problem? He saw Goldfarb's behavior now as more than shameless groveling—it was a life strategy to avoid *this.*

They were talking. His face twitched and trembled from the strain of blankness. *Open mouth and show teeth, let eyes pop and blaze wide like the Maori warrior faces New Zealand's All Blacks put on before every match. No scenes! They want to feel good about letting you go. Don't let them.*

Suddenly, needle-pricks and muscles jumped like creatures trapped under Dane's skin that were trying to escape. He laid his hands on his face to hide the tics.

"Are you okay, Dane?" Sheldon asked.

"Yes, of course." The spasms continued. He pressed his palms on his face.

"We offer a generous severance package," the HR vice president interjected. "You'll receive vacation pay and three weeks salary. If you sign the release today, your settlement will come by mail in ten business days. But you have to sign now." Dane could have written her copy. All that was missing was a 1-800 number.

"I'll take it," he said.

Contemplating the hard stop of four years of employment and the seismic interruption of his career was unbearable, so Dane escaped into the handshaking, door-opening, hallway-walking, bag-filling, everybody-knowing twilight between corporate separation and physical departure as he crossed the divide from inside to out, from earning to yearning.

In fifteen minutes, the separation was final. Dane transformed from dead weight to moving man. His anger was assuaged by the severance package and his fear metabolized into hope as new ex-colleagues predicted that he would land a new job before he wanted one.

He said good-bye to Goldfarb, who called Sheldon and Nadine "bastards" under his breath. The door of a young Croatian art director in the next office was closed and she was sobbing behind it. She had been recently promoted to art director and purchased an apartment. Now she was unemployed. Nadine and Roscoe had jokingly named her "the little mouse" because she worked quietly till all hours on projects nobody else wanted. On her birthday, she brought in a cake from a Croatian bakery for everyone to share. Yet, despite her sweetness and submissiveness, she was laid off.

Dane hoisted the black trash bag stuffed with his personal effects—a cheap, plastic radio, a poster demonstrating the knee joint in detail, and other medical mementoes—and staggered backward under their unsentimental weight. Shifting the bag in front of him, Dane lumbered unsteadily out of Integrimedicom and down to the street.

AD NOMAD 4
DRUGS, SEX AND ADVERTISING

Case 4-A

EINSTEIN, ICE CREAM & THE CRYBABY OF CAPISTRANO

1. A BRIDGE OVER THE ABYSS

If the layoff was an abyss, a phone call on Dane's last day at Integrimedicom was the bridge over which he might safely cross. A creative director at a new agency liked his book and wanted to meet him.

Dane's need to superimpose structure on coincidence was a side effect of his creativity. In a quasi-religious impulse, he imputed the recent sequence of events to providence and wrapped their randomness in fate. As he dragged his *Glad Bag* into the torrid subway car for one last commute, he interpreted his layoff as good luck, while fellow travelers scorned him for the space his sad sack occupied and the disgrace it meant.

His interview took place the next Monday. Edie Plinkus, the interviewer, had climbed from traffic to creative director. While Dane dressed to impress, Edie's droopy sweats were more à propos of a jog than a job. "I'm competing in a world martial arts meet in California next week," she explained. "I can't wait!"

Dane had learned two principles of social communication, which he applied to interviews: 1. Show interest in others by overcoming a lack of it; and 2. Interact with the other person's interest by discussing a similar pastime.

Determined to respond pleasantly, Dane asked which martial art Edie Plinkus practiced. When she blurted Chinese words with Sino-sinus precision, Dane nodded effusively to mask the vacancy in his eyes. He then confided that he studied *Kung Fu* when he was a cab driver after being attacked by a cohort of cavorting insurance salesmen. Edie Plinkus nodded with naked disinterest before launching a new topic.

"The agency is like a factory," Edie said. "There isn't much creativity."

Dane was crushed. Being considered for this position was no longer a compliment but an insult. He did not realize that Edie was practicing her martial arts on him *mentally*. She turned his exuberance against him by depreciating the job.

"That sounds great!" Dane replied with twice as much enthusiasm. His need for work made him impervious to pain. "Creativity was getting boring...It's so overrated."

Dane's reversal made Edie Plinkus smile. Oh, he was good! Impressed by his *interview-jitsu*, she extended the meeting to expound on commitment, teamwork and long hours. Dane nodded with oblivious fervor as her palaver washed over him. His mind drifted into financial projections: with the Integrimedicom severance package, vacation pay and the first paycheck from this new position, his lay-off could yield his highest monthly income ever!

Edie all but told him he was hired when she stood up and thanked him for coming in. As Dane waited for the job offer, Edie said she would be interviewing all week and would let him know her decision. She had thrown Dane again but this time he had no time to recover. He walked out on two feet; emotionally he was flat on his back.

Two weeks later, the recruiter told him Edie filled the position from within. Dane did not linger on the setback. He phoned recruiters, agencies and former colleagues, lining up interviews. He was sure persistence would land him a job.

The fourth quarter of every year was typically hectic in pharmaceutical advertising. Clients had to splurge on end-of-the-year projects or forfeit their unspent budgets. Agencies could not cope with the work overflow and hired freelancers and billed clients at a higher rate.

This year was different. Dane received no offers. It was a bleak sign of his low market value or an industry slump.

He had one interview in September, another in October and a

third in November. The dearth of opportunity worried him but not as much as the interviews, themselves. Dane approached each meeting with *The Three C's*: confidence (trusts self), competence (has skill), and compliments (likes others). He described his swift career ascent, the DONARAL campaign and other successes; and the good people he had met. The interviewers smiled and politely asked why he had held no job for longer than 18 months. He explained the circumstances: he left Green to make more money and was laid off at Integrimedicom when they lost their clients. The interviewers replied that they needed someone who would stay for years, not months.

Dane was confused. He always believed changing jobs was the norm in advertising but now he was viewed as a vagabond. His career was supposed to be on the upswing and it might be over.

2. THE CRYBABY OF CAPISTRANO

Dane had been jobless for four months when interviews trickled in after the New Year. Tormented by his inability to find work, he viewed even the most distant opportunity as potential salvation. He drove thirty miles in a snowstorm to meet one creative director whose office was ornately furnished and fragrant with incense. Nothing came of it. The next morning, he interviewed with an old friend of Landon LeSeuer. Fred Potter had a kindly face, a scraggly beard, and framed glasses. He wore a loose cable-knit sweater, baggy corduroys, and spoke in a soft voice. In a more efficient world Fred Potter would have been the heir to Mr. Rogers.

According to advertising legend, Fred cried hysterically when he was fired at Green Advertising. Ten years after the fact, Dane searched for blood-shot eyes and salty splotches on Fred's cheeks as if ancient tears left lasting scars. But it was Dane's turn to cry when Fred reviewed his book and confided that there were no jobs at his agency. Fred tried to comfort Dane by saying that the interview was not a waste of time.

"When I was out of work I wrote a book about what to do when you're out of work," Fred confided.

"Did you tell your readers how to find a job?" Dane asked.

"Most books do that," Fred said. "I had a new angle: When you're out of work, you think your job is finding work but the real job is having a good attitude about being out of work."

Dane was tempted to ask Fred to repeat the double-talk but guessed that hearing it twice would only quadruple his confusion.

The "practice" interview ended when Fred handed Dane his card. "If you have questions, please call." The gesture was as empty as the interview. Fred had wasted Dane's time, yet was so nice about it that Dane was not angry. He interpreted this fruitless meeting as a harbinger of imminent opportunities, like the swallows of Capistrano.

3. EINSTEIN AND ICE CREAM

A week later, a recruiter Dane vaguely knew phoned with an opportunity fifty miles away. Dane was intoxicated with hope, although this headhunter had sent him on many fruitless interviews before. The previous failures were not Dane's fault—he once waited an hour before a meeting was cancelled—but the recruiter blamed him anyway. She coached Dane to keep his responses brief, forego extraneous remarks, and give as little information as possible. These "pointers" poked holes in Dane's interview style and *personality*; but he stammered gratefully that he would suppress his verbose tendencies and make her proud.

On a raw Thursday morning Dane presented himself at the agency outside Princeton. He was an hour early. In urgent need of urinary relief, he searched for a filling station. After driving in circles, he deduced that an upscale town like Princeton must zone gas stops in its outskirts. He found a station, filled his tank and voided his bladder, then paid an impromptu pilgrimage to Einstein's home. As Dane gazed at the modest frame house, he reflected that Einstein was his boyhood hero. "Einstein" was even Dane's middle school moniker. What were his classmates thinking—or *drinking*?

Dane waited another hour at reception. Indignation was eroding his upbeat interview disposition. Suddenly he noticed a magazine on a coffee table with the headline, "Top Fifty Agencies in New Jersey." He scribbled the agency information on the back of a résumé. Each number he transcribed raised his self-esteem and confidence. His interviewers wasted his time but he still made the most of it.

Two women finally met him. Each apologized profusely and without conviction for making him wait. The first interviewer was the human resources director. She was an expert in imposing corporate structure on human behavior, which made her skeptical of a New York resident working in central New Jersey. She claimed that the agency was more than a backwater subsidiary of a multinational corporation: it was a community. For instance, she often met employees and their families at a local ice cream parlor on Friday nights. She made it sound like part of the job description.

The creative director in need of copy support was an elegant woman in her 40s, who once worked at Integrimedicom. She described her horse and her renovated farmhouse. Dane simulated interest so well that she offered Dane an assignment. However, before Dane could enjoy the acceptance, the creative director lamented that the hiring process was complicated by the conglomerate's accounting irregularities; reams of paper work had to be filed before Dane could start and months would pass before he would be paid.

Dane left Princeton with dim hope of working there but he had compiled a list of 25 other agencies, so his glacial campaign to find work held promise.

He also looked forward to an interview the following day. It would be his fourth of the month. After the many messages Dane left all over town, a creative director agreed to see him. Dane showed up at the agency at 9 AM. Fifteen minutes later a human resources specialist emerged with a bland apology and escorted him to her office. It was "Bagel Friday" so she ate her bagel and *schmear* and asked, "What are you looking for in a job?"

Cream cheese glistened on the HR associate's lips and chives lodged in her teeth as she questioned Dane with professional detachment. After finishing the interview and bagel simultaneously, she brought Dane to the creative director, a voluble man who wore pungent cologne and a gold Swiss watch. He was busy so he passed Dane to the Alzheimer's team leader, a bald man in dirty jeans and a tee, who asked Dane, "What can I do for you?"

"What can you do for me?" Dane asked.

Medical writers frequently showed signs of the diseases they wrote about. Reflux medication writers had heartburn, statin writers experienced chest pains, and ophthalmologic writers were struck by partial blindness. Did this interviewer have early onset Alzheimer's? How else to explain, *"What can I do for you"* at a job interview?

"I need a job," Dane said.

"We have an opening but it's too junior for someone with your experience," the copy supervisor replied.

Another opportunity, another mirage. Shifting realities were to be expected in an economic desert. Dane left the agency perplexed. Was he close to a new job or as distant as before?

Case 4-B
A PASSION FOR PROSTATES

4. DANE MAKES A HIT

Dane sent cover letters and résumés to every agency he transcribed from the *Pharm Ad* annual. After a few days his cell rang while he was driving Iris home from school. The woman's voice and name were unfamiliar and her voice was splintered by static. She explained that Bill Bevaqua, the creative director at UNIHEALTH, had seen Dane's résumé and wanted to meet him the next Monday at 4 PM.

Dane drove 35 miles to the interview in single digit cold. In blue twilight he entered a concrete and glass building in the middle of a vast parking lot. A plasma billboard suspended from the skylight flashed UNIHEALTH, "SCIENCE with SOUL" and slides of smiling doctors and patients in pajamas. The slide show culminated in the image of a smiling, bald-headed boy holding a teddy bear, along with his beaming parents. The headline read: "They said you could not sell a cancer drug with a smile."

"Can I do this?" Dane asked himself. He did not want to work on cancer but he still rode the elevator to the second floor. The door opened and Bill Bevaqua was waiting there to greet him.

Bevaqua had a square jaw and a round face. His warm intensity conveyed directness and purpose. The creative director led Dane to a small room with a sliding Plexiglas door, called a *fishbowl*.

"People all over are looking for work," Bevaqua began. "I don't hold that against them but I'm not in the business of handing out jobs."

"I'm not here for a handout," Dane replied. "I've always more than earned my pay."

"That's why you're here," Bevaqua said. "Dane, I'll get to the point. Ten years ago, there were seventy launches a year. Last year there were forty. And the number is dropping. Companies are merging, pipelines are shrinking. *Me-2s* are now *Me-6s*." Bevaqua's eyes were wide and horrified as if the dire vision they beheld had faded to black.

Dane's anxiety was rising. Was Bevaqua's prophecy a ploy to make Dane *not* want the job before it was *not* offered to him?

"More agencies are competing for fewer products and less business...We have to work smarter, think better, create—," Bevaqua paused, his lips parted like doors held open for the right adverb to stumble through, "—more creatively!" Aware of his redundancy,

Bevaqua sighed. "I'm no writer. That's why you're here. Let me take a look."

Bevaqua turned the pages of Dane's book with the brisk impatience of a man shoveling snow. To put his work in the best light, Dane provided a context for each concept. Bevaqua cut Dane short. "Let the work speak," he whispered with his forefinger over his lips. He paused often, nodded effusively and guffawed. "This I like. You did this?" He pointed at "The Faces of Premature Ejaculation" and "Make it last!" campaigns.

"Yes! That's me," Dane replied.

Bevaqua stopped flipping the pages and jabbed at one concept with his forefinger.

"I've seen this one!" he said, spinning the portfolio around so Dane could look. It was the weightlifters execution in the "Release the Load!" campaign for SLOJAC.

"That's my work!" Dane said. "I did it at Integrimedicom before the layoff."

"Wait!" Bevaqua finger-licked his way through a physician's magazine and smacked one page excitedly. "There!"

Dane stared at the page: it was "Release the load!" all over again.

"I can't believe it!" Dane protested. "They laid me off and used my concept—for a laxative ad!"

After losing the "greasy stools" and premature ejaculation accounts—along with half its workforce—Integrimedicom scored *Evacumab*, the world's first biologic laxative. It was a gift from the parent agency and Sheldon and Nadine thought Dane's "Release the load" was a perfect concept to launch the genetically engineered stool softener.

If Dane had received credit, his grinning mug would have been on the cover of *Pharm World* magazine. Instead, he looked like a plagiarist.

Bevaqua accelerated through the rest of the book before closing it with a *thwop*.

"I've seen enough!" he exclaimed.

"You have?" Dane stammered. Bevaqua would now dismiss him as a creative rip-off artist.

"This work is excellent. You've captured a world of pain. You're a genius!"

"It is? I have? I am? I mean, thank you."

Bevaqua's ten seconds of praise reversed months of self-doubts. Dane's work meant something again.

The chief creative officer of UNIHEALTH pursed and relaxed his lips several times like he was warming them up to say something special.

"Dane! I'm from Chicago. There are no hills to hide behind. I see the forest and the trees, and never waste time beating around bushes. So this is what I'm thinking. You are one big paradox. Freshness and experience, creativity and logic, wit and insight, age and youthfulness, strangeness and familiarity, all rolled up in that special compound called you!" Bevaqua brought his blue-collar hands together as if pressing elements into one compound, "You think out-of-the-box...*but* you haven't thrown out the box. That's good...because you never know when you have to send back the product!"

Bevaqua's finger twitched in the air. It appeared to transmit a coded message. The executive creative director stared at Dane with his head tilted as if guiding a pinball in his brain out his ear.

"I have two positions to fill," the creative director said. "But I have one in mind for you. I think you'd be perfect for prostate cancer. You have the fresh voice we're looking for."

"I do? Yes, I do. Great!" Dane stammered. The prospect of earning thrilled him after months of unemployment. Even "cancer," which made Dane shudder—with images of careering green and white *Sloan Kettering* vans—sounded beautiful.

"You made premature ejaculation sexy. That's not easy to do. I want you to bring your passion for *ejaculation praecox* to prostate cancer! Of course, it wouldn't *just* be prostate cancer," Bevaqua continued, "You'd have the entire prostate franchise...We're also launching a drug for benign prostate hyperplasia. Ever heard of it?"

"No."

"God, you'll love it!"

Bevaqua grinned at Dane like a man who found a brother in a strange land.

"Dane, my gut tells me you belong here. You're not happy just doing a job. You want to own the job. That's how we are here. We believe in ownership. We don't have employees. We have job owners."

"I've always want to own my job," Dane stammered. "So far I've been just a renter—and sometimes just a squatter."

Bevaqua's large eyes bulged with hypertensive excitement. If words were pinballs, Dane would have earned a free game.

"Thing is, we've got to move fast. The client is nervous. So...okay!" Bevaqua snapped his fingers like his mind was obedience-trained. "I'm totally sold and ready to order one Dane Bacchus for UNIHEALTH but we have horizontal management. Each hire has to be one size fits all. Stretchy, *heheh*! I want you to meet the associate creative directors. Can you come back?"

"Of course," Dane replied.

"So we're on," Bevaqua said. "Ecstatic!"

5. MEETING THE TEAM

Dane returned to UNIHEALTH at the end of the week to meet the cadre of associate directors. The temperature was 25 degrees warmer, snow and ice were melting everywhere and it felt like spring in January. Dane was full of hope until slabs of ice flew off the top of a truck in front of him, nearly smashing his windshield.

He read it as a sign, nature's interactive billboard, for the meeting ahead, but he was determined to overcome whatever awaited him.

Four associate creative directors faced Dane across a conference table. They were smiling. Three of the four had not seen Dane's résumé and would not be working with him. A Russian art director with blond ringlets and a silver goatee looked up from Dane's CV and flashed a mischievous smile.

"So! Says here you write novels, poetry and publish many articles. You write music, sing your heart and soul in clubs and radio. You even invent your very own art form. So...why are you here?"

Dane smiled cautiously. Was this a trick question?

"I'm here for a job," Dane replied.

"Of course you are!" the Russian let out a short laugh and brought his hands together in a loud clap. His smile was blunt as a fisherman's knife, scratching at Dane's psyche to open it like a mollusk. "My point is this: if I did half as much as you, I would not look for job. I would be rich."

The remark opened a fissure in Dane's mind from which scalding anger had been known to overflow. With playful insight, this stranger had located a conundrum of Dane's existence before which he was a stammering idiot.

But Dane contained his rage. He recalled an anecdote from his teaching days. A student described how his homeboys observed July 4th on the Jersey Shore by feeding *Alka Seltzer* to seagulls and watching them explode in midair when the tablets detonated in their guts. "I'm no seagull," Dane reassured himself.

"You're perceptive," Dane replied. "I am a bad businessman to make so little of what I've done."

His rational self-deprecation fell like a gavel over the proceedings. The associate creative directors adjourned the meeting. They had their fun with Dane, though not as much as they would have liked.

For an excruciating week Dane awaited news from UNIHEALTH. On a Friday morning, as he pushed a cart down a supermarket aisle, his cell rang. It was Bevaqua. "You must have paid your references well because they all gave you high praise. Can you come in this afternoon? I'm making you an offer."

Driving 35 miles in snow and fog did not dampen Dane's euphoria. It felt like an excursion. Bevaqua greeted Dane at his *fishbowl* office with an envelope. Dane was so moved that his economic free-fall was apparently over that he could not bear to open the envelope and read its contents. When he brought himself to unfold the letter, he went no further than, "We are pleased..." to avoid bursting into tears. Bevaqua assured him with a paternal smile how glad he was to have Dane on board.

6. LOTS OF LUTS

Before Dane could gather his thoughts in a few sentences of gratitude, the creative director handed him a 300-page, ten-nation study about the link between lower urinary tract symptoms (LUTS) and older male sexuality.

"I need you to write a background report on this by your first day," Bevaqua said.

Dane was stunned. The hiatus between being hired and showing up was the best part of a job—anticipating income without working for it. How could Bevaqua revoke this precious prelude? Was Bevaqua giving Dane an entrance exam to predetermine if he qualified for the position? At UNIHEALTH, Dane not only owned his job; he pre-owned it. Yet rather than protest, Dane immersed himself in his work. After so long on the outside, Dane needed to belong. He told himself that being put to work before his starting day meant he was needed. He wanted to impress Bevaqua and make UNIHEALTH his home.

The multinational study Dane was given to evaluate and summarize was based on data from hundreds of thousands of questionnaires. It provided compelling insights about male urology and psychology. Once Dane perused the findings of this seven-nation survey, he had no doubt about his new job— lower urinary tract syndrome (LUTS) was his destiny and benign prostrate hyperplasia (BPH) was a relevant illness worthy of his study and creativity.

For years, Dane had witnessed older colleagues belly up to urinals with grunts of frustration and resignation in their eyes. It was different than *"micturition inhibition"*—a term Dane coined for the stage fright men had during public urination. This multinational study data explained why many older men had discomfort while seeking relief.

Dane was shocked by how many men worldwide were unable to pee or maintain erections sufficient for intercourse. Less surprising was the macho reaction. Hundreds of thousands of men reported groin pain, yet few admitted that it affected their virility. Retirees in their 60s and 70s, unable to maintain erections for twenty seconds, reported having sex five or six times per week. Dane also noted national differences. Men from Spain, France and Italy claimed the greatest number of copulations while American men admitted to more realistic numbers. Were American men sex-slackers or could they afford to be open about their impotence since they defined manhood in more ways than coitus—by golf, income, cars, hobbies and good cigars?

Dane read with interest, even excitement. He had been handed a global health problem to write about. It could mean years of prosperity. By immersing himself in Europe's strange horizontal charts and numbers with decimal commas rather than points, Dane mastered topics like amount of semen per ejaculation and frequency of maintained erection after penetration. He knew the data so well that it revealed patterns to him. Dane derived great intellectual satisfaction from delving so deeply into the lower urinary tract epidemic afflicting older men. Then it occurred to him that someday he might be one of the men afflicted by it.

"No, this can't happen to you," Dane reassured himself. "Can it?" He urged himself to remain professional and detached. This should be no different than menopause, intermittent claudication or premature ejaculation. Yet Dane could not avoid a creeping apprehension. He knew he could never have menopause and premature ejaculation was in his adolescent past but a thick prostate, slow painful urination and impotence were in the waiting room of his life. Even while he worked, he felt a pain in his groin. For days, he fearfully monitored his urinary stream and counted his erections.

"You're getting personally involved! Don't blow it," he chided himself and continued to do his homework.

When he had absorbed the study, he summarized it in a five page "backgrounder." He spun the data two ways and wrote a version for each. His first variation was titled "Up and Down." It reflected the insight that "When lower urinary tract symptoms go up, sexual appetite and performance go down." The second concept was titled "The Other half," referring to the 50% of men experiencing lower urinary tract pain and sexual difficulties. Dane was pleased. When asked to write one report, he wrote two. In America, it was always better to super-size.

He emailed the two versions to Bevaqua a few days early and received an astounding response. "This is excellent. Bull's eye! Exactly what we were looking for. This was why you were hired. Thanks for making me look so good! Bravo."

7. CUBE WORLD

On his first day of work, Dane missed his exit and went ten miles out of his way before arriving at the office a half-hour late. He shrewdly phoned UNIHEALTH when he first lost his way to win sympathy for being new.

The tactic paid off. Bevaqua greeted him with an ursine pat on the back and a fraternal laugh. "So, you missed that exit. I did that when I started fifteen years ago."

This boded well for Dane. Already he was stepping into the

footsteps of his mentor. He reflected that doing the right thing was less effective than doing the wrong thing in the right way.

After he settled into his cubicle, Dane surveyed the second floor.

The most telling detail was how quiet UNIHEALTH was. Soon Dane learned why. When UNIHEALTH people chatted, their lips moved but they made no sound. Even when he was close to them, they were inaudible. It was *cube-talk*—the evolutional adaptation resulting from the need to communicate privately in a public place.

In a cube-world, where space was shared, privacy was taboo. Only conference rooms and *fishbowls* had doors. *Fishbowls* were small glass-walled enclosures where small meetings took place. Awful things were presumed to happen in *fishbowls* since interactions there were visible but inaudible and passersby could only guess what they were. Being summoned to a *fishbowl* induced anxiety. It was a public pillory and an isolation chamber, a starting point and a terminus.

8. EINSTEIN OF ADVERTISING

The *fishbowls* were also sacred portals where major events, transitions and transformations took place.

Such a transition befell Dane in his second week. An ice storm kept many UNIHEALTH employees at home but since Dane could ill afford another unpaid holiday, he braved the conditions and was nearly alone at UNIHEALTH. It was a great way to get noticed.

Bevaqua summoned Dane to the executive *fishbowl* to discuss a special project. Sounding his usual apocalyptic theme, Bevaqua warned that there were few new drugs in America's drug pipeline, which meant fewer launches and promotions. ""If we're going to stay ahead of the unemployment curve we have to act now," Bevaqua said with blue-eyed, rock-jawed resolve. "Or we'll be selling drugs—*on street corners.*"

Bevaqua told Dane that UNIHEALTH hired a firm to market itself to prospective clients. "They know how to sell products. We'll become the product they sell," Bevaqua said. The marketing firm, headed by a dogmatic eccentric named Bozenfeld, would help the agency formulate an effective marketing campaign. First, the agency would create an offering—a prize, program or object to attract prospective clients' attention and demonstrate the agency's creativity.

Dane assumed that Bevaqua counted on him to create this offering to save the agency. Why else had the chief creative officer briefed him a day in advance? Others might have balked at the pressure but Dane felt that his training, temperament and talents entitled him to this pivotal role. Bevaqua had identified him as the creative stud he was and Dane embraced his destiny as the Copywriter Messiah.

An agency meeting was parleyed. The finest minds of UNIHEALTH across all disciplines struggled as one to comprehend the assignment. These canny professionals, who had imbued countless chemical compounds with metaphors, personalities and animal features, such as faces, bodies, wings and fiery breaths, had to give character to advertising, whose function and effect were less tangible than the drugs it promoted. They had no vocabulary for this and the result was an uncomfortable silence.

While his colleagues grimaced in dumbfounded pain, Dane was inspired. Rather than formulate a metaphor for advertising, Dane posed two questions: What was advertising supposed to do and why did it fall short? Answering both questions would help define the agency's mission and create their unique offering.

Dane reviewed the advertising in which he had been involved. Much of it came from ideas conceived elsewhere. Once adopted, an idea had to accommodate other ideas—from the agency, the client, regulatory and creative research participants. By the time a concept found its way to an audience, it was a monstrous hybrid of communication—a sphinx or harpy.

Ironically, a process intended to produce effective advertising had the opposite result. The most effective advertising was original and pure, forming a coherent impression and creating one recognizable brand, but was this possible in a hodge-podge of compromise and a capricious marketplace?

This question had perplexed Dane since he started in advertising. Now it occupied his every thought. In his car, his cubicle, and his bed, ideas, images and equations tumbled in his mind like lottery balls. One morning in the shower, he had a pure and simple vision—the acorn.

"How strong is your acorn?"

A strong concept was like an acorn...it would grow into an oak. The key was to find that acorn and to let it grow.

But Dane could not stop here. He needed a logical basis for his creative insight, a scientific theory with cool-looking formulas to ground his intuition in the world of observable phenomena. A torrent of new ideas poured out of him. These concepts were so complex and bizarre that they could not be expressed in English sentences, or even in existing mathematical concepts and symbols. Dane had to devise a new math to address the problems of advertising. He drew symbols, gave them values, and scrawled equations to express his theories.

He wrote an equation to describe advertising: Let M=Message and A=Audience. Message=Statement+Graphics. Audience=People+ Market conditions. M is separated from A by line (/R), the "Resister."

The objective of advertising was not to create a relationship between message and audience but to remove the "Resister," a value comprised of incomprehension, indifference and noise. If he raised the numbers of the M and A values, through mutual incorporation (Message clarified and made relevant; Audience educated and informed), until the values on both sides of the equation were equal to or greater than the number of the Resister, he could remove the "Resister"—resulting in the perfect advertising message.

Creating a science on the fly exhilarated Dane. He scribbled equations and proofs in mathematical notation, scratching them out, only to replace them with others. He devised theories, symbols, rules and operations to support his proofs as he proceeded. It must have looked like gibberish but the more he wrote, the more sense it made to him.

He made an effort not to be too grandiose. He did not wish to behave like an art director he knew, who disappeared in his office for days during a pitch. One afternoon Dane looked in and asked the fanatic what he was up to.

"I'm branding the biggest thing there is," the conceited art director boasted. "I'm branding life!"

Dane wished the art gnome could see him now. Branding life was child's play compared to what Dane was doing—which was nothing less than revealing the unifying principle for all advertising.

All morning, he worked out his theory, which he titled "Promotional Equilibrium." He was so engrossed in his calculations that he almost forgot to breathe and had to pace the office to stop hyperventilating. When he had solved his equations and double-checked his work—as if anyone could understand such computations well enough to detect accuracy or error—he wrote his theory and proof as a short paper and rushed to the meeting.

During the creative review, Bevaqua and Karen presented programs with acronyms, such as ROI (Return on Investment), which would include information about UNIHEALTH. Their ideas were dry and business-oriented and Dane worried that he had misunderstood the assignment. But when his turn came, he was intoxicated with adrenaline.

"Programs with acronyms are great," Dane said, "But there are so many of them that they all sound alike. And acronyms are hard to figure out and even harder to remember. We have three to five seconds to overcome the audience's impulse to toss the offering. How do we accomplish that?

Dane scribbled his mathematical formulas on a flipchart. He stepped away from his squiggly notations occasionally to check his work, nodded, then continued to write frenetically, explaining his steps, until he finished the proof for "Promotional Equilibrium." He turned to his audience.

"Any questions?"

Other proponents of mystifying theories might have collapsed under the weight of their colleagues' silent astonishment but Dane was unfazed. He had planned this presentation carefully. *Promotional Equilibrium* was just his opening act. He had his audience where he wanted them—in utter confusion and receptive to any alternative they could understand.

"I propose that we take this concept titled, *How Strong is Your Acorn?* and turn it into a children's book, like *Are You My Mommy?* or *Green Eggs and Ham.* We'll write the ideas in pithy passages with superb illustrations. If it's cute and has a nice cover, it might be seductive enough not to get tossed. Our prospective clients might even read it to their children. But along with the fun stuff, we'll give our prospective clients something unexpected...nothing less than the unified theory of advertising on which our children's book is based, which they can use to produce an acorn of perfect advertising— *anytime!* Do you see? We capture our audience between childlike simplicity and the highest order of conceptual sophistication!"

The silence was back. This time it might have engulfed most thinkers and buried their ideas. Only Dane's hyperactive inspiration protected him from the prospect of professional ruin. A strong, youthful voice broke the hush.

"It's brilliant," said a young, female copywriter—one of the rising stars of the agency. "It's like Einstein meets Dr. Seuss!"

The executive vice president swiftly agreed that it had possibilities.

"I'm so glad you said that," Bevaqua said, "It's deeply profound. Every time I think about it, I get a new thought. It's like replicating in my brain...in a good way."

Dane was ecstatic and relieved. In the ruthless environment of UNIHEALTH he knew that at least he would not be fired for another week. His acorn concept and the "science" behind it were sent to Bozenfeld, the marketing consultant, that evening. He would have final say over which idea was developed into a marketing offering.

The next afternoon Bevaqua called Dane into the *fishbowl* and handed him the email he had received from the marketing guru moments before. Bozenfeld, the marketing maven, had selected "The Acorn" concept and the theory of "Advertising Equlibrium"; he wrote that he believed this was a unique offering, with definite appeal to both sides of the perspective client's brain, and would differentiate UNIHEALTH in the marketplace.

After only eight days Dane was the creative genius of UNIHEALTH. It was a triumph he could ride for at least a few months. His rapture was so acute that he could barely tolerate it. With his theory of "Promotional Equilibrium" Dane believed he had done more than reach his creative apex; he had made an important contribution to the field. He went to the local *Taco Bell* to celebrate with a brace of bean burritos.

Did success go to Dane's head? How could it not? Success is a drug not administered orally, topically or by injection. It enters the brain directly through the eyes and ears and creates insidious craving. Rather than savor his coup, on his ninth day at UNIHEALTH Dane prowled the cubicled halls, stalking his next opportunity. He was addicted to success and craved more. He should have asked himself this: After reaching his zenith, where else could he go?

Case 4-C
FOUR MEN AND A FISH

9. PROFESSIONAL PROSTATE

He received his answer at 9:30 AM Monday morning when the Prostate Team convened. The Prostate Team had three women and Dane. The account director was Sylvia Befunkawicz, a fast-talking, fast-moving woman. The art director was Karen Long, a small, pale woman with large glasses and a perpetual scowl. Karen was one of the associate creative directors who had met Dane during his second round of interviews. The third woman was the traffic coordinator, who was taking a personal day to plan her wedding.

"Welcome, Dane. We're thrilled to have you on the team!" Sylvia Befunkawicz said with a brassy voice that made "thrilled" sound like "irritated."

Immediately, Sylvia launched into a litany of projects. She expected Dane to help with them all.

"Do you have any questions?" she asked.

Dane knew it was important to ask a zinger or at least to make a semi-astute observation.

"There was something in the study that puzzled and intrigued me. Men who had genital discomfort claimed to have sex several times a week."

"Yes. We noticed this discrepancy," Sylvia replied briskly, "A doctor I interviewed called it *sexaggeration* and warned that it might compromise the study. It's unlikely that most men over forty have any sex when half have erectile dysfunction. Nice point, Don! It's great having a prostate on board. You can give valuable insight."

Sylvia's smile implied that impotence was Dane's personal expertise. She asked him if he had further questions. Apparently expecting none, she stood up to leave. But Dane was dissatisfied. He could not let everyone leave that meeting with the idea that he was impotent and had stale insights.

"I have one more question," he said. "*Prosbar* induces chemical castration. But its concept has four geezers on a boat holding a fish. What does this mean?"

"Doctors love that image. It tested extraordinarily well," Sylvia said and briskly walked out of the *fishbowl*.

"I was hired to bring fresh creative ideas to this brand. Was that an over-promise?" Dane cracked.

"You're experienced. What do you think?" Karen Long, the art supervisor, replied.

10. FOUR MEN AND A FISH

Dane received his first creative assignment that morning. It was to write copy for a breakfast invitation card to be distributed at the upcoming national urology meeting.

As copy supervisor of the Prostate Team, Dane was responsible for two drugs. One was *Contruro,* for benign prostate hyperplasia, marketed in Europe and a year away from FDA approval. The second drug, *Prosbar*, treated prostate cancer. Rather than kill cancer cells, *Prosbar* (luprolide acetate) deprived them of the testosterone on which they thrived. It was bluntly titled "chemical castration."

Without testosterone, prostate cancer cells could not replicate, so they died. However, without testosterone, men could experience humiliating side effects—breast development, hot flashes and a loss of sex drive. The aftershock was worse. The testes might shut down the testosterone factory forever, leaving the man a cancer-free eunuch!

Reading about chemical castration made Dane's groin ache. His thighs tingled and shook like he had spontaneous nervous leg syndrome. His flailing leg kicked out the computer power cord, prompting one more visit by the IT guy, who pegged Dane as an annoying freak.

Dane tried to submerge his queasiness in work. The breakfast invitation card he was assigned to write would be slipped under urologists' hotel room doors in the evening. It would invite doctors to attend *Prosbar*'s breakfast seminars where paid experts would tout the benefits of chemical castration. Karen said the card copy should be catchy and appealing because every prostate drug would compete with *Prosbar* for urologists' time and attention.

It was a small, yet agonizing assignment. What would draw a crowd of world-weary urologists to a breakfast meeting about chemical castration, which they already understood in detail? Dane thought hard with no immediate result. He tried every one of his inspiration-inducing techniques. He pulled his hair, boxed his ears, smacked his face, and bit his fingers—to no avail. Then he resorted to a last, desperate measure—he started to think.

What was the deepest prevailing feeling connected to this drug? Sacrifice. The loss of a man's testosterone was the greatest sacrifice he could make, next to his life. What else could inspire such self-sacrifice? Love of country? The surging measures of an anthem stirred Dane's consciousness. Why not suggest to urologists that it was their patriotic duty to learn the latest about chemical castration? Dane envisioned Nathan Hale with a noose around his neck, proclaiming, "I only regret that I have but two balls to lose for my prostate!" He explored this theme with a safe Marine Corps headline: *We're looking for a few good urologists.*

Such a platitude was like salt—it made his creative juices flow. He extended the patriotic metaphor with Uncle Sam: *Wanted: One Urologist.* Then he switched to a "wake up" concept with the headline: *"Make the Prosbar Booth your first stop this morning."* Now Dane was loose enough to spring right out of the box. He thought he'd get edgy with a sexual message to offset chemical castration. He drew a sultry vixen at a counter with the headline, *"Don't keep Prosbar waiting."*

Karen came by his cubicle with her comments. "Your ideas were fresh and some were funny. But you didn't use the brand art—four men and a fish."

"You asked for intriguing," Dane said. "Who is intrigued by four men and a dead fish?"

"The ones who chose the concept," Karen replied impatiently. "Would you just try this again now? We need it in layout today."

Now Dane had to come down from Mount Rushmore and Iwo Jima and consider how to make four old men and a fish interesting and relevant to a convention of urologists. Finally, he had an idea.

Since the invitation must combine men, fish and breakfast, Dane would advertise smoked fish for breakfast. Good food was always a lure and who didn't like bagels and lox to start the day? Dane wrote a smoked fish series. "CATCH NOVA SALMON ON A FRESH BAGEL AT PROSBAR BREAKFAST SEMINAR" and "PROSBAR BREAKFAST SEMINAR: THE FRESHEST DATA AND SMOKED STURGEON."

Dane rushed into Karen's cubicle excitedly. He was proud of how well he had adapted to the new creative requirement, and handed Karen the new breakfast copy with a broad smile.

"Smoked fish? Are you insane?" she asked.

"You said I had to use four men with a fish, promote breakfast, and make it catchy and appealing. I did it all!"

Karen was in no mood to dismantle Dane's enthusiasm.

"We'll just have to use what we had before. Thanks," she said.

Dane returned to his cubicle nonplussed and deflated. His first creative task for Prostate Team was a contained disaster—a trashcan fire. It was humiliating but he wrote it off. How could he make four men and a fish work when the idea was as moribund as the fish in the picture? It symbolized what was wrong with the prostate franchise— which he was hired to fix.

Why should he dwell on a chemical castration breakfast invitation when his *How Strong Is My Acorn?* children's book was in layout? Besides, just that morning, Dane received unexpected high praise. The UNIHEALTH newsletter featured a rave review of his report on the diminished sex lives of men with thickened prostates, calling it a "compelling read" that "holds you from the first sentence and doesn't let go." The reviewer was the agency president, himself, a benign prostate hyperplasia (BPH) sufferer.

11. MINIMUM PI

Later that week, as Dane soared on the backdraft of "the Acorn project" and the sex lives of old men with enlarged prostates, Dane received another assignment. It was patient prescribing information for *Contruro,* the benign prostate hyperplasia drug, the kind of information one might find in a magazine or a drug website.

Karen and Sylvia assumed he knew how to write a consumer PI, so Dane did not ask them how to do it, though it was his first attempt. He would follow his instincts. A standard PI was detailed and clinical but over-the-counter drugs, like aspirin, had simple prescribing information to communicate to average consumers. Dane went home, perused aspirin boxes and crafted his first consumer PI. He was pleased with his resourcefulness until the next Prostate Team meeting. Sylvia turned to Karen and said, "He didn't do what we asked!"

Dane was at the table but Sylvia did not address him directly. As a group account supervisor, Sylvia did not deign to speak to Dane, who was only a copy supervisor. Dane broke through the caste barrier. "You asked for a patient PI so I modeled this after a consumer PI I found on a box of *Advil,*" he said.

Sylvia stared at him in astonishment and turned to Karen. "Is he an idiot? Does he understand English? I don't have time for this."

Karen explained to Dane that he had written a fine over-the-counter prescribing information but unfortunately that was not the assignment. She explained that an OTC package insert was full of warnings because over-the-counter drugs were easy to buy and the FDA did not want consumers to self-medicate. In the case of a prescription drug, side-effects had to be downplayed so patients would want to ask their physicians to prescribe it. She showed him a consumer PI printed by a competitor in a men's magazine and asked him to imitate it.

Sylvia demanded that he stay late until he completed the revised PI and editorial signed off on it. "It has to be done tonight. That was our agreement," she emailed him.

No such agreement had been made but Dane knew he could not cross Sylvia again. He needed to redeem himself. He had relied on his famous *gut* for the consumer PI and it failed. Dane had suffered setbacks before but this one stung worse since it followed his greatest success. He worked in sullen silence.

In cosmology and theoretical physics, a theory as original and elusive as "Promotional Equilibrium" would have carried Dane for years or a lifetime, but in advertising it was beautiful and *unbillable*. "The Acorn Project," only a week old, was already sliding into the forgettable past and Dane had the nauseating sense that his image was slipping from genius to imbecile.

Case 4-D
JOB CASTRATION: PATHOLOGY & TREATMENT

12. JOB REPOSSESSION

The next Monday, when Dane entered the lobby of UNIHEALTH, the "I" was dark so the sign read UN HEALTH. Ordinarily he would have read this as an omen but he had recuperated from his botched PI. He was still ahead on the balance sheet—two victories, one defeat, and a tie: he considered his *Prosbar* breakfast invitation good enough to win if "four men and a fish" had not fought it to a draw. He spent the morning at his human resources benefits orientation. Medical coverage was a principal reason he was working and his family coverage started one month after his first day, which was two weeks away.

When Dane returned from his benefits meeting he learned that Sylvia and Karen had changed his prescribing information copy in his absence. It was a *coup de copy*. Despite his hard work on the piece, his team now made him look incompetent and expendable. He was outraged but how should he respond? Maybe the job could not wait for his return. Or he had made more mistakes. Should he protest? No, he sensed a trap. They wanted him to complain so they could retaliate and sink his reputation even deeper. Dane could not afford the risk.   His benefits had not taken effect and were already endangered.

That afternoon a party was catered in the atrium to celebrate new business. The agency president, a former copywriter, told Dane how much he liked the "acorn" and asked how the prostate franchise was going. Dane told the agency president that it was going well, except that his teammates had just rewritten his copy. The agency president grimaced and looked Dane in the eye.

"Never let anyone write your copy," he said.

"I'm not only an incompetent but a wimp," Dane thought.

It occurred to him that he was in the worst trouble of his advertising career. He always had enemies but even colleagues who loathed him respected his work. They even stole it.   Those seemed like good times now. The Prostate Team encircled him, laid siege to his job and Dane was unable to defend himself. His brilliant, early success had weakened him with false confidence. Since people loved his work, he believed he was immune to attack. Now his team disparaged his competence and made him seem useless by doing his job for him with insidious and ruthless efficiency. UNIHEALTH was doing to him what *Prosbar* did to a man's testosterone production; it gave him an artificial surge, only to shut him down. As Dane wrote about chemical castration he was being professionally castrated.

If the women on his team already criticized and appropriated his work, how long could he last at UNIHEALTH? Dane retreated to the men's room and looked himself in the mirror.   "Fight for your manhood."

He knew he needed to do more than grab his testes and pound his chest. He had to change the terms of the conflict, to switch the issue from job competence to job ownership, which Bevaqua had promised him.

At the next meeting of the Prostate Team, Dane told Sylvia and Karen they were never to change his copy again.

"You might know the client but I am the only one here who has a prostate," he said in summation.

"Awesome!" Sylvia replied. "Let me make something clear, Dane. I will do what it takes to serve our client. I'm sorry you're offended but this is the law here—and in every agency!"

"I'm not offended. Just let me do my job!" Dane cried.

"Believe me, we want you to do your job, more than anything," Sylvia replied with silky insouciance. "And we're still waiting. Please, Dane, do your job."

By acknowledging the effect Sylvia and Karen were having on him, Dane exacerbated the situation. He went to Bevaqua to head off the potential damage. Perhaps as a fellow man, Bevaqua might sympathize with his ordeal. Behind the sliding door of his *fishbowl*, Bevaqua was grinning into space, presumably from inner peace or the goodness of his deli sandwich.

"Dane, I'm proud of how you stood up for prostates everywhere."

"How did you know?" Dane asked.

"It's an open space and your voice carries."

"Can you help me, Bill? It's real bad."

"What do you mean? Are they rewriting your copy?"

"Yes. But it's worse...They're trying to castrate me!"

"I love your intensity," Bevaqua said. "Now channel it. You're new here. Know the turf before you fight for it."

"They're all over my turf. They give me jobs without directions and scold me when the client doesn't like what I've done. Then they take over for me. It's classic castration!"

"Or miscommunication. Your team is new. Teamwork takes time."

"But my reputation!"

"You wrote a great backgrounder and your acorn project has wide support. So you laid an egg with the patient PI. I'd take two out of three."

"But you said I owned my job. Is it being repossessed?"

"It's heavily mortgaged," Bevaqua guffawed.

"That Sylvia Befunkewicz has it in for me!" Dane cried.

"Sylvia is Sylvia."

"That's what I mean!"

"Sylvia is a force of pharma. She's awesome!" Bevaqua continued. "Sylvia has worked late everyday for a year. She has come into the office on 35 weekends and traveled 20 weeks of the year! The woman has unquenchable passion for what we do at UNIHEALTH. Her journey is an odyssey!"

"But I'm no Cyclops!" Dane replied, jabbing his forefinger into his forehead.

"Dane, *Dane*. Sylvia is dedication personified and she doesn't wear panties!"

"How do you know that?"

"Know what?"

"That Sylvia doesn't wear panties."

"Dane, where did you hear that?"

"From you!"

"Dane, let's not go there. Sexual harassment lurks in those innuendoes."

Bevaqua, an expert in reading distress in human faces because he caused so much of it, now discerned his prostate writer's acute agitation. He snapped his fingers.

"You know what I think? Dane needs his spiritual vitamin. I want you to meet someone."

Bevaqua summoned Marjorie. Marjorie was the world's oldest active pharma copywriter—a spry septuagenarian with cropped white hair and *Hipster* narrow black framed glasses on a woven, multicolored lanyard. In her oversized motley sweater and leggings, she resembled an elf that emerged from a dark cubicle with manuscripts of golden verbiage. Marjorie had piety. She gladly toiled day and night with the quiet efficiency of a high end air conditioner. No doubt, Bevaqua meant Marjorie to be Dane's instant role model, Jung's *Wise Old Woman* archetype, and his cross-gender Virgil on a tour of UNIHEALTH hell. If Dane could be like Marjorie—hunting for obscure references, patiently numbering and renumbering citations, playing with asterisks and other superscript notations—he could succeed.

When Bevaqua discharged Dane from the *fishbowl*, Marjorie accompanied him down the corridor between cubicles toward "the copy corner." When they stopped by Dane's partitions, she whispered, "You've lasted longer in this cube than any of your predecessors."

"Is this a good omen or a bad one?" he asked.

She smiled inscrutably. "That will depend on you."

Marjorie slipped away, leaving Dane to interpret her enigma. Did she imply that his cubicle was UNIHEALTH's site for a dark rite of initiation—or human sacrifice? Was he surpassing expectations or were his days numbered?

There was an email from Bevaqua on his computer.

"The client will ask about the data in your backgrounder. See Dr. Mooney, the science consultant. He'll help you."

13. DR MOONEY AND RAIN BREAD

The next morning, Dane left a copy of his statistical analysis with Dr. Mooney, a man in his late 60s, with white hair and a gentle countenance. Later that day, Dr. Mooney reassured Dane that his analysis of the data was accurate. It was the first good news Dane had received since "the Acorn Project" weeks before.

Dane had to pay for it: Dr. Mooney told Dane the story of his life.

Dr. Mooney limped with a dark wooden cane whose handle was carved in the shape of a rat. He immediately explained the limp and the cane, revealing a surprising connection he had with Dane.

"I am afflicted with intermittent claudication," Dr. Mooney confided. "Have you heard of it?"

"Heard of it! I owned it!" Dane replied. "Well, nobody owns intermittent claudication. I only wrote about it. Mainly direct mail for a drug called STRIDALL."

"You wrote for STRIDALL? I've received those mailings. I actually opened and read them. Very informative and entertaining. Well done, my boy! In fact, you were so persuasive I agreed to try STRIDALL, you know a trial prescription. Good stuff!"

Dane did not know what to make of this untimely compliment. He was glad to finally meet someone who received his intermittent claudication letter, mailer and brochure. It meant his work was not entirely in vain, although he doubted it would help him now.

"Sit, sit," Dr. Mooney urged. "I have only one golden rule: *Quid pro quo.* I read your gibberish, now hear mine. It's called the story of my life."

"Sure thing!" Dane said. He welcomed a friend in his current situation, and one who appreciated his copywriting was *lagniappe.*

"I know, you must think I'm Irish with a name like 'Mooney.' But it was a case of mistaken ethnic identity. I'm a Jew. When my dad came from Poland, he found work as a janitor in Irish bars. His name was *Muni.* His employers heard *Mooney,* so he changed it.

"You might also surmise that I was born in a lab and got my first white coat when I was two. But my first job was in a white butcher's apron. Everyday after school and on Saturdays, I helped out in my dad's and uncle's butcher shop.

"My dad and his brother came to hate each other. Sibling rivalry and business partnership did not mix—what's new? They went their separate ways but I secretly worked for my uncle since he paid me more. What a backstabbing little so-and-so I was, right? I made amends later when I bought a house for my dad with the movie rights to my best-selling book on the sex lives of rats."

Dr. Mooney's eyes lit up as he noted the dumbfounded look on Dane's face.

"It sounds like nonsense now but wait! It gets worse. That's what a life is—gibberish that makes sense in the end. So you think I was always gifted in science. In fact, my first love was not the test

315

tube but the tuba. Unfortunately, I got a hernia carrying it and there were no jobs for a tuba player so I switched to trombone. I wrote a trombone sonata and dreamed of doing a duet with Yo Yo Ma. Too bad he wasn't born yet. Anyway, when I prepared for my audition to Juilliard, fate intervened.

"I loved street jazz musicians. When I thought I was good enough, I played my trombone on a corner. I made more playing on Sundays than selling meat on Saturdays. I saved the money for my tuition for Juilliard. It seemed poetic.

"One evening, I'll never forget. My mom had made a delicious pot roast and I went out to my corner...I was playing *All the Things You Are* when two street thugs called me names and started throwing things. They didn't know my ethnicity, so they called me every slur in their pee brain vocabularies. One thug grabbed my cap full of change while the other guy went for my trombone slide. I whacked the second guy with the slide but his buddy jumped me and I hit the pavement. They worked me over and left me lying there bloody with my busted trombone.

"The slide was bent but the damage to my instrument was the least of it. Using my trombone as a weapon killed the music in me. I went into a funk and couldn't play a note. I changed majors from music to psychology.

"To earn extra money, I cleaned laboratory animal cages. I became intrigued by rats, especially their love lives. Understand that I was innocent. All I ever did was study and play music, so copulating rats were a sexual awakening.

"It changed my life. In those days very little was known about the sex lives of rodents. I was a pioneer. For my honors thesis, I studied their sexual stimuli, what turned them on. I wanted to know if male rats were excited by female rat private parts, so I shot 8 mm films of rats having intercourse. Then I exhibited it to other rats—*pay-per-view*. Ha! That's lab rat humor. But make no mistake. I was in earnest. I believed I was on to something. If I could learn what turned on rats, then maybe we could turn it off, reduce rat populations and contagions like the plague. I dreamed of a *Nobel*. Suffice it to say, it didn't happen because the data showed that rats are not sexually aroused by visual stimuli. Yet, ironically, the same rats in heat will hump their cheese. This insight, by the way, was the basis for my dissertation and best-selling book, *Who Humped My Cheese?* Heard of it? They made it into a documentary on *Adults Only Animal Planet*. So I entertained the world but didn't improve it.

"Life was good. I was a tenured professor and a popular lecturer. Still, I was restless. I pined for the excitement of the laboratory. So when I was offered a chance to run clinical trials for a drug company, it was a wonderful new beginning and it led to UNIHEALTH. I've gone full circle. I even played my trombone last year at the agency picnic."

There was clearly so much more to Dr. Mooney that Dane did not dare to ask questions for fear of a sequel. Dr. Mooney concluded his life story when he could remember no more and was called to a meeting.

However, Dr. Mooney's greatest quality came to light on a dark, rainy day. Dane arrived at UNIHEALTH to find employees devouring jelly-filled cookies, strudel, poppy seed cakes and glistening Danishes.

It was a UNIHEALTH tradition. When it rained, Dr. Mooney brought in boxes of pastries and cakes to raise people's moods. These offerings, which Dr. Mooney called *rain bread*, demonstrated his genius for behavioral therapy. *Rain bread* conditioned the UNIHEALTH staff to enjoy coming to work on a rainy morning.

Dr. Mooney's generosity inspired Dane more than his life story. In his act of kindness, Dane saw it was possible to make people feel better in simple ways. He started bringing in cookies or cheesecakes on sunny days. By doing a small thing for people he barely knew, he felt more connected to them.

14. THE FEATS OF BACCHUS

Unfortunately, there were not enough rainy days to uplift Dane's spirit. After his prostate protest speech he learned what it meant to own your job at UNIHEALTH.

Three weeks after his "Acorn concept" won approval, the book was printed and distributed. It was a hit. People at UNIHEALTH read it to their children and enjoyed the pictures. Soon it would be disseminated to drug companies all over the world. Dane was elated.

But when the hoopla abated, Dane returned to his team—the fundamental unit in advertising. Regardless of an agency's size, the team you were on mattered most. It was critical to survival.

Dane never calculated the effect his early success would have on his teammates. Karen, his immediate supervisor, saw Dane's appointment as an insult. Worse, she thought Dane was being groomed to supervise *her*. Bevaqua's support of the "Acorn concept," which she worked on but considered hopelessly irrelevant, confirmed her paranoia.

Dane stumbled into Karen's life as the latest agent of her despicable fate. She had two sisters, both doctors. Karen attended Cooper Union to study art—a brilliant coup—but her adult life had been one long series of attempts to redeem this career choice. She fell into a pattern that started with her family. Just as her parents ignored her achievements in favor of her sisters', Karen's dedication, intelligence and talent were often underestimated as she progressed slowly through the UNIHEALTH ranks while toiling on others' ideas.

Yet Karen's dislike for Dane was more political than personal. She saw him as a vulnerable appendage of Bevaqua, to be amputated with impunity. Karen despised Bevaqua but was too shrewd to attack him directly. If she made Dane look bad, Bevaqua would look worse for hiring him.

Sylvia Befunkewicz, the account director, also despised Dane in an impersonal way. She despised the *Contruro* client. Since she could not tell him, she abused Dane as a surrogate. To Sylvia's credit, hers was a "green" abuse system; abuse was conserved and recycled with no extraneous abuse discharged.

At every team meeting, Dane was treated like an inept and impotent delegate of the middle-aged and elderly male population of benign prostate hyperplasia patients.

"These guys can't urinate or have sex. They're always in pain," Sylvia said. "How does it feel, Dane?"

Dane squirmed. Posing as an expert on a disease of aging men made him indispensable. Even so, it was humiliating to his manhood to tell women that he could not urinate or have sex—especially since he could do both. But since he needed the money, he embellished the false impression.

"It hurts...more than I can say," Dane said.

"What goes on in a man's mind when you're standing there trying to pee and can't?" Sylvia asked with clinical curiosity, like she would use this insight in a marketing report.

"I try to visualize a garden hose," Dane replied.

Sylvia brought out an anatomical model of the male urinary tract with a rubber, an inflatable penis and a removable bladder and rectum.

"I want to introduce you guys to a new gift from our client. It's an anatomical model and it costs several hundred dollars."

Sylvia had a sharp pencil in her hand. She poked a little dark organ just south of the bladder that looked like a chocolate donut.

"See this? What is this, Dane? Huh?" She asked, stabbing at the prostrate.

Dane felt a sharp pain in his lower urinary tract and squirmed.

"It's a prostate."

"Very good, Dane," she said. "And what happens when men have BPH?"

She poked at the rubber penis with her pencil. Dane winced.

"They can't have an erection."

"Right." Sylvia pressed a little bulb in her hand which was connected by a tube to the inflatable penis. The penis straightened and lengthened. Sylvia pressed the bulb in another way and deflated the penis. "Or..."

"They can't maintain an erection."

"Very good, Dane," Sylvia said. "I think we should name our lower urinary tract model. Who has an idea?"

"Since Dane aced the quiz, let's name it *Little Dane*," Karen said.

"All in favor?" Sylvia asked.

Dane was the only dissenting vote. Within an hour—the normal news cycle at UNIHEALTH—everyone knew about *Little Dane*.

Dane brought his grievance to Bevaqua.

"This is harassment!" he cried.

"What did she do?"

"She abused the male anatomical model. She poked at the prostate and penis with her pencil. It was psychological torture!"

"It's plastic, Dane."

"But she named it *Little Dane*! Isn't that mental cruelty?"

"She likes you, Dane. You know how I know? She doesn't poke plastic prostates with just anyone. She's teasing you to see how you react."

Dane had little time to react. His chagrin was replaced that afternoon with unadulterated despair.

Sylvia called Dane into a telephone conference with the client, a Southerner, who described in detail how he grilled a hog head before he changed subject to the backgrounder and references. "Y'all got yaw fingers up yaw butts or what?" he asked.

When the client ended the call to have his teeth cleaned, Sylvia told Karen she needed the background report Dane wrote, fully annotated with references—immediately. Karen asked him if he understood his assignment and dismissed him from the meeting.

Dane had no idea which references he was supposed to use. He had written his backgrounder based on a 300-page clinical document

Bevaqua handed him when he was hired. Now he learned that the seven-nation survey could not be a reference since it was never published—and was owned by the drug company. Karen gave him the number of a woman in medical education and told him to order the references but this contact had left the company months before. Ordering references was a complicated process. When Dane completed the order forms, Karen tossed them in the trash. Another firm had sent the documents.

Dane stared at the tower of articles and panicked. He needed to insert cogent quotations from as many references as he could read in a few hours. He paced, cursed and considered hurling himself from a window—but they were all sealed shut. He overcame his anxiety, read every article methodically and used quotations from seventeen of them. Three hours later, he handed the annotated version of his backgrounder, with highlighted references and a bibliography, to Karen.

His achievement was soon buried under a new hassle. Sylvia was dissatisfied with the patient PI so he rewrote it. Then she changed her mind and ordered him to type out client changes—unintelligible marks in the margins of thirty pages of single-spaced script—and insert new annotations. After Dane completed this, Sylvia rebuked him for omitting a reference. Dane offered to insert it but she said she would do it herself.

The next afternoon, the client gave his verdict on the improved patient PI. He hated it. "How many times we gonna play *PI* ping-pong, people? Writer, you got your head up your proverbial ass, son? How'd you mix up the two damn categories of urination difficulty? You got obstructive and irritative symptoms cross-wired, man. Even a bitty child knows the difference, so what's yaw problem? You put weak stream, insufficient voiding and straining in the *irritative* category when any fool can tell ya they're *obstructive*. And then you listed urgency and frequency as *obstructive* when they're *irritative*— not *irritating*. Damn, it would be funny if it wasn't so damn pathetic.

All BPH symptoms are irritating, y'all!"

When Dane pulled his head out of the client's mouth, he was grateful his brain wasn't put in a jar. To disprove the incompetence his teammates ascribed to him, Dane worked late every evening. Yet his efforts to redeem himself did not relieve the numb sensation in his genitals he was starting to notice with alarming frequency. He diagnosed it as a psychosomatic response to reading about enlarged prostates but this was a facile diagnosis. It was far more serious than that.

Even after his early skirmishes with The Prostate Team, Dane had started losing sexual urges, thoughts and longings. All he felt in his groin was a dull ache. It was a strange sensation. At first, he believed that slouching in a knock-off ergonomic chair cut circulation to his pelvis, pressed the sciatic nerve, or strained his lower back. Yet improved posture and analgesics did not stimulate his libido. His job-induced castration was already in an advanced stage.

15. AN ANTIDOTE FOR JOB-INDUCED CASTRATION

Zach Trench, the youngest group copy supervisor in UNIHEALTH history, had the cubicle abutting Dane's. He was one of the four associate creative directors who had interviewed Dane before his hire. Zach watched Dane suffer the testes-crushing criticism of the Prostate Team, and heard him quietly groaning across their shared partition. After initially enjoying the spectacle, Zach decided to be humane.

As they stood one morning at adjacent urinals, Zach Trench spoke to Dane, who was having a bout of *"micturition inhibition"* and could not void.

"So you're working on *Contruro*."

Dane nodded grimly.

"I worked on *Contruro*. Five writers have been on that account in six months."

"Why is there so much turn-over on the account?" Dane asked.

"It's a pisser," Zach said, quoting the unofficial motto for the Prostate Team. He shrugged, waited for a laugh that never came, flushed, and slapped Dane on the back, which deviated Dane's aim, causing backsplash.

As the two writers washed their hands and studied their faces in the mirror, Zach told Dane that of the five *Contruro* copywriters, two were fired and three were reassigned. The account was a disaster, the client was an animal and Sylvia was "certifiable."

All of this reassured Dane. When he returned to his cubicle he found a sheet of paper with a Web link and a handwritten note. *All of science teaches us nothing more than this.*

Dane clicked on the link. FREE PORN. On the landing page he found women of all shapes and sizes. Instinctively, Dane knew this was no time for porn. He clicked the X on the corner of his screen but the computer froze on the page of naked women.

"What are you working on?" Karen asked. He could feel her coming up behind him. Either she had an instinct for catching him with porn, had been tipped off, or even planted the note with the hyperlink on his desk, herself. It was feeling like a set up and she was ready to pounce. Dane threw his body over the monitor and ripped hard at the ganglion of electric cords in the back of the motherboard to make the monitor go dark.

"What are you doing?" Karen demanded.

"I was stretching and lost my balance."

"Your computer is off."

"It crashed," Dane said.

"It didn't crash. It's unplugged!"

"Well look at that." Dane feigned amazement at the dangling prongs and wires. "I'll have to reattach them."

Karen looked at Dane disdainfully. He set new lows for masculine ineptitude in her mind.

His computer had crashed and was making strange test patterns like early morning TV. An IT guy came by to remove corrupted programs and install new ones. He was a downtrodden sort who loped from one job order to the next. It was conceivable, even probable, that he neither knew nor cared why Dane's computer crashed. Dane asked the IT guy questions to test the depth of his apathy.

"What makes a computer crash?

"Mostly opening email attachments that contain viruses."

"Can it happen when you open a website dealing with urinary problems?"

"You mean porn? No. Not unless you downloaded it. And the IT manual prohibits that," the IT man said accusatorily.

Dane nodded and bit his dry lower lip. He hoped these facial tics would cut off the flow of blood to his embarrassed face. In an office populated predominantly by women, Dane's image would never survive the rumor that he was a sex-obsessed, porn-loving maniac.

16. HOW CONTRURO!

At the end of the week, Dane found a dark, little plastic donut on his desk with a post-it. "It's a complimentary prostate from our client: for inspiration."

That afternoon, Sylvia and Karen called Dane to *the fishbowl*.

"I have an assignment you'll like," Sylvia said.

"It's a game," Karen added.

"Our client wrote a short sentence to describe what the drug does but it's too dry and he's not happy with it," Sylvia said. "He wants the words to pop and sizzle."

"That's what we pay you for," Karen said.

"So your job is to take the same three ideas and six words and write at least twenty more variations without changing the words."

The tagline read as follows:

Contruro—an effective uroselective alpha blocker with a favorable sexual and cardiovascular side effect profile

Dane stared at the words in murderous stupefaction. Should he try to know what they meant before rearranging them, or would understanding get in the way? He could view himself as a moving man who puts chairs and coffee tables where the customer demands or as a designer who sees the relationship of the furniture. At 3 PM, Friday, Dane was in moving man mode. He asked Sylvia by email if the taglines needed to be done by end of day. "Yes," she replied curtly. "That was our agreement."

It was another one of Sylvia's phantom agreements. Hoping one success would redeem him in her mind, Dane worked with alacrity. It was an assignment scripted for his skill set. With his penchant for syntax and redundancy, Dane could move words around a sentence with effortless finesse, devising a verbal array of cadences and nuances. And for dessert, he could create compound adjectives with the word "prostate," which had never been seen or spoken anywhere in the world.

Contruro, the effective <u>prostate-targeted</u> alpha 1 blocker, treats BPH without compromising sexual function or blood pressure.

Contruro, the <u>prostate-preferential</u> alpha blocker, provides effective relief of BPH symptoms without disrupting sexual performance or affecting blood pressure.

Contruro, the effective <u>prostate-selective</u> alpha blocker, is proven to treat BPH with fewer sexual and cardiovascular side effects.

And many etcetera's.

Even Dane, as supple as any verbal contortionist, with a weakness for saying the same thing a hundred ways, could twist the same few words no more.

When he was stuck, tired or uninspired, Dane revived himself with internet porn instead of fresh air. Pictures of naked women were a sexual double espresso when his energy ran low. This attraction to nude photographs exceeded sexual stimulation. He reviewed the thumbnail pictures of naked women in part to make his work-castrated self feel manly, but his palpitations came from transgression and the risk of exposure. If caught, he would lose his job and never be hired again. How would he explain this outcome to Becky and Iris, or live with himself if he failed to provide for them? Yet scopophilia was an occupational illness for a man writing about chemical castration, like black lung in a coal miner.

This site featured an impressive array of women of all ages, races and body types. Dane was surprised to find even white-haired women spread-eagled on the page. He surmised that Dr. Mooney must have secretly provided the link since the women were more mature than those in the usual porn magazines and websites.

Dane felt a luxurious privacy alone at UNIHEALTH that Friday evening. After minutes of naked-gazing, he returned to work refreshed. However, his porn exposure produced symptoms of benign prostate hyperplasia—painful erection, difficulty achieving orgasm, and lower urinary tract discomfort. Dane might have relieved these symptoms if a highly selective morality had not prevented him from doing so. He had no qualms about gawking at nude women on a company computer but had scruples about masturbating in public. These eclectic ethics left him with aching testes.

After three hours on the *Contruro* messages, Dane muttered, "First class verbiage." *Verbiage* was a term account people used that made writing sound like effluent discharge. Dane hated it but he had no better word for thirty arrangements of six words. He printed out the three pages of taglines with the same pride he once derived from the amount of leaves he bagged for his in-laws. He looked for Sylvia, his taskmaster, but she had already gone for the weekend.

On his way out, Dane saw a glow of light from a cubicle. Marjorie, the elderly copywriter, was scrutinizing a layout. She blinked and smiled. "You're still here? Don't tell me you're dedicated."

"I get things done when I have to."

Then Marjorie stretched. Dane saw that her slender arms were graceful and her sweater clung to her torso, revealing shapely breasts. Marjorie assumed a yoga stance. As she moved her head, Dane caught her at an angle and made a discovery. Marjorie looked like a woman he had seen on the free porn website. He said good night and told himself he must be imagining things. Was it possible that after her monkish day job she became that miracle of nature—a granny porn model?

Driving home, with nothing beyond talk radio to consider, Dane wondered why Marjorie posed for a porn website. Was she so poorly paid that she showed her private parts to make ends meet—or merely bored?

Dane rolled into his neighborhood at 10 o'clock. There were no parking spaces, only dog-walkers. Many people had settled in his community lured by the promise of abundant street parking, only to create a vicious scarcity. For two hours Dane circled before squeezing into a spot. He walked into his apartment after midnight.

17. FISHBOWL REVISITED

On Monday, Sylvia ordered Dane to make hundreds of pages of Xerox copies of thirty references.

"But isn't that the traffic person's job?"

"She can't do it. She's planning a wedding shower."

Dane saw no purpose in protest or argument. He did what she asked of him. When Sylvia stopped by the machines to check up on him, he handed her the stack with a flourish, still trying to please her.

"You did these all wrong!" she cried. "You can't write copy and now you can't even make copies!"

"But these are the ones you asked for!" Dane pleaded. He wanted so much for her to say he was good at something to stem the hemorrhage of his reputation.

"I don't have time to explain..." she said, dropping the stack of papers.

"It's not my job to make copies anyway," Dane retorted angrily as she walked away.

Bevaqua, who was in the supply room next to the copy room, pilfering *Sharpies*, overheard Dane.

"Dane, can I have a word with you in my *fishbowl*?" he asked. Dane followed after him, like a boy on his way to the principal's office.

"Four members of your team have complained about you," Bevaqua said. "They allege that you don't listen."

"I thought I was doing well."

'Ditto. That's why these reports hurt deeply," Bevaqua made a fist, which he pressed against his chest. "Do you know your job?"

"Of course," Dane replied.

"There are reports," Bevaqua sighed.

"Reports of what?"

"Serious accusations."

"Accusations?" Dane felt a pounding on his chest. It was his own fist. Unconsciously, he was imitating Bevaqua. "Wait! I never saw reports."

"Of course you didn't. You generate reports of incompetence, insubordination, and incontinence, and I'm the one who reviews and evaluates them."

"I was never incontinent."

"What about incompetent?"

"No."

Bevaqua squinted at the paper.

"I need my glasses. Oh, here they are: incompetence and insubordination," Bevaqua flinched and covered his eyes. "It hurts to read or speak these words."

Dane sank into the chair to absorb his shaking. He felt weak and dizzy. He had *abyss sickness*. It came when you sank to new depths with great velocity. Only weeks ago, Dane had attained a career pinnacle, branding an agency and creating a theory for effective advertising. Now he clung to his job, weighed down by a freight of free-floating remorse for being his sorry self. His family counted on him and he was failing them. His first paycheck had put the brakes on their freefalling finances but at this rate his income stream might soon end. Even his health benefits did not take effect for days. He must save his job at least until then.

"You and I...we don't know what to make of this. We need someone who knows," Bevaqua said.

The executive vice president of creative summoned Karen into the *fishbowl*. She sat against one corner of the table; Bevaqua leaned against the other corner. They triangulated Dane with scowls. On the glass table between them sat a manuscript. Bevaqua regarded Karen gravely, indicating that they were to start their procedure. Bevaqua handed the paper to Dane.

"Dane, have you ever seen this manuscript?"

It was the *Contruro* messaging assignment—six words in thirty different sentence combinations.

"Yes," Dane said. "I worked on it last Friday."

"Do you notice anything peculiar about this manuscript?"

Dane scrutinized the three printout sheets—and grew agitated. They looked fine. They were written on UNIHEALTH stationery. He reviewed the thirty sentences. He believed he had done well on this assignment and nothing he saw now contradicted this impression. So why was he to blame?

"Two large red circles are on the first page," Dane noted, then added a forensic detail. "They smell like magic marker. I didn't do that."

"I know you didn't, Dane!" Bevaqua replied. "That is a red marker, which is color-coded for Sylvia. You're only allowed to use a brown marker. Do you see what is circled?"

Dane read the circled statements several times but could not interpret their encirclements.

"No, I'm sorry. It means nothing to me."

"They have LUTS in them," Karen blurted. "LUTS! LUTS! We told you to remove it from all messages as of last week. So you turn around and write LUTS, not once, *but twice.*"

"Dane, were you aware that LUTS was banned from *Contruro* messages?" Bevaqua demanded officiously.

"I was unaware it had to disappear," Dane admitted. "I was also unaware I put it in."

"So you were totally unaware," Bevaqua concluded.

"It was a Friday evening. I worked on it for hours," Dane replied. "I was told to spice up the statements and LUTS was the spice that came to mind, I guess."

"But you were told to use only the six words in the message. *Six words!*" Karen cried out, displaying five fingers on one hand and one on the other. "And LUTS wasn't one of them."

Dane thought obtuseness, Friday night fatigue, and the omission of a petty detail under pressure comprised an effective three-excuse regimen. However, Bevaqua and Karen's faces showed no understanding or forgiveness; admission of a simple lapse would only feed their firing frenzy. Dane must present his oversight as something other than a blunder.

"Look, I didn't do it on purpose but maybe subconsciously I inserted LUTS because I like the acronym. Even before my first day here I studied LUTS. It's part of me now."

"That is so wrong! " Bevaqua thundered. "We are professionals here. We can't indulge attachments to acronyms, no matter how attracted we are to them. If you were directed not to insert LUTS you should have resisted your impulses."

Seeing how emotional the LUTS issue was to Bevaqua, Dane reversed himself.

"Look, it was a typo, okay? I must have keystroked LUTS out of habit. It was Friday night. I didn't know what I was doing."

Karen grimaced.

"This worries me. You claim you wrote LUTS on purpose. Then you say it was an accident. Who are you? And how can I believe you?"

Dane knew he was cornered so he came out fighting with a desperate last charge—common sense.

"So I inserted LUTS twice in thirty messages. That's less than 7%. Which means I had it right 93% of the time. That's a phenomenal success rate!"

Bevaqua shook his head at Dane with the grief of a father betrayed. "I can't believe what I'm hearing! At UNIHEALTH, nothing less than 100% is acceptable."

Dane was sinking in the morass of their inquisition. He had been so proud of the messages he created from a few boring words and the speed with which he crafted them, yet even his good work was bent against him because the infamous LUTS worm infiltrated two of thirty statements. Bevaqua's grim countenance told Dane he would need something very special to exonerate himself this time—a truly audacious excuse.

"A mistake may have been made," Dane pleaded. "But I don't know your procedures and nobody took the time to explain them."

Dane had few business skills, however devising excuses was one of his best. As a copy supervisor, Dane was expected to know procedure but since UNIHEALTH never provided him with an official procedure orientation, how was he to know? Employees had few rights worth recognizing in pharmaceutical advertising but a procedure orientation was sacrosanct. Procedure, more than logo, slogan and mission statement combined, identified the character of a corporation because it defined how it conducted business. By failing to provide Dane with a procedure orientation, UNIHEALTH failed its own procedure.

Bevaqua and Karen had not anticipated this twist. While they scrambled for a coherent response, Dane filibustered.

"While someone was napping at the procedure switch, I stayed late Friday evening to get those messages done—and I nailed them. That's commitment. But nobody cared enough to stick around and read them. So now you crucify me over an acronym in a sentence. People, is that all we're talking about here? LUTS?"

"We're not talking about a four letter word. There's a big picture here," Bevaqua rebutted, looking as hard-boiled as a ten minute egg. "The word is a *symptom* of a larger problem."

Bevaqua waved his arms in a circle to emphasize the largeness. He showed Dane a page out of the brochure that passed through Dane's hands the previous week. A circle marked one page where the reference number 7 was followed by a 10.

"What happened to references 8 and 9?" Bevaqua asked.

Dane squinted at the document. He admitted that the references in question were non-existent.

"Yes, I skipped numbers 8 and 9, but I want to point out that I was the one who removed the bad references Sylvia inserted. I had no time to follow up."

Bevaqua's eyes narrowed. Dane thought he had been nailed.

"Why was Sylvia doing references?" Bevaqua asked.

"Karen told her to go for it. So she did them wrong," Dane said.

Bevaqua scowled at Karen. Dane had driven a wedge between them.

"Sylvia's been on us about referencing from the get-go. You know how it's been," Karen said.

"Do I ever! Thank you, Dane. You've given me the smoked herring I need," Bevaqua said. "If account people are running around doing references, they can't scapegoat creatives for their mistakes. We're adults, which means we're accountable. We're done here. But Dane needs a procedures orientation. Karen, can you make that happen? I've got another meeting."

Dane had survived. That he measured his job by survival rather than success indicated how far he had fallen—from genius to deadbeat in four weeks. His hire at UNIHEALTH was a fiasco but his family needed health coverage, which would take effect in two days. Bevaqua and Karen may have intended to cut him off before the benefits kicked in, but Dane eluded the trap. He would probably receive his benefits before he got fired.

It seemed an attainable goal but he did not know how sick UNIHEALTH was making him and how his illness would manifest itself in a meeting devoted to procedures.

18. PROCESS MAKES PERFECT

The next morning Dane received an e-mail announcing his emergency procedural orientation. At 3 o'clock he entered a small conference room, where several department heads stood before a blackboard. On the slate someone wrote "Welcome Dane!" in rounded letters with the side of a fat chalk. At the long table, one chair was set. A place card with his name was in front of it, with a pad, a laminated chart and a pencil with the UNIHEALTH logo. No effort was spared to make Dane feel like a first grader.

A hefty stapled document was handed to Dane. It was the text for his tutorial. On page one an anatomical chart of the organization described the process in boxes and arrows. Each box contained a department name and listed its functions, while the arrows showed the procedural flow: client→ account→ production→ account services→ writer→ account services→ writer→ art director→ editorial→ account services. Arrows were the vessels of UNIHEALTH, transporting projects from client need to fulfillment. The presentation could have taken ten minutes but persisted for two hours.

This system was universal but since Dane requested this session to edify his clueless self, he played the grateful screw-up, ravenous for redemption. After pleading ignorance of the process, he feigned astonishment at its miraculous workings. Dane flipped the pages while his tutors lectured. With wide eyes, effusive head nods, and cramping hand, he scribbled the verbose testimony of a procession of department heads.

He raised his hand effusively in response to one slide.

"Yes?" the presenter asked, baffled by Dane's observance of classroom etiquette and his urgent manner. He was, after all, the only student.

"The red tag copy box leads to the blue ribbon editorial review," Dane said. "Does the copy change between those boxes?"

"All queries must be answered and all copy changes made as required by all processors," the presenter replied.

"I mean, does the folder change color from red to blue?" Dane asked.

"No! However, the copy itself receives a blue stamp," the presenter acknowledged.

"Oh, wow. That is so cool!" Dane gushed and nodded his head so hard that he felt vertebrae crack.

Given the choice of being a resentful, remedial delinquent and an enthusiastic partner in the education process, he chose the latter.

However, like many underachievers forced to repeat a pedagogical step, Dane underestimated the psychic injury inflicted by remediation—the punitive boredom as well as the insult to pride and intellect. The conjunction of his tutors' condescension, primary school pedagogy and the banal subject matter made Dane's mind swim from particulars to a larger picture. Process was no longer *how* work was done; it was the work itself. *Kinko's* could produce ads and brochures; agencies sold process. Advertising people created less and processed more. Process was popular; it covered the greater collective ass.

Dane's hand traced the process chart. He fleshed it out, circled the boxes, added lines and shaded spaces, out of which he made muscles, limbs, a head, torso, extremities and sexual glands. In minutes he had created the process incarnate, a complex evolutional amalgam of *Leviathan, Nude Descending a Staircase* and *Mr. Potato Head.*

His stomach gurgled. He was hungry. He had not gone out for his usual Wednesday *Taco Bell* burritos. The traffic manager was pointing with a red laser at a slide projected on the screen behind her. However, she no longer wore clothes. Her body had a pale brown hue and the shape of a bellows. She had been transformed into a stomach. Sloshing sounds issued from her mouth as her body contracted rhythmically.

Dane's gut responded to the lecturing stomach with a growl of its own. "It's all in the process," his stomach said.

Now another department head took the floor. He had a long, curved back and a bulging stomach, and stood on large, waddling feet. His color was brown and pink and he resembled an intestine. The sounds coming out of his mouth were gurgles and flatulent trumpet notes.

Dane's own gut growled again. "Process of elimination," It quipped. "You're being eliminated. What a waste. Gurgle, gurgle."

"You're being rude!" Dane whispered. "You'll get me in trouble."

"Yes, Dane? Did you have a question?" the speaker asked.

"No, no. It's clear," Dane told the traffic manager without looking up.

A woman stood up. The head of editorial had a ruddy, mobile face, the muscles of which contracted like a heart as she spoke about preparing the perfect manuscript. The sounds that emanated from her were *thumpathumapthumpa* punctuated by a whish.

The process was embodied before his eyes.

"Process makes perfect!" his gut growled. *"Process makes perfect!"*

"Shut up, impudent gut!" Dane shouted. "I won't keep listening to your crap!"

The lecture had stopped. The process mavens stared at Dane as individuals offended not for themselves personally, but in behalf of all civilized human beings who embody a process. He must account for his unspeakable speaking. But what could he tell the department

335

heads to make himself seem less offensive or less insane?

"Sorry. I'm trying to write down every word but my hand is cramping. I'm getting impatient with myself."

"No worries," the editor said sympathetically.

Still, Dane worried.

Dozing off and posing irrelevant questions to stay awake or to aggravate people were standard behavior for Dane. Hallucinating talking body organs and conversations with his gut were legitimate cause for concern. Was he losing control of his incorrigibility? Or was this the latest event in the process of copywriting castration that took root as a loss of sexual feeling, grew into rampant porn abuse, and now blossomed as body organ fetishism and delusional fantasy?

19. PART OF THE FAMILY

The highway was congested that evening. His drive would be longer than usual, but Dane did not mind the commute. It helped him flush out the toxins of the office and reflect on the day. As Dane sat in traffic, he considered the procedure meeting that just passed.

It was clear now that Dane had been lied to about finding a home at UNIHEALTH. The best he could do now was to keep it from destroying his real home.

Dane often took pride that he did not bring the job home with him. However, the shame and frustration he experienced at work were powerful and insidious. They stowed away in his mind and subverted his good intentions.

The sickness first affected his nerves. It masked itself as exhaustion and irritability. He behaved erratically at home. Ordinary details of life he usually ignored—Iris's insolent backtalk, Becky's nervous nagging and their chronic lateness—provoked outbursts that made them all miserable.

Home life offered no refuge or relief. When Dane came home evenings, he had time enough to change clothes and eat dinner. Then he washed dishes while Becky helped Iris with homework. Later, Becky fell asleep. Dane sometimes tried rousing her. He had no feeling in his groin but he hoped that her touch and warmth would revive him. After a long day she curled away from him with sleepy protests and Dane stopped trying to awaken her.

To wind down, he played computer games. After his porn experience at UNIHEALTH, it did not take him long to the mature women porn sites on the computer. In the intimacy of the dark bedroom, with his wife close by, this act was more charged.

Once he had done this a few times, he took risks, visited porn sites while Becky and Iris were awake. One evening, Becky came into the bedroom suddenly to ask him a question.

Dane fumbled to shut down the illicit window, found the x, and pressed it repeatedly with his forefinger but the computer balked and he spontaneously stood up to block the screen. Becky had seen enough.

"Dane, are you insane? You'll be put on a list of people who visit these sites. We'll get a virus," Becky said.

"You can't get STDs from a computer," he said. "Not yet."

"You have a ten-year-old daughter. Do you want her to see that? To see her father looking at that?"

"You're right. I'm sorry. It won't happen again."

Dane was ashamed but couldn't stop.

One evening Iris burst into his bedroom with a question.

"Daddy, who invented the telescope?"

She was behind him. Dane could not click fast enough to eliminate the offending windows. He spread his hands over the screen and turned off the monitor.

"What is that, Daddy?" she asked.

"I'm doing homework for my job, Honey," he replied. "The computer crashed."

The window finally vanished but Dane was a wreck. Iris had a ten- year-old's discretion to accept his response and to ask no more.

She had not looked at the images. Instinctively perhaps, she knew better than to confront her father's shame.

"I'm sick," he thought. "I have to stop."

Case 4-E
BELONG OR BE GONE

20. THE UNITHON

At the end of that fourth week, Dane secured his family's health benefits. He attended the procedural orientation and had no further run-ins with Sylvia or Karen. He believed his personal turbulence at UNIHEALTH was behind him.

Then he received more encouraging news, an email from the director of human resources requiring his presence at *Unithon,* an initiation event for new employees.

"*Unithon* is important," Zach Trench told him. "It's treated like a sacred initiation, when every employee passes from probation to permanent. You can't get out of it. HR gets nasty when you blow off their events. They screw up your vacations, benefits and all else that makes this job meaningful. Go. It's a tribal thing. In the end, every new employee says in unison, '*I am UNIHEALTH.*'"

Unithon sounded like the perfect antidote to Dane's hostile Prostate Team environment. He could meet new employees like himself across the many units of the agency. Everyone described *Unithon* as the best corporate function with the Christmas party as a distant second.

When Dane informed Karen that he would attend *Unithon* on Monday, her face screwed in anger. "You can't. You have to be here. We need you."

"Why do you need me in the morning?"

"The brochure is in editorial. We need a writer to sign off."

"But I'll be here later. *Unithon* is mandatory. I don't want to get

338

a bad name with HR."

"Skip it."

Dane felt like a 14-year-old boy telling his mother he wanted to go to a party. He viewed participation at *Unithon* as his right. He looked forward to receiving the agency pin, signifying permanent employee status. Why was Karen so set against his attendance? Was this really about urgent business or did she want to keep him on probation in perpetuity?

Even if Karen's machinations were real, Dane knew his insistence on attending an unbillable company function was obdurate and immature. If the paycheck was so important, he should put all else aside. Yet, he was sick of being left out and determined not to be deprived of an employee experience. He wanted his UNITHON employment to be official. He wanted to belong.

After a heated discussion, Karen conceded that he could make up his own mind about attending the event. Dane, meanwhile, worked out an internal compromise nobody else knew about or agreed on.

That Monday he woke up early to arrive at the orientation at eight o'clock. He almost collided with a truck as he crossed six lanes to reach the exit and was the first to arrive at the venue. He thought if he attended *Unithon* early, he could return to the office by late morning, fulfilling his belonging needs without neglecting his professional duties.

Unfortunately, *Unithon* was not available in *Lite*. A major event scheduled for a day was too important to squeeze into an hour. By 9:30 only a breakfast had been served and social ice-breaking games were in progress. People declared their happiness to be at UNIHEALTH. They proclaimed how great their teammates and supervisors were.

Dane craved that happiness and wanted to extract some of it vicariously at the *Unithon*. It was not to be because his supervisors and teammates did not want him there. With each blissful testimonial, his anxiety increased until it eclipsed the event. How could he forget that Karen expected him? It was primary school revisited when his parents fought. In class, he was like other pupils but he knew what awaited him at home.

When the orientation recessed, Dane phoned Bevaqua to cover himself. He related his whereabouts and asked if it was cool.

"Dane, it's very bad," Bevaqua said. "You were told to be here."

"I thought it was okay for me to attend *Unithon*. Should I come in?"

"Come in right now. There's work to do."

If Dane had gone straight to the office that morning, he would have despised himself for cowardice. Instead he defied orders and hated himself for putting his job at risk. By attending orientation and leaving early, he angered Bevaqua and his team but never attained the love and belonging at *Unithon* or received the UNIHEALTH pin.

"Good, you're here," Karen said when she saw him, "But if I were you I'd steer clear of Bevaqua. He's furious."

21. EXCLUSION

All morning Dane had nothing to do. The urgent needs he was ordered to the office to address had evidently vaporized. Dane waited for something to happen. He wandered the office and passed Bevaqua in the hall. The creative director said hello and betrayed no anger, which unnerved Dane.

As Dane took stock of his unsettled situation, he received an email from the account director for the prostate franchise, letting him know he would not be needed at the client meeting in two days. This event had been planned for weeks. It was supposed to be Dane's first face time with the client.

Dane barged into Bevaqua's cubicle. The creative director was not surprised to see him and told Dane what he wanted to know.

"Your first five weeks have been rocky. If there is no improvement, I'm afraid you will have to find another home," he said.

After his talk with Bevaqua, Sylvia smiled at Dane from across the corridor and passed by his cubicle. Dane lifted his briefcase. The strap looped around one chair arm and the briefcase smacked Dane in the face. Sylvia laughed. She joked that the briefcase was beating him up.

"Why am I being left out of the client meeting?" Dane asked.

"The meeting is focusing on budget and will probably run long," Sylvia explained. "We don't want to distract the client with creative stuff."

This story did not square with Bevaqua's account. That night Dane explained the situation to Becky.

"They're going to fire you," she said.

"Why would they go out of their way to be nice to me?"

"They're toying with you."

Panic overwhelmed Dane. He felt feverish and sick. He would believe anything to stop his insecurity. He argued with Becky but knew she was right.

22. EXIT STRATEGY

There was one other "private space" in UNIHEALTH and people who entered it looked both ways before entering. The phone room was a hybrid of an old phone booth and a coat closet. It contained a chair, a counter and a phone. It was included in the floor plans in the same spirit as restrooms—as a concession to nature's call, in this case, a personal call.

Dane skulked down the corridor, stopped at the phone room and ducked into it. As long as he had the phone room, he had a lifeline to the world and the hope of escape. A light switch was on the wall but Dane dialed in darkness. He was in a race to quit before getting fired and needed to run it discreetly to avoid suspicion. He could not see the telephone so he continually misdialed—a take-out, a laundry, an Indian banquet hall, a funeral home and people speaking foreign tongues.

During his second week at UNIHEALTH, while he rode the popularity of "the Acorn Project," Dane received a call from a Connecticut agency where he had interviewed during his layoff. He never thought he would need to pursue this opportunity. Now, with his job in peril, Dane returned the call, hoping the position and interest in him were still there.

The Connecticut creative director assured Dane that he would add his name to list of applicants for the staff position. He scheduled an interview for the following morning.

If UNIHEALTH suspected that Dane failed to show up for work because he was interviewing for another job, he would be fired summarily, so he planned a hoax. He phoned Karen at 8 AM in a gravely ill voice—weak, coughing and pained. Her voicemail came on, as he predicted, so it would be hard for her to judge his authenticity.

Why did Dane go through this elaborate ruse to cling to a job he believed he would leave anyway? Competitive fire was a factor. He was playing a game of *Quit or Be Fired* with UNIHEALTH and wanted to win. Pride also played a part. Dane preferred walking away to playing the victim. However, money was the prime motivator. His long layoff had persuaded him that later was always better than sooner when it came to losing income. He was determined to squeeze every dollar he could from UNIHEALTH.

Dane's interviewer for the new job was a creative director of art. His index finger was in his mouth for much of the interview as he probed a piece of caramel wedged in a molar. Otherwise, he treated Dane with great respect. He reviewed his portfolio with interest and gave his verdict at the end. "Great book!" he said. "You're what the creative doctor ordered: A fresh voice. I've been stuck with writing chores and it's gotten stale."

During his drive to UNIHEALTH that afternoon, Dane gave himself dry heaves with his reliable gag-reflex procedure. When he arrived at the cube-world, he was confident he looked like crap.

People were surprised to see him as if they were complicit in his conspiracy to leave. He lumbered about the agency to impress everyone that he had showed up sick.

Late the next afternoon, Sylvia handed Dane a project with corrections to incorporate. She demanded that the manuscript be clean by end of day. Emboldened by his interview, Dane told her he would work until no later than 6 PM. When he was ready to leave, he sent her an e-mail reporting that the manuscript was pretty clean.

"Pretty clean doesn't cut it for our client," Sylvia wrote. "It has to be perfect."

"If you wanted perfect, you should have given it to me yesterday when I came in sick or earlier today. I'm not working late on Friday night because you waited until late Friday afternoon to give me the project."

Sylvia stomped off in a rage and Dane almost laughed. But when Dane heard nothing more about his prospects at the Connecticut agency after the interview, his defiance seemed premature. He went into termination-watch mode.

As Dane walked among the cubicles, his colleagues' eyes whispered, *"Dead man working!"*

A week after the interview the Connecticut creative director phoned to offer Dane the job. Dane was so relieved that a salary cut of a few thousand dollars sounded like a raise.

Still, he was compelled to wait for a week while references and human resources paperwork were processed before an offer sheet was faxed. Dane wrote his resignation letter on April Fool's Day and was eager to submit it. Then he thought, "If I resign today, people will think it's a practical joke." So he postponed it.

23. NEGOTIATED RELEASE

Finally on April 2, Dane was ready to resign.

All morning, Dane kept his sights on Bevaqua. He had a pre-resignation edge. It was the discrepancy between his excitement and the blandness around him. He thought everyone sensed his passage, saw the distance in his eyes and the freedom in his walk. The envelope with his resignation letter was warm and crumpled in his back pocket.

After stalking him all morning, Dane tracked down Bevaqua in his cube early that afternoon. Karen was just leaving. Her furtive manner convinced Dane that she was informing on him but he smiled at her because it no longer mattered.

Bevaqua invited Dane in. He had a thick, half-eaten sandwich on his desk.

"I feel like a dentist today," Bevaqua said. "You know, administering pain to people in a reclining chair."

"I have something for you," Dane said with exaggerated formality.

He extracted the warm, wrinkled envelope from his rear pocket and handed it to Bevaqua with a snap of the wrist and a bowed head.

Bevaqua stared at the envelope in his hand and had a moment of *jamais vu*—he seemed puzzled not by what the envelope contained but by what it was.

"Open it," Dane said impatiently.

The letter was concise. Bevaqua read and grimaced. Then he let it drift from his hand to the desktop like a dry leaf.

"Do you have questions?" Dane asked.

"I need to write down my thoughts before I ask questions," Bevaqua said.

"Yes, that is the procedure," Dane cracked.

"Is something on your mind, Dane-O?" Bevaqua asked with a paternal smile. "I'm here for you!"

"You mean, besides my team going behind my back and your threat to fire me?"

"Yes, moving forward, is there anything else you need off your chest?"

"Besides that my team leader and supervisor mentally abused

344

me, subjected me to public ridicule and trashed my reputation by making me look incompetent?"

"Putting all that aside, is something stuck in your craw?"

"You mean, besides your barring me from my employee initiation?"

"That's right. Is something really eating at you?"

"No, I'm good. That does it for me. I'm going."

"Hold on. Don't be hasty. I had a few thoughts, Dane," Bevaqua said, rubbing his thick cheeks with his meaty hands. "I have a little theory that you might not want certain internet usage on your record."

"What?" Dane froze.

"Have a little thing for naked, do we?"

"Are you blackmailing me?"

"Of course not! We're family here, Dane. We understand."

"You were about to fire me!"

"I never considered it. We need you, Dane. You bring your own special whatever. I was making constructive use of your fear."

"Like you're doing now? It won't work. I used porn for research."

"Research? What kind would that be, Dane? Erection research? Eye-popping, drooling research? Female anatomy research? You should be surfing prostates, not naked ladies."

Dane knew he was caught but would not allow Bevaqua to bulldoze him into staying at UNIHEALTH now so he could fire him later.

"Okay. So I looked at websites. My colleagues saw what I was going through and they gave me the link. I needed it. It was all I had to keep me sane and feeling like a man. When you hired me you never told me honestly what this account was like."

Bevaqua turned his head askance and appraised Dane with a cold, incredulous eye.

"So you were self-medicating with porn. I like that," Bevaqua nodded slowly. "But tell me, Dane, did your therapeutic porn come with a fair balance warning? 'This smut may be harmful to your reputation and may cause lasting damage to your career?"

"No, but I never operated heavy machinery when I was looking at it," Dane said. He turned to leave.

"Wait!" Bevaqua blurted. "What if I move you to another team?"

"Another team?" Dane asked. It never occurred to him that Bevaqua would reassign him. He wondered if this was a play to keep him or a ploy to stall him. "What about prostates?"

"It's time to spread your wings. Just think—dialysis, diabetes, allergies."

Dialysis! Diabetes! Allergies! Dane was exhilarated by the intrigue of these therapeutic areas and by Bevaqua's extemporaneous effort to keep him. Maybe he had found a real home at UNIHEALTH, after all—a place where people insulted and threatened you, and made you want to leave before they begged you to stay.

"You think a reassignment could be arranged?" Dane asked.

"I can't guarantee it," he said. "I'll have to get back to you in a few days.

"I don't have a few days," Dane replied, regaining his resolve. "I've accepted another position."

"So, you've made other arrangements," Bevaqua euphemized. "Good luck. You've done good work here."

The two men shook hands and Bevaqua reiterated his praise for Dane. This final meeting ended like their first interview two months before—as if nothing happened in between.

Dane informed Karen of his resignation while she was in her cubicle, glowering at a MAC G6 monitor as she struggled with a layout. "I'm not surprised," she responded to his news as she continued to click away. "I told you it was a difficult account. It couldn't have been pleasant for you. I had fun working with you at times. I hope you find your acorn."

He had been sure Karen was against him but now she deprived him of this certainty. She seemed less an adversary than an observer speculating on outcomes. Dane did not understand how a person could appreciate him and want him gone at the same time. In Karen's view, Dane's UNIHEALTH experience followed a predictable arc. Yet he walked away from her, confused and dissatisfied.

24. NO GOOD BYES

In his final weeks at UNIHEALTH there were two major events. Dr. Mooney sent an email:

> It is with mixed feelings that I must announce my retirement. I will still consult and come to the office on occasion. I love the people at UNIHEALTH (of course platonically, ladies...no sexual harassment intended!) and I will miss you all.

Everyone was sad to learn Dr. Mooney's news since it was widely believed his retirement would be so gradual as to be imperceptible. For a few days Dr. Mooney disappeared. This prompted little concern since he had other clients. Then, one morning in the men's room, Zach Trench told Dane that the venerable Dr. Mooney had been found unconscious in a stall with his pants around his ankles and his hand gripping his penis. He had suffered a stroke.

The UNIHEALTH managers protected their icons. They never disclosed the details of Dr. Mooney's illness to the largely female staff, who adored Dr. Mooney like a lovable uncle. It would have besmirched his image and put every male employee under a cloud of perversion.

Dane recalled the last time he saw Dr. Mooney. It was the day he tendered his resignation. Dr. Mooney stopped by his cubicle to tell him that testosterone converted to estrogen in certain mice, a phenomenon which baffled macho scientists. This apparently useless information made little impact on Dane, caught up as he was in his new freedom. Yet, in retrospect, he pondered whether Dr. Mooney's story of the hormone-switching mice was a parable with a profound life message. If so, what could it be? That virility was impermanent? That hormones could not be trusted?

When Dr. Mooney heard Dane was leaving, he handed him his card.

"Maybe you can use me in your new agency," he said.

Dane found it strange that Dr. Mooney solicited business at the point of retiring. Retirement might not have been his idea. Perhaps he masturbated in the men's room to lift his spirits.

In retrospect, Dane wondered if Dr. Mooney's report on trans-hormone mice was a cry for help. "Of course, how could I be so obtuse?" Dane chastised himself for his insensitivity until he recalled a more damning detail. When they first met, Dr. Mooney told Dane he was taking a free supply of STRIDALL, due in part to Dane's superb direct mail. Could STRIDALL, whose mode of action was unknown, have triggered the stroke?

Dane researched the side effects of STRIDALL in the prescribing information. There it was under "Adverse Events:" a 5% occurrence of cerebral ischemia."

"I made him sick!" Dane told Becky that evening. "If only my writing weren't so persuasive."

"Your writing didn't give the man a stroke. He's seventy years old. You don't know what he ate or his genetic makeup," Becky said. "For all you know he ate steak and cheeseburgers every night."

"He did eat a lot of Danishes," Dane reflected before he was buffeted by another wave of guilt. "No, it's not that easy. Don't you see? I almost killed a man with my writing! A good man."

"It was a free sample. Maybe he didn't take it correctly. Maybe he stopped taking it. You don't know."

This suggestion stopped Dane's hysterical self-incrimination long enough for him to think. Dr. Mooney had only a month's supply of STRIDALL. By now he would have surely run out, well before his stroke occurred. If he was still taking STRIDALL then he and his doctor, not Dane, were to blame.

It rained on the day after Dane heard about Dr. Mooney's stroke. He brought a chocolate mousse cake to UNIHEALTH in his honor. All morning, Dane stopped by the kitchen to see how the cake was doing. After an hour, only a quarter of the cake had been eaten. Dane was demoralized. Even his generosity failed. Later he passed the kitchen and noted that only a quarter of the mousse cake remained. Dane was gratified. He might have failed as a writer at UNIHEALTH but his desserts were a success.

25. LAST WRONGS

Dane had only a few days left when another tragedy befell the UNIHEALTH family. Toby Bowles, a promising junior account executive, was found dead on her kitchen floor.

Toby had become a UNIHEALTH legend, not merely for her unsurpassed work ethic but for her extraordinary effort to lose weight. In the course of one miraculous year, Toby worked her way up at UNIHEALTH from office assistant to traffic manager to junior account executive and down from 300 lbs to a svelte 150. In the process, Toby was involved in a romance that made all UNIHEALTH employees feel warm and hopeful. She fell in love with Vibert, the mailroom manager, and they were engaged to be married.

Dane knew the story of Toby and Vibert from hearsay, but he never witnessed their mutual fondness bud under fluorescent lights during late night projects and blossom into passion at the company Christmas party. There, at the Parsippany Hilton, Toby and Vibert crashed a wedding reception in the hotel's other banquet hall and helped themselves to that party's superior refreshments. When their trespass was discovered and they were pursued by security guards, they dashed across the lobby and bolted from the hotel, carefully holding their heaping platters before them, laughing and exulting in their mischief.

Tragically, this was the last carefree moment the lovers shared.

Soon after this caper of gourmandizing affection, Toby made a life-changing choice. She underwent a lap band procedure because she wanted to lose weight "to be pretty for Vibert." She called the lap band, a "wedding band inside" that bonded her forever to her man. Four months later, her mother found her on the kitchen floor of the Bayonne home they shared. Toby had a thoracic aneurism and died without regaining consciousness.

All UNIHEALTH employees convened in the atrium the day after Toby died. It was Dane's penultimate day and the sky was a shroud covering the atrium skylight. Many colleagues came forward to recall how much Toby grew as a person in the short time they knew her, how she accepted responsibilities and met every challenge.

"She was always the last to leave," Sylvia Befunkewicz said. "And you know if I say so it must be true."

Others recounted that Toby was just hitting her stride and her love of Vibert was the final piece in her personal puzzle. Van trips to Toby's wake were planned.

Dane had no clear interest in attending Toby's wake. He never met the deceased. He had no chance to chat with her, to banter, to share pithy insights and personal dreams. Anyway, Dane was leaving the next day and aimed for an inconspicuous departure.

What incited Dane to crash the wake of a stranger? Even as he separated from UNIHEALTH, Dane needed to belong. Not knowing Toby did not prevent him from mourning her. Rather, it intensified his sense of loss. Toby was all that Dane was not—devoted to her job and agency. Toby's entire life transpired at UNIHEALTH. Dane, by contrast, held on at UNIHEALTH for two months and left when it became unbearable. In Toby, Dane saw his tragic potential and experienced vicariously the belonging he missed. She was the UNIHEALTH employee in everyone. By paying his respects to her, Dane honored all pharma workers with no way out and mitigated his guilt for leaving the agency in a car rather than a box.

Dane drove to the Jersey City funeral home so he could come and go as he pleased and take a private tour into his past. Years before, Dane had taught at the state university in Jersey City. He had once admired the old Gothic houses of clapboard and dark red brick, with their steep slate roofs, turrets and dormer windows, and imagined he could live in their obscure splendor. Now in the late afternoon rain, the gorgeous elements looked like undigested architecture, remote and miserable, foreshadowing the grim event to which he was an uninvited guest.

The mortuary had a black, brick façade. Its awning was suspended over the sidewalk, a jet shroud held aloft by gold posts. "Sitwell and Sons Funeral Home" was inscribed in gold Gothic letters with a ghoulish dignity. Dane entered with others in diffident respect. He confronted three concurrent mysteries—death, the deceased and his motive for coming. Would he be vilified as an emotional vulture gorging on the sorrow of grieving kin and colleagues?

As Dane trudged into the viewing room, he pretended this was only a community gathering. He ignored the sullen drapes, wood-paneled walls and floral aerosol. The open casket rested on a raised bier before a hearth, drawing visitors to the void. Dane wondered if the fireplace was a homey touch or multitasked as a mini-crematorium. Dane had been to one viewing in his life. As the UNIHEALTH contingent filed past the open casket, Dane followed the other mourners and lowered his eyes.

Suddenly, Toby lay under his down-turned eyes, her wide, stiff body in a blue dress filling space but seemingly weightless on black velvet. Toby's freckled face was faithful to the enlarged photograph in the atrium but Dane was meeting her for the first time. *Meeting her?* The embalming fluid, masked by powders and pomades, must have shot to his head. As he struggled to connect with Toby's corpse, Dane was conflicted by two infinite distances—death and the impossibility of knowing a departed stranger.

He felt like a registered imposter, mistrusted and despised. His throat throbbed against his collar. He could barely swallow or

351

breathe. His soon-to-be-former colleagues whispered their farewells to Toby. Dane overheard someone confide that she never looked better. It seemed irrelevant, even cruel, but they knew her and could be pardoned for saying the wrong things. Dane had no words and nowhere to find them. He agonized over what to say to Toby's corpse and wondered if her soul could hear. Was small talk permissible? Or should he tell her lifeless body that he was using her death to bond with the living and to experience by proxy the belonging her life epitomized? Would someone overhear his confession and berate him for it? He knew nothing of eschatology but dreaded the impact a false word might have on the departed and on himself.

"I'm sorry I never met you," Dane muttered to dead Toby. "I'm sorry you died trying to make somebody happy because now they're sadder than ever. But you're lucky because people cared about you. You belonged."

Suddenly, dead Toby's eyes opened. She glared at Dane and said, "Lucky? I'm dead! I didn't think I could feel worse, but congratulations! You've done it. Now get out!"

Dane lurched backward. After the shock of being denounced by a corpse, mortification set in. Did anyone hear Toby's outcry? Was he insane? Clearly his stiff-side manner could be improved. Dane glanced furtively at other mourners for a hint that they had witnessed the miraculous *rigor mortis*. The mourners stared at Dane with disapproval for his pathological immaturity. Bevaqua was impeccably elegiac, as polished here as in the agency boardroom. His bulbous eyes issued Dane a solemn reproach, "Suck it up—with dignity."

Although no one acknowledged Dane's presence, he felt surrounded by appropriate people, trapped by their gravity and his own awkwardness. He could not remain among these strangers but was unable to leave. Then he noticed Vibert seated on a chair, staring at the casket, fingers covering his face. Losing Toby was a vicious blow to the mailroom manager. She would have helped him raise his teenage daughter and they might have started a family together. Now he was condemned to manage the mailroom without the woman he loved. Dane crouched by the bereaving boyfriend and said, "I'm sorry for your loss."

Vibert's eyes were red, despairing but peaceful. "Thank you. I'm sorry, too."

Dane patted Vibert's shoulder and left. Despite himself, he had stumbled on the right thing to say.

The UNIHEALTH office was nearly vacant when he returned. He erased all traces of himself from his computer and set his papers in right angles on the desk for a neat final impression. His departure went unnoticed.

Crossing the parking lot for one last time, Dane marveled at the UNIHEALTH building of glass and concrete in the middle of nowhere. Was it true he had worked here for two months?

Driving in the rain, Dane summarized his UNIHEALTH experience by counting the events between his hire and resignation. It was like looking for patterns in raindrops before the wipers scattered them. His reeling finances had stabilized but his new job in Connecticut would take him even farther from home. He was exhausted and anxious, and still had a dull ache in his groin. Was this how discharged patients felt after a traumatic event?

AD NOMAD 5
SUPERVISORY WARNING

Case 5-A
ROAD WORRIER & CAKE CRUSADER

1. THE ROAD TO WINTON

Dane approached his new job at Mentos Advertising ("Minds Marketing Medicine") with a stoic calculation: he needed the check more than he hated the trek. Each morning started with certain failure. To arrive at work on time, he needed to cover the 41 miles between New York and Winton in under an hour, but Winton was unreachable in less than 70 minutes.

The commute wrecked Dane's faith in maps. Rand McNally drew Route 95 as a wide-bodied anaconda, yet Dane knew it was more annelid than snake—multiple segments stitched into one absorbent traffic organism that sucked hope out of motorists.

In two dimensions, Route 95 appeared direct, even accommodating, but it was chaos in concrete—mangled and treacherous from wheels and weather. Cruising in one stretch, Dane wallowed in congestion in the next. As exhausts wafted to his windshield, he fumed at the dashboard clock. An inch between Winton and New York in the atlas might as easily have marked the distance between Earth and Mars.

Other features of his morning routine compounded his agony. Each morning he drove Iris to school six miles south, then reversed direction, returning to his original starting point at 8:10 AM, where traffic merged from three states. This was where his workday began.

Each leg of the trip had a unique character. When the warped, narrow streets south of his neighborhood were vacant, they were his launching pad. He defied city gravity by making every light, sped across a bridge over a crooked creek called *Spuyten Duyvil*, accelerated on a ramp and careened around a blind curve under an overpass, before injecting his car into the clogged interstate artery. The gouged and glutted Cross Bronx Expressway—phlegmatic as a subway—then widened to the broad New England Throughway athwart lower Westchester and Connecticut's Gold Coast.

After corporate Stamford's lane closures, miles of sun-beaten straightaway ensued, concluded by a last, agonizing lap on a local Winton road, where black and white squad cars patrolled like fuel-injected orcas. Dane could never appreciate the colonial charm of Winton High School with its white cupola or other architectural gems on the scenic route because his vision was impaired by a tardy man's remorse.

2. THE CAKED CRUSADER

Self-examination was a painful side effect of Dane's commute. As he struggled with traffic, he reviled himself.

"Why can't you find work in your area code?" he asked rhetorically. "It was 36 miles to UNIHEALTH; now it's 41 miles to Mentos! Ambitious people go the extra mile, but you're going *five* extra miles!" he ranted. "That's commitment you can be committed for...*Hey, I like that headline.*"

"I must have committed a crime in another life," he mused. "Or maybe I was a centipede and this is an improvement." Gradually Dane's thinking moved from metaphysical to political. "It's a conspiracy!" he raved. "But who's behind it? I bet Goldfarb would know!"

Even when he maneuvered his 4-cylinder Toyota like a stock car, Dane rarely made it to Mentos before 9:15. He went through the glass doors like an outcast. At Mentos, unlike New York agencies, people worked 9-to-5, but Dane could not benefit from a typical work day.

As a new employee, his lateness already showed signs of being chronic, which went unmentioned, but not unremarked. His boss, Dick Spilkus, warned that Connecticut people were uptight like New Yorkers, only more genteel.

Dane was stung by the rebuke. He knew this was no way to start a job, especially not as a supervisor. People reported to him! Was he setting a good example?

However, if nothing else, advertising taught him this: you could not prevent people from judging you but you could influence their judgment. If his tardiness was a given, he must give the people of Mentos something else to talk about. A public relations move was in order. The one he made was from his last job.

"Let them eat cake!" Dane thought.

Rain Bread had made Dr. Mooney an icon, so Dane introduced it to Mentos. Since Dane's image needed urgent care he could not wait for rain; he brought coffee cake every morning from a neighborhood bakery and placed the baked offering on the kitchen counter. John, a retired cousin of the agency owner, who did odd jobs including brewing coffee, showed Dane the plates and utensils. Staff employees moseyed in. "You brought cake?" a colleague exclaimed. "How lovely! Does it have processed sugar? Too bad! I can't eat it. But it's so sweet of you!"

The gift of cake was a crude public relations gesture, yet it communicated multiple messages. It told the Mentos staff that Dane was not a colleague so much as a guest from afar, who had the good manners not to visit empty-handed and thus deserved their consideration. *Cakesmanship*, as Dane coined his action, also provided an escuse for his lateness. People might think, *"He stood in line at a bakery to buy this cake,"* thus transforming his truancy to self-sacrifice.

It did not take long for Dane to idealize his political tactic into a nobler concept. He viewed himself as a missionary, bearing urban sweets to distant *burbs*—a pompous presumption since it was Connecticut, not some far-flung rain forest. The flaw Dane never saw in his plan was that unprompted generosity might be seen as bizarre rather than righteous.

Glucose Diplomacy, as Dane labeled his policy, was overall a shrewd preemptive strike at his colleagues' skepticism. As staid locals, they probably wondered why Dane drove so far for a job. Was he damaged goods? But as long as Dane was sating their collective sweet tooth, they did not insist on an answer.

Dane also knew *cakesmanship* was a gamble. It could get stale and send the wrong message. There was the case of Ivan Blinsky, a language professor Dane knew from his teaching days. Blinsky was a lumbering man with thick lips and bulging eyes, who panted and spoke with a lisp. Blinsky's prestige at the university had dwindled to nothing despite his seniority and Ivy League degree. His classes were often cancelled and his department was eliminated. With no office of his own, Dr. Blinsky tramped across campus in a frayed raincoat and damp sneakers, with a bag of books and a box of donuts, which he handed out wherever he parked his carcass. Dane now understood the stark motive behind Blinsky's sweets. Each donut beseeched, "Don't hate me!" The bribe worked. People did not hate Ivan Blinsky; they pitied him.

Now Dane had one more question to ask himself in traffic: was he turning into the Ivan Blinsky of advertising?

3. THE BOSS

Every job, Dane had learned, began and ended with a boss. He knew this because he had started and ended with several bosses.

Dick Spilkus, the executive vice president/executive creative director at Mentos, had thirty years of advertising experience. A private man with a grave face, Dick spoke softly but growled when vexed. After decades of uncertainty and struggle, Dick had a survivor's irony, which yielded sparks of sardonic humor when his dark mood lifted.

Dane spent time with Spilkus to learn about Mentos but mainly to learn about Spilkus. Dick had the irascible, weary air of an ambivalent family man dragged through life by responsibilities. His son was in a Caribbean dental school and his daughter was a college senior. Dick was always on the phone with industry friends, cadging an entry-level job for his daughter. Editing her résumé was Dane's first assignment and he would have considered it demeaning if it had not given him a chance to bond with his boss.

"You're a good father," Dane said. "I wish my dad did this for me. Come to think of it, I wish I had a dad."

Dick laughed in hiccups in response to Dane's "joke" only to settle into moroseness.

"It's not for her," Dick replied. "She'd rather sit on her ass. My accountant says I have too many people on the payroll. I'm trying to get her *off* the payroll."

The conversation hit a patch of temporary silence.

"So how'd you spend your weekend?" Dick asked Dane.

"It was quiet," Dane admitted modestly. "I went swimming and clothes shopping with my daughter, got a parking ticket, watched basketball on TV and vacuumed."

"Exciting," Dick deadpanned.

"That's my life," Dane replied. "What did you do?"

"Saturday night my wife and I went to the Galleria in White Plains."

"Isn't it a long way to go for a mall?" Dane asked, breaking a rule of office conversation by posing a question to which he knew the answer.

"A forty minute drive," Dick said. "We don't shop. I like to walk around and look at the people."

"Don't you have people closer by you can look at?" Dane asked with reckless indiscretion.

"Yeah, but I see them all the time."

"Aren't there malls in Connecticut?" Dane asked, doggedly trying to make sense of Dick's weekend excursion.

"Our malls are full of teenagers. The people at the Galleria are elegant and upscale."

Dane ran out of questions before the dialogue caused permanent

AD NOMAD   Eric Jay Sonnenschein

damage to his professional relationship with Dick. Spilkus shifted to business.

"I know the creative tools you bring to our shop. That's why I hired you," Spilkus said. "But I need you to manage here. You're supervising a writer and three editors."

Dick summarized the agency's copy department and its problems. In two minutes, Dane noted that the copy department had more problems than employees. His first mission was to reconcile Barbara, the senior writer, and Ralph, the senior editor.

"I want you to interview them," Dick said. "Learn who they are *as people...*"

"As opposed to who they are as plants or insects?" Dane asked. By injecting inappropriate humor in a serious conversation, Dane was playing fast and loose with the rules of office conversation etiquette.

He got away with the wisecrack or so it seemed. Dick responded to Dane's sarcasm by pressing his tongue between his teeth to make a vile, sucking noise.

"Get to the root of the conflict and cut it out. Make them work together," he said. "Advertising is a people business. And one more thing. Make sure Barbara shapes up."

"Is something wrong with her?"

Dick grimaced and stroked his neck to check the closeness of his shave.

"Where do I start? She's insubordinate. Unreliable. Often absent. She's a piece of work that needs working on."

"May I ask a dumb question?"

"Go ahead. Answering them is my specialty."

"If Barbara's so bad, why does she work here?

"A good question gets a dumb answer. I don't know. She has her good points, but I haven't found them. That's your job. Now get out there and manage."

Case 5-B
MANAGING THE MOMENT

4. MANAGE WITH CARE

Managing the copy department was a step up in Dane's advertising career and a step back to teaching. Like any employee who ever smarted from an overseer's abuse, he pledged to do things differently when he was in charge and to rectify every wrong he ever experienced. This was his chance to be the boss he never had.

Dane did not merely embrace the chance to lead and solve problems; he craved it. Judgment and objectivity were instincts that had lain dormant in him since he entered corporate life. Now he could hone them into fine instruments. Dane did not lust for power. His mission was to help people collaborate for a common good. He wished to be a boss he would respect, not resent. In this regard, one item in Spilkus's briefing troubled Dane. Dick expected Dane to boss people around, especially Barbara, the other writer. Why would Dick turn one writer against another, man against woman? Was he giving Dane sanction to bully Barbara like it was his sexist birthright?

Meanwhile, Ralph, the senior editor, had to be reckoned with. He was on probation for fighting with Marie, a tempestuous account executive/traffic manager and former bartender. What did probation mean at Mentos? Dane had no idea.

He would need to make determinations and enforce them, but first he had to investigate. He needed to interview the conflicting parties.

5. THE RETICENT WRITER

Barbara was the first to be interviewed.

She stood at his office doorway like a curious spectator until he invited her in.

Barbara was slow, deliberate and taciturn. Before she opened her mouth, Spilkus's assessment of her ran through Dane's mind with the speed of prejudice. Barbara had florid cheeks, suggesting a penchant for drink. Vaguely overweight, she wore a large flannel shirt to cover her torso. Nonetheless, her pendulous breasts shifted when she moved, suggesting that her modesty had no need for undergarments. One exception to Barbara's dishevelment was a well-cut mass of honey blond hair, the feature she clearly valued most. All told, she seemed a rustic recluse, insouciant of public opinion.

But Dane could not close the book on Barbara yet. As a manager, he had to see the data from different angles. Her appearance might yield alternative meanings, which fairness compelled him to explore.

Red cheeks could result from hypertension or a brisk walk with her pet. Exposed shirt-tails might be a fashion statement, a lack of affectation or no time for laundry. Yet, from all perspectives, Barbara was the most poorly groomed woman Dane had ever seen who was not a dog-walker or panhandler. He concluded that she was depressed.

Dane mused, "How can I manage her when she doesn't manage herself?" And what would management of Barbara entail?

Dane's first ever subordinate stared at him, frankly wondering when he would tell her why she was there.

"I'm Dane Bacchus. I'm a writer and I've been hired to manage the copy department. I'll need your help."

Barbara stared at him without speaking. She apparently did not accept Dane's empowerment, camaraderie, or his appeal for help.

Dane tried outflanking her intransigence with a chat.

"So how long have you been here?"

"Twelve years."

"Were you always in advertising?"

"I was in public relations before I switched to textbook publishing. From there I moved to a magazine. Then I was a medical editor. Now this."

"Are you from around here?"

"A few towns up the road."

"That's great. So you don't have a long commute."

"No. It's convenient, I guess."

Barbara had nothing to prove and less to say. She had worked for a science association and a magazine. She was a writer and editor. Did she have a family, children? She did not say.

The interview encountered a long pause as Dane struggled for another job-related question. The silence deteriorated from awkward to painful and Barbara felt the need to put them both out of their misery.

"I've worked here for twelve years," she said. "I live in the same house in Newster where I grew up with my dog. My brother's a lush who works at a *Valvoline* car center. That's about it. Do you need me for anything else because I have a project going out tomorrow."

"You can tell I'm not very boss-like," Dane said frankly.

"That's refreshing. I guess," she said dryly. "The last supervisor loved to play boss."

Dane was encouraged by her response. Finally, he had said the right thing and the interview was going somewhere. He believed he was gaining her trust and might now obtain candid answers from her about the copy department.

"Dick mentioned a conflict in the department. It's my job to resolve it."

"Good luck."

"Thanks," Dane said, ignoring the badness of her good wishes. "So can you tell me about it? The conflict?"

"One word—Ralph."

"The senior editor?"

"Yes."

"How does he cause conflict?"

"He changes copy without telling me, then justifies it by saying it has to be this way, according to the American Medical Association."

"He doesn't just correct grammatical mistakes and suggest changes for your approval?"

"He changes words—because he feels like it."

"That's outrageous," Dane declared. After one minute he had blown his administrative neutrality. It must have been a negative record, he thought, like a fighter getting knocked out in the first minute of the first round. He needed Barbara to know he was a writer who shared her concerns in order to gain her trust, but not at the expense of objectivity.

"He's an asshole," Barbara explained.

If Dane agreed that Ralph was an asshole before even shaking his hand he knew he could no longer manage the department.

"We have to work with Ralph, so we can't call him an asshole."

"*You* can't but I can," Barbara said.

"So what do you write about here?"

"I work on all the ophthalmology products for Tiny Anderson."

Dane's gut told him Barbara was not impressed by him as a supervisor. She seemed unhappily secure in her role, a status to which he aspired. He considered asking her to speculate about why Dick disparaged her but this seemed a short cut to a cul-de-sac.

"When I talk to Ralph, is there a question you want me to ask him?"

"Ask him what makes him a flaming asshole. He knows everything but I bet he can't answer that one."

6. THE VERBOSE EDITOR

Dane met Ralph later that day. If Barbara was soft, ruddy and round, Ralph was all angles, bone, pallor, and edge. He dressed with meticulous accuracy. Every button was buttoned, the collar was crisp, and pleats, hems and creases were razor sharp. Just as creatives bound their merit in portfolios, the senior editor's appearance was his best editorial work.

Ralph loved to talk but editorial review conditioned him to revise, which made his speech deliberate and slow. He qualified every statement and glanced away intermittently as if checking a teleprompter. Dane had known people to speak in digressions and asides, but Ralph was the first person he met who spoke in clean, annotated copy.

"I hear there's conflict in the copy department," Dane said.

"Really?" Ralph blinked with astonishment behind his metal-rimmed glasses. "May I inquire as to your source for this claim?"

"My source? Dick Spilkus, the creative director. It's common knowledge that you and Barbara have had your differences."

Ralph shrugged. "It's always been my policy not to get involved in office politics. I just do my job. Anybody who has read my journal, emails and letters knows this about me. I'll provide them as sources if you like."

"I don't need backup and I won't read your journal. I'm not accusing you," Dane said. "Dick asked me to solve the problem. All I want is for things to run well."

"That's all I want!" Ralph affirmed with emphatic nods. "I am committed to doing the best possible job and to ensuring that every printed item this agency produces is professional and correct." Ralph's Adam's apple was bouncing in his neck. "My views are documented in my application cover letter."

"Yes. That's great. And now we want the department to be cohesive and cooperative. Barbara said she was upset when you changed her copy without consulting her."

"Oh, she was!" Ralph's eyes widened. His head turned and bowed as if he had been slapped. In profile, his scimitar nose and sharp eyes made him resemble a raptor. "I never did that. It's against my professional standards and against the Mentos editorial guide, which, by the way, I wrote."

"So you're claiming she invented the entire story. You never changed a word."

"I have changed a word or phrase on occasion but only to make it consistent with language developed earlier. I never took creative license or inserted my words in the place of the writer's."

"That sounds reasonable," Dane said to put the editor at temporary ease. He wondered if Ralph was disingenuous, delusional or obtuse—or any combination thereof. How could he deny a conflict with Barbara when she called him an "asshole" to his face? Did arrogance make him oblivious to others? Dane identified Ralph as someone who might not be reasoned with, only subdued. He dreaded such people but occasionally wished he were like them.

"I have utmost respect for writers," Ralph averred. "But as an editor I must be sure that each piece is coherent, correct and consistent."

"Yes, of course."

"You can rely on me. You want things to run smoothly and I will do all I can to help."

Ralph's declarations of unity and support were so emphatic they gave Dane a headache. Each utterance was empty, yet correct—an editorial masterpiece, displaying a strict adherence to rules. Dane studied Ralph for a self-revealing tendency—and found one. While summarizing his background, Ralph mentioned he was a writer before switching to editorial work for a more stable income. The repressed writer inside Ralph might be emerging like a guerilla fighter to take potshots at Barbara's copy.

When Ralph left, Dane was spent.

In his first round as a manager, Dane had settled nothing. He could not even induce the parties to acknowledge a conflict existed. He did not change Barbara's mind about Ralph or prevail upon Ralph to speak candidly about Barbara. The one insight Dane extracted from this muddle was that both Barbara the writer and Ralph the editor occasionally did one another's jobs and did not observe the professional boundaries between them. Dane still presided over a mess.

7. (Y) OUR TOWN

Frustrated by his sputtering attempts at managing his department, Dane fled the office and explored his new neighborhood, Winton's upscale and scenic downtown.

When he started at Mentos, Dane believed working in Winton was a privilege that would reward him aesthetically. It was a lovely town with a long history and distinctive character. Winton was different from anywhere he had ever worked or lived.

A colleague once philosophized that where you worked meant less than what you were working on, yet Winton provided Dane a splendid exile. He found solace from his work anxieties in the quiet, congenial burg. Everyday circa 2 PM, he crossed the slush-covered bridge over the estuary that lifted and fell in the heart of Winton's downtown. The Sasquatch River gave the bedroom community the timeless charm of an old, coastal village. Dane inhaled the redolent, ocean-saturated air and thought how great it was to be in such a novel environment. Winton was not New York but it was somewhere. It was a cultural landmark—colonial Williamsburg without costumes.

This was Goldfarb's adopted home. Dane tried to visualize his downtrodden Integrimedicom friend in this haughty habitat. He traipsed by the YMCA where Goldfarb swam each morning before his commute, then proceeded up the Old Post Road past a ramshackle house standing in the rear of an undulating lawn like a craggy promontory. The spectral manse personified Winton like the Empire State Building symbolized New York. A gnarled elm hovered over the lawn like a demented sentry.

Within a week, Dane had taken in Winton. He had sampled a pastrami sandwich from the best deli in the Connecticut Gold Coast and devoured a slice from a family pizzeria serving pies to Wintonians for fifty years. Other stores on Main Street were generic—a chain pharmacy, a *KFC* and a *Banana Republic*—but Dane deleted these from his image of old Winton as an enlightened upper-class town, unique in Gold Coast County for welcoming Jews and minorities.

Yet, despite a gracious veneer and its unique liberal heritage, which set it apart from other exclusive towns, Winton conferred an aura of entitlement on its residents and issued visitors a tacit guest pass.

Dane felt like a "day worker" in Winton. Yet, pizza remained a great social equalizer and Winton's pizzeria was equal to any in New York. He would not deny himself a succulent slice even when he felt out of place consuming it. His concentration enabled him to shut out all but the mastication of sauce, dough and cheese. And unlike New York playgrounds, where adults without children were barred, Winton's venerable pizzeria welcomed all customers. However, among its regulars—high school students and moms with children in tow—Dane felt like a degenerate, particularly in his old trench coat.

One day while he paid for his pizza, the counterman inquired if he wanted a drink. "No, thanks, sodas only increase my thirst!" Dame replied. The counterman shot Dane a look, took his two bills and slid a penny across the counter, though the slice was two dollars even. Was the penny his way of saying Dane was cheap for not ordering a drink? Dane fumed but swallowed the slight because he never boycotted great pizza.

And so his attempt to integrate himself in his work environs went about as well as his effort to manage at Mentos.

8. THE GLOVE

After his initial departmental probe, Dane agonized over how to make peace in his department. For a week he considered tactics to bring together the two intractable foes. He made no progress until one morning, as he drove to work, a *McDonald's* billboard over Route 95 triggered an epiphany.

He would take Barbara to lunch, forge an alliance and together they would convince Ralph to respect her copy. It was a one-sided start, which was understandable since Dane was a writer, and editorial interference was an abuse he had suffered and wished to rectify. Yet, Dane was optimistic that if Ralph respected Barbara's ownership of her words, she would abide by his editorial judgment. Once these boundaries were established and peace restored, Dane would take Barbara and Ralph out to lunch together and suggest ways they might use their overlapping skills as a team.

After this managerial epiphany, Dane might have been well-advised to call it a day's work and turned off at the next exit since he had used up his allotment of good moments for the day. Just as cruising speed on Route 95 swiftly regressed into mysterious slow-downs, Dane's can-do attitude had a way of reversing itself due to annoyances which cascaded into debacles.

First, his beloved cartridge pen slipped from his pants pocket while he was driving. When he parked in the garage and searched for the pen under his seat, the pin holding the leather wristband to the watchcase popped a spring, allowing his watch to slide off his wrist. If he tried slipping the spring in place, it would jump from his fingers and be eternally lost in the car upholstery. The day was on a downward spiral when Dane took himself in hand.

"Stop the childish compulsion, Dane!" he chided. "You're a manager now."

Dane glanced at his watch and saw that he was late. He stopped obsessing over little objects and got out of the car. It was a small victory over his dark side—and only 9:20 AM, "on time," if he was awarded a twenty minute handicap.

As he dashed to the stairway labeled "EXIT," Dane noticed Ralph, the senior editor, crossing the garage from the other end.

"If Ralph comes in now, I'm not late," Dane reassured himself. He surmised that Ralph was as punctual as he was precise.

Though the editor was a reliable time marker, Dane did not want to talk to him. He raced up the stairs without acknowledging Ralph or waiting for him. Minutes later, the editor appeared in his office with

Dane's gloves in his right hand.

"Did you lose these?"

Seeing his most recent birthday gift in the hand of his underling and potential nemesis stunned Dane. He sensed his managerial stature crumbling.

"I did? Where did you find them?" Dane asked.

"On the stairs."

"Right. Thanks. They must have fallen off my hands—I mean, out of my hands. I was rushing. I was late."

Dane was ashamed of losing his gloves, but more so by how he lost them—by avoiding Ralph. In returning them, the editor let Dane know that he was unavoidable. More importantly, he showed Dane how colleagues should treat one another.

"Don't mention it," Ralph replied. As he turned to leave, Dane felt contrite. He had misjudged Ralph. The editor might have dumped the gloves in the trash or taken them for himself.

"Wait, Ralph. I appreciate what you've done. Can you join me for lunch tomorrow?"

"You don't have to do that."

"I know, but I want to. It won't be fancy, but please be my guest."

Ralph agreed.

Impulsively, Dane had jumpstarted the reconciliation process but not in the way he planned.

Lunch with Ralph held political risk. Barbara would view it as a shift in the balance of power against her. To mitigate this impression, Dane packaged the event in such a way that Barbara would dismiss it. Dane and Ralph went to the Chinese take-out in town and had their lunch on a bench near the marshes along the river.

"You must think I've got a big ego," Ralph confided. "But my whole career has been about reducing the size of my ego. I once edited books until I lost my job. Then I edited articles at a magazine before the magazine folded. So, now I edit ads and promotional brochures. My next career move will probably be editing haikus."

Dane laughed. It was a surprisingly self-deprecating and whimsical remark from someone who seemed tightly wound and serious. Maybe Dane could work with Ralph, after all, and bring about departmental peace.

As they ate, Dane believed Ralph had relaxed enough to discuss his conflict with Barbara.

"So what can we do to make peace?" Dane asked.

"The problems have been overblown," Ralph replied. "You know how people get under pressure. That's all it is."

Faced with the same denial of reality as before, Dane felt cheated and ashamed for having lunch with Ralph. Although his gesture was to reciprocate a kindness, Dane hoped to catch the editor off guard and talk business. Ralph, however, was too canny for that.

Full of remorse, Dane stopped by Barbara's cubicle when he returned to the office. Instinct dictated that he control the damage before she found out about his lunch with Ralph and the reconciliation plan was ruined.

"So you and Ralph had lunch," Barbara said.

"How did you know?" Dane stammered, caught off guard.

"I was doing errands and saw you cross the bridge."

"He found my gloves so I took him to lunch."

"You don't need to explain."

"I intended to ask you out to lunch to discuss the situation."

"Sure."

"Then one day we'll go out together as one department."

"I'll pass. I want to enjoy my food, not throw up."

"Ralph's not a bad guy."

"He's lucky someone thinks so," Barbara said, regarding Dane as if he were obscenely naïve.

9. HOME BOY

Dane returned to his office, closed the door and pressed his head between his palms. How did he ever delude himself that he had management skills? He longed for when he was told what to do and to do it again, when he was manipulated, criticized and abused. Anger was easier than anxiety. Ah, to hear the tongue lash against his ear that reminded him, "Peon! You're not paid to think!"

In the middle of his emotional wallow, Dane received an unexpected call.

It was from Goldfarb, whose glowing reference enabled Dane to land this job. Goldfarb was taking a vacation week in Winton, so they met for lunch the following day.

Goldfarb, always a filmmaker at heart, staged a dramatic rendezvous on the estuary bridge. Dane barely recognized his old partner. Goldfarb looked relaxed and refreshed. His jacket collar was around his face, making his beard look full and his face round under his cap bill. In the city, Goldfarb looked haggard and rustic in an *LL Bean* parka, but in Winton's mist he looked successful and robust.

"How've you been?" Dane asked. "How's Integrimedicom?"

"Nadine's still busting my balls."

"It's a miracle you still have any."

"Speaking of which, I had a hernia."

"How did you get it? Swimming? Riding a bike? Carrying layouts?"

"Athletic sex!" Goldfarb quipped. "Actually they don't know how it happened."

"Are you okay?"

"I needed an operation. It was awful. I don't trust doctors and I didn't want one touching me there! And I'm terrified of hospitals. The *procedure* lasted a half hour but I was sore for weeks. Fortunately, I was able to...you know...have relations after only a month."

Dane could not repress a smile.

"You think it's funny!" Goldfarb remarked. "I've had my figurative balls cut off so many times you can't imagine me having sex.

But I do. It's important to me."

"It's not that. I just remember how mad you were when your wife totaled your car."

"She's a pain. But there are things I didn't mention," Goldfarb said. The ex-partners carried paper bags of take-out from a Chinese restaurant and walked by the river. On damp benches by the marshes, they ate broccoli on brown rice and drank hot and sour soup like they were in Chinatown. They watched the ducks floating in the mist and exhaled cold, smoky air.

"So, how do you like it out here?" Goldfarb asked.

"I can see why you love Winton. It's beautiful," Dane replied.

"How's your new job?"

"It's okay. I'm in management and the people are unmanageable."

"Now you know what you're like!" Goldfarb chuckled. "So you're a boss. Good for you. You'll be a great boss."

"I'm not so sure. So far, I'm not getting anywhere."

"It's hard. People in this business are crazy and they have watermelon sized egos. You know. You've got one."

They laughed, then lapsed into slurping soup out of Styrofoam cups. Brindled mallards bobbed like corks on the green water. As Goldfarb ate his food in his habitat, he looked confident and successful. Dane was nonplussed. This was not the same Goldfarb he thought he knew—a spineless if affable lackey. Clearly, that was just a role Goldfarb played to keep his job. He was an ancient survivor like the Chinese serpent, shrewd and adaptable. At times, Dane wished he could be more like him.

"A boss has power," Goldfarb said. "You can do things the right way for a change."

"I don't know if anyone wants things to be right," Dane replied.

"You can try. What's your alternative? Look around for another job? You've already moved around a lot," Goldfarb said.

"Not always by choice," Dane said.

"Not consciously," Goldfarb replied. "But you can't keep fighting yourself."

"I'm just trying to find my way."

Goldfarb nodded. His eyes were friendly.

"If you keep changing jobs, you may run out."

Goldfarb had never challenged Dane this way when they worked together. He spoke like an advertising veteran of 25 years—and an older brother. Goldfarb's concern comforted Dane but he chafed at the advice. Between Dane and the choice Goldfarb exhorted him to make was the distance between what he had and what he wanted, between striving and surrender. Yet he knew Goldfarb was only being practical. This was his livelihood. What else could he do that would pay him half as well?

"I don't see a way out, but I can't stop looking," Dane said.

"I hope you find it," Goldfarb sighed. "Meanwhile, you're in a good position. Enjoy! Stop looking for an escape. Take each day as it comes and experience the moment."

Dane had been surprised by how Goldfarb looked. Now he was shocked by what he said.

"This is a side of you I've never seen," Dane said. "You sound so positive...like a self-help guru."

"I have my moments," Goldfarb conceded. "Look, I've got to run. We're painting the house so we can sell it."

Goldfarb crossed the bridge with Dane. "Check out *Farmer Moe's*. It's a nice walk," he said.

When Dane returned to the office, Goldfarb's questions took effect. Would he ever run out of places to work? It was fine to fantasize about purpose and destiny but what would he do for money? This was his fifth job in five years. His recent lay off had lasted for four months and his previous job at UNIHEALTH had gone for only two. He had to make Mentos work!

10. THE MOMENT PAYS OFF

Dane followed Goldfarb's advice—about living in the moment, but particularly about going to *Farmer Moe's.*

The pilgrimage to *Farmer Moe's* was uphill and a half-mile east of downtown Winton. This was the grocery whose exotic package goods made Goldfarb salivate—gourmet chips, mango salsas, exotic jerkies, donuts fried in nut oils, cookies baked with whole grain granola, and eggs laid by happy hens from coops with satellite radio. Dane, still traumatized by his long lay-off and yet to receive his first Mentos check, was on a strict one-slice, one-coffee, one-tank-of-gas daily budget. But before leaving empty-handed, Dane grabbed the only bargain in the store—a tin of *Altoids* for $1.50. A woman and her young son were on line behind him. The boy was intrigued by Dane's purchase and reached for the *Altoids* on the shelf.

"No, dear, we don't need *Altoids*," his mother said in a loud voice that mortified Dane.

"That's what you think," Dane said.

The little boy giggled and his mother said, "How dare you?"

"Is that all?" the cashier asked.

"Yes," Dane stammered and bolted from the store.

If *Farmer Moe's* did not work out as planned, Goldfarb's advice about making the most of his new job was more effective.

While performing his ablutions over the course of a week, Dane asked himself, "Can I continue to wander and be at peace?" Rather than hate his predicament, Dane pondered ways to enhance his work experience by being more valuable to colleagues. He resolved not to fly into the future or drift into the past, but to wallow in the present.

This revelation could not have had better timing.

Though the copy department remained a quagmire, Dane's quiet demeanor and *Glucose Diplomacy* were making friends at Mentos. One morning he delivered a cheesecake, creating a palpable buzz. When the production chief noticed Dane's gnarled hand, she gave him her bottle of *Aleve* to reduce the inflammation and his fingers straightened for the first time in months.

Dane also caught the attention of Dirk Ferguson, the agency president, and Tiny Anderson, his second-in-command. Dirk, a small, neat man with coiffed, white hair, was the last man alive to wear polyester suits, but they were well tailored. Dirk had a perpetual wry smile like he had a 24/7 laugh-track in his head. Humor is often a matter of will—if you want to laugh, you will think something is funny. Not much that came out of Dirk's mouth was droll but his wry expression, learned from *The Best of Carson* DVDs, made it seem that way.

"Tiny" Anderson, who managed the most important accounts at Mentos, was a lumbering giant. When Dirk and Tiny stood together they were a sight gag for bored clients. Tiny was a human triangle—large-boned, wide-hipped, with large feet and a small head. He might have thrived as a cartoon animal at children's parties. Instead he managed a group of trade magazines which comprised a major piece of Mentos' business. Barbara, who presumably worked under Dane, was Tiny's writer. When she was writing for Tiny, she wrote for no one else.

Dane sensed that Tiny liked him so he tried to solve his Barbara management problem with him directly. "Barbara is your subaltern. Can you spare her sometimes so she can help me?" Dane said.

"She's my *what*? Subaltern? I love it when you talk dirty," Tiny said.

Dirk Ferguson and Tiny gave Dane a challenge—to name a medical education company.

Naming things was Dane's favorite job. He was so enthusiastic about naming people, places and things that he mispronounced names in order to create new ones. It must have been genetic. As a boy, Dane loved the part in *Genesis* where Adam named the animals of Eden. While his parents fought in the next room, little Dane played Adam in Eden for many happy hours, removing his clothes and renaming the stuffed animals in his sister's room. When his parents learned about his Biblical reenactments, they exercised Godly wrath on him for being nude around his sister and for playing with her stuffed animals. Yet, this trauma did not snuff his love of naming, which found full expression in advertising. At WIF, he named an apartment building, a health spa, and an old pencil factory-turned-condo. Later he gave names to drugs and devices, including *Inphallus*, a cutting-edge condom that gave ED patients erections by transmitting sound waves to their penises.

Dane's alacrity for naming impressed and concerned Dirk Ferguson. He warned Dane about the assignment in his stand-up manner.

"I love your enthusiasm, Dane," Dirk said. "Is there something wrong with you?" Pause for laughter. Tiny guffawed. "Naming a medical education firm won't be as stimulating as *Imphallus*. Unfortunately."

Dirk looked askance and paused for laughter. Tiny guffawed.

"In fact, the name for a medical education firm should be as dry as a martini but as lofty as the Mile High Club." Dirk gave a deadpan look and paused for laughter. Tiny and Dane complied. Dirk smirked and launched the explanatory segment of his monologue. "The winning name will be a real word, relevant to the company's image and purpose, and a compound of smaller words that describe the company. Once you come up with a name that makes us beg for more, run a computer search to be sure the name isn't in use."

"And one more thing," Tiny added, "The name should be similar enough to existing companies to identify its business but fresh enough to catch the eye and intrigue the mind."

"Is that all?" Dane asked.

"If we think of anything we'll tell you," Tiny said.

Dane raced back to his office, shut his door and removed his shirt to channel the spirit of Adam. Moments later he was furiously key-stroking acronyms. Dane entered that meditative state where satisfying work often transported him until discussions outside his office broke his bare-chested trance. Realizing where he was, he put on his shirt. Suddenly, a dapper man he had never met burst into his office and inquired urgently if Dane was the copy supervisor. Dane said nothing while devising a plausible lie, but before he could articulate it, the stranger said, "Oh, good, I have an emergency!"

Case 5-C
MENTAL BENDS & OTHER DISABILITIES

11. MENTAL BENDS

The well dressed intruder was Maurice Minton, Dane's "team" account director, and he had a massive assignment for Dane.

"Let me be as clear as Lake Baikal...that's the world's deepest fresh-water lake," Maurice began, flaunting some erudition recently acquired from his young daughter's latest issue of *National Geographic for Kids*. "This assignment is lava hot, with work to occupy an entire copy department. Dick tells me you are the copy supervisor. In a word, you are *the man*."

"With all due respect, 'the man' is two words," Dane replied, although he did not know Maurice well enough to correct his grammar.

"So they are!" Maurice laughed and clapped his hands. He beamed at Dane like he was the prodigal son. His eyes danced when he announced the importance and time-sensitivity of these jobs. The ten pieces, which included a patient brochure, a newsletter and several letters to managed care organizations, all fully annotated with a bibliography, were *due yesterday*.

Due yesterday! Just when Dane resolved to live in the present, he had to work fast enough to reverse time. For Dane, "due yesterday" was a starting pistol firing in his head. It was a cocktail of agony and ecstasy, when a copywriter showed his creativity and speed and did what he was paid to do.

"So when can I see something?" Maurice asked.

"I'll start now. You should have some pieces tomorrow."

"Excellent!" Maurice thundered. He pointed at Dane. "I'm counting on you, big guy."

As Dane raced back to his office and tried making sense of the wall of work rushing toward him, agony turned against ecstasy like a black widow murdering her mate. He recalled that along with ten new jobs for Maurice, he had to create and research memorable, meaningful acronyms for Dirk's and Tiny's corporation-naming assignment.

It was noon but Dane was too nervous to eat. An unbearable pressure filled his guts and torched his skin. "Restless butt syndrome" caused him to fidget in his chair and he experienced a fizzing in his brain like carbonation. His jaws tingled as if super-heated saliva seeped from his gums while white spots sprinkled his vision like old film leader. All signs pointed to "mental bends," a disease triggered by a rapid shift from normal to high pressure. In an instant he might scream and throw objects. When Maria, the turbulent traffic manager, dumped a heap of folders on his desk, Dane nearly hurled them back at her. Instead, he exercised supervisory restraint and walked to Dick's office for moral support and professional assistance.

What was he thinking?

12. NO HELP FROM ELVES

When Dane entered Dick Spilkus's dark lair, the creative director was practicing his own brand of personal relief by rolling two rust-eaten Chinese healthy balls in one hand while feeding his mouth cheese-flavored nachos with the other. Dick's head vibrated as if sensors in his skin detected Dane's presence and roused him from his "stand-by" trance.

"What is it?" Spilkus demanded with vague irritation.

Dane described the pile of work he had been given. Dick's mouth made a smacking noise, his tongue absorbing tortilla salt from his palate. He managed one pithy word between nacho deposits.

"Delegate."

Far from mollifying Dane, Dick's message exacerbated his nervousness. It was a managerial trick. He subtracted from Dane's burden by doubling it. Now the copy supervisor faced two challenges—to get the work done and to suborn someone else to do it. "Delegation" was the second managerial skill Dane would be tested on after "conflict resolution"—for which he had received an "Incomplete."

"Call Barbara," Dick said. "She works under you. Now get her to work *for* you...and one more thing, Dane."

"What's that?"

"Can you bring a pineapple cheesecake? I've been craving it since you brought in the plain one."

"I'll look into it when I've finished writing the ten pieces by next week!" Dane replied as he bolted from Dick's office.

Dane phoned Barbara to recruit her but she had bad news for him. Dirk Ferguson, the president, had just handed her a major project—to write his son's recommendation letter for a junior year abroad program in Patagonia—and Dirk Ferguson's assignments took precedence over everything.

With a vengeance, Dane returned to Dick Spilkus's dark office for more mentoring in the art of delegation. Dick was rolling a pen in his mouth like a cigar as he stared vacantly at his oversized monitor.

"Barbara's busy working for Dirk."

"Dirk *is* #1," Dick muttered without moving his eyes from the monitor. "You're #2. Do what you gotta do."

"What does that mean?"

"You're the writer. You should know what it means."

"Are there other resources?" Dane asked, unabashedly stalling. He could not face the work until he exhausted every appeal.

"Resources?" Dick asked vaguely as if trying to recall what the word meant. "You mean *like elves?*"

Dane forced a laugh that crumbled into a hacking cough.

"You are our resource. Make us proud," Dick said, maintaining his monitor gaze.

This inspirational charge convinced Dane of two things: not to linger long enough to distract Spilkus from the screen and not to expect help. He left his boss on mental stand-by and returned to his office, where job bags spilling bloated documents, contaminated with marginalia, doodles, circled passages, misleading arrows and stapled scraps, awaited his attention.

Dane's despair spiked. He urgently needed help or his skull would explode.

At last Dane understood why movie characters in crisis often threw breakable objects. It was not action so much as procrastination before taking action. Dane had no glass but a mountain of paper was at hand. He lifted the stack and dropped it on his desk to produce a booming thud. Folders hit the floor and spilled their contents.

"Damn!" Dane cursed.

For his next act, Dane reviewed the contents of each folder to estimate which project would demand the least time and effort for the maximum sense of accomplishment. If Maurice asked about the job status tomorrow, Dane wanted to tell him three jobs were done. Maurice would be ecstatic and the pressure would be off. Manipulating perceptions in this way could provide illusory progress—and superb public relations.

Dane soon realized the jobs were all unique in ways picayune and perverse. Some needed new copy—an easy fix—while others required extensive patchwork of copy from diverse sources, involving laborious puzzle-solving. Dane evaluated and prioritized for a half-hour, extracted three slim folders from the pile and dropped the others on a chair.

Yet even triage did not lighten the load where it was heaviest—in

Dane's head. He pressed his hand against his brow like an eyeshade and supported his cranium like a piece of bulky equipment. He fumbled to organize the work until he fell into a rhythm. That afternoon he did three of the ten projects, and drove home relieved and confident that he would complete the rest on schedule.

13. TIT FOR TAT

When Dane returned to Mentos the next day, he saw what was left to do and freaked one more time.

His feel-good, self-motivational tactic had backfired. The three completed pieces were eclipsed by the remaining seven, which were like epic serial-killer notes—layouts littered with cross-outs, arcane doodles and scribbled instructions to insert pages from other texts. This was not copywriting but code-breaking a puzzle with pieces picked out of a dumpster.

Dane recognized now why he needed to manage. If he did not delegate work, he would have it all to himself, which was tantamount to digging a pit and shoveling dirt on himself. Dane had tried to delegate projects to Barbara but she was always busy and he stopped asking. When he had lunch with Ralph, he violated her trust and forfeited her cooperation—forever. But maybe she forgot about his lunch with Ralph or he would catch her at a hungry moment. If he asked her to lunch and she accepted, he could persuade her to help. He was dreaming! She would never have lunch with him—in her mind, he was contaminated by Ralph.

After an hour of drudgery, Dane overcame his qualms and phoned Barbara for lunch. She agreed to meet him at one and they discussed where they would go.

"I don't feel like a supermarket salad bar," she said.

"What about Chinese?"

She was lukewarm. Dane reassured her that it was open for discussion—but Dick stood in his doorway, so the discussion was over.

"Gotta go," he whispered.

"We'll take my car," she said.

"OK, right. One," he said and hung up.

For no apparent reason, Dick needed to talk to Dane about his Chinese healthy balls, how great they were and how he paid only two dollars for such an ancient and effective alternative Chinese therapy.

"Did you know they're good for arthritis, circulation and brain function?" Dick asked.

Dane nervously consulted his timepiece. It was five minutes to one. Now that Barbara had agreed to meet him for lunch he could not be late or he would never be able to delegate a thing to her; he would be stuck mismanaging himself.

"Yeah, Chinese apothecaries kick FDA ass," Dane told Dick with awkward exuberance. "I wish we had them as pharma clients. I mean, tiger tooth, rhinoceros horn, they're the best."

Dick blinked. His tongue licked cheese powder off his lips. "I want to see those acronyms before you leave," he said.

"Right, great," Dane said.

Dick took exception to Dane's tone. His sensors detected dismissiveness but he needed to pee and his bladder always came before his ego.

It was after one. "Damn!" Dane thought. "She'll think I stood her up. I'm screwed."

He leaped down the stairway a landing at a time down to the garage and stood behind a pillar to escape the potential gossip of passing colleagues. He did not know how to explain his vigil. Ten minutes passed and Barbara did not appear. A woman in a leather jacket finally emerged. She tossed her hair and walked toward him. Was it Barbara? She looked more energetic and focused than he had seen her.

"Are you sure we can't just walk to lunch?" he asked.

"Absolutely sure," she said. "We'll take my car."

Dane weighed this option cautiously. As her passenger, his

supervisory stature would be diminished. Yet, this could be perceived favorably. If she drove, she was in charge. He could not be accused of abusing his power. Her driving also had a practical benefit. Barbara knew Winton better than he did. They climbed into her SUV, twice the size of his compact, and she accelerated from the garage.

"Where to?" she asked.

He suggested Chinese take-out and a picnic near the river—it was his standard lunch itinerary.

"Is that what you did with *him*?"

"I like Chinese food," he confessed. "And I like the river."

After picking up the food, Dane thought Barbara would leave her jeep in the library lot and they would walk to the river. Instead, she took an emphatic right turn and drove in a new direction.

"I won't eat the same food in the same spot where you went with that drip. I'd puke."

She turned right at a sign for the beach. Goldfarb had urged Dane to see the beach where he took long meditative walks. Now was his chance.

The bumpy one lane road twisted among dunes and brambles. The tang of salt water and organic decay permeated the air. Winton no longer seemed suburban, but wild, exotic and secluded.

They sat on flat stones, eating from containers among the dunes and shrubs. Long Island Sound slapped the sand. Gulls coasted overhead and pecked in the muck.

"Damn, the chopstick left a splinter in my lip," Dane whined.

He picked at the splinter with his fingertips but could not extract it.

"I'll get it, "Barbara said. Over his mild protests, she used tweezers from the Swiss Army Knife in her handbag to pry the sliver from Dane's mouth. He was the boss but she had taken him on a field trip to the beach and was now playing school nurse.

"I lost a tooth in the hot and sour soup last week," Dane complained. "Now I'm stabbing myself with a chopstick. I don't know why I go back to that place. It's bad luck."

"Because the food is good," she said. Her approval lifted his mood.

When they paused from their meal, Dane turned to business.

"I need your help with some assignments Maurice gave me."

"I'm overloaded with a job from Tiny," Barbara replied. "I'll do what I can."

A long rodent darted into the brambles behind the dunes.

"Looks like a weasel. It's probably a rat," Barbara observed.

"You're good on animals," Dane remarked.

"I worked for a zoo newsletter," she said. "Did you hear that in Hollywood certain major stars use weasels for sexual pleasure?"

"No," Dane said. "How does that work?"

"They let it crawl up their butts."

"I should have known," Dane said, trying to seem worldly as he spooned in some hot and sour soup. "It's classic Freud. *The Rat Man*," Dane remarked. "He fantasized about using an Asian torture device against his fiancée and his dead father."

She laughed. "Clearly, you were once a teacher."

It surprised Dane that Barbara was so current on weasel sex and Hollywood gossip. He had pegged her as a small-town recluse in lumberjack clothes, who lived with her pets in a dilapidated house and was oblivious to the world. Clearly, there was more to her. When they drove back to town, she pulled into the garage and kept the motor running.

"Thanks for showing me around," Dane said. "I would never have gone to the beach on my own."

"I like showing you around," Barbara said. "Thanks for asking me to lunch. But why did you do it?"

Dane was taken aback. Did their pleasant time not answer the question? He believed his intentions were clear. Since they were not, he felt the pressure to explain.

"You're a colleague. We had business to discuss," he said.

Barbara's face stiffened and her eyes went cold.

"You took me out to lunch because you did it with Ralph. You wanted to be fair."

That was correct and Dane would have readily admitted it if Barbara had not been staring at him so unhappily.

"I already told you how that happened. Ralph found my gloves and I showed my thanks," Dane said uneasily. "I always meant to have lunch with you first."

"Yeah, but you went with him first," Barbara replied.

Her grudge worked like a time machine. It nullified the pleasant hour they had spent and reverted to the conflict Dane believed they resolved. He wished to treat Barbara and Ralph as equals but parity with Ralph was unacceptable to her.

Barbara smoothed her hair in the rear view mirror, then placed her hands on both sides of his face and pulled him toward her, submerging his head in her flannel shirt and pressing it between her breasts. She held him tightly there and rocked her torso sideways to envelop him in their fullness and heat. Dane struggled to break free but her arms were wrapped around his head and neck and her fingers gripped his hair. In urgent need of air, he put his hands on her shoulders and peeled away from her.

"Why did you do that?" he gasped.

"It's one thing you didn't do with Ralph," she said flatly.

She turned off the engine and smoothed her hair in the rear-view. Dane's impulse was to bolt from her car and to run across the garage—to convey that he was an unwilling party to inappropriate contact. His second thought advised against such a conspicuous response. It might raise questions unlikely to be answered in a manner likely to be believed. Despite his confusion, he knew composure was critical. He also knew his professional relationship with Barbara had changed, though he wished it had not.

As minutes, then hours, separated Dane from the event, it loomed larger in his mind, and he needed to pretend it never happened. Toward this end, he phoned her later that afternoon.

"Thanks for having lunch with me."

"Thank *you*."

"I think we made progress."

"Yes."

Rather than clearing the air, this conversation circulated it like an old fan. By not referring to the incident, he extended its awkwardness.

"So we're okay, right?"

"Of course. Why wouldn't we be?"

"That's great," he said, gulping air since had been holding his breath. "I want us to be able to work together, right?"

"Sounds good."

"I mean it."

"Relax."

Barbara seemed willing to pretend nothing happened. Dane's fear was assuaged for the moment. However, over-the-phone pain relief was never more than temporary. Dane's long drive home provided fertile time for his anxiety to grow.

"I'm not managing very well," he thought.

14. STRESS TEST

A few days later, on a Sunday morning, a phone call from Philadelphia broke the Bacchus family's one long slumber of the week. Becky's ailing mother was in a hospital in critical condition with high fever and breathing difficulties. The family was told to come at once.

Within an hour, Dane, Becky and Iris were southward bound. When they arrived at the hospital, two young residents told Becky that her mother might not survive. They handed her a clipboard with a form permitting the hospital staff not to resuscitate.

Becky and her sister insisted that their mother would recover. She had weathered health crises before.

Becky's mother did not die on schedule. She had double-pneumonia. With oxygen and an antibiotic drip, her condition stabilized. Becky needed to stay on so Dane and Iris headed home without her. Along with Dane's long-distance job he would be Iris's sole caregiver for at least a week. Working 41 miles away, he would also need to arrange her after-school pick-up. Between family, job and commute, Dane had believed he was overwhelmed but he was now well beyond that familiar extreme.

That Monday morning, after driving Iris to school, Dane arrived at the agency in time for another status meeting. This small agency had more status meetings than all of his previous agencies combined. Status meetings were typically mundane traffic reports detailing where projects were in the continuum between start-up and out-the-door, whereas Mentos status meetings were "convene-and-ream" sessions to lay blame for the latest mistake.

Maurice called the meeting to order by coughing in his fist and slapping his hands. A jangle of nervous energy insulated in slick moves, Maurice was an executive for a new millennium, with one foot in a corporate corridor, the other in the street. Maurice was buttoned-down most days in black-rimmed glasses, tailored suits and onyx cufflinks. But on dress-down Fridays, he knew how to keep it real in baggy jeans showing designer boxer shorts. His baritone was a tuned instrument for stately cadences delivered with impeccable diction; yet he opened every status meeting asking, "How y'all feelin'?"

This meeting was different.

The man with a belly laugh that could fill an office with mirth paced the conference room in grave silence.

"People, this has gone *beyond* ridiculous."

"Nipel's haircut?" Dick asked.

Some tittered but Maurice brooked no levity.

"Nipel just called. He was furious. He informed me that we inserted the wrong fair balance on the *Flococcin* sales aid—again! We used the atypical gingivitis copy instead of the cute bronchitis copy."

"That's an easy mistake to make!" Dick said. "They're caused by the same *cute* bacteria."

"This is unconscionable!" Maurice's fist hammered the table. "People, we are close to losing this account. We must be more accountable!"

"Aren't you being a tad dramatic, Maurice?" Dick asked as he covered his face with his hands. "The copy for both conditions is almost identical."

"*Almost!* Dick, this is pharmaceutical advertising, not horseshoes! This project is inexcusably late because of our frequent miscues. As creative director, you must ensure that this does not continue. Don Mentos told me it took him ten years to get his foot in the door at Budiheim Pharmaceutical. I assure you that I will not be the one to lose it due to boneheaded bumbling. Okay, people? Let's be professional!"

These meetings made Dane miserable. He believed he was blameless for inserting the wrong fair balance, yet felt accused. He worried about an agency that was in perpetual trouble with a client over trivialities. Although newly hired, he sensed that his job was in jeopardy. Worst of all, Dick made light of Maurice's fulminations, so the collective anguish seemed gratuitous and surreal.

"Tomorrow Nipel will be here with Sandra, his new assistant product manager," Maurice informed the team. "Sandra is a highly successful sales rep. She is an expert in hospital flirtation, doctor dinners, gifts, kick-backs, pay-offs and freebies. I want you all to be on your proverbial toes. Our clients deserve our full commitment."

"Will you be there, Maurice?" Dick asked.

"Unfortunately, I had a previous commitment at my daughter's school PTA bake-off," Maurice said. "But Nancy will be on hand and she and Nipel have forged a strong bond."

Nancy, a large-boned newlywed from nearby North Sasquatch, Connecticut, bobbed her head in accord.

"Epoxy or crazy glue?" Dick asked.

Case 5-D

NIPEL'S GIFT & THE BOSOM BULLY

15. SUMMIT WITH NIPEL

Dane braced himself for his first meeting with the infamous Nipel. The best thing Dick ever said about the *Floccacin* product manager was that he was a buffoon. He usually called him a vermin.

The meeting was for two o'clock. A platter of fruit and cookies tastefully placed on the table multitasked as refreshment and a breastwork between client and agency.

Nipel and his new assistant, Sandra, arrived late enough for the green bananas to turn yellow. Nipel's mouth was curled in a perpetual smile while Sandra resembled a life-sized American doll in a pantsuit.

'I'll say one thing for you guys: you're consistent. You never fail to make a mistake," Nipel said.

"Hah! Hah!" Dick said. "It's no wonder we make mistakes when the jobs turn around so fast they give us whiplash?"

"Mr. Genius Creative Director, I know you're a comedian when I see your layouts."

Nipel's voluble hands and barbs were the stuff of stand-up and demanded laughter. For the *Floccacin* product manager, the agency was more than a marketing partner—it was a captive audience.

"Really, guys! I love your dancing bugs. But we must feed the regulatory beast its favorite dish—*an accurate fair balance*. The fair balance for Bacterial Exacerbation of Chronic Bronchitis is not the same as for acute diaper rash. If by some miracle the patient reads the fine print, he will be confused and treat a disease he does not have!"

"Who'd know the difference? It takes a microscope to read the fair balance!" Dick said.

"Then be happy, Genius Creative Director! Regulatory wants the fair balance larger!" Nipel announced.

"If a patient has both conditions, both fair balances can be right," Dane interjected.

"Acne and bronchitis: what are the odds of these co-morbidities?" Nipel asked.

There was laughter.

"These populations may intersect. Teenagers, for instance," Dane said. "Maybe they're your target audience."

"Teenagers. I like that. You may have something," Nipel said.

"Can we get back on track?" Dick asked testily.

"The point is this," Nipel said. "You creative icons with big ideas suck in boring details but boring details are what we pay you for."

"Good news! We hired Dane. He's a master of boring details."

"Excuse me for saying so but we have bigger problems than the type size on the fair balance—like better ways to reach doctors," Sandra interjected. "I don't want to depress anyone but I went on calls with our reps. *Guess what?* They never opened the detail aids—*not once*. The rep has one minute to talk to doctors. There's no time for fair balance or anything else."

The agency people shifted nervously in their chairs. If clients started to think advertising was useless, they would stop paying for it.

"Mr. Creative Genius, here's an idea," Nipel said. "Design a bug suit for reps to wear. Then they fall down in the hospital corridor."

Everyone laughed. Nipel beamed before turning somber.

"You must have heard the *scuttle bug*. Massive layoffs are rumored. Even my job is not safe. But before I am dead meat, I want to leave my mark on medical marketing....a legacy for *Floccacin* product managers of the future. I see it as a guidebook of medical guidelines for bacterial infections for which our drug is indicated."

Nipel paused to let everyone absorb the magnitude of his vision. Dick had mentioned the guidelines guidebook to Dane. Barbara started it more than a month before Dane arrived and it was presumably near completion. Dane only needed to set a deadline for

Barbara but when he questioned her about the project she was vague about it.

"It will be my Stonehenge, my *Taj Mahal*. Fair balances come and go but the *Floccacin* guidelines guidebook is forever, guys. Don't fail me."

"We won't, Nipel," Dick said in a low, earnest voice, his jaw set with *rock*titude. He turned to Dane. "What's the status of the *Floccacin* guidelines guidebook?"

The room was silent. All eyes fell on Dane, along with the onus of producing Nipel's masterpiece and the weight of eight people's buck-passing expectations. This was his moment to look strong and effective. His facial muscles tightened and nostrils flared. He squared his jaw and said, "The *Floccacin* guidelines guidebook is well underway."

"Can you tell me when it will be delivered?" Nipel demanded.

"In two weeks," Dane said involuntarily, as if the voice spoke through him without his consent.

Everyone nodded. They loved Dane's take-charge style.

For seconds, Dane experienced the warm rush of public approval. He liked how it felt. He knew how to seize a moment! No, he *squeezed* the moment.

The heroic feeling was fleeting. It occurred to Dane when he left the meeting that he still had to complete three of the ten pieces Maurice had given him. They were due in 48 hours.

He needed help. To receive it, he had to be a manager and delegate to Barbara. But he couldn't.

16. THE BOSOM BULLY

The prospect of asking Barbara to do anything made Dane feel sick. He had phoned her to smooth over the awkward moment an hour after it happened, thinking this would make everything normal, but then avoided her for days. The inappropriate contact passed from

AD NOMAD   Eric Jay Sonnenschein

awkward to dangerous as time converted it to myth.

Confusion added smoke to the fire. Dane could not define or explain this unprecedented event. It was amorphous, which made it more frightening. Sexual transgression was the skeleton key to the moment. Barbara's act was aggressive and sudden. She seemed to use her breasts to subvert and subdue him.

Dane had to get over this. He needed to talk to someone. He phoned Goldfarb for advice. In his quarter century in advertising Goldfarb must have witnessed his share of *situations*. At first, Dane described the circumstance to his ex-partner in euphemisms as decorous as thick drapes. But when he thought he heard Goldfarb snore gently, he came to the point.

"She grabbed my face and held it between her breasts," Dane admitted.

Goldfarb's silence was now intense as his cinematic mind arranged the bodies and set up the lights.

"She turned on your engine before she turned off hers," Goldfarb quipped.

"But I didn't do anything."

"Your face did it all."

"My face was there, if that's what you mean."

"It was *there* all right. How were they? The breasts—were they large?"

"It's irrelevant."

"I can't help you if I don't know the facts."

"They covered my ears."

"Oh, yeah! Did she say anything—before, during, or after?"

"She mentioned weasels—."

"I was thinking more along the lines of *'Give it to me!'* Weasels... Interesting."

"Does it mean anything?" Dane asked.

"I think it means *you* are the weasel...So how did it feel to get an old-fashioned *facial*? Good, right? Exciting?"

"It was suffocating. I was turning blue."

"Do you think she was part of a conspiracy to undermine your power by making you faint? She'd leave your body in her vehicle with evidence...like her bra!"

"I don't know," Dane bit his lip. "It's a cancer in my mind."

"That's why she did it."

The worst could not be confided on a company phone between sheet rock walls. Barbara's act thrust itself into Dane's bedroom. He was tormented by guilt, unable to forget the shameful exhilaration of illicit contact. Amateur psychologist that he was, Dane tried to exorcise the lewd memory by simulating it in a controlled setting. When Becky removed her bra before bed, Dane asked her to put on his flannel shirt, then rushed to her, knelt at her feet and plunged his face between her breasts, to relive the taboo in the sanctity of marriage. Becky recoiled at his violent urgency and said her breasts were tender. Dane apologized, more repentant than ever for imposing Barbara's sexuality on his wife.

"What should I do? Go to HR?" Dane asked the sagacious art director.

"And say what? That you were attacked by her breasts? They'll fire you—if they don't have you committed first," Goldfarb replied.

"That's what happened!" Dane insisted.

"No one will believe it. Listen. This woman is your *bosom bully*. It's been going on for years but guys are too macho to admit it. A woman uses her breasts to provoke and intimidate. Look at me, don't look at me, let me put it in your face, but don't dare touch them!"

"I can't do a thing?"

"Relax! What did we say about living in the moment? There's a lot worse out there than breasts in your face. Lie low and let it blow over. I worked with a guy who had a bosom bully. He went to HR but she turned the tables and claimed he made *her* uncomfortable. Who do you think they believed? Then other women came forward and said he stared at *their* chests. Then they found a *Juggs* anthology in his office. He said it was planted but did anybody believe him? They made his life hell with *in-your-endo's*. His *Secret Santa* gave him two plastic jugs and someone hung a bra from his office door. Then his wife left him. He had to go for therapy twice a week to keep his job. Then he was downsized. Last I heard he was selling lingerie at a *Lord & Taylor* in Paramus."

"*Oh, no!* I' saw that guy...when my wife was buying a nightgown."

"Right. Don't let it happen to you! Keep your face away from her."

Goldfarb's confirmation that the situation was serious reassured Dane. He realized it wasn't all in his head. Even so, he was in a predicament. When he hung up with Goldfarb, the phone rang with the extension he dreaded most.

"So are we on for lunch?" Barbara inquired.

Dane panicked. "We were having lunch? I'm sorry. I didn't realize."

"I thought you mentioned it. I wondered if you had free time."

Free time! Dane panicked. *Breasts! Face! No!*

"I wish I did. It's a bad time, worse than bad. They dumped a ton of work on me."

"I've been there," she chuckled. "It's disappointing."

There was no sign in her voice of insinuation, accusation or innuendo. Maybe they had bounced back from their moment to being colleagues again. Dane felt he could reach out to her professionally.

"I've got a stack on my desk," Dane said. "Can you help?"

"Sorry, I can't. I'm swamped," she replied.

Just like that Dane was back in a familiar place—buried under his work-load in his one-man managerial delusion.

"No problem," he lied. "I'd better get back to work. Can't stop until it's all done. So can we do it another day?"

"Sure," she said.

Dane exhaled. She sounded friendly. Maybe everything was alright.

17. BAD BOY

That night Dane had a nightmare. He was selling lingerie in a *Kmart* when he woke up, shouting, "Black bustiers are not 20% off. This is a white sale!"

His first panicky thought was that he had awakened Becky and she would wonder about the content and meaning of his cry. He looked to his left. Becky wasn't there. She was out of town. Dane was alone with his bad dream, which somehow made it worse. He needed reassurance but had none.

Since sleep was no longer possible in his agitated state, Dane worked until daylight to complete the last of Maurice's ten projects. While he wrote, he paused and glanced at the bed next to his desk. He imagined Becky curled up in repose—her serenity and innocence intensified his guilt.

"I didn't do anything," he whispered to her photograph on his desk. "I never wanted it to happen. It was so fast." He turned back to the screen and continued to work.

Later that morning, Dane showed Maurice the ten managed care pieces he had completed ahead of schedule by working evenings and weekends.

"Well done and I raise you a bravo!" Maurice said, in a manner strongly suggesting that Dane was making his mark as a "Mind Marketing Medicine."

"You've done so well that I have one more thing for you to do!" Maurice handed Dane another voluminous job jacket.

"But first, let's celebrate!" Maurice declared. He brought his hands together, his eyes darted left and right, and he pulled his miniature Italian espresso maker off the shelf. "You must try this coffee. It's *Kona Volcano* blend. The beans were roasted on a lava bed. It puts fire in the belly!"

Just as Dane waited to receive Maurice's caffeinated appreciation, the phone rang. It was Dick, calling for Dane.

"Come to my office," Dick said curtly.

Spilkus was glaring at his flat screen in the dark when Dane arrived.

"Where are the company names you never showed me?" he demanded in a low, sullen tone.

"I showed you everything," Dane replied, unsure of Dick's reference.

"Don't play dumb, Dane. You know you're not supposed to give *anybody anything* until I see it."

"Dirk and Tiny needed more names and fast. I said I had to run them by you first but you were out and they couldn't wait."

"Yeah, right, okay," Dick relented. "I saw 'em. They're pretty good names. Sit down. I have to give you your first month evaluation. You've done everything we've asked of you and well. There's only one area where you've let me down. What about the pineapple cheesecake?"

"I...They don't have it...I mean, if I look around New York for a cheesecake, I may have to come in late. Or call in sick."

"No, no, that's okay," Dick said. "Go back to work."

18. ACTING OUT

Dane's reward for completing ten pieces in a week was to receive an eleventh. Maurice promised it would be easy but the dark, faxed pages were cluttered with illegible comments and deletions. Sections were crossed out with instructions such as "See A," or "Use ventilator copy." Meanwhile, the deadline for the Nipel's guidelines guidebook rolled toward Dane. Dane had no idea what the book should look like or how long it had to be but he assumed Barbara was writing it because he was too busy to think otherwise and the job folder was on her desk. Although Dane wanted to trust Barbara to "own" Nipel's guidelines guidebook, the "manager" in him worried that she was not keeping up with her payments.

"By the way, how is that guidelines guide book going?" he asked.

"What?" she answered.

"You know: the *Floccacin* guidelines guidebook. You've had it for awhile."

"I have?"

"Yes. That's what Dick said."

"Oh that. I started it. It's coming along, I guess."

"That's good. We're delivering it in two weeks."

"Oh."

"Is that a problem?"

"I don't think so."

Barbara finally conceded that one section of Nipel's guidelines guidebook was done but she had not looked at it for weeks.

"Can you work on it?"

"I'm busy on other stuff. But I'll try."

Her reassurance was enough to soothe Dane's nerves. He hung up and looked at his watch: it was 2:30. Iris was getting out of school and he had to pick her up. It was Friday and she would wait for him at school, since she had run out of friends to go home with.

Since Becky was out of town looking after her sick mother, Dane acted as a single parent. He woke up Iris every morning, prepared her lunch, drove her to school, and rushed after work to pick her up in the evenings at a friend's home. Dane needed to collect Iris as soon as possible because her friends' parents, while sympathetic, did not want their children wasting study time with a friend when they should be doing homework.

Dane had explained his situation to Dick. He thought his boss was a family man and would sympathize. Dick told him to do what he had to do but seemed to resent Dane for leaving.

To compensate for any bad impression he was making, Dane carried a briefcase filled with references and documents containing annotations and footnotes for Maurice's job. He would work through the weekend and was confident of getting it all done. He passed

Dick's office and wished him a good weekend. Dick was talking with Ralph, the senior editor.

"So, why is there always a problem with the references?" Dick called after Dane.

Dane stood transfixed. He could not ignore the question and walk out because Dick's imperious tone demanded an answer. He was playing boss again, catching Dane off-guard for an unforeseen mistake. How could he complain about references! All Dane had done of late was to search for, cite, collect and highlight supporting documents.

But the barb did not aggravate Dane as much as their taunting smiles, which epitomized his managerial status. He was outflanked and outranked by boss and subordinate—Dick the snoop and Ralph the rat. Ralph seated with his legs crossed at a casual right angle especially rankled Dane. What right did Ralph have to be at ease while Dane was on edge? Ralph had promised to come to him with his problems but preferred going over his head; Dick, meanwhile, purported to seek harmony while playing the editor against the writer. Dane was no copy supervisor! He was a copy slave!

"All I do day and night is to write and reference these pieces. So what's the problem?" Dane barked at Dick.

"Ralph says the references are a mess," Dick said.

"He never told me that," Dane replied. "Ralph, you said you'd come to me with problems and we'd solve them together. But you're not man enough to do that. You're a weasel who goes behind my back."

"Stop! Dane, get the hell out of here!" Dick said.

Dick broke the incantatory flow of Dane's anger like a referee ordering him to a neutral corner. Dane knew he had transgressed more than his norm and felt vulnerable and weak. Four weeks of winning friends at Mentos unraveled in two minutes of unfiltered vitriol. He retired to his office and sat shaking at his desk. When he believed all was calm he returned to Dick's office to apologize.

Dick seemed to expect Dane although his eyes barely moved from one spot on the monitor.

"I don't know what that was about but it was unacceptable. You attacked a colleague," Dick said.

"I'm sorry. I snapped," Dane admitted.

"Ralph's a mess. How will I get any work out of him now?"

"He'll get over it."

"You also attacked me."

"I didn't say a word to you."

"Not directly. But this is my office."

"I'm sorry. I have worked non-stop on ten projects since last week. Plus, I have family concerns," Dane explained. "When you criticized me about the references, I thought Ralph had complained behind my back. I snapped."

"Pressure comes with the job. You need to manage it," Dick admonished him.

"Ralph shouldn't go over my head," Dane countered. "If he had a problem he should have come to me."

"It was my fault. I asked him," Dick said.

"So *you* went behind my back," Dane parried.

"Listen, I should fire your ass now. The only reason I'm not is that I once made the same, stupid mistake. When I was at Green, an account guy stormed in my office. He said my layouts were crap and had to be redone. I'd been working for weeks day and night on them and I knew he was busting my balls, so I told him to fuck off. He said he'd have me fired so I threw a heavy object at his head. Dane, your work is great but don't let this happen again or I'll fire your ass."

"Thanks, Dick. I won't."

On his way home, Dane tried to block out his thoughts by listening to a radio interview. A crime writer described shooting a friend in the face when they were teenagers. Dane felt better. At least he had not injured or killed anyone!

Reflection was how Dane normally processed his traumas.

Thinking diffused the pain. However, he could not bear now to reflect on how he nearly lost his job for no good reason so his body reflected for him. His hands trembled. He tried to steady them by tightening his grip on the wheel but that merely displaced the shaking to the rest of his body. He shivered uncontrollably and the car careened. "Asshole!" he shouted. "You almost got yourself fired. From a place where you're liked. And for what?"

19. REPENTANCE

On Monday, people regarded Dane as if he had stepped off a wanted poster. Nobody ate his cake. The only one who liked Dane better than before was John, the owner's tough-guy cousin, who said good morning for once. Everyone avoided Dane until Dick Spilkus and the president, Dirk Ferguson, called him to the conference room. Dane expected the worst but they only asked Dane to write a promotional ad for the agency.

"You have to rebuild fences," Dick told him later. "People were hurt by what you did. They said, 'Dane seemed like a nice guy but now I'm not sure. How could he treat his boss that way?'"

Dane meant to convey remorse but Dick's fence-mending suggestion aggravated him. He had lost his temper and transgressed corporate decorum but committed no atrocity. He had vented his rage on Ralph and "Ralph rage" was commonplace at Mentos. The senior editor was on probation for fighting with people so why should Dane apologize to people for fighting him?

More ridiculous still was Dick's claim that Dane was resented for abusing his boss. He had not lambasted Dick but even if he had, why would colleagues hate him for it? Did they not secretly wish they could yell at the boss to restore fairness and balance to the universe? Maybe they once had such a desire but renounced it so long ago that they now regarded the impulse with horror like a perversion locked in their hearts. In corporate life, insubordination was a dangerous fantasy workers rarely acknowledged, while free speech was diluted water cooler banter. Shouting in Dick's office was honest and real, which only made it more despicable.

Dane believed he owed himself the biggest apology. After building good will and a solid image, he revealed "Not-so-Great Dane." People at Mentos would never again see him as 'the cake crusader' but as an obstreperous hothead. He must reassure them that what they had seen Friday was an aberration so they would feel safe with him.

He also had to make things right with himself. Dane examined his recent loss of control. "Why Mentos?" he asked. He explained his outburst with familiar theories—a fear of success, a will to fail, a sense of inadequacy that undermined potential happiness—which clarified nothing. No doubt, he succumbed to the workload and was tired, confused and angry with his role at Mentos. Yes, the blow up was long coming, but it erupted only because the vapid atmosphere at Mentos was conducive to emotional violence. Excessive civility yielded low external resistance, causing internal pressure to explode. Yes, that was it!

This wealth of viable theories should have freed Dane; instead it only added pressure. If the moribund environment at Mentos resulted in a loss of control, Dane remained in constant danger. A colleague could be avoided but an entire office? He must imagine excitement at Mentos or its low energy would trigger further eruptions. Yet, how could he imagine excitement at Mentos without inducing a hallucination?

Fortunately, painful introspection soon yielded to a new challenge and a fresh opportunity to rehabilitate his image. Dick asked Dane to collaborate on a branding campaign for another major client—a producer of blood products for patients with genetic disorders. Most doctors and patients were unaware that an enzyme deficiency triggered lung tissue destruction resembling emphysema. While doing concept development, Dane interviewed patients who had all been misdiagnosed and mistreated by doctors their entire lives. Their genetic disorder was often discovered only after their breathing capacity was shot. One patient spoke between gasps on a ventilator to which he would be attached for the rest of his life.

The information Dane gathered inspired him. He conceived a campaign based on camouflage—how a rare thing can masquerade as a common one and go untreated until too late. Nature abounded with such examples so images and headlines came easily. Dick was enthusiastic. The clients liked the concepts, as well. Dane was elated and relieved. A week had passed since his outburst and his good work was making people forget his bad behavior.

20. NIPEL'S GIFT TO POSTERITY

There was no time to celebrate this positive reversal. On the afternoon of his triumph, Dane accompanied Dick and Maurice to Musgrove Pharmaceutical to meet Nipel and Sandra.

"I have bad news and good news," Nipel announced. "Musgrove Pharmaceuticals just announced they will lay off 10% of their employees. The good news is you may not have to see me next week."

"Don't say that, Nipel. We love you like a brother," Maurice said.

"I never speak to my brother," Dick said.

"But do not be sad. I can bust your balls until then," Nipel said before turning to Dane. "So how is the great guidelines brochure coming?"

"Great," Dane said.

"Excellent," Nipel replied. "I've waited too long for it...If my last day comes, I want to hand the one who fires me an enduring legacy...I will look him in the eye and he will know he can stop my income, destroy my career and mutilate my self-esteem but he cannot kill my contribution. "

"That's beautiful, Nipel," Maurice said. "We will make your dream come true."

"When?"

"Easter weekend's coming up. How about next Tuesday?" Dick said.

"Brilliant!" Nipel replied.

This reference book, which had languished as an afterthought for months only to become Nipel's gift to posterity, was now a hot job. Barbara claimed to have produced only a few new chapters and Dane had never seen them. Now it was his job to deliver a manuscript more ponderous than any he had ever attempted in order to redeem a client's fragile career and make his dubious dream of immortality come true—*in a few days.*

When the meeting was over, the agency people waited for the elevator. Dane fended off an attack of *mental bends* by admiring the Musgrove Pharma décor. It was aesthetically pleasing by drug company standards—pale green carpets, sable drapes, art deco wood paneled chevrons and brass railings. Even the elevator was richly appointed with dark mirrors, wood panels and polished brass controls.

"This place is nice," Dane remarked casually to mask his nerves.

"You don't get out much!" Dick quipped. The others laughed.

"I appreciate design," Dane defended himself.

"So why do you look like a dog's lunch?" Dick asked.

The others laughed enthusiastically.

Dane did not know how to respond. He wore khaki slacks, a corduroy jacket and a cream colored tie, and looked no better or worse than usual. He did not know why Dick insulted him or why the others laughed but it converted his panic into anger.

Dane was able to delay the *mental bends* until he returned to the office, where he suffered another "bubble brain" attack. He tried to treat himself. He stretched, threw folders and slapped his cheeks but the pressure remained unbearable. Unlike other hard projects, where he saw bulging reams of paper slide from flimsy folders and knew how screwed he was, Nipel's guidelines guidebook tortured him because of all that he could not see. He did not know where the document was, where to start, how much was done and how much was left to do.

Dane knew his first move was to supplicate Barbara for help. She had refused him before but he was in panic mode now. She must have a faint sense of duty or, failing that, a trace of compassion. Wouldn't the same woman who cared for a dog help a copy supervisor?

She picked up the phone on one ring.

"Hello?"

"It's Dane."

"I know. Your extension came up."

"Yeah. Heh, heh!" Dane laughed like it hurt.

"So are we on for lunch?" she asked.

Dane panicked.

"Lunch? Today? It's four o'clock!"

She laughed. "We weren't on for lunch. I'm screwing with your head."

"You're not alone. Remember Nipel's guidelines guidebook? It's due in a few days. I need your help."

"I can't," she said. "I'm doing a project for Tiny Anderson."

"You can't do it?" Dane demanded. "It was your project. You've *got* to do it."

"I can't," she yawned. "I have no time."

"But it all has to be done in two days and it's your job."

"I can't help you. I'm working for Tiny."

Dead air enveloped the impasse like dark matter no one dared to explore. A massive project needed to be done and he could not make her help him with it.

"Can you send me the work you did on it?" he asked.

"Sure," she said.

That afternoon, evening, and the next day Dane did nothing but write the *Floccacin* guidelines guidebook. By Thursday evening he was almost done, which would have been fine if the finished product were not due the next day.

21. A GOOD FRIDAY MORE—NO LESS

That evening, Becky received a call from the hospital where her mother was being treated. She had been moved into ICU. Her vital signs were poor as a new infection raged. She was on an antibiotic that Dane wrote about months before, which exacerbated her suffering.

When her mother was admitted to the hospital, Becky stayed with her for a week. After she stabilized, Becky limited her trips to weekends. Now with this setback, Becky could not wait for the weekend. Dane drove her to Penn Station Friday morning. And since Iris was on spring break, she accompanied Dane to Mentos.

Iris was delighted to go to work with Dane. She had been to every job he ever had. Iris loved art and always did something creative when she spent the day with him. She usually made friends with Dane's colleagues, especially art directors and production people, and left every agency with a bin's worth of supplies.

It was a fresh spring morning. Iris enjoyed the long, boring trip to Winton by controlling the radio. Although Iris's boisterous company made the trip more fun than it had ever been, Dane was under a cloud his daughter could not dispel. A holiday weekend approached and he was under enormous pressure to complete Nipel's guidelines guidebook. Dane had worked hard on it and it was almost done, but no one had seen it and Dane could not predict his colleagues' expectations. Would they make him work all day and night? He hated having his ten-year-old languish in an office all day.

Iris soon made friends with the Mentos staff, who bestowed on her their abundant office supplies, which she greedily accepted for her amusement. Dane had no permanent name plate near his door so Iris created one with pencils, markers and copy paper. Her zeal made Dane wistful. Iris made his job seem so enjoyable when he knew it wasn't, and he felt responsible for protecting her from that fact. He wished they could have fun together but a barrier had been erected between work and play.

Dane applied himself to the last pages of the guidelines guidebook with zealous efficiency, inspired by Iris and his desire to spend more time with her. He finished the document late that morning and handed it to Maurice's junior account executive, who received it cheerfully and said, "Well done."

"I hope so," Dane said. He and Iris strolled across the bridge over the Sasquatch River and went to the pizzeria, where they ate slices sitting in a red leatherette banquette. Among the other adults with children, Dane finally felt he fit in. After lunch, they strolled up the curving main street when rain poured down amid the sunshine. Dane and Iris played tag with the rain, running and laughing from awning to awning. It reminded him of when she was five and they played hide and seek.

When they returned to the office, Dane waited for feedback on Nipel's guidelines guidebook, Iris meanwhile crouched on his office carpet, putting the last flourishes on her special name plate for Dane. It featured his name in rounded letters festooned with flowers and other motifs. They taped the sign next to his door. Dane's office neighbors stopped by to compliment the artist but after they returned to their jobs, the dullness of Mentos set in and Iris was bored.

"Daddy, how long do we have to stay?" she asked.

"I don't know," he replied.

The assistant account executive walked in, nervous and upset, with Nipel's guideline guidebook in her hand.

"This is full of mistakes," she cried.

Dane was shocked by her harsh response. He thought he had done a good job and expected her to be happy that the guidebook was finished so far ahead of the end-of-day deadline. He flipped through the manuscript to review the mistakes. The pages had typographical errors mostly—registered signs not in superscript and extra spaces between some words.

"These aren't major," Dane said. "They're easy fixes."

"So fix them," she demanded.

Dane raced to correct the manuscript. Time was accelerating and he was trying to catch up, while mindful of Iris's growing boredom. He wished more than anything to complete the project and have everyone sign off—or have the arbitrary deadline extended. He hoped the agency would close early in observance of Good Friday.

"Daddy, how long will you be working?" Iris asked.

"I don't know, honey. Not long," he lied. "I'm sorry."

"It's okay. I'll be back."

She wandered off while Dane worked furiously to make the changes to Nipel's legacy.

A team meeting was called for three o'clock and it was 2:50. Dane glanced up from his screen and wondered where Iris was. He searched for her among the cubicles on his floor without success and became nervous.

"Iris!" he called.

"Daddy?"

She was in Barbara's office, sketching his bosom bully while they chatted.

"What are you doing?" Dane demanded. It was unclear to whom he addressed the question.

"Look, Daddy. I drew this. Do you like it?"

It was a sketch of Barbara. Iris made her look many years younger and as innocent as Iris.

"Yes, it's very good, but you shouldn't disappear like that," Dane reproached her.

"Don't worry. I didn't eat her," Barbara said.

The team meeting was in the conference room on the second floor near Dane's old office. Dane and Iris took the stairway.

"What were you and that...lady talking about?" he asked.

"Barbara? Nothing. School. She's nice."

"Yeah. She's great," Dane said.

Iris gravitated to the art studio while Dane entered the

conference room across the way where many group inquisitions had taken place.

Maurice called the session to order with a cough and a clap of the hands.

"This team is on a losing streak and it must stop. I'm serious, folks. We are professionals!" Maurice bellowed. "We should be able to do what needs to be done. We have been working on the guidelines guide book for ages. And I hear it's still not done!"

Dick turned to Dane with shock and betrayal configured on his face.

"Aren't you on this? I thought we discussed it."

"I've been working on it non-stop for days. I finished a draft this morning and submitted it."

"It's full of mistakes," the hysterical assistant screamed.

"They were typos. I already corrected them," Dane replied.

"Editorial still needs to see it," she insisted.

"So give it to them!" Dane retorted.

"They won't have it back in time. We need it for the printer on Monday!"

"That's your process. I've done all I can," Dane said.

"What am I hearing? You are copy supervisor!" Maurice boomed. "This is *precisely* what I'm talking about. This irresponsibility is destroying us like a cancer."

"I'm not irresponsible and I'm not a cancer," Dane replied. "I've met every deadline and this is no exception."

"We need this by Wednesday," the nervous assistant shrieked. "Editorial can't see it before Monday. That means everything has to be out the door Monday afternoon if we're having it bound!"

"This is inexcusable," Maurice said. "You knew the deadline."

The attack intensified. Dane felt like a bombarded target. He had three options. He could bolt from the room, duck under the table or stand up for himself. As a copy supervisor, he could not retreat so he shot to his feet.

"I won't take the fall for this, do you hear me? I've worked my tail off meeting impossible deadlines, handling crisis after crisis," Dane spoke out. "The guidelines guidebook was Barbara's project a month before I was hired. I took it on at the last minute because it had barely been started. I wrote most of it in two days with no help—so don't yell at me!"

"Sit down! I am the team leader," Maurice demanded.

"I will not sit down. I've done nothing but work hard since I got here but instead of support and encouragement, I'm scapegoated. There might be fewer crises with better management!"

"That's enough," Dick blurted sternly.

Dane and Maurice continued to shout and point fingers at each other while the other team members looked on aghast, until Dick adjourned the meeting.

"What was that all about?" Dick asked Dane.

"He was abusing me."

"He was being firm," Dick replied.

Dane realized he had done what Dick warned him never to do. He left the conference room downcast and depleted.

"Daddy, look!" Iris showed him a clear plastic triangle someone in the studio had given to her. "It's so cool. And check out this stylus. It can draw on the screen."

Iris was laughing and socializing with art directors. Neither she nor anyone in the studio knew what had transpired in the conference room. Dane tried to lose himself in her happiness but it reminded him of his forbidden outburst and intensified his guilt.

The office was quiet for the rest of the day. Dane completed the corrections to the guidelines guidebook before he and Iris left at sunset.

"Daddy, let's go back to the Bahamas this summer so we can swim in the ocean. It's so beautiful there. You can see fish swimming around you," Iris said.

"Okay, honey," he replied.

The happiness in her voice tore away at the instability he had brought into her life. It was like her sixth birthday party when he vowed to get a job and keep it for twenty years. That was a promise he should not have made. As Winton faded in the rear, he asked himself why he lost his cool knowing it would cost his job. This was no momentary lapse and it was pointless to reconstruct the scene. In a way he could not articulate, the event seemed inevitable.

That weekend provided merciful distractions. On Saturday Dane drove Iris to her art class and took her shopping for spring clothes. On Sunday they drove to Philadelphia to visit Becky's mother in the hospital. It rained hard all day. The sky was dark, the hospital was bleak and Becky's mother had tubes running up her arms and in her nose. A strong antibiotic drip made her body tremble. Becky's mother was glad to see her granddaughter and thanked Dane for visiting. Dane and Iris drove home when visiting hours were over, unaware that they had said their last good-byes to her.

22. DON'T TAKE IT OUT ON THE CHEESECAKE

Dane hoped the wet weekend would wash away his recent misconduct at Mentos and it would be forgiven if not forgotten.

He went to work on Monday in a mellow mood, prepared for the fallout. Eerily there was none. One executive gave him an assignment and told stories of the bad old days in advertising. Dane had meetings with other executives to discuss new projects. No one seemed to know about his recent tantrum and Dick never called him in to discuss it.

Had Dane reached that American Nirvana where talent was a license for bad behavior? Had he entered the same caste as the crotch-grabbing, hung-over copywriter who spoke at *The Institute of Design* orientation? An inner voice told Dane he would never be so lucky.

The next day, Dane bought "rain bread" for his colleagues at Mentos. In the bakery display case he saw a cheesecake with pineapple topping. Was there ever a more fortuitous symbol of redemption? Without hesitation, he bought this as a special gift for Dick along with the *babka* he purchased for everyone else. All morning he looked for Spilkus in his usual haunts—the dark office and hallways—but did not find him.

During the lunch hour, Dane walked over the bridge to send his taxes from the Winton post office. It was raining hard. When he returned, an account executive phoned about a new project. They were chatting amicably when Dick called on the other line. Dane explained to Dick that he was being briefed on a project and asked if he could get back to him.

"Come now," Spilkus replied.

Dick's cold tone intimated that Dane's sins were neither forgiven nor forgotten but Dane entered the creative director's dark office covered in fear-repellent. He believed he possessed a weapon against which Dick was defenseless. Dane opened the cake box and flapped its lid to let the scent of sweet ricotta permeate the room like delicious nerve gas. Dane felt invincible. He could keep his job forever!

Spilkus's eyes bulged angrily at his monitor but his nostrils twitched and flared at the rich aroma suffusing his office. Mrs. Mallory, the human resources director, occupied the couch. She was lactose intolerant and impervious to Dane's offering.

"Look," Dane announced. "Here it is! The pineapple cheesecake you've been craving for a month. I finally found it. *Bon appetit!*"

Dick's eyes ogled the cheesecake. His mouth gaped with delight, only to fall in a downward twist as bad timing churned potential pleasure into wrath.

"It's too late, Dane. We're letting you go," Spilkus said. "I warned you we'd have zero tolerance for another outburst. Maurice is devastated. He says he can't work with you. Your work is outstanding but your behavior is unacceptable."

"Most people here like me," Dane pointed out with unusual cool for someone being fired. He believed his pineapple cheesecake was protecting him. "The people I fought with have other conflicts. And you told me when you hired me I'd get writing help, but that never happened. I did the work of two or three people, nights and weekends. And when I got it done, I was abused. Is it strange that I lost my temper?"

"None of it excuses you," Dick said. "You're out of here."

"What about my projects?" Dane pleaded, as he started to realize that the power of his pineapple cheesecake was not working. "People depend on me. What do I tell them?"

"You tell them nothing. You're gone," Dick replied in monotone.

"What about Nipel's guidelines guidebook?"

Dane haggled to keep his job while Dick's eyes said, "You're fired" with implacable cruelty. Dane knew he sounded pathetic but could not resist. A half hour earlier he had projects, relationships, a niche at Mentos, but he was no longer a mind marketing medicine. Now that he was terminated, people would ask, "Where's Dane?" Dick would tell them, "He's gone" and that would be it.

Mrs. Mallory, the human resources director, liked Dane and was delighted by Iris, with whom she had chatted the previous Friday. Although lactose intolerant, Mrs. Mallory was moved by Dane's gift of cheesecake. She dabbed her eyes at the pathos of his situation.

"Dane, I'm not involved in hiring and firing. That's management's role. But when Dick told me you were being let go, I made an exception. I defended you and asked Dick to give you a second chance. You've made many friends and good impressions at Mentos. Of course, there was the incident some weeks ago but advertising is rough and tumble—and you tumbled. But now I've become aware of behavior that far exceeds...I could not believe you could do such a thing."

"What is it?" Dane demanded. He could not bear the suspense.

"It's come to our attention that you had improper contact with a female employee."

"What?" Dane groaned.

"...Physical in nature...We have zero tolerance..."

Dane's momentary numbness was followed by an aftershock.

"I was the victim! *She* made inappropriate contact! She grabbed my head and..." Dane stopped before describing what Barbara had done, for fear that even uttering the words would incriminate him. He adapted a rule he learned in his creative writing class: "Show, don't tell."

"She did this!" Dane thrust his palms backward toward his face and shook his head vigorously, his hands repeatedly slapping his face.

"I couldn't breathe!" Dane yelled. "I was gagging. I had to pull myself free, do you understand? She did it to me!"

Mrs. Mallory, a sedate woman in her 40's, stared at Dane incredulously. Dick had warned her about the likelihood of such an eruption, yet nothing could prepare her for its appearance and effect. Meanwhile Dick, who had been glancing furtively at the pineapple cheesecake, now gazed at it with unabashed longing.

"I don't want to play a game of *he said, she said*. Here is your last check. We've given you two weeks severance for the excellent work you've done," Mrs. Mallory replied.

Dane knew his job would officially be over once he grabbed the check so he let the HR director's hand extend the envelope in midair to postpone the inevitable. He refused to accept that he was fired until they acknowledged the accusations against him to be false. They were depriving him of his income but he would not be denied a respectable story to tell his wife. Becky would accept anger, fatigue, numbing work and a long commute to explain his leaving Mentos but how could he explain inappropriate contact—even if he was the unwilling recipient?

Mrs. Mallory finally inserted the separation envelope in Dane's hand. He opened it.

"The position for which Dane Bacchus was hired has been eliminated."

It was simple, sterile and unspecific, without condemnation or complaint. He was not terminated; the job was. After his initial relief at the vagueness of its wording, Dane reread the letter, stunned by its finality. Dick was impatient. Perhaps he wanted to be alone with his pineapple cheesecake.

"It's not hard to understand, Dane. It's over. You're fired. Get out!"

"What about the cheesecake?" Dane asked.

"What about the damned cheesecake?" Dick demanded. "Take the damned cheesecake!"

"Can't we eat cheesecake and talk this over like men?"

"There's nothing to talk about. I told you not to act out again and you did. Now go!"

It was all too much for Dane. He was trying to say, "I'm not a bad guy. I brought pineapple cheesecake," but Spilkus was not biting. He preferred to kick Dane out in the rain, to remove him from the payroll like he did with his children. Suddenly Dane picked up the cheesecake box and shuffled on tired feet toward Dick. He held the open cake box over the creative director's desk while Spilkus stared listlessly at his monitor so the fragrance would wind around the creative director and make him forget all else.

"Here, take your cheesecake!" Dame insisted.

Spilkus saw Dane holding the dessert like a sacrificial offering and lashed out against his own weakness.

"Get that out of my face!" Dick shouted. He swung his arm like he was hitting a backhand shot in tennis, knocking the cheesecake box out of Dane's control. It flipped and hit the floor.

"Oh dear," Mrs. Mallory said. "Dane, you should go now. We don't want more scenes."

Dane stared at the capsized box that hid its delectable contents like a cardboard hut.

"I'll clean it up," Dane said.

"That's all right. The cleaning people will do it," the HR woman said.

417

"No, let me," Dane insisted.

Dane crouched on the floor and gently lifted the box, to make a grisly find.

The pineapple cheesecake lay upside down with its yellow topping smeared across the felt carpet. Dane had intended to rescue the dessert and slide it back into the box but it was flat, separated in pieces and melting into the carpet fibers. Dane knelt over the cheesecake like it was a beloved corpse and tried molding it in a circle with his palms, but the cheese was too soft. He stared at his sticky hands covered with ricotta and fruit bits. He wanted to clean his hands but how was it possible with no towels or napkins? Should he lick off the cheese or wipe his hands on his pants? The cake could not be saved. The mess could not be cleaned. Dane wanted to cry. It was one thing to fire him but why did Dick waste his cheesecake? He should scoop the cheese into a ball and smash it in Dick's face, stuff it in his mouth and nose and make him gag.

"Get him out of here!" Dick railed.

Dane felt a gentle hand on his shoulder, urging him to rise.

"Come, Dane. Someone will clean it," Mrs. Mallory said gently.

Mrs. Mallory escorted Dane to the men's room, so he could wash his hands, and then back to his office, where he relinquished his key and Mentos ID, slung the strap of his battered briefcase over his shoulder, and removed Iris's paper name plate from the door. Iris had been so happy here just days before and had made many friends. What would he tell her? 'Daddy was fired for shouting!'

He drove the final 41 miles through fog and a driving rain, contrite and crestfallen for the Mentos fiasco. He anguished over telling Becky that he was unemployed again—after only forty days. His stint at Mentos had a strange trajectory. Normally, his jobs began with high expectations and ended in disillusionment, whereas Mentos started with doubts he attempted to overcome—could he handle the commute and the job?—and ended in the certainty that he could not. In between he tried harder than ever before to succeed but never did more than hang on.

On the stretch between Greenwich and New Rochelle, Dane's brain numbed to his predicament. He found comfort from an unlikely source. A song he had not heard for ages came on the radio and he sang along. "MacArthur Park is melting in the dark, all the sweet green icing flowing down. Someone left a *cheese*cake in the rain..." He never understood what a cake was doing in the rain or how it could melt—until now.

What was wrong with him? He had a disease, like rheumatoid arthritis, which flared up unpredictably and uncontrollably. Maybe he was infested with demons or under a curse. Yes, it was a curse. That was the only way to explain his failures.

At the last exit in New York before the bridge, Dane pulled up at a light near the bus station. A man crossed in front of his car and walked down the street. The pedestrian carried plastic bags in either hand, wore weather-beaten sneakers and a frayed raincoat, and waddled like a duck. Was it Ivan Blinsky, the donut-giving professor from the university? Dane had not seen Blinsky for years. He did not know if he was even alive but if he was, this would be the time he trudged back to the city after his evening classes.

At the chance sighting of his academic ally, Dane was stricken by guilt but also saw a chance for redemption. Blinsky had given Dane more than donuts. He had spoken highly of Dane throughout the university, enhancing his reputation, which resulted in more courses for Professor Bacchus to teach. Out of gratitude, Dane drove Blinsky into the city from the suburban campus after classes. One evening Ivan hinted that he would appreciate a dinner invitation but Dane did not extend it. Becky did not expect a guest and Dane doubted they had enough food for Blinsky. Besides, Dane had seen Blinsky eat donuts and wished to avoid an encore performance with meat and mashed potatoes. He left Ivan at the station and their friendship faded.

Blinsky's improbable appearance now punctuated and explained

419

the Mentos disaster. It was cosmic retribution for how Dane had treated Blinsky. Yet, now he could make amends.

At the green light, Dane rolled slowly down the street after the lumbering figure with the bags until he was a few yards in front of him. He pulled up to the curb, jumped out of the car, and met face to face with the man who had not come to dinner.

"Ivan Blinsky?"

The man's eyes bulged much like Blinsky's but were devoid of recognition and full of fear. Dane was oblivious to these warning signs and continued to unburden his troubled heart.

"I remember your donuts, Ivan. I appreciated them, too, even though I don't like donuts. Your generosity inspired me. Now I see what you went through. I know how it feels to give and give only to get taken. I'm so sorry if I offended you, Ivan!"

"I'm not Ivan and I don't know what you're talking about!" the man cried. "Just leave me alone!"

Dane peered through the darkness at his interlocutor, who was not Blinsky but an albino man frequently seen walking a small, black dog in the neighborhood.

"Here! Take the money!" the albino dog-owner cried. "Just stop talking!"

The frightened man dropped bills on the pavement and fled, as recommended by police mugging guidelines. Dane was stunned by this reaction. Had he cultivated a criminal aura by violating the natural corporate order? He noticed a police car idling a few blocks away, so he dashed to his car and sped away.

He found street parking with miraculous speed, only to sit in the car for a half hour, steeling himself before going home. He was so full of regret that he needed to discharge it in stages. First, he phoned the headhunter who had set up the Mentos job to apologize for being fired in less than three months, thus forfeiting her commission. She forgave him and surmised that Mentos let him go to avoid paying her. The recruiter added that Mentos must be a tough place to work since they always needed people.

When Dane told Becky the news, she told him not to worry; he'd find something else. She added that she was glad he no longer had to drive so much. Dane felt somewhat better. When he tucked Iris in for the night, she asked if his not working meant they wouldn't go on vacation, which made Dane's guilt flare anew.

A few days later as an act of contrition, Dane brought the car to the dealership service center for maintenance. He needed to spend money responsibly to absolve his immature behavior. The dealership service department was a great place for penance-spending since repairs routinely cost six hundred dollars. The mechanic found metal wedged in Dane's front tire near the inner tube. If that shard had penetrated a millimeter deeper, the mechanic said, a highway blow-out would have occurred and Dane would have been injured or dead.

Dane and Becky viewed this as a sign that his Mentos firing was good luck. But Dane's remorse lingered. He reflected on Goldfarb's warning. How could he keep moving from job to job? *Worse, what if he could not find another one?*

AD NOMAD 6
UNDER A COLONIAL POWER

Case 6-A
A NEW FRONTIER

1. MID-CAREER CRISIS

The eighty mile commute was no longer on his agenda but Dane's confidence was a wreck.

This termination was his worst; his first old-fashioned sacking. He was no longer an innocent victim of random job-kill and his misbehavior would cost him thousands in lost wages. Even the Labor Department might deny him unemployment benefits for being fired with cause.

Mentos was a black hole in his career, two unmentionable months yielding an incriminating secret. Dane had omitted jobs from his résumé because their brevity might denigrate his dedication, but insubordinate outbursts were corporate crimes. No one must know he was a hothead who ranted at account people—until they learned it for themselves.

Dane wondered if he would work again. The experimental phase of his career had passed when he could job-hop with impunity because he was inexperienced and full of potential. His frequent moves could no longer be viewed as missteps of a free spirit seeking a home but as the mayhem of a depraved corporate orphan unlikely to find one.

He once envied copywriters with five years of experience as specified in job listings. Now that he was one of them, experience should have been a precious ally but it wasn't. Advertising was a compromise, so why did his quest for security leave him twisting?

Recoiling from uncertainty, he dove into the nostalgia of his university files. There, he pored over lecture notes and talks he had delivered to colleagues who acclaimed his eloquence and erudition. He discovered his essay on the American Frontier—a personal treasure. *Niche and Nichelessness* explored the impact of the westward expansion on the American psyche, a topic apparently irrelevant to his current predicament, but which spoke to him now like wind on the prairies. Was he not a restless pioneer who refused to settle when his freedom was threatened?

Why had he ever left the university life? There he was appreciated. Dane did some career math: he had one teaching job for ten years; not one advertising job for even two. His next move was apparent: return to academia and write off advertising as a spastic detour.

Just then, Dane found the jewel of his academic career—his one publication in the university's peer-reviewed journal, *Episteme*. He turned the magazine's textured pages until he came to the title page of *Humbaba and the War in Iraq: Gilgamesh Revisited* with his by-line across the top. He read the piece ecstatically until he made a ghastly discovery.

The last two lines of his academic *chef d'oeuvre* were deleted! One sentence dangled with no predicate—like a severed head—and the last sentence was omitted entirely. The power of his argument was wasted, his masterpiece destroyed. At first, Dane suspected his own absent-mindedness but he located the hard copy in his files and it was impeccable. Through incompetence or spite, his university colleagues had polluted his academic posterity!

Dane's teaching nostalgia was officially over at that moment. He had been a talented and dedicated instructor but the fate of his scholarly masterpiece was a bitter memento of the disrespect and poverty that plagued his academic career.

Instinct urged him to shun personal reflection even if it was the turnpike to truth. Truth was out of his price range. He must aim at a more accessible target—the next job.

2. VOICE OF REDEMPTION

Throughout this career free fall, Dane heard a small voice in his head. It belonged to Albert Griffin, his first headhunter. Dane recalled that Griffin had sent his book to another agency when he accepted the Mentos job.

Dane dialed Griffin's number with trepidation. In their most recent chat, the recruiter had slammed the phone on Dane for grabbing the Mentos job while declining an interview Albert arranged for him with a Canadian agency. While Dane pleaded financial duress, Griffin accused Dane of selling out for a soul-killing, time-wasting, career-annihilating dead-end in of all places, Winton, CT! In retrospect, Griffin was right—but did such an admission come too late?

"Hey, Albert, it's Dane," he said.

"The Connecticut nutmeg!"

"I'm not in Connecticut," Dane replied.

Griffin was silent. Dane closed his eyes and cringed.

"I can't believe you called," the recruiter said with his trademark hush of excitement. "You won't believe this. The Canadians still haven't filled that copywriter position. Do I have your book?"

"You submitted it," Dane said.

"Oh...Right."

"But I want to include some great stuff I did in Connecticut," Dane added.

"Great! Be here by five o'clock and I'll send it tonight," Griffin demanded. "This is *hot*. They loved your book three months ago. They'll love it even more now."

Dane was paranormal about doom. However, a greater force seemed to be working now in his behalf. How often did an opportunity linger for months? As he raced to Albert's office, he cried out in the street an improvised headline of thanks, "From the depths of Mentos, redemption is *heaven-sentos!*"

3. HORIZONTAL MANAGEMENT

It was a splendid day in late April when Dane interviewed at the offices of Georgian Shield, an award-winning Canadian agency, located in the Dole, Osborn and Adelman building, the cradle of advertising's golden age.

Georgian Shield was an award-winning subsidiary of DOA Worldwide, the last advertising network with a Madison Avenue address. Dane viewed this interview as a commentary on his ability— and ascendancy. He was vying for a senior creative position at the agency that epitomized creativity; that told the world to *dream in color* and *to invite a dog to dinner*; where Goldfarb was once a proud professional before his groveling and pandering period. The best part was that Dane felt he belonged here. Despite his professional pratfalls, Dane retained the swagger of an advertising genius of global stature. He believed he was an opinionated maverick who put an imprint on all he did and raised the quality of everyone around him—and was prepared to say so during his interview.

Merely doing business in this hallowed landmark signified success. In the marble atrium even security guards had class. Dane did not wait in line for a galoot in a bad blazer to ask for ID and to call his party. A pretty woman in a short skirt, with long, black-hosed legs crossed on a high stool, flashed a smile, asked Dane to speak his name into a camera and wished him luck like she knew he really needed it.

This was how advertising was meant to be, Dane mused. This made all of the compromises, mediocrity, sucking-up, idea theft, interminable hours and insufferable meetings half-bearable. At least here you were pandering *somewhere*, not in a *pre-fab*, rehab, glass-and-concrete   complex at the nexus of two interstates between a *Pathmark* and a wetland.

As Dane emerged from the elevator, a wall-sized monitor assaulted his eyes with a Cannes award-winning commercial produced by the Brazilian office of the most creative network on the planet. Dane watched women in thongs doing a samba on *Volkswagens* while shooting water cannons at SUVs. Dane knew he would never contribute to such "killer," award-winning work, but being close to it might enhance his creativity via mental osmosis.

Managers at Georgian Shield took pride in their award-winning *horizontal interview* process. In retrospect, Dane thought the process was called *horizontal* because it left the candidate horizontal—from exhaustion. Yet it was an effective way of giving everyone ownership of the hiring of new colleagues to ensure the best fit. Dane was slated to meet several key people. Dane's first interviewers were Juan and Jeremi. Juan, a short, nasal art supervisor, described how uplifting it was to shoot commercials for a drug that gave hope to dying cancer patients. Jeremi, a large, scowling woman, told Dane what it meant to grow up in Muskatoon, Manitoba where sheep herded down Main Street and they called it a parade. Juan and Jeremi nodded at Dane's book without comment.

Then Rupert McIntosh, the head of the New York office, a dapper man with a goatee, discussed his career and last year's Thanksgiving *turducken,* before describing the job for which Dane was considered. It would feature frequent trips to the client's corporate headquarters in Luxembourg and research sessions in Singapore, Paraguay and Zimbabwe because it was vital to learn how gastroenterologists worldwide felt about prosthetic rectums.

Dane was gang-interviewed for six hours by ten people, including a global strategist, an office manager, an intern, two accountant executives, a receptionist, a mailroom worker, a deli deliveryman, a cleaning lady and a newly-hired art director named Ron, who sat in a dark office and spat organic sunflower seeds into a green waste basket because he heard it benefited both his prostate and the environment. Ron had no clue why he was interviewing Dane, so Dane asked himself questions and answered them, while Ron watched with tentative amusement.

By the fifth hour, Dane was depleted. He had been offered no refreshment and his brain had used up the caffeine from his morning coffee. He strained to listen to his interviewers, to present his work and to explain his wispy ponytail. Meanwhile, the award-winning office manager chose not to bring Dane the bottled water she promised in order to test his reaction to adversity. It was all part of the award-winning *Yucca Flats* candidate assessment process.

Finally, a short man with a red mustache bounded into the room. His face was ruddy and perspiration droplets rolled down his hypertensive cheeks. This was the award-winning creative director from Canada. He shook Dane's hand.

"Ay. Dane. Nigel Hogbine here—there...and everywhere. Ho! Ha! *Sawrry*. I use Beatles' references as *mood-freshener*. Good meeting you. You've got a great science bag," he said.

Bag? That must have been the Canadian word for "book" or portfolio.

To put Dane at ease, Nigel Hogbine told him he had been voted the student in his senior class most likely to resemble his name. Dane's look of astonishment prompted Nigel to explain. "I s'pose they thought I looked like a hog. Ha! Ha! The laugh was on them, *ay*? My family's name wasn't originally *Hogbine*. They changed it from *Hawriceck*. My father thought *Hogbine* had class!"

Dane chuckled nervously as Nigel flipped through his book. The creative director went "Ummm" several times and closed it. "Like I said the first five times I saw it: *first-rate work*. So let me tell you about us. Georgian Shield is the number one creative shop in Canada. Now we have clients in the States. We need the best talent we can find. Thanks for coming in."

Nigel shook Dane's hand and left the room as fast as he entered. When Dane left the DOA building, he had no job.

"You're their guy," Griffin gushed the next day. "It's between you and another guy."

"If I'm the guy, who's this other guy?" Dane asked.

"There's always another guy. Sit tight. You've got the inside track."

Dane went through a book of stamps sending "Thank you" letters to everyone who interviewed him and waited. Two weeks later Griffin called. "Don't tell your wife but I heard unofficially you're their man...the favorite...you've got the lead along the rail on the homestretch."

"*Ye-e-e-e-e!*" Dane whinnied skeptically.

"If you take a job on a cruise line I'll kill you," Griffin said.

"I won't."

"This is big. Georgian Shield is a subsidiary of the most prestigious agency network in the world. They just won the Ad Council Award of Newfoundland. The fact that they like you means you're an international star. Don't blow it."

"I won't," Dane said. But he wasn't sure what there was to blow.

4. LAST HURDLE

A month had passed since Dane's gang-interview. Albert Griffin phoned Dane every week to remind him he was their man, he had the inside lane of the fast track and the job was his to lose.

Still nothing happened.

Then, one unemployed Monday when Dane wondered if he should buy life insurance and have himself killed over a parking space, Albert Griffin phoned.

"What did I tell you? They're making you an offer," Griffin said. "They would have made it sooner but they didn't think they could pay you."

"Did you tell them I work for food?" Dane said.

"You do but I don't," Griffin said.

Later that afternoon, Griffin left a message. The offer would be faxed.

No fax came. Dane was losing hope when Griffin called.

"The president and executive vice president want to meet you in a two-way-no-holds-barred web-chat. Tomorrow at noon at the Madison Avenue offices."

The next day, Dane sat on the tenth floor of the most prestigious agency network in the world. On a large monitor, two Canadian men, one rotund, the other youthful and fit, fired questions about his hobbies.

"So, Dane, play hockey?" The fit man asked.

"No."

"Knock-hockey?" The rotund man asked.

"Not recently."

"Hmmm. Do you skate at all?"

"Poorly. But I swim."

"Very good! Well, thank you for coming in."

Dane left the cradle of advertising despondently, believing he had blown the interview. Why was he honest about not playing hockey, the Canadian national sport? And who swam in Canada but seals and polar bears?

Later that afternoon, Griffin called. "So how did you do?"

"Okay. But I don't know."

"*You did great.* They just sent over the offer."

Dane fell to the floor in abject gratitude for this sixth or seventh chance. His Connecticut debacle was rectified and he would again provide for his family. He was working in New York at a Canadian subsidiary of a multinational corporation. Life was worth living after all.

Case 6-B
GROWTH FACTORS

5. ADVERTISING JUST HOW HE PICTURED IT

After six weeks Dane had the Georgian Shields job. It came with an office on Madison Avenue, no less—in the heart of Manhattan, a block away from Rockefeller Center.

Dane always fantasized what it would be like to have a great career and get up each morning, loving his life because his work mattered. Finally, he was *in* the world, not clinging to the rim of a spinning centrifuge that flung unwanted souls like flecks of spit.

The horizon line where reality met expectation, where images and ideas evoked by a phrase like "Madison Avenue" matched the experience, were rare—and this was it.

This job, this office, this building, this window, this street enveloped Dane. He even imbibed creativity from the DOA office ventilation. His humble gratitude for this miraculous career boost evolved into more grandiose emotions. Ensconced in his Golden Age of Advertising office, in a position that waited for him for months, Dane's gut, which had been silent since Dane scolded it during his hallucinations at UNIHEALTH months ago, now told him that fate had fingered him for a higher purpose.

Each morning he used the Ogden Adelman board room toilet. It was identified by a bronze plaque on the door emblazoned with the name of the legendary agency founder and Hall of Fame copywriter. In the Adelman john, the bowl was full of aquamarine disinfectant before the day's first flush. The brilliantly tinted water seemed to sanctify its imminent pollution. To absolve his trespass of this historic place, Dane sat on the can with a tiny book of Adelman's sayings. Dane had received it as a keepsake at his human resources orientation, along with a tote bag, a key chain and a tee-shirt. The measure of Adelman's genius was that in an industry that masticated copy and evacuated copywriters, his ideas were immortal. He gave a sleazy trade respectability and raised hucksterism to an art.

"Effective messages speak to the heart and the gut," Dane read.

Rumination and evacuation occurred simultaneously, producing inspiration. Dane wondered if the great Adelman ever sat here. If so, was it possible that Dane absorbed his genius transdermally through his butt cheeks? Reading Adelman's epigrams reinforced his faith that he was called to Georgian Shields to carry out an important mission. He pledged to produce memorable advertising, to think strategically and to settle for no less than the best. Reading the master's thoughts while sitting on his seat challenged Dane to address each creative problem with one overriding question: "What would Ogden think?"

6. TALKING, CHEWING & CHOKING

On his first day, he sat in a web conference with Sally Takamitsu, the account director in Toronto. Dane would be writing for Sally's client, *Grovil*, a topical biologic compound that healed diabetic foot ulcers. Sally had product-driven black hair, a smooth, round face and a rapid-fire delivery that emphasized adverbs, prepositions and conjunctions.

"Hello, Dane, I just want to tell you HOW VERY excited we are to have you ON BOARD. We have SO much for you to do. AND I can't wait to tell you all ABOOT it."

An appetizing lunch was served but Dane felt uncomfortable tucking into a thick sandwich while people watched him masticate on a monitor.

When he managed to sneak a bite, Sally asked him a question. Dane chewed vigorously, while holding up his finger to indicate that he would swallow imminently and be right with her. However, seeing how perturbed Sally was at the delay, he gagged on his sandwich.

"Oh, dear!" Sally said. "*Sawry!* Can someone give him water like immediately?"

Unable to stop coughing, Dane gave himself a *Heimlich* by punching himself in the solar plexus. The meeting proceeded.

Later that afternoon, Nigel Hogbine chugged into the New York office to interview a young art director candidate.

"Welcome aboard," Nigel said, shaking Dane's hand. "Liking your first day, *ay?*"

They went to at a neighborhood pub, where they drank *Guinness*, ate chicken wings and discussed *The Newsroom* and *Slings and Arrows*, two brilliant Canadian television series Dane admired. This was advertising at its civilized best. Dane thought he was respected, even liked. What was wrong with this picture?

7. NEW HIRE EUPHORIA

Dane always had to hype a job to himself. His "new hire high" helped him perform at a peak level of competence and enthusiasm for weeks or even months. If he believed a job was a turning point toward greatness, he fooled himself into putting in long hours and doing ridiculous amounts of work.

It was an unwritten rule that a new hire must love his job. Colleagues expected no less because they relied on new hire exuberance to help them cope with their old-timers' *ennui*. A new hire reminded veterans how they felt once upon a time when their positions meant change, novelty, a paycheck—before redundancy and boredom set in.

However, Dane's current euphoria exceeded his norm. This job triggered a mythic hallucination. He believed his hire was due to providence, that he was The Chosen One, whose portfolio bedazzled all who beheld it.

On his second day at Georgian Shield-New York, a courier dropped Dane's luminous portfolio on his desk, warped and discolored with an irremovable label. Dane's sacred book had suffered water damage in the Georgian Shield mailing room in the long months of deliberation before his ultimate hire.

This sign might have returned Dane to earth—if he had wished to go there—but he saw Georgian Shield as a promised land for advancement. In other agencies there were talent vacuums to fill but peers and overseers were always present with knives aimed at his back. In Georgian Shield-New York, Dane was apparently

435

autonomous and unchallenged; his supervisors were across the border and he was their man in America.

At last, Dane had a clear shot at making his mark on advertising.

8. PARTNERS

In keeping with Georgian Shield's tradition of creative teams, Dane was paired with Ron, a handsome, but diffident young art director. Ron holed up in his dark office with blinds drawn and talked to no one but his girlfriend, who phoned him incessantly with problems related to female ailments and their miniature dog.

Ron's low profile was a personality trait and career strategy. He had studied advertising at a special graduate school before enduring lean times in New York. Having never experienced the conservative redundancy of pharmaceutical advertising, Ron was eager to learn for the sake of some security.

Dane often sat in Ron's office to develop rapport. "Relationships matter!" he repeated to himself. If Georgian Shield believed in partnerships, Dane resolved to be the best partner ever.

Ron was an advocate of spiritual and physical cleansing, exotic spas and therapies. He was a fitness fanatic, who took vitamins, drank bottled water, and had toxins removed from his body by submerging his feet in ionized water.

One Monday, Ron came to work exhausted. He had spent Sunday from dawn to dusk learning spiritual techniques, like turning his inner eye on his internal organs. In this workshop Ron learned to read the minds of *things*, which were inanimate but not stupid.

"If things have feelings," Dane remarked, "floors must be bitter because we walk all over them."

"You're laughing now," Ron replied as he stared at his screen. "But things get the last laugh. Do you know why they break? Because they know we're just using them."

Dane thought Ron was either insane or a brilliant politician. This outburst of "Pan*thing*ism" could be Ron's way of warning Dane not to demean him. Dane made a note to himself, "Treat Ron like a human being."

That afternoon Ron's computer crashed. Yet his faith in the consciousness of things never wavered. When Dane barged into Ron's office the next morning, he found the young art director hugging his motherboard with his eyes shut. Only when the IT guy came later that day with a new cord did Ron leave his office.

While Ron's girlfriend nurtured his spiritual and physical needs, a retail department store executive gave him career guidance. On tennis courts and in hot tubs his mentor tutored him on "how to work the work environment." These tutorials were paying off. Dane noted how his partner's voice quavered with reverence when he received a call from a supervisor. "He's really good," Dane thought.

Dane perceived early on that he and Ron were treated differently. Dane agonized through multiple interviews and weeks of job limbo, while Ron was hired fast and paid to do nothing for months. A week after Dane started, Ron went on a two-week vacation during which he and his fiancée wallowed at a healing mud spa while Dane waded through a morass of tiresome projects.

A man less paranoid than Dane could have easily inferred that Ron was more highly valued than he was.

However, seven years of advertising experience had taught Dane that it was premature to resent a new partner after a few weeks. He speculated that Ron was doubtless an amazing art director despite his inexperience, and had hidden qualities, besides. He was right.

When Nigel came to town, he invited Dane, Ron, Juan and Jeremi to dinner. At midnight, they emerged from the restaurant in a driving rain. Everyone looked for cover or a cab except Ron, who got drenched by dashing across the street to buy Nigel an umbrella so the creative director would stay dry while walking several feet to his hotel.

Even Nigel smiled with embarrassment at Ron's obsequious kindness. "What can I say?" he asked.

Servility was Ron's special power. Dane acknowledged that he could not compete with his partner in fawning and groveling and it would be unseemly to try. He also knew he would need to forget Ron's kiss-ass brown-nosing or he would be unable to respect or work with him.

The hitch was that Dane was cursed with a superb memory. The more he tried to forget Ron's sycophancy, the worse it plagued him. The mental acrobatics he needed to perform this feat depleted his new hire euphoria and forced him to reevaluate the heroic myth of his hiring. Perhaps, the Canadians had waited so long to hire a copywriter that Dane was handed the job by default.

Dane found himself again in an agency where he would be underestimated and undervalued, which translated into working harder and longer hours. Yet his inspiration was so high and his ambition so sensitized, that he viewed his undervaluation as a gift—a motivational power tool. He knew more than his supervisors about what needed to be done. If he was the only one who knew how good he was, he would disarm his detractors.

9. HEALING: THE PATH TO DOMINATION

Dane's account, *Grovil*, was the major piece of business in Georgian Shield's New York office. *Grovil* was an ointment containing a laboratory cloned growth factor that promoted tissue growth in diabetic foot wounds. Dane spent long hours reading about the disease, the drug and how to induce medical insurers to pay for it despite its steep cost.

First, he immersed himself in the story of diabetes and its impact.

Twenty million Americans had diabetes and many diabetics had foot ulcers that did not heal. These wounds often went untreated, even unnoticed, because diabetes caused neuropathy—nerve damage. Since healing was compromised, diabetic foot ulcers often were badly infected. Infection spread and tissue died. At that point, a surgeon had to debride—cut away—the gangrene and the open wound was wrapped in moist dressings until it healed. However, once infection invaded bone, amputation was often the only option.

Along with their other contributions, the ancient Egyptians were great innovators in wound care. They gave dry and moist bandaging to the world and were the first to apply salves to wounds. Egyptian wound care, with refinements, remained the first line of treatment for diabetic foot wounds.

Grovil was a major breakthrough. By cloning growth factors, Grovil stimulated the regeneration of healthy tissue. In clinical trials *Grovil* was proven to accelerate wound healing when compared to conventional wound management.

However, *Grovil* cost several hundred dollars for a small tube and doctors were reluctant to prescribe it. Most diabetes patients could not afford *Grovil* out of pocket, and insurance companies would do almost anything to avoid paying for it. After three years on the market, *Grovil* had barely scratched the wound-treatment market with twenty million dollars in sales. At this rate, *Grovil* would never be profitable or recoup the drug company's significant investment. It needed to be re-launched, remarketed and reintroduced to resistant physicians.

Dane's first assignment was to write a brochure to explain to doctors how to prescribe *Grovil* to their patients while inducing insurance companies to pay for it without fraud.

His second project was a series of *mood boards*. Mood boards were a research tool to assess which message and tone would be most compelling to patients and physicians. Each mood board was a poster conveying a theme supported by icons and phrases. The five *Grovil* mood boards had five themes, selected by the client and account team according to marketing objectives and audience insights. The themes were "high science," "medical emergency," "speed of action," "drug as hero" and "peer approved." Each concept addressed a product benefit or a medical issue linked with *Grovil*.

439

After a week of perfecting headlines and subheads and shuffling icons, Dane, Sally and the clients tested the mood boards at a research facility. The theme that resonated best with the greater number of physicians and patients would become the re-launch campaign theme.

10. RESEARCH, REVELATION, REJECTION

At research, Dane finally met the account director, Sally Takamitsu in person. Sally draped her body, arms and hands on anyone whom she wished to persuade of anything. The most frequent recipient of her soft-skinned attention was the *Grovil* marketing director, a conservative family man who responded to her unsolicited heat with crisp resistance.

Doctors and patients, fifteen total subjects, reviewed the five mood boards. One diabetes patient was an affable, obese man. He knew he damaged his health but he could not help himself. He would eat a healthy salmon dinner at home, only to sneak away to his friend's house and put away several large cheeseburgers. His diabetes was uncontrolled and he had foot ulcers.

"So what would you say was your favorite mood board?" the moderator-psychologist asked him.

"They're all awesome," the diabetic glutton gushed. "Can I take those *M&Ms*?"

"Sure, help yourself."

The diabetic man submerged his fist in the candy dish, filled his hand with M&M's and slammed them in his mouth. He sloshed them around between inflated cheeks, swallowed and reached for more candies.

"But which was your favorite concept?" the moderator asked.

"It's so hard. They were all really good," the diabetic said. He shoveled deep handfuls of M&Ms into his mouth, chomped twice and swallowed.

"Try to tell me. Did you like the medical emergency?" the

moderator asked.

"Oh yeah. Can I have a *Coke*?" the diabetic asked.

"Sure," the moderator handed a *Coke* can to the diabetic, who flipped the top and downed its contents in a fluid motion.

"So can you tell me why you like the *medical emergency* concept?" the moderator asked.

"'Cause my life is one big, fat medical emergency. Ha! Ha!" the uncontrolled diabetic said as he belched the carbonation.

Behind the two-way mirror, Sally gave *high-fives* and thumbs up to everyone. "I told you medical emergency was the ticket!"

Then the interview took a turn. The diabetic sat back in his chair, his eyes glazed and his mouth agape. He did not look well.

"So what do you think of this message?" the moderator asked in his soft, officious voice. No answer. "What do you think of this mood board?"

The diabetic man's mouth went slack; eyelids drooping, his eyes rolled back. He keeled over on the chair, coughed and spewed a geyser of vomit.

"Are you all right?" the moderator asked the sick man in the same bland, middle register. Then he broke professional character and spoke to the two-way mirror. "We need an ambulance and a mop."

They changed interview rooms. Doctors came in the afternoon. They were not golf-playing demigods of popular stereotype but hard-working, weary men, beleaguered by teeming caseloads of hopeless patients. These physicians sighed when asked to comment on the mood boards as if they were being asked to take a test for which they had not studied.

"Doctor, do you agree that diabetic foot ulcers are a medical emergency?"

"Nah! Diabetic foot ulcers can go on for years, usually do," one doctor replied. "I know—the drug company's going to try to take away my license for saying that diabetic foot ulcers aren't as serious as cancer or stroke. Even if diabetic foot ulcer were as serious as the plague, I'd need data to believe '*Grovil* reduces the risk of amputation.'"

Another doctor sorted through the mood boards like he was tossing bad cards. He smirked and chuckled.

"Doctor, what do you think of medical emergency?" the psychologist-moderator, a vulture for responses, asked.

"It's wonderful. That's what you want me to say, isn't it?" the doctor stared at the two-way mirror, where he suspected the drug company people were watching him.

"We want you to tell us what you think," the moderator insisted.

"What I think?" the doctor mimicked and smirked. "Okay. The drug company would probably accuse me of malpractice for not using *Grovil* early in the healing process, but my patients can't even afford the co-pay for *Grovil* if the health plan approves it."

"Doctor, do you think your patients would benefit from *Grovil*?"

"Maybe, but my patients can't even read their prescription bottles! I had a patient bite into a hemorrhoid suppository! Now *that's* a medical emergency!"

"Doctor, does *Grovil* sound like an effective therapy?"

"Oh, yeah. It's wonderful." The doctor said, waving at the two way mirror where the *Grovil* team watched. "You hear me? I said your product is terrific! But it's too damned expensive!"

The doctor turned to the moderator. "Have I been helpful?"

One by one, every doctor reiterated the financial issue with *Grovil*.

After three days of research no theme was a clear winner. The team convened to discuss their learnings.

"Maybe, we should consider the economic angle as a concept," Dane said.

"Cost isn't urgent or sexy," Sally said. "And it's incredibly *boring*!"

"Are diabetic foot ulcers sexy in any way?" Dane asked. "Cost is the major barrier and we don't have one message to address it."

"It's a good point," the Grovil marketing director agreed. "But the price isn't coming down."

Sally had quickly worked herself into high dudgeon.

"Well, I think it's so outrageous and out of line for a copywriter to try to direct strategy. This is my job. Time and again the most powerful message has proven without a *doot* to be medical emergency. Amputation grabs people's attention. If doctors and patients see how close diabetic foot ulcers are to amputation, cost will be swept aside!"

Sally adjourned the meeting, and whisked the client off to another room to show more data. Dane drifted off to research a men's room. When he returned to the research area, he opened a side room door by mistake. Sally was on the table with the client standing between her legs, gasping hard. Sally turned to the intruder and screamed, "Get out now!"

"It's urgent!" The client gasped.

11. THE IMPORTANCE OF BEING URGENT

After five research sessions in three cities, involving twenty subjects—twelve doctors and eight patients—Sally, the *Grovil* marketing director, and the research psychologist concluded that "medical emergency" was the message doctors and patients preferred and would be the platform for the *Grovil* re-launch.

"How bogus does it get?" Dane muttered. "In my notes 'medical emergency' came in fourth...*Fourth!* Out of five messages."

"That was in Edison, New Jersey," Ron adduced. "Maybe people felt differently in Houston and Milwaukee."

"Doctors are the same everywhere. They don't like people telling them how to do their job. Why do we bother with research?" Dane asked.

He knew the answer. Research resulted from the usual suspects: due diligence, hand-holding and covering your ass. If the campaign did poorly because of a flawed marketing strategy, the product manager blamed research.

However, in this case, research indicated a clear direction, which the *Grovil* marketing team deliberately ignored. If the data were interpreted correctly, the manufacturer would lower the drug's cost, sell more units, heal more wounds, make more profit, establish a leadership role in the diabetes community, and everyone would be served.

But Sally's urgency concept was in the way.

Dane coped with this frustration in his usual way. He made a short pilgrimage to the Adelman toilet to use the commode and read what his mentor, Ogden Adelman, had to say on the subject.

"What do I do now, Ogden?" Dane asked.

"Even the best creative can't make a product do what it doesn't. If you try, it will be exposed as fake," the voice of Adelman spoke from page 70.

"Yes, I know," Dane replied as his crisis deepened. He read one of Adelman's adages on Page 90. "When you're in a box, bring scissors."

Dane was surely in a box. It was the essence of advertising. When people said, *"Think out of the box!"* It was no injunction to be original but a taunt, as in "Think out of this box if you can."

Heal now or amputate was a good message. If doctors did not take a *wait and see* approach to cancer or heart disease, why would they wait for a foot wound to turn gangrene? The problem was that doctors would not listen. No one cared about giving poor patients quality care if Medicaid, HMOs and Medicare did not pay for it.

And even if amputation was a legitimate threat, the FDA would never let *Grovil* use it as a promotional message because there no clinical data to prove *Grovil* reduced amputations—and there never would be, since medical ethics forbade a clinical trial where participants risked amputation to test a claim.

Such obstacles aside, Dane relished the creative challenge

because it was his alone. In most agencies, people swarmed on a project such as *Grovil* like garter snakes in a mating ball, but Dane's bosses were in Canada and he was unopposed in New York. Ron knew cars, skateboards and breakfast foods, but nothing about drugs. He nodded passively at whatever Dane said. Dane believed Ron was his reward for every art director who ever domineered over him.

Dane and Ron perused the creative brief and brainstormed. How could *Grovil's* faster healing be linked with lower risk of amputation without saying it? Dane imagined a closet full of shoes with only left shoes. Ron proposed a crossing sign whose man icon had a truncated leg. Such urgent visuals allowed headlines to be suitably vague. Dane considered a macabre testimonial: A ballet slipper, a photograph of a girl in a tutu. The headline would read: "Your left foot has done so much for you...how sad to see it go."

Ron designed a time bomb strapped to a foot; a dynamite stick protruding from a diabetic ulcer.

Then Dane hit the message to incorporate urgency *and* cost. An elderly couple slow-danced; a dotted line circumscribed the man's foot like a perforation for coupons. The dotted line around the foot implied amputation without stating it. It might also multi-task as a peel-off game. The reader would peel the strip off the foot and receive up to $50 off his next tube of $300 *Grovil*.

Advertising was fun again. The creative ideas were abundant and the Ron's executions were superb. All was going well. So what had to happen next?

Case 6-C
THE GOOD FIGHT

12. THE BAD OLD DAYS

Nigel, the creative director, was going on a vacation cruise to Iceland to bathe in volcanic waters. Since his ship was leaving at the end of the week, he needed the concepts Dane and Ron were working on by Friday at 1 PM in order to review them before his departure. Ron and Dane were on schedule. Ron e-mailed Nigel *PDFs* of their concepts as they went along. Then on the eve of Nigel's vacation, the creative director made an unexpected request.

He asked Ron to draw the concepts with markers on paper and fax them to Toronto. He said he wanted to see bare ideas without computer images and tasty fonts. It was how concepts were done twenty years ago, he said, when he was starting out.

"Why is he going nostalgic on us now?" Dane wondered. Creatives often whined about the *good old days* before computers made layouts so easy that clients expected finished ads before there were any ideas in them. The grousers were mainly copywriters who envied art directors for the uncanny powers computers rendered them.

How wickedly ironic it was that Nigel, an art director, wanted to turn back time. Ron was stricken.

"Nigel," he pleaded, "I haven't drawn anything since art school eight years ago."

"Don't worry, lad. I don't expect a finished comp. I want thinking, not execution. You'll find it helpful, too. *Ay?*"

"But it will take forever."

"Trace the images or do stick figures," Nigel suggested breezily. "Look forward to seeing them. Get them to me by noon so we can talk. I'm out of here before one."

Nigel's quest for purity of concept was laudable but if he wished to emphasize that ideas mattered more than pretty layouts, he might have chosen a better time. Was he making the New York creative team work twice as hard for laughs? He may have wished to humble Ron by exposing his poor draftsmanship or to test Dane's ideas without an art director's beguilement. Whatever Nigel's motive, asking Ron to do computer-less comps was like Pharaoh ordering more bricks with no straw.

Dane reminded himself that drawing concepts by hand was as authentic as the building they were in. He tried to relive the excitement of De la Femina and Travisano creating a campaign at 8:30 AM, a half hour before the client showed up for a presentation. Dane should have been thrilled to have this classic advertising fire drill. Then why was it making him sick?

Watching Ron, the cocky *click-meister,* slowly move a marker over tracing paper and a magazine image agitated Dane. It was torture to observe someone competent in one respect look so hapless in another.

"How is it coming?" Dane asked Ron.

"I hate this."

"Art directors are expected to draw."

"It's not the same," Ron replied as he focused with dead eyes and a slack jaw on the tracing. "Artists specialize like doctors. Some guys illustrate comps all day. They're fast and accurate. Me doing this is like an ophthalmologist setting a broken bone...He could do it but not like an orthopedic surgeon."

"You're right. It's my nerves talking instead of my brain."

"I like how you said that," Ron laughed.

It was the first time in a month that the two men had had such a long conversation.

By 12:45 PM the next day, Ron had completed forty concepts. He knelt before the fax machine to supplicate it to work and faxed the traced sheets to Nigel. When no response came at 1:15 the partners phoned Toronto but could not get through. At 1:30, Nigel phoned. "So, boys, where are the concepts, ay?" he demanded.

"I sent them at 12:45," Ron said.

"I never got them."

"OK, we'll send them again."

"Do it now. I'm leaving," Nigel replied casually.

Dane and Ron faxed the concepts as fast as they could but Nigel left without reviewing their work. He would not return for two weeks and testing was in three. It was a first for Dane. Either Nigel was the coolest boss or the worst.

"We missed the boat," Dane said. "I hope Nigel doesn't miss his."

13. A SURPRISING REVERSAL

Nigel was a cunning manager. Like an ace bombardier, he dropped his payload with precision from high above and blew creative peasants to smithereens. He found the weakness on this team and exploited it. By changing the concept format at the last minute and leaving before he reviewed his team's work, he shut down the *Grovil* project until his return. Dane and Ron would be idle for two weeks and have themselves to blame.

After six weeks, Dane saw the first threat to his autonomy as the senior medical writer in the New York office. Because he and Ron failed to deliver the work on time to Nigel, they might be perceived as incompetent numbskulls in need of micromanagement. They handed Nigel a pretext for seizing control of their creative output. Ron's lack of formal art training had snuffed Dane's best shot at advertising stardom.

But in advertising, failure could be as fickle as success. Dane's and Ron's second chance came swiftly since Sally, the account director, and Julien Pellicule, the vice president of client services, were not playing Nigel's game. They could not wait for his return to evaluate concepts. They needed to see what they had in advance of the important client review, and asked Dane and Ron to show their work without Nigel's input.

Sally was skittish. She needed Nigel to tell her a concept was good. Since he was in Iceland she was lost. And when Sally was lost, she was more demanding and critical than usual.

"I don't get this one. I don't get this one, either!" she screeched. Despite her caviling, Rupert McTavish, the head of the New York office, and Pellicule were impressed by the work Dane and Ron showed. They agreed that everything could be better on a computer. "I know!" Ron blurted, "I'm sorry for this but Nigel insisted on drawings."

Account people were once again Dane's unlikely allies, putting him back in control.

He and Ron executed the ten concepts the top account people wanted by week's end. Everything was working perfectly. The concepts would be done before Nigel returned from Iceland and he would be too late to change them before the client meeting, two days after his return. Then there would be only two days to refine the concepts before research.

Dane and Ron braced for Nigel's return, sensing he would be unhappy about being bypassed. They also expected him to review their work immediately and overhaul everything. However, the first day of Nigel's return passed without comment. Had he forgotten them? The next day Dane had a personal day off, scheduled weeks in advance and signed off by ten people. He and Becky were going to Iris's day camp to see her in a musical production. If Nigel wanted to put his imprint on the work he had apparently run out of time. Or had he?

Dane and Becky had to leave at 10:30 to make it to Iris's performance by noon. At 10 AM, Nigel phoned Dane at home to discuss the concepts. Becky stared at Dane while Nigel held Dane on the line. Dane explained to Nigel that he was on the way out and had to cut the call short but Nigel was oblivious. Finally, Dane blurted, "Nigel, I have to leave now." He reminded Nigel that he had signed the form that granted him a day off.

Later that afternoon Nigel phoned again. After reviewing the concepts he wanted to change everything. He had rewritten headlines and inserted new visuals. Dane felt doomed—again! He and Ron would have to work all night to make Nigel's many changes before the client presentation—and there would be mistakes.

Dane and Ron had misinterpreted Nigel from the start. When

the creative director absconded for Iceland without reviewing their work, they thought he had confidence in them. But he only let them think they were free so he could make them do everything his way at the last moment.

However, Nigel also miscalculated. He expected the creative team to flounder for two weeks so he could enter at the last moment to rescue the account from disaster. Only he ran out of time to make his big play.

"You're meeting the client tomorrow morning at 9:30 AM so you can't change everything tonight," Nigel conceded. "We'll see what can be done later to add ideas."

Dane relaxed and smiled to himself at this rare victory. Maybe he *was* The Chosen One and this *was* the Chosen Job. Dane was savoring the moment too much to assess whether this was a legitimate battle for independence, a freakish anomaly or another mythic hallucination.

14. WHILE THE MOUSE IS AWAY

After a successful presentation in which the client liked all that he and Ron presented, it was Dane's turn to take a vacation. Before he left, he finished and reviewed with satisfaction the concepts to be submitted for research. He knew his concept would win since they were all his. He was a monopoly like cable TV and would soon take his place among advertising geniuses he admired as the creator of a landmark campaign.

With such an unassailable position, he gave no thought to research while on vacation. When he returned, he scanned his emails for the research results, more from sporting curiosity than an urgent need to know. Which of his creative children had won? He didn't care because he loved them all. Dane opened the file titled "Research Results" and stared in disbelief at two concepts he had never seen. No one was there to explain this puzzling turn of events until Ron sauntered in after ten.

"Where are the concepts we worked on?'

Dane had been in the business long enough to forget what could happen when one goes away for a week.

"It was terrible," Ron said quietly. "After testing in North Carolina, three concepts did well—the bomb strapped to the foot, the guy in the wheel chair and the dancing couple. But the client wasn't comfortable."

"They weren't comfortable! What does that mean?" Dane yelled. "They had hemorrhoids?"

"Sally said they weren't comfortable. That's all I know," Ron stared at his monitor.

"Sally!" Dane shouted. "I bet *she* made them comfortable."

"Nigel made me go with him to Toronto to brainstorm. He said we needed five new concepts. When we got there, Nigel, a writer and I went to a Starbucks. They talked a mile a minute and ignored me. They came up with five ideas and I spent the day and a night finding pictures and doing layouts for them."

Ron showed Dane the ideas Ron and the other writer created: a man with pencil points for feet; another with feet severed from his legs; and a wheel-chair-bound woman with a stump for a leg. The worst was a contortionist holding a foot with four amputated toes next to her face.

"It's a freak show," Dane growled. "I'm gone for a week and this happens...and you let them do it?"

"What could I do, Dane? Nigel's our boss," Ron said sadly. "I was their slave."

Dane suspected that Ron was too good a sycophant to be a passive victim but he could not accuse him. Half an ally was better than none.

"Do they think this inflammatory advertising will be approved by the FDA?" Dane asked rhetorically. Ron was silent.

"This is how they view us. We're second-class," Dane said.

451

"They're getting even with America for taking most of their hockey teams."

Dane took a week off believing he could not lose; when he returned, he learned he could not win. He understood how Haile Selassie must have felt when Ethiopian soldiers hurled spears at Mussolini's tanks, or how people in Guernica felt when the Luftwaffe bombed them. Or how heads of state felt when they were ousted in a *coup d'état*. Dane understood everything but what it meant to be an employee of an advertising agency.

"We still have one concept in the mix," he told Ron. "We'll win this war."

"You think so?" Ron asked doubtfully.

"You've got to believe it, Ron," Dane said. "Did you spend all that time and money in advertising schools so people could hijack your opportunities? Are we together on this?"

"Sure," Ron said, nodding tentatively. We're partners."

15. BORDER WAR

So began the *Grovil* Concept War between the Toronto and New York offices. Over a two month period, this regional conflict would be waged in offices, conference rooms, and hotels; in memoranda, emails and text-messages; in bars, restaurants and corporate cafeterias; and in various echelons of *Grovil's* pharmaceutical company and Georgian Shield. It would be characterized by fierce backstabbing, silken threats, and ruthless innuendoes. In the end, one concept would remain, in the front section of endocrine magazines everywhere.

Nigel still had two concepts in the mix. His first-string idea was a massive, red circular ulcer on the sole of a big foot. The client titled it *Pepperoni foot*. Nigel's second concept was a tasteful variation of the first. It depicted a foot with a small wound and a large exclamation point. Dane's and Ron's *Dancers* came in as the third entry. It showed an elderly couple waltzing in their den. A dotted line circumscribed the man's foot to imply potential amputation.

Early reports that trickled into the New York office had pharma executives choosing the New York team's *Dancers* to Toronto's *Pepperoni foot* by two-to-one. The clients viewed the concept of two old slow dancers as a touching evocation of the target audience performing an activity that required feet. Meanwhile, the perforation encircling the foot conveyed a subtle warning of amputation without scaring anyone or besmirching the drug company's tasteful reputation.

Each affirmative update sent Dane into internal transports of fist-pumping exultation, while Sally and the other Canadians reviled the client and defied Dane to show emotion.

One Friday afternoon Nigel and Sally held a telephone conference call regarding the *Grovil* concepts. Sally sullenly announced that the client decided to pass on *Pepperoni foot*.

Nigel was furious with the clients.

"Sally, make sure the client tests all three concepts."

"Nigel, it's impossible."

"Work your guile. Nothing short of our award-winning reputation depends on it."

Nigel urged Sally to write the client a letter to remind them how well *pepperoni foot* tested.

"When their advertising bombs, the agency should cover itself against fallout!" he declared.

Dane was beaming at the success of *Dancers* but Ron was troubled by the Nigel's hostility toward the New York team.

Undaunted by their setback, the Toronto office poured more resources into *Pepperoni foot*. The top brass at Georgian Shield invited the clients to a dinner party in the Toronto Skydome. They wined, dined and lavished perks on them, but the clients were impervious to their seduction. They wanted the old dancers with the perforated foot.

Dane believed the popularity of his and Ron's concept proved his usefulness to his Canadian employers. Was he not hired because he knew how to create for American tastes? He also believed the concept competition was over and won, despite signals that the Toronto office hated his *dancers* on principle.

He had underestimated the ego of Georgian Shield. If the winning concept was made in America by Americans, how could Georgian Shield justify their invasion of the American market by claiming they were more creative than their American counterparts? They viewed the *Grovil* clients as obtuse for preferring an inferior American concept and repudiated Dane's idea as an insult to their authority and aesthetics.

To a casual observer, this was a popularity contest between a big, ugly, injured foot and two old dancers with a cutout foot in which victory meant no more than ads placed in magazines targeting physicians and diabetics. But nothing less was at stake for Nigel, Sally and the Georgian Shield team than Canada's manifest destiny to infiltrate and dominate American advertising. They would never concede defeat.

16. BIG PEPPERONI FOOT IN YOUR FACE

The *Grovil* war dragged on. According to rumors, Nigel and Sally finally convinced the *Grovil* clients, after extravagant backstage maneuvers, to submit Toronto's *Pepperoni foot*—with a smaller, more tasteful, pebble-sized pepperoni ulcer—*and* the preferred American *Dancers* to quantitative testing—the ultimate *mano-a-mano* of concept research.

The stalemate required a cease-fire, so Nigel and Sally called for a web-chat sit-down with the New York creative team.

Sally waved at Dane and Ron. She wore a tight satin top which left little to the erotically susceptible imagination. With every movement she made in her chair, Dane had the impression that he was watching a private conversation between two breasts behind a curtain.

"Hello, there, guys," Nigel began. "First let me say, 'Good work.'"

"Thanks," Dane and Ron answered glumly.

"Yes," Nigel said. "It hasn't been easy. This client is not who we thought they were."

"They're morons!" Sally blurted.

"So, guys," Hogbine continued. "We're going to quantitative testing with these two ads...Now which one do you think works better?"

"*Dancers*," Dane said.

"Dane, are you choosing it because it's your own work?" Nigel asked. "We're too professional to let our egos get in the way."

"No, I'm totally impartial," Dane exaggerated. "*Dancers* appeals to our target audience. They're lovable, old people—not obese, donut-eating idiots.   Dancing is aspirational. Why use expensive goop on your feet if all you do is lie in bed and watch reruns—just cut off the dead dog and be done with it, right?"

"Dane, do you know what you're saying?" Sally asked as she shivered, making her breasts jiggle and sway.

Dane suspected Sally of trying to distract him with seductive motion. She expected him to have an erection, lose his concentration, concede the point and run to the men's room to masturbate. Not this time! Dane Bacchus was a professional.

"We recommended the foot ad," Nigel said. "We think it has *FSC*, *First Strike Capability*."

"That's a cold war term!" Dane replied. "Who are you? *John Foster Dull Ass*?"

"Quite right," Nigel replied. "It's our homage to America's golden age—the 1950s."

Ron squirmed. His mentor, the upscale retail store executive, had advised Ron that if he was ever caught in heavy fire between a colleague and a superior, he should always side with the superior.

"Nigel, Sally: both are great concepts. We can make them both work," Ron pleaded.

Nigel nodded with paternal satisfaction and turned sternly to Dane.

"You disagree, Dane. So let us explain why we think the foot works better."

Nigel thrust the large presentation board against the camera and jabbed the large festering sore with his long finger.

"This is foot-in-the-face advertising. The foot is so real, you can smell it. The viewer sees foot, identifies with foot and seeks medical attention for foot. It's an icon, indelibly stamped in the audience's collective bipedal brain. That's branding. That's how we do it at Georgian Shield."

Nigel withdrew the foot. Now Sally strutted to the easel and held the *Dancers* concept aloft.

"This concept is off strategy," she said, "It's soft, not urgent. Old folks slow dancing: where's the sizzle? Their cold, flaccid bodies don't even touch!"

"And here's another thing," Nigel jumped from his seat, wagging his forefinger. "The perforated line around the foot gives pause. But we don't want doctors to pause. No, no. We want them to slather *Grovil* on feet!"

In case they did not understand his point, Nigel scooped a gob of *Vaseline* from a jar and rubbed it all over the foot image on the presentation board.

"Guys?" Sally asked. "Are you writing this down?"

Dane pointed to his forehead. "It's all going in here."

"I hope you'll keep it there, Dane," Nigel said. "We can't confuse clients with choices."

"They always choose wrong," Sally said.

"And we can't give them second rate," Nigel added.

"Maybe they like our ad because it's good," Dane suggested.

"That's a comforting misperception," Nigel shook his head. "This client is like an abused child. They like bad advertising because that's all they've ever known. They hired us to break the vicious circle."

After the meeting, Dane went into Ron's office.

"How could you do that to me?"

"Do what?"

"You caved. You told them both concepts could work. What happened to unity? To partners-for-life? If we don't hang together, we'll hang apart."

"We shouldn't be fighting. We're all on the same team. They pay our salaries. We should work with them," Ron pleaded.

"If getting along is what you aspire to, you're dead," Dane said.

"No, Dane. That's how to stay alive," Ron countered. "They like us. They praised us. They want us to be on their team. But if you fight them, they won't listen to anything you say."

"They won't even listen to the client so you think they'll listen to us?"

Ron went silent and stared at the monitor, preparing his summation.

"Look Dane. I want do great work and make a name, but this situation is making me sick," Ron said. "Last weekend, Ilona and I went up to Connecticut for an ionizing detox. The water turned black in thirty seconds. *I'm toxic.* The therapist said it's stress. If we keep fighting I'll be dead."

17. THE MOTHER OF ALL RESEARCH

Quantitative testing went forward.

The objective was to learn what people thought of an ad while they flipped through a magazine. The test measured several indicators: if they stopped on the ad, for how long, how much they recalled, if they understood the message and were compelled by it.

While quantitative testing seemed more scientific than qualitative, its methodology was arcane and so technologically sophisticated that it defied outside observation and quality controls to verify the accuracy of its results. When Dane raised this point, he was asked to observe the operation first hand.

He woke up at 3:30 one morning. A waiting livery car drove him to an office park in the Princeton corridor of New Jersey, where an unmarked van with dark windows took him the rest of the way to a warehouse facility in a cornfield. Dane had a déjà vu. It looked like the same facility where, as a university instructor, he graded essays for standardized tests.

Sally and the psychologist, Dr. Vaughn Foozner, were waiting for Dane.

"This is not a research facility. It's a *reality simulator*," Foozner said. He was bald, bearded, wore a diamond stud in one ear and was a hybrid of Blackbeard and Rasputin in a lab coat. "We simulate the milieu where magazines are read."

"It's so exciting," Sally said.

The *reality simulator* was like a movie set. Subjects were observed in a space modeled after a public restroom. Participants were issued a magazine slimmer than the newsstand variety and led to stalls with doors equipped with hidden webcams. Seated on chairs simulating toilet seats, the subjects leafed through the publications. Pages were coated with sensors that recorded the interval between each turn of page. The ad whose page was open for the longest cumulative time would be judged "more impactful."

"Are they really using the toilet?" Dane asked.

"The commode simulates a favorite reading place," Dr. Foozner said. "If they need actual relief, we give them a bathroom pass."

Throughout the morning, patients with diabetes filed into the *reality simulator* with their magazines and were escorted to stalls. Some balked at the scenario. One man asked, "Do I have to...perform?"

"No, just read," Dr. Foozner said.

"Where's my cup?" another man asked belligerently. "No cup, no urine sample."

"No urine sample is necessary. Just read," Dr. Foozner said.

"But I don't have to go," a woman brayed.

"That's fine. We don't want you to go. This isn't a real bathroom."

"So why is it here?"

"We want you to read the way you normally do."

"But I never read in the toilet," the woman insisted with increasing agitation.

"Pretend you do!" Dr. Foozner said.

It was slow going that morning.

After lunch, Dane noticed that the new research subjects looked stiff and pasty.

"Are these people okay?" Dane asked. "They look sick."

Sally laughed. The psychologist grinned.

"They're not sick," Dr. Foozner said.

"They're *read dummies*. Robots," Sally said through her giggles.

"I prefer to call them *virtuo-sapiens*," Dr. Foozner said. "They're the latest innovation in advertising research psychology. We've programmed them to behave like normal American consumers. They're culturally coded to detect verbal and visual hot spots in ads and to allocate their interest accordingly."

"We like bacon and eggs," one *virtuo-sapien* said to the other in the research room.

"Have you seen the latest *Hard Copy*?" replied the other.

"The cold weather gives me morning stiffness," the other replied.

"You have divine hair."

"I'm worth it."

They reminded Dane of an installation Dane once saw at the Whitney Biennial—two Styrofoam heads protruding from a barrel of Styrofoam peanuts conversed in perpetual non-sequiturs. Dane was impressed by Dr. Foozner's cultural literacy, but appalled that he used an art concept for scientific testing.

"How can machines simulate human emotions?" Dane asked.

"They do it all the time," said Dr. Foozner. "We have a very small statistical margin of error."

"The client adores this *process*," Sally piped in. "You saw how slow research was with humans, ay? They're too stupid. These *read dummies* never waste time and they know exactly what they think."

Test numbers came in two weeks later; a half year after Dane and Ron faxed the first thirty concepts to Nigel. *Pepperoni foot* scored a 70, while *Dancers* scored a 64. Dane was disappointed. Rather than an indisputable victory, the outcome was a statistical dead heat, within the margin of error. Still, Dane had reason to be sanguine. The inconclusive result meant the client could choose *Dancers*, which had been their favorite all along.

The *Grovil* clients visited the Georgian Shield New York office for a meeting. It was clearly important because it was catered by a midtown deli.

Sally, Nigel, Dane and Ron sat across from the clients.

"We're going with the foot," the marketing director announced.

"That is a wise choice," Nigel said.

The clients explained their decision. What ultimately swayed them was a different set of numbers than test scores—production costs. They thanked Ron for researching the comparative figures for turning *Dancers* and *Pepperoni foot* into ads. According to Ron's estimate, a close-up photograph of a foot would cost $40,000 and require minimal casting and talent fees, modest production values, a small amount of make up and no wardrobe. Meanwhile, a photograph of two dancers would cost $60,000 and involve time and expense for casting, wardrobe, props, make-up and more intricate lighting.

Normally, $20,000 was not nearly enough to influence an important branding decision by a Fortune 500 corporation with a global presence and an immaculate image. But Sally and the new *Grovil* product manager had gone through a significant portion of the advertising budget by scheduling and canceling research meetings all over the country in order to have sex trysts in 4-star hotels. They needed to cut corners somewhere and the launch ad concept was convenient.

After the meeting, Dane looked for Ron so they could vent together about their defeat. Dane was able to express his antagonisms openly to his partner because Ron was such a brownnoser that he adapted to anyone, even Dane. But Ron could not be found.

As Dane passed a conference room he heard Nigel talking behind a closed door. "Well done, Ron. I won't forget this."

"No problem, Nigel," Ron replied. "I always thought the foot was a great idea."

Dane was dismayed. He had believed he was making progress in liberating Ron from his inner wimp. Unfortunately, sucking-up as a coping behavior, done repeatedly for years, was too much for Ron to overcome under duress. His groveling had risen—or fallen—to the level of betrayal, leaving Dane isolated and alone against his overseers.

Case 6-D
GOING ROGUE ON THE TENTH FLOOR

18. DANE MEETS "THE OTHER GUY" OR WINTON REVISITED

Now that the *Grovil* campaign was settled, the New York office was due for a hiatus of peace and analgesic monotony. Still, there were changes afoot.

One Monday morning, Dane found a frowsy woman with a large belly wandering about the office in slippers. She held a tumbler of *Diet Pepsi* by the neck. Her wide eyes and hayride hair made her resemble a comic-strip heroine looking for her mommy. She was looking for a straw instead.

Dane guided her to the kitchenette, a few feet away.

"Are you a client?" he asked facetiously.

"No, I'm a freelance writer. Hi, I'm Dotty."

Dottie Wacker extended her hand with the plastic container dangling from it and Dane shook her *Pepsi*.

"You'll be seeing a lot of me," Dottie said. "Nigel said I could work from home but I had to get out of there. A woman on my floor wants to kill me. Her boyfriend's always flirting. It's not my fault he thinks I'm *hot*."

Dane was sure she was joking and almost laughed—but she wasn't, so he didn't.

"I would have started last week," Dottie went on, "but I had to go to Staten Island twice last week to see my dentist. Boy, that was no fun with the ferry and a bus! I know, you're thinking, 'Why doesn't she fix her teeth locally?' My Staten Island dentist needs me. He looks forward to my check-ups and cleanings. And now that I have a root canal, we're practically married!"

Dottie Wacker's mysterious appearance did not need clarification. She was Nigel's "gift" to Dane for his unwillingness to fondle *Pepperoni foot*. She would be assigned to projects Dane could have worked on in his downtime and take *his* billable hours.

The new freelancer presented another danger, as well. Dottie had worked at Mentos before Dane arrived. She was the "crazy lady" copywriter whose legend Mentos people recounted around the water cooler. Dane wondered if Dottie knew of his notoriety—and would spread it around New York.

As it turned out, Dottie had no time for his Mentos stories. She had an anthology of her own.

"They promised they'd make me creative director," Dottie whined. "They had so much work for me that they put me up in a motel for a month. I was like a little mole, working night and day. I never went out. When the project was done they said it was the best slide kit completed in less than two weeks that they ever saw!

"So when I finally got back to New York, my goldfish and plants had died while I was gone. I gave the bill to Mentos and they said they'd pay it. Fine! So I was a little reverse-commuter again. One morning I got off the train and stepped on somebody's discarded sandwich. Suddenly I felt the ground go squishy under me. The sandwich must have been full of mayonnaise. I slipped on it and fell right on my back. So I picked myself up and left the station when a dog ran up to me and peed on my new pumps. That was it! The cosmos was sending me a message in bold caps: GO HOME! How could I create in such circumstances? I'd be worried sick all day what would happen next! So I took the next train to New York and hid under the covers. Mentos didn't understand. They were such users."

"Insensitive cretins," Dane agreed.

"Plus—they were always renovating. The construction workers were animals. They made sexual noises and comments. I get a lot of that. Men think I'm hot. It was a nightmare. They squeezed balloons obscenely. And then...They filled condoms with Elmer's glue...and cut the tips so they dripped...and dangled them outside my office window!"

"Did you complain?"

"*Yes!* The Mentos people laughed. They thought I was making it all up!" Dottie replied.

"So you quit?" Dane asked.

"No, I told them I had to take off some time to ride my horse. I was a champion eques*trienne*, see? That's important to me. So after six months they said they couldn't hire an associate creative director who rides horses—for insurance reasons. Can you believe it?"

"It's hard."

"They showed me the documents. So I asked if they could get a rider to cover a rider. They said it was a Mentos policy not to change insurance policies for four years. Since they had just put this one in place I would have to wait three more years. That's too long not to ride a horse, don't you agree?"

"Yes," Dane said, although he had never been on a horse. "So how did you get this job?"

"Georgian Shield called my headhunter and I interviewed with

Nigel. But they gave the job to someone else—to *you*. So a few months later Nigel called. He said he needed a job done super-fast. It would take up all my time, even weekends. I told him, 'Sure thing! That's my specialty.' And here I am."

Dottie was the "other guy" Griffin always mentioned against whom Dane always had "the inside track." This was the first time Dane met someone he had competed with for a job. Nigel was notifying him that this hiring mistake could be rectified and that #1 could be replaced by #2.

19. THE RELUCTANT PATRIOT

Dottie Wacker's appearance darkened Dane's mind. He viewed it as a direct threat. What did he do to deserve it? No more or less than the best creative effort of which he was capable.

Under the incidental attack, Dane perceived a pattern of evil. He was now reasonably sure the Canadian agency did not hire him because he was a world-class talent. He was an intelligence asset to undermine American pharmaceutical advertising.

When Dane refused to be a subservient, self-hating hack, they brought in another mole, Dottie, many times more submissive than Dane, to exert pressure on his job.

With his position under siege, Dane raised his fight to a higher level of abstraction and assumed a new role. He became a cultural patriot and viewed his mission as that of ambassador and defender of his country's advertising.

He was on his own. Few people knew America's advertising was under assault. It was lonely and thankless to be the solitary sentinel against an imperialist invasion. Dane seriously considered renouncing patriotism. He had fought for his ideas against hostile supervisors. Did he ever win or even draw? He could not recall even one idea for which he had won the good fight.

However, a patriot does not battle for gratitude, for gain or even for victory—but only for the cause he believes to be right.

One afternoon, as Dane overcame his natural inclination to take a nap, he heard a gentle knock on the door.

"May I come in?"

There was Ben Franklin poking his jowly face in the doorway. With a twinkle in his bifocal eyes, Franklin inquired, "Is this where I find Dane Bacchus?"

"It's finally true," Dane thought. "I'm officially insane."

He slapped his face, so life-like did Ben appear to him. He wished to expel this apparition but Dane's hero was not going anywhere.

"I-I," Dane stammered.

"I'd say the 'Aye's' have it then!" Franklin quipped. "May I speak with you? I won't take much of your time. For time is the stuff life is made of, isn't it just as true now as ever? You look busy...or, should I say, weary—of course, the latter presupposes the former. In any case, let me tell you how proud we are of your vigilant efforts. You are a patriot, dear fellow, and your country will always be indebted to your service and sacrifice."

"Ben, when will the sacrifice end? I want to fight for what's right, but I have a family to support and bills to pay."

"I, too, wagered all, my lad. Now ask yourself if the reward was worth the wager."

"Yes!"

"Then I'll be off. It's been good chatting with you, friend. Remember: Right is on your side; just make sure your left flank is defended."

Ben chuckled and Dane laughed.

"You've been dead for over two hundred years, Ben, but you've still got it," Dane praised his hero but Ben's avuncular presence had passed.

Now Dane knew what he must do. He loved his country's advertising and knew he had to fight for it—or lose it forever.

"Are you okay?" Ron asked. "You were talking to the door."

"Oh, yeah! I was reading copy out loud to see how it sounds," Dane answered.

"We have a web chat in the Adelman room," Ron said, waiting impatiently for Dane to gather his accouterments.

Dane noted that Ron was usually telling him what he had to and where he had to be. He was a hybrid of boss, secretary and messenger.

20. THE AGONIES OF DA FEET

As with any war, the *Grovil* spoils went to the winners, Nigel, Sally and their collaborator, Ron, while Dane, on the losing end, experienced subjugation in its most pernicious forms—for instance, he revised ad copy with the new *Grovil* product team.

While Ron was at the shoot for the *Big Foot* photograph, Dane and the *Grovil* product team—a former salesman, a chemical engineer, and a former pharmacist—played in a verbal sandbox, noodling words and phrases. For an hour they deliberated over what to call a podiatrist—should he be dubbed a podiatric doctor, a foot specialist or a podiatric specialist? Another lengthy debate raged over the relative merits of "mend" and "heal." Dane tried to abridge the discussion by touting his credentials—an advanced degree in English, over a decade of teaching experience and a list of professional publications. This stopped the argument for seconds like a comma, a semi-colon, or a dash, before it resumed with renewed intensity. Dane fought word by word in two paragraphs of rubble—like a defender of Stalingrad. When he counted the words from his original copy there were only eight survivors.

Dane faced another indignity of the fallen. It was his job to hand-write clients' copy changes on a layout, after which they were incorporated in a new layout and returned to the client for review. When a layout was finally approved, Dane transcribed every change from every round of layouts onto a final manuscript. In this way the copy on the final layout matched the final manuscript. Dane recorded every copy change twice, a redundancy which he worked late every night to complete. He pleaded with Toronto for a shortcut only to be told that redundancy was part of the Georgian Shields process, which was immutable and inviolable.

One night as Dane moved his eyes between layout and manuscript page on screen, he abruptly stopped, as if a spring snapped in his neck.

It was the first warning sign of a massive epiphany. His skin radiated with heat. A powerful energy surged through his body, making it impossible for him to be still. He paced to discharge these internal forces but they overwhelmed conventional responses.

Dane stared into the abyss of his life and yelled.

"Deluded again! This always happens! Behold the international creative superstar, in reality, a miserable clerk! It's your time to make it, Boy! Hallelujah! Your breakthrough, screw ya! Here you are every night moving shit from one page to another! *Pepperoni foot*'s a muvvah fuggah!"

"Are you okay?" A squeaky voice inquired from the other side of the half-open door. It was Dottie Wacker.

"I'm fine," Dane said. How much did she hear? He didn't care.

"I didn't mean to intrude but I heard screaming," she said, her face round and bright as a balloon. "I thought you had a heart attack. Want some *Pepsi*?" Dottie thrust the big plastic bottle toward him.

"No. I'm fine. Thanks," Dane said. Then, out of a perverse self-destructive impulse, he chose to explain himself to her.

"I was just having my usual fun in the mud-pit-salt-mines-slave galleys of advertising. You know, reviewing minute changes on the last of twenty drafts of gibberish until I'm seeing triple and my mind is aspic."

"Wow, that's exciting," Dottie replied. "Okay, you have a good night."

Dane laughed. Even his complaints made no sense to anyone. He experienced a new species of freedom. As he passed the

Rockefeller Center skating rink he shouted at no one in particular on the empty street, "Who cares about the Great God, Ogden Adelman! Not my partner for life; he's an enemy spy! Not Nigel and Sally. They eat pepperoni with their feet!"

21. DANE IN GETHSEMANE

The rage building in Dane was unbearable. His acknowledgement of how badly this job was going gave intelligence to his anger.

"I understand the problem but what do I do?" He pleaded with his mind for answers while squeezing his head.

He had to counterattack but his taskmasters in Canada were beyond his range. He needed a closer target—and found one—in Ron.

Dane's partner was a superb target. Ron made out beautifully in the *Grovil* War. How did he manage it? Dane recalled the time he looked for his partner and heard him plead to Nigel about his true affection for *Pepperoni foot*.

Admittedly, it was only a misdemeanor back-stabbing, an acceptable level of boot-licking and ass-covering that was natural in the advertising culture. However, this was no isolated incident or first-time offense for Ron, but symptomatic of a pattern of treachery— and a substrate of evil.

Ron and Dane had always been going in opposite directions at Georgian Shields, so their clash was inexorable. While Dane sank from senior medical writer to backroom drudge, Ron catapulted from tyro and agency pet to unofficial liaison between Dane and Toronto, transmitting Nigel's and Sally's wishes to Dane. Now he stopped by Dane's office each day to tell him the agenda—like he was boss. Youth was served and Dane was the butler.

Ron's only flaw as a scapegoat was that he was rarely around. He was shooting the *pepperoni foot* ad. While Dane made minute changes all day long or listened to clients jabber over the meaning of *a* and *the*, his hatred for Ron grew in absentia. Much of this rancor was envy-based. Dane resented Ron for receiving the best assignments and perks and for selling him out to obtain them. Yet, what aggravated Dane most was that Ron's ass-kissing strategy was trouncing Dane's proud professionalism.

His crisis had almost reached crescendo.

Where was Ben Franklin now when he needed him? Where had Adelman's aphorisms led him but to a big, ulcerated foot?

"You idiot!" he muttered.

"What is it, Daddy?" Iris asked. They were eating dinner at the table and Dane was involved in one of his internal dialogues.

"Nothing," Dane said.

"You have to change. Learn how to kiss ass!" Dane's inner voice chided him.

Ass-kissing was his last frontier. He had done "loud," he had done "modest" and "confident" and "humble." He had used threats and guile and negotiation—everything but unadulterated ingratiation.

Dane tried *systematic desensitization*, a technique for modifying behavior. He printed a photograph of unappealing buttocks on his home printer, which he taped to his bathroom mirror, in order to practice kissing it. If he could kiss an ass in two dimensions, he hoped to be able to do it metaphorically in real life. However, each time he approached the photograph with a pucker on his lips, he had cold sweats, nausea and acid reflux in his mouth. Once he trembled with a small seizure. Would he ever conquer this psychological frontier?

When Dane realized that he was incapable of even beginner's ass-kissing and would never develop this craft, he conceded that Ron had a rare and prodigious gift—and hated him more.

22. THE FIRST PLAGUE: RATS

In the Adelman washroom, Dane muttered his latest vow.

"Ron, you turned against me and sold me out. You conspired with Toronto and shafted my concept. Worse, you prostituted your talent and dishonored American advertising when you helped *Pepperoni foot* get produced. But the worst thing you've done, Ron, is to injure my soul with your ass-kissing genius. You've gone too far, Ron, and now you will pay!"

Dane lit a match and put it out on his palm, then spat on the burn to seal his oath. He would now execute his plan.

At a specialty hardware store, Dane purchased hi-tech wire cutters designed for untraceable sabotage. The blades were formed to resemble the gnawing of rats.

One late evening as Dane pored over more inane copy to be corrected in triplicate, he sneaked into Ron's office with rat-blade cutters, snipped the computer power cord and left.

As Dane walked across town to his train station, a fire engine passed with sirens ringing. Dane used the commotion to discharge adrenaline by shouting, "Hey, Ron! Let's see if a machine really has a soul!"

Ron was not expected in the office until the following week. He was out on *Pepperoni foot* business and taking a long weekend at an herbal spa with his fiancé and their miniature dog.

When Ron returned the following Tuesday, Dane had a warm smile for him in the kitchenette.

"Hey, dude! You've been missed."

"Yeah, right," Ron grinned and hurried to his office. For ten minutes nothing happened. Suddenly, Ron appeared in Dane's office, his face ashen and desolate. "My computer is down. The wires are cut."

Dane's mouth and eyes gaped wide with simulated pain and he teared up. He feared that Ron would suspect him and converted this fear to fake empathy.

"Are you sure?"

"There's no power."

"Let me look." Dane studied the ragged snip of the power cord with consternation. "What kind of animal would do this?"

"I don't know. My *G-7* never hurt anyone!" Ron cried.

Dane stayed with Ron to steady both of their nerves. He believed that if Ron were left alone he might suspect his partner.

The IT guy, Oscar, diagnosed the problem.

"Looks like you need an exterminator, Ron," Oscar said. "You got a rat with a taste for power cords."

"Rats?" Ron said. "How is it possible?"

"You keep food in your drawers?"

"Only dry tofu flakes and toasted lentils!"

Dane could have kissed Oscar for what he said next.

"Yep, they're partial to those. I guess it depends on the rat. You got yourself a real *Whole Foods* loving rat."

Ron was silently hysterical. His mouth quivered and his eyes were wet and glassy. He blinked into space as if transmitting an SOS to aliens, while he tried to make sense of this tragedy. Having so much on his mind nearly crashed his thought process.

"It's weird," Oscar explained to Dane. "People attract rats that like what they like. I guess it's evolution. Rats are the ultimate social animal."

"Yeah, you're right about that," Dane replied.

Dane's vandalism surpassed his intended effect. Ron sat in his dark office, slumped over the sleek swan-necked monitor. He believed his beloved *Macintosh* was not broken but injured. He also suspected his *Apple* could reveal his assailant's identity, not with its powerful processor and operating system, but with its soul. Dane sympathized with Ron as his strange, passionate beliefs were dashed. He wondered if Ron suspected him. If so, he had no proof, and his mentor, the high end retail executive, would warn him against making unsubstantiated allegations. Ron could also be trusted never to divulge his theory that his computer was able to identify its assailant. He wished to avoid sounding like a freak to Nigel and Sally, his supervisors and supporters.

Ron left for the day. A memo from Canada warned everyone to

remove food and beverages from their offices. This was good news for Dane. The home office apparently believed rats were the culprits and held Ron responsible for the severed power cord. Dottie left that evening with a shopping bag full of her goodies. She had stashed Pepperidge Farm cookies and tumblers of diet soda in every office she occupied. "How do they expect me to work without snacks?" she asked.

Dane was the caring colleague that day. He asked everyone if he could help with anything. He told Rupert, the Georgian Shields New York chief, that he had exterminating experience. He offered to spray and set traps in Ron's office. His kind offer was noted and declined. Dane's positive attitude was a diversion. He knew he was a prime scapegoat for any debacle and ran on nervous energy to skirt suspicion.

23. THE SECOND PLAGUE: CONNECT THE DOTTIE

For a few weeks, Dane was contrite about his sabotage. In the moments after Ron's discovery, Dane trembled with anxiety at the impact and criminality of his act and agonized for days at the possibility of being exposed. He admonished himself never to repeat such a deed for any reason.

But remorse faded fast. When Ron returned from his R&R, he was handed a fat, new pitch. As soon as Dane heard the news, he barged into Ron's office in a controlled rage to learn more. There, he found Dottie Wacker curled up in a chair, looking fluffy and content in laundered sweats. She sat close to Ron, who barricaded himself behind his 28-inch monitor.

Dottie had been assigned to collaborate with Ron on the prestigious project.

When Ron glanced at Dane in the doorway, he blushed and stammered like he had been caught having sex with Dottie. He assured Dane that he had no say in her getting the assignment. Ron

472

was so flustered that Dane made light of the situation and left.

Yet Dane's equable response to Dottie's usurpation was no match for his current drudgery. As he reviewed manuscript pages against pages of layout, his appetite for revenge sprang like an animal without memory of its last meal.

He revised his view of Ron's nice-guy diffidence. He now characterized his sensitivity as a masquerade. What was so great about an art director who was quiet and behaved? Dane reverted to a 1960s attitude: people were part of the solution or part of the problem. Ron was part of the problem and Dane resolved to deal with him—*again*.

Dane noticed how excited Dottie was to work with Ron; she looked at least two years younger in his presence. Ron, for his part, avoided Dottie, even when she was a few feet away, by hiding behind his monitor. Dane quickly identified Dottie as his next weapon against Ron.

Dane sympathized with Dottie, whose curriculum vitae of professional abuse—overwork, arbitrary firings, repeated and unwarranted insults about her work—was written on her puffy face. But since she was hired to pressure him, her presence was aggravating. She was slow, inefficient and made every job seem twice as hard as it was. Dan viewed Dottie's hire as an insult to his ability. However, his objection to Dottie was not about efficiency or pride—it was straight survival. On the surface, she was the nicest downtrodden wretch you ever wanted to meet. She shared cookies, cheese doodles and 64 oz. plastic bottles of diet soda with anyone. But kindness was the grinning mask of a gritty foe. Dottie threatened Dane's livelihood. She was the runner-up for his job and would snatch it if he was fired— a strong possibility at the rate things were going.

Feckless as she seemed, Dottie's devastating weapon was a lack of ego. She was a human filet—self-esteem had been gutted out of her. Ego is heavy machinery. Without it, Dottie was more flexible and less sensitive to inconsideration, slights and excessive demands. Dane worked long and hard but Dottie could work longer and harder. Dane resented his unpaid overtime but Dottie was grateful for it. Dane resented arbitrary changes to his writing whereas Dottie shrugged when a whole project was rewritten. Dane worked to live; Dottie lived to work. Had she attained higher consciousness or a nadir of groveling?

Dane's punishment did not end with Dottie's pitch assignment. It was only the first lash. Nigel did not intend to slap Dane once for his *Grovil* stand but to pulverize him. He assigned Ron to work with Dottie on other projects. What a fuss she made over her new status! She stopped by Dane's office with bright rouge circles on her cheeks and mascara lashes shooting outward like black quills protecting her damp, glistening eyes.

"Have you seen Ronnie?" she asked Dane.

"No, I haven't seen Ronnie," Dane replied like a father on a '50s sitcom. "Should I take a message?"

"No. I'll check his office later," Dottie giggled and pranced off.

Dane did not think she was deliberately taunting him about her encroachment. She seemed genuinely excited about working with someone, *anyone*, especially a man.

One afternoon, Dane broke away from a marathon copy review with the *Grovil* product team, while they tortured ten words of pharmacy coupon copy to verbal death. Dane had to talk to Ron about a short creative assignment. When he opened the door, he found Dottie snuggling up to Ron, her legs folded on a chair. She was looking over his shoulder at the monitor. She had overcome his last barrier and intimacy suffused the recycled office air. Dane felt like he was interrupting a date. Dottie confirmed this by blushing—right through her blush.

"Sorry, I didn't want to bother you," Dane apologized.

"Oh, that's okay," Dottie said as if she were hurrying to drape a sheet over her naked self. Even in her shame, she looked so beatifically happy that Dane felt sick.

He had to get rid of her.

A major conflict had surfaced over the iconic foot that was photographed for the *Grovil* campaign. The client believed its brand foot looked neither old nor wrinkled enough for the target audience to love. Nigel disagreed. He thought the iconic foot was neither smooth nor dainty enough to arouse doctor and patient fantasies.

While mediating the conflict between Dane and Toronto, Ron won a reputation as a conciliator. When he was dispatched to massage the client's foot conflict, Dane set his plan in motion.

At a card and novelty store in the neighborhood, Dane found what he was looking for in the alternative card section in the back. The cards there were bold and intimate in nature…composed to say sweet generic nothings that stalkers might wish to say to their beloveds.

Dane discovered a perfect card for his purpose. Crimson on plush, porous rag, the card cost $7.95 so you knew the feeling was genuine.

Its illustration, exquisitely drawn and sumptuously colored by an artist with an affinity for Gustave Moreau, depicted a unicorn, pure and white, with his manly erectile horn, and a woman, clearly naked on his back, her virginal, white body covered by auburn ringlets. The message read, "You have a secret admirer."

This red card incorporated every value Dane had in mind: mythology, mystery, animal passion, even bestiality. But he wondered if it was too flamboyant. He studied another card on the shelf. It showed a knight on one knee, holding in his arms a woman faint from passion. The message read: "I wish I could tell you how I feel."

"If I only knew, myself," Dane muttered. He purchased the card.

Before Dottie Wacker came in one morning, Dane placed the envelope on her chair and waited. He knew she would not ask him if he wrote it because she wanted it to be from Ron.

He never saw Dottie that morning and was deprived of her reaction. He did not know if his mischief had its calculated effect. He was not certain that she found it or took its message seriously. For all he knew, he had misread her and she was gay.

That afternoon, Dottie popped her face in his doorway. Just the face, gaily painted like a sagging kewpie doll, with multiple circles— round blue eyes circumscribed by black kohl and hoops of red rouge on her cheeks. She opened the door wide to show off her tartan skirt and white blouse; *eureka,* she was a school girl again! Dane wanted to pump his fist. Instead, he smiled and said how chic she looked.

"Meeting a client?" he joked.

"No. Have you seen Ron?" she asked eagerly.

"No. But if I do, I'll tell him you're looking for him."

Dottie smiled demurely and thanked him.

When Ron returned, Dottie kept as close to him as she could without physically touching. If he bolted for the men's room, she escorted him to the door, under the pretext of using the lady's room nearby, and waited for him to come out. Ron was known for liking his space but Dottie would not let him have it. He was her secret admirer and she could not keep a secret.

The week passed and Ron avoided his office whenever possible. He was "around," roaming the halls. One day, Dane went to the Adelman washroom and opened the unlocked door. Ron was seated on the closed seat, tired and forlorn.

"Please, don't tell her I'm here," Ron whispered urgently, as if he needed not only to avoid Dottie's physical attention but her surveillance.

"Have you noticed Dottie acting strangely lately?" one of the young women in the office asked Dane. "If I didn't know better I'd say she's hitting on Ron. Am I dreaming?"

"No and yes," Dane answered both questions, leaving the questioner bemused.

Finally the situation erupted. The entire staff heard sobs rolling out of Ron's office like sirens bewailing a fathomless agony.

"You can tell me how you feel!" Dottie cried out, as if answering

the card. "What? You don't know what I'm talking about? I can't take it anymore. You're so unavailable. How could you lead me on like this? You don't love me. You used me," she cried. She bolted for the lady's room, covering her face full of tears.

The staff gathered outside Ron's office and stared through the half open door. Ron was stunned. He looked at the crowd with sheepish bewilderment. He hated attention and his mentor from the upscale retail store chain tutored him to be a man of mystery and intrigue—handsome, debonair and inaccessible. Now this was impossible. Ron was in a full-blown scandal, accused of toying with an older woman's feelings. He was humiliated to be romantically linked with Dottie. Fortunately for him, even the agency staff's urgent need for juicy human interaction and the faintest whiff of gossip could not induce them to believe he took advantage of Dottie. They surmised it was a mistake, albeit an entertaining one.

The situation also yielded a bumper crop of human resources fodder, which portended problems for Dane. What would happen when all parties were called in to explain the misunderstanding? Dottie would present the anonymous love card. If Ron saw it, he would deny seeing or sending it. Management would believe his confusion, suspect mischief and focus their inquiry on Dane, the consummate culprit candidate.

Dane needed to make the card disappear but first he had to find it. Since Dottie was hyper-sentimental, she probably kept it near her bed so she could kiss it before falling asleep. However, since Dottie was always at work, it was just as plausible that she kept the missive close at hand in her office—on the desk, in a drawer, or in her coat closet—to inspire her writing of bullet points.

Finding the card in Dottie's office and disposing of it gave Dane his best chance of avoiding implication in the scandal he fomented. He would need to search at night when darkness and solitude were allies. The task was complicated by Dottie's tendency to stay late. She turned the corporate office space into a second home by sporting sweats, slippers, going bra-less—and padding around with a mug of hot cocoa.

It was Dane's good luck that Dottie's romantic reversal ruined her appetite for thankless work that evening, and she left at eight. Once Dottie was gone and the hallway was dark, Dane sneaked into her office and rummaged through her desk, bookcase and shopping bags huddled on her floor like plastic homunculi, waiting for a bus. But he could not locate the red card. Out of desperation, he flipped through a stack of articles she was using for a piece on hormone replacement therapy, titled "The Power of Women's Hormones," and glimpsed a red sliver obtruding from the pile. How poetic, he thought, that she used this card to mark a page on sexual response! He slipped the red square under his shirt and burned it in his bathroom sink.

Nigel and a corporate harassment specialist flew in from Toronto to settle the love spat. They had a long meeting with Dottie in the conference room. She referenced the letter, Nigel asked to see it, and she ransacked her office vainly hunting for it. Dottie cried hysterically and speculated that Ron must have stolen and disposed of it to "deny his feelings." Hmmm...Nigel and the harassment specialist had a theory: either Dottie was delusional or Ron had tampered with evidence, which made him appear more culpable.

An office interaction consultant was brought in to huddle with Nigel and the harassment specialist. These conspicuously clandestine proceedings shredded Dane's nerves and gave him palpitations. He hid in the men's room, where he repeatedly splashed water on his face. One colleague came to the men's room twice and noticed Dane.

"Face clean yet?"

"Messy *udon* for lunch," Dane replied. He knew this excuse would only work once; if he was seen there a third time, he would be a prime suspect for anything. Dane skulked to his office and kept his head down with a tedious referencing task for which he was grateful.

Dane was not summoned that afternoon and he assumed no one suspected his involvement in the affair. He believed he had won. Ron and Dottie would be terminated for mutual harassment and inappropriate collegial relations—and Dane would pick up the loose business.

He never foresaw what followed.

24. THE THIRD PLAGUE: BLACK FEET

Just before Dane left for the day at 6 PM, Nigel, the corporate harassment specialist and interaction consultant called him to the conference room.

"Do you know about Ron and Dottie?" Nigel asked with glinting blue eyes that claimed to know who Dane really was.

"Ron and Dottie?" Dane asked blankly. "No, I didn't see anything. They were very professional."

"They've had a misunderstanding," the corporate harassment specialist said. "And they're distraught."

"Really," Dane said. "I thought they communicated well."

"Dottie believed Ron had, err, feelings for her. So she...ummm, tried to reciprocate. She was terribly mistaken," Nigel said.

"Creative partnerships are complicated," Dane observed. He enjoyed this moment despite being scrutinized and tacitly accused. "When brains overheat, bodies ignite."

"Hmmm," the interaction consultant interjected. "Dottie mentioned a red card. Something romantic. But it's *hmmm* disappeared. Do you know anything *aboot* it?"

"No, I don't."

"We have two people in bad shape," Nigel said. "They can't work. Ron wants to go to Brazil to be healed by a holy man."

"Ron always had a passion for spiritualism and fitness," Dane remarked.

"And Dottie is in a depression. She wants to ride her horse."

"She loves horses."

"Two of your colleagues' lives are in shambles and you're not in the least upset," the harassment specialist observed. She, Nigel and the interaction consultant stared at Dane with reproachful suspicion.

"I have faith they'll bounce back," Dane replied.

His three inquisitors' scowls dissolved into shared resignation. They suspected mischief but had no basis for accusing Dane. They decided not to investigate or to seek retribution. Instead they made healing the priority. Ron received a week of paid sick leave in which to recover from post-traumatic stress. Dottie, meanwhile, was moved to a remote office down another hallway, where she could work with minimal interaction.

The winter holidays suspended office politics. Petty machinations were obscured by parties and gift-giving.

After the holidays, Ron reappeared depleted but free, with a box containing his career mentor's Christmas gift. It was a portable ionizing foot bath and detoxification kit, to purge toxins from his body at work and on the move. The kit included a tub for two feet, a battery pack and chemicals.

"You'll see," Ron promised. "I'm going to be a different person."

"That's great," Dane replied.

Dane researched detox foot baths and how they worked. A person's feet were placed in a basin wired to charge water with ions at the push of a button. The positively charged ions attracted negatively charged ions as well as acid wastes in the body, which were drawn down and out through 4,000 pores in the feet. Since feet had the highest concentration of pores in the body, they were deemed exit doors for detoxification. The ionizers were also diagnostic. A user could identify which toxins were in his body by the color of the water: red meant too much iron, blue, too much nickel, and black, an overload of copper. A person could ionize himself several times until the water was clear.

According to Dane's sources, ionizers were quackery. Of course, 40% of people who used placebos felt better. The improvement was psychological, not physiological. This was good news for Dane. If Ron believed in ionizers, he might believe in almost anything.

Dane went to work.

While Ron was out, performing his "rising star" routine, Dane went to a magic and novelty store where he had once purchased a Viking horned hat and a clay drum for a poetry performance. It was a hunch but he found there a bottle of "delayed reaction" ink that was invisible but gradually gained color after mixing in water.

Late one evening, when everyone had gone home and Dane was legitimately alone in the office, transferring changes from a layout to a manuscript, he entered Ron's office and lined the plastic sides of the detox foot bath with the invisible delayed reaction ink.

The following day, Dottie showed up in Ron's office to apologize and to ask for his friendship. Ron smiled and appeared relaxed. When Dottie left, Ron immediately felt the need to detoxify himself. He pulled his detox foot bath from under his desk, filled it with bottled water, pushed the button to activate the ions and submerged his feet. Within two minutes the water was black.

Ron appeared in Dane's doorway with a stricken look on his boyish face.

"I'm a dead man, Dane," Ron groaned.

"You're exaggerating, right?"

"I'm toxic!"

"Maybe your feet were dirty."

"I wash them twice a day."

"Maybe your designer socks bled dye."

No. I'm toxic. It's the only explanation. I've been eating nothing but raw vegetables and soy milk."

"That'll do it," Dane said. "Just add stress and stir. It's a recipe for a nervous breakdown. Take it easy."

"You're right," Ron said. "You're a good friend."

Ron took off another day. When he returned, he tried the detox tank to see if the rest had done him good. The water turned black within 30 seconds. Tears blurred his eyes. He said he had to take another sick day, to find out what was wrong with him before it was too late.

25. RON DOWN

The black water in the ionizing foot bath convinced Ron that he was too toxic to perform on a daily basis, or even to be around other people. He wanted to resign but was persuaded to take a leave of absence—and work from home.

Dane had no partner and little work. One half year after starting at Georgian Shield, his promising career move was at a *cul de sac*. His colleagues were remote because Dane challenged Georgian Shield procedures and showed jovial disrespect for Nigel Hogbine, calling him "Hogtied," inflating his cheeks to simulate Nigel's jowls, and waddling around the office with Nigel's slow gait like he had a load in his pants. His colleagues laughed but spies tattled on Dane's antics to Nigel. Now everyone was afraid to associate with Dane and he was one man who *was* an island.

Once more with feeling, Dane had shown poor judgment. He led a revolution in which he was the sole insurgent. The other Americans behaved like Canadians. They respectfully disagreed with the mother office but were discreet about it. If they had been American colonials, they would have turned Tom Paine over to the British and watched him hang next to Nathan Hale.

Despite his mischief and discontent, Dane's predominant mood was penitent. Rumors circulated that Ron had a nervous breakdown and an inflammatory ailment. He was on medical leave and under heavy alternative medication—a St. John's wart drip and an herbal colonic purge.

One afternoon Dane received a call from an Arizona area code. Ron was phoning from a healing spa and cryogenic center with a unique guarantee—if you didn't recover, they froze your corpse.

"*Dane, I'm worse than toxic,*" the art director whispered

hoarsely. He sounded truly ill.

"You can't be. What's worse than toxic?"

"My body is a hazardous waste site."

"What are you talking about?"

"My doctors wear hazmat suits."

"It's probably the latest style in hospital wear."

"No. I'm really sick. I got ionized water therapy from one of the four leading therapists in the world. The water went from yellow to red to brown to black...*in 30 seconds.* My kidneys, bladder and prostate are all a mess. *I'm 30 years old!* Then the liver toxins started coming out—brown and disgusting. After that, white foam bubbled up. It was my lymphatic system. My immunity is so wiped out that my body is defenseless. Then I saw the red flecks. That's serious blood damage."

"There's no such thing as blood damage."

"I had black flecks, Dane. *Black flecks.* Heavy metal in my body..."

"Ron, you're healthy," Dane said, as if the truth could waltz in at any time and defeat all the lies.

Ron whimpered.

"You got rid of them, right?" Dane asked.

"No! The therapist said in her six months of practice, she never saw anything like it. I was like radioactive. She gave me another treatment. The water went from yellow to orange to green to brown to black in twenty seconds. My gall bladder's leaking. My joint cartilage is jelly. She ionized me four times and the water always turned black in thirty seconds or less."

"So does this mean you're not coming back?"

"I may not be around long enough to come back. Maybe I can art direct in a less stressful place...like the Amazon."

"You think there's IT support in the rain forest?"

"I don't know. Bye, Dane."

Dane's crisis of conscience was replaced by relief. He had

experienced intense guilt for making Ron believe he was ill, but now that Ron really was ill, Dane was no longer culpable. In fact, making Ron think he was sick might have saved his life.

Case 6-E

A FRESH BREATH OF ASTHMA

26. BACCUS BECOMES CASSANDRA

When *Grovil's* accountants reported that Sally and the marketing director had spent 25% of the re-launch budget on first-class airfares, four star hotels, and world-class spas in American cities and the Yucatan, the budget was frozen and projects were put on hold. Only when the first wave of *Pepperoni foot* ads appeared in every endocrine publication in the world did the extent of the misappropriation became fully known. The *Grovil* re-launch, whose brand character was a wrinkled foot with a fake ulcer, was a corporate embarrassment. The brand's reputation was so badly harmed that it was said that even *Grovil* could not promote its healing.

Fortunately, Georgian Shield New York hardly missed a breath because the parent agency handed it a major piece of business—an asthma medication. *Aleige*, an expensive and powerful new biologic drug, mitigated the severity of asthma attacks by reducing the amount of allergy-producing IgE antibodies in the body.

When Dane heard *Aleige* would be handled by Georgian Shield, he believed an advertising god had put him in the cross-hairs of magnificent fortune. He already had extensive experience with this drug. After Green Advertising he had worked briefly at an agency that launched *Aleige* and he knew a good deal about this drug and about allergic asthma.

Dane barraged Nigel with phone calls and emails, pleading to be assigned to the *Aleige* team. He tried to convey his knowledge and enthusiasm to everyone concerned and even to those who could have cared less. For weeks he received no response.

Finally, the *Aleige* campaign started and Dane was allowed to participate.

"Before we start, I need you to understand something incredibly important, *ay?*" Nigel told the multinational team. "It's actually my favorite acronym yet: BYAO, which is short for *Bill your asses off!* If you even think about the product, bill it. If you take a dump, bill it."

"All right!" the Georgian Shield creative department shouted in unison.

After a few torrid days of creative fervor, Nigel papered the conference room walls with a vast number of concepts. At the creative review, he dashed from corner to corner, tearing concepts from the walls. He balled them up, mashed them into pucks and smacked them with a toy hockey stick he had brought for the occasion. Nigel shouted, "He shoots!!" When he hit someone, he added, "—*he scores!*" Those concepts Nigel liked he scribbled over with headlines of his own. Dane had a Canadian déjà vu of a Madison Avenue cocktail. It required every milligram of his maturity not to bolt from the room.

During the second intermission of Nigel's hockey-style creative review, Dane said, "I could really use a *Molson!*"

A few concepts escaped Nigel's unique abuse. He liked one that showed a man on a deck chair on an iceberg; the line read, "This way or the *Aleige* way." He also gushed over allergy sufferers snuggling with allergic triggers, including cats and mold spores, with the headline, "Can't live with them, can't live without them." However, the big winner was "Zap the Triggers," in which allergens like cats, dogs, mites, dust and a woman with a tennis racket were in balloons to be zapped by a pop gun in the lower left hand corner.

"You can't say *Zap the triggers,*" Dane pointed out.

"Can't say it? Oh yes I can! *Zap the triggers! Pow.* Zap the triggers!" Nigel cried out. He removed a concealed squirt gun from his pocket and aimed it at Dane's temple, then pulled the trigger. Water ran down the side of Dane's face.

"See, I said it and did it. *Zap the trigger!*"

"Shooting squirt guns at people, wow, that's real mature," Jeremi, the copy supervisor from Muskatoon, Manitoba said, "Where can I get one?"

From across the room, Nigel threw an open magic marker at Dane but missed, hitting Dottie Wacker in the face and leaving a smudge on her forehead. Dottie, always a sport, said, "I never went to church for Ash Wednesday so this works for me."

"You can't say *Zap the triggers!* because it's inaccurate," Dane explained. "*Aleige* doesn't eliminate allergic triggers or prevent allergies. It intercepts IgE antibodies in the blood stream before they can land on mast cells and trigger the release of inflammatory agents. By reducing the number of IgE antibodies that can link with receptors, *Aleige* helps to reduce the severity of asthma attacks. It's like reducing the number of enemy paratroopers in a battle by shooting them out of the sky."

Dane liked the paratrooper analogy but Nigel looked at him with his mouth agape. The room was silent.

"That is so fucking *b-o-o-o-o-ring!*" Nigel said. "Is everybody as bored as I am? Can I have a show of hands of people who lost their pulse during Dane's explanation?"

Everyone in the room raised their hands. Dane lifted his hand to make it unanimous and prove he was a team player.

"People will prefer asthma to your message, *ay?* Your high science explanation won't sell one little shot of *Aleige,*" Nigel said.

"But yours won't sell any either because the FDA won't let you say it," Dane said.

"Oh, they won't, won't they?" Nigel set his jaw indignantly before stepping back and clearing his throat. "I'll tell you something, Dane," he resumed in the same rasping hush he saved for his reading of the *Night before Christmas* at the annual holiday party. "We don't have to be so goddamn literal. *Zap the triggers!* will do nicely in research."

"People may like *Zap the triggers!* because they understand it but what they understand is misleading and incorrect."

Dane's protest provoked Nigel to go on a personal creative rampage. By the next day, he had an entire studio executing concepts, which ranged from a dust mite made of glass crystal to a photograph of barbed wire with the headline *Allergies Achtung!* presumably to target Nazi sympathizing asthma sufferers.

Dane viewed these concepts as creative mass-suicide. Nigel continued to misstate the drug's mode of action, to be clever at all costs, and Dane warned him of the consequences. Dane spoke truthfully, though not for heroic reasons. He deployed truth as a weapon of reverse psychology. He knew no one would listen to him, least of all Nigel. The more honestly he spoke, the more likely the creative director would do the self-destructive opposite.

"With all due respect to the Georgian Shield way," Dane said with quiet rectitude, "if you pick *Zap the triggers!* the FDA will force you to withdraw the advertising. I've seen it happen and it can be devastating."

The room was quiet again. Nigel stared at Dane.

"That will never happen. I will not that happen," Nigel said.

27. KEN OF THE SPIRITS

Nigel presented *Zap the triggers!* with the agency's recommendation and nearly lost the account. He came to New York and summoned Dane.

"Partnerships are mysterious," Nigel said. "I have put two people together and it was unstoppable. Other partnerships don't work. I'm splitting up you and Ron. He'll work from a spa with a new writer on new business and you'll be paired with Ken Blair."

Ken was Nigel's American friend. He was a short, quiet man with a red nose, matching red cheeks and blue eyes. He hailed from a great lakes town in Minnesota, where his mother and father, show business folk, had retired. When the flu hit Georgian Shield New York, Ken recounted that people in his hometown rarely called doctors or bought medicine. When they fell ill, they went to the liquor store. Ken was still compliant with this treatment plan—especially when he was healthy. It was Ken's gift to make all he did and said seem wholesome and good—including his love of alcohol. He had discovered the essence of great advertising.

Ken was once a creative director at consumer agencies in Hong Kong, Singapore, Sao Paolo, Los Angeles, Toronto, and New York. Now he toiled in the studio on tedious brochures, fixing type, correcting typos, spending twice as long on such tasks as younger colleagues. However, time was unimportant to Ken. He had no children or family. On rainy weekends, he took long walks searching for old haunts—a cigar shop in Chelsea where they once rolled cigars, a Flatiron hat shop where they once sold derbies, and an apothecary where he once bought Horehound cough drops to soothe his throat after cigars.

Dane knew Ken's partnership was another of Nigel's punishments, but he resolved to like Ken to spite Nigel. When he noticed Ken had a spaced out gaze, he assumed his new partner was a profound thinker—or having a blackout. Dane appreciated that Ken discussed advertising thoughtfully—in terms of message, words and signs—but he also knew about Ken's relationship with Nigel and suspected him of spying.

28. PRESENT & RESENT

One afternoon, the *Aleige* team drove out to the client corporate campus in New Jersey to present work: a patient brochure written by Dottie and a testimonial brochure Dane wrote about allergy sufferers who found relief with *Aleige*.

Dottie was also in the presentation because Nigel put her there. After her romantic meltdown she was reinstated as Dane's #1 challenger, as Nigel continued to undermine his position. At the multinational creative briefing, which he conducted over a telephone, Nigel divided the work among all of his creatives. He singled out Dottie, "You're doing the patient brochure, *ay?*"

"Ay okay, Nigel. You the man," Dottie replied.

"Neat. And we need it next week, so can you work over the holiday weekend?"

"*No problemo*, Nigel."

This association between Nigel Hogbine's flabby ass and Dottie's puckered lips enraged Dane. He wished to reach into the phone line and rip out Nigel's windpipe. Patient brochures were Dane's specialty. He was a recognized master of the fourth grade reading level and could transform it into fierce poetry. But Nigel Hogbine was vindictive and ruthless. He acknowledged Dane's dual mastery of primary school rhetoric and the allergic cascade by assigning the brochures to frowsy, feckless Dottie, who would be poaching Dane's assignments in perpetuity due to her amazing adaptation—a willingness to bend over and be impaled by Nigel's demands.

En route to the drug company's secluded corporate campus, Dane had a quasi-allergic flare up triggered by Dottie's presence. As the only writer in the agency who understood *Aleige* and asthma, he viewed Dottie as extraneous; he alone should present work to the client. Dottie, meanwhile, saw herself as an associate creative director of copy, fueling Dane's animosity. As he drove the car, he studied Dottie in his rear-view. Her blond, troll hair was washed and she wore a business suit and pumps instead of her trademark sweats. Her distended belly hiked Dottie's skirt up to her solar plexus and she looked like a wayward, middle-aged parochial school girl. Yet, in her own eyes, Dottie was Dane's buttoned-down boss presenting to *her* client.

Dane was the first to present. He told the client, a pretty woman, seven months pregnant, that he believed his testimonial book, based on real patient transcripts, would be the most important selling piece for *Aleige*. It would persuade doctors and patients in a manner that ads and commercials never could. Each of the patients in the book was an ordinary person with asthma: a black mother of four, who nearly died in pollen-rich South Carolina, before she found a prison job in Arizona and asthma relief with *Aleige*; a private school boy who nearly died from asthma but now played ice hockey after taking *Aleige*; a stock broker, with two inhalers on her desk, who nearly died of asthma on her brownstone stairs before she found *Aleige*; and the extraordinary case of Oscar Simono, MD, an allergist who spent his childhood breathing into paper bags and whose face swelled to watermelon size when he put a banana to his nose—until he found *Aleige*. Dane assured the client that this testimonial brochure would be an asthmatic's classic, to be read from one exacerbation to the next and passed from generation to generation like a volume of fairy tales with an inspiring message of hope provided by *Aleige*.

The client was transfixed by Dane's enthusiasm. Pharmaceutical executives usually loved their product. If you loved their product, they loved you, too. The pregnant client told Dane she was impressed with his vision and eager to see his next draft.

Dottie was up next. She presented her patient brochure in a nasal voice. Her words stuck in her mouth like peanut butter. The pregnant client stared with revulsion at Dottie's distended belly. She seemed appalled by this feature. She may have believed Dottie was a pregnant imposter stuffing a pillow in her blouse to win points with her or to make a joke in poor taste about pregnancy.

For once, Dane observed a personality clash that did not involve him. It felt great. Dane watched the female marketing director's loathing of Dottie gather force. He saw what it looked like when someone could not stand to be in a room with you. The client glared at Dottie, propped her chin under her palm, glanced at her watch with rising frequency, realized she was late for something, and cut Dottie off in mid-sentence. Dottie had a high tolerance for abuse. She said it was no big deal.

Despite her brave disclaimer, Dottie's *Silly Putty* ego was flattened and disfigured. Dane sympathized with her, yet also felt vindicated. Finally, someone confirmed his impression that "the other guy" was incompetent. He hoped Dottie would give up or get fired and leave the field to him. She was another human being trying to make a living but she had been threatening his living for nearly a year—and he wanted her gone.

29. CIRCLE OF TRUTH

When the group returned to the office, news of their success had preceded them and there were congratulations all around. Dane was surprised by the glory. It was as if the agency was overjoyed that the client actually liked something they were doing.

Dane had client love and understood its power in advertising. He finally appreciated why an account guy had his client's dead father's golf shoes enshrined in a display case.

He also sensed that this was the right moment to ask for a raise.

His annual "Circle of Truth" review was imminent though nobody mentioned it. Did his supervisors think of firing him? Or did Georgian Shield, ordinarily fastidious about procedures, forget about this one because it might result in spending more money?

After he had called human resources and left Nigel numerous messages, receiving no response, Nigel acquiesced to reviewing Dane.

It was a cold, rainy day in June when Nigel descended on the New York office. That afternoon he called Dane into a conference room and set up a PowerPoint presentation. The first slide showed a circle with people inside it. Then the people were outside the circle and a question mark was inside. Nigel narrated the slide presentation in a deep, cavernous voice, as if it were a public television documentary.

"We have a procedure for finding out how we're doing at Georgian Shields—the *Circle of Truth*. Each employee is evaluated by peers, supervisors and underlings. We call it a circle because a circle has no sides and only one center. All viewpoints are equal and important. You have worked with many people and each one has a unique perspective on you. Together they tell us who you are as an employee, a colleague and a professional."

Nigel cleared his throat. "And now we come to you, Dane Bacchus. This is your circle of truth."

Click. A slide showing Dane's ID photograph, read:

"It was an interesting year for Dane Bacchus. There was the *Grovil* launch. The *Aleige* testimonial brochure. Miscellaneous projects. Click. Another slide. The word "Problem" had red licks of fire sprouting from it.

"But we have a problem!" Nigel said. He did not click to the next slide. He wanted Dane to linger on the mysterious problem.

"Problem? My work is the one thing our client likes, so you guys have the problem."

Nigel stepped back and clicked. The slide had several words with checks next to them: Quality of Work, check. Creativity, check. Client relations, check. Productivity, check. Responsibility, check.

"Yes, your work is top drawer," Nigel said. "But your colleagues say..."

Click.

"Dane is stubborn!"

"That's good, right?" Dane exclaimed. "Nigel, you said you're stubborn."

"True, but I'm stubborn like titanium. You're stubborn like pig iron."

"I am not pig iron! I am enriched uranium."

"No, Dane. You are degraded plutonium!"

"Okay. Just to show I'm a team player, I'll agree that I'm degraded plutonium. But I still deserve a raise."

"Dane, your insight and knowledge are besmirched by your stubbornness. So what can we do?"

Click. The word "CHANGE" filled the slide.

"Dane, you must change, *ay!*" Nigel said.

"But how can I? If I weren't stubborn I wouldn't be successful."

"I'm *sawry*, Dane. I can't recommend a raise to someone perceived as stubborn. It's just not how things are done, *ay.*"

Clearly they were going in "Circles of Truth."

Nigel smiled with twinkle-eyed intransigence.

"I will review you in six months. If things change we will talk *aboot* a raise."

Dane went to his special place, the Adelson rest room, for quiet time. He felt betrayed by Georgian Shields. He had miscalculated again. He thought personality was irrelevant in advertising, that being good was what mattered. *Wrong!* The churlish copywriter at *The Institute of Design* orientation, who scratched his gonads and worked at the best agencies, must have been the lucky exception.

Dane's only consolation was the law of advertising averages. Good and bad news took turns. If things were going your way they would soon go against you, and vice versa.

30. DOTTIE GOES BATTY

The good news was waiting in Dane's office when he returned. The client left a voice mail with her congratulations: the senior vice presidents in the respiratory division loved his *Aleige* testimonial brochure. Now the *Aleige* product brochure job folder, Dottie's baby, sat on his desk. An account massacre had just occurred. The pregnant client phoned Toronto and threatened to fire the agency if Dottie was not removed from the account. Dane was asked to take over her project.

Dane's rival was finally eliminated. The runner-up, the "other guy," no longer shared his job.

Dottie had not yet been notified of her dismissal because no one knew how she would react. People were comfortable with abusing her by assigning her massive quantities of work to be done in inadequate amounts of time, but they had no idea of what to expect if they took work away from her. She was a job-junkie with a limitless craving for vile assignments and the concomitant adrenaline rush. Sudden drudgery-deprivation might result in severe work-withdrawal, which could be difficult to watch.

Reasons for their circumspection were soon confirmed. Dottie dashed frantically from office to office, checking everywhere and with everyone for the job folder on which her life, livelihood and identity depended.

"Have you seen my patient brochure?" Dottie asked as she lifted herself on tip toes to identify the code numbers on the folder occupying his desktop. Dane did not answer.

"That's my job folder! What is the patient brochure doing here? Are you working on it?" she demanded.

"They want me to be familiar with it since it's going into research on Monday," Dane replied.

"They gave you my patient brochure?" Dottie asked. Her large eyes squinted and widened, flexing to resist tears.

"Yes."

Dottie looked sad and resigned—normal vital signs. Otherwise, she appeared to take her demotion well. Yet, just beneath her composure, Dane sensed injury and indignation about to erupt.

Suddenly, Dottie burst across the room and reached over his desk. Her fingers clawed for the folder. In the split second of her assault, Dane hoisted the folder and used it as a shield, but she grasped its edges, tugged hard and tore it apart at the seams. Twenty-five drafts of manuscript spilled from the folder as Dottie wrestled with Dane for the dismembered plastic covers.

"Get off of my folder! Get off!"

Ken entered the office.

"What's going on?"

"Dottie's having trouble letting go," Dane gasped. The entire staff stood outside, straining to see the action from the half-open doorway.

Flailing with nails slashing, Dottie tore at Dane's face and shirt. When he released his half of the tattered plastic folder, she held it to her bosom, closed her eyes and let tears flow.

"My patient brochure," she whispered. "The job folder is empty. Where are the back-up rounds? How will I know the changes? Where is my brochure? My brochure?" she whimpered.

"Look on the floor," Dane said.

When Dottie realized her job folder was ripped apart and its contents were strewn about her feet, she collapsed in sobs on her 25 drafts. "He took my patient brochure! My patient brochure."

"What happened?" Rupert McTavish, the office head, asked.

"Dottie didn't want to let go of the brochure," Dane said.

"Can you blame her?" Rupert asked reprovingly. He regarded Dane like he was the cad who seduced the pregnant client into hating Dottie.

"It's business," Dane said. "The client requested the change."

"Right. And you care about the client!" Rupert said.

"Don't you?" Dane asked.

That afternoon, the staff catered to Dottie's nervous breakdown. They gave her sips of ginger ale and Thai left-overs from a client luncheon. It was like her birthday. Dane ruminated on the unfairness. If he had thrown a fit—come to think of it, he had—he would have been escorted out and terminated. Yet, after Dottie's violent fit, people still viewed him as the transgressor. Dane, meanwhile, felt no responsibility or remorse for Dottie's situation. He was the staff writer. He was hired first; Dottie came later. Prior to this patient brochure, she had done all of the taking. When she regained her composure, Nigel would find her something else to do.

During the next few days, Dottie occasionally conferred with Dane about a project, pretending nothing had happened. With each visit she was more agitated, going from sighs to pants to raising her voice. With Ken watching intently from his desk across the room, Dane responded carefully to Dottie's outbursts. He had to treat her kindly like she was an addict in work withdrawal. Soon she burst into his office with a layout, crying, "If you're making the changes, make them all!" Dane and Ken looked at one another, wondering if she would explode again more violently than before.

"I can't work this way!" she cried.

There it was, like an exposed, beating heart, the ego Dottie pretended did not exist. Dane felt like a detective with a confirmed hunch. Dottie's flash of ego revealed who she was behind her, "Aw shucks, walk all over me!" façade. Her obsequious flexibility was her aid to survival, how she managed to get work away from him. By revealing it, she conceded the fight was over.

Case 6-F
COMING TOGETHER & APART

31. A VISIONARY MOMENT

The next week Dane escaped the recycled air of the office to spend two days with the clients, changing and testing the patient brochure. He drove alone to the same New Jersey town where he had been a professor for ten years.

The meeting was in a luxury hotel complex near the interstate highway. A cadre of twenty top research and product management professionals assembled in a plush meeting room. A laptop on one long table projected manuscript pages on a screen. Key decision-makers suggested changes to the prose pell-mell but nobody led the discussion or transcribed changes on screen.

"Someone needs to input the changes," the product manager said.

"I'm the copywriter in residence. I will be your scribe." Dane said.

The room filled with laughter.

Dane felt at ease. As the *Aleige* people called out alternatives to sentences, Dane key stroked the changes and asked, "Is this what you want to say? Or how about this?" He changed the order, moved clauses and asked for comments and suggestions. The participants chattered, offered opinions, argued and came to consensus.

Years earlier Dane had taught remedial students how to write in computer labs. He strode from student to student, screen to screen, helping them to develop ideas and to write and organize sentences and paragraphs for optimal impact. Now he performed the same function for an older student body—with a significant difference. His college students rarely enjoyed composition, whereas *Aleige* team reveled in it.

During breaks, drug company people treated Dane like an esteemed colleague, which felt good but very strange to him. For years, clients had seemed like implacable monsters, always demanding more work and later hours. For once, he met them as people.

He talked with Carla, from regulatory, who turned two-hour copy reviews into all-afternoon marathons by demanding that obvious statements be explained—and often deleted. Carla had her reasons for making everyone miserable. When she was a pharmacist, a customer came in with gunk on her teeth. She begged Carla for something to remove it. The woman showed her the box the gunk came from—it was a hemorrhoid drug. The woman had followed instructions by breaking the capsule before inserting it, only to insert it in the wrong end.

"That's why copy has to be idiot proof," Carla concluded.

A voice cried out, "Look, it's Dr. Simono!"

Dr. Oscar Simono, a hero of Dane's testimonial book, entered the room to comment on the product brochure. Dr. Simono was a paid consultant and his response would not be in the research report. Still, he was an asthma expert who had self-injected *Aleige* for years.

"Maybe he'll do his trick!" someone exclaimed.

Dr. Simono was highly allergic. Touching a banana skin or

inhaling the scent of a strawberry swelled his face to twice its size. He casually peeled a banana and chomped.

"This banana was like a loaded gun but now it's just a banana. Thanks to *Aleige*. Say, you should use that as body copy," Dr. Simono said. The executives gave Dr. Simono a standing ovation. He was a genius.

Suddenly, Dr. Simono staggered backward, panted and gripped his chest. Before the respiratory brain trust's astonished eyes, his face grew red and large like a balloon filling with water.

"What's wrong? Call a doctor!"

The heady ambience trembled with apprehension. How could this happen? The attendees believed they were witnessing the death of Dr. Simono, their beloved advocate, and a public relations debacle. Did they need to report this to the FDA? Why did Dr. Simono insist on daredevil stunts? Did he think he was the Knievel of Allergies?

An allergist, waiting to be called in to give his opinions on the patient brochure, revived Dr. Simono with a shot of Benadryl. Dr. Simono would live on to perform more death-defying fruit stunts. But what caused his collapse? Dr. Simono admitted that he had not taken his *Aleige* for three weeks. He ate the potentially deadly banana to test how long a dose of *Aleige* remained effective.

The spectacle of life and death was not disruptive. It stimulated a burst of creativity from the group.

Page by page, Dane orchestrated the complete rewriting of Dottie's brochure, which had taken her a month to write. He was like a maestro using an orchestra of creativity-starved business people to write a twenty page brochure. After ten hours, the drug company cohort was exhausted but in good spirits and ready to go home.

During the process, Dane realized that his peak advertising experiences happened when people created together. The usual agency-client relationship—one party submitting, the other receiving—was adversarial. Work went back and forth like a tennis ball, and projects were completed only when both players were sick of the game. When agency and client collaborated like partners and shared the project, revisions and approval were simple.

"This was great," he told the drug company executives when the brochure was completed. "We wrote this together. Now we know it's right and we can sign off. This is how all work should be done. Together."

They raised their soda cans and plastic coffee cups and toasted, "To the future of advertising!" then applauded, before breaking out for the night.

32. OLD SCHOOL DETENTION

The next morning Ken came to the facility to present new work with Dane. They started late. Dane explained a piece and read the headline. Then he described the photograph as it related to the copy.

"I'll do the art!" Ken blurted.

"Oh, okay," Dane said.

Ken spoke quickly and softly.

"We selected PMS 450 because that is your primary color and we thought it breathed well, as opposed to the target audience. Heh! Heh! Then we chose elegant type because the product offers high end relief...and...the subjects are shot in soft focus..." Ken went on to explain the colors, design elements and photograph without vocal expression or eye contact. When he was done, his hand was across his chest, his face was crimson, and he was gasping for air.

"It looks like you've got another *Aleige* patient," Dane cracked.

The client laughed. Ken's eyes widened as he sucked in enough air to come out of his panic zone.

When their presentation was over, Dane and the client moved on to the brochure revision session but Ken waved at Dane to come back. He seemed to need help standing up.

"You stepped on my lines," Ken said.

"I did? Not intentionally."

"You explained the photograph. We've talked about this."

"I mentioned it to explain the relevance of the copy," Dane said.

"You're not supposed to describe visual content. You're supposed to read the copy."

"Clients don't need me to read copy, Ken. They know how to read."

"The photograph is part of art. That's my domain," Ken insisted.

"Your domain, my domain. We shouldn't see it that way, Ken. We work together. You can read the copy and I can discuss the art. It's the same concept."

"You laughed at me," Ken said.

"You had us worried there so I tried to lighten the mood. If the clients laugh, they'll keep us," Dane reassured his partner. He was still imbued with his revelation of the previous evening—creative unity— everyone working together.

But Ken did not share his experience.

"I need to be assertive. I have to do this," Ken gasped.

33. BUTT WHAT?

The two-day client contact gave Dane confidence but he could not shake his discontent.

The office he shared with Ken was like a cell. Their desks faced one another and every time Dane looked up, Ken was there. Ken tried to be gracious. That was the problem. Dane felt Ken trying. Ken resented Dane's phone conversations with Becky. He left the room or his red round face puckered in strenuous efforts to concentrate. When Dane said he was sorry, Ken replied, "Not at all" without meaning it.

People were nervous. The *Aleige* account was now a skeleton with only a few projects left on the bones. Dane and Ken stayed busy creating kits and newsletters. On morning, they presented the latest work to the new account supervisor.

The presentation was informal and took place in their office. Dane recited the headline and started to explain it but realized that there was nothing to explain—they had used the same headline before. Ken followed with a description of the art. Dane commented on the symbolism of a woman staring in a mirror when Ken shouted, "You did it again!"

"Did what?"

"You interrupted me."

The account person looked bewildered. Dane was stunned and humiliated. As the account person left, Dane closed the door and turned to Ken.

"Don't do that again!"

"I warned you not to interrupt!" Ken replied.

"I added a thought," Dane said. "And if I did interrupt, you still had no right to shout at me—even if you were my boss, which you're not. You barely know what you're doing."

Ken's shoulders twitched like a wind-up toy ready to run.

"I have to be a presence," Ken said as if he were coaching himself. His fists were clenched. "I need to assert myself."

Ken charged Dane.

For years Dane had been swimming and lifting weights. When Ken, a short, angry man, collided with him, he bounced off of his chest, staggered backward against his desk and shouted. "So you think I'm going to run from you? Not so fast!" Ken charged again and stopped short. He stood up to Dane, belly to belly, forehead to chin, like a bilious baseball manager confronting an ump.

"Save face or save your job!"

Two forces competed for control of Dane's body—physical instinct and economic survival, the law of the street versus the employee manual. Instincts honed in playgrounds throbbed in his fists. He itched to cock his right shoulder and punch Ken's presumptuous red face. He had never retreated from a fight, even against superior numbers and men of size. It was how he nipped victim-hood in the bud. Was it not his second amendment right to bear arms when his arms were literally *his arms?* Yet, as juiced as he was with adrenaline, the rule of the workplace froze his shoulder and pinned his arms to his sides. Physical contact would put his livelihood and family's welfare at risk.

"Get out of my face!" Dane snarled at Ken, hoping *anything,* even his breath would force his partner to retreat.

"Why should I, Dane? Huh? Going to beat me up?"

"Just back off!" Dane replied. He now understood the anxiety of the big man against a smaller man. He must neither advance nor retreat.

"Are you going to hit me, Dane? It's what you want to do. Go ahead. But if you do, you'll get fired. *Fired!*"

The dread of capitulating to instinct tightened Dane's body till it twitched. He could not abide Ken so close, yet the smaller man stood firm against him. Dane would not risk harm to Ken by hitting him but he needed space and his energy surged to be released. He bowed his head and bumped Ken's forehead. Ken staggered backward and flopped on the floor. His face contorted like a fist and he jabbed his forefinger at Dane. "You head-butted me!"

He crawled to his feet and bolted from the room. Dane was dismayed. He barely touched him.

"He hit me! He hit me!" Ken shouted.

Ken disappeared and Dane had the office to himself. Rupert, who headed Georgian Shield-New York, and Juan and Jeremi, the creative supervisors, interviewed Dane to file reports. Dane recounted that Ken shouted at him and violated his personal space.

"Ken's afraid to return," Rupert told Dane. "He thinks you'll hurt him."

"Let's get this straight. He bounced off of me! He was the bouncer. I was the *bouncee!*" Dane insisted.

Rupert, Juan and Jeremi had never heard this terminology on *Law and Order* and Dane doubted they believed him, so he did not plead his case. Any emotional display would confirm Ken's version of the event.

The next day Ken phoned Dane.

"How are you holding up?" he asked Dane sympathetically as if they were best friends trapped in a bad situation. Ken's friendly tone puzzled Dane. Ken had worked on detergent accounts but failed to see that some stains do not wash out. He was oblivious to the fact that he complicated Dane's life by misrepresenting their argument as a fist fight. In two days Ken returned to his desk and he and Dane were looking at one another again like nothing had happened.

But the Georgian Shield East was too quiet and Dane suspected trouble. The following Tuesday started typically. In the DOA lobby, Dane announced himself to the camera, "I am *Utu Mabootu*, the world's tallest albino pygmy." The security guard looked away dyspeptically as she had done the previous 100 times he used this alias.

Nigel stopped by Dane's office at 10 AM and asked him to come to the conference room. He offered Dane a seat and regarded him sternly.

"Dane, we have to let you go. I warned you that your behavior needed to improve, so you beat up Ken."

"I didn't beat him up. He ran into me."

"Please sign this statement and you will receive a month's severance."

Dane's first impulse was to ball up the document and shove it down Nigel's throat but instinct told him this might be his last income for some time. Dane walked the hallway to his office. No one so much as cast a glance in his direction. They did not seem to know was happening to him, or if they knew, he was already absent to them, a departed figure.

Dane collected his stuff and phoned Becky. As he waited for her in front of DOA Worldwide, Ron approached. He noticed that Dane carried more than his usual paraphernalia so he asked if he had a doctor's appointment. Dane told his ex-partner he had been fired. Ron bowed his head and said he was sorry, then extracted a card from his pocket and handed it to Dane.

"I think this might help you."

It was a card for an ionizing water detox spa.

"Why, Ron?"

"Dane, you may be toxic."

"I'm not toxic. This agency is toxic."

"No argument there. But you *can* save yourself."

AD NOMAD 7
NOMAD'S LAND

Case 7-A

FREELANCING: FUNCTION, FREEDOM & FAKING IT

1. FREELANCER

Dane could not sleep off his Georgian Shield nightmare. In a recurring dream, a voice whispered, "No billable hours...you didn't move your bowels..." He sat up in a sweat. When he drifted back to sleep, Ron appeared in a dream wiggling his black toes, asking, "Why did you do it, Dane?"

"Not my feet! I'm not toxic!" Dane woke up screaming.

Becky cradled his head in her arms and cooed, "Everything's going to be all right." But Dane was not all right. He guzzled quarts of coffee to fight fatigue, yet remained a zombie.

"Return to your true calling!" Dane urged himself but the dark monitor mocked his uninspired eyes. Instead of writing, he watched cartoons, took long showers and derived fresh air, mental stimulation and a sense of accomplishment from grocery shopping with Becky.

Dane had been damaged by jobs before but at Georgian Shield he sank to new moral depths and was deeply ashamed. Advertising was a livelihood, not a license to ruin lives. His business cost was too high: he was evolving into a predatory life form he hated and barely knew.

Ron's advice haunted Dane. He needed to renounce pharmaceutical advertising and find work that was simple and good, like serving coffee at Starbucks, helping folks find stuff at Home Depot, or selling orthopedic running shoes to people with bad feet.

However, after three idle weeks, a crashing wave of bills washed away Dane's scruples and he relapsed into income addiction. He forgot how despicable drug advertising had made him and craved the paycheck. His job lust had become unbearable when the phone saved him. "The right person is needed right now!" a headhunter demanded.

Urgency and immediacy were Dane's best friends. He took a

freelance gig fifty miles away. During a ninety minute drive staggered by traffic lights, he passed an endless tract of homes, condos and malls, and marveled at the wealth and stability in which he barely participated.

His first project was an overdue report on insomnia which needed swift completion. Due to the short deadline and long commute, Dane was allowed to write from home. To prove himself, Dane promised the first draft in a ridiculously short time. The job was so hot that he stayed up writing for 48 hours.

Dane applied the Stanislavski method to medical writing. By forgoing sleep, he entered the mind of an insomniac to make his content more authentic. But his sleepless binge triggered a facial twitch and scrambled syntax. On a night's rest, his sleep-deprived prose read like gibberish key-stroked by a gorilla in the mist.

After a torrid week, Dane returned to the agency to revise his report. He took respite from the agency's air conditioned tedium on the corporate campus grounds. It was an Elysian field for stellar think tanks, where cerebral people were meant to walk and talk intellectual trash and play games with the world's fate.

The think tank market had crashed, leaving the splendid grounds to Dane, who took unworthy advantage. He padded on pebbled paths across a plush lawn hemmed by geometric hedges, imbibing the scent of blossoming gardens, while manmade geysers from nozzles between black stones, ejaculated refreshing mist at his skin. He traversed Romanesque foot-bridges over petal-strewn ponds, where fat mallards floated like popped corks. In this idyllic setting Dane's mind started to mend. He had a revelation. "Work is good," he whispered.

When the insomnia project was put to rest, the agency partners offered Dane a permanent position. He declined their offer because the commute was long and he could not commit to a full-time job. However, this brief assignment produced in Dane a life-changing discovery.

Work *was* good. It was corporate life that was corrupt. To

reconcile integrity with income, he must forswear full-time employment and the tainted aspirations of job ownership, stability and security, which all led to evil. When earning a day's wage, Dane harmed no one. As a temporary employee, he would have no wobbly ladder to climb, no weak position to defend, no empty title to grab, no dubious promotion to covet and crave. It would be all work and no politics. A new career path opened before him.

Dane became a freelancer.

2. STEAMROLLER OF RELIEF

Like an endorsement from destiny, Dane received a call the next day from Pharmation, an agency in NJ owned by the same network as Mentos, where Dane had been fired for inappropriate shouting. He felt like a fugitive returning to the scene of an unsolved crime. To alter his appearance, he devised a limp and borrowed Becky's eyebrow pencil to color in full eyebrows.

Toby Tutweiler, the imposing creative director who interviewed Dane, specialized in consumer advertising but inherited pharmaceutical accounts in a merger. She despised any drug that could not be smoked or snorted, and deemed medical advertising a wasteland in desperate need of creative salvation.

For some reason, Toby identified Dane as The Chosen One who would save drug advertising from borrowed interest, visual puns and boring headlines. Dane was flattered but baffled by Toby's faith. Was she too zealous to know that no one would change drug advertising without first overhauling the drug industry, the FDA and molecules, themselves?

The next Monday, Dane was helping Becky identify ripe melons in a supermarket when Toby called his cell. A client had rejected the agency's creative. Could Dane come in by noon?

At 11:59 AM Dane was in the office of a recently fired creative director, feverishly writing concepts and headlines for a slow-release opiate that provided steady relief.

It was a challenge. Opiates filled the marketplace and every gentle, airborne metaphor from butterflies to parachutes had been used to sell them. The only feature that distinguished this pain medication from others was its long, steady delivery of relief, which prevented breakthroughs.

At 5 o'clock Dane was beckoned to a room, where senior creatives, who identified him as *Toby's mole*, reviewed his ten ideas. They gave grudging kudos to his zipper with missing teeth and liked the freshness of his mountain flattened by a steamroller.

At 8 PM, Toby strutted in like Patton in pumps, reviewed the team's work and hated everything but Dane's broken zipper, which she liked for its bite but discarded for its sexual innuendo.

"What about the steamroller?" Dane blurted. "We can sell steamroller toys...*errr*...like *Hess* trucks...The concept has legs...I mean, *wheels*...No! *Tracks*."

Toby's look swiftly demoted Dane from savior to stooge.

"The target audience is in constant pain," Toby countered. "Do you really think they'll be motivated by toy steamrollers?"

"What if they have children or grandchildren?" Dane pleaded.

The creative brain trust snickered.

"Miraculously, I still have an appetite after seeing this crap," Toby said. "I'm getting dinner. When I return, I'd better not be nauseous."

"That's setting the bar pretty high, don't you think?" a writer cracked as Toby walked out.

When the scent of Toby's hair product was a whisper in their noses, the white-haired elder of the creative cadre, who misidentified Dane as "Dean," warned, "You realize, we're not leaving this room till she's happy."

The brain trust nodded with collective gloom. *What were the odds of that happening?* As if condemned to a circle of hell even Dante could not have imagined, the men slumped at the table in stupefied resignation. Occasionally someone expectorated an idea that hung like smoke before dissolving in silence. These hardened creatives were at ease with drudgery and discomfort, like pit-masters slow cooking their own brains.

It was nine o'clock on a Monday evening and Dane was in a familiar place—despair. In his dull neighborhood, everyone turned in early and parking would be impossible to find. He earned a per diem rate so technically he could leave and be paid. The only snag was being hired back. To be exempted from this torture chamber gracefully he needed an exit strategy. Fortunately, he had one in reserve—his finely-crafted limp. He stood up and shuffled about the room, dragging his leg ostentatiously. No one noticed. He hobbled some more and suggested with a soft voice wavering with pain that he should probably leave on account of his leg.

"Do you think with your leg, Dean?" the white-haired elder asked irascibly.

Dane admitted that he did not.

"Then would you take a seat?"

Apparently, the only way to escape this room with impunity was to think his way out. Dane disseminated ideas like his mind was a conceptual yard sale.

"Ball-peen hammer!" he shouted.

"Too painful, Dean," the white-haired elder said.

"A feather with the drug's logo!"

"Too light for a strong narcotic," another writer opined.

"A vacuum cleaner sweeping a carpet of nerve-endings!" Dane shouted as if struck by divine revelation.

"That sucks," an art director yawned.

"We did it three months ago," another writer piped in.

Pressure thinking and metabolizing large bodies raised the room temperature to perspiration drip point. Dane wiped wet beads from his forehead, prompting the white-haired creative leader to stare at him.

"Dean, what's that on your face?"

Dane thought the group leader was mocking him or posing a trick question.

"What? You mean my eyes, nose and mouth?" Dane asked peevishly.

"There's a brown streak over your eyes."

After a confused moment, Dane recalled the fake eyebrows of his disguise, which he had scribbled on frantically that morning. How could he explain it? He had to think fast—*again*—and it was becoming harder to do after a day of thinking about a slow-acting opiate.

"It must be the organic brown soap my wife made me use," Dane said.

"Glad to hear it. I thought it was shoe polish, only you missed your shoes," the white-haired elder said. Raucous laughter filled the room. The creative thinkers kept it going like a fire on a cold night, until they forgot what they were laughing about.

Hours passed. Toby arrived.

"So what do you have for me?"

She rolled a toothpick with her tongue while the men displayed the finery of their minds: a steamroller, a steam iron, a locomotive engine with a smiley face, a lace curtain, a fire extinguisher, a lawn mower, hedge-clippers, a meat tenderizer, a ball-peen hammer with a fur handle...

Toby glowered but it was unclear whether her reaction was due to aesthetics or indigestion. She burped.

"You can do better," she said as she left for the lady's room.

Giggles and monosyllables festooned the silence. Some creatives expressed concepts with their fingers. Dane gave the limp another chance. In his earlier demonstration, he had dragged the leg, whereas this time he swung it from the hip like a sickle severing weeds. The white haired supervisor stared at him. "That's not the same leg you were dragging before," he said.

Dane paused with unease. Someone was paying more attention to his mischief than he was. Should he say the pain traveled or that the inflammation was symmetrical like rheumatoid arthritis? It was too risky. These medical writers would know he lied or would fact-check it.

"No, it's the same leg," Dane bluffed. "You must have seen me limp in the other direction."

"Dean, if it bothers you, sit down," the leader suggested.

Dane was getting used to the idea of circling his neighborhood all night or sleeping in his car, when Toby returned at midnight. She stared at the doodles on the wall and settled on Dane's *steamroller flattening a hill.*

The next day, everyone took credit for the steamroller concept and conveniently forgot that Dane created it. Toby summoned Dane to her office.

"It's slow so you don't need to come back."

"Did I screw up?"

"You tell me! I hired you to remove cheesy metaphors from drug advertising," Toby said. "So you gave me a steamroller and a toothless zipper."

"I thought you liked them." Dane replied, lowering his mortified eyes.

"I hated them. The client loves them!" she cried.

"That's great! I saved your business!" Dane replied.

"But at what cost? Because of your shitty creative, we'll have to live with a steamroller flattening a hill for years! I'd rather lose the client than produce this *drek!*"

She peered at Dane as if his soul were a bad clam she needed to pry open regardless. "Don't you want more than success?"

"I'll tell you when I have some," Dane replied honestly.

During the long drive home, Dane felt used and abused. It was a familiar sensation but not one a freelancer was supposed to feel—in particular, when working on a pain medication. Belittlement and inadequacy went with a staff job; freelance was supposed to be different. Dane had never been fired faster—and for doing what he was told. As he drove, he composed his anguish. "It's the way of the freelancer," he told himself. "You did the assignment. You were paid. You are successful."

3. REVIVAL

That night the phone rang.

"Hello there!"

The buoyant voice belonged to Paula, Dane's born-again Christian, high-fashion, art director friend with whom Dane had briefly collaborated at Integrimedicom.

"We're partners again!"

Paula and Dane were teamed on a secret pitch for a ground-breaking drug—at Pharmation—of all places. It was a second coming for Dane but with a major difference. Once again, Dane occupied the office of a recently fired creative director but this time Paula was in the office across the hall, distracting him with her Mary Magdalene evangelism. She wore stiletto heels and a short skirt that exposed the full length of her brown, sleek legs. Spaghetti straps held her silken top over her firm breasts. Bangles jangled around her neck, wrists and ankles. She played angelic synthesizer music on her computer while she and Dane explored concepts for a pitch so preliminary that nobody knew what it was for.

"So, tell me about this pulmonary hypertension," Paula said.

"The vessels in the lungs are constricted so blood doesn't flow through them," Dane explained.

"So it's a big bad disease and our drug is the good guy that's fighting it," Paula summarized.

"Something like that," Dane replied.

"Just keep it simple, *Sugar*, and tell a story," Paula advised.

She propped her legs on the desk, stroked her thighs and scowled at her feet.

"I'm not sure about these toenails. I like 'em brighter," Paula mused. "Ya know, Jesus loved feet."

"I thought he washed them."

"Well, he wouldn't wash 'em if he didn't love 'em." She wiggled her toes and laughed.

While Dane struggled for a headline, Paula searched the internet for pictures.

"Check this out," Paula said.

Dane thought she found an evocative image for a new concept. Instead, she was browsing a Christian singles website for eligible men. Her mouse rested on one with a long face and bad hair, who could have been Dane's double.

"What about this guy? He's a single dad with two teenage kids."

"Contact him instantly," Dane advised. Paula was less sure.

"He snorkels. I don't trust the piety of a man who is always underwater. I want a fisher of men, not a fish."

Later, as they brainstormed for ideas no one was asking for, Paula broke the silence.

"So Dane, why do you hate Jesus?"

"I don't hate Jesus."

"But you don't love Jesus."

"Love of deity doesn't come easily for me," Dane said. "It's nothing personal."

"But it *is* personal. Jesus loves you...And you know what it is to feel unrequited love."

"Jesus can handle it. Can we talk about *endothelin-A* receptors now?"

A large female account executive with blue framed glasses walked in. Paula showed their new concepts.

"The disease is a shark. See? It's all dangerous and blue. We're the skin-diver with the harpoon," Paula explained, as she pointed at the salient features of the ad with a child's exuberance.

"You're so brilliant," the large woman with blue framed glasses told Paula, then shot Dane a dirty look.

One afternoon, Dane walked in while Paula was proudly showing off their concepts to a pugnacious senior writer who greeted Dane each morning with, "Hey, Stupid!"

The churlish writer was consistent. "Bye, Stupid," he cracked before walking out.

"What's wrong, Sugar?" Paula asked, sensing Dane's agitation.

"If you show our work to people, they'll steal it and we'll be out of work," Dane snapped. He was enraged and viewed Paula as a traitor.

Tears filled her eyes. She reached for him with two bare arms and hugged him.

"*Oh, Dane!* Do birds keep secrets? No, they sing every morning and the Lord finds them all the worms they can eat. You must believe."

Blockage and suffocation characterized pulmonary hypertension—and Dane's and Paula's creative process. They were stuck on artery metaphors—sewer pipes, sink-traps, rubber tubes. Dane even proposed rigatoni stuffed with cheese.

"I am so empty!" Paula cried. She cranked the sound on her computer. An angelic choir of synthesized castrati blasted plainsong from her speakers.

"I hear a rumbling in my brain," Dane replied nervously, hoping to preempt her prayer and proselytizing. Too late.

"We need the Lord's salvation!" she cried. "Let us pray for inspiration!"

Falling on her knees, Paula reached high to the heavens, seeking divine intervention for bad medical metaphors.

"Oh, Lord, fill my mind and spirit with your never-ending creativity."

Agency staffers were drawn to Paula's doorway as if the bangles that jingled on her wrists were church bells ringing. They witnessed Paula in a tight miniskirt, tan arms reaching skyward in voluptuous supplication, fusing church and state, science and faith in spark-inducing paradox. When Paula stopped humming her hymn, she opened her eyes as Pharmation employees applauded. She laughed, reached for the heavens, and cried, "Praise the Lord!"

"Praise the Lord!" they responded.

Dane wondered if he should pass a hat. When the crowd scattered, Paula declared, "See? People need to believe." She clasped her hands and looked upward. "Please, Jesus, help Dane believe!"

Perhaps her prayer was answered. Or Dane compensated for his lack of faith with a creative revelation of his own. Primary hypertension stopped women's breathing, so Dane visualized a woman in a binding corset. He believed Paula would love this image since she often wore lingerie as business attire. Instead, she cried.

"You're leaving me!"

"I don't know what you're talking about."

"Don't lie. God knows what's in your heart."

"I have no plans."

Evidently, Paula did. Dane was soon relegated from his office across from her and to a cubicle at the far end of a vast, open space. The truculent writer who called Dane, "Stupid!" everyday was in and out of Paula's office. He and Paula feasted on Dane's headlines now while Paula turned every status meeting into a prayer service with one theme: "Believe."

Staff people avoided eye contact with Dane until a group surrounded him at the water cooler and fired paper clips, hissing, "Antichrist." Paula came to Dane's rescue. She warned his tormentors that the antichrist was not a person but a failure in all people to believe. Dane was saved but when the time came to present the pitch, Paula stayed on and Dane was discarded.

He was starting to think freelance was a less stable version of full-time employment— steady abuse without a steady paycheck.

4. WHAT'S MY PRODUCT?

It was uncanny. No matter how often Dane got the shaft he always fell into a new dumpster.

He received a last-minute assignment to write copy for *Info Med*, a small agency with a unique method to sell drugs, titled *Informational Promotion*. Dane's challenge was to figure out what *Informational Promotion* meant, since no one told him.

Dane hoped the Fed Ex parcel from *Info Med* would explain, but the materials featured sultry close ups of sensual women with two-word headlines like "Invigorating Information," "Hard Facts," "Dynamic Data," and "Influence Interest." After careful analysis, Dane concluded that *Informational Promotion* was for erectile dysfunction. He created ten new headlines and body copy to incorporate this theme.

Dane met the men of *Info Med* to give them their $500 worth of creative.

Cedric Mann-Dingus, the creative director, a large-boned Englishman with a rosaceous nose, introduced Dane to his associates, Gino and Lance. Cedric was from the celebrated Mann-Dingus family that once amassed and bankrupted an advertising empire. Gino, the marketing director, was short and nervous, with craving eyes. Lance, the data manager, had black framed glasses and spiky hair, like a dad in a Disney movie.

The *Info Med* brain trust faced Dane across a table. With dour gravity, they stated that his work was outstanding but did not convey their novel idea.

"Out of ten copy platforms you couldn't use one?" Dane asked dejectedly.

"The abundance was lovely," Mann-Dingus replied. "But none were quite, *mmm*, right."

"Can you describe your product?" Dane asked.

"We have to ladder up to that," said Lance.

518

"First we put a stake in the ground," Gino said.

"What makes your method unique?" Dane asked.

"Don't go there," Gino said.

"That's the *'Ah hah!'* moment!" Lance added. "We serve it up with sex."

"If we tell you the *Ah hah* for shits and giggles," Gino said, "you'll go, *'Huh?'* It's that brilliantly simple."

"Like the bloody wheel!" Mann-Dingus brayed after clearing his throat.

"What's like the wheel?" Dane asked.

"The Sumerian sod who invented *that* was a *bona fide* bloody genius," said Mann-Dingus. "But he didn't make a shekel because he had no patent."

"What would friggin' Hammurabi say 'bout that!" Gino pounded his fist in his hand.

Like a Chilean tree that harvests moisture from fog, Dane's mouth gaped to help his brain absorb meaning from these words. Yet even this novel adaptation did not help him understand *Info Med's* method.

Gino squirmed like he was gagging a fart.

"Here's the problem.   When I present our *informational promotion* modules to clients they tell me...*Yeah! So you do ads, brochures and newsletters differently...is that it?* No, damn it, that's not it."

"*Do* you produce ads, brochures and newsletters?" Dane asked.

"Yeah, but you're missing the point!   He's missing the point!" Gino repeated convulsively.

"*What is the point?*" Dane pleaded.

The three men pelted him with buzz-words.

"It's *drive acquisition.*"

"Ramped up to *motivate conversion.*"

"Then we deliver on it with *relationship through subtraction.*"

"And sexy it up with *brand magnetism.*"

"Are the naked women part of your method?" Dane asked.

Lance pointed excitedly at Dane. "That's the *Ah!* before the *Ah hah!* Like Niagara before the falls."

Dane yanked at his hair follicles but pounding his head on the table was faster and more effective.

"Will nobody tell me what this is about? *Please*?" he supplicated.

An hour passed and nobody explained the meaning of *informational promotion.* It was as if the men from *Info Med* expected him to know. Dane regurgitated key phrases. "DNA? Free radicals? Serotonin between synapses?"

"Bigger. And remember: *sex*," Gino said.

"Is it the *Pharmasutra?*" Dane guessed.

"You're miles away," Richard said.

Dane slumped. Digging for metaphors gave him a mental hernia. Maybe knowing the product and what it did were irrelevant. Maybe he had lost his gut instinct.

"Do we tell him?" Gino asked. The others nodded.

"Thank you," Dane responded gratefully.

"It's sperm fertilizing the egg," Gino said.

The three men stared at Dane in suspense: would he get it?

"A million ideas swim to the brain but only one gets in," Lance added.

"The women in your ads...the sperm is for them?" Dane asked unsurely.

"Bingo!" They boomed in unison.

"Now here's where it gets tricky," Mann-Dingus brayed. "How do we say this without animated sperms!"

"That is *so last year*," said Lance.

"Been there, done that," Gino said.

After extended foreplay, the men from *Info Med* had injected their proprietary idea into Dane's mind. Now they watched his face to see if he "got it" while they popped *Altoids* to prevent the possible taste of defeat. Dane's eyes widened. He *had it* and everyone felt it.

They pumped their fists and cheered before he opened his mouth.

"Life starts with conception!" Dane proclaimed.

Their mouths opened. They seemed to taste the idea. Then they puffed their cheeks as if swishing it around, only to purse their lips to spit it out.

"That's not it," they said.

"See? Conception: it's a double-entendre...It's perfect. It ties your sexual theme with your creative theme," Dane pleaded.

The more energetic his sales pitch, the faster Dane sank into their unreceptive grimaces. They wanted to love it, but couldn't. It was Dane's turn for despair. He saw himself forever spewing words inadequate to an ineffable idea.

"How about this?" Dane snarled. "Tell your clients to jerk off for more ideas. You're experts in that!"

The *Info Med* men stared at him in astonishment. Dane had the imploding sensation that he had blown his fee.

Mann-Dingus wagged his clubbed forefinger.

"That's it! I've been trying to say it for years!"

Dane had solved the impossible problem of creating a message for a product he did not understand. It was a shame that he was too demoralized to experience satisfaction at the feat. He had brainstormed before but was never hit by one until now.

He staggered to the parking lot. It was dark and he had no idea where he was. As he made his way slowly home on secondary roads through a long string of small suburban towns with their stop signs and traffic lights, his mind raced over the incessant talk, the unspeakable product, the irrelevant sexual imagery. It led him to one conclusion: he couldn't do this anymore. His advertising career was over.

Case 7-B

FREELANCE VS. STAFF: COMPARATIVE PATHOLOGIES

5. DOMESTIC REHAB

Dane retreated to domestic safety. He helped Becky with groceries. He moved on to cleaning the house. When he had a taste of housework he wanted more. Cleaning and straightening gave him a sense of control and achievement.

He thought Becky would be pleased and he was right. At first, she appreciated her husband's willingness to do chores, since it relieved her of the drudgery. But Dane's restless domesticity, always seeking new dirt and clutter to remove, became a nuisance. She had to take swift, decisive action.

"You're not doing it right," she scolded. "You're vacuuming without dusting. So you're only half-cleaning."

'It's better than nothing," Dane replied. "You're getting all procedural on me. Just like advertising." Dane clasped his head as if it were that simple to wring out the bad memories and feelings.

Becky had limited sympathy for Dane's angst. She viewed his strange passion for housework as a pathological waste of talent that could destabilize the family. If he believed he was the better home-maker, how would they survive? She sat with him as he blew on his soup and stared in his eyes.

"Is housework how you want to spend your life? She asked earnestly. "Then hire yourself out as a maid."

Dane received the message. When put in professional terms, housework lost his interest. His ultimate fulfillment would never come by eliminating dust-bunnies and cooking French onion soup. He was an amateur. If advertising no longer satisfied him creatively, at least it paid.

He considered all that he had learned in his three freelance jobs: work was good but he should expect no lasting reward or security from it; faith was important; and he could solve problems in a state of ignorance. Why should he quit now? He was on a roll! He made calls and someone called him back.

6. RELAPSE

Form Icon was a young New York agency teeming with energy and people. Every square foot of converted loft space was cluttered. Roaches poised on walls like ornate thumbtacks as rats sniffed and bellied among the wastebaskets brimming with day-old take-out.

Work stations with low partitions signified the egalitarian décor of *Form Icon*. Privacy was effaced by communal voyeurism. Colleagues stared at colleagues when they looked up from their monitors. At venerable agencies like Green, prestige was marked by the number of tiles in your office ceiling. At *Form Icon*, two planks of counter-space signified as much status as you were likely to get.

Last-hired staff and freelancers were issued desks abutting boilers and restrooms or obstructing aisles like plaques and tumors. In deference to his experience, Dane sat behind a rolling cart near a lady's room, like an attendant without towels. When he made eye contact with women seeking relief, he felt like a contestant on his own private game show, *What's Her Business?* Monte Hall would ask, "Is it number one or number two?" One female employee's dour look implied she read Dane's filthy mind; he blushed and did double penance when stench and disinfectant wafted through the open door.

Dane's cart was eventually given to a new full-time employee while he was relocated to a small conference room with six other temporary creatives.

There was no room for Dane, yet somehow he fit in. His personality offended no one, and his writing was respected—and routinely dissected. At *Form Icon*, Dane had a career-defining insight: people changed his writing *because* they liked it. Advertising's cruel affection was better than the alternative: If your work was despised, they made *you* rewrite it—or fired you.

As a freelancer, the workday was easy but getting jobs and being paid for them were not. Dane was diligent about having timesheets signed and tracking his paycheck. The burden of a full-time job was replaced by constant change. The job was not stable but cyclical with identifiable emotional phases—anguish (no work), gratitude (gets work), resentment (works too hard), disgust (work gets trashed) and anguish (assignment over, looks for work).

After a month, *Form Icon* offered Dane a staff job. The Los Angeles office needed a New York writer. Dane would replace a young man who wrote excellent bullet points but who disappeared for half of every workday. The creative director, Michael Moran, a garrulous, blue-eyed Ivy graduate with the shifting focus and feline reflexes of a bartender, told Dane he had the perfect blend of talent and experience to nobly discharge the duties of New York writer for the LA office.

"Such as—?" Dane asked.

"The usual," Moran said, stroking his jowls while previewing his words. "But instead of 9-5, you'll work 12-8." Dane knew no one in the industry worked eight hours. He would rise in the morning, take his daughter to school, wait until noon, and work until midnight.

"I'll never have dinner with my family," Dane lamented.

"Have breakfast," Moran guffawed.

"We don't have time for breakfast," Dane muttered. "I'll never sleep."

"You can do this job in your sleep," Moran insisted. "Look, don't bust my balls. I'm giving you a golden opportunity. There's no travel but you'll cross the great divide between day and night, where darkness is visible."

Moran observed a moment of silence to appreciate his soliloquy. He knew the middle-aged freelancer had no better offers. Dane accepted the staff position—three months after renouncing full-time employment forever. Yet in his heart he remained a freelancer.

7. STAFF INFECTION

When Dane deliberated over taking the staff job, everyone said it was a "no brainer." With a permanent position, he would "own" his job and be respected. When he accepted the offer, he was congratulated. An hour later, he received an email to appear at dawn outside a homeless shelter to pose for the agency's edgy Christmas card. Attendance was mandatory.

After completing his human resources paper work, Dane had his first fringe benefit—he returned to his cart outside the lady's room.

This was just an appetizer. The main course of Dane's full-time position was a tripled workload. Within a week, Dane had familiar staff symptoms: tight deadlines; late nights; endless rounds of picayune changes. Normal quitting time—6 PM—was his mid-afternoon. The end of his workday was midnight—or later. Six o'clock meetings occurred like a parody of a family dinner; the black phone console on the conference table was a plastic roast in effigy. Projects were added, subtracted, multiplied, divided, grafted, amputated, resurrected and reconfigured for the morning after. Dane was sucked into the vortex of full-time pharma.

Once again, Dane worked for long-distance supervisors whose faces he never saw. The account people in Los Angeles were distilled into voices barking demands. Dane was a writer with five critics. His copy came back to him with five sets of changes in a web of lines, hash marks and word balloons. "Track Changes" must have been invented by a computer software genius intent on driving wordsmiths insane. Dane tried to sort out the revisions but after hours of text-forensics, he concluded the changes were arbitrary and accepted them without comment.

Meanwhile, Moran flew between coasts and into spasmodic, red-eyed rages. "There's a fucking conspiracy to get me fired!" he shouted.

"Can anybody join?" muttered Jon, a sex-addicted art director in the next cube, who designed porn websites in his downtime.

Late nights, long-distance accusations and data manipulations battered Dane. He awoke one Saturday morning with a hand twisted in a claw. That afternoon he drove Becky and Iris to buy shoes. Seeing them leave a shoe store with boxes under their arms and smiles on their faces made the fourteen-hour work days worthwhile. However, as he waited in the car, Dane realized his fingers were red and swollen and he could not make a fist. Was this arthritis or a sign of heart disease?

For weeks Dane's body revolted. His morning stiffness was so intense that he required ten minutes to roll out of bed. He could not lift a shirt over his head or grip a toothbrush. Aching knees forced him to shuffle backward. Dane had described inflammatory diseases often enough to know he had one. Some jobs hurt his pride but *Form Icon* was hazardous to his health.

Dane received cortisone shots in his hands and electro-stimulation in his elbows. He wore splints over both wrists while he keyboarded, ate, relieved himself and slept. On restless nights, his splints smacked him in the face, resulting in a black eye and facial bruises, which made him resemble a battered spouse.

One evening, the account head, a nervous woman named Nelly Gukos, demanded that Dane turn three pieces he wrote into two. Between six and eight o'clock, Dane worked feverishly to complete the assignment in order to be home before midnight. At 8 PM, Nelly phoned with a new thought. She asked for the two pieces to be turned into five by the end of the night, Pacific Coast Time. To meet the new deadline, Dane would have to work all night—and for what?

He exploded.

"I give you 100% and it isn't enough!" he shouted. "My predecessor gave you 25% but he was never around for you to torture!"

"The client comes first!" Nelly declared indignantly.

"The client will come first—*to my funeral!*" Dane said.

"Is that a death threat?" Nelly demanded hysterically. Clearly, she wished to come first to his funeral. Two account executives, one creative director, a traffic coordinator and two client samples of a schedule IV sedative were required to sedate her.

The next day, Moran waved his forefinger, like a blunt instrument, in Dane's face.

"Are you trying to get me fired?" Moran yelled.

"Are you trying to kill me?" Dane replied.

"That's horseshit!" Moran bellowed. "Hard work kills no one. I saw a North Korean on CNN set the world record for non-stop working—sixty hours straight—and he was smiling!"

"He had gas! Look at me!" Dane pleaded. *"My hand is a claw. My arm and back are a mess. My wrists are in splints. I need twenty minutes to get out of bed."*

"It takes me a half hour!" Moran retorted competitively.

"You have a drinking problem."

"So do you. You don't drink enough!"

"I can't hold a glass! Or put on a t-shirt or hold a toothbrush."

"If copywriting is too strenuous," Moran sneered, "look for an easier line of work—like opening doors at ATMs!"

All that prevented Dane from being fired was that he had an easy act to follow. His predecessor rarely worked a full day while Dane put in sixty hours a week. His west-coast overseers complained about his attitude but did not order his removal.

Dane had hit the pharmaceutical advertising lottery—a job so undesirable that he could not lose it. While his position did not make him proud, it gave him leverage to vent his sickness on his California overseers. When they berated him because the studio confused colors on a chart, Dane chided them that he was no art director.

However, he overestimated his clout when it came to creative fulfillment. His only chance to put new work in his book came in business pitches. The problem was that he had no art partner—*again*. Dane produced more headlines and stick figures on copy paper.

During creative reviews, Dane's kindergarten stick figures were jeered at by colleagues.

Dane complained to Moran, who responded with eye-bulging desperation.

"I'll be fired *any second* now and you're bitching about *your lack of creative opportunity?*   Listen *Vincent van Gogh-Fuck-Yourself...it's not my problem!*"

"Excuse me for needing job satisfaction," Dane insisted. "I can't be a flunky."

"Oh yes you can. *Watch me!*" Moran growled behind clenched teeth. "You're not supposed to like your work. It's work, not *fun...*"

When Dane had his first paper route at age ten, these were his father's words to him before he ran off with a restaurant hostess.

Moran once boasted to Dane that his strength was not intellect but greasy guile—a claim he often verified. He diverted himself from his chronic job insecurity by keeping Dane off balance, praising Dane's professionalism when he called in sick, only to demean his talent by changing his copy. When Moran particularly liked Dane's headline, he made a point of spoiling it by inserting another verb. When Dane pleaded for the reinstatement of his verb, Moran fired a terse email. "If you continue to harass me when I work with your copy, you will exhaust my patience."

Despite the compromise and mediocrity Dane had endured over time, he continued to view himself as creative. He believed he had the skill to find the right words and the strength to stand by them. How gutless would a writer be not to defend his copy? "Be passive or get fired"—Moran's ultimatum—reduced Dane to a survival mantra of "Don't care," "Grab paycheck" and "Shut up." Dane's creative core was at risk. Could he let Moran mutilate his words without disabling his ability to find them?

Yes, he could! A voice in Dane reminded him that by changing his copy, Moran paid Dane advertising's highest compliment. As Dane processed this enlightenment and made peace with his Inner

Prostitute, a headhunter phoned. Like psychic buzzards, recruiters sensed work distress from great distances. Was Dane happy in his current situation? No, Dane admitted, he was not happy.

Dane interviewed for a new job, which provided immediate pain relief. When he returned to *Form Icon*, a creative review was in session. Moran and Seamus Mallarky, the executive creative director of *Form Icon*, were praising his stick figure concept. "Good work, Dane. Glad you could join us," Moran barked ironically.

A young stranger was in the room. Dane sensed the newcomer's presence with the visceral instinct that detected a rodent darting into a crack. On closer observation, the stranger's face betrayed inappropriate excitement. Dane identified him as a new hire. As questions festered in Dane's Petrie dish brain, Moran introduced the neophyte with his peculiar grandiloquence. "Our body creative has been deficient in the *cogitato,* the *penetrato*, and the *resonato* that youthful enthusiasm can infuse. I believe that all of the above are incarnate in *this* man. Please welcome Jon, our new writer on the LA business."

The hire of a new writer for Dane's account was not only news but a special bulletin. Of greater human interest was the new writer's utter lack of advertising training and experience. He never attended *The Institute of Design*. He never saw his work go up in flames and out a window. Dane felt more insulted than threatened. Did Moran think Dane could be replaced by a tyro?

Moran took Dane aside.

"Our usage of your talents has been suboptimal, for which I take full discredit," Moran admitted. "You have so much to give that is going—*ungiven.* You're a teacher to your core. That's why I want you to mentor young Jon."

"Great!" Dane replied. "If I do a good job, will you fire me sooner?"

"Wrong. We hired Jon to help you. So you won't have to stay late."

"How can he help me if he knows nothing?"

"You'll teach him."

"If he's my assistant, why wasn't I part of the hiring process?"

"It's a great question to which I have no answer," Moran admitted. "You're right. We should have told you. But things have been crazy and we forgot."

Moran's plan to have Dane collaborate in his own elimination was so guileful that he pimped it as a promotion. He upgraded Dane from the cart by the lady's room to a windowed office. Dane instantly identified his office and title as the trappings of a powerless cog. He watched Moran mentor young Jon, walking and talking with the neophyte as he punched his arm and flicked his forehead. Moran had found his ideal junior copywriter and they bonded in full view. Moran even installed his protégé at Dane's cart by the lady's room, a sign that he was on the fast track for advancement.

A major pitch for a blockbuster drug put *Form Icon* in creative delirium. Dane went into his art director partner's office to work out concepts and headlines only to find Moran's protégé expressing *his* ideas.

Dane observed the preparations for his own termination. With anger and defiance, he set out to show Moran—and the world—that he was no passive, overpaid, unwanted has-been. If *Form Icon* didn't respect his expertise, he would quit before letting Moran fire him. So he quit. In his letter to the agency partners, he cited his reasons for leaving: long hours, weird schedule and no creative outlet.

After he submitted his resignation, Moran charged into his office.

"You blamed me, didn't you?"

"It had nothing to do with you," Dane said.

"You don't get it, *Great Dane*! Some people in this agency are looking for any reason to fire me. You gave them one!"

After that awkward moment, Moran disappeared. Dane thought he was in the L.A. office but when he received no surveillance emails from his boss, he asked the porn-loving art director if he knew

Moran's whereabouts.

"The street. Moran got canned," the art director reported. "I thought you knew. He was ranting that it was your fault. If I were you, I wouldn't stick around. And by the way, awesome, Dude!"

The art director gave Dane a *high-five* and offered him 25% off on his next porn website design.

Initially, Dane was flattered. He had no clue that he deserved such a lavish gift or that his departure was significant enough to blame on anyone. However, pride was an unstable element in Dane's mind; it swiftly degraded to worry. Moran was volatile, divorced with children, in need of constant income; in short, he was the Hollywood prototype of a man who goes berserk. Only his job had prevented him from attacking Dane on numerous occasions. Now that such restraints were gone, would he not indulge his proclivity for violence?

Dane requested a meeting with the agency partner, Seamus Mallarky. With rotund dignity, dark, middle-parted hair, round-framed glasses and a bow tie, Mallarky was the dapper New York entrepreneur incarnate. He greeted Dane with the courtesy of a seasoned diplomat.

"So you're leaving us," Mallarky declared with a hint of rue. "*Form Icon* wasn't all you thought we'd be."

"I had to leave," Dane said. "You hired someone much cheaper to replace me."

The agency partner did not contradict Dane.

"So what can I do for you now?" Mallarky asked, while blowing a few stray hairs off his forehead.

"I want you to know Moran had nothing to do with me quitting and I hope it didn't get him fired."

"The two phenomena are unrelated. You have my word," the agency potentate said, strumming his lips with his finger.

"The problem is Moran thinks they *are* related. I heard he's angry being out work. I worry he'll do something desperate. You know Moran."

"I've known Michael Moran for twenty years. So what's your point?" Mallarky stroked his round cheeks, lifted his glasses off his nose and widened his eyes.

"Don't you think he might come back one day for revenge and— *go pharmaceutical*?"

"Go p*harmaceutical*? What are you talking about?"

"You know—bullets instead of bullet points."

Mallarky laughed, shook Dane's hand and said, "No worries, Dane Bacchus. I'm sure Michael Moran will land on his two big feet!"

Despite Mallarky's reassurance, Dane's worry was unwavering.

He cut short his two weeks notice and took his family out of town for a vacation. He told no one where his next job would be, hoping Moran would lose his trail.

8. A LOW POINT IN A HIGH PLACE

Prior to Moran's firing and his own resignation, Dane had proven he was more than word fertilizer by getting hired to his highest position ever.

The title of Associate Creative Director assuaged Dane's injured pride. After accepting the offer, his ego was further massaged when he was invited to lunch at a French restaurant to meet his new colleagues. Dane was never welcomed to an agency with such pomp but never started a job with such misgivings.

For one, he was the only man on a team of seven women. The second problem was that he would supervise a science expert who knew he had been hired to offset her creative shortcomings. Could Dane avoid her wrath and sabotage? What if other team members remained loyal to her?

When Dane settled in, his new agency felt less like a promised land than a final resting place. The offices had the exhausted air of an abandoned factory, cavernous and cluttered with empty cabinets and obsolete equipment. Through ceiling holes, bundles of insulation, wires and tubes dangled like herniated guts. Women, who predominated on staff, worked in cubicles, with their backs to the corridors so they were easily spied on. "To watch their backs," employees hung curtains from shower rods across their cubicle entryways and propped mirrors near their computers. Dane interpreted these customs as quirks and ignored them. Whenever he felt queasy about his new workplace, he reminded himself, "I am a group copy supervisor!"

Dane's worst fear was directed to his supervisor, Cindy, the one interviewer who objected to hiring him.

A Tarot reader once advised Dane that to succeed he needed to make an ugly woman feel beautiful. Dane tried to fulfill this prophecy with Cindy, a gargoyle with blue framed glasses. To induce Cindy to like him, Dane tried to make her feel important by checking in with her regularly to let her know what he was doing. Despite Dane's courteous attention, Cindy showed no interest in his activities. She much preferred to detail her ailments, felt and imagined, and her fear of dying at her desk. She popped vitamins addictively to prevent this grisly fate.

Making Cindy like him was proving to be Dane's toughest career challenge. However, after she related certain adverse events from her career, he no longer took her antipathy for him personally. Cindy once had a boss who called her to his office each morning for two years to shout in her face for no good reason. It was a trauma from which she never recovered and for which she exacted revenge by transference to male subordinates.

When Dane came to Cindy's office in his second week, she said, "Ummmm, errrr, Dane, I have heard complaints about you. Your radio annoys people."

"But it's on so low I can barely hear it," Dane said.

"It's too loud," Cindy insisted.

"I can't wear ear pods because the radio gets no reception close to me and I have no windows."

"Are you Maria in *The Sound of Music*? Turn off the radio," Cindy barked.

After this scolding, Dane did not visit Cindy as often. However, after his second week, his confidence ran high. The client had praised his work and his paycheck was the largest to date. When he knocked on Cindy's door, he believed she would say, "Bravo, Dane!"

Cindy descried Dane out of the corner of her blue glass frames. "I'm glad you came in. We need to talk," she said.

"Is it about the brochure? The newsletter? The video script? They all went well."

"No," Cindy sighed. "Dane, we have high hopes for you which you seem determined to dash."

"What is it this time?" Dane blurted.

"Don't take that tone with me. People complain that you talk loudly on the phone. Don't you know how to behave?"

"Someone complained about my phone calls?" Dane asked in disbelief.

"Your obtuseness is what disturbs me most," Cindy replied. "Surely, you have worked in other offices. We want your creativity and intelligence, but how long can I tolerate your bad attitude and behavior!"

Dane was shaken. Apparently, he was failing to make Cindy like him—to such an extent that he could be fired.

"I don't know what to say. This is new for me," Dane said.

"Get off your high horse, Dane," Cindy replied coldly. "I've been in this business thirty years and I've heard about you."

"I haven't done anything wrong," he protested without conviction.

"I think we've talked long enough," Cindy said.

The next week Dane was summoned to a conference room and fired. Cindy said that he caused too much trouble. Dane's best paying position lasted 27 days.

It was his worst career misstep of all time. The calamity

happened so swiftly that Dane could not make sense of it. He became a job pathologist and autopsied the fiasco. The cause of firing was clear: Dane had overreached. His fabled gut had failed him.

Case 7-C
A SERIOUS SIDE EFFECT OF COPYWRITING

9. CHILLING IN THE HOT ZONE

In business, no consideration is given to casualties of work felled by injury or disease. No special ramps are mandated by law for people incapacitated by the brutality of their occupations. The wounded must move on with their damage or be left behind.

In his year long, full-time job relapse, Dane paid a spiritual forfeit. His self-confidence was shot; his emotional health was fragile. He needed to return to the freelancer's fold and uphold its code: to work solely for financial ends.

He received a call from Barber & McGill, an agency with a dark reputation and a sexy slogan: "The Hot Zone." The founders envisioned their agency as a foundry of ideas, but the office layout was a dark maze of crooked hallways, unexpected stairways, fluorescent lights and shadows.

Dane's boss, Dahlia Woods, was a prim woman, whose large, thick glasses covered half of her face. Dahlia had over 700 emails on her computer but rarely answered them. When she was not with clients, at research or in meetings, she walked briskly with folders under her arm like a professor heading to her next class.

After the trauma of his dismissal from the highest position he ever attained, the solitude and inactivity at "The Hot Zone" made Dane feel lonely and useless.

From his office, Dane overheard staffers bemoan problems, miscommunications and unreasonable expectations. It was a long psychiatric group session. Everyone cringed at the prospect of long nights and firings. They lamented agonies endured, calamities survived and damage done. They regurgitated desperate pitches, implacable clients, futile sacrifices, inexplicable losses and unjust recriminations. People produced materials without clarity or direction; shot at moving targets and missed. If things were not done badly, they were not done at all.

In this apocalypse, Dane saw that his only salvation was to sell the novel he had just completed about a dysfunctional family, receive stellar reviews, sell the rights to Hollywood and become a celebrated author.

He dispatched 300 letters to agents and editors. Within a few weeks, the book, titled *Toad in the Toadstools*, which had taken seventeen years of writing and revision to complete, was rejected by 300 agents and editors, based on letters and sample pages.

After this swift and resounding repudiation of his slowly-gestating creative passion, Dane faced his writing choices: he could do what he loved and earn nothing or make a living doing nothing.

Despite his idleness and perfunctory tasks in "The Hot Zone," Dahlia asked him to stay on for three more weeks. Dane was cheered by this approval and believed Dahlia liked him. One morning, she told Dane she would be at research in Philadelphia.

Dane recalled the days when he and Goldfarb attended research in Philadelphia; the morning trains; the client praising him for being the one agency person to arrive at 8 AM; his concept, "I get around" defeating "A woman and a dog." Dane had a staff position and a future then. In hindsight, it was his golden age.

"Is it the research facility on Walnut Street?" he asked Dahlia. "I've been there."

"Too much chatter," Dahlia scowled and walked off.

Dahlia's rebuff hurt Dane's feelings, even though he knew he should not take it personally. He was paid to work, not to talk. He would be a more valuable resource with his mouth shut. Dane no longer expected to be creative; why should he be congenial?

As he resigned himself to his situation, he was saved by the phone.

A small agency, *The Butcher Block*, inquired if he was available for freelance. Dane had interviewed at *The Butcher Block* the previous summer. The creative director loved his work and set up a second interview with the account team. It went smoothly until the agency owner, an East Asian scientist, arrived late, wearing pajamas and sporting a bamboo cane. After yawning and glowering, the Asian genius rose to his feet and smacked the desktop repeatedly with his cane until splinters flew.

"You change jobs too much! What for? You got fire-eating ants up you pants?" the Asian genius rebuked Dane. "We take pride in what we got here. We like family. So why we hire you?"

"First of all, I have nothing in my pants…I mean, I have stuff in my pants, but that's not a problem—and neither is my working different places. I've learned a lot by moving around and my experiences can benefit your agency," Dane said. Despite his inspired ad lib, Dane went home that hot afternoon with a heavy portfolio, no job and his lucky sports jacket soaked in dog day sweat. From that day forward, *The Butcher Block* symbolized for Dane a place where he had his head chopped off.

Circumstances had changed at *The Butcher Block*. Now Dane was needed there and he was offered a higher freelance rate than he was receiving at "The Hot Zone." This simplified his decision.

"I'm leaving," Dane told Dahlia as she strutted to a meeting.

"Is there a reason?" she asked.

"Yes, but I don't want to chatter too much."

Dahlia looked at him nonplussed and walked away.

10. THE BUTCHER BLOCK

The Butcher Block was in a spacious loft space in Chelsea. It had won *Pharm World* Magazine's "Micro-Agency of the Year" title that year due to its reputation for innovation and diversity. The charismatic Cambodian scientist who owned *The Butcher Block* hired attractive, young people from all over the world. It was Madison Avenue, the United Nations and *Babes in Toyland* in one.

Dane believed *The Butcher Block's* reputation for doing things differently until he noticed their campaign for an arthritis drug had the same headline—*Go Beyond*—that Barber & McGill used for a kidney failure medication.

"You're here for the money," he reminded himself.

In his first week, Dane wrote letters, brochures, charts, guides, reminders and coding documents for an insurance kit for doctors. It demanded little flair but permitted Dane to create materials and show his speed and skill. Within a week he submitted a dozen pieces for review. Although Dane made a concerted effort to write concisely, the client complained that there too many words, and had the pieces stripped down to bullet points, icons and illustrations.

The client's logophobia aside, Dane enjoyed himself. The female employees at *The Butcher Block* were stylish and attractive, and they smiled frequently, though not specifically at him—but who was keeping score? It was like working in the pharma version of the Playboy mansion.

There was one problem: Beatrice, his newly hired supervisor.

Beatrice had many fine qualities. She was refined, sensitive and charming. She had once been a radio correspondent until she lost her job and crashed into medical advertising. Beatrice might have been cast by Hollywood as a town librarian with a steamy past. Her face was pale and worn, yet she retained a hint of youthful allure. She adorned her graceful body in tasteful elegance and her voice had a warm ring that softened insults. Yet, despite her demure dignity, Beatrice warned Dane of her dark side at the agency Halloween party when she wore a witch's costume and laughed ghoulishly in his face. Dane thought she enjoyed her role too much.

For a month, Beatrice had the best quality a boss could have. She was largely absent. Since she was on the road with clients, she informed Dane that she had no time to focus on his projects or to review his copy.

However, just when Dane dared to think this freelance job would permit him to write without interference, Beatrice appeared at the office more often and compensated for her prior absence by hovering over him. She complained that he did not show her his work and demanded to see everything he wrote, probing and changing it all. Dane executed her changes but she forgot what they were and accused him of ignoring her directions.

"You signed off on what I did," Dane protested. "Here's your signature."

Beatrice acknowledged her mistake but continued to micromanage him and his work. When Dane stretched or went to the men's room, she pounced. "Are you busy with anything?" She generously provided him with an array of tedious tasks, like proofreading forty pages of prescribing information copy.

"Just make the money," he whispered to himself.

One day Beatrice lectured Dane on a grammatical error she believed he had made. Rather than appease her, he reverted to the English teacher he had been and explained the rule to her. She looked shocked that he knew anything.

"I'm qualified," he told her. "That's why I was hired."

"I thought it was because you're a good schmoozer," she cracked.

Dane knew insults were part of freelancing but Beatrice's misjudgment perturbed him. He was a terrible schmoozer! Anyway, what right did she have to demean his credentials? He had more knowledge and experience than she did. Quickly he stopped himself from dwelling on it.

"It's my job to write," he repeated. "It is her job is to rewrite my writing. Embrace the process."

Suddenly the process stalled. As the drug's approval date approached, the FDA announced the need for more safety data. The launch was postponed.

At first, the client and agency ignored the FDA delay. The creative team continued to work late nights to meet breakneck deadlines as if the drug were going to market any day. This urgency was predicated on denial and panic, not productivity. They believed frenzied effort could save their income source from desiccation.

The Butcher Block entered a black hole. When an account imploded, employees rushed to the disaster because it exerted enormous gravity. More people attended more meetings that lasted longer. Yet, the longer and more frequent the meetings, the less anyone knew. By late afternoon, team members were perplexed about which projects were going out and how late they had to work. The staff was in collective hysteria—a silent, communal scream that obfuscated communication and comprehension.

Beatrice had been out of town so often that she spent half of her salary on kennel fees for her dogs. Now that she was in the office everyday, she walked her pets and ripped Dane's work. His projects, approved after multiple revisions, came under new scrutiny.

Dane rewrote fifteen pieces and Beatrice demanded with a smile that he show her each one. Every draft came back to him bathed in her green ink, with changes ranging from punctuation to word choice to reworked sentences and restructured paragraphs. Dane made the changes, which Beatrice changed again. This sequence was repeated so often that the changed copy reverted to his original. Sometimes Dane substituted his word for one Beatrice scribbled in the margins, but she always detected his mischief, crossed out his word and reinserted hers with a rebuke: "You didn't make this change!"

"You're getting paid," Dane reminded himself.

Yet, regardless how often he repeated the freelancer's creed, Beatrice penetrated the thick skin of his prostitution. A lifetime of pride broke through. He reflected that his ambition and sacrifice to write from the age of 14 resulted in this— not one word he wrote stood as written.

"Don't take it personally," his inner voice instructed him. "Be strong."

To buoy his spirits, Dane played a game with Beatrice to prove her copy changes were arbitrary. When she switched his infinitive to a gerund in one sentence, he changed her infinitive to a gerund in the next.

When the draft came back, Beatrice had switched his gerund back to her infinitive. Dane laughed. Clearly she wanted the copy her way and did not care about making it consistent. He tossed corrected manuscripts on her desk like horseshoes and she ignored his impudence.

Dane savored his moral victory until Beatrice came to his desk with a fresh pile of manuscripts scarred with green ink. She asked him to complete the changes before he left for the evening. As she walked away, she put her lips to his ear and whispered, "I'm thinking things I would love to be able to say but I can't. You probably feel the same way."

She had never said anything remotely personal to him before so Dane suspected her words were a trap.

"No," he said. "I tell you what I think."

"Oh, well," she replied. "I guess I speak for myself."

Beatrice's mischief now escalated beyond word changes. By alluding to her suppressed and forbidden thoughts, she complicated Dane's feelings toward her. Dane was bewildered. Was his autocratic boss coming on to him? Did she imply that she was no tyrant bent on his demise but a warm, vulnerable woman, who respected his writing and liked him, as well? Or was this her way of saying she reciprocated his loathing and arbitrary changes were her way of showing it?

Then he recalled his insight that advertising people changed writing because they liked it. Perhaps he had misread Beatrice all along. Maybe they were *copy-dancing*. He used one word, she another. Back and forth they do-si-do'ed and both made money. Beatrice did not rip his writing to crush him with her power. She was just giving him more billable hours.

Dane's circumstance was now bathed in a splendid new light. He was no longer persecuted. Beatrice was out one day and he missed her green ink. When she returned, he was eager for drafts to come back to him with her *loving* changes.

Just when Dane started to enjoy *copy-dancing* with Beatrice, he received a new assignment. A surly editor sat with Dane and interrogated him for hours about a long document Beatrice wrote. Forty pages were covered with spidery red lines, inscrutable circles, scribbling, cross-outs and queries with exclamation points—and Dane had to answer them all. He had a new theory about Beatrice's recent niceness—it was a set up.

"What does this mean?" the surly editor demanded, pointing to an illegible word.

"I have no idea," he said.

"Wake up, Dane, you're the writer."

"I didn't write this," he said. "Beatrice wrote it. Ask her."

"You're the writer of record. See? You signed off on it."

"I signed off because I was the only writer who stayed late."

"Where is the reference for this claim?" the editor demanded.

"There are no references," Dane explained. "We weren't given any."

"How can a piece be written without references?"

"The drug isn't on the market so there are no published articles about it," he replied.

The editor badgered Dane for these and other evasions. The discussion went in circles until the editor went to dinner.

After his editorial bludgeoning, Dane shambled past a large bookstore on his way to the subway. Inside, a young man was reading for fifty avid listeners. Dane stared at the event through the window with morbid fascination. It was the worst possible nightmare—watching his dream lived by someone else. A piercing sensation in the back of Dane's neck drew tears from his eyes. The motive for all that he had done from the age of fourteen was in that bookstore. Dane had entered advertising because publishing a book seemed an impossible longing. Now he saw it was possible—only not for him. He retreated from the window, stepped awkwardly on broken pavement, and collapsed on the concrete. A woman asked if he was okay. "Never," he said. Ashamed, he lifted himself to his feet.

At a meeting a week later, Dane opened his mouth to speak but no sound came out. He forced a cough to mask his disability. Earlier, he had noted his voice growing hoarse and believed he was becoming ill but now he was mute. Since these meetings were dominated by garrulous people and filled with discussions about minutiae to which Dane rarely contributed, he thought his inability to speak would go undetected. However, some of his colleagues smirked and nodded in his direction as if to solicit his opinion, like fish nipping at the tail of a sick comrade. Suddenly, he felt the need to hide.

"I'm hoarse," he told himself.

Beatrice hovered over his cubicle with green-inked manuscripts in hand but she was only a shadow, eclipsed by her magnified hand holding a manuscript that levitated before his eyes like a blimp.

He tried ignoring the blimp hand. But when he glanced up from the screen, the hand nudged the manuscript in his face. He swatted at it but the hand danced away. He grasped at the floating hand, which performed aerial shows with manuscripts above his head.

Coworkers across from Dane stared with curiosity as he swatted at the air and worried that he was about to "go postal."

Three manuscripts lay across his chair, covered in more green ink. While he stared at the circled words the letters separated into dots, reformed as strands, and trooped off the page like columns of organisms. He did not know what the words had been or how to bring them back. He hoped the next sentence would help him recall the previous one, but the letters on the next line dissolved, as well, pixel by pixel, into dots that rolled off the page.

He blinked and reassured himself that he was only tired. He

picked up a second manuscript and his eyes swept a sentence. The words made sense. Yet, when his eyes moved back from right to left, the ink lifted from the paper like a black stain and spilled off the page.

Dane wanted power over words—but not this. His reading annihilated content! He knew if he mentioned this to anyone he would be finished at *The Butcher Block*. He was supposed to work until the end of the month but for that moment he needed a break. He tossed the manuscripts on Beatrice's chair while she was sitting in it and they landed on her lap.

"Oh, special delivery?" she joked.

He tried to bolt without explaining.

"You made all of the changes?"

"No, I-I-I can't read these."

Her eyes widened. "Is something unclear?"

"Yes."

"You don't understand something?"

"No, it's my eyes. I can't see. It's a blur."

"You should have that checked," she said. "Leave them until tomorrow."

11. A BREAK

The next morning Dane had coffee with Becky and glanced at a newspaper before taking a train to work. He started to read the sports pages with trepidation. The words were there until one by one they disappeared.

"I can't read this," he told Becky.

"What? Did one of your teams lose?"

"I can't read the words."

She believed he was working out a situation for a short story so she improvised along with him. "Oh, have you tried *Clear Eyes*? Maybe your eyes are overtired."

"It's not my eyes. I can see. It's the words—*they vanish*."

"Oh, the words disappear," Becky repeated calmly like she had seen this disease on her favorite hospital show. "Well, maybe you don't like the words and this is how you eliminate them."

She did not know how close she came to a diagnosis.

Dane agreed with her low-key response. He wanted to believe his problem was nothing serious but suspected otherwise. He blamed it on himself, imputing it to over-exposure to advertising. After resolving to work freelance, he had taken a full-time job, and when that was over he subjected himself to repeated pharmaceutical writing abuse until he snapped.

He hid his anguish from Becky and Iris. It was easy to add one more abnormality to his behavior. Blurting silly names and nonsense words, making facial contortions during internal monologues, having vehement arguments with invisible adversaries, and staring into space at a traumatic memory were already staples of his repertoire.

Becky however noticed a break in his pattern. She counted on his loquacity but all he could give now was sullen taciturnity. And rather than talking to himself in a serious manner, he made his cell phone open and close like a mouth and spoke through it like a puppet.

"Hi, my name is *Phoney* and I'm not fake. Ha! Ha!"

Becky emitted a patient laugh to which Dane did not respond.

"I think something is wrong with Daddy," she told Iris.

"How can you tell?" Iris replied.

Becky believed psychiatry was like watch repair. Trusting a stranger to fix something of value was the surest way to break it. She resolved to care for Dane on her own, believing that with proper rest Dane would return to his norm.

12. COGNITIVE CACOPHONY

The worst part of Dane's breakdown Becky could not see and Dane did not confide. When his peculiar reading problem did not improve, he believed he had a bizarre neurological disease that caused words to vanish after he read them. But who would believe him?

For two weeks Dane was afraid to write or read. Eventually, however, he was bursting with ideas and needed to write them down to relieve the pressure on his brain. He put pen to paper and made letters. In a blink they unwrote themselves. His pen cartridges appeared to be spiked with self-erasing ink.

Every hour Dane attempted a new sentence. The words stayed briefly, vibrated, then scattered into dots and spilled off the page. He tried writing on the computer but with respect to his words, the monitor was as incontinent as paper. Dane's fear and desperation mounted. His future must have writing in it. Without it, he was useless. Becky ran into the bedroom and found her husband smacking his head with his blue line journal.

"What is it?" she demanded, exasperated that he was venting like an overgrown infant.

"Look!" Dane held the book open to the page he was writing on. "Can you see anything?"

"Yes. You wrote the same sentence several times and now it looks like a Jackson Pollock. Let me see. I think you wrote 'I'm a sick raccoon' seven times."

"That's right but I can't see it. My own words vanish, too."

"Maybe it's your pen."

"It's not my pen," He cried. "My eyes are erasers. I used to fill pages with verbosity. Now I make entire pages disappear."

When Becky observed him write words, they stayed on the page. "Do you see them, honey?" she asked.

"Yes," he said.

A moment after leaving him alone, she heard him yell profanity. She rushed to the bedroom and found him tearing pages from books he had swept from a shelf.

"The words won't stay!" he shouted. "I've finally done it. I've destroyed the best part of myself. Writing is all I can do!"

Becky wrapped her arms around him as he fell in a heap on the floor, sobbing.

"We'll figure this out. But you can't fall apart."

Dane remembered from his teaching syllabus a book by one Dr. Lucien Paley, a world-renown neurologist specializing in disorders that impaired memory, motor skills, sensory organs and other brain functions. One of Dr. Paley's patients, described in the bestseller, *My Name Is Yorick*, woke up one morning unable to see or feel his body; he walked around believing he was a floating skull. Another patient recalled nothing of his life but knew everything about bony fish, a subject he never studied. Still another patient had no concept of the color "chartreuse," yet painted his entire house in it. Perhaps Dr. Paley could help Dane.

Dr. Paley was now affiliated with a world-class hospital a mile from the Bacchus apartment. When Becky phoned his office she learned that Dr. Paley had recently returned from a book tour. After much pleading, she managed to speak to the great man and explained Dane's illness.

"Yes, it sounds quite upsetting," Dr. Paley said. "Yes, I have seen disorders of this kind. You were right to contact me. When can you bring your husband in so I can have a look?"

Becky was trembling. "Anytime."

"Your husband is a writer," Dr. Paley remarked. "That raises the stakes, doesn't it?"

"Yes. Please help him."

"I'll do what I can; you have my word."

That afternoon, Becky brought Dane to the neurology clinic of *The Psychiatric Institute,* where they waited in an open room with large glass windows providing river views. Dane felt uneasy among other patients. Unlike a dermatology clinic, where most diseases were hidden under clothes, the neurology clinic revealed a multitude of afflictions. One patient had a facial tic, another flipped through a magazine, cursed, closed the publication and reopened it. A third patient bounced in his chair as if riding a horse, then jumped to his feet and twirled around until he became dizzy and fell back into his seat.

"I want to go," Dane whispered.

"Don't you want to get better?" Becky asked.

"I'm not like these people."

"Hullo. You must be the Bacchuses!"

Dr. Paley stood before them, a warm, radiant man with wooly white hair springing from his head. With a clipboard in one hand, he extended the other in salutation and ushered them to his office.

"It's a delight to meet you, Mr. Bacchus. Your wife has told me that you are a writer who has become a hyperactive editor, eliminating words as soon as you create them."

"Yes, I'm the *verbinator*," Dane said and forced a chuckle.

"Oh, that's a good one!" Dr. Paley laughed. "May I use it for my next book?"

Dane winced.

"Of course, I'm joking," Dr. Paley slapped Dane gently on the leg. "But perhaps we can collaborate."

Dr. Paley drew Dane out in amiable conversation before subjecting him to a battery of tests: an eye chart, simple recognition exercises—pictures on paper—and identification of images flashing on a monitor.

"So, you say it's a reading problem," Dr. Paley said. "Let's read something close at hand, say, my most recent book. The type is rather large."

Dane read a paragraph with ease. However, when he returned to the top, the paragraph was gone.

"You know, Dane, you are in some ways quite fortunate to have such a poetic disease! A writer for whom words disappear. Of course, the brain is ironic by nature."

"Doctor, I don't feel lucky."

"Of course not. I suppose I feel a special affinity with your condition because I—Well, enough about me. First, let me reassure you that it is not unusual for stress to incapacitate us. Powerful chemicals are released in the brain which can create imbalances. Are you able to recall an incident which caused you great pain?"

"Yes," Dane said. "My last ten years."

"Oh, I see. Can you be more specific?"

Dane summarized his decade of employment, culminating in the winter night when he passed the *Barnes and Noble* reading.

"I bent over and wept," Dane said.

"Absolutely! It's quite normal," Dr. Paley nodded fervently as his eyes misted behind his Franklin glasses. "I don't know how I could cope if I were not published from time to time."

Dr. Paley put Dane's head in a new brain-imaging machine, a contraption resembling a hair dryer. After an image was made, the doctor studied it on a monitor. It looked like a tie-dye hallucination of blue, green, red, purple and blue. Dr. Paley gasped. Pointing at certain sectors, he exclaimed, "Yes, we've got something! See that!"

He turned to Dane.

"Dane, do you see this area right here? It is your prefrontal cortex. Do you see that blue swiggle that looks like toothpaste? Yes. Well, that is precisely what we were looking for...the smoking gun. Those neurotransmitters are not firing. A diagnosis at this time may be premature but this is extraordinary. Dane, you have an acute case of *cognitive cacophony*. There have been only a few reported cases in the world. How does that make you feel? Hmmm?"

"Don't tell me, there is no cure!" Dane cried.

"Yes, well, buck up! The exciting part is how it came about. Your cognitive dissonance with your work must have degenerated to an inflammatory stage where you no longer retained what you wrote and read. It was as if your neurotransmitters walked off the job in protest. You had an autoimmune response to language—your psychic defense. Your words had been annihilated so often by others that your short term memory eliminated them in a preemptive strike. This protected your cortex from permanent damage. One disease protects you from a more serious one."

"Doctor, I appreciate you're trying to put a good light on this but tell me honestly: will my words ever hold the page again?"

"Dane, one can't be sure, of course, but I feel that you will pull through. You see, your current difficulties have a special meaning for me. When I was in medical school, I too experienced a serious emotional block in my studies. Words and ideas that always frolicked in my fertile mind were cold and dead. I was so frightened that I kept it to myself. But I studied my symptoms and diagnosed the illness. It was severe burnout, what is now called scorched brain syndrome...I cured myself with fish oil supplements and a steady diet of Bach cantatas and *Monty Python*. I was my first clinical success! And you will be my most recent one."

Dane played with a life-size model of the brain on the medicine table while Dr. Paley left the exam room to consult with Becky, the primary caregiver, in his office.

"So how have you been coping?" the world acclaimed neurologist asked Becky.

"Doctor, I studied psychology in college and have a mother's common sense. I've done all I can for Dane by reading with him and taking dictation when he wants to write. I know it's not enough."

"On the contrary, you've done extraordinarily well given the circumstances," Dr. Paley replied supportively as he approached her. "Cognitive disorders are tragic. Learning and understanding, which are ordinarily sources of human meaning, identity, and pleasure, are disrupted and become agents of pain and frustration. Your husband has endured a terrible trauma. He believes he is a failure. You can help him in many ways. First, you must administer 'winner therapy.' That is, you must continuously tell him that he is a winner. Secondly, you must not permit him to read anything but perhaps *Curious George* and the Amelia Bedelia books. If he needs to write, you must become his hands. I can see that you have lovely hands. If he feels closed in, take him to the zoo. I have drawn strength from a world-class zoo and we have a fine one in New York. By watching animals, perhaps he will reconnect."

On the word "reconnect," Dr. Paley felt the irresistible impulse to reach for Becky's shoulders. He drew her to him and attempted to plant numerous kisses on her face. However Becky, a loyal wife and an expert in protecting her makeup from smudging, pulled away from the amorous neurologist.

"Dr. Paley, what are you doing?"

"I don't know," he gasped. "I can't know everything. But it felt right."

"Doctor, what are you thinking? You just said Dane has been through a trauma—that he feels like a failure. How can this help him?"

"Technically, it can't hurt him. You see, he suffers from *cognitive cacophony*, which is on a different circuit altogether from cuckoldry."

"You're sworn to do no harm and I'm all he has. He would be devastated."

"Yes, well...perhaps you are right, but how can we be sure?" Dr. Paley made a second advance on Becky's position. He lunged for her but she moved nimbly behind a chair and swatted away his groping hands.

"Doctor, you are a world-class healer, not a two-bit heel," Becky pleaded.

"Yes, well I have my dark side," Dr. Paley replied, stroking his forehead to restore his internal calm. "Now please run along and do as I prescribed. In a fortnight we shall see."

For two weeks, Dane was on a regimen of "winner's therapy," writing by dictation, having children's books read to him, and going on outings to the Bronx Zoo. There he reconnected with gorillas, baby lemurs and ancient elephants grabbing gobs of hay with their trunks and dropping turds from their rumps. "If they can be happy, why can't I?" he mused aloud.

"Because you're human—and a winner!" Becky answered.

"I am?"

One morning Dane was driving with Becky. He had been on the toilet all night with food poisoning and was exhausted. After dropping off Iris at her art class, they headed to Starbucks. Dane turned to Becky. "I'd like to know more about diarrhea," he said.

Becky took her eye off the road for a moment to look at him and nearly hit a curb.

"What did you say?"

"I want to understand diarrhea better than I do," Dane repeated. "I know it's watery stools...but I want to know more."

"Maybe diarrhea is offered in continuing education somewhere. We'll check online," Becky said.

"You think?"

Becky sensed in Dane's perverse curiosity a hopeful sign. His morbid interest in diseases, so intrinsic to his medical writing, was stirring again.

As she read the paper in the café, Dane said, "I think my mental illness is improving."

She smiled. "Yes, darling. It is. You're a winner."

When they returned home, Dane eased a medical encyclopedia from a bookcase and flipped through it without a moment of perturbation. Becky squeezed his shoulder and whispered, "You're back!"

One day, only weeks after the appointment with Dr. Paley, they were shopping for clothes on a busy commercial street when they passed a large bookstore. Dane stopped to stare in the window.

"Are you sure you should be doing this?" Becky asked with alarm. She thought he would have an attack of *cognitive cacophony* on the spot as the book titles vanished in his sight.

"Can we just go in?"

"You want to go into a bookstore?" Becky asked.

"I miss it. I want to look at books."

When they returned home, Dane started writing on his computer.

He finished a page without stopping, then closed his eyes, counted to sixty and opened them. The words were all there, round and solid.

"Oh that is good news. I'm so pleased," Dr. Paley said during Dane's follow-up, "It may be too early to make a rash prognosis, but I think, Dane, that you have turned a corner. This is a superb outcome."

Although similar cases had been documented, Dane's specific condition was never diagnosed or named.

"I am writing a paper about this. And with your permission, I would like to name it *Dane Syndrome*."

Dane was pleased. If his name and achievements did not stand the test of time, his pain would live on forever.

"And now you must promise me, you must see this as a wonderful gift, an opportunity to enjoy your writing to its fullest. See this as a second chance, Dane. Never let yourself become so dissonant with your talents that they become a source of pain."

Case 7-D
DANGERS OF SELF-PROMOTION

13. SELF PROMOTION AND PERSECUTION

Dane emerged from his eponymous disease with fundamental questions about his life: where was he and what could be salvaged from what was left? He started his advertising career late in his life and it lasted for ten years. He was experienced, perhaps too experienced and expensive to hire. He might seem more rigid and less compliant than a younger person. A fearful thought occurred to him: was his advertising career over?

Despite his uncertain situation, Dane followed Dr. Paley's advice. For four hours a day he wrote stories and revised drafts of books to which he never thought he would return. When he had been writing inane copy he chided himself, "Is this how you want to be remembered—or forgotten? Face your destiny like a man!" He saw himself as a prodigal writer who had betrayed his life's purpose and longed to return to it. Now he was back and enjoying the homecoming. To a point.

That point was his bank account. His lack of income perforated his confidence. Creative writing might be his life's work but he could not earn his living at it, and writing without income made him feel like a parasite.

Freelancing regularly had provided balance but he received no calls. Business was slow. At first, he ascribed it to the general economy but came around to blaming himself. Agencies had merged into super-agencies with oceanic databanks filled with résumés of former employees. Dane had worked everywhere and was in every databank as a bottom-feeder with good copy and bad attitude.

Undaunted, he sent his résumé to 25 agencies with warm and friendly notes outlining his availability—and received no response. He went on job search engines and found that the same agencies that ignored his emails were listing jobs. Did human resource people keep busy by posting empty job descriptions or did they prefer any unknown to him?

Dane contacted people in the industry, although such queries seemed futile. If agencies were busy they would phone him; if they were not, no amount of calling them would induce them to hire him.

After two months, he was sufficiently desperate to resort to temp agencies, which took a 35% cut of Dane's paycheck and added layers of bureaucracy. The recruiters asked if he had a website. Dane had always shown his book at interviews, but he was informed that hiring wasn't done like that anymore. Clients perused a website, and if interested, met the candidate.

Dane designed his website. He scanned and uploaded ads he had worked on and organized the site according to every form of advertising he had done. He also hyperlinked samples of his longer work so recruiters would know that he did not inflate his experience.

In a week, his website was complete. Dane had evolved from hard copy to the digital age. His self-promotion now matched his expertise. Potential employers could experience his work without experiencing him. It no longer mattered if he was "hard sell" or "soft sell," or resembled an employer's despised relative or colleague. He would no longer get in the way of his own excellence. If recruiters failed to find him assignments, it was now officially their fault.

The internet immediately worked for Dane.

Within weeks, an agency with a windfall of new business offered him a month-long freelance opportunity. His supervisor was a woman with a sense of humor and the projects were interesting. He was so highly motivated that he offered to finish a project over a weekend.

That Saturday, Dane received a call on his cell. It was odd that anyone phoned him on a Saturday evening since he had no social life. He thought it must be his supervisor checking on his progress. She would be so happy when she learned how far along he was that she would offer him a full-time position.

"Good evening, Dane. This is Georgette Giaconda. From *The Butcher Block*."

"Oh, hi," Dane said. He had not heard from *The Butcher Block* in over a year. No doubt, they remembered his efficiency and wanted him back. What did he know? Suddenly two agencies would compete for his services.

"Dane, I'm sorry to bother you but the agency owners and the client are breathing down my neck. Our client's promotional materials are on your website and they want you to remove them immediately."

Dane struggled to understand.

"There's a lot of stuff on my website. I may have mentioned the work I did for your client. I'm a writer."

"That product is not on the market yet, so the materials are not in the public domain. Our client hired a consultant to surf the internet looking for mentions of the drug and they found materials on your website. They want you to remove them immediately."

Dane felt harassed by the urgency and vexation in her tone. When he arrived home that evening, Dane told Becky, "*The Butcher Block* wants me to remove something I wrote for them from my website."

"Doesn't a drug company have more to do than police a copywriter's website?"

"It should but maybe I'm more important than we think."

"You couldn't be more important than I think," Becky said as she kissed him on the cheek.

Dane smiled. It was one of the nicer things Becky had said to him in awhile. He did not suspect that Becky was giving him a dose of "winner's therapy" to prevent a relapse of *cognitive cacophony*.

That night Dane removed the product's name and packet insert hyperlink from his website. This piece of unreadable prose, over which he had fretted for weeks, contained clinical data and marketing strategy. Key points were highlighted, analyzed and commented upon. The piece reflected his analytical ability and grasp of science...*Now he couldn't use it.*

The next day was a cold, blustery Monday. Dane was eating lunch in his car when his cell rang. It was Georgette Giaconda.

"You didn't take the prescribing information off your website. The agency partners and the client are furious. They want it removed in 48 hours."

"I deleted it last night," Dane stammered. "It's not on my website. The hyperlink is gone."

Dane sensed that something had gone horribly awry in this new universe.

"It's still there!" she cried. "I'll send you the link."

Dane raced to his cubicle. He was so nervous he believed he would explode. Now this trifle buried on a back page of his website protruded like a tumor from his skull. He was the target of two colossal entities that could crush him—a drug company and an agency.

He clicked on the hyperlink. The troublesome webpage was still listed on the search engine. Dane had removed the hyperlink but the file remained in his document gallery. He called home and talked Becky through the removal of the file. Now when he clicked on the hyperlink, it yielded an error message. Dane believed his troubles were over. He phoned Georgette with the good news.

"It's still on the cache, Dane. Anybody can read it!" she shouted, "It's the damned PI. How could you do that?"

Dane *googled* the drug. His webpage was listed and the PI was in the cache file, faint but legible.

"I'm a writer," Dane defended himself. "I put samples in my book. This is no different."

"Everyone puts samples in their book on the down-low," Georgette growled. "But the internet is open to everyone. You've been irresponsible and put us all at risk."

"How did I know the internet would fling my web content across cyberspace?"

"Well it has and we could be in serious trouble. You violated the non-disclosure contract you signed. You are in breech of contract. It's like stealing. We want to avoid legal consequences."

Breech of contract! Stealing! Legal consequences! For the rest of the day, Dane wanted to vomit, tear off his skin and walk out of it— into a new one. He repeatedly typed the drug name on the subject line to make it vanish but it popped up each time to hound him. He paced as if he could out-walk his responsibility, but it had him in its talons. Due to his poor judgment, he could be stripped of all he had worked for and loved; his family would be ruined.

Dane phoned Georgette and contritely reported that he had done all he could. She transferred him to Lorenzo, the IT director, who explained that the cache was not permanent but the normal removal process could take two to six weeks and they had only a day. He sent Dane a link for emergency removals. Dane needed to insert *metatags* in his website but how to do this surpassed his comprehension.

At 1 AM, Dane lay on top of his covers in his underwear, shivering in the cold, presumably to kill himself from overexposure, when the phone rang. Lorenzo said they had to fix the problem immediately. Dane sat in his shorts at his computer in the cold room as a peculiar penance while Lorenzo talked him through steps that were slow, delicate and treacherous. Dane divulged his website password to Lorenzo, enabling the IT director to enter Dane's website and insert the metatag that would abort the poisonous page. After an hour operation, Dane's website code rejected the metatag.

At 3 AM, Lorenzo was at an impasse and said he would resume in the morning. Dane agonized whether a drug company would sue an impecunious writer and he managed only a few hours of sleep.

As he drove to work, *The Butcher Block* IT director phoned with an update: all efforts to insert the metatag had failed. The problem required another solution.

"Is there anything I can do?" Dane asked.

"You've done enough," The IT director replied. "Just pray."

Dane took this seriously. All day he mumbled prayers like, "Oh, Lord, free me from the hyperlink! Delete the package insert and deliver me from pharmaceutical affliction!" When Dane was not praying and trembling, he evacuated his bowels or tried to lose himself in work.

However, all of the prayer, work and defecation in the world could not contain the fire of damnation stoking Dane's paranoia. Copyright infringement, misuse of proprietary information, penalties, litigation and ruin stormed his consciousness like a posse of psychotic burglars, sacking peace of mind and slaughtering hope. In pacing the office, he wished he could walk out of his body and his life.

That evening after work, he went to the pool where he had spent many happy hours, and tried to relax and forget his circumstances. As he swam lap after lap, thoughts of his transgression crept into his mind. He summarized his offense. He posted an old packet insert from a year ago for a product that never launched. It included annotations revealing a sales strategy the client planned against its competitors.

They would make him pay.

Dane switched from a relaxing stroke to a suicide speed. If he swam enough laps with sufficient effort could he end his misery with heart failure? He tried to annihilate thought and devolve into a fish but this was not the ocean and the lifeguard whistled the end of lap swim.

At home Dane saw an email from the IT director. After much hesitation he opened it. Lorenzo had inserted the code. The offending web page and package insert would be gone in 48 hours.

Dane rejoiced at his reprieve. Even so, he clicked on that web page repeatedly for days to see if the offending document was finally gone. It slipped slowly down the list, page by page, but whenever he found it, he could not swallow. What if the pharmaceutical company lawyers saw it? Would they or *The Butcher Block* sue? He checked his website and found that there had been hundreds of hits. Becky speculated that the client's lawyers were probably circling over Dane.

Finally, the offending page was gone.

Dane believed his troubles were over until he received a notification from the attorneys of the pharmaceutical company. They threatened him with further legal action.

"I don't know what to do," Dane said. He was twisting and writhing from agitation.

"First stop squirming," Becky said.

"They could take away everything I've worked for and care about. They want to kill me."

"Maybe if you lie low for awhile, they'll forget about you," Becky said.

Dane had always believed that running from a problem never solved it but here was an exception. To protect his family, he needed to leave them and disappear. If he had not been so depressed and panicky he could have seen his connection with an Iranian journalist he met, who fled his home ten minutes before the secret police came to arrest him. Dane was eluding a less violent but equally destructive corporate tyrant.

He shut down his website and boarded a bus for Canada. Before he left, he told Becky to tell his pursuers he had disappeared and had not been heard from.

14. FLIGHT AND FIGHT

After two buses and a stop in Niagara Falls, where he considered jumping, Dane arrived in Toronto 24 hours after leaving New York. He played tourist for a day, wandered around the downtown area, loitered at the Eaton Center, went to the university, took a bus to Greektown, and made a pilgrimage to De Grassi Street, the mythical home of the teenage soap opera he used to watch with Iris. He saw Cabbagetown because he liked the name and checked in at a rundown motor hotel near the university, where his room had a broken window and a door that did not lock.

By his second day, the novelty of Toronto had faded. Weary and alone, Dane stopped playing tourist and saw his situation for what it was. He was in hiding in a city that was not his own. Toronto was a cleaner, quieter version of New York where most people were busy and productive and Dane was a vagrant.

Disoriented and depressed, Dane stood on the corner of Dundas and Yonge, at the center of the great city, when he heard a peculiar sound. He turned toward a whiny voice and saw a limbless man on a skateboard—a bust on wheels—twirling his shirt sleeves in circles while he crooned, "Sometimes when we touch, the honesty's too much..." A small crowd gathered in a semi-circle around the limbless man, who sported a long, thick beard. A coffee can stuffed with currency paid tribute to Canadian generosity and the public's tolerance for off-key crooning.

Yet the torso singer's income stream had more than one source.

A man in business attire and *Bally* slip-ons winced as he passed the limbless beggar, then stopped with a business proposition. "If I give you a dollar will you stop singing for five minutes?"

"Two minutes," the torso singer said, squinting at the man to measure his resolve. "I've got my public to perform for."

When the dapper pedestrian smiled wryly, the limbless man called his bluff by resuming his song in mid-verse with pitch-putrid effect. The businessman calculated how far from the dreadful voice he would be in two minutes and slipped the money in the can. The torso singer had played a street version of arbitrage, in which he derived his income from both singing and silence.

The torso singer observed a few moments of silence, then resumed his act. By rolling his shoulders, he twirled his pinned up sleeves as he sang. It was like a dance. Within fifteen minutes, ten other pedestrians had dropped money in his can—four in exchange for the man's silence.

The limbless man was a shocking paradox of disability and competence and Dane watched him intently. Yet morbid fascination was not the sole motivation for Dane's gaping. Under his beard, which seemed as long and thick as a surrogate limb, the street performer's face looked familiar to Dane, although he could not place him.

The street singer liked to be listened to but expected to be paid; he took exception to Dane's freeloading fascination.

"This isn't a free show, *ay*," he said.

"Maybe not but the street is free," Dane answered.

"A wise guy, *ay*?" the limbless performer replied.

"I know you're working and you deserve to be paid. You're amazing," Dane put a Canadian and American dollar in the can.

"So you're from the states, *ay*?" the limbless song and dance man asked. "What did you do? Sex with a minor? Steal from drug dealers? Kill your mom?"

"I put a drug company's package insert on my website."

"Drug company, ya say?"

The skateboard serenader squinted at Dane like he vaguely recognized him, too, and needed just one clue to identify him.

"Puppy Man! Is that you, Dane Bacchus?"

Dane did a double-take of the talented stump man and his mind erased the beard from the face.

"You don't remember your old door-locking friend, Austin Weebler!"

"Austin? What—!" Dane was too surprised to formulate a question.

"It's my coffee break. Go and buy us coffee and donuts and we'll talk!"

Weebler told Dane to take ten dollars from the can and buy refreshments at the *Tim Horton's* across the street. The errand done, Dane drank his coffee and helped Austin slurp his.

"What happened to the rest of you, Austin?"

"That's a strange tale," Weebler began cheerfully. "You remember I was in the hospital. Well, I got better but I couldn't handle good health. I turned back into a lab rat. You know, testing side effects. Long story short, I lost circulation in my extremities, got necrosis in my arms and legs and they had to amputate to save my life. Anyway, that's what they said. I think they did it so I couldn't pop more pills or inject more injectables."

"So how did you get here, Austin?"

"The drug companies paid me a settlement but I had to leave the States," Weebler began. "It was too painful for my family and everybody to see me like this and I got sick of their heartbreak and pity. So I came here to start over. And, hey, it worked! I really *am* a new man, Dane. I'm bigger through subtraction. In Toronto, I'm *Stump*, the singing torso on a skateboard. So why are you here?"

Dane explained the website and the threatened lawsuit.

"Screw 'em, Dane. They're messing with your head. They've got too many problems to go after you. While we're chatting, that drug company's probably been sold or merged, or gone bankrupt. What time is it? Shit. Back to work."

"But Austin, why do you do this? You've got enough settlement money to live on, right?"

"The money's good but I don't do it for the money, Dane. I always wanted to sing for people and this is the first time I can get away with it. And—you saw—I make people happy... especially when I stop."

Weebler a.k.a. *Stump*, invited Dane to watch him work. After an hour, he suggested that the unpaid intern try making some money. Between sets, Austin explained his technique. "It's like drug advertising, Dane. You have to be bad enough to get paid." Weebler urged Dane to incite a love-hate reaction. "Dig deep!" he exhorted Dane as the tide of lunchtime street traffic gathered.

"I don't have to dig deep," Dane replied. "I have a gift for making people hate me."

"Yeah, I noticed that at Green," Weebler said.

"I'll read my poems," Dane said. "When I used to read them at work, people begged me to shut up."

"There you go. My bad songs and your bad verse: what a team!"

"My poetry isn't bad," Dane sulked.

"Of course not! But people think all poetry is bad," Weebler observed.

As casual as a street sign indicating a dead end, *Stump* Weebler's statement was an elegant equation for what went wrong in Dane's life.

"We'll make a fortune," Austin said. "They'll pay anything to make us stop."

"If the cops don't stop us first," Dane remarked.

"I'm too pathetic for the cops to mess with. You're borderline."

Out of the briefcase Dane carried to feel like somebody—sort of— he extracted a literary magazine he kept with him to feel creative— sort of. It contained two longer poems, which he proceeded to read in a loud voice and an affected accent, with his head thrown back.

"I am the great white male...love life, give me a nickel...think upon time, lend me a dime...think about eternity...give it to me free."

Some audience members winced or looked askance, while many others laughed. A few listeners even nodded and gave Dane a *thumbs up*. A significant number of spectators put money in the cup. Some loitered in a circle around Dane and asked him to read more or to re-read a line they didn't quite get.

"See man? You're a natural. Look, more people. You're on, ay?" *Stump* Weebler said during their next break. "Forget about advertising. Stay here and make an honest Canadian dollar."

Dane started his next set when a familiar voice was raised above the crowd, "Oh, God, it's Dane Bacchus...the *Grovil* man *groviling* for spare change."

Dane was reading a short poem and managed to be heard over the heckler's disruption. When he had finished, he identified the rude audience member as Nigel Hogbine, his former boss from Georgian Shield. Nigel was inebriated.

"So advertising didn't work out for you, *ay*? You've put out a tin cup in the streets of Toronto, *ay*? How touching! And you found the perfect *Grovil* mascot, ay? This is what can happen to you if you don't use *Grovil, ay*?" Hogbine asked. People in the crowd laughed and put their hands together for Nigel. They believed he was in the act.

"You know this guy?" *Stump* Weebler asked.

"*Know me*?" Hogbine yelled. "This man owes me! He ruined my career! Because of this man's arrogance we lost *Grovil!*"

"Maybe the black box warning had more to do with it," Dane said.

"They should put a black box on you! You lost us the business and they blamed you on me!" Nigel cried.

"You fired me!" Dane shouted. "It's time you moved on—with your miserable life and down the street."

"That's one more of your award-winning headlines, *ay*? This man ruined me with cheap clichés," Nigel taunted.

"You did a good job of that, yourself, with 'Allergies, Achtung!'"

Nigel staggered toward Dane with his arm cocked to pummel him when *Stump* Weebler twirled his shirt sleeve around Nigel's leg like a lasso and snared the cuff with his teeth. In seconds, Nigel sprawled on the pavement.

"Help!" *Stump* Weebler cried. "This bully is attacking me!" Under his breath, *Stump* told Dane it was nice catching up and it was his cue to exit street right. "Go home, Dane, the drug company won't mess with you."

Dane bolted as Nigel struggled to free himself from the mayhem.

The furies of Advertising Past pursued Dane with drunken invective and sirens screaming, but after running several blocks, Dane outpaced them—for the time being. He knew that despite *Stump Weebler's* sleeve-twirling interference, Nigel would sort things out with the police and Dane would eventually be flushed out of Toronto and deported to his corporate execution.

As he caught his breath a few blocks from his performance and collected his wits to make a next move, a voice called out his name.

"Professor Dane?"

Dane took off again, acknowledging his name by running from it. Could even his distant past be haunting him?

"Professor Dane. It's me. Roderick Von Dronk."

Dane recognized the voice, stopped and looked in the direction of the man running after him.

"*Global Poet*?" Dane said.

Roderick Von Dronk, Dane's former student, stood before him like a human non-sequitur. Von Dronk signed all of his essays and tests as *The Global Poet* when he was a student in Dane's English class. Practical study meant nothing to Von Dronk. Money had not been invented so far as he was concerned. He lived for poetry. In his mind it was not a skill or talent but a spouse with whom he had an enduring love.

After the international incident with Hogbine, Dane was cautious about meeting anyone from his past.

"I gave you a good grade, didn't I?" Dane asked.

"I don't remember, Professor. Grades were meaningless to me."

"Right, right," Dane muttered.

"I saw you back there reading your poems with the amputee. I didn't know you wrote poetry. You were good."

"Thanks, Global Poet," Dane muttered. "So why are you here?"

"I could ask you the same," Von Dronk pointed out. "But with respect for your age, I won't."

"Thanks, Roderick, because I couldn't tell you."

"I came to see my Russian girlfriend," Global Poet explained. "We found each other on a poetry chatline. Her user name is *Chernobyl's Child*. She is a sonnet, full of dignity and radiance. Her smile is rhyme."

"That's, that's—beautiful, Roderick. But see, I'd better keep moving. In fact, I need to go home, to New York."

"I was going back today," Von Dronk said. "I have my aunt's car. You want to come along?"

That was how Dane escaped Toronto.

The disgraced copywriter and the Global Poet drove the width of New York State a few miles in front of a massive low pressure system that bore down on them from the west. When they careened southward through the Catskills, the low pressure overtook them. The ineffective wipers of Roderick's old car smeared dirty rain across the windshield from mud flaps of passing trucks.

"Can you see the road?" Dane asked.

"The poet's medium is enchanted blindness," replied *The Global Poet*.

"That's brilliant but I think you should pull over."

Dane wrapped a towel around the defective rubber wiper. It seemed like a good idea until the terrycloth disintegrated, adding fiber shreds to the visual chaos. After slowing to a mist, the rain came down in sheets as they crossed the Tappan Zee Bridge. The terrycloth around the wiper swept waves across the glass, turning all visual cues into flashes of white, red and green. Dane shouted in terror as *The Global Poet* clutched the steering wheel with more hope than conviction that he was driving in the right direction. Cars on all sides blasted horns of warning and rebuke. The bridge was finally crossed, the road was before them and the rain faded to a mist. They were alive. Dane was calm. He felt that whatever awaited him at home would be a comfort.

Von Dronk dropped Dane off in upper Manhattan, near the entrance of a park and a subway station. Dane called home to warn Becky and Iris of his proximity.

Iris came to a park plaza where Dane waited near ping-pong tables.

"Darling," Dane whispered.

"Daddy?"

"Over here."

She let out a cry when she saw him. To escape identification in Toronto, Dane had shaved his hair and wore wet, muddy clothes and a baseball cap.

When the pharma company called Becky, she said Dane was out of the country. She never heard from them again. But Dane was not content to be left alone. He struggled to understand why. Dane scoured the internet for drug industry news and learned that the company which pursued him had been sold to a foreign conglomerate.

Dane was free.

Case 7-E
WHY REVENGE is SWEET—AND SOUR

15. UNDER THE GUN

Business improved when he returned.

He received a call from Grayson, Upshire, and Newby, known across the industry simply as GUN. GUN was the most feared and fabled agency in drug advertising. After years of sending in his résumé to GUN with no response, Dane would now learn about this mystique from the inside. In the first hour of his first day, he received an assignment to write a four-page brochure. He found his sources and wrote the brochure in a few days. The GUNNERS, as they called themselves, liked his resourcefulness and extended his assignment for six weeks.

Dane's term at GUN followed a typical progression—various assignments were done fast, revised faster, and reviewed until they were finished, leaving less work to do. At the start of his sixth week, Dane was told to find reference publications for a project. He worked on this assignment for two days, only to be told there was no money to order articles GUN did not already own. Then the account team said new support documents were unnecessary. Before leaving one night, Dane told Patricia, a staff writer supervising his work, that the reference materials he was able to find for free were in a folder on his desk if she needed them. They chatted briefly. He said it was a shame so much work and time were wasted, wished her good night and left.

The next morning the head writer for the account, an affable man in his 30s who liked beer and football, called Dane into his office and asked him to close the door. Closed doors were usually objects of dread in Dane's emotional lexicon. As a freelancer, though, he could not be fired, which allayed his anxiety. Also, he had acted in such an innocuous manner in six weeks at GUN that he felt confident he had offended no one. To the contrary, Dane thought he might be offered a full-time position.

"Dane, what happened yesterday between you and Patricia before you left?"

Dane still had the capacity for surprise—and was filled to capacity at that moment. He sensed he was in trouble but not why.

"Nothing. I went to her office, I said I was leaving and that the references I worked on were on my desk if she needed them."

"I believe you," the copy chief said. "But she went to my boss and said you threatened her. He wants you out of here immediately."

"But what did I do?"

Dane was stunned. He had been dismissed before but always for a reason, so he tried to find one now. He rifled through his memory of interactions with Patricia—words, responses, a cold look, a remote sign of her resentment—and found nothing. In movies, falsely accused people often appeared stupefied. Now it was his turn.

"I was respectful. I never even went into her office," Dane said.

"You're a big guy. You're fit. Some people could find that intimidating."

"Me?"

"Listen, we'll pay you to the end of the week," the copy supervisor told him.

GUN compensated Dane generously and promptly for his swift evacuation but Patricia's lie galled him. He thought of contacting the creative director who believed the defamation but did not know what to say. Should he threaten the man or try to persuade him with good will? In the end, would a supervisor who believed his underling's lie have an open mind and concede an error? Dane doubted he could win so he did not look back. He was on to the next job.

But the next job did not come. The media said it was the economy. Dane did not take it personally. Drug companies were slow to initiate projects. Mergers outnumbered new drug applications and FDA denials and product recalls surpassed approvals. But rationalizations gradually ran out.

The dry employment spell evolved into a slow siege. Dane feared that his advertising life was *really* over. Each morning he was so anxious he could barely face the day. He was wracked with guilt as his family slid toward poverty. He searched for work by reaching out to people he knew and by scanning employment search engines--without success. Doubts crept into his routine. How could a person with his proven ability to write fail to find work? Had someone cast aspersions on his name?

He remembered the incident at GUN.

When he was dismissed months before, he deposited his fat paycheck without protest. Now he was convinced that Patricia's calumny had spread like oil and polluted his career. To get hired again in advertising, he must restore his reputation. He must track down his detractor and make her recant her slander.

It was a difficult objective with significant impediments. Conventional communication was unlikely to succeed. What was the point of phoning or sending emails that would identify the sender but receive no response? Dane's only satisfaction would result from confronting his accuser. The sixth amendment afforded him that right even if GUN did not.

Dane returned to the office building GUN occupied early one evening and stood before the security desk. He wore a blond wig, trench coat, heeled shows and rouged cheeks to impersonate Loni Loomis, whose ID he pinched between two painted nails. Loomis was a former employee of another agency where Dane had freelanced. The ID was issued to Dane so he could come and go freely, only he never returned it. Loomis had resigned from the agency to work closer to home before a stroke erased her long term memory.

Beads of perspiration trickled from Dane's hairy armpits and made him feel unfeminine. He gambled that the guards would see the faint resemblance between Loni's picture and his disguise and accept a freakishly tall woman more readily than suspect a transvestite.

They glanced at Loni's ID and let Dane pass. The moment revealed to him one of human nature's secrets: in a woman, ugliness can have the power of beauty.

Dane took an elevator to the tenth floor to confront his accuser.

The ID card was only good for access to the building. It did not open the GUN lobby doors because it lacked the proper magnetic strip. This did not matter to Dane. He had no intention of entering the GUN offices. Patricia Holmes occupied a windowless office in the middle of the floor; if she saw him there and cried out, he would be trapped. His plan was to lure her outside GUN's offices to the elevator bank, where she would be isolated and alone. He used a phone outside the glass doors to dial her extension and affected an Asian accent when she answered.

"You *awdah* take-out from *Happy Wok*."

"I did?"

It was a calculated risk. Patricia did not order take out from *Happy Wok*, but at six o'clock she was probably hungry. Dane timed this operation for when GUN people working late had their dinners delivered.

Dane spoke softly. A six-foot four transvestite in a blond wig with an Asian accent holding aromatic Chinese take out in a greasy paper bag might raise suspicions of passersby. There were none.

"Yeah, you did. *Pushy Ho?*"

"Patricia Holmes! Doesn't anyone speak English?"

Dane was nervous. He had made her angry. Would the scheme work? He knew food was often delivered to the wrong floor and it was highly probable that Patricia's order had been pilfered by a colleague.

"Okay," Patricia conceded irascibly.

Dane pushed a button so an elevator car would be waiting when she came. It was the only private place he could think of. He would draw her into the elevator with the promise of food and speak to her there.

"What are you doing there?" Patricia called out from the glass doors when she saw the take out bag dangling from the delivery person's manicured hand. Dane's false accuser was angry but her hunger was stronger. It drew her to the bag of take-out in Dane's hand. When Dane saw her striped jersey and dark painted toenails peaking from the espadrilles that constituted her uniform, he pulled the bag inside. Patricia stepped into his trap. He pushed the "door close" button and handed her the take-out bag.

The bag was in her hands, the elevator started to move and she saw before her a 6'4" transvestite—this was not what she expected.

"What the—"

"I'm sorry for doing this. I would have tried to phone or email you but you would have blown me off or called the police, right? I just want to know why you told your boss I threatened you when all I did was mention where the references were on my desk."

"Who are you? I never worked with you!"

"Don't pretend you don't know me. Do I look familiar now?"

He pulled off the wig and revealed his face.

At first, Patricia was startled by the wig removal. But she quickly recognized Dane.

"You! The freelancer. Why are you here? What are you going to do?" Patricia demanded.

"I'll ask the questions. Why did you try to ruin my reputation? Do you realize that when you lie about someone it's like assaulting them and the people they love? My family needs me to provide and you threatened that."

"I don't know what you're talking about! I told my boss we didn't need you. Now let me go. You're in trouble. Your family—!"

The elevator had stopped in the basement. Patricia reached for the elevator button but Dane clasped her wrists. She screamed.

"No, stop! Don't do that," Dane shouted.

Panic overcame him. Patricia's scream was another false accusation and this one would destroy him and his family. He beat her with the wig at first but to little effect. Then he stuffed the wig against her face to smother her cries. Patricia kicked and struggled but he pressed her against the elevator side and finally she stopped struggling.

"What have you done, Dane? What will you do now?" Dane muttered repeatedly. He lifted her and spilled her into the dumpster, then covered her in books and papers. He hoped she was alive and that she would forget.

Dane pressed the sub-basement level where he bolted from the elevator. He stuffed the wig in his canvas bag, walked slowly, turned a corner and hustled down another corridor, seeking an unguarded exit. He found a maintenance uniform on a hook outside a closed mail room. It was past quitting time and anyone working late was at dinner and oblivious. Dane slipped into the jumpsuit, put on a *Mets* cap so the brim shaded his eyes, and opened a fire door, setting off an alarm. He walked briskly down a narrow street behind the office tower, crossed a wide avenue and fled in a cab.

When he arrived home, he ate dinner with Becky and Iris. Becky wondered why he was nervous. Dane said he had been stricken by terrible remorse for never visiting his mother's gravesite since her death three years before.

"But you didn't go to her funeral," Becky reminded him.

"She didn't invite me," he said.

Iris rolled her eyes. Was this her father's insanity talking or was he making a macabre joke?

"You know what I mean. I didn't go to her funeral because I didn't know she died until later. I need closure."

"Are you all right?" she asked.

"No. But if I do this one thing, I think I will finally be at peace."

"How long will you need?"

"Only a few days," he said.

Dane packed a few personal effects in a gym bag and left that night. He told Becky and Iris he needed to travel by night so he would be at the gravesite at dawn to mark a symbolic new day.

He could not risk them knowing more if the police questioned him. His mother's grave was in Pennsylvania. Dane went to Maine.

16. MENTAL IN MAINE

Dane bought a bus ticket to Hartford, where he boarded the next bus out for Springfield, Massachusetts. From there he rode to Boston and onward to Portland, Maine. He stayed in Portland long enough to know it was not obscure enough for him to feel safe there. He bought a shrimp roll from a street vendor and took the next bus out, eastward to Camden, Maine. Even Camden seemed too familiar and close. He kept riding until he ran out of energy and fear in an obscure town called Mathias, Maine.

On a scale between significance and oblivion, Mathias tilted toward the latter. It was a few square blocks of retail and two intersecting county roads, one leading east, the other to the beach. Dane found a rooming house near the center of town. It was a cluster of corners, gables, dormers, and turrets, owned by a large woman in thick glasses, a tent dress and sneakers. Leaning on a cane, the proprietor waved at Dane from the porch though he was a few feet away.

"You've come a long distance," she said kindly. "I'm legally blind but I see that much."

"Portland."

"You will find rest and sustenance here," she said with biblical eloquence. "It's $50 a night. How many days will you be staying?"

"Only a day or two," Dane said.

"You can give me $50 now and tell me more tomorrow morning. We have complimentary coffee and you shouldn't miss it. They say it's the best in town."

Dane's hostess processed Dane's check-in before rising slowly from her seat like a pullout sofa unfolding on rusty hinges. The long ordeal made the woman's wrinkled eyelids open and shut like accordions. Vertical at last, she poked her cane against the unvarnished floor before leading Dane up three flights of creaking stairs to his room. The brightness and space of Dane's first resting place in two days exposed its decrepitude. Former homespun touches were reminders of present poverty and neglect. The wallpaper, once green and patterned, had stained to sepia. The brass bed frame was tarnished and the mattress was soft and lumpy as moist pizza dough.

"It's cheerful," Dane said politely.

"I want you to feel at home. But no funny business."

"Funny business?"

"No women. And no self-abuse."

"Oh. Don't worry..."

"I have good reason to worry. Yes, I do. You see, I had a visitor who thought it was fine to play with himself in the bathroom. I turned him in. And you know what? He was wanted in Vermont for sexually abusing a 90-year-old woman. Can you imagine? That could have been me!" She paused for Dane's reply.

"Not you! You're too young!" Dane replied to avoid offense.

"If I had my say, he would have fried in an electric chair until his hair sizzled and his eyeballs popped like blood-soaked corks. That's all he's good for in my book. But they extradited him."

"Unbelievable! Well, that's our system," Dane said, hoping to abridge the discussion.

The woman clobbered the floor with her cane. "There's a brass recital at the church, if you like that sort of thing...And if you're hungry, *Chuck's Chowder Hut* makes chowder the way I like it—piping hot."

"Thanks. Sounds perfect."

"Not perfect. But good. I like my soup hot and my cider cold. I have no use for tepid." She squinted. "You know what else I like hot?"

"No, I have no idea."

"Guess."

"I don't want to presume."

"Go on. Guess!" the woman growled, her myopic eyes flaring like nuclear events.

"Oh, okay. Umm. Oyster stew?"

"No. Try again."

"Uh, this is hard. Lobster bisque?"

"No! Try again."

The woman looked so eager that Dane felt an enormous pressure to get the right answer.

"Umm, hot toddy?"

"No! A hot bath! Haha! I was sure you'd get that."

"You're full of surprises."

She smiled beatifically.

"Well, run along. The night is younger than I am. Ha! Ha!"

When she left, Dane threw himself on his bed to be released from the stiffness of two days of bus travel. Instead, he sank into the Venus Man-Trap mattress and was swallowed alive.

He studied the wallpaper as if were an old textbook and made out the design—alternating elephants and sunflowers—then struggled out of the bed with his sore back to make the recital.

The church sanctuary had the musty funk of rectitude. The red carpet was threadbare in spots and the white walls were more appropriate to a clinic. Red velvet pads on the wooden benches had worn away in circular buttock depressions. Dane hoped the brass would blow away his depression, but the polyphonic fanfares sounded like musical preludes to an execution.

He left during intermission and meandered down the dark commercial streets of Matthias before returning to the boarding house. Dane ascended the arthritic porch stairs and opened the heavy, belligerent door of the lodging house, dark but for the perpetual office light. He padded down the hallway when a voice barked from behind.

"Who are you?"

"I'm your guest. From faraway?"

His hostess squinted and lurched at him with her cane.

"Who are you?"

"Your guest!"

The cane cracked down across his shoulders. Instinctively, he snared the cane in his hands, while the proprietress kicked and screamed, "Intruder! No one violates my peaceful home!" She flailed at Dane before a heavy weight caved in on him, belonging to another guest or handyman.

The police sorted it out. They asked if he needed medical attention.

Dane declined help despite bruised ribs and a swollen face. He wanted as little fuss and documentation as possible. His hostess gave him ice, aspirin and piping hot chowder, served with profuse apologies.

"Ever since we were robbed 22 years ago I have been a different person. I used to be trusting. I was gracious. No more!" Her face quivered and contracted. Her large body quivered. Sobs and tears poured out of it like a wrung sponge. When she stopped, she wiped her face with her sleeve.

"Can I make you something? How about a nice mayonnaise and relish sandwich?"

Dane laughed through his painful ribs. He felt safe because his hostess owed him for the beating. According to his personal sense of justice, Dane believed his physical punishment in Maine was a sign that his New York trouble might be over; the landlady's assault was a karmic down payment on his crime.

"Can I get change to make a long distance call?" Dane asked. His cell battery had discharged and he wanted to talk to Becky and Iris.

The woman opened a drawer to a trove of nickels, dimes and quarters. With ten dollars in nickels and dimes, he called from a payphone.

"Did anybody call?" he asked Becky.

"No."

"Anybody come?"

"No."

For Dane, such a simple question provided a respite but failed to solve the underlying problem. The police had not come yet, but they would. He had transgressed and must be punished.

While Dane contemplated his fate brewing in New York, his shabby room, with its flabby mattress and revolting wall paper, made him feel like an outcast on the verge of a desperate act. The behavior of his hosts added the kind of local color guaranteed to make visitors homesick. During his second afternoon, he returned to his room after lunch and discovered someone else's feces in his toilet—a result of poor hospitality or worse plumbing. What did his sheets have in store? He slept on his covers and nearly froze to avoid finding out.

Staying in the room was no worse than leaving it. Dane navigated the dark, decrepit halls and stairs. He often encountered there the cane-wielding proprietor, who glowered at him like he was an escaped convict. However, her maternal feelings were aroused when she heard Dane's "sniffle." She referred him to *Chuck's Chowder Hut* and gave him a zigzag of directions he could not recall or follow. When Dane asked a passerby the location of *Chuck's*, the man smiled at Dane as if he were telling a vintage insider's joke. "*Chuck's* been boarded up for years," the man said. "The proprietor's been in a hospital for the criminally insane. He was lucky to get that after what he pulled." One night after a football game, Chuck spiked his famous chowder with a "date rape" drug and assaulted the high school cheerleading squad.

When the anticipation of great chowder was withdrawn, what was left for Dane in Mathias but insanity? The townsfolk appeared to exist there for the reason Dane lingered—a vain hope of security in its oblivion.

On his third night, Dane was awakened by a flashlight in his face. He shouted.

"I thought I heard you yelling in your sleep. I wanted to be sure you were all right," his hostess said.

"I shouted because you shined a light in my face," Dane said.

At that moment, Dane made up his mind to leave Mathias.

He took the next bus to Boston and a train home. He missed Becky and Iris and felt guilty for exposing them to the consequences of his mistakes.

He phoned from the subway station down their street. Iris met him on the plaza near some ping pong tables. He wore sunglasses, a raincoat and a tilted baseball cap.

"Daddy?"

"Iris. I missed you. Just walk ahead and let me in. I'll walk in the service door and come up through the basement."

"Daddy, why are you acting so weird?"

"Don't ask obvious questions," he replied in a quiet growl that made other commuters turn before they walked up the stairs to the street. "Just walk ahead of me."

Yes, Dane was home.

Case 7-F
MENTALOSCOPY: AN INVASIVE, HIGH-RISK PROCEDURE

17. THE RECKONING

For weeks Dane woke up in the middle of the night expecting a violent knock on the door. He thought he should wait outside his building to be arrested like Shostakovich the composer did when he believed Stalin's police were coming for him. But no one came for Dane.

One day, the Bacchus buzzer burped. It was mid-morning and Dane expected no deliveries or repairs. He peered out the window at the street below, where a black car was double-parked. When the doorbell sounded more insistently, Dane squinted in the peephole. Two men stood in the hall and looked back at him.

Dane trembled. The dreaded moment had come. Just when he was willing to face the music, the musicians showed up. Clearly, he was tracked down and would finally have to account for what he did to Patricia Holmes in the freight elevator.

"Dane Bacchus? We'd like to ask you a few questions. May we come in?"

He opened the door. Two men in raincoats entered and took seats at their dining table. One man was larger, younger and had a crew cut. The other was short, portly and bald. Becky looked at Dane searchingly. What was this about? He could not face—or tell—her. And then as he looked around the table at the impassive visitors and his stricken wife, words of remorse poured out of him.

"I did not kill that woman. I only threatened her when she falsely accused me of threatening her. Actually she started screaming before I threatened her. The dumpster was not my idea. It was just there!" Dane broke down in sobs.

The men looked at Dane nonplussed. No one spoke.

Dane was now both fearful and confused. His breathing was shallow and his hands were shaking.

"Mr. Bacchus," the man in the crew cut said. "Take a deep breath."

"I'm trying," Dane said. "I'm allergic to stress."

"I'm Agent Dempsey," the taller man said. "This is Agent Hardman. We're from Washington. We came to ask you a few questions related to your work as a pharmaceutical copywriter."

"You're from Washington? New York dumpsters are outside your jurisdiction?"

"Most of the time," the bald agent replied. "To be honest, we didn't understand a thing you just said."

"Oh, that's uh, well, I'm sorry," Dane stammered. "I'm writing a story and I have a problem separating fantasy and reality, right, honey?"

He glanced at Becky, who nodded along with consternation in her eyes. Dane gave her a reassuring smile. If these agents were from Washington, they came on federal business, not on a local matter. The pressure was lifted from Dane for the moment. It was exhilarating to answer questions from Washington because he felt sure he had broken no federal law. He was in a giddy mood.

Dane did not know that Patricia, whom he lured with Chinese take-out and flogged with a cheap wig, awoke in the service elevator dumpster covered in magazines and *mu shu* chicken. She climbed out of the canvas dumpster and realized an hour had passed. When she told her supervisor she had been assaulted in the service elevator by a tall, transvestite delivery man who once worked for GUN as a freelance writer, he waited for the punch line. When it did not come, he stared at her like she was foaming at the mouth. Patricia laughed and said it was a joke. She knew pursuing the complaint would be a false move. People would say she used drugs and drank. She could not risk police involvement, a blood test and probing questions. She let the incident pass as one more reason to be paranoid.

The federal agents sat at the Bacchus kitchen table, opened briefcases and removed papers. "We came to speak to you about your timesheets at..."

Was Dane being investigated for padding timesheets? His joy that these were not NYPD detectives gave way to fresh panic. "I'm being investigated by the IRS!" he thought. In the hierarchy of situations to be feared, a visit from IRS agents signified top level trouble—and he was in it.

"Gentlemen, if you're from the IRS, I have to tell you upfront that my billing was always accurate," Dane pleaded. "They tried to corrupt me. They ordered me to bill my time on the toilet but I wouldn't do it. You want to know why? Because I don't spend that much time on the toilet. I do my business and I'm out of there!"

The men looked at Dane incredulously. They neither believed nor cared to hear about his toilet estimate. Overall, the inquiry did not seem to be starting well. The agents looked unconvinced and unhappy with Dane's performance. Dane knew he had to defend himself but not to the point of obstruction. He wanted these G-men to go away—satisfied. If they left mad, they would be back with a vengeance. He scrambled for something else to say that might please them.

"If you want to see my tax returns, you're welcome to them. They're clean, too, in style and content. My wife prepared them. She's very meticulous. Okay, okay! I'll admit it. I claimed my printer cartridges as an expense—occasionally. But that was only a few hundred dollars. You know, printers are cheap but they really nail you with the ink. And, oh yeah, I itemized oil changes when I used my car for work. I'll write you a check—with penalties, if you want."

Dane reached for his pen and checkbook to show his good faith. He hoped they would be appeased, if not pleased, by his coming clean, but the visitors' faces remained as hard and impassive as before. Agent Dempsey scratched his short hairs and rubbed the corners of his mouth with his hand. He, in particular, seemed disappointed in Dane, as if he initially had high expectations of him but no longer viewed him as a credible witness—*of anything*.

The agents closed their briefcases almost in unison.

"Mr. Bacchus, we're not here to hear about your IRS returns; or about your time on the toilet, or about a woman you may or may not have assaulted and thrown in a dumpster," Agent Dempsey admitted.

Dane swallowed and tapped his foot but tried to conceal all emotion as they perused his face. Alas, it was too late for that act.

"So wh-wh-wh-y are you here?" Dane stammered.

"Mr. Bacchus. You've been padding your timesheet for years..."

Dane's mouth was opening to protest but before a word could escape, Agent Dempsey interrupted him.

"We're aware it's standard industry practice. Just one small scam in a range of criminal activities. Sure, we could make an example of you. You might be convicted—or exonerated. Either way you'd spend your last dollar defending yourself."

Dane's body was a burning edifice he wished to flee. Advertising was bringing plague after plague upon him. Becky held his hand.

"We're not interested in ruining your life, Mr. Bacchus," Agent Hardman said. "We want you to tell us what you know."

Little Dane, the tiny, old man in Dane's soul who reminded Dane of his innermost fears and dreams, now came out of hiding, which suggested the worst was over. These agents had dropped Dane in a deep hole, only to toss him a flashlight. They would not destroy him. Yet, if he failed as an informant, with nothing but inconsequential crap to relate, would they think he was holding out and mete out twice as much vengeance?

"What I know about what?" Dane stammered. "I was just a

writer."

The two men glanced at one another knowingly.

"Mr. Bacchus, in the past year many important drugs have been withdrawn from the market or been given "black box" warnings for harmful side effects," Agent Dempsey explained. "Others have been proven ineffective. And still others have resulted in multi-million dollar lawsuits and settlements."

"Yes," Becky interceded. "It's in the papers everyday."

"Yes, Ma'am," Agent Hardman said and turned to Dane. "Mr. Bacchus, we ran every name associated with pharmaceutical advertising through our computers and your name was associated with more bad, dangerous and discredited drugs than anyone else in the country."

Every misgiving Dane had in the past ten years crashed down on him. Every warning and adverse events section of every package insert of every drug he ever worked on—each patient who contracted cancer, had fevers, suffered from priapism or bleeding—was on his conscience. They were no longer mere mouse type on onion skin paper. These were people with faces, bodies, *dreams* and a lot of pain. They suffered and died while he made a decent, middle-class income to send his daughter to day camp and give her piano lessons. How venal he was!

"I didn't know!" Dane expostulated but they all knew he did.

Agent Dempsey opened his briefcase, removed a document and pushed it toward Dane. "Does this look familiar?"

"It's my résumé," he stammered.

"Why don't you start at the beginning?"

Dane described his descent into advertising. He explained his aspiration to be a great writer, his struggles, disappointments, poverty; years of teaching and classroom abuse by bored and indifferent students. He recounted his desperate decision to try advertising as a career with little prospect of success and his belief that truth was key to the effective promotion of drugs and devices.

"I told colleagues and superiors—drugs are not corn flakes. These are potent substances with the power to heal—or kill. When doctors prescribe them and patients swallow them, trust must be an ingredient."

Dane stopped. The silence in the room was like a precipice. He dared not go further. He watched for signs on the agents' faces that he affected their emotions but they remained dour and intractable. Becky looked at Dane with an admiration he had not seen from her in a long time.

"My supervisors ordered me to write what the client wanted, to hell with accuracy or facts, but I wouldn't do it. I always made sure of my facts and never wrote anything without clinical support."

The agents grunted. One wiped his forehead; the other removed his glasses and rubbed mucus from his conjunctiva.

"Mr. Bacchus, did you know of any instance when the advertising agencies deliberately lied about a product to mislead the public?" Agent Dempsey asked.

Dane recounted the bogus research he attended: the male transvestite discussing a woman's hormone replacement therapy; simulators with fake toilet bowls and *virtuo-sapiens* for *Grovil*. He detailed the *Refluxydyl* GERD conspiracy and the purple folder. The agents nodded at this *intel*. Agent Dempsey told Dane that they were aware of this conspiracy. He extracted a photograph from his briefcase and showed it to Dane. "Do you recognize this man?"

"It's Landon LeSeuer, my old boss."

"LeSeuer has increased GERD medication consumption on every continent but Antarctica," Agent Hardman remarked. "We're looking for him now but he's somewhere in Mexico."

Dane thought he had exhausted his anthology of tales of corruption, yet the agents stared at him implacably, expecting something more and different. Dane had no choice. He gave himself a *mentaloscopy*, an exhausting purge of his proverbial guts, full of unfiltered, free-associating verbiage, hoping to provide the unsuspecting lawmen the answers they demanded.

His interviewers appeared to witness Dane's *mentaloscopy* with discomfort. When he started to describe how an account director and product manager misappropriated the *Grovil* campaign budget to pay for their *sexcapade*, Agent Hardman, whose eyes had shut, slumped in his chair.

Dane was first to notice since Agent Dempsey's eyelids were also lowered.

"Don't fall asleep," Dane pleaded. "I'm getting to the good part. With all the sex..."

Agent Dempsey, now awake, tried rousing his slumping partner, Agent Hardman, whose unresponsive body tumbled to the floor.

"He needs medical attention!" Dempsey said.

The agent pulled out a special phone and an ambulance arrived within five minutes. Now Dane was genuinely afraid. Agent Hardman had suffered a heart attack while hearing his story. As paramedics wheeled away the fallen agent, Dane was a jittery, jabbering mess, profusely apologizing to Agent Dempsey for his partner's distress. Agent Dempsey tried easing Dane's mind but did not have enough time for such an undertaking. He thanked Dane for his cooperation, handed him his card, and said he would call if he had more questions.

It sounded like a cordial conclusion but Dane worried.

"Do you think I'll be charged with anything if he's seriously ill or dies...like obstruction of justice, attempted murder or involuntary manslaughter?" he asked Becky.

"Honestly, Dane, you see something negative in everything. What did you have to do with his being sick?"

"He had a heart attack while I was talking. Doesn't that implicate me?"

"You're a medical writer and should know better! Who has a heart attack or stroke from listening? The worst that could happen to someone listening to you is mental exhaustion. You did your duty. His genes and diet did the rest!"

"I'd better check my umbrella insurance policy to see if it covers this."

When Dane discovered that his umbrella policy had lapsed during his long lay-off he had another nervous collapse. Only a long session of Becky's "winner therapy" eased him back to functionality.

Over the next few weeks there were no calls or visits from law enforcement agencies. Dane relaxed, which allowed his imagination to run rampant. He speculated that he had initiated a case against drug company corruption that would result in broad and lasting reform. He would be a star witness and whistle-blower, like Daniel Ellsberg or John Dean. While he awaited his subpoena to a congressional hearing like it was a black-tie invitation, Dane imagined the statement he would make and the grilling he would face. He would speak at a long table in a credible and monotonous voice, taking measured sips of water from a tall glass, while attorneys whispered urgent messages in his ear.

"How could you, a smart and educated man, do such a stupid thing?" the bilious committee chairman would badger him in a self-righteous drone.

"Sir, I wanted to make a difference for millions of people who need drugs but don't even know they're sick. I was misled."

"And why should we believe a word you say, Mr. Bacchus, when you admit that you lied for years about the efficacy and safety of medications millions of Americans take?"

"I always wrote the truth, sir," Dane said. "Others may have changed my words but every medical statement I wrote was fully referenced by reputable medical sources."

At this point another member of the committee would intercede.

"I just want to say, Mr. Chairman, how impressed I am with the eloquence and candor of this witness. Mr. Bacchus, you are a credit and inspiration to every sell-out writing hack who ever lived."

"Thank you, sir."

When the hearings were over, the media would gush over Dane's

586

poise and swimmer's physique. Articles would reference his erudition and dignity, his baldness and his ponytail. He would sign a six-figure book deal to write a cautionary tale on the dangers of prostituting one's talents. It would be optioned to Hollywood; a major motion picture star would win an *Oscar* playing him and would thank Dane, his wife and his agent.

No agents from Washington contacted Dane and he received no subpoena.

The federal government passed on Dane's knowledge of bloated medical advertising spending. Congress and the White House concluded that the billions spent on medical advertising had minimal impact on health care costs; hospitals and drugs were reasonably priced; and health costs were out of control because too many people wanted care and premiums were too low.

"Why didn't they call me?" Dane asked forlornly. He could not shake the feeling that he had done something wrong and missed another opportunity.

"You should be happy," Becky said. "You're in the clear. You did nothing wrong."

"Yeah, right," Dane replied.

Nothing wrong! Becky's innocent words sprang on him to twist in his mind and taunt his heroic delusion. How could he be a hero when he was possibly a murderer? Was Patricia Holmes dead or alive? He did not know. When the federal agents left without asking about the woman in the dumpster, Dane was so relieved that he experienced a remission from guilt, as if acquitted of a crime that might have never happened. The local police were also strangely disinterested in Dane's assault. Weeks passed and no one called Dane or knocked on his door to ask suspicious questions. Was law enforcement lulling him into complacency before pouncing on his guilty ass when he least expected?

Or did Patricia Holmes wake up and resume her hateful life?

As time passed, with no work and no committee hearings in

Washington to distract him, Dane fixated on Patricia Holmes in the dumpster. He asked himself repeatedly, "Is she alive or dead?"

The lapse between crime and punishment did not comfort him. It was the perfect growing environment for his guilt. He replayed the elevator scene repeatedly and asked himself why he had done such a stupid thing. He might have taken a life, ruined his own and destroyed his family. He could not live with, speak of, or act upon what he had done. He was immobilized by a deepening sense that he was unfit to live in this world.

Dane's days were quiet but his dreams were full of law enforcement, sirens screaming, roof lights spinning, his door bell ringing. Dane found himself watching reruns of "Law and Order" episodes. He did not leave the apartment, even to go swimming, which had been his only means of exercise and relaxation. Becky saw him deteriorating but did not want to sound alarms. With all that happened in the past year, she was afraid to ask Dane what he was going through and why. She told herself he was undergoing post-traumatic stress and watched for signs of improvement—which did not come. Finally, she broached the matter.

"What's wrong, honey? You've been acting very worried. Why should you be? You're off the hook."

Dane looked at her with terror. "No, I'm just on a different one."

He told her about Patricia Holmes, the dumpster, how he impersonated a woman with amnesia impersonating a Chinese take-out delivery person.

"So, there was no record of you being in the building?"

"No."

"And we haven't heard anything on the news about a grisly midtown office murder? Or a missing pharmaceutical writer?"

"No."

"Well, those are good signs," Becky said.

"But I still don't know. And I don't know how to find out."

"Let me call the agency and ask to speak to her. Then you'll know for sure and we'll go from there."

Dane's search for the main number of GUN took a half hour. The rest took five minutes. When Becky hung up the phone, she told Dane, "She lives. But what an unpleasant woman! She belongs in a dumpster."

Case 7-G
LIVING YOUR DREAM VS. DREAMING YOUR LIFE: PERSPECTIVES AND PRIORITIES

18. FATHER KNOWS LESS

At his worst moments in advertising, Dane swore he would gladly walk away from the business if he found a way out of his troubles. Now that his problems were behind him, he accepted those terms. During despondent months of unemployment he reminded himself, "At least you're not being sued or in prison for attempted murder."

Crisis-free, he faced a slow alternative to annihilation—joblessness, loss of savings and the prospect of never again earning an income. Society was fast to expel people from the workforce. For years Dane was told he lacked maturity and experience. Now he struggled against the perception that he was old.

"So you're not in the Advertising Hall of Fame and you're not a Hollywood caliber whistle-blower," Becky said. "You're still a wonderful husband, father, and writer. Why don't you appreciate those gifts?"

Dane heeded his wife. Advertising had fed him and could starve him, but it could not stop him from being a husband, a father, and a writer. He should enjoy his family. This was the time to start.

One afternoon, Dane, Becky and Iris went on a rare family outing to the Metropolitan Museum of Art.

It was summer and Iris had no dance classes, homework, community service or friends to be with. For the first time in years,

Dane and his family had time to be a family

Iris was sixteen. College was a year away. Seated on a cushioned bench in the 20th century gallery, Dane watched his daughter's profile as she sketched from a painting she admired just as she had done in elementary school. Ten years before, as a tiny prodigy, Iris's hypnotic focus on her work endeared her to adult museum goers. They crowded around to see what line she would draw next, as though watching a six-year-old make art were a mini-tour of Lascaux, drawing them closer to the mysterious core of the creative process.

Now Iris was almost a woman, yet her face remained soft and full. She could still summon the rapture of a child as she coiled over the sketchpad and moved her fingers nervously over her drawing.

"This is nice," Dane thought. "This is what I have been missing."

However, even nostalgia, presumably nailed to the past, would not be still for Dane. While he watched Iris reenact her old pastime, his mind strayed to the raw day before her sixth birthday when he and Becky bought her a crimson dress for a party he could not afford. Iris's joy and excitement had crushed him then because he knew the insecurity of her happiness—on his account. He had vowed to support her and promised that if he found a job, he would work at it for twenty years until Iris was an adult. Only ten years had passed and Dane had come up short. Yet, he had paid the bills and kept the family going. They thrived; his work was not in vain.

Now, ten years later, Dane suddenly felt disoriented, like he had been dropped among strangers.

Dane had met men who traveled extensively and did not know their families. Dane was not like them. He came home nearly every evening. He was no traveling salesman, sailor or astronaut, yet he might as well have stepped in from a space station—he saw his wife and daughter in the museum gallery as if for the first time in years.

Becky had changed although her refined beauty was intact. The machinery of age had not altered her skin and muscle, and despite a few character lines, no signs of struggle marred her features. She and

Dane were rarely apart, yet he barely recognized his wife.

"Where have you been?" he muttered to himself.

As Iris drew on the floor, a man in a trench coat and goatee approached. He looked over her shoulder and commented. Was this a famous artist, like the Russian master who once told Dane and Becky their six-year-old was a prodigy? The Russian master spoke through a woman translator but this man was alone. He squatted close to Iris and continued to smile and chat.

Iris turned to her parents and Dane received the cue that this man was no Russian master but a middle-aged pickup artist, or worse—a sex trafficker! Was Iris appealing for help?

Dane was jolted from timeless fatherhood to the gritty present. Iris was no longer a precocious six but sweet sixteen. This was a new, potentially sordid situation to which he must react. He could give *The Virgin Spring* a happy ending!

Dane shot up from the padded bench and approached the man.

"She's sixteen. Get lost before I call the guards." The man fled.

"Daddy, he wanted to buy my drawing."

"That's not all he wanted to buy," Dane said.

"You're exaggerating, Dane," Becky said.

"I'm protecting my child," he said.

"She doesn't need a bodyguard."

Dane felt hurt because his good intentions were misunderstood until he realized his intentions were incoherent.

"I guess I suck at this," he concluded.

"At what?" Becky asked.

"At this. Everyday father stuff."

"You don't suck. She needs you as her father."

Dane thought Becky was being kind. Other people in the gallery stared at him as if he did not belong in a civilized place. As the defender of his teenage daughter, he was more pariah than the art buyer/pervert. He strived to be a caring and attentive father but was clearly ill-equipped and poorly prepared.

19. DELUSIONS OF GRANDEUR MEET GENERAL RELATIVITY

Dane's attempt to save his daughter at the museum masked a wider chronic problem. He believed his mundane life was a hoax and a grander destiny lay beyond. He felt just as surely that fatherhood would not lead him there. He shifted his focus to writing.

For ten years he yearned to return from advertising Babylon to creative writing. His longing was portrayed in sepia images of a distant home; it flashed before him at a book store and triggered *cognitive cacaphony*. Advertising was exile. How far had he strayed? Would he find a way home and would a home still be there?

Now he could live out his destiny as an artist, his *true self* and write his novel, free of constraints. Each day he hoped to regain the passion for work that made all else, including money, insignificant.

Dane had discipline but he missed the essential. At his keyboard he waited for inspiration. It was a process whose sequence he knew by rote: compression, frustration, and explosion. But inspiration did not come. "I've lost it!" he whispered to himself.

While he bravely sat vigil for his muse, he reflected on the museum outing, how Iris sketched Millet's farmers, only to slam shut her sketchbook in frustration—like she had done as a child. She was still a child—and would need his help for the foreseeable future.

He still had a purpose as a father and a husband. From that thought, the wish to be the old-fashioned dad he had been for years grew in Dane. While he waited for genius to appear like an Aztec god, his role of father, husband and colleague grew more real to him than the "true self" behind them.

Although he was awkward in day-to-day parenting, he might still excel as the stereotype 1950's father who disappears by day, returns at night and does errands on weekends! Peering down at his old manuscript, he longed to be the breadwinning dad again. It made him feel needed—and he *needed* that.

If only he had that pride and contentment again! But first his attitude toward work had to change. Dane always believed a job was a nuisance. He wanted to be left alone to save time and energy for "what mattered."

Now the job mattered. He must find one and hold on to it. But to do this he must change. He did not need to become a sycophant. All he needed was a professional attitude.

These cravings for a work routine sent Dane's mind on a tour of his job history. His longest stop was the time he collaborated with Goldfarb. Dane recalled the afternoons above the rooftops of Soho, seeking inspiration by staring at water-towers. He saw Goldfarb perched on a window sill, soaking in the warmth. Beyond the brainstorms, client meetings and trips, he saw Goldfarb as the epitome of professionalism—someone who did not expect praise, a raise, or respect and who did not backstab or lie—but just came into the office everyday and did his job.

Dane phoned the number he had for Goldfarb. In the middle of the first ring, Goldfarb answered, "Hello!" in that hard and weary voice that expected the worst and was ready to deal with it.

"Hey, there, it's Dane. How's it going, man?"

"Dane, so how are you doing? You working?"

"Sort of."

"Oh. Freelancing, right?"

"Yeah, what about you?"

"I'm still here. It's hard to believe. I'm just waiting to be fired."

"That's what you said five years ago."

"It's still true. I blend in with the walls. They probably don't know I'm here."

"You're too modest. You're an amazing survivor, like the Chinese dragon."

"Yeah—speaking of Chinese, you want to meet for lunch sometime? There's a good Sichuan restaurant down the street."

Dane was enthusiastic. The restaurant was located near Goldfarb's office, which had moved to the fringes of midtown, near the river.

"It'll take me awhile to get down there," Dane said.

"Aren't you working in midtown?"

"No. I'm home."

"Look, don't bother, Dane. We'll meet when you're working again, okay? Something will turn up. It always does."

The brief conversation with Goldfarb only increased Dane's longing for a job and a commute—the whole, tiring, miserable life he used to hate.

Did Dane crave re-entry to the work cycle due to a perverse desire for what he no longer had? This was Becky's interpretation. It was sound but not entirely correct.

Dane's brain was trapped in the gravitational field of a working-stiff existence. Experience, like matter, imposes gravity, warps space, bends time, and determines the paths of objects. The longer and more intense an experience, the more it shapes our psyches.

The writing of books was once Dane's destiny, until the working man routine, with the gravity of ten years, bent him. Each morning he woke up anxious and lost because his new life followed the curve of the prior one.

One morning, he stared at his novel to find his way into it, and said, "Admit it, you've changed." He made himself a wager. He would write and look for a job, and devote himself to the one that came first. He had played this game ten years before, at his daughter's sixth birthday party.

20. LAST BELL OR FINAL CALLING?

At around the time when Dane was about to explode from conflicting tendencies and a hemorrhaging bank account, the Bacchus family had an unexpected boon.

Becky's unmarried aunt died, bequeathing to her a substantial sum. Dane always dreamed of freedom from financial pressure and the fantasy arrived, but happiness did not come along for the ride.

The inheritance was substantial enough to protect the Bacchus family from foreseeable homelessness but it would not allow Dane to retire. However, the modesty of the windfall did not bother Dane as much as its existence. Money worries had been with him his entire life. They were all he knew. Self-denial belonged to him; it was part of his identity.

"If we live off of this money what will be left for Iris?" He asked Becky. He had made sacrifices to spare his daughter the humiliating deprivations he suffered in his youth—going out to dinner with people and being unable to order, for instance—but his sacrifice was no longer required.

Yet despite Dane's misgivings, financial security was like a vacation, it dilated his imagination. He awoke one morning, brimming with energy and enthusiasm, turned on his computer, and accessed his novel. The words made sense, the story flowed, and his characters had life; everything delighted him, and the project mattered.

The wager was over. His old creative self was victorious over the "salary man." He could work in his proverbial cave and write tomes destined to become artifacts found in jars by illiterate goatherds in the next millennium.

That afternoon, after hours of writing, Dane received a call from a recruiter. It was Albert Griffin, the man who sent Dane on his first interview, who found him his job at Integrimedicom and another at Georgian Shield. Albert sounded jovial and familiar, like no time had elapsed since their prior contact. He asked Dane if he was still at Georgian Shield. Dane said he had not worked there for three years. "Oh," the recruiter said blandly. He asked Dane if he had worked at two agencies where he knew of openings.

"I worked at one and interviewed at the other," Dane replied flatly.

It was a recruiter-repellent response. Griffin's dejection was palpable, his silence made it official: Dane's advertising career was being lowered in the ground. At first, Dane was at peace with losing his advertising career forever. Why did he need it when he had a small nest egg and his old creative self?

When the split second passed, finality set in. Dane was crossing over from currently unemployed to totally retired, with no long term means of income. Becoming the one native-born, English-speaking cab driver in New York was his only logical career move.

Griffin, who always seemed to have a descrambler for Dane's brain, broke the silence.

"I have a position open at a rising agency in Flemington, N.J. Interested?"

"They sell cars and furs in Flemington."

"So buy a car and a fur at lunch. Your wife will love you for it. Don, they're winning business right and left."

"It's too far."

"There's a train, Dean. The office is across from the station. New Yorkers work there. You'll fit in."

"That's ridiculous," Becky rebuked Dane when he described the opportunity.

"I know," Dane admitted. "It's the only call I've had in months."

"Something better will come," Becky said. "You have talent and experience."

"What if talent and experience are irrelevant?"

Griffin phoned back the next day.

"I'm about to send out your resume. But listen, can you tell me about your science background? They asked specifically about that."

"This is ridiculous. I've been writing medical copy for twelve years," Dane replied. "How much more science background do I need?"

"Right, I know," Griffin replied. "What about a science degree or college classes you took?"

Dane frantically flipped through the rolodex of his life and finally blurted, "I won four county science fairs in middle school. Does that count?—my name was in the paper!"

"I'll see what I can do," the recruiter said.

When Griffin did not phone back, Dane surmised that the opportunity fizzled. He struck it from his mind but it would not stay out, since other headhunters called about the same posting. Dane gave them all permission to represent him and none called back.

Dane might have interpreted this lack of interest in him as a cosmic rejection. Rather, he viewed the recruiters' calls as empty distractions from his true calling and their failure to follow-up as a sign for him to pay his bet: between creative writing and advertising, creative writing won.

Meanwhile, his bank account plunged by four thousand dollars per month. He sat at his computer and lost himself in his work, but finances always found him. Financial doom loomed, crowded him and smothered inspiration. He wrote a sentence only to stop at the thought of poaching his family's nest egg, of leading them on a slow descent into destitution. He glanced at the monitor. In 24 point type a message read, "Get a job."

A month had passed since Griffin had called about the agency in Flemington, when the recruiter called again. Miraculously, the position was still open. Was Dane still interested? Was he ever! With his nose-diving bank account, this car dealership Mecca forty miles away sounded familiar and close.

"That's great!" Griffin exclaimed with life-affirming enthusiasm when Dane agreed to the interview, as if the entire universe rejoiced in Dane's good sense. "Can you be there at 11 AM on Friday?"

Dane was invigorated. That was two days away. If the interview went well, he might start the week after next. He started to count prospective paychecks and calculate when his bank account would stop spiraling and start to climb.

Becky resisted.

"It's too far. Don't go to the ends of the earth for a job. *We don't need it."*

Becky believed these words would soothe and sway him, releasing him from the cycle of necessity that complicated his life. But Dane's old dreams were riddled by premonitions of old age, uselessness and poverty. Now that he had earned money, he could not waste this ability.

"I can't use up your inheritance," he said. "That money is for you and Iris. You may need it if something happens to me."

"Something *will* happen to you if you drive all over for a job," she argued. "That money is yours, too. You can use it as seed money for the career you always wanted. When you sell the rights you'll pay it back."

"What if nobody buys my book? Then we're stuck."

"And what if you believe in yourself like I believe in you? Don't go to the ends of the earth for a job you don't want or need."

"I *do* want it and need it. When I make money I can relax and do other things. When I have no income, all I do is worry"

Becky looked so disappointed that Dane had to say more. She was trying to help but he felt he needed no one's help.

"Look, honey, I'll always love writing and I would love to be an author, but it may be too late for that dream. So if I can still make money and help us, how can I turn my back on that?"

Becky regarded her husband with sad acceptance. When Dane put his first advertising portfolio together years before, she reluctantly sipped a cup of soup in a towel for one of his concepts because he was so determined to get a job. She could not stop him now from trying again.

"Okay," Becky relented. "You can write at work and think in the car. But it's a long trip.

"I've done it many times," he reassured her.

On the day of the interview she made him coffee.

"Be careful," Becky said before he left for western New Jersey.

"How do I look?" he asked. He had worn his lucky, bright orange, silk tie and his green jacket. The tie knot was askew. She adjusted it.

"Very handsome," she said.

Becky kissed Dane and watched him walk down the hallway and around the corner. A few minutes later she looked out the window and watched him put his portfolio on the backseat, get into the car and drive off.

Dane went over so much in his mind as he negotiated the turnpike, then switched to Route 78, an interstate he had that morning to himself. He felt invincible, resilient. There was still so much left in him.

His thoughts turned to the interview. It would be his masterpiece. His responses would be brief and his small-talk minimal. He would refrain from jokes, extraneous remarks and critical comments about former employers. And once the job was his, he would work late whenever called upon and without resentment, and would be cheerful and patient, regardless how obtuse people were. It was Dane's serenity prayer.

The stand of leafy trees bordering Route 78 was more fence than forest edge, and the green signs were now miles apart. Dane had been on the road for over an hour. He sighed: what a long commute! If he got the job he would need to sleep in the office after a late evening. Dane did not like these subversive thoughts. What would he do if he was not hired? The idea was intolerable. He must succeed!

Dane experienced a surge of pressure through his body. His throat narrowed to a straw. He was choking. Dane fumbled with his collar, tore the connective thread, freeing a button which dropped to the car floor. "Damn!" Pressure intensified. Dane slipped his hand behind his tie and tugged to free his throat. He leaned forward and braced himself on the wheel while he steered. He had had jobs like this before and where had they led him? All his life he had put his dreams on hold. Why was he running? *"You're too young to retire,"* he answered his own question. *"You'll outlive your savings and what will you do then?"*

He dropped his left arm and steered with his right hand. Not having a job might be the best thing that ever happened to him. Maybe sitting at home at his desk was living his dream and he didn't know it. "Give it a chance," he thought. "Turn back." His arm stopped aching. It was probably just nervousness and adrenaline, he thought.

Route 78 was notorious for poor visibility on clear days. Even with glare-repellent *Ray Bans*, Dane struggled to see the next green sign in the sunlight. He could not miss his exit since the next one was ten miles farther and would cost him twenty minutes to circle back. As Dane headed west, an eastbound eighteen-wheeler clipped a van in the passing lane. The van skidded into the median and the truck lumbered after it across the grass toward the westbound lanes. Dane saw the two metal behemoths in his periphery. He believed guardrails and a wide median would block oncoming traffic but the vehicles barreled toward him. Instinctively, he veered two lanes to the right and rolled to a stop on the shoulder. Brakes screamed and crashing metal thundered behind him. Dane saw the fiery wreck in his rearview, laid his head on the wheel and gasped for air.

□

Made in the USA
Charleston, SC
19 May 2012